HIGHER JUSTICE

Book One of the True Justice Series

D. E. Heil

D1608194

TALKING HEADS

"What's the American public to do?" Chris Morrison, one of the hosts of the morning news program asked. "Begin carrying machine guns and hand grenades to the grocery store?"

"Of course not," Tom Littleton, his co-host, replied. "The President has to make sure Homeland Security is doing their job, but he's not."

"So you're going to blame it all on the President?"

The commentators of *Monday Morning Alive* were bantering back and forth to provide entertainment under the guise of news. Along with all their competitors, they had spent the last few weeks discussing the horrific events of recent months.

"If Homeland Security can't protect us, is it any wonder more and more people are roaming around with guns?" Tom asked.

"Do we really want people taking the responsibility for their own security? Someone will get hurt."

"Hundreds, maybe even thousands, of citizens were saved from injury or death but it's still not right," Tom replied.

"Congress is trying to pass common sense gun control laws to keep firearms out of the hands of terrorists, but the President is blocking their efforts," Chris said. "The Senate only needs 33 more votes to override his veto. He's hiding behind his interpretation of the Second Amendment."

"What good will more laws do?" Tom asked. "How many more innocents must die before Congress does something worthwhile?"

"So what do you suggest? Everyone begin carrying guns like the Wild West and have rivers of blood run in our streets? That's not the answer."

"Of course I'm not suggesting that everyone arm themselves. We still have police to protect the public," Tom replied hotly. "But on the other hand, we don't have a clue how many terrorists may already be on American soil."

"It's up to the government to stop these coordinated attacks," Chris said as he leaned forward to emphasize his point. "They're being carried out with military precision by people we think are bankers, doctors, or computer experts. Why don't we know who they are or what they're planning? Where's our intelligence community? Parents are afraid to send their kids to school."

"Some people are afraid to go to work because they wonder if they'll ever come home. That's hurting the economy."

"Worry about whether they'll come home? More folks are worrying about whether they'll have a home and family to return to."

"So what does Congress have to…"

"Wait!" Tom said as he put a finger to the microphone in his ear. "We have a breaking story!"

Chris dropped his finger from the microphone in his ear, and without uttering a word, he began to type furiously on the keyboard in front of him.

"It's being reported that there has been a shooting in a church in Nebraska during morning services," Tom reported as he continued to keep his finger to his ear and listened intently. "An unknown number of gunmen entered a small rural church, and without warning, began to shoot indiscriminately into the congregation gathered there. A large number of people have been injured but it's too early to report on any casualties."

"That can't be right!" Chris suddenly exclaimed with a look of utter astonishment on his face as he vigorously jabbed his finger toward his computer screen. A small drop of spittle flew from his mouth, and he shouted with great anguish cracking his voice, "It says right here that Nebraska doesn't allow guns in churches! Something has to be wrong! That can't be right!"

"Yeah," Tom said incredulously as he stared at the side of Chris' head. "There is definitely something wrong here..." His words trailed off without comment about his colleague's state of mind.

CHAPTER 1

POOR CHOICES

Amanda Freundin, a lifelong resident of Curtis Bay in the heavily industrialized area comprising the southern portion of Baltimore, giddily tottered home after a long night of partying with three of her girlfriends from school. As usual, she had partaken of the greatest portion of the Robert Mondavi Chablis the girls preferred. Her lime green flip-flops softly smacked the coarse-grained concrete as her ample bosom defied the chill winds by threatening to fall out of her low-cut V-neck sweater. A pink hooded fleece sweatshirt was loosely thrown over her shoulders more as a fashion statement to accompany her fashionably torn jeans than to offer warmth.

Like a small child on a warm summer day she meandered from one scraggly tuft of dying grass to another giving each a glancing kick then giggling hysterically at her own nonsensical antics. The fact the grass was growing in the numerous cracks scattered throughout the neglected concrete sidewalk instead of in a flower-studded meadow did not seem to faze her at all.

It had been easy for the slightly overweight fourteen-year old dishwater blonde to persuade Marty Donsbach, the forty-two year old maintenance man at the apartment complex where she lived with her alcoholic father, to buy wine for her. Marty was always willing to do little favors for the ninth grader. Because of her street-honed survival instincts she only spoke with him in the company of others.

She snaked aimlessly back and forth down the broken sidewalk in the desolate section of town she called home, totally oblivious to the danger lurking ahead.

John Dugan was six-foot two inches tall and 170 pounds of pure evil wrapped in a disarming personality. Greasy blonde hair hung in stringy clumps from beneath a black rayon watch cap perched rakishly on the side of his head. His stained, skin-tight denim jeans were bleached white on the front of the thighs and fashionably torn at the corners of the rear pockets. His chest muscles bulged seductively from beneath a well-fit white tee shirt that was partially concealed by an unbuttoned long-sleeved flannel shirt and the open front of a navy blue jacket.

He studied the desolate urban landscape before him as though he were surveying his personal empire. Like most career criminals, Dugan lived with the delusion he owned or somehow controlled the streets he prowled.

A swirling tornado of multicolored leaves blew down the deserted street signaling the beginning of winter. Seeing them, a shiver slithered down his back, causing him to dig his head deeper into the collar of his jacket.

"I need some, Man," Wayne Varecci, Dugan's toady cohort, spewed venomously as he leaned uncomfortably close to Dugan's right ear.

Varecci was of average height at five-foot ten inches tall. His protruding abdomen made him look squat and ill shaped with thick, short legs jutting from beneath a baby-blue hooded sweatshirt. His thick, short neck caused it to appear that his ears were growing out the top of his rounded shoulders.

Both men, barely out of their teens, had been hardened far beyond their years by growing up on the unforgiving streets of Baltimore's poorest neighborhoods.

"You always need some, you horny bastard," Dugan said through a tight-lipped sneer.

His mind flashed back to disgusting images of Varecci's past escapades, causing his stomach to churn with repugnance. Even the most liberal member of the American Psychological Association could not consider Varecci's sexual perversions remotely acceptable or non-violent.

Dugan glanced around the dirty, darkened alcove of the abandoned storefront the pair had sought protection in to partially deflect the biting late October wind. Faded, golden lettering was barely legible on the glass front of the door. It announced to the world that Yancy's Fine Tailoring was open six days a week. Dugan smiled silently to himself. Apparently, Yancy hadn't bothered putting a 'closed' sign in the window when he abandoned the business over twenty years ago.

"Here you go," Dugan said as Varecci's beady eyes followed his gaze toward the silent, seemingly abandoned rail yard.

"Amanda looks like she's got a good load on tonight."

Their eyes met as they silently acknowledged each other's intentions.

"I don't know about Amanda. She may have some incurable disease that'll make the Little Guy turn black and fall off," Varecci said playfully as his menacing grin glowed in the muted light reflecting off the dusty windows of Yancy's derelict shop. Dugan stared at him with disgust then remembered to smile. Varecci craved frequent verification that he was witty and Dugan was willing to play along to keep the dimwit happy.

"Beggars can't be choosers," Dugan hissed from between smirking lips. "Besides, she's the answer to your prayers. Or aren't you interested anymore?"

He noted the sudden snapping motion of Varecci's head and the hard, wicked glare in his eyes as he took offense. Dugan immediately and silently stifled his minion's rebellious attitude with a cold, hardened stare of his own. A slight shifting of his weight forward as though assuming a fighting stance, combined with a minute straightening of his carriage to accentuate his height advantage, established his unspoken dominance over Varecci.

"How do you want to handle this?" Varecci mumbled, accepting his place in the social hierarchy. A thin, crooked smile appeared on Dugan's lips signaling his acceptance of Varecci's surrender.

Varecci's hooded eyes furtively darted away to avoid Dugan's piercing stare then riveted on the chunky figure tottering steadily toward them.

"Follow me and you'll see," Dugan hissed menacingly.

Dugan and Varecci slunk nonchalantly onto the sidewalk in a fluid, unhurried motion. Years on the street had taught them to move swiftly but smoothly. Subconsciously they had learned the human eye and mind focus on sudden, unexpected movement. The more subtle their approach, the less wary their victims would become making it easier for the hard-edged young men to draw near their prey.

Amanda was startled when the two disheveled men seemingly appeared out of nowhere. The illuminated cones of dust-diffused light streaming directly downward from ancient streetlamps offered only limited visibility. Between the gauzy cones of illumination dancing shadows fooled the eye like a camouflaged optical illusion.

"Hey Amanda. What's a nice girl like you doing out on a night like this?"

Dugan kept his most disarming smile carefully fixed on his face. He knew his smile was one of his greatest assets. He also knew deep down that God had to be displeased when he used his gift as a weapon against his fellow human beings. Of course, he never gave a damn what God or anyone else thought of him so he was able to easily dispel any guilt he may have ever felt.

It took a second for Amanda's alcohol befuddled eyes to recognize Dugan's face. Her flashing smile instantly communicated the crush she had on him since they first met three weeks previously.

"Hey Dugan," Amanda bubbled.

"Varecci," She slurred as she disgustedly acknowledged Dugan's lackey without looking directly at him. Varecci's face darkened, highlighting his bloated, unshaven and pockmarked cheeks.

"Listen, you skanky little…"

Before Varecci could say more, Dugan interrupted by addressing Amanda with a twinge of false sincerity in his voice, "You've been out partying without me again Amanda. I'm hurt."

She knew he was only joking with her, but the doleful pouting of his fleshy lips was irresistible to the fourteen-year-old blonde.

"The night's still young Amanda. What do you think we can do?" Dugan slyly crooned as he flashed a smile.

Amanda's alcohol-limited attention was completely focused on Dugan. He wanted to keep the young girl's attention focused on him, which allowed Varecci to slip silently and unnoticed behind the unsuspecting teen. Dugan's heart began beating furiously because of the anticipated carnal pleasures permeating his mind.

"Amanda darling," he said while breathing heavily from between barely moving lips, concentrating on performing his best Marlon Brando impersonation. His eyes searched leeringly into hers as his hips moved forward with his hands following a split second later. He was proud of the moves he was making. They were working perfectly to charm the gullible youngster. She was totally absorbed by his presence. Her reaction confirmed his long-held belief that he should move to Hollywood and become an actor.

Amanda felt herself succumbing to Dugan's advances and began moving closer to him; all too willing to show him how much she wanted him. His hands began to gently fondle her golden hair. They could feel each other's breath on their faces.

"Now," Dugan said simply and calmly.

Instantly Varecci's huge hairy arms encircled and crushed Amanda's to her sides. She momentarily froze as her mind raced to make sense of what was happening to her.

"What the hell!" she yelped while jerking her head back in an attempt to crush her tormentor's nose flat against his ugly face. "Varecci, you BASTARD!"

The evil lurking in his soul was instantaneously revealed when Dugan's affable smile distorted into a contemptuous thin line.

He deftly flicked a snot-streaked blue and white kerchief from his back pocket and stifled the stream of profanity gushing from her cavernous mouth. The demonic look on his face was indelibly etched upon her mind as he cruelly jammed the rag past her teeth while her tongue vainly struggled to deny it access.

"Gag, you whore, it's all you deserve," Dugan muttered gleefully as terror grew in Amanda's tear-rimmed baby-blue eyes.

"Crank her arm up. I've got her head."

Casting a casual glance into the dark rail yard, Dugan's ominously calm voice directed Varecci like a puppet on invisible strings. "Drag her down to the creek."

An overwhelming sense of helplessness smothered her soul.

 Damn! Not again! Amanda thought as she struggled with all her might to escape the horrors she knew awaited her.

CHAPTER 2

HOMEWARD COMMUTE VIA CURTIS BAY

"Yes Honey, I know. But these babies don't realize they're inconveniencing us by being born in middle of the night," Robert Fogler chuckled softly over the cell phone as he spoke with Irene, his lovely wife of 28 years.

Over their years together he had made a habit of calling her when he would be arriving home in the middle of the night to avoid startling her with the noises he made while pussyfooting into their house.

Robert may have felt much older than his 52 years, but he looked like an athletic 40 year old. His 6 foot 3 inch frame carried sinewy muscle with only a hint of paunch around his midsection. With close-cropped hair showing a slight smattering of gray and creamy ebony skin, the accomplished African-American could easily have been featured on the cover of GQ magazine.

"I am tired. I've been up for almost 36 hours and the last one was a difficult delivery," he uttered, barely above a whisper. Then he amusingly listened to the subdued complaint she murmured through the cloud of sleep that fogged her mind. He could almost recite it verbatim because it was the same grievance he had heard many times during their numerous years together.

"I am not too old for this," he protested. "Besides, what would I do if I gave up delivering babies?"

A gentle smile spread across his lips. He could tell by the silkiness in her voice that she was imagining him smiling in the darkness of the night. People could communicate without saying a word, knowing each other's thoughts, when they knew each other since age five as Robert and Irene had.

"You go back to sleep and I'll be home in 15 minutes," he said. "I'm going to hang up now because the old railroad bridge is coming up and the cell phone coverage is spotty down here."

"I love you too," he quietly replied to the muffled words of affection she had murmured. He kept his voice low and sultry, so not to rouse her from the half-asleep stupor she was obviously still in. His mind drifted toward his arrival home because there was little he enjoyed more than sneaking into bed to lay beside the roasty-toasty warmth of her body.

Just as he snapped the silver receiver of his cellular phone closed and reached to place it into the black plastic cup holder of the car's center console, a fleeting blur of motion caught his attention on the crumbling sidewalk running along the right side of the cheerless street.

His senses immediately went on high alert when a second rapidly disappearing swirl of motion caught his eye in the stygian depths of the rail yard and he fully realized what was unfolding before him.

His right foot eased the brake pedal toward the floor causing the heavy vehicle to slow to a crawl.

One was tall and thin with stringy blonde hair hanging from beneath a black watch cap. He was wearing a dark coat, he recited to himself. *The police will want positive identification.*

The other one was of average height with a big belly straining against his baby blue hooded sweatshirt.

His eyes scanned to the right, tunnel vision limiting his visual field. Then he saw it. A lime-green flip-flop was lying upside down in a scrubby patch of dead weeds at the edge of the sidewalk.

Robert began to gain confidence; secure in the knowledge he could recall so much of what he had seen. His brain raced to embed other details in his mind's eye as he simultaneously formulated a course of action.

The blond guy had the chubby girl's hair in both fists and was pulling her behind him. The fat toad-like one had the girl's left arm cranked up behind her back. His other hand held the belt loops of her blue jeans so he could drag her.

But where in the hell did they go? This damned rail yard goes on forever, he thought to himself as he struggled to remember the layout.

Suddenly he had an idea.

He hit the gas pedal of the powerful vehicle, immediately exhilarated by the surging momentum of the revving engine. With a deft flick of his wrist, he jerked the wheels to the curb where he had last seen the trio.

The right front tire of the shiny black Mercedes SUV jolted over the low curb and ground to a halt. Its halogen headlights threw a brilliant bluish glare deep into the black depths.

The coating of grime covering the street billowed into a swirling cloud of putrid red dust, which immediately overwhelmed the German-made automobile. The filthy haze ominously obscured his view between the railroad cars. As the sooty filth slowly settled to the ground, the unearthly yellow glow of the solitary streetlight lent a surreal air of unreality to the scene unfolding before his eyes.

Where the hell did they go?

His groping right hand flew to the cup holder where his phone was securely housed.

Like a man possessed by demons he flipped the phone open, held the emergency button for the requisite three seconds, then held the chilly plastic receiver to the side of his head. A pre-recorded message informed him the call could not be completed, making him wince.

He had driven into the dead zone and was now out of contact with the outside world.

Frantically, he held the illuminated screen at arm's length trying to decipher the glowing words without reading glasses. The dancing letters swirled in his blurred vision.

Damned my old eyes!

Squinting to force his sleep-deprived eyes to focus, he recoiled with horror when an absence of glowing bars confirmed he was out of touch with the rest of the world.

What the hell do I do now?

His options flashed through his mind. None of them were appealing.

A windy, rushing sound began resonating deeply in his head as time began speeding by like a runaway freight train. In the distance, a lonely train whistle sounded ominously in the night.

Damned! I'm going to jump into deep shit with both feet this time, the tall, ebony skinned man thought as his hands suddenly moistened with sweat. *I'm getting involved with something that's none of my business. But I have to.*

No I don't.

The hell I don't...

He tried to talk himself out of becoming personally involved, but he couldn't. He'd always possessed a conscience that wouldn't allow him to walk away from another human being in trouble. This wasn't the first time his conscience had gotten him into trouble; and it obviously wouldn't be the last.

He propelled himself from the Mercedes with wild abandon. Only when his feet hit the broken macadam of the street did he realize he was acting rashly.

The damned adrenaline is trying to get the best of you. Slow down, he thought as he struggled to remain calm.

He was not the type of person to panic in tricky situations but the taste of fear on the dry, cottony-textured surface of his tongue told him he was in trouble.

Just leave; it's the right thing to do. Call the cops; they can handle it better than you can.

All of the lessons he had learned as a physician and first-aid responder, as well as the instructions from the self-defense courses he'd taken on his own time and paid for himself, screamed from the recesses of his mind to get back in his vehicle; but he couldn't force himself to leave. His conscience wouldn't allow him to abandon anyone in trouble.

Activating the 9-1-1 emergency response system was the first action to take above all others when confronted by a crisis situation; or so they had taught him over and over again.

What they don't tell you in the safe, secure environment of the classroom is what the hell to do when you're alone and the damned cell phone won't work. How could there be such huge gaps of cell phone coverage in a city the size of Baltimore?

He fumed as he resisted the urge to fling the phone across the street and into the reflective waters of the Chesapeake Bay less than half a football field away.

In a fit of indecision and near panic, he leaped upward toward the driver's seat of the high-riding SUV. The non-slip pads glued to the top of the running board gave his foot a firm grip, allowing him to put all his strength into his skyward momentum. His body was split between gaining a better vantage point and returning to the safety of his vehicle in search of cell service. When the top of his head smashed into the unforgiving steel of the doorframe, his knees buckled and his hand went limp, allowing the cell phone to fall silently to the floor of the vehicle. An electrical convulsion of tingles rocketed throughout his entire body, reminding him of the sensation his sinuses experience when biting into a chocolate covered peppermint patty.

He didn't feel his body bounce off the seat or flop unceremoniously onto the gritty blacktop because the sudden, unexpected compression of his cervical spine momentarily snuffed out the electrical signals from his brain. The weighty darkness of unconsciousness fell upon him as willful thought and vision were swept away into a contented, satiny blackness.

It took a full five seconds for his mind to return to semi-consciousness.

The world around him appeared as a spinning collage of bursting colors interspersed with momentary explosions of dazzling brilliance followed by interminable gaps of dark nothingness. For a long time he dared not move. Finally, he struggled to right himself by pulling on the running board as his vision began clearing with agonizing slowness.

The fleeting memory of the blonde girl being dragged into the rail yard quickly displaced all other thoughts and caution from his mind. With his forehead resting gingerly on the running board, he suddenly felt the weight of the entire world on his shoulders.

He knew deep in his heart by the time the police got there the girl would be dead or wishing she were. The desire to help her jolted him back to near-consciousness.

With slow and deliberate movements, as though he were doing it for the first time, he pulled himself to his feet.

One agonizingly slow-motion movement after another lifted him out of the abyss of blackness that threatened to engulf him with each passing moment. Waves of nausea unceasingly racked his guts. His faltering mind was still groggy from the concussion he had inflicted upon himself.

Glancing around slowly, he realized the uninhabited and alien-appearing landscape surrounding him offered no assistance. The darkened fronts of the desolate, lonely bars lining the sooty, dingy street that polite society had long ago forgotten only added to his feeling of abandonment.

Industrial areas were almost always abandoned at this time of night. This forsaken hellhole was certainly no exception. Time seemed to hold him like an invisible vice as the fetid air of this God-forsaken part of the city crushed in around him.

You know you should go for help but there's just not enough time if you hope to have any chance of saving that child from only-God-knows-what.

His muddled mind began to reason with itself, trying to sway him from the crazy idea forming in the back of his head. He felt the heat begin to rise in his forehead as a cold, clammy sensation settled between his shoulder blades.

With a brilliant flash of intuition awakening him from his stupor, he realized that in a matter of minutes the three would be impossible to find in the millions of dark, silent hiding places scattered about the railroad yard. He knew he must act now if the girl was to have any chance of rescue.

You're on your own; so don't just sit there. Get moving.

He was now resolute and deliberate in thought and action. The fear and indecisiveness ruling his body just mere seconds before was replaced by resolve as he methodically began to prepare himself for battle.

Ignoring his matching alligator skin briefcase and wallet sitting on the passenger seat, he pulled his well-worn and weather-beaten bomber jacket from the front passenger seat where it had strategically hidden the pistol residing there.

After hurriedly shoving his arms into the pile-lined sleeves of the battle-originated garment, he noticed with an almost zen-like perception that the black leather jacket barely covered his broad shoulders. Rousing himself from his momentary lapse of concentration, he zipped the heavy brass zipper to his throat.

It's better to be wearing a dark colored jacket than glow in the dark with your white shirt exposed. Well Lord, when you led me to get training and carry a pistol for self-defense you sure knew what you were doing.

Leaning into the SUV just enough to reach between the driver's seat and middle console, he grabbed his Sig Sauer P220 from a kydex holster secured amidst the snug confines of the tawny leather seats. The weight of his upper body slumped onto the seat as it gave way to an unbearable fit of fatigue.

For driving comfort, he always removed the in-the-waistband holster he wore while working. A custom-crafted leather holster hand-made by the late Lou Alessi was tremendously comfortable standing but tended to gouge the hard steel of the pistol grip into his tender ribs while driving. To alleviate this uncomfortable problem he had purchased a specially rigged holster and installed it between the seats. A casually thrown coat or newspaper kept the pistol hidden as required by the laws governing his concealed carry permit.

Like most physicians, he did not like the inconvenience of carrying a pistol but the situations occurring in hospitals required him to be ready for anything. With an air of desperation he jerkily stepped away from his car.

The Sig he firmly clutched in his right hand was considered to be top-of-the-line in defensive pistols by law enforcement professionals. When your life is on the line, he had correctly reasoned, cost is of no consequence.

My instructor told me that if I needed to use a handgun for self-defensive it would probably be in semi-dark conditions. He was right!

He also said that the day might come when a reliable pistol may be the only friend I have with me. Unfortunately, he was right again.

Robert's Sig was chambered for the powerful .45 ACP round that had carried the U.S. armed forces through decades of fierce battles as the primary pistol cartridge of America's fighting men. Tonight, he was thankful for the destructive capabilities of the large caliber because he knew the likelihood of everything going smoothly was remote.

Flicking a tear of fear from the corner of his eye, he cleared his conscious mind, took a deep breath, and said a desperate prayer for guidance. A fleeting search for alternative answers flashed across his mind.

"Shit!" He muttered under his breath when he realized there were no alternatives. He was out of options and time.

Drawing a slow ragged breath into his suddenly oxygen-starved lungs, he shuffled on heavy, leaden feet into the swirling darkness of the seemingly abandoned yard. He held his only hope for success in the slippery palm of his sweat-soaked hand.

CHAPTER 3

BAD CHOICE

Moving cautiously while simultaneously analyzing every tiny sound reaching his attentive ears, Robert slinked furtively in the shadow of a gondola railcar carrying scrap steel. The smell of the rail yard was unique and puckered his nose. The matted dirt stank after having decades of heavy industry settle upon it. The gritty odor of gravel and the astringent aroma of diesel fuel mixed harmoniously with the musky, almost fish-like redolence of peeling paint and rust.

He hunkered beside the aged vehicle of burden to survey his surroundings. It took a few moments longer than he expected for his eyes to adjust to his shadowy surroundings. The almost total darkness found in the midst of the yard surprised him.

Only the faint twinkling of a smattering of stars was visible overhead. There was no appreciable illumination from the fading sliver of a moon. He found himself wishing the puny, orange-tinged glow of the filthy streetlights carried this far.

Just as he was beginning to be able to differentiate indistinct forms in the darkness, he caught a fleeting glimpse of stooped figures clumsily disappearing like limping Will-o-the-wisps between railroad cars.

That has to be them!

Most of the cars were open-topped with ancient barn-red paint flaking off their rusting steel skin. These brutes were designed to haul raw materials for industry, mainly bituminous coal or iron ore. However, the aged relics he hid behind were no longer up to the rigors of long hauls from distant coalfields. These octogenarians had long ago been relegated to short hauls toting waste metals. If they failed at that job, they were then carried to the smelting furnace by their surviving brethren and relegated to the mountain of soon-to-be-recycled scrap metal.

He cautiously approached the area he had last seen the trio, making sure to keep his form low to the ground while shuffling his feet just above the surface to avoid tripping.

Keep your ears open. They'll be of more use than your eyes.

A tiny scraping sound reached his ears, immediately riveting his attention to an area obliquely to his left where Amanda Freundin's feet and fingernail-studded hands flailed desperately in an attempt to escape Varecci's stench.

"Quit struggling or I'll let Varecci have you all to himself. And you don't want that, believe me," Dugan hissed into her ear, taking extra care to maintain a vise-like grip on a fistful of her hair so she couldn't smash his finely featured face. "He really likes it the more you struggle. It excites him."

Amanda went limp and Dugan thought his ruse had worked.

In a flash, she managed to free her left hand while spinning her body to the right and sunk her stiletto sharp fingernails into Varecci's face. His pustulous flesh separated in long, bloody welts from his right eye to the corner of his tainted mouth.

"You BITCH!" he roared like a wounded animal as his meaty fist smashed into her chest. Her breath whooshed out like compressed air being released from an overly inflated balloon.

Robert's head swung slowly and deliberately toward the trio as his ears pinpointed their exact location while the muzzle of his Sig tracked their movements.

He could only see specter-like forms in the murk, but he could clearly hear scuffling feet rolling diesel fuel-saturated stones on the railroad bed. His acute hearing was trying to verify there were only three of them. He hoped he had not missed seeing others when they vanished from the street.

"No yelling!" hissed Dugan.

"But..." Varecci whined as Dugan yanked a wad of Amanda's yellow hair toward the ground with a vicious sweep of his entire body. She gasped and whimpered pitifully as he smashed his knee into her back effectively pinning her to the ground.

"Quit your damned sniveling and pay attention! We're not going down to the creek. This is as good a spot as any."

Robert hurried in a shuffling gait, keeping his upper body as low as he could while trying to stay in the deepest, darkest shadows.

A rustling in the gravel brought his undivided attention to an area only twenty yards ahead of him. He stopped in his tracks.

Hell! They may be armed too! I didn't think of that!

He intelligently decided he was not able to confront two assailants under these circumstances regardless of how well he was armed.

I'm way the hell in over my head.

He spun around to make a stealthy retreat and accidentally glanced the Sig off the side of the railcar he was standing beside. The clang of metal against metal in the stillness of the night attracted more attention than a waiter dropping a tray full of wine glasses in a busy restaurant.

He instantly realized the folly of his actions.

Oh Shit!

"What the hell was that?" Dugan demanded, his ears striving to fix the location of the disturbance.

Varecci was too engrossed with beating Amanda to hear Dugan's words. He reveled at each wet, pounding blast his pummeling fist made when it contacted the delicate flesh of the hapless girl. The hollow sopping sounds held his rapt, though limited, attention.

Varecci's puny mind made it impossible to comprehend anything occurring outside the perverted pleasure he derived from the overwhelming aphrodisiac of dominating another human being. No minor disturbance would deter him from his planned rape and mutilation of their prey.

Seeing that Varecci didn't comprehend what was happening, Dugan grabbed his wrist. He could feel the piercing hatred of Varecci's searing glare searching quizzically for him in the darkness.

Robert sensed they had stopped and were listening to pinpoint his location in the shadows. He knew the moment of truth was at hand and moved forward toward the heaped mass of humanity with smooth, sure strides.

It was too dark for Dugan to fully comprehend the significance of the apparition sliding from the shadows beside the rail cars, but he knew it meant trouble. He reached for the Raven .25 ACP automatic pistol residing in his back pocket while simultaneously shifting his grasp from Varecci's wrist to the collar of his sweat-soaked sweatshirt.

Using his grip on Varecci's collar, Dugan jerked him around to face their opponent. He used the small silver-colored pistol clenched in his fist to point toward the dark form descending upon them. Robert was only thirty feet away and closing rapidly.

Varecci, seething with out-of-control anger over having his fun interrupted, swung a vicious punch to the back of Amanda's head, instantly stunning her into unconsciousness. As she collapsed into a rumpled heap Varecci rushed straight toward Robert in a blind rage.

A warning sounded in Robert's adrenaline-charged primeval mind allowing him to sidestep Varecci's attack a split second before he made contact. The move saved him from being bowled over by the much younger and stronger man but he was knocked off balance.

Holy hell! He just about had me! That was way too close. Create distance! Create distance!

Robert clawed madly at the side of the rail car with his left hand and almost spun wildly out of control in his haste to escape. The inky blackness of his surroundings removed any visual landmarks, which further disoriented him.

Varecci twirled in his tracks and promptly renewed his attack. Robert was forced to step backward, his hand sliding along the length of the car to avoid tripping.

As he stumbled backwards, the voice of his self-defensive shooting instructor echoed through his mind as though the words were being whispered into his ear:

When your assailant is attacking at bad breath distance, raise your gun up to chest level using both hands, making sure you keep it held close to your body so he can't grab it, square your body to the line of his attack and gently press the trigger.

The blinding muzzle flash of Robert's gun discharging in the near-total darkness temporarily blinded both of them and effectively disoriented Varecci because he did not feel the 230-grain Speer Gold Dot enter his belly just below the solar plexus. The bullet angled downward through his guts before exiting his turgid body just above his right kidney.

It was not an immediately fatal wound.

Robert's classroom training in self-defensive use of the handgun began to return to him in a flood of mental recollection:

Create distance between yourself and your attacker. Your superior skill from training will carry the fight to a successful conclusion. Regardless of whether he's armed or not, an attacker doesn't have to be skilled; he only has to be lucky. And the closer your assailant is, the luckier he becomes.

Varecci struggled to sort the bewildering bits of information flooding his limited mental faculties. Robert took full advantage of the lull in the action to put as much distance between himself and Varecci as he could before ducking between two fully loaded cars.

He began standing up to better assess the situation when Dugan fired his first shot.

The bullet ricocheted from one steel wall to the other in the confined space between the two rail cars where Robert had taken refuge. The slug barely missed his head twice during its zigzag flight.

Still blinded by his own muzzle flash, and now disoriented by the report of Dugan's gun, Robert frantically sought an escape route.

In his unsighted state, he turned and ran headlong into the rusted steel ladder attached solidly to the side of railroad car. During the day, workers checked the car's contents from these sturdy ladders. Tonight, this one caused Robert's second concussion of the evening.

At the instant his head collided with the ladder his legs sagged as a mushroom of exploding light erupted in his eyes. His left hand instinctively flew forward in a desperate attempt to arrest his fall. It found the bottom rung of the ladder and he clutched it frantically.

Realizing what he was grasping, Robert spontaneously formulated a plan as he one-handedly hoisted himself upright. Raising himself to his full height, he grabbed the highest rung he could reach. He pulled himself up until his foot was able to find purchase on the lowest rung.

Go quickly but silently if you hope to survive tonight. Hiding is your only chance!

Keeping the Sig firmly clasped in his right hand he used his right wrist to pull himself up to the next level.

If I can get above them maybe they'll lose track of me and that'll give me time to think.

Robert's hastily implemented plan failed before it began.

"There's the son-of-a-bitch!" Dugan screamed when he saw Robert's shadowy figure faintly sky-lighted against the starry background.

The instinct of any predatory animal in the wild is to pursue and kill any prey that is running away. The adrenaline-fueled predatory behavior of the younger man was triggered by the sight of Robert's fleeing figure and was further aided by the modern rendition of fangs; the .25 caliber Raven.

Dugan was impulsively driven to pursue Robert as pent up anger and bloodlust fogged his mind.

Firing the silver-colored pistol one-handedly, he rushed at Robert with savage abandon. In his homicidal haste he failed to notice that Varecci had begun climbing the ladder in pursuit of their prey. The electrifying exhilaration of the predator's pursuit engulfed Varecci in a shroud of invincibility common to young, testosterone-charged males.

Varecci was halfway up the ladder when Robert crested the crown of the railroad car. Scrambling to his feet on the ten-inch wide lip running completely around the top of the car Robert looked back down the ladder he had just stepped off of and was horrified to see Varecci reaching for his foot with one hand while clinging to the ladder with the other.

It was precisely at this inopportune moment that Dugan, in the midst of stepping down from a rail of the train track, triggered a 50-grain .25 ACP round. Dugan's bullet flew low; hitting the dull-minded Varecci in the hand he was using to hold himself to the ladder.

Varecci recoiled in shock and searing pain while staring dumbfounded at his wrist where the tiny slug ripped a path of destruction through brittle bones and stringy tendons.

Unthinking, he grasped his damaged wrist with his other hand to soothe the inferno erupting from its mangled joints. In the unreal slowing of time that occurs during times of severe mental stress, Varecci watched in horror as his bloated body peeled away from the ladder. His comic attempt to grasp the ladder with his uninjured hand was futile.

He tumbled clumsily out of control between the gondola cars and landed heavily with his rib cage straddling the steel rail of the tracks. A dull thud and sickening cracking sound occurred simultaneously followed immediately by an agonized, guttural scream. The three smashed ribs he suffered were not life threatening but the combination of this injury plus a blood-gushing bullet wound through his intestines rendered him incapable of standing.

Varecci was out of the fight.

One down, Robert thought as a smile of relief crossed his lips. His elation was short-lived. Dugan, using a two-handed hold on the tiny pistol, unleashed his final bullet at the shadowy figure tottering precariously on top of the car.

Robert felt the buzz of disturbed air from the bullet as it flew by his forehead.

Once again, his mind heard his instructor's voice whispering in his ear:

If your assailant is more than ten feet away you have to take careful aim and slowly press the trigger to make your shot count. Taking your time to precisely place one vital hit is infinitely better than wildly scattering bullets throughout the countryside.

Taking the advice of the voice reverberating through his mind Robert stood to his full height on the lip of the railcar and took careful aim using the outline of the gun instead of the night-obscured sights.

With a deliberate press of the crisp, three-pound trigger he sent a 230-grain .45 caliber Speer Gold Dot into Dugan's body, hitting a mere six inches to the left of his aiming point.

The bullet entered one inch above Dugan's right collarbone, angling downward to exit just below his right shoulder blade. The rapidly expanding bullet nicked the subclavian artery on its destructive path through his body. A wound to this vital artery, only half of a foot from Dugan's violently pumping heart, offered no opportunity to apply a tourniquet or otherwise staunch the pulsating gush of blood that immediately began soaking through the tightly woven fibers of his shirt.

The sudden disruption and severing of the nerves running from Dugan's neck into his right arm caused the silver gun to slip from his grasp. The lightweight zinc alloy pistol barely made a sound when it tumbled to the gravel-strewn ground.

Dugan knew instantly that he had been shot when the blinding muzzle flash and the almost-simultaneous thump of the heavy metal bullet smashing into his chest assaulted his senses. Adrenaline charged blood pressure forcefully expelled spurts of blood from the severed artery like a fireman's high-pressure hose; blood vital to carrying life-giving oxygen to nourish his now-starving brain. He did not know that his dying brain held only enough oxygen to operate for approximately 15 seconds before ceasing to function.

Dugan's sense of self-preservation had always served him well in surviving life on the streets. Without conscious thought his body pivoted 180 degrees and began pumping his legs as fast as his feet would move. Shards of gravel crunched noisily with every stride carrying him farther from the danger threatening his life.

Dugan never gave a second thought to his injured accomplice as he twisted his way through the maze of silent trains sitting idle. After detecting the sticky stream of warm blood snaking its way into to his shoes, his thoughts became fixated on the rapidly growing wet spot saturating his flannel shirt and jeans.

Robert focused all his attention on Dugan running between the trains and toward the run-down neighborhood beyond, but failed to notice the rapid, successive clamor of railroad cars jerking each other into motion.

Beginning with the train engine surging forward to supply forward momentum to move the train, each car began yanking its neighbor from a dead stop to a violent, lurching start, which then instantly slowed to a barely perceptible creep.

If he had understood the significance of the reverberating peal of heavy metal couplings smashing against each other, and it had sunk into his concussion-befuddled brain, he may have realized the train he was standing on was beginning to move.

Through a foggy bank of consciousness he slowly became aware of a slight tremor emanating upward from the steel skin of the railcar through the leather soles of his shoes. The trembling only occurred intermittently but grew stronger with each passing second. Thinking it may be Varecci renewing his attack, Robert focused his attention down the ladder as his fatigued eyes struggled to penetrate the murkiness under the gondola's belly.

With a sudden crash and jolt the open railroad car he was standing on lurched forward with a violent start, jerking itself from beneath his feet and sending him into an intractable free fall. His uncontrolled six-foot tumble into the car was not mitigated by any attempt to save himself.

The visual illusion caused by the car being partially full with heaps of discarded scrap steel added to his inability to discern where his body was in time and space. Clumped in uneven mounds, the soon-to-be-recycled waste created differing hues of mottled shadows scattered about the half-filled car. The distorted fluidity of the sky further confused his senses as he desperately tried to make sense of what was happening to him.

Robert landed upside down with a sickening crunch reverberating through the center of his chest when his upper back hit the corner of an ancient Maytag washing machine. Before his mind could register he had been injured, his head slammed onto the mangled tire rim from a 1964 Ford Fairlane, causing his third concussion of the evening.

His exquisitely crafted Sig P220 slipped unnoticed from his grasp and landed beside a mutilated lawnmower engine. The tool Robert had used to save his life and that of Amanda Freundin would be melted down as scrap metal when it reached the foundry.

Robert would never know he was knocked unconscious or that the hapless Varecci was sliced in half by the gargantuan silvery steel wheel belonging to the same railroad car he fell into. Ironically, both of the former adversaries had their lives irreversibly altered in the same irretrievable instant.

Amanda eventually awakened, beaten and bruised, having lain unconscious throughout the entire gunfight. After struggling to her feet she unsteadily staggered home to a warm bed with no recollection of Robert's involvement.

Two days later, railroad workers would find Dugan's and Varecci's grotesquely bloated bodies.

The police investigating their deaths would never uncover the truth linking the events leading up to their demise on that fateful night. Robert's disappearance and abandoned vehicle only added to the mystery.

CHAPTER 4

A RUDE AWAKENING

The train slowly meandered its way from the Baltimore railyards toward Virginia where the foundry and final destination for the scrap metal was located. In the outskirts of Washington, D.C., the train stopped to take on additional cars before continuing its journey. It was here that Robert Fogler, fourteen hours after he had fallen into the railroad car, awoke in agony.

Damned! My head feels like I've been out drinking for a week. I can hardly move I'm so stiff.

When he attempted to sit up a spasm of lightning-like pain shot from between his shoulder blades into his head. The pain was so great he did not notice or care that he was cutting his hands on sharp edges of scrap metal as he struggled to his feet.

Ow! Ow! My arm is numb and I can't move the damned thing!

Peering over the rusted lip of the gondola car he realized he did not know where he was. With Herculean effort, his stiff, uncooperative joints finally allowed him to laboriously crawl out of the car. His slashed hands dripped congealing drops of bright red blood onto his pants and the inside walls of the rusty metal hulk.

He did not know where he was going; only that he was in dire need of help. As he staggered across the railroad yard, a seemingly deserted neighborhood appeared on the far side of a chain link fence. The silvery diamond shapes of the woven metal fence separated the putrid brown of the railroad property from the mottled gray concrete sidewalks and grayish-black macadam street.

There must be someone there who'll help me, he thought groggily.

When he staggered closer to the fence his spirit plunged.

How the hell am I supposed to get over this thing?

Searching feverishly up and down the gray metallic fence, his eyes fell upon a ragged two-foot square hole cut in the fence many years previously by teenagers wanting to access a desolate place to drink beer.

After falling onto his hands and knees he flopped onto his belly and managed to crawl through the hole, miraculously avoiding most of the pointed wires jaggedly protruding from the edges. Only his scuffed leather jacket kept his belly from being severely cut by broken beer bottles scattered on the ground. His bare hands and knees did not fare as well.

Standing upright was almost an impossible task. He was hurting from his head to his toes. His hands began throbbing insufferably; shards of broken glass were now embedded alongside as well as in the cuts he received from the ragged edges of scrap metal in the railcar.

A blinding headache accompanied by tunnel vision began affecting his eyesight. He used his bloody hands to shade his hypersensitive eyes while squinting against the horrendously bright sunshine. The urge to vomit was overwhelming.

Robert was suffering external auditory exclusion with all sounds picked up by his ears appearing muffled while an almost intolerable din clanged inside his skull. His incredibly stiff upper back caused him to lurch in a rocking gait that would have made the Hunchback of Notre Dame appear nimble. Shuffling on unsteady legs he agonizingly staggered down the sidewalks of unfamiliar streets. His mind swirled in a tornado of befuddlement.

He looked for someone to help him but no one was to be found on the deserted streets. His injuries finally overcame him as the pain became too much to bear. Collapsing in the shade beside a foot-worn granite stoop leading up to the sun-bleached wooden front door of a crumbling red brick house, he closed his eyes for a moment to rest his pain-racked body; too weary to travel any farther. Unconsciousness mercifully enveloped him and cradled him in the boundless black depths of sleep.

CHAPTER 5

CHAUNCEY

When he awoke, it was cold and dark. There was a man talking to him and pushing his shoulder to awaken him. Robert could only stare dumbly at him and demand gruffly, "What the hell do you want?"

Slowly, the man's swirling facial features came into focus. It was the kind, gentle face of William Collonem, a thirty-two year old social worker at the Bethlehem Mission for Homeless Men. William's six foot five inch frame carried 320 pounds on it. The huge, intimidating size of his body often went unnoticed because of his constant, comforting smile.

"Can you hear me?" William asked patiently with a smile purposefully affixed upon his lips.

"Yes I can hear you. What the hell do you want?"

"I want you to get in the van so I can take you to the mission. It's going to be real cold out here tonight, cold enough to kill you. We have hot food, a warm bed, and biblical guidance waiting for you there. Are you OK?"

"I hurt real bad. I need a doctor."

"Let's get you in the van. We have a doctor who visits the mission on Tuesday afternoon, that's tomorrow. If you're in really bad shape we can take you to the emergency room. Did you get beat up?"

Getting no answer, William tried again, "Where are you all hurting?"

Robert still did not reply.

Seeing the man did not understand him, or could not respond, William helped him painstakingly gain his feet and led him to the van.

Must be drunk as a skunk to be this unsteady, William thought sadly.

"Have you been drinking?"

"I don't think so."

"You don't know?"

"I don't know. Who are you anyway?"

"I'm William. Are you diabetic? You're pretty unstable on your feet but I don't smell any alcohol on your breath."

"I don't know."

"What's your name?"

A quizzical look came over his face. "I don't know."

"You don't know your own name?"

"I can't remember. Please, I need help. I really hurt," he whined pathetically.

William was used to men occasionally showing up at the mission offering a false name to avoid being identified for past crimes. Having a man deny knowing his name was a much rarer occurrence.

"Come on; let me help you into the van."

He glanced toward the street and saw a white eleven- passenger van in desperate need of a car wash with "Bethlehem Mission" emblazoned on the side in large blue block-style lettering. A solitary cross of faded light blue paint adorned the passenger's door.

As William assisted him into the van, William's helper, an intern from Alexandria Community College named Scott Haldeman, asked him, "What's your name?" as he held a Ticonderoga #2 lead pencil poised over a piece of dog-eared lined yellow paper attached to a clipboard.

A dry mouth and cracked, thickened lips caused him to slur his reply, "I don't know."

"What's your name?" Scott asked with irritation and impatience in his voice.

I have to talk to him about the inflection and tone of his voice, William thought sadly. *Any affront to these guys can get the snot beat out of him in a skinny minute.*

"What's your name?" Scott repeated with increasing irritation in his voice.

Robert stared at him with a blank look on his face, "I don't know."

William sensed it was time to intervene.

"Just put down Chauncey, he looks like a Chauncey to me." The note of finality in his voice combined with a stern look as he glared down at the smaller man motivated Scott to take the hint without comment.

"Besides, we don't have another Chauncey at the mission so it'll help avoid confusing him with anyone else. Especially since he doesn't have a last name," William added consolingly.

Thus Robert Fogler became Chauncey.

Chauncey became a man without a past or legal name. Not named by his mother but by a large man named William from the Bethlehem Mission for Homeless Men. Chauncey had suffered total amnesia caused by a rapid succession of multiple head injuries and could not remember anything before being awakened by William.

"Grab a seat in the back of the van, Chauncey," William directed. "We still have a lot of men to pick up and it's better if they don't have to trip over you to get to an open seat."

As an afterthought William added in a mentoring, almost fatherly tone of voice, "Chauncey, you have to realize that the men who will share this van and the mission facilities with you are hardened by life. They're used to fighting for every scrap of food, clothing, and dignity they possess. They defend their territory, or even what they perceive as their territory, with sudden and devastating violence. Many of them are mentally unstable. Don't give them a reason to fight with you. Some of these guys will kill you before you know what happened."

Chauncey stared at William with no sign of comprehension on his face but finally gave a little nod of his anguished head. William's friendly smile broadened slightly before he turned away to continue his search for other derelict men to save.

Chauncey looked at the person he was to sit beside in the rear seat of the van, and was relieved to see a very docile older man whose face beamed above a warm, toothless smile.

Wanting to take William's warning to heart Chauncey decided to make friends with this seemingly harmless man. "Hello, my name is Chauncey," he said as he extended his tattered right hand. He fought back an obvious wince when a burning pain shot from his right shoulder blade to his fingers.

"I don't think you want me to shake your injured hand, man. It looks bad," the old man slurred indistinctly through puffing lips as he struggled to speak without the benefit of teeth. "My name is Wilbur. Do you have a last name?"

"No, I don't. Only Chauncey. And that's not my real name. William gave it to me when I couldn't remember my own."

"That's OK. I only use one name too and I don't want to explain why," Wilbur said. "I don't care about little things like being around people not having a name as long as I get me a good meal and a bed to sleep in."

"William said he'd feed us and give us a warm place to sleep. I need a doctor. I hurt bad."

"Yeah, that's too bad," Wilbur murmured absentmindedly, his attention consumed by the sight of another homeless man entering the side door of the van. The new arrival was well known to him.

"Be glad there are only two seats back here. This guy is pure trouble," Wilbur whispered as he gestured toward the man entering the van.

Chauncey, hugging his tormented right arm to his chest, glanced nervously at the man whose head had just poked into the van. Cautiously leaning closer to Wilbur, he asked, "Who's that?"

"That's Malik," Wilbur replied in a barely audible whisper.

Malik was a hulking, ill-mannered alcoholic smelling of filth, urine, and sweat. He glared with unblinking eyes at Chauncey and Wilbur before slumping onto the middle of the seat in front of them.

"Keep an eye on that one," Wilbur whispered to Chauncey. "He's a mean bastard."

Hearing him, Malik turned around to resume his menacing glare. Wilbur's fear was short-lived because Phillip, a man who had been sharing a steam grate with Malik, entered the van, stumbled, and landed heavily on the seat, jostling Malik in the process.

Chauncey watched in horror as Malik instantly launched into a vicious attack. He first hit Phillip in the middle of his chest then immediately threw a vicious right hook to his outstretched chin.

The blow to Phillip's chin glanced harmlessly off his whiskered jaw, doing no permanent physical damage. He quickly recovered and retaliated with a right cross to Malik's nose. The cartilage of Malik's nose snapped while his blood splattered across Chauncey and Wilbur's chests.

Chauncey sat transfixed as William Collonem launched himself into the van, savagely grabbed Phillip by the collar of his coat, and ejected him onto the sidewalk. When William's head reappeared at the van door it merely took a hand gesture to instruct Malik to follow him outside.

Only when Malik reached the van door did the realization hit him that he was about to be banned from the mission. He balked, shook his shaggy head slowly back and forth, then began backing up to return to his seat.

In a flash, William snatched a large handful of Malik's overcoat with his right hand and an equally sized handful of hair with his left. He easily pried the large man from the van and tossed him toward the steam grate as though he were nothing more than a plastic sack of garbage. Malik landed face first on the frigid sidewalk, bloodying the palms of both hands and ripping the knees out of his pants.

Chauncey stared in stunned amazement as William pointed his finger at the two prostrate forms lying on the ground and began spitting words at them with a venomous tone, "You bastards want to fight, go ahead. But you're not going to do it in my van. You can spend the night on that steam grate and I hope it keeps you warm enough to keep you alive. If not, then good riddance to both of you. If you do survive, I'll check back here tomorrow afternoon and see if you're ready to begin acting like human beings instead of animals!"

"He's different when he's mad," Wilbur observed in a quiet, awe tinged voice as he continued to stare at the spectacle unfolding before his eyes.

Turning on his heel, William spun his huge body agilely around, slammed the sliding door of the van closed, and unhurriedly took his place in the driver's seat. He motioned calmly with his index finger for Scott Haldeman to occupy the passenger seat. Scott obeyed immediately; reaching for his safety belt before his buttocks even hit the seat then swinging the vehicle's heavy door closed right away.

Malik, his broken nose bent at an awkward angle, blood running in an uninterrupted stream over his chin and pooling on the front of his dirt-stained nylon coat, sat beside an equally astounded Phillip on the cold, hard concrete in stunned silence, watching in dismay as the van pulled away.

Chauncey sat silently throughout the entire ride lost in his misery. Everyone, including Wilbur, paid him no attention.

CHAPTER 6

THE BETHLEHEM MISSION

To Chauncey, the ride in the van seemed to continue interminably and the seemingly endless number of stops plagued him mercilessly.

William, whom Chauncey quickly decided was not a very good driver, jerked the van to a sudden stop or bolted forward in a jackrabbit start at each stop, sending spasms of almost intolerable pain through his body. Even mandatory stops at red lights or stop signs resulted in agonizing convulsions of misery; each of which took Chauncey to the brink of unconsciousness.

In making their usual rounds William and Scott would quickly interview homeless people they found loitering on the streets or living under bridges. Most of the neglected souls they discovered were homeless waifs well known to them. The "usual customers" were often waiting for the van on street corners much like an employed commuter waits on a bus. The accepted custom of opening the van door, giving Scott their name as soon as it slid open, and entering in an orderly fashion went smoothly with those who knew the routine.

The homeless men who were not known to William had to be subjected to a short interview before being allowed into the van. Women were left on the street with instructions that the van for the women's shelter would be coming shortly.

He was amazed at how many homeless people refused the mission's offering of shelter. These hardy individuals, many of them suffering mental illness, chose to live in freedom on the streets. Scott gave them a brown bag lunch containing a ham and cheese sandwich on pasty white bread, an apple, and a non-descript chocolate candy bar with nuts. They had their choice of steaming black coffee or hot chocolate in a large Styrofoam cup topped with a shiny plastic lid.

Finally the van stopped and William turned in his seat. He then raised his voice to make sure everyone heard him, "We're here. File out of the van one at a time. There's no reason to push and shove. Nobody's going anywhere any faster than the whole group can move. You will all be processed together so help each other to speed up the procedures. Anyone who wants to fight or tries to smuggle alcohol or drugs into the mission will be immediately thrown back onto the street and into the cold."

He nimbly swung his bulk out of the van and took a position next to the side door. As the door slid open William continued his litany, "Go up the front steps and someone will assign you your job then direct you to the showers.

"After you're showered and dressed in clean clothes you can proceed to the dining hall. At precisely six o'clock the religious services will begin. The services will be officiated by the Reverend John Yates, the director here at the Bethlehem Mission. You will be courteous, pay attention to what is being said, and show proper respect, which means no talking during the service," he continued in a staccato voice.

"They always make you listen to the minister before they feed you. Just obey the rules and everything will be OK," Wilbur whispered into Chauncey's ear in a friendly, mentoring tone. Chauncey leaned away the best he could to avoid vomiting from the horrific, putrid odors wafting from Wilbur's toothless mouth.

The men began filing out of the van in a relatively orderly manner. Most of them were familiar with the workings of the mission having been there many times before. Chauncey had trouble getting out of the van. His open wounds and tormented joints had stiffened, increasing his misery.

William, seeing the problem Chauncey was experiencing, helped him step down from the van.

"It's a good thing tomorrow is Tuesday. The doctor will be in so I'll put you on the list to see him. I don't want you getting blood over everything so I'm going to excuse you from any assigned chores."

"Thank you," was all Chauncey could say from between pain-clenched teeth.

Chauncey's eyes followed the steps of the mission upward to the massive carved wooden front doors. The structure had once obviously been a government building. The twenty-three granite steps were foot-worn in the middle with the ends retaining their original squared-off edges. The stucco façade was painted white with six large columns holding up the portico's roof in the grandiose staging of hexastyle architecture.

Chauncey laboriously ascended the stairs. Each step increased his agony. The acidic odor of bleach and pine-scented disinfectant cleaner slammed into his nostrils as soon as he stepped into the cool, dimly lit lobby. Nausea overwhelmed him.

Slowly turning his body instead of his head to avoid worsening his headache, he surveyed his surroundings.

"Chauncey, you have to keep up with the group. Do the best you can. I'll meet you after you're showered. Make sure you work lots of soap into those wounds to get the dirt out, then I'll bind the cuts so you don't bleed all over your clean clothes," William said with concern in his otherwise deep, rough voice. He had obviously volunteered to be Chauncey's guardian angel while he was healing and unable to fend for himself.

He managed to shower but thoroughly cleansing himself was difficult considering the limited range of motion of his joints. While removing his clothes, he found cuts and abrasions over his entire body. He was shocked to find a ten-inch laceration running from the top of his left thigh to the knee. He gently worked the scant bubbles of the cheap, harsh brown soap he had been given into his wounds and obediently scrubbed lightly in all directions.

After the soap washed the grime away, stark light radiating from the bare bulbs illuminating the shower area caused shards of glass embedded in his palms and knees to sparkle like diamonds. He carefully plucked the fragments with his fingernails then tossed the shimmering slivers of variously colored glass into a dark green plastic trash can in the lavatory area adjacent to the showers.

After dressing in newly laundered but detergent-stiffened clothing Chauncey shuffled bewilderedly down the starkly lit hallway to the dining area.

He was glad the men moved down the hallway as a group. Being able to concentrate on the back of the man in front of him helped steady his faltering gait.

The dining hall had tables set end-to-end forming long lines from one side of the huge room to the other. Lines of chairs were neatly arranged on either side of the tables; six chairs per ten-foot table giving each man approximately three feet of table space. Such spacing had been closely analyzed by the mission director and was found to reduce the number of fights triggered by territorial instincts.

White lines painted on the floor assured the tables were in their correct place. This attention to detail guaranteed that six-foot aisles between tables were maintained. Guests bumping into each other or jostling another's chair as they carried their tray of food to a place at the table was a major precipitator of vicious, often-bloody fights.

A tall, thin, slightly balding man in his mid-thirties stood on a small riser at one end of the dining hall observing the men as they filed into the room. Trustees of the mission, usually bent and shuffling old men who were allowed to remain year-round as resident workers, offered guidance to seat the men systematically so they took the next available seat at the table.

Because of the orderly manner in which the men filed into the dining hall they were all seated within minutes waiting impatiently for the Reverend John Yates to begin his sermon and the food to follow. Tantalizing smells wafted from the kitchen causing the famished men to salivate.

Reverend Yates didn't hold anything back. He sermonized on every topic affecting the homeless men's lives. Some men paid token attention to his moralizing while others sat in bored silence. Most were staring at nothing in particular with a blank expression on their weathered faces.

And then there was Chauncey.

He found the words of John Yates absolutely fascinating. The concept of Heaven and Hell placed the four hours of the life he could remember into a workable framework. He now had a template to begin forming his future around.

Chauncey did not look upon the message as pontification but rather as personal counseling. The impact on him was so significant that when he sat with his food in front of him he could only pick at it because he was so deep in thought and introspection.

From the moment he first picked up his tray he had problems holding it. His hands had few areas not sliced or inflamed by cuts. He obviously had missed a number of glass splinters because touching those areas sent a nauseating bolt of pain shooting from his hand into his arm. He was relieved when he was finally able to send the tray down the conveyor belt to the dishwashing area without dropping it.

In the recreation area Chauncey gingerly set himself at the end of a light tan naugahyde couch smeared with smudges of filth embedded so deeply they could never be wiped away. A strategically placed lamp saturated the arm of the couch with a flood of light bright enough to read by.

The short-cropped commercial-grade carpet beneath his feet may have come from the factory with a mottling of dark-hued colors to cover up stains but the huge smattering of blotches contaminating the floor covering gave it an unintended camouflage appearance.

The instant Chauncey tentatively picked up a dog-eared magazine with his damaged fingers from the scarred end table abutting the couch, his eyes began devouring the words from the front page to the back. Feature articles, advertisements, and every sidebar were read word for word in a frenzied quest for knowledge. Neither the type of magazine nor the topic of the article mattered to him. He only wanted to absorb the thoughts and ideas conveyed in the writing.

Chauncey was so consumed by his passion that he did not notice the towering figure of William Collonem standing in the doorway with Reverend John Yates.

"Where did you pick him up?" the reverend asked in a low, conversational tone so the men didn't overhear him. In reality, it would have been nearly impossible to yell over the clamor of the television set or the ruckus rising from around the ping-pong table.

"Over by the old library on Mulberry," William replied as he continued his vigil of Chauncey.

"And he claims to not know his name or anything else?"

"That's the story I got."

"He sure gobbles up everything he can read. Has he paid any attention at all to the TV?"

"None. Few of these guys even touch those magazines unless it's to kill a fly that's bothering them."

Reverend Yates smiled knowingly.

"Maybe he's telling the truth, and that's why he wants to learn as much as he can. You don't think he's an extraterrestrial who needs to learn everything about us before launching an intergalactic invasion, do you?"

William chuckled softly.

"I don't know what to think about him. But I'm going to make sure Doc Reynolds sees him tomorrow. The poor guy is really hurting; and it's not just his hands."

"If you can, speak with the good doctor before he sees Chauncey. I would like to get his opinion of the man's mental condition. Keep an eye on him if you would, eh William?"

"You know I will," was all William was able to say before Reverend Yates disappeared down the hallway on the way to his office.

CHAPTER 7

DOCTOR REYNOLDS

"So what do you think, Doc?" William asked as soon as Chauncey had left the room.

"I'm not sure what to think about his mental condition if that's what you're asking. Physically, he's a mess. I removed the rest of the glass splinters from his hands and knees the best I could. There may still be some imbedded in there but it'll have to work its way out. I gave him some antibiotic ointment to apply to the wounds and he'll need to keep bandages over them for a few days until the skin begins to scab over. After that he should be OK as far as his cuts are concerned."

Doctor Reynolds looked directly into William's eyes.

"His musculo-skeletal complaints are something else all together. It looks like he took a pretty savage beating the best I can tell. He has bruises all over. Did you know he had a cut between his shoulder blades? That's not the type of wound a man can inflict upon himself. It wasn't very deep so I just put a few butterfly bandages on it instead of stitching it up. He told me he's grateful for the aspirins and extra blanket you gave him last night."

"Yeah, I saw him tossing and turning all curled up in a ball. I figured he was chilled through from lying on the sidewalk out there. I've seen it before," William replied.

"I'm sure you have. Did he tell you about the nightmares he had? He has crazy dreams about people shooting at him and babies in the hospital with tubes running in and out of them. The part about the numbers was pretty strange also."

"No, he didn't tell me about any of that. What was so strange about the numbers?"

"It almost sounded like phone numbers but it was all jumbled up. He seemed to get very agitated when he was telling me about the numbers. I guess it's like those dreams where you're trying to run away but can't."

"Could you make anything out of his dreams?"

"No, he couldn't remember specifics. You know how that goes. Is there anything that stands out about him in your estimation?"

"Well, he seems confused but that's not unusual for these guys. His mind seems to wander quite a bit also. Once again, not too unusual for our guests here at the mission."

"So you finally decided to use some of the psychology they taught you in college?" Doctor Reynolds asked chidingly referring to William's near-useless degree.

"Yeah, I guess so," William replied good-naturedly. "What do you think about those headaches he complains about?"

"They appear to be migraines; or at least a pretty severe tension headache. The headaches may be related to his neck and upper back pain. I know a pretty good chiropractor, Sarah Collins, who operates a clinic over in Northwest. She's a good friend and her husband's an orthopedist on staff at the hospital with me. She may be willing to take on a charity case if I ask her to. I'll give her a call."

"Thanks doc, I appreciate that."

"I know you do William. Sometimes it seems as though you've adopted these men to take the place of the family you lost."

As soon as he said it, he knew he shouldn't have. The sudden downward casting of William's eyes and the sagging of his shoulders verified he had said the wrong thing.

"I'm sorry William…"

"It's OK doc. Thanks for your help, I'll see you next Tuesday."

Not knowing what to say, Doctor Reynolds muttered, "Yeah, see you then," before turning and walking down the deserted hallway.

William spun around and yelled after him, "I'll keep Chauncey around here for a few days to let him heal up a little. Call me as soon as you can with that chiropractor's number, OK doc?

"Good idea. You'll be hearing from me," he replied without breaking stride.

CHAPTER 8

CHAUNCEY'S TALENTS

"Chauncey, I need you to stand here and check the boxes from this shipment as they come off the truck. We want to be sure we're getting everything we paid for. Can you do that?" William asked as he held out a dark brown clipboard and yellow #2 lead pencil.

"Yes I can," Chauncey replied with an eager-to-please tone in his voice.

"The mission usually has enough food donated to feed the men we take in nightly as guests," William explained. "But cleaning supplies and paper products have to be purchased from a supplier with monetary donations."

As instructed, Chauncey diligently checked off each box as it came off the large, white-sided delivery truck. Tyrone and Samuel, two of the mission's trustees, kept two hand trucks busy off-loading the delivery van; slowing only enough to allow Chauncey an opportunity to see what they were taking to the mission's storage room in the basement.

After the last of the boxes were off-loaded and stored in the basement of the mission, William returned and silently gestured with his hand for Chauncey to give him the checklist.

"Everything there, Chauncey?" he inquired cheerfully. William loved seeing the men work cooperatively. He knew it was good for them and offered them the best chance of becoming productive members of society.

"Yes, everything's there but the numbers don't add up," Chauncey said as winced from a jolt of pain that shot down his arm when he handed the clipboard to William.

William pretended not to notice him flinching.

"The boxes are all there but the numbers don't add up correctly? What doesn't add up? Aren't all the boxes there?"

"The numbers on this side of the paper," Chauncey explained, pointing to the right hand column where the charges for the items were listed.

"What doesn't add up?"

"We ordered three cases of toilet paper and we received three but they're charging the mission for four," Chauncey said as he pointed to the discrepancy with one of his undamaged fingers. "Everything else is OK."

"We'll get this straightened out with the cleaning supply office. The driver doesn't have a clue about this stuff. He only drives the truck," William confidently proclaimed while looking askance at Chauncy.

"Has this ever happened before?" Chauncy asked skeptically.

"I don't know. And I bet John doesn't know either. He's so absorbed with the day-to-day operations of the mission he usually doesn't have time to sort through paperwork with a fine-toothed comb."

William looked thoughtfully at the invoice in his hand, and then glanced at Chauncey with a sly look in his eye.

"Hey Tyrone! Can you handle it from here?" William asked the trustee who had just emerged from the basement.

"Sure, we only have to break down these boxes and put the stuff where it belongs," he answered matter-of-factly.

"Come on Chauncey, let's see if the good reverend has a minute to spare."

William knocked loudly on the wooden door to John Yates's office. It had obviously been covered with innumerable coats of variously shaded paint; each of which showed through assorted nicks and gouges on its battered exterior.

"Come in," John said in a calm, even voice that flowed like a comforting mist from behind the closed door.

"John, I have something for you to see if you have a minute," William boomed as he opened the door and sauntered into the room.

Chauncey followed William into the sparsely furnished office. At first glance, the office looked clean and well organized. Closer scrutiny revealed that it was only clean. Boxes holding piles of loose papers were neatly tucked beneath every table and desk in the office. Chauncey suspected that a door on the back wall of the office led into a closet holding more of the mission's neglected paperwork.

"John, would you please look at this invoice from the cleaning supply company?" William asked as he held the paper out to Reverend Yates. "Do you see anything not quite right about it?"

John took the invoice from William with a quizzed look in his eye; then he scanned it from top to bottom. "What's your concern? It looks pretty much like the one we get from them every week."

"Chauncey noticed that we were charged for four cases of toilet paper but we only received three. He asked whether this type of mistake happens often. I think it's a fair question and should be answered."

John's disgusted look told William he did not want to be bothered by trivial oversights. Without saying a word, he reached beneath the computer desk and pulled out a cardboard storage box filled to the brim with loose papers.

Searching through the jumbled mess, John finally found a yellow invoice matching the one he held in his hand.

"Let's look at last week's and see."

Holding them both at arm's length, one invoice in each hand, John squinted slightly to see the squirming numbers. Disgustedly, he laid one of the invoices down to pick up his gold-rimmed reading glasses lying upside down on his food-stained desk blotter. Taking a minute to scrutinize the invoices, he deliberately laid them down side-by-side on his desk.

Without a word, he once again rummaged through the overflowing cardboard storage box in search of another invoice. Triumphantly raising one from the bowels of the clutter he earnestly searched it for discrepancies.

"Well Chauncey, it looks like you've stumbled onto something here. Each week's supply order has one item we're being charged for but did not order nor receive. There definitely seems to be a pattern," John said with disappointment in his voice.

"Chauncey, I'll handle this but I have to know how long these shenanigans have been going on. Would you be willing to go through all these bills I haven't had time to? I should have made time but I didn't," he said as his voice trailed off while his shoulders slumped noticeably in resignation.

"Of course I'll help. I don't know what I'll find let alone what I'm looking for but I'll try," Chauncey said enthusiastically.

For a split second John's furrowed brow, which seemed to be a permanent fixture chiseled on his otherwise finely featured face, was overwhelmed by a smile of relief. Trying to keep up with the avalanche of paperwork and petty bureaucratic drudgery deluging his office was the bane of his existence. He had gone to Theology College and worked diligently for his degree in counseling to help people in need, and not to shuffle papers around his desk all day.

Forgetting his problematic workload for just a second, John's true calling shone forth as he remembered to inquire about Chauncey's well-being. "How are you feeling today, Chauncey?"

"I'm hurting terribly, but thank you for asking."

"Did Doctor Reynolds call with information about his chiropractor friend?"

"Yes, I have an appointment with a Doctor Sarah Collins tomorrow evening after her regular office hours; that's when she does her charity work. It's on the bus line, and William said he'd give me bus fare. He generously offered to pick me up in the mission van when I was done. He said he might be out all night checking on the people who refused to come inside."

"Yes, William is very generous with the mission's gasoline fund," John said with a joking tone to his voice as he threw a teasing glance at William.

"Well, that settles it," he continued with a tone of finality. "William, will you find a place for Chauncey to work undisturbed? And Chauncey, please concentrate on these cleaning supply bills first. I'd really like to know how far reaching this problem is so I can rectify it immediately. Please find out if there are any others."

With those words, Chauncey became the mission's bookkeeper.

CHAPTER 9

POROUS SOUTHERN BORDER

Muhammed Shah was unimpressed with the kaleidoscope of colors bursting from the Arizona desert as the breathtaking panorama swept past the windows of the Ford Econoline van. He was more concerned with the increasing dampness in the sweaty seat of his pants as his buttocks pressed into the sweltering plastic seat.

He was an unassuming man dressed in worn blue jeans and a slightly wrinkled short-sleeved dress shirt purposefully donned to blend in with the thousands of immigrants illegally crossing into the United States from Mexico every day. His natural walnut-hued skin allowed him to mingle unobtrusively with his fellow travelers. A day-old haircut and shave from a barbershop near the Mexico City airport offered a local touch of authenticity to his new identity as Jesus Jimenez, a citizen of Mexico. A tattered, sun-bleached green and yellow John Deere cap was pulled low over his eyes to complete his disguise.

I haven't been able to get the taste of this accursed land out of my mouth since arriving here, he thought disdainfully.

For what seemed like the ten thousandth time in the last three hours, he allowed his gaze to survey the other eleven passengers crammed in the van with him.

In three days we will arrive in Baltimore and I will be done with all but three of these chattering baboons, he thought, looking upon them with condescension while his deceptive, gracious smile never wavered.

Of course, I have to remain sociable until I have what I need to complete the mission Allah has ordained for me. It was only by His Grace that I was able to arrange a meeting with infidels who work at the Aberdeen Proving Grounds in Maryland - the location of the only remaining store of mustard gas from the American's World War I.

Without warning, the gringo driver jerked the steering wheel to the left to avoid colliding with a meandering armadillo; violently slamming the sun-wrinkled man seated beside him into Muhammed's shoulder. The man looked at him and shrugged his shoulders with his palms skyward in a submissive gesture of apology for the driver's actions.

The passengers relaxed when the van resumed its monotonous trek with the familiar hum of balding tires on scorched asphalt droning endlessly in their ears.

Thank you for allowing my border crossing at Nogales to proceed without incident, Mohammed prayed silently. *You are obviously allowing me to establish your rule over the people of the United States and to punish them for their shameful ways. It is by your will that the American politicians are too stupid to close their country's borders to the couriers of their destruction.*

Ignoring the rancid flatulence wafting throughout the van from one of his ill-mannered travel companions, Muhammed suddenly felt at ease. A satisfied grin spread across his craggy face as he settled back into the cramped seat to tolerate the rest of his journey in thoughtful silence.

The foolish infidels from the American's Department of Homeland Security don't even know I am the key to their destruction. I am the chosen one, the only person who knows the identity and location of all our followers who have been secretly living in Washington, D.C. for many years.

He looked out the dirt-streaked window impassively and smiled broadly.

It is I, Muhammed Shah, who has sole discretion on how to use these human resources to demolish the infrastructure of American society.

His furrowed brow relaxed and he began to snore gently as his head slowly settled upon his chest in sleep.

CHAPTER 10

ILLEGAL IMMIGRANTS AND MUSTARD GAS

"Commander, how did you meet these people?" Abdul-Haq asked Muhammed, trying to avoid having the doubt in his heart from being heard in his voice.

"It is none of your business," Muhammed said. "But I will tell you because I want you to be familiar with the operation we are about to embark upon."

"Thank you, Commander."

"Jose Padilla, Juan Martinez, and Jorge Diaz were in the group I was with when we came across the American border with Mexico," he said while staring intently at him. "They work on a construction crew that cleans and repairs air ducts in the buildings of the Aberdeen Proving Grounds."

"And why is that important to our mission?"

"Because, you fool," Muhammed replied haughtily. "The only remaining stores of mustard gas in the United States are stored in the Edgewood area of the Aberdeen Proving Ground in Maryland. It is being stored under heavy guard until a disposal plant can be built to neutralize what remains from America's World War I."

"That war was a long time ago."

"Yes it was, but the mustard gas is still potent and the Americans want to be rid of it," Muhammed replied. "Luckily, lawsuits from environmental groups have stopped the expected completion of the disposal facility which is good for us because we have an important use for the gas."

"And what is that?"

"It is none of your business," Muhammed said menacingly. "You will be informed of your duty and nothing else."

"I'm sorry sir," Abdul-Haq stuttered. "I---"

"Never mind," Muhammed said disgustedly. "Just be thankful the Americans are inept and stupid."

"I am, Commander," he said sheepishly.

"The environmental extremists have aided us for many years," Muhammed said with a tone of superiority in his voice, eager to flaunt his knowledge. "First these groups complained about the proximity of schools and communities to the proposed disposal plant so the government fitted the schools in the area with overpressurization devices to protect students and staff in the event of a catastrophic fire or explosion during incineration."

"That must have taken much money and a long time to complete."

"The Americans have too much money and they waste it," Muhammed said disgustedly. "The schools were protected and the local community was prepared for such an occurrence by undergoing training, planning sessions, installing additional emergency equipment, and other programs which were put in place to assure that no tragedy would occur during disposal of the gas. The news reports were very clear in explaining all the details."

"The fools," Abdul-Haq said heartily to ingratiate himself with his commander.

Without responding to Abdul-Haq's comments, Muhammed continued, "A disposal plant is the only way to neutralize the gas that would be acceptable to the American public but the environmental groups continued filing lawsuits to delay its construction."

"You are very knowledgeable."

"It was through the reporting of these lawsuits in the newspapers that I learned everything we need to know about where and how the mustard gas at Aberdeen is stored.

"And what role will these Mexicans play in your plan?" Abdul-Haq asked then immediately realized he had once again voiced a question he should not have. "I'm sorry sir---"

"Do not worry," Muhammed said. "Quite simply, they are our burglars."

"I am sorry, sir, but it sounded like you said they are our burglars."

"That's exactly what I said," Muhammed said as he puffed his chest out proudly. "I have promised each of them five thousand dollars to steal canisters of mustard gas from Aberdeen Proving Grounds for us."

CHAPTER 11

STEALING MUSTARD GAS

Muhammed, Abdul-Haq, Jamaal, and Hamza were standing idly in the empty interior of a dimly lit garage on a seedy side street in Dundalk, Maryland that Jamaal had rented under an assumed name. A solitary, bare bulb hung from a beam in the center of the vast, unused space illuminating the grease stained concrete floor with an eerie, anemic glow. The bare concrete block walls emitted a bone-chilling dampness even though it was late spring. Gasoline odor permeated from the pores of the decrepit concrete and made Muhammed nauseous.

Taking a deep breath in an attempt to calm his rebellious stomach, Muhammed strode to the center of the group.

"Now that we have gathered I want to explain what is to transpire tonight and why you will be doing the work Allah has ordained for you," Muhammed said commandingly.

"We have waited years for you to gather us together and reveal our destiny to us," Hamza said respectfully.

"Yes, it was important to keep each of your identities secret; even from each other," Muhammed responded. "It was necessary so you would not be able to identify your colleagues in case you were captured by the infidels and questioned. I alone have been entrusted with that information and am the key to open the secret of your years of hardship."

"Praise be to Allah that you have been sent to unite us to do his bidding," Abdul-Haq said. "Living with the infidels and their decadent ways has tested our faith many times."

"I am sure," Muhammed said as he raised his chin to signal his superior rank. "Now it is time to divulge the reason for us being here."

The three men attentively looked at him.

"The tools we need to accomplish our mission have been delivered," Muhammed said expansively. "We are here tonight to assure we are the only ones who are aware of that fact."

The three men stood silently and stared intently at Muhammed. He made them wait in silence for a few moments to underscore the privilege his superior rank afforded him.

"The plan involving the Mexicans was quite simple," Muhammed explained. "The only question was whether these infidels could fool the security people at Aberdeen."

"Commander, was it possible for these Mexicans to just walk out of the Aberdeen Proving Grounds with canisters of mustard gas? They are not very sophisticated or educated."

"Of course not you fool!" Muhammed sputtered angrily. "They work in an unsecured section of the same building where the mustard gas is kept. Unguarded air ducts connect the secured and unsecured areas of the building."

"And they can gain access to the secured area?"

"The plan was very simple," Muhammed continued without acknowledging the question. "They simply unscrewed the steel mesh grate blocking access between the heating systems of both areas."

"And do they know what they have stolen?" Abdul-Haq asked innocently.

"Do you think I am a fool?" Muhammed spat. "They only knew they were to take the cylinders that look like propane tanks painted with yellow and red stripes."

"Were they sure those are the cylinders containing the mustard gas?"

"The newspaper had a picture of the cylinders in the article about the environmental group's lawsuit to halt construction of the disposal facility."

"Surely the cylinders were big and heavy," Hamza said. "How did they get them past the guards?"

"It was simplicity itself," Muhammed replied. "They use crawlers, similar to those used by mechanics to work beneath automobiles, to haul tools and cleaning equipment through the air ducts. It was a simple task to load the mustard gas cylinders onto the crawlers and roll them past the steel mesh barrier."

"But weren't they seen removing the distinctively painted cylinders from the air ducts?"

"After reaching the area of the building they are authorized to be in, they spray painted the cylinders to match the other equipment used to clean the air ducts."

"Excuse me for being so inquisitive, Commander," Hamza asked sheepishly. "But didn't the scent of spray paint alert the guards or other people in the building?"

"It is a very good question Hamza and one that I too thought of. It is very good you are inquisitive; you will be a valuable asset," Muhammed replied with an obvious tone of approval in his voice as he looked disapprovingly at the other two men for not being as insightful.

"The workers used large fans to vent air from the ducts to the outside; they are normally used to stop fumes from chemicals used to kill mold and sanitize the ducts from sickening the building's occupants."

"It is a brilliant plan, Commander," Jamaal said in an attempt to ingratiate himself with his superior.

"Simplicity leads to brilliance," Muhammed agreed as he mentally congratulated himself for developing such a plan. "At the end of the day the workers simply hid the newly-painted cylinders beneath the rest of the equipment in their truck."

"Were they not stopped and searched as they left?"

"The canisters blended in with the other equipment they use every day in their labors."

"How many of the gas cylinders did they steal?"

"Ten in total but they only stole two per day otherwise they would have obviously been leaving at the end of the day with more equipment than they arrived with in the morning."

"Wouldn't the guards inspect the steel mesh grate and see that it had been removed?"

"After the workers replaced the grate, the duct surrounding it was painted. Painting is one of the contracted services for which they have been hired," Muhammed said smiling. "It looked the way it was supposed to appear after it had been cleaned, repaired and re-painted."

"And when are we to receive the mustard gas?"

"I already have it in my possession," Muhammed replied with a large smile on his face. "Each day they left the cylinders in the garage of a deserted house owned by our supporters. I picked up the cylinders after they left. They never saw anyone."

"So what are we going to do when we meet them here in half an hour?" Hamza asked innocently. "Pay them for their thefts?"

"No you fool," Muhammed said. "We are going to kill them."

"Won't someone miss them and ask questions about us?" Abdul-Haq asked with a trace of uncertainty in his eyes. "Surely they will have told someone about their theft, the money they expect to be paid, and about you."

"Yes, they may have told the people they live with. Their wives and children live with other illegal aliens in a rented house in Aberdeen," Muhammed said with a wicked grin. "I have already dispatched four men from another cell of true believers to kill everyone in that house then burn it to help hide the identities of the corpses. The authorities will suspect they are drug-related murders."

"And what would lead them to think the murders are drug related, Commander?"

"Because our men will leave a small amount of cocaine and heroin hidden in their vehicles parked in the driveway," Muhammed grinned, very proud of his clever plan.

"Will the authorities dig deeper for more information on the residents of the house?"

"No, they will have no identification in this country," Muhammed said. "They are illegal aliens living in the shadows of society. They have no documented job, do not pay taxes, and do not have their names on anything, not even an automobile. They do not exist."

"They will kill the children also?"

"They are infidels, Hamza," Muhammed said with deadly malice in his voice. "Are you unwilling to do what is necessary to complete our mission?"

"No sir," Hamza said with conviction. "It is Allah's will."

"Commander," Jamaal asked hesitantly. "Do you have plans for the mustard gas?"

"Yes Jamaal," Muhammed said quietly. "I have formulated a plan to use it on thousands of infidels at a Christian festival known as the Hallelujah Gathering. Of course, none of you will be participating in that operation. It is not what you were trained for."

"Praise be to Allah," the three men said in unison.

CHAPTER 12

SARAH COLLINS

The petite but athletically built thirty-four year old director of the District Spinal Care Clinic deftly flicked a wisp of her short-styled auburn hair from her eyes and forced a smile onto her face to energize her fatigued mind. After all, her day was winding down and she had a relaxing evening scheduled with her husband.

When she entered the room the tall, handsome, middle-aged African-American man lounging in one of the two chairs in the treatment room was casually studying the anatomical charts prominently displayed on the pink walls of the room.

"Well Chauncey, you've been under our care for four months now and it's time for a re-examination," she greeted her favorite patient as she bustled into the exam room.

After poising her pen over a clipboard, she began firing questions at him in rapid succession while writing furiously.

"How are your migraine headaches these days?"

"I haven't had one in about two months, thank God," Chauncey said with relief in his voice. "I didn't realize how much they hurt my ability to concentrate and work until they disappeared."

Sarah always marveled at how well this previously homeless man spoke. His diction was far above most of her other patients. As a matter of fact, he spoke more eloquently than most people she knew.

"I'm glad you can concentrate again," Sarah said with a smile, "especially since you're my bookkeeper now."

"I agree," Chauncey said as he returned her smile. "But you have to remember I was initially hired as a handyman so it wasn't as important to be headache-free for the first two months of my job."

"That may be true," she said. "But I'm always happy to see someone make progress and be relieved of horrendous symptoms like you had."

"And I'm very glad you were here to help me," Chauncey replied. "But I still feel funny about you treating me for free."

"Chauncey, all of my employees and their immediate families get chiropractic care for free as a benefit of the job," Sarah said. "And it's not all unselfish."

"What do you mean?"

"I mean that chiropractic is preventive health care," she replied evenly as she looked directly into his eyes. "It means my employees will not get sick as often and they'll be healthier while on the job and I like healthy, productive employees."

Chauncey smiled at his boss to return her broad grin. His admiration for Dr. Collins went beyond the normal employer/employee relationship because she had faith in him and gave him a chance when no one else would.

"Are there any areas of pain you're still having?"

"No, except for that stiffness between my shoulder blades," Chauncey continued. "I still wake up with a lot of stiffness in my upper back every morning but it loosens up in a half-hour or so."

"If you jump into a steaming, hot shower as soon as you get up, and let the warm water beat on that area, does it help you get moving faster?" she asked while continuing to write without looking up.

"Yes it does. And it stiffens up again just before bedtime."

"That's called the arthritic profile," she said. "You have some degeneration in that area, that's the type of wear-and-tear called osteo-arthritis, and you'll probably fight that battle for the rest of your life."

Chauncey nodded his understanding without saying a word, his face exhibiting no emotion at hearing the bad news.

"Just remember that seeing me for treatments will help to stop or at least slow down the degeneration as well as keep you moving with less stiffness and pain," she continued as a perky smile spread across the smooth, unblemished skin of her face. "I guess you'll have to work for me forever so we can keep you as healthy as possible."

Chauncey was amazed at how her entire face seemed to beam wholesomeness when she smiled.

"How about the shooting pains down your right arm?" she asked.

"They've been gone for about two months also," Chauncey replied. "Well, not totally gone. Occasionally it still flares up a little but an adjustment usually takes care of it. Will it ever go away totally?"

"Maybe, maybe not," she replied noncommittally. "Life in general, and gravity in particular, are constantly beating up on you. The areas still giving you trouble, especially if they recur on occasion, will probably plague you for the rest of your life. Once again, regular care will help keep it under control as much as possible. That's the best that can be hoped for," she explained in a calm, matter-of-fact voice.

"How's your new apartment working for you?" she asked to avoid having him dwell on bad news.

"It's great," he replied. "The mission was terrific in helping me get a place of my own. They fed and housed me until I could take care of my health problems- thanks to you- then helped me get this job. But I'm glad to be able to leave there. Having some privacy is really nice."

"Do you see William anymore? You two were pretty close."

"Oh yes! He comes over for lunch on Tuesdays and Thursdays," Chauncey replied, warming to the conversation. "He insists on bringing food, but it's not necessary."

"He's a very proud man," Sarah said. "He's just trying to be friendly without being a burden."

"Reverend Yates joins us when he can," Chauncey continued, thinking on what she said about William as he spoke. "I think they're both glad for an opportunity to escape from the pressures of the mission for a while."

"It's nice you have time to visit with your friends," she said.

"What's nice is having my apartment and this office only a few blocks away from each other so I can go home for lunch," Chauncey said. To change the subject he asked, "You have a big night tonight, don't you?"

"Yes, one of Josh's partners in their orthopedic practice is retiring and they're having a big party downtown," she replied. "The dinner is a dual celebration because they'll be officially welcoming Josh into the practice as a full partner. He signed all the papers and made everything legal and binding last week so now he has full partner benefits.

"And it's a personal celebration for Josh and I because the house we have been rehabilitating for the last two years is finally finished. I am so glad to have all the workers out of my house. Maybe now I can have some peace and quiet."

"You must be very proud of him."

"I am proud of him. As a matter of fact, he's waiting in the parking lot for me to finish so why don't we concentrate on getting you examined?" she asked, flashing a twinkling smile as she spoke.

Chauncey returned her smile, hoping that someday he would find a woman his own age as nice as Sarah.

Chapter 13

JOSHUA TOBIN, M.D.

Joshua Tobin, Sarah's loving husband, settled onto the plush leather seat of his BMW 550i. He knew she wouldn't leave her office until after the last patient had been treated.

I hope those are her last patients, Josh thoughtfully mused as he watched three well-dressed young men walk out of Sarah's office door before settling onto the tanned leather of his car seat to dream of a bright future.

It's been a long day and it's going to be a long night. Sarah can wake me when she's ready, he thought as he settled deeper into the comforting confines of the caressing leather and closed his eyes.

One of the men walking nearby, Tobias Masterson, was an eighteen year old patient of Sarah's who was recovering from an auto collision he had been involved in three weeks earlier. The other two men, Marias Phillips and Rolondo Hammon, were also eighteen years old and had grown up with Tobias.

The three men were almost inseparable growing up. They were cousins but looked so much alike they could easily be mistaken for brothers and often were. Each of them was almost six feet tall and weighed close to 200 pounds with closely cropped hair adorning the tops of their rounded heads. The various gold accoutrements each wore around their necks, pierced through their earlobes, or capping their front teeth were often the only distinguishing features to easily tell one from the other. Usually, if you saw one of the three, the other two were not far away.

The three cousins had a lot in common including long rap sheets for crimes ranging from simple theft to assault and battery. They almost always committed their crimes as a gang of three.

While growing up in their neighborhood, it was common knowledge that if someone started trouble with any one of the cousins they would assuredly have all three to contend with. The men were not overly well endowed with intelligence, but they were always willing to stand up for each other and that attribute alone was what had gotten them through scrapes with the law or other street thugs.

As they left Sarah's office that evening the three street-wise young men had only one thing on their minds.

A gorgeous, well-endowed girl had invited them to a graduation party in Chevy Chase. Her skin was as smooth and velvety as a rose petal and glowed like a piece of freshly unwrapped Godiva chocolate. The contrast of her luscious skin against the brilliant glow of a taut fitting white halter-top still haunted their daydreams.

"How the hell we supposed to get to this party?" Marias asked pensively. "Chevy Chase is way the hell on the other side of town."

"We need us a ride, Dawg," Rolondo pointed out before exiting the front door of Sarah's office. "He's right, Chevy Chase is way on the other side of the beltway and it ain't right for us to show up there on foot."

"That ain't right for sure, Home," Marias replied. "What if we meet the girl of our dreams? It ain't right to take a lady home on the Metro."

The three threw their heads back in unison as they laughed uproariously at Marias's sarcastic joke. In the back of their minds, however, they knew he was right.

"It ain't right, for sure," Rolondo intoned solemnly.

"We could have gone with Harold if Tobias didn't have to get his neck fixed," Marias suddenly added with irritation in his voice.

Tobias, angered by Marias's comments retorted, "Listen man, my neck hurts pretty bad. If it was you, you'd be cryin'. Besides, my lawyer said if I don't keep all my appointments, I won't get no money. You want that man? You want me to not get any money?"

"You been there every day you supposed to be, for sure," Marias said. "But you ain't ever been there on time. I heard that bitch at the front desk yellin' at you."

"She wasn't yellin' at me," Tobias replied jokingly. "She in love with me and want me bad, Man."

The three cousins burst into laughter once again.

"Besides, it don't matter none. My lawyer say I only have to be there, he didn't say when."

"If you had the damned money we'd have a ride, right?" Marias asked in a conciliatory tone.

"Yeah Dawg, we'd have a ride," Tobias replied in a manner accepting of Marias's peace offering.

Suddenly Tobias stopped in his tracks, his gaze focused across the parking lot on a shiny new metallic dark blue BMW 550i sedan. "There's our ride, Homes," he said as a broad smile broke across his lips revealing a mouth full of pearly white, evenly spaced teeth.

No spoken word was necessary. They had performed carjackings many times as a well-organized team and each knew the roles that had to be taken.

"I'm taking the passenger side because of my neck. It's the easiest and I don't want to be in pain at the party," Tobias announced with finality.

"So where do I go?" Rolondo asked hesitantly. "I don't want to pull open the driver's door. I always take the passenger side."

"Well, today you're taking the driver's door and you damned well better pull it plenty hard, I don't want Marias not being able to get him out of the friggin seat."

"Why doesn't Marias take the driver's door? He can handle it fine," Rolondo whined as he looked pleadingly at Marias.

"I always take the back. I like to pull them out and throw their sorry ass on the ground," Marias stated matter-of-factly. "And I'm good at it," he added with an obvious hint of pride in his voice as he puffed out his chest and shifted his weight to appear slightly taller.

"Just do what I tell you," Tobias said with venom in his voice. "Or don't you want to get to that party tonight?"

"Damned!" Rolondo muttered dejectedly. "Let's do it," he grumbled as he stepped in the direction of the 550i with a sauntering gait.

"Make sure there's nobody around. I don't want any witnesses screwin' things up," Tobias needlessly reminded his cohorts.

They knew he was a perfectionist and expected him to worry about details they considered unnecessary. He had shown signs of Obsessive-Compulsive Disorder since he was six years old and they surely didn't expect him to change now.

"It looks good and deserted," Marias crooned contentedly, more to console Tobias than to make a strategic observation.

"Look at that dumb-shit," Tobias said with a smile. "He just sleepin' like a baby. Not a care in the world."

Josh Tobin was totally unaware of what was going to happen to him in the next few seconds. In the end it did not matter; he was not a man of violence. All his life he had depended on others for his personal protection. He had always been able to live in the best neighborhoods with low crime rates and frequent police patrols. When the three hardened young men mentally checked off items during the victim selection process, they could have not done better than choosing a person like Josh Tobin. It was victims like Josh who made it easy for criminals to overcome them.

He was almost always oblivious to things happening in his immediate environment. Tonight was no different. He was only vaguely aware of Marias Phillips walking past his car. Only when Rolondo, following Marias by a few steps, yanked the driver's door open did it shock him from the murky depths of his nap.

"What the hell--" He began to sputter feebly, but was silenced at the sight of the deeply blued Smith and Wesson Model 19 .357 magnum revolver in Marias's tightly clenched fist. It's heavy, blunt faced barrel gave it a sinister appearance similar to the truncated snout of a venomous snake. The revolver, famed as the choice of lawmen for over two decades, had been in the possession of Tom McAdams, the sheriff of Prairie County, Illinois only three weeks previously.

No other possessions from Sheriff McAdams's burgled rural home had traveled to Washington, D.C.; however, the huge black market price fetched in areas where guns, especially handguns, were outlawed made it very profitable for the burglars to transport stolen firearms great distances.

Josh's vision could barely follow the blur of fluid motion as Marias's gnarly left hand grabbed a fist-full of his carefully coiffed blonde hair and jerked him out of the car headfirst.

"Give it up! Give it up!" Marias yelled in a commanding voice with his spittle-flecked mouth only inches from Josh's left ear.

Josh was so confused by the swift, savage attack that he did not understand what he was supposed to be giving up. The surprise attack had worked too well; the victim was completely disoriented and incapable of cooperating even though he was more than willing to do so.

As soon as Tobias saw Marias pull Josh from the car, he ripped opened the passenger door with his right hand and sprang into the passenger seat. Even before his buttocks hit the leather seat his eyes locked on the ignition switch. "I got the key! I got the key!" he chanted gleefully over and over again in a crazed fit of joy.

Marias was too engrossed in humiliating Josh to hear Tobias's gleeful gibberish.

Josh's buff tan calfskin wallet was jammed in the cup holder of the console between the two unblemished, leather bucket seats and it immediately caught Tobias's attention. Grabbing the wallet in his left hand, he began thumbing through it with his right, stuffing wrinkled, green cash and credit cards into the depths of his right front pants pocket. Tobias was too engrossed in pillaging his newly found treasure to pay attention to what was going on outside the car; he then tossed the empty wallet under the front seat.

"I got the money! Let's go!" Tobias yelled to his cohorts but Marias could not hear him because he was too engrossed with manhandling Josh.

"Give it up! Give it up Mutha Fucker!" Marias continued to bellow in a maniacal attempt to coerce Josh into handing over his wallet. His frenzied, shrieking voice rose in volume and shrillness with each repeated stanza.

Josh, in a surreal daze, was trying to comprehend what was happening to him. His mind reeled as he worked feverishly to grasp the reality of the situation and find a way out of it. In the protected cocoon of his sheltered life, he had incorrectly been taught that criminals were nothing more than fully-grown, misunderstood children who had not been treated correctly or fairly during the formative years of their childhood.

Marias was far from being a misunderstood child. Rather, he was a consummate life-long criminal who resorted to bursts of unrelenting violence to get his way.

Incorrectly assuming he could take control of the situation by acting like an understanding parent speaking to a misbehaving child Josh attempted to stand up and look Marias in the eyes.

"Don't look at me Mutha Fucka! What the matter wiff you!" Marias yelled insanely as a spritz of spittle flew from his mouth.

The situation escalated to lethal proportions. His lack of respect for Josh as a worthwhile human plummeted immensely while his disgust rose precipitously.

"Give me your money, Mutha Fucker!" Marias yelled.

They only want money.

Josh's befuddled mind was finally able to comprehend a portion of what was transpiring around him.

All I have to do is give them money and they'll leave me alone.

"What the matter wiff you Mutha Fucka?" Marias shrieked shrilly, his voice on the verge of being incomprehensible from rage as his clenched right fist, still clasping the blued steel Model 19, smashed into the fleshy tip of Josh's nose.

Josh slumped to his knees. If it had not been for Marias's unrelenting grasp of his hair he would have fallen to the ground in a crumpled heap.

Josh's mind wandered wildly as warm, sticky rivulets of blood coursed down his face. His ability to think rationally was diminishing rapidly and his once brilliant mind was now powerless to comprehend the scope of his swiftly deteriorating situation.

Still using his left hand full of Josh's hair, Marias tried unsuccessfully to lift him and force him backward toward the rear of the BMW, its dark blue metallic paint now splattered with variously sized droplets of Josh's blood.

"Get him between the car and those bushes," Rolondo excitedly instructed from his vantage point at the driver's door. "We don't want anyone seein' him like that and gettin' us in trouble."

"This fuck's too heavy."

"Lift him up, Dumbshit."

Marias savagely jerked Josh to a partial standing position making it easier to forcefully walk him backwards toward the brushy fencerow separating Sarah's parking lot from the pharmacy's lot next door.

Josh, his mind feeling like a piece of driftwood tossed mercilessly in an effervescent, storm-tossed sea, stumbled backward as he tried to regain his feet.

I can talk to these guys---I know I can, he thought desperately.

Pain induced nausea tore at the lining of his stomach and threatened to progress to vomiting with each passing second. Even with Marias lifting him by the hair of his head he was not able to stand vertically. His knees stubbornly refused to fully extend. A slight bend at his waist caused him to bear his weight precariously on the balls of his feet.

This time, when he began to speak, the blood dripping across his lips sprayed onto the front of Marias's pale pink silk shirt.

Marias went ballistic.

"What the fuck a'matter wiff you Mutha Fucker? What the fuck you do? What the fuck you DO? This my new shirt, you shit! I jus' got it today! What the fuck'm I gonna wear ta the party now?"

In his semi-conscious state, it appeared to Josh that Marias actually wanted an answer.

Suddenly a not-so-brilliant flash of intuition careened into Josh's befuddled mind.

If I buy this guy a new shirt, he'll leave me alone!

Marias released his grip on Josh, allowing him to fall heavily to his knees.

"I can buy you a new shirt -- and pants too, I have lots of money!" Josh said in a garbled voice as his head sagged toward his chest, suddenly feeling much too heavy to hold up.

Mustering the last of his strength he laboriously raised his eyes and looked at Marias with a sheepish, boyish grin spreading slowly across his puffy bloodied lips. With his neck craned back his head began bobbing side-to-side like an animated bobble-head doll as he tried to keep his assailant in focus through the watery mirage dancing before his eyes.

Smiling through blood-drenched teeth because he was sure he had hit upon a solution to his dilemma; he fought to focus his eyes on Marias. What he saw made him stop his friendly, disassociated chatter and stare in disbelief.

There stood Marias as if in a fencer's stance, pointing the Model 19 single-handedly at Josh's chest. For Josh, time seemed to slow to a near-standstill. He vividly saw the leisurely contraction of the muscles in Marias's trigger finger and the slow but steady blanching of the skin over his knuckles.

His mind snapped back to reality and he made a final, desperate move to save himself by throwing his body wildly to the right.

It was a valiant but futile effort on his part because all he accomplished was to redirect the 125-grain Federal hollow-point bullet to strike below his left clavicle instead of dead center in his chest. The bullet plowed through the second rib on the left side, shattering it into multiple sharp bony fragments that began ripping an ever-widening swath of devastation through his chest cavity. The gilding metal covering of the bullet peeled back from the soft lead core, increasing its destructive path.

The energy from the speeding projectile propelled the now-jagged edges of the disrupted metal and bone fragments through the rubbery, pulsating walls of his aorta. The tattered remains began fluttering like the tail of a kite in a high wind with each powerful beat of his heart. Life-sustaining oxygenated blood, now liberated from the guiding confines of the artery, began dumping into the depths of his thoracic cavity.

His blood pressure began plunging rapidly toward zero because the bright red blood now lay useless in a pool instead of being pumped to his brain to deliver its life-giving cargo of oxygen.

In a surreal bastardization of reality Josh did not feel the impact of the bullet.

A massive gushing sensation of warmth spread gently throughout his chest filling him with a sense of well-being and contentment. Quickly, a searing stab of pain between his shoulder blades replaced the rush of warm, pleasant comfort as his body acknowledged the disruption of major blood vessels. The flash of scorching pain instantly segued into a growing sense of serenity. With dissociated interest he realized he was falling forward.

Small gray stones covering the parking lot stood out vividly on the black background of the asphalt and fixed Josh's undivided attention. The visual clarity of the diminutive rocks increased with each millisecond as he focused his attention with laser-like intensity on each and every one of them. The pebbles began rushing toward him at warp speed.

He did not feel the slightest amount of pain when his nose crushed against the unyielding asphalt surface. The cartilage of his nose broke loose from its moorings and was forcefully driven into the recesses of his skull.

In agonizingly slow motion, he sensed his body settling onto the surface of the surprisingly cold, hard parking lot. In his mind's eye he imagined his body being absorbed by the unforgiving ground.

Toasty warmth spread throughout his body like butter melting on the nooks and crannies of a hot English muffin fresh from the toaster. He eagerly yielded to his growing desire to actively pursue the growing, unbelievably brilliant white light overwhelming his thoughts and mind.

The all-consuming warmth peacefully and silently lulled Josh Tobin into the eternal slumber of death.

The number of people a trained and skilled person such as Dr. Joshua Tobin could have helped over a long and productive life would never be known. A highly educated but deceased physician is no more an asset to society than any dead individual, regardless of education or their station in life.

"Let's get the fuck outta here!" Rolondo shrieked frantically as he swung his bulk onto the driver's seat of the BMW. Marias heaved himself into the back seat with a satisfied grin on his face.

"Did you see the look on that dissin' mutha fucker's face when I smoked him? It was great," he beamed.

"Great! What the matter wiff you? What the hell we do now?"

"We drive outta here real slow without makin' a fuss so we don't attract no attention," Marias said. "Then we get me a new shirt. This one's trashed."

CHAPTER 14

SARAH'S ORDEAL

"Damn this traffic! It's getting worse each week, I swear!" Ellen Murgen vented into her cellular phone.

"It's aggravating for sure," Stacey Johnson, Dr. Collins's receptionist sweetly crooned into the phone. "But don't you hurry and get into a wreck."

"I really appreciate it, Stacey," Ellen said.

"Dr. Collins is running a little late herself so if you're only fifteen minutes late it won't be a big deal," Stacey reassured her. "But if you're going to be later than that give us a call back and we'll just schedule you for next week. There's no use stressing you out any more today than you already are. OK?"

"I'm so glad to be able to work without pain and my entire life is back on track," Ellen continued without answering Stacey's question. "I know she's had a long, tiring day but it feels like I'm starting to go downhill. She's told me many times that if I catch problems early they're much easier to take care of."

Patients often wanted to maintain a conversation while they're in traffic to help the time go by more quickly and Ellen was obviously in a mood to chat. Stacey, however, was busy and anxious to finish her work so she could go home at a reasonable hour.

"We'll see you in fifteen minutes and get you taken care of," Stacey pleasantly replied, gently putting an end to Ellen's unnecessary chatter.

Stacey turned toward Chauncey's gray steel desk and said, "Chauncey, will you please find Dr. Collins and tell her that Ellen Murgen is going to be about fifteen minutes late because the traffic is bad?"

Chauncey lifted his gaze from the stack of tally sheets from which he was gleaning the daily statistics. Stacey noticed that his eyes were red and bloodshot, and he had to force a smile onto his face.

"I'm sure it will be fine with her," Chauncey said tiredly. "But just to be sure I'll tell her so she knows what to expect."

When Ellen wheeled out of traffic into the almost deserted parking lot of Dr. Collins's office, she scanned the lot for a convenient place to park. Even in the fading light of late afternoon it was easy to see there were plenty of parking spots in the middle of the lot affording an uncomplicated entry as well as effortless exit.

As soon as her car came to a full stop, she placed the gearshift into the "Park" position and climbed out of her car, being careful to place both feet on the ground before using her arms to push herself out of the driver's seat, straightening her skirt as she stood up. With an awkward heaving motion she swung the heavy car door closed, glanced briefly toward the brushy fencerow in front of her car, and simultaneously clicked the "Lock" button on the keyless remote. A mellow "beep" sounded and the brilliant halogen headlights automatically clicked on, which clearly illuminated a well-dressed man lying face down in a parking space 15 yards in front of her car.

Ellen Murgen was horrified to see the spreading pool of dark red blood flowing from him and slowly meander its way toward a storm drain.

Frantically casting her eyes left and right she made a mad dash for the lighted security of the office doors screaming hysterically as she ran.

Bursting through the front door in a terrified frenzy, she ran directly to the reception desk and blurted to Stacey, "There's a man- a dead man, I think- lying in the parking lot. He's bleeding- a lot! Oh My God!"

Her wild-eyed look spurred Stacey to immediately dial 9-1-1 with a manic outburst of energy. She did not need, nor did she want, to seek verification of what Ellen had seen.

"Chauncey, lock the front door please," Stacey instructed the perplexed bookkeeper as he stared in wide-eyed amazement, trying to comprehend what was happening.

Before he could move to lock the door, Sarah burst from the hallway leading back to the treatment rooms.

"What's wrong?" she asked as she and Dr. Joseph Holmes, her associate doctor, ran side-by-side from the back of the office. "What's going on?"

Sarah glanced at Ellen and saw she was too hysterical to offer an explanation.

"What's happening?" she asked, looking directly at Stacey.

"There's a dead man in the parking lot in a pool of blood," Stacey reiterated with all the information she had received from Ellen.

"Oh my God! Josh!" Sarah shrieked as she bolted for the door. She clawed at the door handle in a paroxysm of fumbling fingers and her face drained of all color. Her ashen complexion added to the anxiety felt by everyone in the room.

"Oh my God! Oh my God, NO!" she repeated over-and-over again, her voice becoming more hysterical and louder with each word.

Before rushing into the night, Sarah spun toward Dr. Holmes with a fierce look in her eyes and ordered, "Get examination gloves and as many clean towels as you can carry. Hurry!"

Dr. Holmes, assessing the situation in a flash, turned to Stacey and ordered, "You heard her. Get the gloves and towels and hurry! I'm going after her!"

Chauncey had already bolted out the front door in hot pursuit of the distraught Sarah by the time Dr. Holmes joined the exodus from the office.

Scanning the parking lot from the top step of her office, Sarah immediately identified the prostrate figure laying in the dazzling radiance of Ellen's headlights. Her eyes verified what her heart had known all along.

"Oh my God! Oh my God! No! No! NO!" was all she could repeat to an unhearing and uncaring parking lot.

She darted into the deepening shadows without hesitation. The billowing tails of her white laboratory coat lent silent testimony to the speed with which she propelled herself across the asphalt. Chauncey sprinted after her in a surprising burst of unexpected speed, which shocked the much younger Dr. Holmes.

"Sarah! Wait!" Chauncey called in a firm voice as he clutched her arms in a resolute, unyielding grasp. "You don't know if they're still in the parking lot. It may be dangerous. Let me go first."

He gently passed the sobbing, almost incoherent Sarah into the arms of Dr. Holmes where she slumped onto his chest. His encircling arms clutched her tightly to him to keep her rubbery legs from collapsing. Her feeble efforts to protest his grasp only further drained her ebbing energy, adding to her inability to capably support herself.

Chauncey cautiously made his way toward the fallen man, casting wary glances throughout the parking lot as he went. It was almost impossible to see into the lengthening shadows scattered throughout the lot.

I wish I had a flashlight and a club, he thought as he warily wended his way toward the prone form of Josh Tobin.

In a sudden fit of renewed vitality Sarah broke away from Dr. Holmes's supporting arms. Her headlong rush caused her to awkwardly bump into Chauncey and almost knocked him over as he warily made his way toward the prostrate, unmoving body of her husband.

"What the hell---" Chauncey exclaimed loudly as he stumbled out of her way and struggled to keep himself from falling.

Ignoring Chauncey's shocked exclamation she threw herself beside Josh's limp, apparently lifeless body before lifting his head gently onto her lap. His listless neck allowed his head to roll within her lap while his unseeing, slightly glazed eyes rolled back into his head.

An ambulance arrived with its red and white lights flashing as Sarah was rocking back and forth on her haunches, moaning an incomprehensible wail of grief while cradling Josh's head to her bosom. The ambulance pulled beside the throng of onlookers who had gathered around the fallen man.

The ambulance crew was accustomed to seeing a crowd of onlookers staring at and surrounding the sick or injured person. As usual, it irritated them because it made their job much more difficult.

"OK folks, move out of the way so we can work here," commanded Rosemary Scroggins, a petite woman with her jet black hair pulled back tightly into a bun and dressed in the dark blue uniform of an EMT as she pushed her way toward the victim.

"Come on folks, cooperate so we can get some help to these people," Harold Croft, Rosemary's partner added. Harold's six-foot five-inch frame carried two hundred and thirty pounds and the sheer presence of his towering body made most people take notice and follow his instructions. His shaven, bald head gleamed above those of most people and added greatly to his commanding demeanor.

The crowd parted just enough for them to see Sarah and the dead body of her husband. The gurney was moved as closely to the victim as possible then left sitting unused behind Sarah who continued her incessant rocking without acknowledging their presence.

"We're too late to do anything for this guy," Harold said as he leaned down and whispered into Rosemary's ear. "Let's just wait for the coroner and homicide unit."

"She's the one we have to take care of now," Harold continued whispering to Rosemary as he nodded toward Sarah. "Let's make sure she's stable then we'll play it by ear to see what we do from there."

After surveying the scene Rosemary silently nodded in agreement then moved toward Sarah.

"Honey," Rosemary spoke softly to Sarah as she kneeled beside her and placed her hands comfortingly on her shoulders. "Why don't you come over here and sit down so we can examine him. It will be better if you give us room to work."

"He's my husband and he's dead," a grief-stricken Sarah moaned to no one in particular.

"I know Honey, but you have to let us do our job," Rosemary gently urged Sarah.

"I should have been here with him. I could have helped him and he wouldn't be dead if I had been here," Sarah wailed pitifully.

Rosemary nodded to Harold to help by taking Sarah's arm as she tried to respectfully pry Josh's head from her grasp.

"That's it Honey, let go and we'll take good care of him," Rosemary's soothingly convincing voice prompted Sarah to cooperate. "You can't help us anymore except by going over to the ambulance and sitting down."

Sarah slowly opened her arms and relinquished Josh's head to the care of Rosemary then allowed Harold, who exhibited an unexpected gentleness in his touch, to help her to her feet.

After struggling to stand at her full height she shrugged away from his supporting arms.

"You'll take good care of him, I know you ..." Sarah never finished the sentence.

The sudden loss of blood pressure to her brain caused by blood rushing to her feet when she rapidly stood up combined with the emotional stress of seeing her husband's lifeless eyes staring into nothingness was too much for her to handle. Without another word

Sarah swooned backward, freefalling to the rear. She tumbled over the edge of the gurney and her feet flew skyward.

Rosemary and Harold both lunged in an attempt to break her fall.

Before either of the EMTs could reach her, the unprotected back of her skull smashed onto the hard, unforgiving pavement next to where her husband's blood ran into the storm drain. The cracking sound of her cranium hitting the ground sent shivers up the spine of every person within hearing distance.

Sarah Collins immediately became a victim in dire need of the EMT's life-saving medical attention.

"Oh shit!" Rosemary said as she rushed to Sarah's aid. "There's going to be hell to pay for this one."

"And a hell of a big pile of paperwork," her bureaucracy-savvy partner chimed in disgustedly.

CHAPTER 15

GOOD-BYE TO JOSH

Sarah was kept in a drug-induced coma in intensive care for four days to reduce swelling of her brain. After her vital signs stabilized, she was moved to a private room for ten days of recuperation and observation. Josh's brother Jeremy, known to his family as J.T., visited her hospital room daily regardless of whether she was conscious or not.

"I feel terrible that I wasn't able to be at Josh's funeral," Sarah sighed as she looked lovingly at her brother-in-law.

"You were unconscious in intensive care for four days for crying out loud," J.T. replied with empathy in his voice. "You were comatose until the day after Josh was buried."

And we're all damned glad we didn't have a double funeral, he thought while keeping a toothy smile plastered on his face.

"But I wish I could have at least visited his grave."

"You will when you're strong enough; I'll take you to the cemetery myself," J.T. said with conviction. "You've been in the hospital for a total of fourteen days. This is the first day you're really cognizant of what's happening around you. You have to regain some strength before you try anything too strenuous. Besides, there's nothing you can do there that you can't do here."

"Yes there is," she replied firmly, barely able to stifle a sob. "I can cry with him there."

"You'll have time," he reminded her. "It may seem like you have to rush things but you really don't."

"Without going to the funeral, it doesn't feel like he's really gone," she said, dabbing at her eyes with a tissue. "I can't seem to accept the fact I'm never going to see him again."

She sobbed gently while groaning deep in her chest.

"Now's the time to grieve," J.T. said gently. "If you don't grieve now it will just take you longer to get back to a normal routine."

"I don't want a normal life; I want my Josh," she said as she began sobbing heavily.

"I didn't say a normal life. That will come with time. For now let's settle for a normal routine. Grieving is a process that has to unfold in its own good time."

Sarah looked at her brother-in-law with a look of awe on her face.

He's just like a big brother to me; a smart, handsome, comforting big brother who is wise and always knows exactly what to say.

"You seem to have a good idea of how these things work."

"I've had too much experience in this type of thing considering my past employment and such," he added evasively as his mind wandered into the past.

"Do you regret working with the C.I.A.?" Sarah asked with trepidation, knowing it was a delicate subject and he was not supposed to ever talk about his association with that federal agency.

"Not at all," he said. "It actually led me into some very advantageous situations."

"Such as---" she prompted, suddenly interested.

"Well, we moved to Northern Virginia so I could commute into D.C.," he said. "I wanted a nice place to raise the kids and we certainly found it there."

J.T. continued conversing in a level, calm tone while looking intensely straight ahead as though he were viewing the last few years of his life on the institutional gray wall of Sarah's hospital room.

"Northern Virginia is definitely a nicer place to raise a family than D.C. will ever be.

"The crime rate there is certainly lower than it is in D.C.," he continued. "The Commonwealth of Virginia trusts its law-abiding citizens to carry concealed weapons and it's reflected in lower rates of murder and other violent crimes."

J.T. was sorry he brought up the crime rate in D.C. as soon as it was out of his mouth. Sarah's eyes lowered and her chest began heaving with deep, racking sobs of grief.

"There are a lot of good churches there also," he continued on quickly, trying to change the subject. "We attend a big Catholic church on Maple Street with a growing parish of young families. St. Boniface offers everything we need to get the kids started on a good moral and principled life."

"You're fired up about a Catholic church?"

"I'm not too fired up about the Catholic Church as a religious organization but you know how Stephanie is. She and the kids are deeply involved in church and school activities."

"Having a good church and school to be involved with really helps foster a feeling of belonging," Sarah said seriously. "It's what makes an area worth living in."

J.T. noticed that her sobbing had subsided and she was concentrating on their conversation.

"The kids are especially getting into the church," he said when he realized he was making headway in pulling her out of her doldrums. "They have a youth ministry group that organizes a Youth Retreat every summer."

"That sounds interesting," Sarah said, leaning forward with peaking interest.

"They go for an entire week to a place in West Virginia for a Christian get-together called the Hallelujah Gathering," he added. "Some of the parents use their week of vacation to volunteer as chaperones."

"They probably have a nice vacation," Sarah noted. "Especially if the kids are teenagers; they can be hard to keep happy on family vacations at that age."

"The kids really love it because they're on their own for a week; even though they're really not," J.T. explained. "The chaperones keep a close eye on them."

He saw that she was very interested in his litany about the kids and their Youth Ministry activities.

"What church do you attend?" he asked in a conversational tone hoping to draw her into the conversation.

"I don't really attend a church," Sarah replied. "At least I haven't for a while. I was raised Catholic like Stephanie but I fell away from it while I was in college."

Sarah took her turn to stare at the wall as though it were a movie screen playing the story of her planned but recently shattered life.

"Josh and I planned on moving to Northern Virginia to be closer to you and your family," she said as she looked directly at J.T., hoping he would understand they had wanted to establish stronger family ties.

"You talked about that when you visited last time," he said pleasantly. "You were looking at Loudon County if I remember correctly."

"Oh yeah," she said sheepishly. "We did talk about that. I forgot."

Then she looked at the folds of the sheets covering her svelte body under a thin sheet of starched cotton cloth, "We wanted the same things you have. A safe place to live and a family."

Sarah began to sob softly but continued, "We planned on having kids, you know. Three. He wanted three. He said it was a nice number."

"Stephanie and I are content with two," he said. "That was enough for her to handle since she was raising them mostly as a single parent because I wasn't home a lot of the time."

"Two weren't enough for Josh because they would barely replace us on this planet and four seemed like a number that a Catholic girl like me would want to have," Sarah continued, not giving him a chance to interrupt. "He liked to joke about my Catholic upbringing but he really didn't care."

"Josh didn't care about what religion anyone was," J.T. added hesitantly. "He never thought much about religion or God in one way or the other."

"I actually think he wanted our kids to be raised Catholic; he said it was a good training ground for the Protestants," Sarah said, hoping he would pick up on the wry humor in her statement.

She flashed a brilliantly white, even smile as she visualized a picture of Josh in her mind's eye. They both sat in silence; each lost in their personal thoughts.

A minute later Sarah looked at him and cautiously said, "I remember you holding my hand when I was going in and out of consciousness."

She watched J.T.'s eyebrows rise in astonishment at being caught caring about another woman who wasn't his wife. "I think you were really concerned about me."

"I was--- we all were--- are," he stammered.

"I never had a big brother that really cared about me, you know," Sarah said. "And whether you like it or not, you're now that big brother."

"Well, thank you for bestowing the title of Honorary Big Brother on me."

"Thanks for accepting," Sarah said as a girlish grin broke across her face. "It's easy nominating you for the position considering how close you and Josh were."

"What about Chauncey?" J.T. asked, hoping to deflect Sarah's attention from being focused on her dead husband. "He rode all the way to the hospital in the back of the ambulance with you, you know."

"I didn't know that."

"And he called me every day to ask how you were doing while you were in intensive care because they wouldn't let him in since he's not family. After they put you in this private room he came to visit every day, but only while I was here. He usually just sat quietly in that chair in the corner and watched you and the monitors hanging over your bed- never saying a word- and then he would use hand signals to let me know he was leaving. If he wanted to talk he'd motion for me to meet him in the hallway."

"I didn't know that either."

"Yeah," J.T. continued, happy to make Chauncey the center of the conversation. "The ambulance guy said he even hung the saline bag and other paraphernalia like he knew what he was doing. Are you sure he doesn't know more about his past than he's letting on?"

"No, I don't think so. He's pretty straightforward. There's really nothing shifty about him that I can tell."

"Well, keep an eye on him. He seems too good to be true."

"Aren't you just the most trusting soul?"

"Well, distrust of my fellow human beings has kept me alive on more than one occasion," he said distractedly as his eyes fell to the floor, staring at nothing.

"Have you heard anything about the guys who killed Josh?" Sarah asked, trying to pull him out of a dark reverie of his violent past.

"Yeah," J.T. said, snapping his thoughts from the past to the present. "The police grabbed them on the Beltway near Chevy Chase. They pulled them over in Josh's BMW for going 90 in a 65 zone."

"Can they prove they were the ones who killed Josh?" Sarah inquired, leaning forward with great interest.

UH-OH. This is the first time she's cognizant enough to bring up the topic of Josh's killers. Well, it had to happen sooner or later. I wish it were later---

J.T. became visibly uncomfortable and shifted nervously on his chair.

"Are you sure you're ready to talk about this?"

"Yes," she said firmly. "I eventually have to learn what happened and now is as good a time as any. Now, tell me what happened."

"When the cops stopped the car they saw one of the guys was nervous and became suspicious," he said as he again moved uneasily in his chair. J.T. was obviously ill at ease with the topic of Josh's killers and stopped talking until he could gather his courage.

"Are you sure you want to-"

"And---"Sarah said as she mimed with her hands for him to continue.

"And they found a .357 magnum revolver and a shirt with Josh's blood on it in the trunk. The revolver, shirt, and car all had blood on them. One of the guys even had blood on his hair."

Sarah sat with a stupefied look on her face. "They found the gun?" she asked in astonished disbelief.

"Yeah, ballistic testing confirmed it was the one used to kill Josh."

"There's no question? It was the gun?"

"Yeah, it was the gun," he said. He was stunned to realize she was fixated on the gun instead of the men who did the killing.

"How did they get the gun?"

"They bought it off a drug dealer in Northwest," J.T. said. "It had been stolen from a house in Illinois or Iowa; one of those Midwest states starting with an 'I' a few weeks ago."

"And that's legal?" she asked with ferocity in her voice and gaze.

"Of course it's not," he said, taken aback by Sarah's intense questioning. "They all had felony convictions on their records. They weren't allowed to possess, or even be near, a gun."

"They?" Sarah asked incredulously. It had just dawned on her that more than one person was responsible for the death of her husband.

"Yeah, there were three of them."

"What are their names? Who the hell are these animals?" she asked as her eyes took on a vicious, burning quality.

"Marias Phillips was the guy who actually shot Josh. They found his fingerprints on the revolver."

He was not anxious to continue so he allowed her plenty of time to digest the information.

"He was driving around without a shirt?" she asked innocently, trying to envision the sequence of events in her mind.

"No," he said evenly. "Apparently they stopped and robbed a clothing store so he could get a clean shirt."

"They what?" Sarah asked, astonished at their gall.

"The guy needed a new shirt because they were going to a party and he couldn't show up with blood on the one he was wearing," J.T. explained calmly as he watched her closely.

"And how did the police figure this out?"

"They found the price tags from the store in the trunk with the bloody shirt and gun along with some other clothes with the price tags still attached."

Sarah was assimilating this information when a flash of astonishment appeared on her face.

"Was anyone hurt in the store robbery?"

The look of dread on her face was agonizing to J.T. because he knew the private hell she was going through. She obviously had to confront the truth of what transpired regarding her husband's death but he was not sure she was strong enough.

"They pistol-whipped the clerk," he said factually after taking a deep breath. "And gave him a concussion and fractured skull."

"Will he be OK?"

"He's in this hospital somewhere," he said. "I don't know how he's doing, but at least he's alive."

"Yeah," she answered with a distracted tone in her voice. "At least he's alive. Who else was involved when Josh was killed?"

"Rolondo Hammons was the one who pulled Josh's door open to get him out of the car; his fingerprints were on the door handle and steering wheel," he answered in a guarded tone.

"Who was the third guy? What is his name?" Sarah asked in a commanding tone.

"His name is Tobias Masterson," J.T. said, waiting for the tid-bit of information to settle in her churning mind.

It hit like a nuclear bomb at ground zero.

"Tobias Masterson," she said repeating the name in a confused, uncomprehending tone, allowing the words to fall heavily off her tongue. "TOBIAS MASTERSON!" she shrieked in recognition and amazement.

She sat bolt upright in bed, the heavily starched sheets falling unnoticed to her waist.

"That bastard is a patient of mine- was a patient of mine- he---" she stammered as her face reddened and her mouth worked up and down, suddenly incapable of uttering another sound.

She broke down in a torrent of tears, which quickly drenched the front of her lime green nightgown allowing her bra to show through the thin saturated cloth. Her sobs came in gasping, raspy spasms sucked through her tightly constricted larynx.

"I was helping that son of a bitch and he killed my husband?" she asked with anguish in her voice and a look of incredulity on her face.

"He didn't kill him directly but since he was involved in a felony that resulted in the death of a person, he was charged with murder; the same as the guy who actually pulled the trigger."

He realized with a jolt that his directness in describing the murder of her husband might have been too much for her to handle this soon after her ordeal.

"Listen Sarah, I---" he stumbled in a halting, uncertain tone.

"NO! You listen! This is shit! A bunch of criminals who have no right to own a gun kill my husband in cold blood. For what? A car? I would have given them the damned car!" she screamed irrationally.

J.T. could only shake his head, unable to think of anything to say.

"What the hell! It's ludicrous. It's past ludicrous! What the hell am I supposed to do now?" she asked in a nearly incoherent, furious tone as she flicked her head back and forth in an agitated display of anguish.

J.T. didn't answer because he had no answer to offer. It was a legitimate question she had asked, and it had no answer that would make any sense to her or anyone else.

In a brisk move that startled J.T., she sat bolt upright on the rumpled mattress. "I'm going to see Nadine," she said with conviction. "She'll know what to do."

"Who the hell is Nadine?" he asked in a confused tone as his brow furrowed even deeper.

"Nadine Brand. My old college roommate," Sarah answered simply as though he should have known. "She was a school teacher for a few years but now she raises horses full-time."

"Why don't you find a young college roommate; those old ones get a little saggy after a while."

"What in the hell are you talking about?" Sarah asked, not believing what she was hearing.

"Young college roommates are much more exciting than those old ones," J.T. stated in his dry, quirky sense of humor.

"You're a pain in the ass, Mr. Tobin," she said laughingly with a look of disbelief on her face as she heaved a pillow at his head. He caught the pillow and laughed along with her.

"OK, OK. So where does this Nadine live? I'll take you there."

"She lives about two and a half hours west of here in the mountains of Virginia on a horse farm. I'll have to call her for exact directions."

"When do you want to go?" he asked.

"Tomorrow. As soon as they cut me loose from this place," she answered.

"But I'm going to L.A. tomorrow. I fly out first thing in the morning. I can't get out of it because it's business and all my meetings have been scheduled for weeks."

"I'll go by myself. I'll be OK."

"I know that but I'll feel better if you're traveling with someone."

"I'll take Chauncey."

"Chauncey? Can he drive? Does he even have a driver's license?" he asked in an unsure tone.

"If he can't drive then I will. Besides, who cares if he has a driver's license? They're giving driver's licenses to illegal aliens for crying out loud! At least he's a citizen."

"As far as anyone knows, at least," he added with a heavy tone of skepticism in his voice. "Who's going to watch your practice?"

"Joe Holmes is watching it."

"He's your associate, isn't he?"

"Yeah. I called him this morning and he's handling it just fine. When I got hurt he jumped right in, took control of everything, and now he's buying my practice," she said plainly.

"What?" he asked with shock in his voice.

"Do you really think I could go back to my practice? Seeing that parking lot where Josh died at least twice every day? I just can't do it," she said as rivulets of tears began coursing down her face.

"Yeah, I guess you're right," he acknowledged, not quite sure what to add to the conversation.

"I called him early this morning to get the ball rolling," she said between sobs. "I have him contacting a business brokerage firm to value the practice and he's talking to our bank to get financing."

"Can he get financing?"

"He should be able to. He's been with me for almost three years so he has his own practice established and knows how to run the business side," she said as she wiped the tears from her eyes with the corner of the bed sheet.

"That should be a selling point to the bank."

"It's golden," she said with her eyes looking levelly at his. "The staff are trained and dedicated. The patients are familiar with the doctors and facility so it's a viable and vibrant practice. That's what the bank looks at when they make a decision on whether they'll lend money to the buyer."

"I've never had to understand the business side of anything," J.T. confessed. "I collected my paycheck and paid our household expenses out of what money we had to work with."

"Well, the business side of life is interesting and a royal pain in the ass at the same time," she confessed. "With it being an active practice I can get more money for it. If I didn't have Joe already in place the practice would dwindle away to nothing in no time at all and be worthless."

J.T. was stupefied and didn't know what to say so he changed the subject.

"So you're off to see Nadine."

"I'm off to see Nadine. But only after I take a nap," she stated matter-of-factly.

CHAPTER 16

VIRGINIA-BRED ROCKY MOUNTAIN HORSES

Sarah's former college roommate, Nadine Brand, had been a loner since her husband left her for another man. She spent her days on the horse farm she received in the divorce settlement, raising and training Rocky Mountain horses.

When Sarah arrived at Nadine's farm, "The Shire," she found her busy in the barn finishing the morning tasks necessary to maintain a healthy herd.

"Why did you name this place The Shire?" Sarah asked after exchanging greetings.

Nadine's chuckling laugh bounced her slightly protruding, jelly-like belly.

"It's from the book *Lord of the Rings* by J.R.R. Tolkien," Nadine replied. "The main characters are Hobbits, little hairy human-like critters with a very formal social structure."

"So you named your farm after hairy little critters?" Sarah asked with a chuckle and smile.

"Kind of," Nadine replied as her belly continued to bob up and down with her laughing. "Hobbits have seven named meals during the day and take life with a smile and great attitude. The Shire is the village the main characters live in."

"That sounds like it's something worth emulating," Sarah said with a grin.

"Yes it is, in my estimation at least," Nadine said as she continued to laugh gently. "That's the way I want to live; plenty of meals and a great attitude."

"The Shire," Sarah repeated, mulling the name over in her mind.

"That name on the sign over the entrance of my lane reminds me of my lifestyle goals every day," Nadine said seriously. "We all need a little reminder of how life is supposed to be, you know."

She had a faraway, knowing look in her eye as she spoke. Suddenly she snapped back to the present and locked Sarah with a penetrating stare.

"That guy who drove you up here," Nadine said. "He didn't hang around very long and barely said anything at all while he was here. What's his story?"

"I'm not sure what his story is," Sarah replied plainly. "He works for me and the rest of his story is way too long to go into now. But he's turned out to be a really good friend when I needed support from the people around me."

"Well, now you have another really good friend to take care of you," Nadine said. "I'm honored to have you visit when the shit hit the fan."

Sarah wasn't ready to discuss her situation so early in their visit. She quickly changed the topic.

"So why did you decide to breed this type of horse?" she asked. "I thought everyone raised race horses."

Nadine gave another deep-seated belly laugh as she marveled at Sarah's naiveté of the world of horses. It seemed that Nadine took every opportunity she could to laugh.

"That's easy," Nadine replied after regaining her composure. "The Rocky Mountain Horse is really from the grass roots of this country. They're as American as Mom and apple pie."

"So it comes from Colorado, or what?" Sarah asked innocently.

Seeing she was serious and really didn't know anything about horses, let alone the Rocky Mountain breed in particular, the teacher in Nadine came to the forefront.

"No, their name has absolutely nothing to do with the Rocky Mountains out west. In the early 1800s, the breed originated in the hill country of Kentucky. The 'Rocky' name came from old-timers who claimed a single colt was brought to Eastern Kentucky from 'some place west of the Appalachians' around 1890," Nadine said, talking enthusiastically about her favorite subject, while a slightly crooked smile creased her sun-wrinkled face.

"So they're a working horse?"

"Originally, and because of the reality of the times, the surviving horses were the strongest and hardiest of the bunch. They led a hard life then, unlike these guys," Nadine said with a little chuckle as she pointed toward her herd.

She suddenly became very serious.

"The Rocky Mountain Horse is strong today because the people in the Kentucky hills could only afford a horse that survived without much care during the harsh winter weather. They either made it to maturity to reproduce or they didn't. The stronger genes survived in the herd."

"The survival of the fittest," Sarah said jokingly. "What a unique concept."

"The Rocky Mountain Horse has had a colorful history," Nadine continued conversationally. "Today the breed is a much sought after horse. Equestrians like them because they're gaited. That means they're easy to ride without a lot of up and down bumping and the horse has a good disposition."

"A good disposition?"

"Yeah," Nadine laughed. "Until you've had a horse get nasty with you and bite, kick, or otherwise beat you up you don't truly appreciate an even tempered horse."

"They are really pretty, that's for sure," Sarah stated in an attempt to show her approval of her friend's passionate love of her horses. "They have such pretty coats; the sunlight just shimmers and glitters off them."

"Yeah, they are pretty," Nadine agreed. "But they don't all have the same coloration that mine do."

"How's that?" Sarah asked.

"All of my horses have chocolate-brown bodies and flaxen colored manes and tails," Nadine continued. "That combination of colors is highly coveted; that's why I'm trying to breed it into my herd."

"So you want to breed the most popular coloration of horse so they're worth more?" Sarah asked, striving to better understand the situation.

Nadine exhibited a not-so-subtle air of pride in her voice and posture as she continued.

"These horses are the center of my life right now," she said. "I made a conscious effort to put all my physical and mental energy into them. I had to, it was either that or I knew I'd go crazy."

Knowing she was moving into dangerous territory with her comments, Nadine continued with caution, "Have you thought much about where your life may be heading?"

Knowing there was no use trying to avoid this conversation, Sarah replied directly to her question without missing a beat.

"I've already contacted a real estate agency about selling my house in Washington," she said, looking Nadine directly in the eyes. "They were really nice about everything and understood I wasn't able to handle much of the details so they arranged to have an auction company sell the furniture and such from the house."

Nadine noticed she had a look of longing in her eyes as she spoke.

"Did you ever go back to your house?" Nadine asked. "Since Josh was killed, I mean."

"I know what you mean," Sarah snapped as she continued looking directly into Nadine's eyes.

"No, I haven't," she admitted as her shoulders sagged noticeably. "I had Amy, a friend of mine from D.C., go in and take out all my personal belongings."

"It's good to have friends who are willing to help in times like these."

"Everything from my clothes to my toothbrush came out in cardboard boxes and brown paper grocery bags," Sarah said wistfully. "What I didn't bring with me is at a storage facility near my brother-in-law's place."

She looked away and stared into the baby blue sky, visualizing in her mind's eye what her house and furnishings had looked like.

"I just couldn't go back to that house again," Sarah said while continuing to look at the sky. "There are too many memories there."

"It's always a difficult time," Nadine said consolingly.

"I wanted to keep it in my memory as a happy place Josh and I shared," she said as she dabbed at a small tear that had formed in the corner of her eye. "I don't want to remember it as an empty shell of what was once my life."

"That was a good idea."

"After my personal stuff was out, I had J.T., my brother-in-law, go in and take all of Josh's stuff out," she said while wiping another tear from her eye. "His clothes were donated to The Salvation Army and his books and professional stuff were sent to his Alma Mater so students can make use of it."

"That was good thinking," Nadine said.

"I told J.T. not to give anything of Josh's to anyone we know. I don't want to see his favorite tee shirt on any of the relatives," she said with steel in her voice.

"That makes sense," Nadine confirmed, trying to assure her friend she had done the right thing.

"If I couldn't say good-bye to Josh at his funeral then I certainly wasn't going to subject myself to the emotional trauma of seeing remnants of the life we'd shared together scattered hither and yon," she declared. "I want to act like he was just a pleasant memory and move on with my life without delay."

She looked at Nadine, her eyes searching for emotional support from her old confidant.

"And you're on the right track," Nadine said seriously. "You seem to be making some very sound and reasonable choices without going overboard."

"That's why I escaped to your 'Home for Wayward Roommates'," Sarah said with relief and a smile, ready to drop the subject.

Nadine took the hint and commenced to steer the conversation away from Josh to Sarah's new chapter in her book of life.

"You came here right from the hospital. How are you feeling physically?" Nadine asked with concern in her voice.

"I'm OK. I really got hurt in that fall and I was in deep trouble for a while," she replied. "But I'm fine now. With that kind of injury there's always concern about permanent brain damage but that doesn't seem to have happened. Thank God. I have enough problems to deal with."

"If you spent that much time in the hospital, it must have been a pretty horrendous fall," Nadine said.

"I just can't get too physically active until all of the stuff inside has a chance to heal properly," Sarah replied, trying to put on an air of bravery she truly did not feel.

"Let's go sit in the shade so it doesn't tax you too much," Nadine said as she motioned for Sarah to follow her toward an umbrella-covered table and matching chairs. "We can talk more once we're more comfortable."

Sarah had arrived at The Shire just before lunchtime as Nadine was finishing her morning training session with the horses. Unknowingly, she and Chauncey had arrived at the most advantageous time because midday was used as a rest period for both Nadine and the animals.

The two former roommates visited for a few hours over raspberry iced tea and lunch-type finger foods. A large sugar maple tree in the front yard provided shade as well as a convenient place to hang bird feeders. The antics of ruby-throated hummingbirds kept them enthralled throughout the warm afternoon. Watching the miniscule birds flit about helped fill in the otherwise uncomfortable periods of silence that occurred in their conversation.

When it was time for the evening feeding of the horses, Nadine excused herself and went into the house to strap a floral-carved El Paso Saddlery holster onto her ample waist. It held a silvery stainless steel Smith and Wesson Model 60 revolver with five-inch barrel.

Taking a moment to organize her thoughts and gather her composure at the outside door leading to where Sarah sat peacefully under the sugar maple enjoying the peace and quiet of the farm, Nadine steeled herself for the scenario she knew was about to unfold.

Straightening herself to her full height, Nadine nonchalantly pushed the screen door open and strode purposefully toward Sarah.

"OK, we're ready to get these critters fed and put away for the night."

When Sarah saw the gun resting on Nadine's right hip she froze in place; her eyes glued on the Model 60. Nadine saw fear register on her face and immediately tried to console her.

"Sarah, it's OK."

"What's OK? That's a gun!"

"Sarah, you're looking at this gun like it's a snake that'll jump off my hip and bite you," she said as soothingly as she could. "You have to realize it isn't the gun that's evil. The men who killed Josh were evil. This gun and all of the others I use on this farm are used for good."

"What good can possibly come out of a gun?" Sarah shot back angrily, her eyes blazing with fury.

"Do you like to watch those horses run out there in the pasture?" Nadine asked levelly as she calmly waved her arm toward the pasture.

"Of course I do. We've been watching them all afternoon."

"Do you see that little guy running with his mother? The tiny pale chocolate colored guy with the blonde highlights?" Nadine asked innocently.

"Yeah, he's really an active little bugger. His poor mother must sleep well at night after keeping after him all day long. What does he have to do with you carrying a gun?"

"He has everything to do with me carrying a gun."

"How?"

"When we get them into their stalls, remind me to show you the long scars down his right flank and across his lower belly," Nadine said as she looked piercingly into her eyes. "Three coyotes tried to pull him down while two more kept his mother busy across the pasture."

"But they obviously didn't succeed," Sarah said evenly.

"They almost succeeded and would have if I didn't have my rifle handy. I had to kill two of them," Nadine said without a hint of regret in her voice. "The others ran for the hills where they probably killed a deer or went over the mountain and took a lamb from my neighbor's herd."

"You've killed things?" Sarah asked in horror.

"Sarah, God gives the good people of this earth the OK to kill the evil things," she continued as she reminded herself to keep her temper under control. "It's what keeps evil from overcoming good."

Before Sarah could reply, she continued.

"You can debate if coyotes are evil or just animals doing what they were put on this earth to do," Nadine said. "I've seen the results of when the neighbor's sheep were torn to pieces, having their guts eaten while they're still alive, and not actually dying until hours later when the sheepherder found them and put them out of their misery."

"That's horrible," Sarah gasped as her hand flew to cover her mouth.

"Yes it is," Nadine said as she looked levelly at her. "I will protect my animals and myself against any and all predators; whether they walk on two legs or four. Now I have to take care of my horses. You can join me if you want to or you can stay here."

With that, Nadine turned decisively and walked to the stables to begin her evening chores. Sarah was still in shock and taken aback by what Nadine had said.

Nadine would never know how long Sarah stood with her feet rooted solidly to the ground because she did not look back. Instead, she continued striding purposefully toward the barn.

Don't look back. Whatever you do, don't look back. She has to face this and you better not give her an out by starting a discussion because you'll only lose the argument then she'll never benefit from figuring out this whole shitty situation for herself.

Sarah felt she should be mad at Nadine for her attitude about guns and killing, regardless of how righteous she felt about it, but she wasn't. She knew deep down in her soul that Nadine was right.

Nadine unhooked the fence latch and let herself through before striding into the barn and out of sight while Sarah stood dumbfounded. She could only stare vacantly at the gaping door opening where her friend had disappeared. Her mind began working through a maze of confounding principles trying to sort out her conflicted emotions.

In the scheme of nature, Nadine's attitude made sense. Her words had appealed to Sarah's sense of righteousness and touched her natural instinct for self-preservation; and it all made perfect sense.

Sarah stumbled numbly after Nadine before leaning exhausted with her elbows resting on the wooden railing, being careful to avoid the steel wire strands of the electrified fence. She was feeling too confused and befuddled to follow her into the stables.

While Sarah watched the horses coming in for their evening inspection and feeding, her mind wandered in many different directions. It was as if she were not in her body, but rather observing the scenery surrounding her in a bizarre bastardization of reality.

She wondered about the frailty of life and the tenacity of humans to cling to it.

She looked at the setting sun and wondered how many millions of people would be watching that same sun teeter on the horizon before disappearing for the night. Out of nowhere, the thought popped unexpectedly into her mind that some of them would be watching it set because they had successfully defended themselves from evil people.

Before she realized it, searing tears began coursing down her cheeks. While she concentrated on the gush of tears dripping off her chin, sobs rooted deep in her core began racking her body with spasms of grief. She valiantly tried fighting against the urge to cry but soon succumbed to her emotions.

Damn him! Damn you Josh! Sarah thought through tearful sobs. *What the hell was the matter with you? Why didn't you defend yourself? Why didn't you learn to take care of yourself?*

What would have happened if I had been with you? We'd both be dead because neither one of us put any thought into being able to fend for ourselves.

"We had so damned much education between us. We're both doctors for Christ's sake! Why didn't we take time to learn how to defend our own lives? We gave other people lives worth living but were just too damned stupid to learn to take care of ourselves," she wailed at the top of her lungs without realizing she was verbalizing her thoughts.

"Now look at us!" she bellowed at the setting sun, not caring she was loudly cursing a man who had died weeks earlier.

"You're dead and I have no life at all!" she screamed in a rambling, cracking voice. "My life is being sold without me being there and I don't even have a place to call my own!"

"Damn you Joshua! Damn you! Damn you! DAMN YOU!"

Nadine heard the outburst and knew it was a necessary part of the healing process. She was actually ashamed to admit to herself that she felt a tiny bit of fear as she listened to the enormous amount of anguish and anger springing from the raving woman leaning on her fence.

Nadine was familiar with the mental healing process. She had gone through a similar soul cleansing when her husband left her. She knew it would continue until Sarah exhausted herself so she resigned herself to just talk calmly to her horses. They seemed to understand and went back to their feed buckets with only the occasional sheepish glance at her.

When Nadine finished with her nightly chores it was almost too dark to see the path back to the house.

Giving her horses a final pat on their long, silky necks she closed the last gate separating the pasture from the open yard. She slowly made her way to where Sarah clung desperately to the top rail of the wooden fence.

Even though she could not see her face in the gathering gloom, she knew she looked like Hell warmed over.

"Come on, I'll get you some soup and put you to bed," Nadine directed. "You'll feel better in the morning. You're not even taking a shower tonight. You need rest more than anything."

Sarah turned dazedly without replying and followed her back to the house, not saying a word or even attempting to walk beside her.

When they got back to the house they removed their dirty shoes outside the front door and went into the kitchen. Without saying a word Nadine removed a large plastic storage bowl of vegetable soup from the refrigerator, ladled a substantial amount into two mottled brown earthenware bowls, and heated them in the microwave.

"This is my mother's recipe and it's a closely-held family secret," Nadine said, probing with conversation to determine if Sarah was ready to open up.

Seeing she was not ready to talk, Nadine said, "Put two pieces of that whole grain bread into the toaster. When it pops up you can spread some of that organic butter I buy from my neighbor on it. It's heavenly; especially on a chilly night."

Sarah obeyed Nadine's instructions robotically and without comment.

When the soup was steaming Nadine set the bowls onto woven placemats to protect the finely finished surface of the ancient walnut table. "This table has been in my family for three generations. My great-grandfather made it with hand tools."

Sarah smiled feebly at her in acknowledgement but remained silent.

She picked up the ornately stamped stainless steel spoon set beside her bowl and was preparing to plunge it into her soup when she noticed Nadine had bowed her head. Hesitating slightly, she set the spoon back down and bowed her head slightly.

"Dear Lord," Nadine began, "thank you for the beautiful day and the ability to visit with dear friends. Thank you for keeping us safe and giving us health. Thank you for the food in front of us; please use it to nourish our bodies to do Your work, Amen."

"Amen," Sarah mimed uncertainly.

How long has it been since you've done something as simple as giving thanks for your life and food? Sarah wondered. *It's been quite a while,* she concluded.

The meal was eaten deliberately and in silence. Both women were tired from a long, emotional, and active day and were not eager to talk unnecessarily. When they were finished Nadine washed the dishes and Sarah dried then Nadine helped her carry her suitcase upstairs to the guestroom.

"The only bathroom is the one downstairs. Use this light to see in the middle of the night," she said as she pointed toward a yellow plastic flashlight setting upright on the dresser. "Those steps are pretty steep and it's totally dark out here in the country."

"If you need anything, don't be afraid to wake me up. I'm usually up a few times a night listening at the window to make sure everything's OK with the horses," she said as she turned and left the bedroom without any further comments.

Sarah's head barely hit the pillow when she fell into a deep sleep. Only when the sounds of rattling dishes and clanking of heavy pots roused her from slumber did she realize it was morning, or at least some version of it because it was still dark.

When she was finished dressing she held the flashlight firmly in her right hand and grasped the handrail determinedly in her left before descending the stairs one at a time. She was glad to get safely to the bottom without falling. A quick left turn took her into the bathroom.

After brushing her teeth and hair she deemed herself presentable and went to find Nadine.

When she got to the kitchen Nadine was nowhere to be seen. Glancing at the white enamel rimmed clock over the stove she saw the bold, black hands pointing to 5:15 a.m.

What an ungodly hour of the morning. Why don't country people sleep later? And where is Nadine?

Then she noticed a faint glow snaking from beneath the door to the Florida Room.

Why would anyone call it a Florida Room when the house is located in Virginia? she wondered.

Slowly and as quietly as possible, Sarah nudged open the stained wooden door leading to the Florida Room, the front entryway to the house. It had obviously started out as an open porch when the house was built over 100 years ago but was later enclosed. A bank of double pane insulated sliding glass windows lined its entire length from one end of the room to the other.

For times of cool weather, a solitary propane gas stove stood against the wall farthest from the door, ready to radiate warmth from its ceramic diffuser. In warmer weather, the windows slid up to reveal wire mesh screens. This allowed the cool air descending from the mountainside to supply a gentle cross-ventilating breeze. An eclectic collection of furniture modeled around an outdoors motif gave the room the panache of a Western-style hunting lodge.

Nadine was sitting sideways in an overstuffed chair enjoying her second cup of coffee as she peacefully observed her horses through the steam-rimmed windows. She had a woolen red blanket with white fringes thrown carelessly across her lap.

In the inky darkness of early morning, Sarah could see row after row of yellow tipped bluish flames hissing gently from the propane heater's diffuser, which offered the only source of light and heat in the room.

"Good Morning," Nadine said quietly as though she did not want to disturb the peacefulness of the new day. "You slept pretty well if all the snoring I heard coming from your room is any indication."

A wicked smile formed on her lips knowing that she was continuing a running joke she and Sarah had perpetuated since their college days as roommates.

"I don't snore! Never have and I never will!" she retorted as she mischievously returned Nadine's smile.

Nadine laughed heartily.

"The coffee's on the kitchen counter. It's decaf. If you need the real stuff we'll have to get some at the store today because I don't keep caffeinated beverages in the house."

"Decaf is fine. I get too worn out half-way through the day if I drink caffeine," Sarah replied as she covered her mouth with the back of her hand to stifle a yawn.

Nadine gave another chuckle as she watched her trying to wake up.

"Cups are to the right of the sink in the cabinet. Milk is in the fridge and sugar is on the table. Help yourself."

Sarah made her way to the sink and tugged at the burnished brass handle of the cupboard revealing a diverse array of multi-colored coffee mugs. She chose a white ceramic mug with a homey Christmas winter scene plastered on its side and poured a cup of steaming, thick black coffee. She added a dollop of cold, clear well water from the tap to weaken the obviously strong brew to make it palatable.

"Well, you still like coffee strong enough to take the enamel off your teeth, I see," Sarah said chidingly. "And you obviously prefer an eclectic assortment of coffee mugs. What happened to that nice set I gave you as a wedding gift?"

"My ex took them with him. I guess his boyfriend liked that style and decided they needed them more than I did."

A wan, mocking smile crossed Nadine's lips.

"Have you gotten over that mess or are you just putting on a good front?" Sarah asked cautiously.

"I've gotten over it. At least the best I ever will. When a woman chooses her mate she thinks it's for life. No one will ever be quite as important to her as the one she chose. It's not easy for a woman to lose her true love," she said philosophically.

A pall of icy silence smothered the room when the reality of what Nadine said hit them both in the same terrifying instant. They could not look at each other nor did they have anything to say for an uncomfortably long time.

Simultaneously but separately, and without a word being spoken, they decided to allow the painful pause to linger until it died by virtue of its own weight.

"Breakfast will be in about an hour," Nadine said, no longer able to stand the discomforting stillness. "If you need something right away you can make yourself some toast. There's whole grain bread left from dinner; otherwise, we'll have bacon and eggs in a bit. By the time we're finished with the breakfast dishes it'll be daylight; then it's off to tend to the animals. This is your last free meal. If you don't work around here you don't get fed."

Nadine flashed an impish smile, which Sarah returned enthusiastically.

"Some good honest work and sweat will be good for me," she stated emphatically to acknowledge Nadine's joke. "And I like to eat so I better work to your complete satisfaction."

After a few minutes of quiet contemplation and coffee sipping, Sarah asked tentatively, "Are coyotes dangerous to humans?"

Nadine shot Sarah a sideways, furtive glance, not quite sure where her line of questioning was going.

"They can be at times. Why do you ask?"

"When I think of coyotes I always envision good old Wiley Coyote. I never would've dreamed they could be as cruel as you say they are. Since you carry a gun, I started wondering if you actually feared them."

"It's not just the coyotes. I've had to shoot a rabid raccoon, and a fox that was killing my chickens. That revolver is a tool around here, the same as a shovel or rake. It has a specific job to do, otherwise it doesn't rate a place on the farm. You never know when you'll need it. But if you need it, you'll need it badly, and you better have it with you and not sitting in a drawer or in the truck. That's why I keep it strapped to my belt."

Nadine sat up straighter and continued on a topic she had put much personal introspection and thought into.

"As a matter of fact, the venison in the soup you ate last night for dinner was a doe that walked out of the woods while I was riding my horse in the back pasture last deer season."

"That was venison? Why didn't you tell me?"

"Why? Food is food. Besides, you didn't ask. You couldn't tell the difference between it and beef, because you ate it all, so you obviously liked it."

Sarah smiled, "Yeah, I did eat it all, didn't I?"

"You sure did and you had seconds also," Nadine said, once again seeing the smile on Sarah's face she remembered from the happy-go-lucky days of college.

They let the conversation drop for a minute but Sarah was obviously not satisfied with Nadine's answer. She asked in a serious tone, "So, do coyotes attack humans?"

"Yes they do. Recently there was a tragic incident where a small girl was killed in her front yard. There are about 30-35 coyote attacks on humans in California every year."

"That's terrible!" Sarah exclaimed as she raised the back of her hand to her open mouth in a subconscious gesture. The horrible picture of a child being torn apart by a pack of coyotes seared itself on her mind.

Seeing that Sarah was deeply and emotionally interested in the subject, Nadine continued after flicking a stray strand of gray-sprinkled jet-black hair out of her eyes. "The incidence of coyotes attacking humans is increasing rapidly, as a matter of fact."

"Why?"

"In a nutshell, coyotes are more frequently targeting humans as a food source. The experts seem to think they're getting bolder."

"Why are they getting bolder? What's it mean they're getting bolder? And how do you know this stuff?" Sarah asked with an interesting combination of aggression and disbelief in her voice.

"Look at it this way," Nadine said evenly. "If you're going to live in the city you better know the rules: don't cross the street against the traffic light, don't look like a goof-ball tourist in the Big City for the first time, etc. It's no different here in the country. You better know what you're up against and play by the rules or you're going to get hurt."

Before the last of her words were out of her mouth, Nadine saw a cloud of sorrow cross Sarah's face. Not wanting to allow her friend to fall victim to a deeper funk, she quickly forged onward with the conversation.

"If I remember correctly---" Nadine continued, strenuously searching her mind for a long-forgotten statistic. "There are four well documented steps coyotes go through in becoming acclimated to humans. At first, they're rarely, if ever, seen in the daylight. They're totally nocturnal because they're not sure about their human neighbors."

122 · D. E. HEIL

"That makes sense. Animals are shy and run from humans."

"Then they begin foraging for food during daylight hours," Nadine continued, ignoring Sarah's comment. "They're testing how much they can get away with. Since humans are most active during daylight hours, the yodel dogs get used to seeing humans while they hunt for food. Familiarity allows them to begin losing their fear of humans."

"Yodel dogs?" Sarah asked quizzically.

"It's a local name for coyotes because of the howling they make at night; it sounds like they're yodeling. Didn't you hear them about three o'clock this morning?"

"I didn't hear anything after my head hit the pillow. It must be this clean country air," she kidded with a girlish smile brightening her face.

"Oh right, I forgot. You couldn't hear anything over your snoring."

"You rat!"

"OK, back to coyotes attacking humans," Nadine said with a chuckle, returning to the subject they were rapidly drifting away from. "Coyotes are what are known as 'opportunistic feeders,' meaning they'll eat anything that'll fit into their mouth. It isn't long before coyotes become habituated to humans, and begin feeding on pets."

"Pets?"

"Yep, good ole Fido or Tabby becomes coyote food."

Sarah interrupted, "They can't eat many cats and dogs, can they? We'd hear about it all the time if they did."

Nadine laughed deep in her belly.

"Yes they can, there's a documented case where a coyote den was uncovered in the center of Erie, Pennsylvania and they found 51 dog collars. Cats usually don't wear collars so they have no idea how many fed that city-bred pack."

"So what about them attacking humans?" she asked as though she was being kept in the dark about this aspect of the coyote's eating habits.

"After the coyotes begin eating cats and dogs, they move up to killing them while they're being walked. Even getting so bold as to kill them while they're on their leash and the human owner is right there."

"No way!" Sarah said.

"I'm serious!" Nadine replied non-apologetically in a somber, earnest tone.

"It's at that point the coyote becomes more aggressive toward humans. It may be because they see humans as an impediment standing between them and their food. That's easy to understand considering most dog owners won't stand idly by while Fido is being eaten off the other end of the leash."

"Wow!" Sarah exclaimed after taking a few moments to absorb all she had heard.

After taking enough time to process all the information, she timidly asked, "So can you stop coyotes from attacking humans?"

"Yes," Nadine replied cautiously. "If you stop them from progressing up the ladder of aggressive behavior toward humans then they'll stay on the lower rungs of the food chain below people."

"At what point do you have to teach them the lesson?" Sarah asked hungrily as she leaned forward with anticipation.

"Well, it's better if you teach them the lesson as soon as possible. You probably won't see them when they're hunting nocturnally but if you harass them in the daylight by shooting or trapping them you'll force them to stay active only when they'll avoid human contact."

"And if you wait until they're eating your pets?" Sarah asked seriously.

"Then you've lost your opportunity to teach them the lesson. At that point they're way too familiar with humans and you'll have to fight them off when they're much too close for comfort. It's better to keep them in fear of you early in the game. Why?" she asked with a quizzical look on her face. "What are you getting at?"

"Because I want you to teach me to shoot," she replied cautiously, half expecting Nadine to refuse her request.

"Just so you can shoot coyotes?" Nadine asked with a slight, crooked smile beginning on her face as she set her empty coffee cup on the scarred oak end table.

"So I can teach predators that they better leave decent folks alone," she replied with a glint of steely resolve reflecting in her eyes.

CHAPTER 17

SARAH LEARNS TO SHOOT

"Wow! We sure finished quickly!"

"I think you put more energy into shoveling those stalls because you're motivated to get started shooting," Nadine chided her dear friend.

"There may be something to that," Sarah admitted as she gently hung a manure-encrusted shovel on a rubber-coated hook suspended from a ceiling beam in the barn. "But it really felt good to be doing some manual labor again. I didn't realize how sedentary my life had gotten."

After a light but filling lunch under the sugar maple tree, Nadine excused herself and reappeared from the house carrying a revolver nestled securely in a dark brown canvas handgun rug and a rifle housed in a jet-black leather case.

"I'll carry these if you'll carry the shooting bag," she said, handing a large dark blue nylon bag full of gear to Sarah.

Shrugging the rifle case over her left shoulder and turning on her heels Sarah said, "Let's go down behind the barn. There's a big dirt pile back there. It makes a good backstop to catch the bullets after we shoot them."

"Why do you need to catch the bullets?" Sarah asked jokingly, a tinge of stress tainting her voice. "Don't you think I'll hit the target?"

"Oh, I'm sure you'll be hitting the target soon enough but the bullet goes right through the cardboard and paper targets we'll be using. You have to catch them in something. Dirt is a real good bullet catcher."

Sarah picked up on the seriousness of Nadine's attitude so she remained silent.

The horses in the pasture watched them intently until they disappeared around the corner of the barn then lost interest and returned to munching flakes of compressed hay from the ground.

Nadine detoured into the rear door of the barn and reappeared with an old yellow, brown, and black striped horse blanket. She walked determinedly to an area where bare patches of earth showed between islands of well-matted grass and unceremoniously dropped the blanket on the ground. After kicking the blanket flat with the scuffed toe of her work boot, she gently removed a blued Ruger Single-Six .22 caliber handgun from its protective brown rug and placed it gingerly on the blanket.

"See this little gizmo here?" Nadine asked as she pointed at the revolver's right side.

"What's that?" Sarah asked.

"That's the loading gate," Nadine replied. "By flipping it open with your thumb, like this, it renders the revolver incapable of firing. That's the condition it will always be left in when we're not shooting it."

"That must be an old gun," Sarah observed. "It's all shiny along the edges."

"It's not that old. The shiny spots are where the bluing has worn off from it being carried in a holster," Nadine replied patiently. "This was one of my favorite woods bumming revolvers before I got the .357 Smith so it's ridden in a holster almost every day for a year or more."

"Woods bumming?"

"It's a term for when you're just bumming around the woods with no particular goal in mind; just taking a nice relaxing walk in the woods."

"Like hiking?"

"Just like hiking," Nadine replied. "Except that you carry a handgun for personal protection or to plink a little for the fun of it to sharpen your shooting eye."

"Plink?"

"Yes, plink," she said with a broad smile appearing on her face. "It's a term meaning to shoot at an old tin can or other target of opportunity."

"But all the safety rules of shooting still apply when you plink?"

"You bet they do. Even when you're plinking in the woods instead of on a formal shooting range, you still have to observe all the rules for safety's sake."

"Are we going to go plinking someday?"

"Someday," Nadine replied as she slid the rifle out of its black leather case. "Right now let's get you started correctly on the range we've set up here."

"What kind of gun is this?"

"This is a Marlin Model 39," Nadine replied patiently. "It's a .22 the same as the Ruger."

She then took the blue nylon shooting bag from Sarah, set it beside the firearms, and spun to face her. Nadine's graceful movements belied her bulky build.

"OK," Nadine began, "Now we're all business. Shooting is a serious activity and we'll treat it as such at all times. It only takes a split second of inattention for an unintended discharge to occur and you can never call that errant bullet back."

"Here are the rules of the shooting range," she continued without waiting for acknowledgement. Sarah stared at her attentively.

"Always have all gun barrels pointing downrange. There is no reason to have them pointing in any other direction. Our targets are down there and nowhere else," she said pointing toward the dirt piles.

"When we go down to the targets, the actions of all guns will be opened, and the guns left lying on this horse blanket," she said as she pointed toward the blanket on the ground.

Sarah's eyes began to widen as she listened intently to the instructions.

"That way we know that all guns have their actions open when anyone is downrange. If there is any breach of these rules we will immediately put the guns away and suspend shooting until we review the rules of the range."

Nadine's determined look left no doubt in Sarah's mind that she meant every word she said.

She continued unabated, "No one is to touch any gun, for any reason, while someone is downrange. If we have to fix something or adjust the sights there will be plenty of time after everyone is back behind the firing line."

"There are the four Rules of Gun Safety. They are never to be broken," she stated with a stern expression on her face.

"Number one," she said, "is to always keep the muzzle of your gun pointing in a safe direction. This is important because if you always have your gun pointed in a direction where it's safe for you to shoot; you'll never hurt or kill anything you don't want to."

"Number Two," she continued in an authoritative tone. "Always assume that every gun is loaded. If you treat every gun, even when you 'absolutely know' it's unloaded, as being loaded, you'll treat it with the respect it deserves. It's when you begin taking your gun for granted that unintended discharges happen. Please note I did not say 'accidental discharge.' There are no such things as accidents in gun handling, only stupid actions by the operators."

"What do you think number three is?" Nadine asked her pointedly.

Sarah was taken aback by the question and could only look at Nadine with a blank, puzzled stare. She hadn't planned on being tested before she was given the information.

"Keep your finger off the trigger until you're on target and ready to shoot," she said without waiting for Sarah to answer. "If your finger is not on the trigger it can't fire the gun. If the firearm discharges then something pulled the trigger. It's as simple as that."

"When you're on target and ready to fire, move the manual safety to the 'off' position," she said as she motioned with her finger without touching the rifle. "Always be careful to keep the muzzle of the barrel pointing down range toward the target backstop when you move the safety to the 'off' position as a safety precaution. Remember gun safety rule number one? This is one instance where it's applicable."

"That only leaves number four," Sarah said, anxious to complete the instructions and begin shooting.

"Keep your pants on, Missy," Nadine said evenly. "The safety rules are much more important than the actual shooting. A monkey can pull the trigger. It takes forethought and a conscientious effort to do so safely."

"Rule Four is to make sure of your target and what's beyond it. That's why we're shooting into a dirt pile. We know it'll stop the bullets."

Nadine flicked an errant strand of hair from her dark brown eyes.

Sarah began babbling on, asking one question after the other. Nadine tried to hide a smile she felt spreading across her face when she noticed the slight hint of nervousness in Sarah's voice.

Being a little nervous is good. It means she doesn't have a cavalier attitude going into this.

After getting their eye and ear protection in place, Nadine raised her voice so Sarah could hear over the sound-deadening earplugs and muffs.

"Now pick up that rifle and we'll get started."

"But I want to learn to shoot the pistol!" Sarah complained.

"And you will," Nadine replied calmly. "But first you have to learn the basics of sight picture, breath control, and trigger press. That's much easier to do with a rifle."

Sarah smiled at Nadine, realizing she was being a little too impatient. Nadine was gracious and seemed to expect it and accepted her eagerness.

Either Nadine was an exceptionally good schoolteacher and has tons of patience or she remembers what it was like when she first began to shoot. It's most likely a combination of both, Sarah thought.

When Nadine instructed her to do so, Sarah scrunched down behind the rifle, her heart beating wildly with excitement. As she was sighting down the barrel, Nadine gave more detailed instructions to her.

"Take a deep breath, let half of it out, hold it, and slowly press the trigger straight back."

Just as Nadine finished her instructions, she heard the signature report of a .22 long rifle cartridge being fired.

PpHTTTT.

The sound was muffled so well by the hearing protection Sarah wasn't sure if she fired the shot. Raising her head up to see the target she asked anxiously, "Did I hit it?"

"Look for yourself," Nadine replied as she handed Sarah a binocular.

It didn't take her long to find the hole in the lower right corner of the target.

"Yahoo!" Sarah hollered wildly, scaring Nadine with her blood-curdling yell.

After Nadine regained her composure, she returned Sarah's smile.

Thank you Lord. Giving her early success in learning to shoot helps keep her enthusiasm peaked.

If she can learn the difference between using something as simple as a gun for good or evil, then she may be able to make some sense of her situation.

"I want to shoot again," Sarah said simply as she snuggled onto the horse blanket and settled in behind the Marlin. Then she looked up at Nadine.

"If I do well with these guns, can I shoot some of the bigger ones tomorrow?" she asked.

"I have a plan on how you can progress all the way up to shooting my biggest guns proficiently," Nadine said patiently. "It may take us a few days to work our way up the power scale but we have time."

CHAPTER 18

ARI-1 COURSE

Each evening, after the animals had been cared for and dinner was in the oven, Sarah and Nadine would retire to the Florida Room with "Sundowners," the adult beverage of choice consumed after the day has ended and the guns are put away. Today, they were enjoying Kahlua and cream over ice.

"So what are we going to do tomorrow after we're done with the morning chores?" Sarah asked tiredly.

"Well, well, you seem to have a certain enthusiasm for this country life all of a sudden," Nadine said as she smiled at Sarah.

"Yeah, I guess I do. The last week has been great. I never realized I had spent my entire life living in cities and hadn't experienced true country living. Do you think I'll ever be able to go back?" she asked jokingly.

"No I don't," Nadine replied seriously.

"Really?"

"You may have enjoyed the lights and fast-paced nightlife of the city when you didn't know any better, but now you do," Nadine replied with a hint of devilishness in her voice.

"You are a wise old sage, Madam!" Sarah said cheekily.

They both rolled in their seats as they broke into uproarious, schoolgirl-like laughter. After calming down and taking a long draw on her drink, Sarah said with a dead serious tone to her voice, "I didn't think I would ever be able to laugh like that again."

"I knew you would. I just wasn't sure it would be this soon. Time truly is the greatest healer but sometimes it takes way too long to heal."

"Yeah," she said absently.

"So what do you want to do tomorrow?" Nadine inquired quickly to change the subject.

"I'd like to go to wherever they sell ammunition," Sarah said, then stopped for a moment to take a sip of her Kahlua and cream. "I want to replace your ammunition we've shot and I want to buy a bunch more so we can shoot it all up. Shooting relaxes me and I really enjoy it. I truly think it's therapeutic."

Nadine smiled knowingly.

"I know what you mean. When my ex left me all I had were my horses and my guns. It was the only thing I knew to be real and I could trust. So I rode and shot all day long for weeks on end. And lo and behold, somewhere along the line my life began to return."

"So you think I should shoot and ride horses for a few weeks?" Sarah asked with a hint of incredulity in her voice.

"Well, kind of," Nadine replied levelly as she glanced at the pasture from the comfort of the Florida Room. "What worked for me may not work for you. Not only are we two distinctly different people with disparate ways of working through our emotions, but your situation of losing your husband is vastly unlike my predicament. You may need a different set of circumstances to get yourself back on track."

"So what do you suggest, Oh Sage One?" Sarah asked with a broad smile on her face.

"Well, though I'm not a psychologist and I don't even play one on TV---," Nadine replied sarcastically. "I think that since shooting is a healing activity for you, you should take the ARI-1 course."

"What's that?" Sarah asked with great interest.

"It's the 101 course offered by the Armed Response Institute. ARI-1 is a 40-hour immersion course that teaches you how, when, and when not to use deadly force. It's a mainstay for lawyers and cops because it goes well beyond the stuff they teach in law schools and police academies about using lethal force."

Sarah looked at Nadine incredulously. "So! You think that since I've decided shooting is fun I need to learn to kill people?"

"Honey, you didn't want to learn to shoot to put little holes in paper," Nadine said in a level tone, trying to broach a delicate subject. "You want to learn to protect yourself from the coyotes and other predators in this world like the ones who killed Josh."

Nadine did not tread lightly enough.

Sarah glared menacingly at her, stood up defiantly, and slammed the yellow-fringed throw pillow she had been cradling on her lap onto the couch before stalking out of the room.

Nadine looked despairingly at the ice in her glass and let her go.

Well, maybe she wasn't ready for what you just dumped on her. What do you do now? Priority number one is to get dinner ready, she decided. *I'm starved.*

After checking on the progress of dinner, she decided the roast would be ready in twenty minutes.

I may as well make another Kahlua and cream then check my e-mail.

When the oven timer chimed the roast was cooked perfectly, the baked potatoes were soft, and there was no sign of Sarah.

I may as well dine alone. I'll set a place for her in case she cools down enough to eat. What the heck! I'm going to open that bottle of Foxhorn Cabernet I've been saving. It'll go great with the roast.

And I may as well catch up on reading this month's Today's Horse magazine. I guess I've gotten used to having Sarah here to talk with during dinner and have neglected my usual meal routine.

Just as she was beginning to clear away the dirty dishes Sarah appeared silently and stood at the doorway.

"Is there enough left for me?" she asked in a guarded but friendly manner. She forced a waxen smile upon her lips. Her eyes were red-rimmed and puffy, and her nose showed signs of redness from repeated wiping.

She's trying to make amends. That's a good omen.

"There's not only enough for you but it'll probably carry us over for lunch tomorrow," Nadine said as she smiled broadly in a gesture signaling her acceptance of Sarah's unspoken apology. "Sit down; it'll be easier for me to serve you since I know where everything is. Do you want wine with your dinner?"

"Yes, please," Sarah replied quietly.

Nadine sat with her as she ate, reading her magazine to avoid staring at every bite she placed it in her mouth. She began eating daintily, placing each forkful in her mouth with great care and chewing slowly, but progressed to a steady cadence as she hunched slightly forward over her rapidly emptying plate.

It's nice to see she's hungry. It's a good sign.

After she was sated, Sarah carefully placed her knife and fork side by side on the dirty plate, then slid it deliberately to the side of the table. Gently lifting her napkin from her lap she folded it with great care and placed it on the table then looked directly at Nadine.

When Nadine sensed Sarah's eyes locked on her she slowly looked up from her reading to meet her gaze.

"So tell me more about the ARI-1 course, Oh Sage One", she said with a smile on her face. "What do they do?"

"They teach people when, how, and when not to shoot in self-defense," Nadine replied. "And they teach you what to do and what not to do in the aftermath of a self-defensive shooting to deal effectively with the legal system."

"Who teaches it, some old, broken down Rambos?"

Sarah was immediately sorry for the sarcasm in her voice and was ready to apologize but Nadine continued without acknowledging her rudeness.

"No Rambos there, it's all either retired or active-duty police officers teaching the course," she replied in a matter-of-fact manner. She wasn't going to let Sarah control the tone of this conversation because it was too important for her emotional healing to treat the topic lightly.

"The Armed Response Institute is owned and operated by a wild, funny guy. Oh God, you wouldn't believe the number of jokes this guy knows!" she said while blushing and gently shaking her head back and forth.

"So they're a little off-color at times, I assume?" Sarah asked surreptitiously.

"That's an understatement, but they are funny," Nadine confessed.

"Any way, the owner is Sam Heydt. He's one of the cops who travel nationwide to train other cops. There're no Rambos there; just professionals."

"So there's a bunch of testosterone-fired cops teaching the course. What does a woman do in that type of environment besides make lunch?"

She was again embarrassed by her own sarcasm. "I'm sorry, I don't know why I'm being so mean. Maybe it's because I'm scared of what's happening to me and how my attitudes are changing so quickly."

"Don't worry about it. It's a legitimate question," Nadine replied then continued, "There're no testosterone-fired teachers in that bunch. Well, they obviously have the testosterone to be real men but they're more courteous and accommodating to their female students than a woman would be. They understand this type of training is basically out of character for women, at least until the women understand their role in protecting the weak among us."

"Sammie, that's the name he goes by, once told me he went to bat for female FBI agents in court because they couldn't pass their firearms proficiency test. Apparently, the more petite hands of the females needed a smaller grip on their handguns and they couldn't handle the large-gripped firearm the FBI was issuing to its agents."

"That's chivalrous of him, but did it do any good?"

"The FBI changed the equipment so it fit smaller hands and that allowed women to pass the shooting proficiency test," Nadine replied. "Now they're doing good work as career FBI agents. Of course, that situation didn't endear him to the FBI hierarchy but it doesn't seem to bother him. The bottom line is that he goes to bat for women."

"And you think this is what I need?" Sarah asked apprehensively.

"It's not me that thinks you need this. You brought yourself to that conclusion but didn't put it into those terms."

"Say what?" Sarah asked as a quizzical expression flashed across her face.

"It goes back to your Biology 101 lesson with coyotes. You even threw in a healthy dose of Psychology 101 from that Bachelor's degree you got back in undergrad," she replied.

"What are you talking about?"

"This isn't rocket science," Nadine said. "A coyote, the predator, will continue to kill and eat its prey as long as some outside force doesn't stop it. Human predators and coyotes act the same behavior-wise. They'll continue doing what they have always done until someone stops them."

"So the responsibility for violence lies with the predator that hasn't been stopped?"

"That's right. But it also depends on the prey. If the prey has the ability to stop the predator from preying upon them, then the predator will change their behaviors. One way or the other," Nadine said, clarifying her remarks.

"But aren't criminals just a product of a bad upbringing and it's not really their fault?" Sarah asked, knowing her deeply held concept of reality was being brought into question.

"It doesn't matter what their upbringing was like if you're the prey," Nadine said unemotionally. "You're still just a piece of dead meat to them."

"Yeah, but---"

"Yeah, but nothing," Nadine said with an edge of impatience in her voice. "Predators are not sensible and you can't reason with them. Don't think for a minute they're like us. They're a distinct breed and live by different rules. What you consider to be 'reasoning' or 'understanding' they perceive as weakness. Therefore, you deserve to be eaten."

"Are you sure that's the way they think?"

"It's the way the mind of any predator works," Nadine stated with finality. "And you know it."

"It seems so cruel---and cold."

"Predators do not reason with their food, they simply eat it. Like you just did at dinner," Nadine said. "A violent human attacker, the predator, can be expected to react in the same way as a coyote."

"But they're human. Not animals!" Sarah said with a twinge of hysteria creeping into her voice.

Nadine noticed that Sarah's hands were moving in anxious, twitching movements as she spoke.

"Violent attackers tend to be sociopathic, meaning they don't follow the same morals as the rest of society. That's why they're called 'career criminals.' It's the way they live their lives. Either way, you're still going to be eaten by the predator. It's not such a good deal for you, the victim," Nadine said plainly.

"So what do we have to do, put all the criminals in jail?" Sarah asked, her previous anxiety having subsided as Nadine began making sense.

"Or kill them," Nadine said matter-of-factly. "The threat of jail, death, or serious injury is enough to change the behavior of the smarter predators; at least if it's staring them in the face. It's the only way to keep them from preying on innocent people."

"Meaning what?" Sarah asked tentatively, still slightly shocked by Nadine's bluntness.

"Meaning that when a criminal is taken at gunpoint by a police officer or an armed citizen, the message is simple," she replied. "Stop your aggressive behavior immediately or be seriously injured and risk dying."

"So we have to shoot all the criminals?" Sarah asked incredulously.

"No, the majority of criminals understand their options are very limited at that point," she said. "They usually stop their aggressive actions immediately to avoid injury. That's why the vast majority of incidents where good people take criminals at gunpoint either end in surrender or, more likely, the bad guy running away. There are over two million such incidents in the United States each year."

"That's a lot," Sarah said. "If there's so many why don't we ever hear about them?"

"You never hear about them because it ends happily with the criminal running away," Nadine explained simply. "Since that's all the victim wanted in the first place, why get the police involved?"

"But you think you'd hear about some of these on the news."

"There's no news when a criminal runs away; only when they commit a crime and someone is injured or killed," Nadine said plainly.

"So all I have to know is how to point a gun at a bad guy and he'll run away?" Sarah asked innocently.

"Definitely not," Nadine said with a look of horror on her face. "You have to be willing and able to use lethal force, and you can only be confident enough to use lethal force if you know the law is on your side. That's why any citizen who makes the decision to carry a concealed firearm should take a course, like ARI-1, that teaches the legalities and tactics of self-defense."

"But if I live out here, which I just may do someday because I really like it in the country, I won't need a gun unless I go into the woods. There's really no crime out here, is there?"

"Honey, that's denial and you know it," Nadine said soothingly. "Just like the person who won't take a CPR course or buckle their seat belt because 'it won't happen to me' you're refusing to accept reality if you think you'll never need to defend yourself. Pretending that violent crime won't find you, regardless of where you live, is just sticking your head in the sand."

Nadine smiled softly with grandmotherly-like concern showing in her face.

"So you think a course is the way to go?" Sarah asked seriously.

"It's the only way to go," Nadine replied softly. "They teach you how to prevent bad things from happening and how to handle them when they can't be avoided."

"We're never done learning I guess," Sarah said submissively.

"You've paid for many years of college learning how to make a living," Nadine replied calmly. "This is the knowledge that may allow you live. Period."

Nadine saw a look of enlightenment cross Sarah's face.

"OK, what will I need?" she asked.

"You'll need a good quality handgun. It doesn't have to be new; there are plenty of gently used guns on the market," Nadine replied. "You'll also need five to six hundred rounds of full power ammunition. You'll be doing a lot of shooting over the week."

"The week!" Sarah exclaimed.

"Yep, it runs for five days just like a real job. There's a lot of information and it's all new to folks like you. You have to have time to absorb it and then put it into action. That's a big task and one that can't be accomplished in a short weekend."

"What else will I need?" Sarah replied with a tone of acceptance in her voice. "If I'm going to be serious about this I may as well do it right."

"You can visit their website and get a list of all of the stuff you'll need," Nadine said with a smile. "But to make it easier for you I already printed the material while you were upstairs."

"So you were pretty damned sure I'd do this," she said with a smile. "OK, let's see what you have!"

"Yeah, I was pretty sure you'd go," Nadine admitted. "We'll go shopping tomorrow afternoon to get you what you'll need. We deserve a break from farm work anyway."

CHAPTER 19

SHOPPING

The next morning after the farm chores were completed they headed to town. Nadine was determined to buy everything Sarah needed for the ARI-1 course before she changed her mind.

The shopping went quickly.

"That pretty well completes our list. How about some lunch?"

"That's the best idea you've had today," Sarah replied energetically. "Where do you want to go? I'm buying."

"Let's head on over to The Eatery. They have good food and I really get a kick out of how everyone seems to know everyone else in these small towns."

During lunch Sarah dominated the conversation with questions regarding the ARI-1 course, which Nadine answered patiently. After leaving the restaurant, Nadine said, "We better be getting back to the farm and start the evening chores if we want to finish before dark."

Within five minutes of leaving The Eatery and the town of Thompsonville, Sarah saw a 'For Sale' sign beside a long dirt lane perched atop a yellow wooden pole. Her head snapped to the right, striving to look at the property as they passed by. A fleeting glimpse of a small, well-kept white clapboard house surrounded by neatly kept outbuildings was all she needed to determine she wanted a closer view.

"Do we have time to go back and take a little better look at that house for sale?" Sarah asked, already knowing the answer to her question.

Nadine looked at her out of the corner of her eyes.

"So you're on a shopping spree and now even a house looks pretty good?" Nadine asked chidingly.

"No, I'm just open to all options right now. I'll need a place to live, or at least a place to run away to when the real world gets too stressful, and I really like this area. The people are friendly and it has a certain peacefulness about it," Sarah replied.

"You don't have to explain to me," Nadine said as she made a U-turn in front of a dilapidated red barn.

"I know," Sarah said as she blushed. "I guess I was just trying to convince myself that house shopping is OK. You know, that it's not too soon to begin rebuilding my life instead of just staying with you forever."

"Good idea," Nadine said, suddenly becoming very serious. "Are you sure you can find a way to make a living out here in the boonies?"

Before Sarah could answer, Nadine asked her second question, "Are you sure you'd be able to put up with the peace and quiet out here for the long haul? You're a city girl that's used to always having something to do from sun-up to well past sundown."

"Aren't we getting a little nosy?" Sarah joked.

"Cut it out," Nadine said as she smiled broadly and looked directly at Sarah. "You know what I mean. You'll have to be able to make enough money to pay the mortgage on this much property. The taxes alone on a piece of acreage this big are enough to curl your toes."

"Actually," Sarah said cautiously, "I should have a ton of money soon."

Nadine's eyebrows rose considerably but she was too polite to ask any more questions. She didn't have to because Sarah was in an expansive and talkative mood.

"My practice is in the process of being sold. Joe Holmes, my associate for many years, is buying it. We've already settled on a purchase price, the bank is willing to lend him the money, and lawyers are drawing up the papers," Sarah said as Nadine turned onto the dirt lane with the 'For Sale' sign beside it and came to a stop. "My house in D.C. is on the market and it should bring a fair amount of money. We moved into a neighborhood that was being 'gentrified' and rehabilitated the house from a wreck into a showplace."

"Rehabilitation takes a lot of work," Nadine said as she tried to steer the conversation away from the direction she knew it was headed. She failed miserably in changing the topic of the discussion.

"We only had three months to enjoy our showpiece residence before Josh was---."

Sarah's voice trailed off perceptibly. She then took a deep breath and steeled herself before continuing, "And Josh had a two million dollar life insurance policy bought by the group practice he was a partner in."

"That was nice of them," Nadine said innocently.

"It wasn't out of the goodness of their flinty little hearts," Sarah said bitterly. "Josh's partners are listed as the beneficiary on the policy and it's in their contract the money will be used to buy Josh's part of the practice from his widow."

Sarah looked out the side window of the car as tears welled up in her eyes.

"That's the first time I've referred to myself as a widow," she said tearfully.

"So what you're saying is you're filthy rich. At least for the moment," Nadine asked in an attempt to change the topic slightly and help pull Sarah out of her funk.

"Yep, that's what I'm saying," she said as a wan smile broke through her tears. "Assuming everything goes as it's supposed to. You know what it's like when a bunch of lawyers get their fingers into things that involve money."

"Oh yeah, unfortunately I do," Nadine said with a smile. "I've had my share of dealing with the law profession."

"Let's go down the lane a little ways and see what the house looks like. I really can't see much from here," Sarah said.

Nadine drove to the front of the house and gave a courtesy toot on her pickup truck's horn to alert the residents in the house that they had visitors.

It took less than two minutes for a small, grandmotherly woman with a floral print apron covering her below-the-knee length housedress to appear at the front door. She was wiping her hands on a white dishtowel with large yellow daisies printed on it and smiling from ear-to-ear.

She opened the door widely yet stood square in the middle of the doorway. The message was clear; if you're friendly then you're welcome. If you're not, you're in for a heap of trouble so you best mind your manners.

"What can I help you young ladies with?" she asked with a smile.

"Hello, I'm Nadine Brand and this is Sarah Collins," Nadine said. "I live down near Rapine and Sarah is up visiting for a few weeks. She isn't sure if she wants to move to the area but she saw your place and wanted to see it up closer."

Sarah quickly interjected, "Naturally, we'll call the real estate agent to set up a time to visit and get a good look at the property. I'm just not sure exactly what I'm looking for, or even if I'm in the market for a new house."

"Well, I'm a Sarah also. Sarah Schneider is my name but everyone knows me by my nickname, Minnie. Don't ask me where the name came from - it just kind of grew on me!" she beamed.

"You're right, the real estate agent is handling the actual showing of the house but if you want to sit for a few minutes, we can visit until my bread is finished baking."

"Thank you but we don't want to intrude."

"Nonsense, you aren't intruding," she said enthusiastically then pointed toward a small, squat white clapboard outbuilding. "Go get those folding chairs from over there by the springhouse and set them up here by the front door and I'll get us some sweet tea."

Without another word she turned on her heels and disappearing back into the dark confines of the house.

Nadine turned and went to fetch the folding aluminum chairs with Sarah close on her heels. Their eyes flitted observantly over the property as they walked.

"Minnie seems to be fairly old," Nadine observed. "She may have lived in this house all her life. If I'm right, she'll be able to give us a history of this property if we can get her talking."

"We don't have much time; don't forget about the animals," Sarah reminded her. "Besides, we just showed up unannounced. I should have just called the real estate agency."

"Don't worry about it," Nadine replied. "Minnie seems to be glad to have some company."

As Nadine was setting up the last of the chairs Minnie reappeared at the door with a tray holding three glass tumblers and a curved handle clear glass pitcher with daisies painted on the side. The pitcher was filled almost to overflowing with ice and murky brown tea.

"Fetch that little metal table off the patio there, Honey, if you would please," Minnie said as she smiled at Sarah.

Minnie patiently waited for Sarah to get the rickety table set up and as stable as it would ever be.

"Help me set this down, Honey," Minnie asked with a trace of straining in her voice.

Sarah took the slightly rusted metal serving tray with an ancient Coca-Cola advertisement printed on its face from Minnie and set it on the table then inconspicuously held it steady while Minnie served Nadine. She then poured a glass of iced tea for Sarah and handed it to her.

"Sit down there, Honey," Minnie said as she indicated an empty chair with a gnarled, arthritic finger. Finally, she poured and lifted her own glass of tea high in the air and made a toast.

"To your health," Minnie said.

"To your health," they said in unison as they held their glasses aloft.

A quaint smile spread between the three women.

After everyone had taken a deep swallow of their tea and the two visitors nodded their appreciation to their host, Minnie started the conversation.

"Now, what can I help y'all with," she asked in a matter-of-fact manner.

"Well, I'm not sure I'm really in the market for a house right now. Especially this far from where I'm currently living," Sarah said.

"Then why are you even looking for a house? And where are you living now?" Minnie asked boldly.

"Well, I'm living with Nadine right now, you see--" Before she realized it, Sarah had spewed out her entire life history to Minnie.

Sarah never thought she could ever tell anyone everything she revealed to Minnie in the next twenty minutes. Maybe it was because she looked like the perfect grandmother and Sarah needed grandmotherly advice at this very difficult time of her life.

"I'm sorry," she apologized. "I didn't mean to dominate the conversation."

"It's not a problem, Honey," Minnie replied.

"So why are you selling such a beautiful house?" Sarah stammered in an attempt to shift the conversation away from her.

"Well, I'm alone these days myself," she said dully. "My husband died of a massive coronary two years ago and I've been running this place by myself ever since. I'm eighty-two years old and while I do pretty well, I'm starting to slow down."

"You look much younger than your eighty-two years, Minnie," Nadine said.

"And you move like a much younger woman," Sarah opined. "As a chiropractor, I tend to notice things like that."

"You're both much too kind," Minnie replied as she blushed then continued with her story.

"My daughter Susan is sixty-two years old this year and has lived in Florida for the last twenty years," Minnie said. "She and her husband recently moved into a brand new senior citizen's housing development that's still in the process of being built."

"Some of the senior housing facilities I've seen recently are really beautiful," Sarah replied.

"She really loves it and says I can get an apartment in her complex," Minnie continued. "That way we can be neighbors and I don't have to maintain any buildings or cut grass."

"That sounds good to me," Nadine said. "How old do you have to be to get into a place like that?"

Minnie chuckled.

"It's a good deal for both of us because she worries about me, wants me close to keep an eye on me, and yet doesn't want me living with them."

She smiled palely as she looked ashamedly toward her guests.

"I hate to give up this place," she continued. "I was born here and I expected to die here like my husband did, but that's not likely to happen."

"Your husband died in this house?" Sarah asked with repulsion in her voice.

"No, he didn't die in this house, he died at the grocery store while picking up a few items," Minnie replied. "As a matter of fact, I don't think anyone ever died in this house."

"That's a relief, I'm a little uncomfortable about houses where people have passed on," Sarah admitted.

"There were a number of births, but no one ever died here," Minnie reflected, searching the recesses of her mind.

To change the subject, Sarah asked, "How much land do you have here?"

"We have one hundred acres or somewhere thereabouts," Minnie said. "There are fifty under cultivation and roughly thirty in woods, and twenty in overgrown pasture land."

"That's a nice ratio," Nadine offered as she looked at Sarah out of the corner of her eyes.

"Do you see that fence with the cattle standing behind it?" Minnie asked as she pointed with a shaky finger. "That's the property line with the Miller farm."

"They have some nice looking Black Angus cattle there," Nadine observed in a neighborly tone.

"And that fence over there?" Minnie asked, pointing in the opposite direction. "That's the property line with the Sabbatini farm."

"Both of the property lines go straight back to the woods and continue until they hit the National Forest property line," she continued, warming to the conversation. "The Forest Service marks their property real well with little metal tags on all of the trees along the property line."

"It's good to know some of my tax money is going toward something useful," Sarah said with a gentle smile creasing her lips.

"The federal government doesn't want anyone felling any of their trees," Minnie stated with finality.

Apparently, Sarah thought, *Minnie's dealings with the federal government in regards to the National Forest property line did not go smoothly over the years.*

"Have you had trouble with the Federal government over your property lines?" Sarah asked innocently.

"Nothing compared to the War of Northern Aggression," said Minnie with a fair bit of vehemence dripping from her voice. It was obvious that hard feelings ran deep and injustices were neither easily forgiven nor forgotten.

Nadine and Sarah looked at each other and muffled giggles beneath their hands.

"And you've taken care of all this property by yourself for the last two years?" Sarah asked to bring the subject back to the farm.

"Well, I haven't taken care of it all by myself. I've kind of overseen its maintenance," Minnie corrected her. "There's a nice man from down the road who farms the fifty tillable acres. Instead of getting a percentage of the profits as is the usual custom, he pays the taxes on the fifty acres and keeps my grass cut."

"That seems like a reasonable trade," Sarah said, marveling over the simplicity of the arrangement.

"Yes it is, as far as I'm concerned," Minnie said. "And he may be persuaded to continue the agreement if you bought the farm."

"Do you really think so?" Sarah asked with increasing interest.

"I think it's a profitable arrangement for him and it saves me quite a bit of aggravation," she assured her. "It doesn't seem as though you're really in any type of situation to run the place by yourself."

"After helping Nadine on her horse farm for a few days I know I don't have enough energy to take care of a place this size by myself," she admitted.

"And if I may be so bold, I don't think you're really cut out to run a farm as a business," Minnie stated as she thrust her jaw forward.

Sarah giggled politely.

"Minnie, you're so right. I would never consider running a farm as a business. This city girl just doesn't have the experience!"

Suddenly, she became very serious. "I don't really know what I want right now."

"That's a tough situation to be in," Minnie agreed with a barely perceptible nod of her head.

"I seem to need a totally different life than what I had a few short weeks ago," Sarah admitted. "I had my life all planned out and now that's all been shattered. I'm left with nothing, or so it would seem."

"I've been there and done that," Nadine added as her mind wandered back into her own past. Sarah shot her a quick sideways glance and continued with her story.

"One thing I do know; if I were to buy a place like this, even if I only used it during the weekends, I would keep it as a viable, working farm."

"That's what it was meant to be and should be kept as one," Minnie agreed.

"The history is too deep here and it's a good place to raise a family," Sarah agreed. "I could never allow a fine farm like this to fall into disrepair."

"For a city girl, you seem to have a firm grasp on what a good piece of land deserves and what it can offer the right person," Minnie said with a warm smile directed at Sarah.

"That's why I would keep it a viable operation," she declared. "Even if it cost me more money than I made out of it." Sarah surprised herself with such a strong statement and was even more astonished that she meant every word of it.

"How would you keep it as a working enterprise if you aren't here all the time?"

"I'd find someone to farm the land like you've done," she replied, looking Minnie directly in the eyes. "I don't see any livestock in the pasture so I'd renovate it to support either horses or cattle. I'm partial to cattle for some reason."

"Probably because you're tired of shoveling out the stalls at my place," Nadine said chidingly.

"That may have something to do with it," Sarah joked back and they all laughed uproariously.

"There are farmers who would watch your livestock while you weren't here," Minnie said. "The local growers are usually looking for additional income and most of them are honest, hard workers."

"Is there any tax advantages to keeping the property as a farm?" Sarah asked, her business acumen peaking.

"The agricultural designation definitely reduces taxes," Minnie replied. "I'm impressed by your grasp of the importance of watching overhead expenses for an agricultural operation."

"I've run my own business for a number of years," she reminded her.

"And you think you can keep tabs on the business aspects, keep the place in reasonable shape, and still have time to relax here?" Minnie asked with a heavy dose of skepticism in her voice.

"It depends on what you call relaxation," Sarah replied as she smiled. "Farms and lounging around don't seem to go hand-in-hand."

The women again broke out in laughter. Nadine was laughing hard enough for her bulbous belly to bounce deliriously.

"I know what you're getting at, Minnie," Sarah said, suddenly very serious. "But you have to know me. I can't sit still for more than ten minutes. I need to keep moving."

"A farm will keep you moving, that's for sure," Minnie replied.

"Relaxation to me would be to have a day that starts at five o'clock, involves manual labor all day long, and ends at half-past dark," Sarah said. "No mind boggling paperwork, no major decisions regarding another person's life, not having to put up with ten staff members bitching because four of them are going through PMS at the same time. Now that's relaxation!"

Minnie looked at her incredulously then burst into uproarious laughter.

"Your daily grind must be a real hum-dinger!" she bubbled. "After all that, shoveling horse shit must be relaxing!"

Nadine and Sarah sat stunned for a split second then began laughing until their sides hurt.

"Minnie!" Sarah said still laughing. "To hear such a prim, proper lady like yourself put my situation into such succinct terms is hilarious!"

After visiting with Minnie for another hour, Sarah and Nadine reminded each other they had to get back to care for the horses.

As they were driving down the lane from Minnie's farm, the delicious scent of freshly baked bread wafted throughout the pick-up from the warm loaf sitting between them on the seat.

"Minnie was elated when you said you'd call the real estate agency and set an appointment to see the rest of the property," Nadine said. "I think she can see a lot of herself in you when she was your age."

"You mean beautiful and worldly?"

"No, I mean full of piss and vinegar."

They both laughed boisterously until they couldn't speak. The rest of the drive to The Shire was made in silence.

She's really thinking deeply, Nadine thought. *I don't know what she has going around in her mind but I'm certainly not going to interrupt. She needs a lot of quiet time, I think. Besides, there's nothing I can add that would be helpful right now anyway.*

Sarah continued to be strangely quiet and contemplative during the evening chores. Her mood continued throughout the evening as she ate dinner with a minimum of small talk.

After clearing and washing the dinner dishes, Sarah said, "I'm going to bed. I didn't realize how exhausting this has been. Maybe it's just the fresh country air, what do you think?"

"I think it's the two huge slices of Minnie's homemade bread with apple butter you wolfed down at dinner and not the fresh country air making you sleepy," Nadine said jokingly.

"Maybe that's it!" she replied with a chuckle. "Good night."

When she reached the kitchen door, she stopped and spun to face Nadine and fixed her with an intense gaze.

"Tomorrow after we do the morning chores, can we shoot the guns we haven't shot yet?" she asked.

"Of course we can," Nadine replied. "But it's supposed to get pretty hot tomorrow afternoon so we better get the shooting done early to stay out of the heat."

"Will it be too hot up on the mountain to take a hike after we're done shooting?"

"No, as a matter of fact, it's usually cooler up there," Nadine offered as a questioning look crossed her face. "Do you want to take a little walk up there?"

"If you don't mind. I would actually like a few hours to myself and see if I like the woods," she stated succinctly.

"It's a fine idea. Just remind me to give you my compass," Nadine said in an encouraging tone. "As long as you don't go over the crest of the mountain you can take a northern compass reading and it will always bring you out to the road because it runs east and west."

"Thanks," Sarah said as a gleeful smile spread across her face.

Now what's that all about? Nadine thought as she watched Sarah walk away.

CHAPTER 20

SARAH'S REVELATION

In the morning, Sarah entered the Florida room in the dark and had the coffee ready long before Nadine made her appearance.

"Well, well, it looks like you're getting the hang of this country living," she said as she settled into her easy chair.

"It really feels great to get an early start on the day!" Sarah beamed.

What's up with her that she's so upbeat and vibrant at this hour of the morning?

"So what are your plans for today?" Nadine asked tentatively.

"We're going to take care of the animals as quickly as we can then we'll shoot the rest of your guns, have lunch, and then I'll take a walk up the mountain so you can have a few moments of peace," Sarah said brightly. "You need some personal time."

"Bullshit! I don't need any personal time and you know it!" Nadine joked.

"OK, I need some personal time," Sarah admitted. "Do you think I'll need a gun while I'm up on the mountain?"

"You can carry a gun with you if you want to, you're certainly proficient," Nadine replied. "Take your pick."

"What about the legality of carrying a gun, even if it's in the woods?" she asked with concern in her voice.

"Virginia allows 'open carry' so long as it's in a holster and in clear view," Nadine replied. "Besides, when you're on my property you're legal."

"What else will I need?" Sarah asked, realizing the seriousness of being in the woods alone.

"Usually, there isn't anyone up on the mountain at this time of year so you should take your cell phone."

"Can I get reception out here?"

"You may not get a signal until you're near the top," Nadine informed her. "But it's better to have it than not."

"Is there any drinking water on the mountain, like a stream or anything?"

"You'll have to carry water," Nadine said seriously. "Never trust untreated water. Most of the surface water has parasites in it these days."

"What do you want for dinner?" Sarah asked unexpectedly.

"We haven't even had breakfast yet and you want to start dinner?" Sarah laughed.

"I wasn't thinking of starting dinner," she said, showing a full set of even, brilliantly white teeth in a broad smile. "I was thinking of buying you dinner. There has to be a decent restaurant that has a wine list around here someplace."

"D'amato's is over in Spinale. It's only about twenty minutes from here and they have a really good lasagna special on Wednesday nights."

"Italian it is!" Sarah gushed enthusiastically. "Can we finish with the horses and still have enough time to get over there before they close?"

"Yes, we'll probably have time to get showered after doing the evening chores and get over there with plenty of time to spare."

"Let's plan on it then."

"Are you sure you'll have enough energy left after climbing the mountain?" Nadine asked seriously.

"For a dinner with wine served on white linen tablecloths, I'll find the energy," Sarah said with finality.

"It sounds like a plan!" Nadine replied cheerfully.

The morning chores went quickly. By 9:00 a.m. Sarah and Nadine were behind the barn situating their shooting gear at the firing line. The ritual of setting up the gear and range had become an organized, efficient task for the two women.

"What would you like to shoot?" Nadine asked as she began unpacking various pistols, revolvers, and rifles.

"I want to pick up where we left off the other day," Sarah said without hesitation. "I want to learn to shoot the larger pistols we haven't shot yet."

"Pistols it is then," Nadine said with a smile.

It pleased her to see Sarah so enthusiastic about shooting. She had worried that she and Sarah would no longer have much in common since they had gone their separate ways after college but the shooting sports gave them common ground on which to renew and build their relationship.

"Let's start with this Glock nine-millimeter," Nadine said as she picked up a black, plastic-looking pistol.

"What are those funny sights on that pistol?" Sarah asked with a questioning expression on her face.

"Those are XS Sight System's 24/7 Big Dot front sight and express rear sight," Nadine offered.

"They're a lot different than the other sights I've used so far."

"These sights are for fast shooting in emergency self-defensive situations," Nadine patiently explained. "These were developed in Africa for hunting dangerous game."

"In Africa?"

"Yes, in Africa. If an elephant or rhinoceros is bearing down on you with the intent of stomping your miserable human carcass into the ground, you have to be able to shoot fast and accurately at very close range."

"Cool!" Sarah exclaimed.

"They called them 'express sights' and on dangerous big game rifles they used a big, round front bead made of elephant or warthog ivory to pick up the reduced light in the thick, brushy areas where that type of game is hunted."

"Why elephant ivory?" Sarah asked.

"Actually, they preferred warthog ivory because it didn't turn yellow with age like elephant ivory."

"So why don't they use warthog ivory since it has a proven track record?" Sarah quizzed Nadine.

"Modern technology allows the use of tritium, a low-level radioactive material, to put a glowing light into the sights."

"Why's that important?" Sarah asked.

"It's important because most violent encounters, or attacks, occur in low-light situations if not in total darkness," Nadine replied. "The glowing sights allow you to place the front sight on your assailant and get your shot off as soon as possible. Remember, this type of shooting is only in life threatening situations so it's a last ditch effort and you better be on target."

Sarah sighted downrange with an unloaded gun to try the sights. "They're real easy to see and line up," she said.

"Speed and accuracy are everything when you're faced with a violent encounter," Nadine explained.

"I like these a lot," Sarah opined.

"And the glowing sights are very helpful for finding your pistol in the dark," Nadine pointed out. "It's much better than fumbling blindly around your nightstand drawer in the middle of the night."

The shooting session went smoothly until Nadine observed, "It must be close to noon. The sun is straight overhead and my belly is growling."

"I'll make lunch," Sarah said enthusiastically, "if you'll get me a compass and any other stuff I'll need for my foray into the wilds of Virginia."

"It's a deal," Nadine said as she laughed deeply at Sarah's mocking reference to the mountain behind the farm.

As soon as lunch was finished and the dishes washed, Sarah took her leave.

"I'll be back by five o'clock to help with the evening chores," she called over her shoulder as she turned toward the mountain.

"I'm going to take a nap while you're gone," Nadine called after her. "You wear me out."

Sarah laughed and gave a carefree wave with her hand above her head before strolling out of sight with long, confident strides.

"I hope she knows what the hell she's doing," Nadine said to herself before shuffling into the cool innards of the house for her afternoon respite.

Nadine awoke after a thirty-minute nap then sat under the sugar maple tree in her front yard with a tall, frosty glass of ice water within easy reach.

Maybe I shouldn't have let her go hiking alone. She doesn't have any experience in the woods. She shouldn't have any trouble from wildlife but there's always the chance she'll fall or twist an ankle.

The searing heat of the afternoon sun was losing its fierceness and began mellowing as the day slid toward evening. Nadine's worrying made her antsy and she made more trips to the restroom than necessary to burn off her nervous energy.

I should have warned her about the methamphetamine laboratories that occasionally spring up in the wilderness areas around here. The owners aren't afraid to shoot someone to protect their investment.

Fifteen minutes before her deadline, Sarah appeared at the edge of the pasture. Nadine exhaled a huge sigh of relief when she spied her walking with purposeful strides across the meadow.

"Hello, Lady of the Mountain!" Nadine greeted her as she struggled to fight her way out of the chaise lounge she was reclining in.

"Hello, Flatlander!" Sarah quickly quipped. "I've made some decisions and some plans."

"Well, well, and what may they be?" Nadine asked as she handed her a frosty, sweating glass of freshly made iced tea.

Sarah paused to remove the lemon wedge from the rim of the crystal clear glass before guzzling most of the murky tea in a cascade of gulps.

After wiping tiny droplets from her upper lip with the back of her hand, Sarah began excitedly, "I've decided that I'm definitely interested in Minnie's place. I called the real estate agent from up on the mountain. By the way, you're right; I had to be almost at the very top before I could get any cell phone reception."

"Anyway," she continued without letting Nadine get a word in edgewise, "she agreed to show me the property tomorrow and called Minnie to make sure it's OK."

Before Nadine could reply Sarah continued, "I asked the real estate agent if she knew any foresters and she gave me the phone number of her cousin. I hired him to make an appraisal of the timber on those thirty acres. If the property line is as well marked as Minnie says it is, it should be easy to get an accurate appraisal."

Nadine's mouth dropped open. "My, my, aren't you just the little business woman---."

Sarah blushed and started where she left off without skipping a beat, "I also had the real estate agent recommend a colleague from a competing agency. I called and hired him to get some background information on the value of similar properties that have sold in the last few years."

"You're going to steal that land from a nice, little old lady! Shame on you!" Nadine gasped with a display of fake surprise on her face.

"I'm doing no such thing, you witch! And you know it! That farm has been on the market for almost a year. Apparently its way overpriced and I want to be able to make a realistic offer for it. If I have a few figures to show Minnie where it's overpriced she may get to Florida while she can still enjoy it!"

"So you don't think that Minnie's just some robber baron waiting for a star-struck Yankee to come along and overpay for her idyllic plantation?" Nadine chided her friend.

"No I do not," Sarah said seriously. "She truly is a nice lady. I tend to think that either her daughter, or the real estate agent, or both for that matter, want to get a lot more for the place than it's worth."

"You may be right," Nadine agreed. "It wouldn't be the first time grown children put their interests above those of their dear, old mother."

"That's the way I have it figured," Sarah said defiantly. "It would be much easier for her if poor, old Minnie passed away before she had to put up with her living in the same development."

"And you're going to set Minnie straight so she can retire to Florida and aggravate her daughter until she takes her final breath. Is that it?"

"Something like that," Sarah replied flatly. "Is there any more of this iced tea? It's the best tasting I've had in a coon's age. How do you like that hillbilly lingo, eh? I've been practicing."

After getting her refill of iced tea, Sarah sat in the shade with Nadine under the sugar maple then continued detailing her plans. "Now for the best part; I really had to think this one out since you brought it up the other day."

"What did I bring up?" Nadine asked in confusion, totally baffled by what she may have said to put Sarah into such a whirlwind of activity.

"You asked me the million dollar question," she explained. "I hadn't considered if I could stand to live out here in the country full time."

"And the million dollar answer is?"

"The answer is 'no'," Sarah answered pointedly. "I couldn't stand all this peace and quiet."

"What?"

"I'd go crazy in a few weeks but you already knew that because you know me," Sarah replied evenly. "But on the other hand, I can't ever see myself living the fast-paced, heavy-on-the-nightlife lifestyle I used to; so I had to find a compromise."

"You're not one for compromise either," Nadine added accusingly as her eyebrows rose in a ruffled frown.

"No, I'm not, but that doesn't mean I can't meld the best of both worlds and make it work," she said, speaking quickly as though afraid of losing her train of thought. "A colleague has been looking for a doctor to take over control of his satellite practice in Northern Virginia. I have my Virginia license because Josh and I had been planning to move there one day to raise a family."

"You mentioned that," Nadine said, not wanting to dwell on the subject.

Sarah fell silent for a few seconds to regain her composure before forging onward.

"I called him and asked if the position is still open and if he wanted me to take over that clinic," she said with so much excitement she was on the verge of babbling. "He was ecstatic because he knows I can run a profitable operation."

"And he just happened to have this position open?" Nadine asked skeptically.

"He's going to open it," Sarah replied plainly. "He hasn't been able to get a decent associate to make that place work in the five years he's owned it. He always hires screw-ups who don't understand what it takes to make a practice profitable."

"So he's going to fire the guy he has working for him now?"

"He was thinking of firing him anyway. Don't worry about it."

Sarah took a minute to regain her composure once again, still breathing rapidly as she contemplated the lifestyle changes she was considering.

"I insisted that I only work Monday through Thursday," she said, having organized her thoughts and was once again warming to the topic. "That gives me three-day weekends to spend at the farm."

"What about the other three days of the week?" Nadine asked. "Can a practice run profitably with it being closed three days out of seven?"

"I'll hire another associate as soon as I get the practice up and running," Sarah said. "It's important to have a doctor covering the entire week."

"And how long do you estimate it'll take you to get the practice up and running to your satisfaction?" Nadine asked incredulously.

"That'll take me about two months, I figure," she said as she turned the plan over in her mind.

"So you're going to work in Northern Virginia?" Nadine asked in astonishment.

"And spend my weekends out here on the farm," she said as her breath continued to come in excited gasps. "I already have my brother-in-law Jeremy, I call him J.T., looking for an apartment for me."

"Now let me get this straight," Nadine said slowly as she tried to digest all that Sarah had just explained to her. "You're going like a possessed woman and I just want to make sure all the pieces fit. You're going to work in Northern Virginia and then spend your weekends out here?"

"Yep! An apartment in the suburbs, very busy and congested suburbs, I might add. Then I'll have a farm out in the country for long weekends. No grass to mow or maintenance to perform at the apartment but all kinds of chores to do on the farm."

"And if Minnie won't sell you the farm at a price you'll accept?"

"Then I'll find another farm. She doesn't have the only one that's for sale, I'm sure."

"And you think you'll be able to keep up with all the demands of a farm only working it during the weekends?" Nadine asked in a voice heavy with disbelief.

"Exactly," Sarah said. "Remember what Minnie said about the guy she has farming the cultivated land? He also cuts her grass and that's the biggest job needing to be done on a weekly basis with the entire property."

"Honey, there's a lot more to running a farm than harvesting crops and mowing the grass," Nadine said in a condescending tone.

"Every other job can either be hired out to a professional if it's too big for me or I'll be able to work on it over a number of weekends," she continued on undeterred.

"Oh, by the way, I also called the County Extension Service and I have them helping me determine if the farmer is taking advantage of Minnie's generosity."

"You are something else!" Nadine said as her eyes flew wide open.

"I may be able to get someone else to farm the fifty acres with a deal more profitable for me, maybe pay the taxes on the entire property instead of just covering half the taxes, and still have enough left over to pay someone to cut the grass," she explained.

Nadine could only stare wide-eyed. "You certainly are a business person if I ever met one!"

"It's only thinking things through and discovering all the possibilities that may occur then picking the most likely to succeed," Sarah stated flatly.

"Oh, and another thing. When I talked to J.T., he told me I could establish residency in Virginia within 183 days then I can apply for my concealed carry permit."

"So what are you going to do between now and then?"

"I'm going to take three weeks' vacation before I start work at the clinic," Sarah beamed triumphantly. "Until then I'm going to ARI-1. I called while I was up on the mountain and gave them a credit card number to hold my reservation so now I'm all set for the course."

"You've been busy today," Nadine said with a smile.

"If you don't mind, I'd like to keep your place as my base of operations until I'm able to get everything settled," Sarah said with a questioning tone in her voice as she scrunched her face up in a cute, girlish expression.

"Of course, you're welcome to stay whenever and as long as you want to, you know that," Nadine replied sincerely. "Besides, I have to see how this is all going to play out."

"Will you come with me to look at Minnie's property?" Sarah asked as she changed subjects without taking a breath. "Two sets of eyes are better than one and you know what to look for in the outbuildings."

"I wouldn't miss it for the world!" Nadine said enthusiastically. "I love helping you spend your money."

They laughed giddily, smiled at each other, then allowed their conversation to lag into silence as each concentrated on their iced tea and allowed their minds to drift.

CHAPTER 21

SARAH'S LIFE MENDS

"It was nice of you to come along to the hardware store to help me find the fixtures I need for those leaky faucets at the house," Sarah said to Nadine as they drove down a lonely two-lane country road. The daisies and tiger lilies lining the roadway were in full bloom and gave a picturesque quality to the unraveling scenery.

"I'm happy to have time to catch up with you," Nadine said. "You've been way too busy trying to get your apartment and farmhouse together at the same time."

"And rejuvenate a practice. It was in shambles," Sarah added tiredly. "Taking on that flagging business was more than I'd bargained for. It took the better part of the winter before I was able to hire an associate to work the weekends and that put me behind getting settled at the farm."

"How about the farm?" Nadine asked. "Was that more work than you had bargained for also?"

"No, it actually came together pretty well and within expectations. I'm thinking of remodeling the entire house once I get settled in a little better. I just want to keep it functional for now."

"Were there many things that needed attention?"

"No, Minnie took pretty good care of the house but there are definitely some repairs she put off doing."

"And your apartment's working well for you?"

"It's great," she said, brightening noticeably as she warmed to the discussion. "It's a nice area with lots of stores. I can get just about anything I need within a fifteen minute drive."

"How do you handle making the switch from the routine you have here at the farm and when you're living in the city?"

"I get up at five o'clock or so to run a mile around my apartment complex then shower and begin my day feeling invigorated," she said. "Then I dash off to church or to the office depending on the day."

"Church?" Nadine asked incredulously.

"Believe it or not, I actually go to church two mornings each week," she replied. "I joined St. Boniface, the church J.T. and Stephanie go to, and began attending morning service."

"You? In Church?

"Yes," Sarah replied huffily. "Me in church. Is that such a terribly hard thing to believe?"

"It's certainly not something I would have expected from you in the past."

"Well, it's me now," she said with a smile. "I even join women from the church on Thursdays for breakfast at the Double J Diner before dashing off to the office."

"Interesting. If you want to, you can come to dinner at my place tonight and fill me in on the details," Nadine said with a disarming grin. "It's not as hopping as a visit with your church buddies but the food is plentiful."

"I'll bring the wine," Sarah replied. "And I have a loaf of nice crusty French bread from a little bakery around the corner from my apartment."

"That sounds like it'll go well with the chili I have slow-cooking in the crockpot," Nadine said cheerfully. "And if you want to go to the Baptist church down in Rapine with me this Sunday, it would give you a chance to meet some of the people from around here. It's time you began expanding your sphere of friends in this area."

"You? Going to church?"

"We all change as we go through life, don't we?" she said as she flashed a knowing smile.

They just crested a hill when Sarah saw a Golden Retriever puppy run from the side of the road at the bottom of the grade and begin trotting in circles while wagging his tail furiously and barking energetically at their vehicle.

"Watch out!" Sarah screamed as her right hand flew to brace herself against the dashboard of the pick-up truck.

Nadine slammed on the brakes hard enough to throw their bodies against the seat belts. The heavy vehicle glided gently to a mildly jolting stop. The last Sarah saw of the prancing floppy-eared canine was of him disappearing below her line of sight in front of the truck.

"Oh my God! You hit him!" she screamed as she battled clumsily to free herself from the restraining shoulder harness. Her fumbling fingers finally found the door handle as she awkwardly hurled herself out of the truck.

Before she could fight her way past the swinging door and front fender she was met headlong by the trouncing form of an out-of-control-with-delight puppy whose roly-poly body shook with each bounding leap.

She was so elated to see he was unharmed, she stooped and almost scooped him into her arms but froze when she saw how filthy his matted coat was.

"He's a mess!" she said with disgust.

"Is he OK?" Nadine asked when she ran panting from her side of the truck.

"He's fine," Sarah said simply. "But look how muddy and knotted his hair is!"

"And he stinks!" Nadine said as she shielded her nose with the back of her left hand. "Does he have a collar?"

"No, at least I can't see one," Sarah said, unwilling to search through the smelly mass of hair surrounding the puppy's mane.

"That doesn't surprise me," Nadine said evenly. "Most farm dogs don't."

"How do we find who he belongs to?" Sarah asked as she squirmed to avoid having the odoriferous beast's prancing paws soil her fashionable jeans.

"There's a farmhouse down the road about a quarter mile," Nadine said as her searching eyes spied a building on the horizon. "It looks like that's the most likely candidate. Let's load this little guy into the back of the pick-up."

"How are we going to do that?" Sarah asked skeptically. "I mean, without getting all smelly and muddy."

"There is no other way," Nadine said succinctly. "We can't leave him here in middle of the road to get run over by the next vehicle that comes along."

"That's not an option," Sarah replied in agreement. "Let's get smelly and muddy."

Sarah enticed the puppy to follow her toward the back of the truck while Nadine lowered the tailgate with a resounding metallic thud.

"He's obviously well fed with all that fat on him," Nadine said as she stood watching the frolicking dog. "I wonder if he was dumped out here because he's too active."

"Forget about him being fat," Sarah said with an exasperated tone in her voice. "Which end do you want?"

"I'll take the back," Nadine said. "The front seems to be preoccupied with jumping on you."

"Good choice," Sarah said as she reached down to grasp the overactive canine while trying to keep her face away from his flailing front paws and lashing tongue.

"He's going to jump out of there," Nadine said critically after dumping him on the tailgate. "We better tie him to the load tie-downs on the sides of the truck if we expect to get him to the farmhouse."

"Another good idea," Sarah replied as she reached for a coil of jute rope riding in the bed of the pick-up. "I better ride back here with him so he'll stay calm. Please try to avoid as many bumps as you can."

"Put those tarps over here for him to lie on," Nadine instructed as she pointed to the other side of the pick-up's bed. "You'll want to squat on your feet to help absorb the bumps you're so worried about."

Sarah's bouncing ride in the ribbed steel bed of the pick-up was much wilder than she thought it would be. The stiff springs of a pick-up truck like the Ford F-150 were designed for carrying heavy loads and transmitted shock waves from every pothole in the crater-rutted dirt lane directly to her legs.

This is lunacy but he's calmed down just knowing I'm here. The poor little guy is just lonely. He must have been frantic being alone out there.

"I see someone down by the barn. I'm heading down there," Nadine yelled out the driver's side window of the truck hoping Sarah could hear over the whipping wind.

When she hit the brakes Sarah lost her balance and flew into the rear window of the truck. Before they slid to a complete stop on the dusty lane, a man with a creased, weather-beaten face dressed in light tan Carhartt coveralls appeared at the door of the unpainted barn wiping his hands on a grease-smudged red rag. He needed a shave and did not look happy at seeing the unexpected visitors.

"Hello!" Nadine greeted him without stepping out of her truck.

"Hello," the man answered in a grizzled voice. "What can I help you with?"

"We found this puppy roaming around on the hardtop road and wanted to find his owner before he gets run over."

Sarah remained silent while the puppy tried to climb into her lap and share his stench with her. The man kept flicking his eyes toward her but did not address her.

"He's not our dog," he replied as his ogling eyes flitted over her again.

"Do you have any idea who may be missing a dog from around here?"

"Nope," he replied noncommittally. "And I don't want him around here."

"There's a problem with this dog?"

"With any stray dog," the man replied as he stuffed the greasy rag into his back pocket. "He was probably dropped off by someone from the city. They think some 'kindly old farmer' will take their rejects in," he said with a heavy dose of sarcasm in his voice. "But feed costs a lot of money we don't have so I don't want him around here."

"If you don't know who owns him, I'm not sure what to do with him then."

"I don't want him," the man said again. "Just keep him away from here so he's not chasing my steers. That'll kill my livestock and I can't afford to lose any."

"We'll figure something out. Thanks for your help."

"What do we do now?" Sarah asked as she hung over the side of the pick-up to address Nadine without having to raise her voice.

"We go to the hardware store and see if any solutions to this problem show up."

"Well, I'm riding with you," Sarah said as she began dismounting the pick-up. "I can't handle riding back here. He'll be just fine."

The rest of the trip was uneventful but the puppy began straining wildly at the rope tether and yipping loudly when Nadine and Sarah disappeared into the double glass fronted doors of the hardware store.

Sarah continued checking on the puppy every few minutes while they were in the hardware store. Each time the pup saw her he would begin his gyrating antics anew.

By the time we get out of here she'll have added an additional twenty minutes to our shopping trip just from checking on that puppy so many times, Nadine thought.

The clerk who assisted them seemed to have an uncanny ability to identify the various rusty bits and pieces of plumbing they brought and replaced them with shiny new parts from huge bins scattered throughout the store.

"Will you ladies need any tools or adhesives to finish these jobs?" he asked politely.

"No, I think we have everything we need to get things back together," Nadine said as she flashed him a warm smile.

"I'll just ring up your items then," he said as he walked behind the ancient wooden checkout counter situated to the right side of the front door. A state-of-the-art computerized cash register perched prominently at the farthest end seemed oddly out of place in the old country-style store.

While Nadine was placing their purchases behind the seat of the pick-up, she noticed Sarah was greeting the puppy with as much enthusiasm as he welcomed her.

"Well, that's rather telling," she crooned with a sly look in her eye.

"What do you mean?" Sarah asked.

"You know exactly what I mean," Nadine replied. "He's your dog and now you have to figure out what to do with him."

"Rex is not my dog," she retorted snippily.

"Rex?" Nadine replied. "You gave him a name and still deny that you've just adopted a stray hound?"

"He's not a hound," Sarah said testily. "At least I don't think Golden Retrievers are considered to be hounds."

Sarah broke down laughing and looked at Nadine with pleading eyes.

"OK, so we've adopted a dog."

"So what are you planning to do with this non-hound retriever named 'Rex?'" Nadine asked. "And what is this 'we' stuff?"

"I figure I'll be responsible for his feed bill, veterinary costs, and all other expenses," Sarah said thoughtfully. "He'll live with me when I'm at my farm on the weekends and he can live with you when I return to work in the suburbs, if that sounds OK to you."

"I think that will be OK," Nadine said thoughtfully as she weighed the ramifications of what she was agreeing to. "As long as he doesn't chase my horses or chickens. If he does, he loses his happy part-time home."

"It should work out well because he'll have the run of two different farms with a changing cast of owners taking care of him."

"Well," Nadine said in resignation. "Let's head over to the feed store for all the stuff you'll need to care for him."

"Yeah," Sarah consented. "We'll need a lot of brushes and dog shampoo. I think we'll have to use scissors to cut most of that matted hair off him."

"We'll probably get enough hair off him to knit a Chihuahua," Nadine joked.

"A big, fat Chihuahua," Sarah added with a chuckle.

In the next six months, Rex grew into ninety pounds of energetic, brilliantly glistening Golden Retriever. Daily grooming with Nadine's horse brushes contributed greatly to his radiant coat. He remained trim even though he had an astronomical daily caloric intake of puppy chow because his self-appointed job of protecting the farms from intruders of all types kept him busy twenty-four hours a day.

CHAPTER 22

COYOTES WILL BE COYOTES

Sarah and Nadine were just settling down after stacking hay and tending to the horses at The Shire. They had hurried with the chores to save time at the end of the day to shoot pistols on Nadine's range behind the barn.

"We only managed to fit in a half-hour of shooting, but it was a welcome break at the end of such a busy day," Sarah said. "I was glad to get a chance to sight in my new gun."

"That's why a lot of folks like to end their day with a little bit of target practice," Nadine replied. "It's relaxing and a whole bunch healthier for you than watching TV."

"How's dinner coming?" Sarah asked. "I'm starting to get hungry."

"The hot Italian sausage has to cook in the spaghetti sauce for at least another forty-five minutes," Nadine said. "Why don't you mix up a few sundowners and we'll sit under the maple tree."

"That's the best idea you've had all day," she replied. "The weather tonight should be just about perfect to sit outside though we may need some light jackets later."

After mixing their drinks they settled into Adirondack chairs facing westward to watch the sun as it dipped toward the horizon. The first few minutes were spent in silence as they absorbed the peace and quiet of the evening.

"You did pretty well out there on the range today," Nadine said after a few minutes had gone by. "Your shooting has really improved."

"Chauncey and I set up a range at the edge of the woods on the back of my farm," Sarah explained. "We shoot .22s at least once a week."

"I didn't think Chauncey was allowed to handle a gun," Nadine stated.

"He can't buy or own a gun because he doesn't have positive identification to prove he's not a felon," Sarah explained. "On the other hand, since there's no proof he is a felon there isn't any prohibition against him handling firearms."

"That makes sense," Nadine said in agreement. "How do you pay him if he doesn't have a last name or social security card?"

"There are millions of illegal aliens working and getting paid in this country every day," she replied without further explanation.

A moment of silence enveloped them as they searched for a topic that would not be of such a sensitive nature. Suddenly, without warning, Rex lunged from beside Sarah's chair where he had been lying peacefully and ran hell-bent for the woods on the far side of the pasture.

"What the hell's up with him?" Nadine asked. Then she heard them.

"Coyotes!" she yelled, starting forward.

"Oh no!" Sarah cried. "He's going after the coyotes. They'll kill him if they get hold of him!"

"Grab a gun and let's go get him," Nadine bellowed with a twinge of fear evident in her voice.

Sarah bolted for the range bag she left on the side of Nadine's porch. It only took her a few seconds to locate the Para Ordnance Companion she had been breaking in with target ammunition.

"It's lucky I sighted this thing in with the Cor-Bon Pow'RBall ammo I plan on carrying for self-defense," Sarah yelled over her shoulder as Nadine raced inside to retrieve her .222 Remington rifle.

"You go - I'll catch up," Nadine yelled without looking back as she ran into the recesses of the house.

Sarah thumbed six of the fat .45 ACP cartridges into a magazine and shoved it into the butt of the pistol, racked the slide, and flipped the safety upward into the 'on' position with her right thumb. She dumped a handful of the stubby cartridges and an empty magazine into the left rear pocket of her jeans in case she needed them.

Racing across the yard, she contemplated turning the electric fence off but decided against it.

It'll take too long. I better just slither under the wire.

Jamming the Companion into the rear waistband of her jeans, she slid onto her belly and hurriedly inched her way under the fence. Three of the horses stood nearby and watched her with bored amusement.

Stay low! If you touch that wire with your back it'll light you up.

With only the lower half of her body left to pull beneath the electrified fence, she placed her left hand into a warm, steamy pile of fresh horse manure. In an unthinking, reflexive action she pulled her hand up at the same time she raised her body to get away from the offending material.

SNAP!

The electric jolt hit the side of her lower back with a mind-numbing detonation of pain that dazzled her nervous system like a jangled mass of quivering spaghetti. It took her a few seconds lying flat on her belly in the fragrant meadow to regain her composure.

Crawl like a soldier on your belly using your elbows to move forward. Move slowly. Keep your butt low. Don't let the pistol touch the wire or it'll fry your ass.

Just after Sarah cleared the fence and stood shakily on the other side, looking vacantly at the smeared manure covering the front of her shirt and jeans, she heard the snarling and yipping of coyotes interspersed with Rex's barking. It only took a few seconds for Rex's growls of bravado to turn to yelps of pain and terror.

Oh shit! They're killing him!

Fear caused Sarah's heart to beat faster. Her legs began pumping up and down as she haltingly sprang into a run.

Calm down and run faster. Don't let excitement make your heart beat faster and use your oxygen more quickly. You run a mile every day, you can make it! Lengthen your stride!

I'll never get there in time!

Run faster! Must run faster!

The edge of the woods loomed forbiddingly in Sarah's path like an impenetrable wall of black vegetation.

Damned it's dark in there!

Her flying feet took her past the slightly brighter border of the pasture and into the shadowy realm of the forest.

At least it'll be easy to find them with the racket they're making. Unless they kill Rex then it'll be quiet and I'll never find him.

Sarah's legs pumped with renewed vigor as she dodged between trees and vaulted over fallen logs. Vines tore at her arms, face, and neck as though they were alive.

There they are! Oh shit! There're six of them!

It only took a split second to realize that every time Rex tried to flee or attack one of the coyotes the others lunged in to rip at his unprotected belly and hindquarters.

Oh no! He's covered with blood!

Trying to ignore the gore staining Rex's golden coat, she slid to a stop behind a locust tree, her breath coming in wheezing gasps as watery snot ran from her nose onto her upper lip. Her mouth and throat were dry as crunchy leaves.

Rest the side of your hand on the tree to steady your aim or you'll miss for sure. You're breathing much too heavily for accurate off hand shooting. Don't rest your gun on the tree, just your hand.

No sooner had she steadied herself than two of the frenzied coyotes immediately launched into a full throttle charge directly at her. Their brilliantly white canine teeth hung like opposing daggers and seemed to glow in the deepening shadows of the forest.

Don't fixate on them, get your pistol up and ready!

The thoughts had barely formed in her mind before the Companion came up to eye level seemingly on its own volition. Sarah subconsciously allowed her training to take over. Her actions were governed by the lessons she ingrained into her muscles and nervous system with redundant drills.

Taking aim on the smaller of the two coyotes, a reddish-brown female with a white-flecked face, Sarah unleashed a .45 caliber pill of devastation.

BAM!

The model 1911 variant pistol bucked in her hands as a 165-grain Pow'Rball bullet left the muzzle at 1,225 feet per second and slammed into the female's right shoulder between her neck and shoulder blade. The bullet ranged lengthwise through her body burrowing a path of destruction as the Pow'Rball expanded to .68 caliber before coming to rest against her diaphragm.

The result was instantaneous.

She fell onto her nose with her hind legs pumping wildly but uselessly at the carpet of fallen leaves littering the forest floor in a nervous reaction caused by instantaneously meeting death.

The second coyote, a large grayish-black coated male, continued his attack, coming in fast and low to the ground. Using the tree for cover, Sarah smoothly aligned the front sight with the crown of his onrushing head.

Concentrate on the front sight. Press the trigger smoothly to the rear. Don't jerk it.

The .45 automatic bucked in her hand but Sarah's practiced response had the big bore pistol back on target in a millisecond.

Don't think about where your first shot hit, just shoot again. Front sight- BAM!- front sight- BAM!- front sight- BAM!- front sight- BAM!

The evenly spaced roar of the gun's muzzle blast reverberated throughout the wooded hillside. At the sound of her fifth shot the large male ceased to be a threat. The slugs had expanded and dumped all their energy into the yodel dog's vitals. Not a single organ in his thoracic cavity was untouched by the barrage of deadly missiles catapulting through him.

Holy shit! Both coyotes fell within 5 yards of me!

Don't let your mind wander," she admonished herself. *Look for more threats. There were six of them and you only stopped two.*

Her well-learned precautions were commendable but unnecessary. The four remaining coyotes had disappeared like will-o-the-wisps into the gathering murkiness of the rapidly approaching dark.

Sarah allowed herself a quick glance at her pistol and the gravity of her situation fell upon her like a ton of bricks.

Holy shit! It's at slide lock!

The gun's empty! Reload now! Reload!

Her left hand flew to the butt of the pistol to catch the magazine as she hit the release button with her right thumb.

You don't have any loaded magazines! You have to recharge the magazine!

Shove the gun into your waistband to free up both your hands so you can reload.

After using her right hand to jam the Companion into her waistband, her left handed off the empty magazine to her right, then flew to the rear pocket of her jeans to retrieve the loose cartridges she dumped there in her fervor to run to Rex's aid.

Keep looking around while you load the magazine. Don't let your guard down.

Put three cartridges into the magazine from the gun then slam it home so you at least have a loaded pistol then load the other one from your pocket until it's full.

Keep your eyes scanning for the threat to return. Don't bet your life on the coyotes continuing to run away. They could come back just as quickly as they disappeared.

Even with her mental admonitions to remain alert in a 360-degree circle around herself, she realized she had been concentrating on watching Rex limp aimlessly in circles when a sudden rustling of brush behind her caused her heart to jump.

Shit!

She snatched the Companion from her waistband and slammed the half filled magazine into its butt, briskly racked the slide with the strength and speed only possible when danger has the nervous system on high alert, and pivoted from her waist in a continuous blur of motion.

"It's me," Nadine gasped as she laboriously puffed each breath through pursed lips. She was preoccupied with pushing her way through the heavy underbrush, her hands and the knees of her jeans caked with horse manure.

"What's going on?" she asked as she slumped heavily against a poplar tree beside Sarah. "What's happening? What are you shooting at?"

"The coyotes ran away but Rex is injured," Sarah wailed as hot tears began streaming down her sweaty, brush-scratched face. "And I'm beginning to shake like a leaf."

When he heard the voices of his masters Rex ceased his aimless meandering and hobbled up to the two women with an obvious limp hindering his movements.

"Oh my God!" Sarah wailed. "His muzzle is ripped and half his ear is torn off!"

"Oh shit!" Nadine exclaimed as she bolted upright. "Look at his side!"

"Oh no!" Sarah bawled from deep within her throat. "His intestines are falling out!"

She flew to Rex's side while stuffing the .45 into the waistband of her jeans just to the right of midline in the small of her back where it wouldn't be in her way. The coyotes had slashed a foot long gash in Rex's left side.

"OK, we'll need some bandages," Sarah said as she stood up and tore her flannel shirt open, buttons flying in all directions. "We can use this to tie around his middle to hold his intestines in and keep them as clean as possible."

"Oh my God!" Nadine wailed as she unthinkingly threw her manure-encrusted fist to her mouth. "This is horrible!"

"Shut up and give me your shirt," Sarah ordered.

Nadine, realizing in a flash that she was panicking in a situation demanding a cool head, immediately followed Sarah's example and ripped her shirt from her back as the buttons pinged off the crispy leaves on the forest floor.

"What else do you need?" she asked.

"I need you to run back to the house, grab a cell phone to call the veterinarian and get your truck. Meet us at the woods edge out in the pasture," she said. "I'll have to walk Rex out of here because he's too heavy for us to carry."

Nadine turned and ran back to the pasture as fast as she could move, the Remington rifle bouncing wildly against her back as it flailed about on its sling.

"Don't worry, Rex," Sarah crooned to him in soothing tones. "I'll get you out of here."

His loving and trusting eyes met hers and she had to turn away to avoid breaking down in tears.

"Stand still now," she said calmly. "And let me tie these shirts around your middle."

He cooperated by standing placidly while Sarah tied the shirts tightly around his middle. He whimpered pitifully when she tightened the second shirt around his midsection.

"I know boy," she said quietly. "It hurts but we'll get you taken care of."

"OK boy," she said soothingly. "Now let's walk out of these woods and get to the pasture while there's still enough light to get a better look at you."

By the time they got to the pasture it was almost pitch dark under the canopy of trees in the woods.

Thank God we got to the pasture when we did. If it took any longer we'd be stumbling around the woods in the dark. This is not the time to get lost.

The coyotes began howling from half way up the mountain. A shiver slithered down Sarah's back as Rex began whimpering pathetically and moved closer to her.

"Rex, lay down," she said, pointing to a grassy spot beside where she had flopped on the ground just outside the edge of the woods. "I'll finish loading my magazines and make sure we have enough firepower to keep those bastards at bay."

Keep talking to him in subdued tones; it'll keep him calm. Hell, it'll keep you calm.

Suddenly the headlights of Nadine's pick-up truck flashed across the pasture and began bouncing wildly toward them. Sarah stood up and began flailing her arms high over her head. The radiant glow of her white bra bouncing frantically in the glowing illumination of the headlights allowed Nadine to feverishly guide the pick-up truck directly to them.

"Put this on," she called as she threw a shirt toward Sarah. "Then help me spread this horse blanket on the ground and we'll use it as a litter to lift him into the bed of the truck."

It was a difficult maneuver for the two women to lift ninety pounds of dead weight into the bed of the pick-up but the Golden Retriever tolerated the handling with only a single, muted moan when his bulk thumped onto the hard steel flooring.

"OK, let's tie him to the sidewall of the bed to keep him from panicking and jumping out then we'll be on our way," Nadine said. "The vet is expecting us."

"Let me spread this other blanket over him to keep the wind off," Sarah said. "He shouldn't be stressed any more than necessary in his weakened condition."

As they leaped onto the front seat of the truck Sarah said, "Drive safely, there's no need to speed on these winding country roads."

"Yeah, running into a slow moving tractor won't do us any good," Nadine said in agreement.

The journey to the veterinarian's office was uneventful other than Sarah frequently turning around to watch Rex through the sliding rear window of the pick-up's cab.

Bursting into the reception area of the veterinarian's office, Sarah almost ran headlong into a stately woman bustling out to greet them.

The veterinarian, Maggie Sjostrom, was a tall, willowy twenty-six year-old woman of Norwegian extraction with her long blonde hair pulled tightly into a bun on back of her head. The combination of blonde hair and white lab coat caused her pasty complexion to wash out in the flickering glow of the fluorescent bulbs in the reception room.

The young veterinarian was not the least bit alarmed to see two women, one with the butt of a .45 automatic peeking out of the waistband of her jeans, arrive in disarray at her office with an injured Golden Retriever.

"Let me guess," Sarah said in the manner of a greeting. "You're the junior member of the practice so you get the privilege of covering evenings over the weekend."

"Is it that evident?" Maggie asked with a flashing smile.

"I've been there and done that," Sarah replied.

"I graduated last year but I'm perfectly capable of handling all manner of animal emergencies," Maggie assured her.

"I have no doubt you are," Sarah replied with confidence in her voice. "The best I can tell, he has a gash on his left abdomen with protruding intestines and lacerations on his muzzle and left ear."

"OK, I'll check him out after we get him up on the exam table," she said as she looked past Sarah and out into the parking lot. She saw Nadine lowering the truck's tailgate and offering solace to a sick looking but friendly Golden Retriever.

Rex slowly raised his massive head and licked Nadine's hand.

"I'll get a transport board. It'll be easier for us to use than the blankets you have him lying on."

Sarah and Nadine heaved the transport board with Rex securely strapped to it onto the stainless steel examination table. The penetrating light from the bank of halogen bulbs suspended above the table allowed Dr.Sjostrom to determine his wounds were serious but not life threatening.

"This will go much faster and easier if you help me," she said looking into the eyes of the women to see their reaction. "Do you think you can do that?"

"I'm a Doctor of Chiropractic and have been through all the courses for this type of work but it's been years since I've worked with any of the gooey parts," Sarah said evenly.

"And I always help Mitch when he comes to work on my horses so I'm used to the 'gooey' work as my esteemed friend here refers to it," Nadine replied with a smile, her attitude relaxing in the presence of Maggie's confident demeanor.

"Good," Maggie said with enthusiasm. "Let's get started."

"I'll need to use a general anesthesia to knock him out otherwise he won't let us work on him; particularly when we get around that muzzle area," Maggie said while looking at Sarah. "And he may bite us, any of us, when we try shaving around his mouth and nose."

"What are your names?"

"I'm Sarah Collins and this is Nadine Brand," she responded while slightly nodding her head toward Nadine.

Maggie strung a vinyl bag of clear solution from a stainless steel stand, positioned the stand at the head of the table then inserted a small needle into a vein in Rex's right front leg. She then carefully measured a minute amount of clear fluid into a syringe and injected it into the plastic tube.

"He'll begin to relax in about three seconds," she said. "Then we can shave the hair from around the wounds, clean them up with antiseptic, and sew them up."

Before she was finished explaining the sequence of events Rex closed his eyes and began breathing deeply.

She moved down to the belly area and shook her head.

"What a mess," she said. "But it's not as bad as it looks."

"Meaning what exactly?" Sarah snapped with a little more edge in her voice than she would have liked.

"Meaning," Maggie continued, nonplussed, "That there's only one small hole in the intestines. That's not bad at all considering how long and ragged this tear in his belly skin is."

"That's good then," Nadine said in an attempt to appease Sarah's fear.

"It will take about ten minutes to shave his belly, another ten to suture the intestine and cleanse the area, then another ten to close him up," Maggie said evenly.

"Let's get to it then," Sarah said with resignation sounding heavily in her voice.

Twenty-five minutes later Maggie snipped the last thread from Rex's belly.

"Now let's have a look at his muzzle and ears," she said simply before moving toward his head. "In another fifteen minutes we'll be done and have an almost-like-new dog resting comfortably."

"Let's finish up," Sarah said flatly.

"Sarah, can you please hold this oxygen mask near his mouth and nose?" Maggie inquired pleasantly. "Just keep it about an inch from his nose so I have room to work."

"I'll follow your lead," Sarah said with conviction. "Just tell me what to do."

Maggie examined Rex's muzzle and nose more closely.

"I'll have this cleaned up in a few minutes," she said.

With sure, smooth movements Maggie proceeded to shave the hair from the damaged areas, disinfect the wounds, and then sutured them with deft hands.

"Now we have to move him to a temperature controlled kennel to recover. Call about three o'clock tomorrow afternoon to check on him and he'll be ready to go home the day after if all goes well."

"Thank you, Maggie," Sarah said before breaking down in a torrent of tears with great sobs violently shaking her shoulders.

"Nadine," Maggie said as she ignored Sarah's meltdown. "Help me move him into the kennel then take Sarah home and let her get some rest."

CHAPTER 23

ANOTHER SHOPPING SPREE

"I don't know about you," Nadine said as she wheeled her F-150 off the hardtop road and onto the dirt lane leading into The Shire. "But this has been one harrowing day and I'm too pumped up to go to sleep right away."

"I could use a hamburger cooked over a campfire," Sarah said. "And a couple glasses of red wine as an appetizer would be nice."

"I have some smoked hot-pepper cheese and crackers to go with the wine while we wait for the fire to burn down to embers," Nadine replied with a laugh. "I don't need you drunk as a skunk before the fire's ready for cooking. I'll turn off the slow cooker and we'll have the spaghetti tomorrow. Besides, sauce is always better if it sits overnight."

"I'll call Chauncey at my place and let him know what happened," Sarah said with fatigue evident in her voice. "He worries about me if I'm out too late."

"You two are something else."

"And what's that supposed to mean?"

"I mean that the two of you are like two spinster sisters fretting over each other," Nadine said evenly. "And don't you try to deny it. You two are almost inseparable."

"Well, we do look out for each other," Sarah admitted. "But that may be changing. He has a girlfriend over in Sharpsville."

"Oh really!" Nadine exclaimed. "And how long has this been going on?"

"Oh, he's been seeing her socially at the Baptist church there for a while," Sarah said. "Her name's Annie. I don't know her last name."

"Well good for him," Nadine replied enthusiastically.

Two hours later they were vacantly staring into the embers of a dying fire with full bellies and the remnants of a bottle of Merlot sloshing in the bottom of their glasses.

Sarah shifted in her chair and had to use her right hand to move her holster around the plastic arm of the folding aluminum chair to get more comfortable. The Kydex holster held the relatively new Para-Ordnance Companion .45 she used on the two coyotes that rushed at her in the forest. It was stoked full with fresh ammunition.

Nadine carried her Glock 19 that was none the worse for wear-and-tear since Sarah borrowed it to complete the ARI-1 course.

It was a great comfort to both of them knowing they had a means of protecting themselves and their animals immediately at hand especially considering the events that had unfolded earlier in the evening.

Sarah was eyeing Nadine's AR-15 leaning against the woodpile, its chamber empty but its thirty round magazine full and ready to load a .223 cartridge with the flick of a wrist.

"So what do you think?" Nadine asked with no particular topic in mind. The silence was irritating her and she wanted to begin a conversation.

"What do I think about what?" Sarah asked with a bit of irritation in her voice for having her quiet reverie interrupted.

"Oh, I don't know. Coyotes, country living, life in general. The usual stuff," Nadine finished, not sure if she really wanted to chat now that she knew Sarah was agitated.

"I think these predators; whether they're coyotes or otherwise, are beginning to really get on my nerves," Sarah stated emphatically.

"Well, you have to learn to live with them one way or another," Nadine replied.

"No, I have a right to be here. They're going to have to learn to live with me and I'm going to set the rules."

"And how do you propose to do that, Oh Master of the Universe?" Nadine asked with a chuckle.

"I'm planning on instilling the fear of Man back into those animals. At least the fear of Woman, as the case may be," Sarah said with a steely smile crossing her lips. "What's the name of that black rifle sitting over there?"

"The AR-15?" Nadine asked, trying to figure out what Sarah was talking about.

"It's a Bush something," she continued, racking her fatigued brain for more information to describe the rifle.

"Yeah, it's my Bushmaster. At least Bushmaster is the brand name. The type of rifle is called the AR-15, the semi-automatic civilian version of the M-16 the military has used for the last 30 years," Nadine filled in as she wondered where Sarah was going with this conversation. "Why are you interested in the AR-15?"

"I'm interested in it, Oh Nosy One," Sarah said, mimicking her. "Because I think I want one."

Before Nadine could question her further, Sarah verbalized a question of her own. "Where do you learn all this stuff you know about guns?"

"I read a lot."

"No--- seriously."

"I am serious," Nadine replied. "I subscribe to Women and Guns magazine, I'm a member of the National Rifle Association so I get the American Rifleman magazine, and I'm a member of the Second Amendment Foundation and get their Gun Week bi-weekly newspaper as a perk of my membership. Why do you ask?"

"I want to know more than I do about guns and shooting," Sarah explained simply. "I know it's fun because we shoot for recreation and a serious responsibility because of my ARI course but---" she hesitated while her mind searched for the correct words, "I want to know which guns are best for different situations."

"That's easy enough," Nadine said simply. "All it takes is some study. Why do you bring this up now? Because of what happened to Rex?"

"Because after all the shooting was done, and the coyotes had run away, I got scared," Sarah said with her voice rising as her emotions took control of her. "Those coyotes actually came for me! A human being! They're not supposed to try and eat me! I'm at the top of the food chain for crying out loud!"

Sarah was visibly shaking again.

"You're only at the top of the food chain if you have bigger teeth than the other predators," Nadine said in a soothing voice in an attempt to calm her down.

Sarah took a moment to gather her thoughts and relaxed her jangled nerves by taking a deep, cleansing breath.

"That's what I'm talking about," she said in a much calmer voice. "I wasn't so sure if I did have the biggest teeth in the woods; at least for a few terrifying moments out there. Why do I keep shaking like this?" she asked as she held up her trembling hands.

"It's a delayed reaction to the adrenaline leaving your system after a frightening situation," Nadine said calmly. "Every time you think about the event your body experiences the same reaction it did during the crisis."

"Luckily, I had my .45 with me," she continued in an even tone without acknowledging that she heard Nadine's explanation.

"But even with it I felt the coyotes could have taken me if they all attacked at once. I ran my pistol dry just killing two coyotes. What if the others would have attacked instead of running away?" she asked with a quivering voice.

"You're not just traumatized about Rex getting attacked," Nadine realized in a flash. "You had to face the reality of being attacked and you were alone."

Sarah could only drop her head and stare at her hands with a dumbfounded look on her face. A solitary tear dropped onto the front of her jacket.

"You and your .45 did a great job, just like you trained for, and that's why you practice frequently. You never know when the stuff will hit the fan," Nadine said soothingly as she tried to assure her everything was OK.

"The .45 did work well in that situation, at least against the two that attacked me," Sarah said analytically. "But I'm not sure I could have placed all my shots quite so accurately if the whole pack had attacked."

"Your training would have pulled you through," Nadine said half-heartedly.

"After running the situation over in my head a few times I've decided I need something with more firepower than what my pistol offers," she continued. "I want greater magazine capacity than a concealed carry type of pistol offers."

"I can't argue with you wanting another gun," Nadine said. "Exactly what do you expect from an AR-15?"

"I want to be able to shoot any coyote that shows its face on my property or anywhere near it," Sarah replied with conviction. "I may even want to start hunting them to keep their numbers down so they don't get bold enough to attack me or my animals."

"Well, it's a good type of gun for predator hunting," Nadine said as she scrunched her face in thought. "There're a lot of folks that use it for coyotes with excellent results."

"And I assume it's good for human predators considering the military has used it for over thirty years," Sarah surmised.

"Yes it is," Nadine confirmed. "A number of police agencies use it successfully and have gotten almost 100% one-shot stops with it when using hollow point ammunition. That's the same type ammunition you'd use for coyotes."

"What's 100% one-shot stop mean? And where did you learn all of this again?" Sarah asked, showing genuine interest.

"I told you," Nadine said. "I read gun and shooting magazines. I'll even buy you a subscription to a few if you promise to read them."

"Thanks, I'll read them. I promise," she said with a chuckle. "Now, what's this 100% one-shot-stop stuff all about?"

"It simply means that cartridge, when using hollow point bullets, usually takes only one shot to make the aggressor cease their hostile actions."

"So you only have to shoot the bad guy once?" quizzed Sarah.

"Usually," Nadine said. "But remember, in your ARI class they taught you the idea is to stop the aggressor from being hostile."

Nadine took a deep breath and continued with the lesson reminder.

"The objective is not to kill the aggressor even though they may pass away from their wounds," she said. "You only want them to stop being violent and trying to hurt you or a loved one. That's why you should keep shooting until they stop their hostile actions."

"Keep shooting until the threat ceases to be a threat," Sarah confirmed.

"Exactly," Nadine replied. "This particular cartridge and ammunition combination, when fired from a rifle, usually takes only one properly placed round to stop their aggressive action."

Sarah was listening intently, so Nadine continued.

"For example, take your coyotes this afternoon. If they had stopped attacking Rex and ran away you wouldn't have had to shoot them," Nadine explained. "Instead of leaving they started attacking you, which required you to use deadly force against them. Only then did they stop attacking."

Nadine was sure her explanation was sufficient and would satisfy Sarah's curiosity for a while. She was wrong.

"That's what I'm getting at," Sarah said.

"What are you getting at?"

"When those coyotes attacked me, Rex was useless," Sarah replied. "He couldn't even help himself anymore."

"He had his guts hanging out for crying out loud!" Nadine whined loudly in defense of Rex's honor.

"That's my point," Sarah continued unabashedly. "I was on my own and wasn't sure I was armed well enough to handle that many coyotes."

Sarah looked at Nadine and saw the confused look on her face so she continued.

"Don't you see?" she pleaded. "We're usually alone most of our lives. Especially you and I. We're women, and we're on our own with almost no chance of help arriving to get our Skittles out of the fire if anything terrible happens."

"Go ahead," Nadine said as Sarah's message began sinking into her fatigued mind. "I'm following you now."

"So what would happen if human predators like rapists and murderers for two examples, decided they want to treat us like prey? Are we really armed well enough with just a handgun? Or do we need a rifle handy also? Especially out here on the farm where the shooting distance may be more than a few feet. I'd rather take on a predator across the yard than at bad breath distance."

Sarah looked at Nadine with unwavering resolve in her eyes.

"I've thought of that many times," Nadine assured Sarah in subdued tones. "That's why I keep various firearms scattered around my farm. A good gun strikes me as being the best form of feminine protection a woman can have in certain situations."

"I've seen at least two down at the barn," Sarah admitted as she smiled at Nadine's joke.

"I haven't had an experience like yours, and I hope I never do, but I've tried to learn from other people's situations so I don't get into the same trouble they did," Nadine said plainly. "Re-inventing the wheel is not my idea of fun especially when my life or that of my loved ones are on the line."

Sarah smiled at the tolerance and patience Nadine showed her on what seemed like a daily basis.

She'll always be a teacher. When she left the teaching profession years ago, she certainly didn't quit being a teacher.

"So what do we do now?" Sarah asked.

"We go shopping," Nadine said matter-of-factly. You won't be happy until you get yourself an AR-15."

"So, where do we go to buy one?" Sarah asked innocently. "I'm not familiar where many gun stores are around here or what's all involved in buying a gun like this."

"The Conestoga Trading Post has the best selection of ARs that I know of in this area. It's as good of a place to start as any," Nadine said as she mulled the list of local gun dealers around in her mind. "And all you'll need is a government issued form of identification so they can do a background check and enough money to pay for it."

"Oh! I have that in my purse if they'll take a personal check," Sarah replied happily as her eyebrows rose in surprise.

"They open at ten o'clock in the morning. I'll pick you up about nine."

"I just wish they weren't so ugly," Sarah said dejectedly. "Basic black has never been one of my favorite colors."

"Then you're in luck," Nadine said with a laugh. "Now you can get them in every color from aqua to desert camo."

"Cool!"

The next morning when Nadine wheeled into the front yard of Sarah's farm, Chauncey was coming out of the barn, his hands filled with wrenches of various sizes.

"Hello Chauncey!" she greeted him.

"Hello Nadine," he said cordially. "It's nice to see you again."

"Is Sarah around?"

"She's in the house waiting for you," he said. "She'll be out in a minute. She's been chomping at the bit to get moving this morning."

"She's on a mission."

Just then Sarah came out of the house with her purse slung over her shoulder and a spring in her step.

"See you ladies later," Chauncey said as he waved with a wrench-filled fist and smiled at Nadine. "I gave her a list of things I need from the hardware store. Please don't let her forget to pick them up."

"Don't worry," Nadine assured him. "I have a hardware list myself so I'll make sure we get there."

Sarah strode directly to the passenger's door of Nadine's truck, placed her hand on the handle, then turned and said excitedly, "Let's go!"

CHAPTER 24

CHAUNCEY GOES TO
THE HALLELUJAH GATHERING

Chauncey threw his duffel bag into the back seat of Sarah's Chevy
1500 Crew Cab. It was Thursday and he had just commuted on the
Metro to Northern Virginia from his apartment in Washington, D.C. to
work at Sarah's suburban office.

"Sarah, would it be a major inconvenience if I took off from
Wednesday to Sunday the first week of next month?" he asked. "J.T.
asked me to help chaperone his church's youth ministry camping trip
to the Hallelujah Gathering. Dr. Holmes has already given me
Monday and Tuesday off."

"So you're finally taking my advice and vacationing for a few days
to recharge your batteries, eh?" Sarah asked emphatically. "You can
catch up on everything when you get back. I've told you that before."

"I know you've told me to take some time for myself," he replied.
"But I enjoy my jobs so much, and with the long weekends up on the
farm it's like I'm always on vacation. Seriously!"

"I'm really glad to see you and J.T. getting along so well," she
said. "I think it does both of you some good to have someone to chum
around with."

"Well, as you know, I've been visiting his church during the latter
part of the week when I'm out this way and help him a little with the

kids at youth ministry. The priest even knows my name," he said. "But then I attend the Baptist church near the farm on Sunday. It gives me variety in my spiritual life."

"Not to mention that Annie attends the Baptist church," she said with a smile.

"Well, that may have a little to do with the variety part," he said as he averted his eyes sheepishly toward the ground and tried to stifle a grin.

"So tell me about this Hallelujah Gathering."

"It's a weeklong Christian event up in West Virginia," he replied. "The farm where it's held has camping facilities and everything."

"That sounds interesting," she lied. "I'm sure J.T.'s kids will enjoy it."

"They went last year and couldn't wait to get back this year," he said.

"You won't be sleeping on the ground, will you?" she asked when the chiropractic angle of the trip sunk into her mind. "You might wake up with your back in a major snit."

"No, I won't have to sleep on the ground," Chauncey laughed. "Most of the chaperones wouldn't tolerate that very well. The youth ministry group has camp cots for us. The kids will be on air mattresses with sleeping bags on the ground."

"Well, have a good time," she said with a chuckle. "Just don't get lost in the wilds of West Virginia."

"It should be an experience," he replied without knowing how true his prophecy would be.

CHAPTER 25

THE HALLELUJAH GATHERING

"So what have you gotten me into, J.T.?" Chauncey asked as the church van loaded with camping gear pulled off the interstate onto a two-lane state road.

"You got yourself into it," J.T. replied with a chuckle. "I just asked you if you'd be willing to help chaperone the youth ministry group at the Hallelujah Gathering."

"Well, you've been here before, what can I expect?"

"The Hallelujah Gathering is an annual event that's held on the five hundred acre farm owned by Peter Giovanni," J.T. replied. "It's a mixture of Christian rock concerts, lectures, and good old-time revival meetings for all denominations. It's geared toward teenagers but the adults get a lot out of it."

"Is the campground right on the farm?"

"Peter has set aside two hundred of his acres for the actual events like revival meetings and concert stages," J.T. explained. "And he keeps about a hundred acres for a campground and concessions."

"They don't use the entire farm?"

"No, the rest of the property is the actual working farm and it's off limits to the Hallelujah Gathering participants," he replied. "It's a rule that's strictly enforced to ensure no one is hurt by animals or machinery."

"That makes sense," Chauncey said. "Do we have reservations at the campground or do we just take what's available when we get there?"

"Actually, we aren't staying on the farm."

"We're not?"

"We're staying on the Hager farm across the road from Peter Giovanni's place."

"Why?"

"It's very crowded in the campground Peter has set aside and that makes it miserable in this sticky, humid weather," J.T. replied. "We'll use the concessions at the Gathering but it's much nicer camping at the Hager's. They also have fewer campers so it's easier to keep track of the kids. That's important."

"Peter's campground is full?" Chauncey asked. "How many people will be attending this event?"

"The first weekend is the busiest with about seven thousand attendees," he replied. "But it'll fall off to half that for the rest of the week."

"It's going to be a mess with that many people jammed into such a small space."

"I told you it would be interesting," J.T. said as he laughed to himself.

CHAPTER 26

RADICAL ISLAMISTS AT THE GATHERING

"You have taken good pictures, Omar," Muhammed Shah, the commander of six terrorist cells secretly living in the United States, said approvingly to his newly-acquainted soldier. "They will give us the information we need to carry out our mission."

"Thank you Commander," Omar said with humility in his voice if not in his heart. "It is very informative to combine the knowledge gleaned from the satellite pictures taken off the Internet with the ones Samir and I took from the ground."

"How did you get such good pictures and detailed information on the property where the Hallelujah Gathering will be held?"

"It was simple, Commander," Omar said as he puffed out his chest proudly. "Samir would drive down the valley in a van with darkened windows and I would be in the back with a camera taking pictures out the partially opened window."

"And these aerial photos?"

"I took those from the top of the mountain overlooking the farm where the Hallelujah Gathering will be held," he explained. "They have been preparing for the event for months so it was easy to see where the various buildings, tents, concert stages, and campgrounds will be located."

"It was not difficult to get to this vantage point?"

"No sir, the road winds across the top of the mountain," he explained. "There are many places to pull to the side and take pictures without being seen."

"You have done well, Omar," he said. "Allah will be happy with your work."

Omar smiled broadly at the praise his commander was bestowing upon him.

"And you have mapped the prevailing winds?"

"Yes Commander," he replied enthusiastically, sure he was due more praise. "We dispensed puffs of talcum powder from a plastic bottle to monitor the winds all along the dirt road bordering the property where the Hallelujah Gathering will be held."

"According to the arrows you drew on this map, the winds blow from the dirt road directly across the grounds where the infidels will be performing their barbaric worship ceremonies?"

"Yes, Commander," he replied proudly. "The winds always blew the same way every time we tested them."

"Allah is smiling upon us," Muhammed said. "We will kill and injure many thousands of the Christian infidels. It is especially important since most of them are of warrior age."

"Commander, is it too early for you to tell us the plan?" Samir asked respectfully.

"It is time to give you the details," Muhammed said. "Three dark colored vans will be stolen to transport cylinders of mustard gas. The vans will move from the head of the valley under the cover of darkness down the dirt road you reconnoitered. The van I will be driving will have four mustard gas canisters and the others will carry three. Each vehicle will stop at a designated landmark and begin placing cylinders approximately every thirty meters as you move down the road."

"Will thirty meters be close enough to cover the entire grounds with the gas?"

"Yes, the eddying winds will swirl the gas around so it is spread far and wide."

"Won't the gas just rise up into the sky and be rendered useless?"

"No, Samir, the gas is heavier than air and will hug the ground as it is carried along. That is the way it was designed for use in the American's World War I."

"And what landmarks will be designated to begin dropping the cylinders, Commander?"

"The first van in line will be driven by Jaafar with Basel in back handling the gas cylinders," Muhammed informed them.

Pointing to a spot on the map with a gnarly forefinger, Muhammed continued, "He will stop here at the dead tree with the bark peeled off. You can see it on this picture right here. Basel will then jump from the van and place the first cylinder upright at the base of the tree. Remember to keep the tanks upright so the gas is released upward to get maximum dispersal."

"Will we be opening the cylinders to release the mustard gas immediately after setting them on the ground?" Basel asked seriously.

"Yes," Muhammed replied. "I want the gas to begin drifting across the fields as soon as possible in case there are problems."

"And what will I be doing, Commander?" Omar asked.

"You, Omar, will be in back of the second van with Samir driving," Muhammed replied as he motioned in Samir's direction. "He will stop here at this small machine shed to place your first cylinder then set the other two every thirty meters."

"That leaves you and me, Commander," Waseem said.

"I will be driving the third van with you in the back," Muhammed said. "We will stop here to place the first cylinder at the edge of the campground where the tents begin. Then we will place them every thirty meters. The mustard gas should cover the entire Hallelujah Gathering. I am particularly interested in the gas reaching the campground and concert areas."

"And the gas will be carried across the Hallelujah Gathering grounds by the wind," Omar said in astonishment.

"The plan is simplicity itself," Samir said with equal astonishment. "And when will this take place, Commander?"

"Satuday evening at ten o'clock," Muhammed said definitively. "Over 7,000 infidels will be gathered at the Christian rock music concert or moving about the grounds. It is the main attraction of the weeklong event. The gas should totally cover the entire Gathering at a time when the attendees are tired and most vulnerable. That fact alone will add many more casualties to the count."

"How did you learn about the specifics of what transpires at The Gathering?" Samir asked inquisitively.

"I looked it up on the Hallelujah Gathering website. The fools put information that is very important to our success on the Internet," Muhammed said with a laugh rumbling deeply in his belly. "They advertise their weaknesses!"

Muhammed continued, "They begin their day with a sunrise worship service and stay busy all day long. This leads to inattention and makes it more difficult for the infidels to think or react while under stress of an attack."

"That is excellent."

"Yes, Omar," Muhammed said expansively. "Such knowledge will allow us to add hundreds more casualties to the tally because of their inability to act swiftly in an emergency."

"Praise be to Allah."

CHAPTER 27

EVENING AT
THE HALLELUJAH GATHERING

The day had been grueling.

J.T. and Chauncey were hot, sticky, and exhausted from being up since 4:30 a.m. to monitor the activities of the teens from the St. Boniface Youth Ministry group all day.

"So how did we get campsite duty?" Chauncey asked to avoid having to stand up from his folding aluminum chair and begin working again.

"The other counselors wanted to hear the rock band tonight," J.T. replied wearily. "After getting up at 4:30 for the sunrise service then sweating like a Missouri mule all day long, I was happy to have a little quiet time and just do camp chores without having to keep tabs on all the kids."

"And all that mud! I'm so sick and tired of wiping it off my shoes I could scream," Chauncey said emphatically. "Thanks for including me on the camp prep team."

"Not a problem," J.T. replied with a smile. "We really didn't have a choice. Everyone else was dead set on seeing the concert."

"From what I understand, the band is the most popular Christian rock group in the world," Chauncey said. "Apparently a lot of people attending The Gathering are here just to hear them."

"Yeah, Peter says there are an additional 1,500 people here today just to hear the concert," J.T. replied. "Thankfully they're not camping overnight or we'd be crowded right out of this meadow."

"At least there's a nice breeze coming down off the mountain now," Chauncey said as he lifted his face toward the surrounding ridge to allow the chilled draft sliding from the highlands to cool his feverish face. "Jason said we could expect a cool wind to pick up in the evening."

"It always blows down off the mountain in the evening because when the sun goes down the air cools," J.T. replied.

"And cold air falls while hot air rises," Chauncey said, finishing his sentence.

"That's why the evening winds are almost always moving from west to east in this valley," he said picking up where Chauncey left off. "The cool air slides down off the eastern face of that mountain before continuing across the road toward Peter's farm."

"So we get first dibs on the cool air," Chauncey said with a satisfied grin augmenting the peaceful look on his face. "We better get moving if we expect to have this campsite set up when the kids get back."

"Yeah, they'll be hungry so we better make sure we have a fire going for hot dogs," J.T. said.

"Should we divide and conquer or do you think we'll get things done faster if we work together?"

"We may as well work together," J.T. replied. "We'll probably be more efficient and if we get done before the kids return we'll just relax and wait for the onslaught of teenage energy."

"That would be good," Chauncey said. "I don't know how late I'll be staying up tonight; we old guys need our sleep."

"Most of the kids will fall asleep shortly after eating," J.T. replied. "Once their bellies are full, they should sleep like a bunch of logs."

J.T. reluctantly heaved his aching body out of the captain's chair then said, "We should get ice to fill the coolers because when the concert lets out, the concession area will be flooded with wet, muddy, smelly, hopped-up-on-soda kids."

"That's a great idea, especially when you put it in those terms," Chauncey said as he propelled himself from his chair. "Oh brother! Am I stiff!"

"Well, keep moving so you don't freeze in place Tin Man," J.T. joked. "Apparently age and grace do not necessarily go well together."

"You wait, youngster," Chauncey chided him back. "You'll have your turn to be this old."

"In that case, I'll race you to the concession stands," J.T. said with a chuckle.

"You calm down and we'll just mosey on over there," Chauncey replied while he returned J.T.'s laugh. "We have to conserve our energy to carry all that ice back here. You'll learn things like that with a little more experience."

"Yeah, right," J.T. said with a chuckle. "Hey! Let me show you something experience has taught me. Come on, let's go."

"Do we need a flashlight?" Chauncey asked as he looked up the hill. "We've sat here so long it's gotten pretty dark."

"I have my SureFire light in case we need it but that moon is half-full and should give us plenty of light to see our way through the meadow."

The two men walked stiffly up the slight rise leading from Hager's meadow to the Gathering campground. When they reached the top of the rise J.T. stopped, raised his arms so they were held out straight from his body, and began twirling in a circle.

"Uh! Oh! Now he's lost it," Chauncey said jokingly as he laughed lightly.

"I haven't lost it," J.T. said as he slowed his twirling then stopped and looked directly at Chauncey. "Can't you feel it?"

"Feel what?"

"See this little rise in the road between the Hager and Giovanni farms?" he asked. "It directs that wind you were talking about upward and makes it seem cooler than the slightly lower areas surrounding this little knoll."

"Now that you mention it, it does seem a little cooler, or is it just my imagination now that you've put the idea in my mind?"

"It's not your mind playing tricks on you," J.T. replied. "I always like to stand here for a few minutes and let the nice cool breeze wash the stench of the day away."

"It is a nice, peaceful place to take a rest," Chauncey said agreeably.

"Usually there's no traffic on this road after the activities start but here comes a convoy," J.T. observed as he stood looking up the otherwise deserted road.

"There are only three vehicles," Chauncey noted as his gaze followed J.T.'s stare. "Does that constitute a convoy?"

"I guess not," J.T. replied. "But we'll stay here enjoying the breeze until they pass then we'll go get the ice. I really hate having my quiet time disturbed."

"Life's rough all over."

"So I hear."

Both men watched in silence as the vans got closer.

"I thought they were traveling together," Chauncey said conversationally. "But that one pulled over and stopped by the edge of the campground. Maybe they're visiting someone."

J.T. remained silent and continued watching the vans intently.

"There's someone getting out of it," J.T. said. "Maybe you're right and they're just visiting."

"Maybe... but see- he's watching the other vans."

"Yeah," J.T. said softly.

"Now the second van is stopping beside that old shed," Chauncey said quizzically. "And the guy from the first van is unloading a canister and setting it up on the side of the road."

"If they're delivering propane tanks to the concession area you'd think they'd pull right up to the stand to avoid a lot of heavy lifting.

They sure as hell wouldn't be leaving them in a deserted field," J.T. said suspiciously. "What the hell's going on here?"

"I don't know but now there's a guy getting out of the van by the shed."

"And the van now at the front has pulled all the way down to that old, dead tree," J.T. noted. "Peter said he was going to cut that tree down this year but he obviously didn't get around to it."

"I'm sure there are a lot more important things that need to be done on a farm than chopping down dead trees."

"I'm sure there are."

"Now someone has gotten out of each of the vans," Chauncey said observantly. "They all seem to be unloading cylinders and leaving them standing upright on the side of the road."

"There's something strange here," J.T. said as internal warning bells began clanging alarmingly in his mind.

"There's definitely something strange here but I can't put my finger on it," Chauncey said as he took a curious step forward. "They look strange."

"Holy shit! They're wearing gas masks," J.T. whispered in an urgent voice. "And the guy by the tree just ran away from that canister like he expects it to blow up."

"What is it? What are they doing?"

"Chauncey! It's an attack! That's some type of gas!" J.T. cried breathlessly through hushed tones as he stooped down and began pawing at his left pant leg. His groping right hand surrounded the polymer grip of a Glock 26 then gave it a jerk to free it from the DeSantis ankle holster that had kept it concealed all day long.

Thank you Lord for letting Virginia and West Virginia have concealed carry reciprocity otherwise I wouldn't have been armed. Thank you for allowing me to tolerate the sweat and discomfort of having this ankle holster on my leg all day.

This was not the first silent prayer that had flitted across J.T.'s mind today and it certainly wouldn't be the last.

"Go to the Hager farmhouse and tell Jason to call 911. Our cell phones don't have reception way up here in the mountains," J.T. instructed Chauncey in muffled tones as he kept an eye on the vans with laser-like intensity. "Tell them to expect casualties so they can put all the region's hospitals on alert to handle a potentially large number of patients. The types of injuries are unknown at this time. Go!"

Chauncey took off running, taking care to lift his knees high like a broken-field running back to keep from tripping over the uneven ground.

J.T.'s mind reeled with scenarios trying to formulate the best plan of action to most effectively handle this threat.

Shit! You're on your own again. Calm down. You've been alone on a lot of assignments and you came through just fine. Focus on your mission. Take the closest ones first then move on to the others in a systematic manner.

J.T. moved forward in a shuffling crouch with his knees bent to keep his profile closer to the shadows of the dirt road's uneven surface. He held the Glock low and pointed toward the ground, its Tenifer surface slick under his glistening, sweaty hands. Ten rounds of Cor-Bon 115-grain hollow-point bullets were ready to be launched at 1,350 feet-per-second to perform the work they were designed for.

I better work myself up this side of the road until I'm directly across from the van then take them out as efficiently as possible. What is that gas? It's thick and yellow. Maybe its chlorine, that's a common gas they may have gotten hold of. No, chlorine's not dense enough and it'd dissipate too quickly in this wind. This stuff is hugging the ground.

It took him less than ten seconds to cover the uneven ground to the van parked beside the dead locust tree.

Whatever it is they're afraid of it. They're really backpedaling away from the canisters as soon as they open them. It must be really nasty stuff.

J.T. lifted his feet just enough to avoid rolling the stones littering the surface of the road to avoid making noise that may alert the men in the van to his presence. He was able to get close enough to see the driver and suddenly a plan popped into his mind with crystal clarity.

He's looking over his shoulder watching the other guy unload the canisters. He can't see me. I can probably work my way around to the back and get the drop on that guy then I'll deal with the driver.

I hope to hell there are only two of them in there!

Shuffling sideways and being careful to never cross his feet by sliding his forward foot sideways then slipping his back foot up next to it before repeating the sequence, J.T. inched his way around the back of the van. Just as he was about to begin moving around the bumper with his Glock at the ready, Basel leapt into the back of the van and Jaafar drifted forward.

What the hell!

A fleeting glance over his shoulder assured J.T. that the occupants of the other vans had not seen him.

The bastards are too busy doing their dirty work to notice me but that won't last long.

When the van stopped, Basel sprang out then twisted to snatch the second gas cylinder from its moorings in the back of the van as J.T. fired two rapidly triggered rounds from only eight yards' distance into the side of his chest just below the armpit.

BAM! BAM!

The first round smashed the fifth rib on its way to ripping through both lungs and tearing the aorta at the top of the heart to shreds. The second whizzed through the spongy space between the fifth and sixth ribs to tear a walnut-sized hole through both lungs three inches from the destruction wreaked by its mate.

Basel fell to the ground, rolled onto his right side, and then flexed into a quivering fetal position. J.T. did not waste time admiring his handiwork but instead took two steps forward. His Glock was held in an unwavering two-handed grip as he smoothly swung the black pistol to his left and settled the front post sight onto the juncture of Jaafar's neck and chest. The flat, pug nose of the black gun spitting a volcano-like flame was the last earthly sight Jaafar's mind registered.

J.T. fired only one round into the hollow of his neck where his breastbone gave way to the soft, fleshy waddles of his throat. The hollow point bullet soared through the delicate dermis and met just enough resistance as it punched through the tough, cartilage rings of the trachea to begin expanding. Its nose mushroomed from .355 to .401 inches by the time it perforated the rear of the trachea and collided with the soft tissues covering the front of the cervical vertebrae. The continually expanding .423-inch chunk of lead and gilding metal pulverized the body of the sixth cervical vertebra and shattered into smithereens. The meteoric shower of sharp, needle-like bony shards and broken metal masticated the spinal cord into a mass of useless, gooey pulp.

Before he could trigger a second round, Jaafar caved in upon himself and collapsed across the console of the van as his flexor muscles went into spasm; twisting his hands and feet into useless claws. It would be minutes before the lack of oxygen from his now unresponsive lungs rendered his brain void of electrical activity.

No time to waste. I have to turn off those gas canisters.

Not bothering to waste time checking whether Jaafar was still a threat, J.T. spun on his heels and bolted toward the only gas cylinder Basel was able to open before his demise.

Making certain he stayed upwind and out of reach of the escaping gas, he jammed the muzzle of the Glock into his waistband to free the use of both hands. Grasping the gray, perforated metal valve he twisted mightily.

A frosty, deadly fog continued spewing into the moist, humid air. The rapid release of escaping gas, contained for decades under tremendous pressure, froze the valve and frostbit his hands as soon as he touched it. Ignoring the skin being torn from his fingers by the frigid metal, he doggedly completed his task. It took four complete revolutions of the valve to stem the flow of gas from the cylinder.

Tossing the sealed cylinder to the ground, he snatched the Glock from his waistband.

OW! Damned! My hands really hurt! Ignore it. You have more work to do. Your kid's lives depend on what you do in the next few minutes.

CHAPTER 28

CHAUNCEY ALERTS JASON

Chauncey was puffing like an old steam locomotive by the time he reached Jason Hager's front porch. The rickety planking hadn't seen a coat of new paint in three decades and the flaking patch that remained was of an indeterminate color. Long longitudinal cracks had formed in the planks but were now filled with compacted mud.

Wrapping his left hand around the grimy white column supporting the roof, Chauncey swung his rocketing body toward the front door. He was surprised to see that the dirty, mustard-yellow wooden door boasted a surprisingly ornate and clean leaded, beveled glass window. A single, bare bulb hung from the peeling paint-flecked ceiling of the hallway making it easy for him to see into the house.

BANG! BANG! BANG!

Chauncey's closed fist pounded against the frame of the door surrounding the sparkling glass window. He only waited a few short seconds before beginning his incessant pounding again.

Jason Hager vaulted into view at the far end of the hallway from what Chauncey guessed to be the kitchen. He was obviously agitated by the pounding on his front door. His long, forceful strides caused his heavily cleated boots to smack noisily off the polished wood floor of the hallway.

"What the hell do you want?" he yelled into Chauncey's face as he burst through the ill-fitting door. "Don't you know enough not to pound on people's doors? You'll break the damned thing then I'll charge you for it! And what the hell can be so important at this hour of the night?"

Chauncey had a difficult time getting his words formed because of the dryness of his throat from running across the meadow. Jason's furious outburst only added to the problem.

"There's an attack against the Gathering, a gas attack, and they're trying to kill the kids," he finally managed to force out of his mouth. "J.T. has gone after them and sent me to tell you to call 911."

"What the hell---"

"Call 911 damn it!" Chauncey screamed at him.

He saw Jason was perplexed by his claim and would need verification before acting.

"There! Up there on the road," he yelled as he pointed impatiently back the way he had come. "They're opening gas cylinders and the wind is carrying it across the fields toward the crowds at the Gathering."

Chauncey did not get the chance for further explanation before two shots rang out from the direction he was pointing followed by a third less than two seconds later.

"Call 911. Please!"

Jason Hager was not very bright but once he understood the gravity of any situation, he always acted swiftly and decisively.

"Mary Anne! Call 911 and get the sheriff up here. Now!" he bellowed over his shoulder to his wife in the kitchen.

"You have to tell them to alert the hospitals," Chauncey said as he forcefully sucked in another breath. "They have to know to expect a lot of injured people so they can prepare."

"Mary Anne! Tell them to call the hospitals. There may be a lot of hurting people showing up there soon," Jason bellowed toward the kitchen. "And we may need a lot of ambulances; I'm going up there to see what the hell's going on."

"Did she hear you?" Chauncey asked with a tinge of horror in his voice.

"Mary Anne! Did you hear me?"

"Yes I heard you, you pain in the ass," a rough, tired female voice answered from the kitchen. "I'm dialing the phone now."

"Come on," Jason said to Chauncey as he snatched a twelve-gauge side-by-side shotgun with the bluing worn off its receiver from behind the front door. He expertly slung its cracked walnut stock under his right armpit and pushed the opening lever with his beefy thumb. "We're going to see what the hell's going on!"

Before shuffling out the door, he grabbed a dog-eared cardboard box of shotgun shells off the shelf of the coat rack hanging from the wall and began shoving them into the open tops of the button-down pockets of his sleeveless flannel shirt.

CHAPTER 29

J.T. MOVES ON

"What is that?" Omar asked Samir as he leaned into the side door of the van after placing his second cylinder upright on the ground.

"There is a man shooting into Jaafar and Basel's van," Samir said as he pointed directly down the road in front of him.

"Then we must hurry," Omar said as he whirled and grabbed the third cylinder before he jumped from the van. "This is the last cylinder we have. I haven't had time to open the second one yet. I will open them both after I place this one in its spot."

"Don't bother putting it up the road; just place it here," Samir yelled but it was too late. Omar had already begun running up the road with the canister hugged securely to his chest with his knees bending precipitously under the tremendous weight.

He had a spot visually marked as the location where Muhammed wanted the cylinder to be placed. Grunting loudly, he slammed the bottom of the heavy cylinder to the ground but it landed on a hummock of grass and fell silently onto its side. Bending from his waist to lift the hefty canister he suddenly felt a sharp, stabbing pain in his lower back like a red-hot knife being driven into him just above his right buttock.

It had been two years since he'd last suffered from lower back pain but he knew immediately the searing pain was from a herniated disc. He grabbed desperately at his low back but stayed bent forward because he was unable to stand straight. Severe, unrelenting pain froze him in his tracks rendering him unable to move.

His misery was short-lived.

Before he could do anything more than raise his head to face the threat he knew to be bearing down on him, he heard the shot that signaled the end of his agony.

The nine-millimeter Cor-Bon round was loosed from a distance of ten yards by a specter of death zooming out of the stygian darkness of the night. The impact of the bullet whacking into his upper chest at slightly less than 1,350 feet-per-second knocked him to his knees.

The brilliant, blinding muzzle flash temporarily blinded J.T. but he was able to make out the figure of Omar kneeling on the ground beside the fallen gas cylinder.

J.T.'s second shot, fired in rapid succession after the first, smashed the glass goggle of the gas mask covering Omar's left eye; his body began to crash to the ground in a crumpled heap as his legs buckled uselessly beneath him.

Before the crash of the first shot striking Omar finished echoing across the valley, Samir threw the van into drive and smashed the accelerator to the floorboards. By the time the second bullet pulverized Omar's brain, Samir was accelerating the 2,000-pound instrument of death directly at J.T. in his desperate attempt to escape.

J.T. spun toward the sound of the racing engine and snapped off a round sending it uselessly through the windshield on the passenger's side, shredding the headrest of the seat Omar had occupied less than four minutes previously.

With the headlights blinding him, he threw himself wildly to the side of the road as Samir's van missed him by mere inches. He landed face down on the stony shoulder, scraping the palm of his frostbitten left hand into the sharp-edged gravel. His right hand resolutely gripped the Glock even as jagged stones tore strips of skin from his knuckles.

He did not wait to evaluate his situation before rolling into the grass on the side of the road. Only when he was sure he was safely out of danger as the van whizzed by did he attempt to stand up. Taking a second to orient himself and reevaluate his situation, he astutely determined he should turn off the solitary gas cylinder spewing gas in huge, billowing plumes.

Remembering the freezing metal of the first gas cylinder, he tore his shirt off and used it to protect his hands from the ice-covered valve. As he worked, he kept an eye on the third van. Just as he gave the valve a final twist, he saw the van begin careening wildly toward him with a plume of nearly invisible dust flying from its rear tires.

Dropping his wet, chilled shirt between his feet, he once again snatched the Glock from his waistband and took aim at the lurching vehicle.

Just as he was pressing the trigger, Muhammed swerved perilously to the left, throwing up a shower of stones and dust. The evasive maneuver caused the bullet to crash into the passenger's side window. Before the exploding glass finished falling from its frame, a second slug entered the passenger's door. A third poked a dimpled hole in the sliding door and buzzed between the two men seated in the van.

J.T. did not waste time watching the taillights of the fishtailing van disappear into the night. Instead, he twirled to face where they had left cylinders in the field. He grimaced when he saw four plumes of dirty, yellow gas gushing across the grass. The leading edge of the plume had almost reached the tent city of the campground.

He began sprinting toward the spurting canisters but reversed direction to snatch his shirt from the ground.

I'll need this if I want to get all those turned off before my hands give out.

As he stooped to pick up his shirt he took one last look to survey his surroundings and rethink his next move.

It's always so silent after a gunfight...

BOOM! BOOM!

The sound of two distant shotgun blasts reached his ears just as he finalized his plans.

I better get those valves shut off, then try to find a way around that cloud of gas to warn the people at the concert. I don't know who's shooting down there but I hope it's the good guys.

He was barely able to finish shutting the valve on the last cylinder. His badly blistered palms gushed an increasing torrent of slick, red blood making it difficult to grasp the slippery metal.

CHAPTER 30

JASON HAGER STEPS FORWARD

"See there," Chauncey said with gasping breaths as he and Jason Hager stopped at the edge of the dirt road. "See the yellow gas moving across the field?"

"What is that?"

"I don't know," Chauncey admitted. "J.T. thought it was some type of poison because they're wearing gas masks."

"Here comes one of the bastards," Jason said excitedly as he pointed at the headlights lurching wildly toward them.

"Did you see that? He tried to run someone over but they jumped out of the way or else they got hit and was knocked down, I'm not sure which."

"That must have been J.T.," Chauncey said worriedly. "I hope he's OK."

"Well, let's stop that bastard and find out what's going on," Jason said as he stepped onto the road and began flailing his right arm above his head in a futile attempt to flag down the van. His grizzled left fist grasped the shotgun as it hung by his side.

Samir did not care that he had failed to run over the American who killed Omar. If he had wanted to, he could have swerved and ended his meddling ways but he was not interested in killing a single man. His goal was to escape.

Allah will be pleased with what you have been able to accomplish and will forgive you for escaping to fight another day.

Samir steered the van to the left side of the road where Jason Hager stood waving his hand back and forth as he strode nearer and nearer to the center of the road.

Fool! You will die!

With an uncharacteristic flash of intuition, Jason realized the van was not going to stop. He began running toward the side of the road as fast as his stubby legs would take him.

"You're not going to run me down you son-of-a-bitch!" he growled as he spun around to face the van and raised the shotgun to his shoulder. He concentrated on a spot in the center of the windshield where he guessed the driver's face would be. The shot was similar to picking a single bobwhite quail out of a flushing covey.

With the flat face of the dark blue van rocketing out of the darkness and bearing down on him, its chromed grill glittering dully in the reflected moonlight, Jason Hager calmly slapped the forward trigger of his shotgun.

BOOM!

The shatterproof glass of the windshield remained largely intact but developed a twelve-inch circle of spider webbing in the center of its glittering surface. In the center of the spider web was a small, three-inch hole completely devoid of glass.

Sensing he was in danger, he took four hurried steps farther from the road. Carefully gauging where it would pass by, he stopped, faced the oncoming vehicle, then slipped his finger to the rear trigger of the antique side-by-side and fired the second barrel into the side window as it sped by. A shower of debris caught Samir in the side of his head and neck.

Both shotgun blasts were not as effective as Jason would have liked because the soft lead pellets deformed on impact. When the flattened metal penetrated the van's glass, it lost most of its momentum but retained enough force to shower Samir with a blinding wash of lead shot and glass particles. He was stunned and disoriented when he swerved across the yard, barely missing Jason Hager.

"Damned! He's gonna run into my tractor!" Jason yelled in an anguished voice.

Samir's van missed the once shiny green and yellow John Deere by mere inches and imbedded itself into the cushioning boughs of an ancient blue spruce on the other side of the worn tractor.

Breaking the shotgun's action open, Jason fished two fresh shells from his shirt pocket and plunked them solidly into the chambers before snapping the action shut with an angry flick of his wrist.

In a fit of rage, he rushed to the driver's door and ripped it open as he muttered, "You son-of-a-bitch! I'm gonna smash your ass up and down this mountain---"

"Jason! Calm down and be careful," Chauncey yelled as he ran to his side. "He may be armed."

"He ain't shit!" Jason rebuked him loudly. "Get your ass out of there you miserable son-of-a-bitch piece-of-shit!" he screamed in a nearly incoherent screech as his rage fed upon itself, fueling his escalating anger with every passing second.

He grabbed Samir by the front of his blood-covered shirt and yanked him out of the van with his left hand while keeping his finger on the trigger of the shotgun with his right. Samir pitched head first from the driver's seat and spun uncontrollably to the ground. With a heavy thud, his limp body belly-flopped on the scraggly grass of Hager's front yard.

Pointing his dilapidated shotgun at the middle of Samir's back Jason said venomously through clenched teeth, "Don't you dare move before the sheriff gets here or I'll blow a hole through you so big a groundhog kin get lost in it."

Chauncey cautiously walked up to Jason and stopped beside him. They both stood dumbfounded and stared at Samir's unmoving form then slowly looked at each other.

In a flash, Muhammed's van sped by with Waseem's shattered body lying motionless on the floorboards. As the escaping van hastened by, Chauncey and Muhammed locked eyes for a split second, each one etching the other's features onto their mind indelibly before it disappeared into a cloud of dust.

CHAPTER 31

DELIVERING THE WARNING

The dirty, yellow gas continued to slowly roll over the uneven ground, wrapping itself around tents and working its deadly way toward the Grand Stand where the concert was being held. It was still concentrated enough to be visible to the naked eye but was becoming thinner and more difficult to see as it slowly meandered across the fields.

Damned! The gas is between the concert and me!

I have to warn the people in the campground and at the concert. But how am I going to do it without breathing the gas myself?

The shots he fired had alerted everyone and many were looking in his direction trying to see what the commotion was all about.

Oh no! There are a lot of campers staggering around gagging.

Checking the direction of the wind, he bolted toward the south side of the campground while keeping the specter of gas in sight.

It's so quiet. The band has stopped playing!

They probably heard the gunshots and stopped the concert. Good!

When he got as close to the campers and the Grand Stand as he could without inhaling the gas himself, he began yelling, "Hey! Hey! Run! There's poisonous gas coming your way! Run! You have to get out of there to save yourself! Run!

Oh Lord! They don't realize which way to run! They're just milling around! Oh no! They're freezing in place because they're confused. Oh Lord! Give me guidance...

In an unexpected flash of inspiration, J.T. realized that if he fired his last two rounds it would get their attention centered on him so he could convey his message via voice commands and hand signals.

It only took a split second to snatch the Glock from his waistband but it took three precious seconds for his damaged hands to prepare to fire it.

Oh man, this is going to hurt

Ignoring the searing pain shooting up his arms like lightning bolts, he took a firm grasp on the pistol and fired two evenly spaced shots into the soft earth at his feet. Looking toward the campground and Grand Stand he saw everyone looking directly at him.

Now's my chance!

Raising his hands high over his head and waving them back and forth he hollered as loud as he could, "Run to that side or that side to avoid the poisonous gas!" His hand and arm signals pointed right and left to correspond with his voice commands.

At first everyone just stood motionless and stared in wide-eyed confusion.

It's a natural reaction for people to just freeze when they're unsure what's happening. I have to be more specific with my instructions.

"Don't run with the wind. Run to the sides this way and that way," he bellowed at the top of his voice. Again, he used hand signals to give visual clarity to his verbal instructions.

Keep it up! You have no other options. Keep it up.

He continued to scream his warnings over and over again. He never felt so inadequate and hopeless in his entire life.

Don't let despair overcome you. You have to fight to the end. You have no choice.

Slowly, some of the campers closest to him began to understand when they saw others coughing and wheezing as the gas overtook them. And like a huge herd of wildebeest they ponderously began turning and moving toward gas-free areas, guiding others before them as they went.

They're helping each other! Of course! It's who they are. Since they were small children these people have been taught that serving others is what God wants them to do.

That's quite a bit different from what the bastards who did this are taught.

"Yes! Hurry! Keep moving in that direction or that direction!" he continued yelling as he feverishly directed them with hand and arm signals.

"Yell warnings to the others so they'll understand what they have to do to save themselves! Tell them about the poisonous gas coming toward them!"

And they did.

Like a droning buzz resonating from an angry beehive, the warnings spread throughout the crowd rising to a crescendo as more and more people began understanding the gravity of their situation and spread the word. Motivated chatter rippled through the horde in an uncontrollable flood.

The unintelligible babble was being transformed into motion as the message spread.

It's working!

Then he heard it.

A booming voice over the speakers at the Grand Stand announced, "We have gotten word that poisonous gas is being carried by the wind and is moving this way. To avoid breathing the gas you are being instructed to move quickly at a ninety-degree angle to the wind. You must move that way or that way as quickly as possible. Leave your blankets and coolers so you can help others. Hurry!"

The guy on the stage is using his hands and arms to signal to the crowd which way to run so there won't be any confusion. Just like I was doing! Thank you, God!

Yes! The band has a better view of what's going on from the stage. He can see and hear me from up there while the crowd down below can't. He heard me and used hand signals like I did!

By this time, the deadly gas had dissipated enough to become almost invisible and was rapidly swallowed by the darkness of night.

I've done all I can do here. I better get back to our campsite and set up a command center for our church's group. That's where they'll return.

If they don't come back then at least I'll know whom to look for, he thought as a great sorrow fell upon him.

He began staggering as he made his way back across the field. The strobe effect from the flashing red, white, and blue lights of emergency vehicles racing up the road added to his disorientation.

I guess Chauncey made it to Jason's and raised the alarm. Now I have to flag down the police and explain what happened before going back to our campsite.

A unique combination of fatigue and vertigo knocked him to his knees before he could take another step.

CHAPTER 32

ONE WEEK AFTER THE GAS ATTACK

"How are your hands?" Chauncey asked after he and J.T. sat down in the Tobin's living room.

"They're healing pretty well," he replied as he held up his hands. "These bandages can come off in another week or so."

"You look like you have mummy hands. Are your hands so bad that you need that many bandages?"

"It's more to keep the burn salve off anything I touch than it is to protect the wounds at this point. That nasty stuff gets onto everything and you can't get it off."

"Your hands must have been badly burned."

"The doc said my hands were only frostbitten by the cold of the metal valve and I didn't really come in contact with the mustard gas at all. So it's not really a chemical burn but the damage is the same as if it were burned."

"They figured out it was mustard gas pretty fast."

"Yeah, when that many people were injured they analyzed it as soon as possible so they'd know how to treat their injuries," J.T. replied. "I spoke to the doctor quite a bit about it and he filled me in on a lot of things I didn't know. Then I contacted some old friends and got some additional information that's not available to the public."

"Tell me about it, at least as much as you can."

"Well, mustard gas is an odorless gas that was used extensively in World War I," he explained. "The investigation showed this was left over from that war and was stored at the Aberdeen Proving Grounds in Maryland. That's where these canisters were stolen from."

"Did they figure out how it was stolen?"

"That's not public knowledge, sorry."

"That's OK," Chauncey said with a knowing smile. "What else can you tell me?"

"Mustard gas is very powerful and only a very small amount is horrendously injurious to the human body but the symptoms may not show up for twelve hours."

"That's why the people who came in contact with it didn't die right away."

"That's right," J.T. said. "The stuff stays active for several weeks. Peter Giovanni has been instructed not to allow humans or livestock onto those fields for at least six months. Further testing will show when it's no longer active."

"Will he be able to survive financially without being able to use those fields?"

"He said he can manage to keep the farm by getting on the road as a truck driver for six months," J.T. replied. "He had to sell the cattle he was planning on putting back onto those pastures because he doesn't have enough feed for them on the unaffected acreage."

"Did you find out what mustard gas does to create so much damage?"

"The doctor said it causes the skin to blister but only after four to twenty-four hours after exposure. That's why they suspected my hands were suffering from frostbite instead of contact with the gas. The damage occurred immediately," he said as he held his bandaged hands up.

"How many have died so far?"

"So far we've lost eighteen," he said, his voice catching as a tear escaped from the corner of his eye. "And the doc thinks the fatality rate may go as high as sixty or more."

"So we'll know how many casualties we suffered in about two months."

"No," J.T. said simply. "Anyone that had more than fifty percent of their body exposed may die over the next few years. Then there's the carcinogenic aspect that may take years to develop into cancer."

"I'm just glad none of the kids from our group were injured," Chauncey said. "It was our good luck they were all on the side of the crowd farthest away from where the gas was released."

"It certainly gave them extra time to get out of there before the gas drifted in," J.T. said with a slight quiver in his voice. "And for that I am eternally grateful."

Chauncey could only stare at the floor. He was at a loss for words.

Regardless of the valiant efforts of J.T., Chauncey, Jason Hager, and all of the police, EMTs, and hospital personnel involved in the Hallelujah Gathering incident, a total of 57 people died and another 453 suffered lung and skin injuries over the next two months.

How many victims will still be added to the list can only be guessed.

CHAPTER 33

THANKSGIVING PLANS

"What are you doing about Thanksgiving?" Nadine asked Sarah as they entered the lower pasture at The Shire after an early morning horseback ride in the crisp chill of October. "Do you want to spend it with me?"

"Thanks for the invitation but I've already accepted an invite from my brother-in-law to join his family for Thanksgiving," Sarah replied. "They told me to bring Chauncey. I think they're under the incorrect assumption we're having an affair."

"Oh really!" Nadine gasped.

"Speaking of Chauncey," Nadine said. "Have you been making any headway into finding out anything about his identity or past, you know, especially since that terrible situation that developed in West Virginia at the Hallelujah Gathering and all?"

"No I haven't," Sarah admitted. "The hypnotist was only able to ascertain that he could remember jumbled sequences of numbers but it's not clear whether they're telephone numbers, a social security number, or a combination to a safe. Hypnosis was worth a try but wasn't very helpful."

"Are you sure Chauncey was really under hypnosis and not just faking it?"

"No, he was under," Sarah replied tiredly. "Dr. Hambra has a good reputation and he believes Chauncey was definitely under. He said it's a sign of superior I.Q."

"What about fingerprints?"

"We've run into a catch-22 situation with fingerprints," Sarah said with exasperation weighing heavily in her voice. "The police won't run his prints to see if he's in the NICS system which would at least give us his real name."

"Why not?"

"Because he hasn't committed a crime."

"Well, have him apply for something, anything that requires a background check," Nadine said. "Then they'll run his fingerprints."

"There's where the catch-22 comes into play," Sarah replied. "Most applications, like applying for a concealed carry permit for instance, require you to provide truthful information under threat of jail. They always require your signature at the bottom of the form to make it a legally binding document and providing false information is a felony."

"So he can't get his fingerprints unless he commits a crime," Nadine said as she organized the situation in her mind. "But if he makes up a false name to get his background and fingerprints checked then he'd be charged with a felony."

"Exactly."

"But at least he'd know who he is," she said. "Even though he'd be in prison for committing a felony."

"It's not funny Nadine," Sarah said with irritation still evident in her voice. "I have an attorney checking into it to see if we can find a way around the catch-22."

"Life's a bitch and then you die," Nadine replied. "It seems that attorneys have to be consulted about every damned thing these days."

"Even when you die the government and attorneys still get a piece of your estate. Just like a pack of vultures cleaning up your remains."

"Why are you worrying about who Chauncey is? Are there problems?"

"No," Sarah said as she rolled her eyes in exasperation. "But his lack of identity is beginning to get me wondering what I'm involved in and it's burdensome for him."

"What do you mean?

"I mean that total amnesia from a head injury, assuming it was a severe beating he suffered, is extremely rare."

"What about emotional amnesia?" Nadine asked. "The beating may have come afterward and has no bearing as a cause for his condition."

"Once again, it's a very rare occurrence."

"So your question is?"

"Does Chauncey really suffer from this super rare situation," Sarah said as she chewed on her lip as she searched for the correct words. "Or am I being duped into helping an impostor move anonymously into another life?"

"Chauncey's not a mass murderer, at least he doesn't seem like one, if that's what you're getting at."

"What does a mass murderer act like?" Sarah asked in an agitated tone. "Ted Bundy was supposedly the nicest guy until he threw unsuspecting girls into his Volkswagen, bound them hand and foot with duct tape, then killed them."

"I see what you mean," Nadine said as she began gnawing thoughtfully on her lip just as Sarah had done.

"That's why I'm footing the bill for an attorney to help me find out who Chauncey really is. It will give both of us some peace of mind knowing who he is."

"Are you starting to get second thoughts about Chauncey? Is there anything I should know about?"

"No, not at all," Sarah said with firm conviction. "It's just that it's very difficult to live in our society without an identity. I don't want him living in the shadows like an illegal all his life if he doesn't have to."

"And that's the only problem with Chauncey?"

"That's the only problem I know of," Sarah replied.

"Which you have basically turned over to the attorney," Nadine concluded. "So the only thing you have to deal with immediately is how to convince your family you're not having an affair with Chauncey."

"That and how to find time to bake pies for Thanksgiving dinner," Sarah said with a look of mild trepidation remaining on her face.

CHAPTER 34

MUHAMMED'S REVENGE

The three men sat in the sparsely furnished but immaculately clean kitchen with two of them on one side of the yellow floral Formica-topped kitchen table. The third sat across from them in a haughty, detached manner, silently pecking at the keyboard of a laptop computer. None seemed to notice or care that the chairs were of a non-matching olive green.

"You have called for us, Commander?" Haady asked.

"Yes Haady," Muhammed replied as he looked up from his computer screen. "I have need of your and Bishr's skills."

"What do you want us to do, Commander?" Bishr asked submissively.

"You two have been very helpful in the past," Muhammed replied. "You disposed of the van with the bullet holes and blood in it and you found a fellow true believer to oversee Waseem's burial and keep the cause of his death secret."

"You asked that both those tasks be handled discretely and efficiently," Haady said. "It honors me to have you say you are pleased with the completion of our assignments."

"I am pleased, as is Allah, I am sure," Muhammed replied with aloofness in his voice. "That is why I have asked you to help with these tasks."

"What are those tasks, Commander?"

"These men who interfered with our blessed work at the Hallelujah Gathering; this Jeremy Tobin and his friend, Chauncey," Muhammed said haltingly as he chose his words carefully. "They must be punished for their meddling."

"Their meddling must be avenged," Bishr and Haady said in unison.

Muhammed looked at both of them from below hooded eyelids until they became uncomfortable under his unwavering gaze.

"It is your task to find out about these men," Muhammed said slowly as he laid a short stack of newspaper articles on the table in front of them. "The newspapers and television say that Jeremy Tobin lives in Northern Virginia. I want you to find his house and gather information about him and his family."

"And the other one?"

"And him also," Muhammed replied with deliberation. "His name is Chauncey and he gives two addresses. One is in Washington, D.C. and the other is a farm near a town called Thompsonville."

"Does he have a last name, Commander?"

"None of the news articles mentions a last name for him."

"And how are we to gather information on these two men?"

"You are to wait until the cover of darkness and take the trash they put on the street curb for disposal," Muhammed said. "There is much to be learned from what these Americans discard."

"Are there other ways besides taking their garbage that you would have us do to gather information on them?"

"Start with their trash," Muhammed said. "Only if it does not give us the information we need will you resort to riskier methods such as stealing their computers."

"We will report back to you regularly, Commander."

"I expect you will," Muhammed said menacingly.

CHAPTER 35

VALUABLE TRASH

"It was very easy to look in the telephone book on the Internet and find Jeremy Tobin's home address," Haady said to Bishr as they slid onto the torn front seats of a dirty brown Toyota Corolla.

"And it was even easier getting directions to his house," Bishr responded as he jammed the key into the ignition switch. "Now all we have to do is drive by the house every evening until they place their trash out for pick-up."

"Will we take it as soon as we see it?"

"No, you fool," Bishr replied. "We must wait until the middle of the night when the chance of us being discovered is very small. Even then we will try to replace the plastic bags with similar bags so they are not missed. Jeremy Tobin cannot know we are interested in information about him and his family."

Two days passed before the men saw what they had been looking for.

"Good!" Bishr said as he slowed the Toyota to more closely inspect the trashcans. "They are using Glad Trash Bags with the red pull strings."

"That is a good thing?" Haady asked quizzically.

"Yes," Bishr replied gleefully. "It is one of the brands of bags I bought and have in the trunk. All we have to do is crumple old newspapers to fill the bags and make them appear full to replace the bags we take away."

"I counted three bags that were visible and two trash cans," Haady said. "Assuming there are two full bags in each of the cans that makes a total of seven bags we will need."

"Then we will fill nine bags in case they put out more trash before we return."

"Will all those bags fit into this small car?"

"No, that is why I have borrowed a van with a side door from Abdul-Qaadir, a man I work with," Bishr said slyly. "I told him I need it to move my girlfriend to a new apartment."

"What is your plan?"

"I will drive the van with the newspaper-stuffed trash bags stacked just behind our seats," Bishr said enthusiastically. "You will very quietly get out of the van, open the side door, and begin loading Jeremy Tobin's trash into the back portion of the van then I will hand you the bags we stuffed to replace the ones you took."

"It will be like an assembly line in a factory," Haady said with amazement in his voice.

"And very efficient so we can quickly be gone with that which we seek," Bishr said with a satisfied grin on his face.

CHAPTER 36

THANKSGIVING DINNER

"Watch those pies, Chauncey," Sarah called out as he tried to balance a third pie on his outstretched arms. "I've been up half the night baking and I don't want them splattered all over the driveway."

"Don't worry about me," Chauncey replied. "And don't forget the wine."

"I'm not forgetting anything," she shot back.

"You two sound like an old married couple for crying out loud," Stephanie Tobin called from the front porch where she stood holding the door open for them.

"I'm not good at very many things," Chauncey said jokingly. "But I'm real good at complaining and bickering."

"I can see that," she replied with an air of joviality. "It's nice to see you again Chauncey."

"And it's nice to see you too, Stephanie," he said as he sidled his way past her and into the house. "Do you want these in the kitchen?"

"Yes, if you would please. You can put those pies on the counter there," Stephanie directed as she pointed him in the right direction. "And Sarah, you can put the wine over on the microwave hutch if you can find any space."

After helping her guests unburden themselves of their contributions to the Thanksgiving Day feast Stephanie said, "Let's go into the living room. There's someone I'd like you to meet."

Stephanie led the way to the sunken living room, descended the two steps with the grace of a ballet dancer, and turned to face them after planting her feet directly between a tall, lanky man and a much shorter, more compact man with a handlebar mustache.

"You know J.T.," she said as she took the arm of her tall, lanky husband. Then with a flourish of her left hand she said, "And this is John Myers, J.T.'s friend. John, this is my sister-in-law Sarah and her friend Chauncey."

"Hello Sarah, it's a pleasure to finally meet you," John said with a slight bow as he extended his hand toward her. "And it's an equally pleasant honor to make your acquaintance, Chauncey. J.T. has told me quite a bit about you. He says you're a good man to have around in an emergency."

"J.T. is much too kind," Chauncey said uncertainly, not quite sure how to proceed with this new acquaintance.

"And I've heard about you also, Sarah," John continued. "I understand you have an excellent reputation as a chiropractor and recently acquired a farm up in the mountains. What is it you named your farm? It's a unique name but I can't remember what it is."

"I call it Predator's Bane," Sarah replied, also a little unsure how to react to him. "And it's a pleasure to meet you, John."

"How did you arrive at that name?" he asked inquisitively as a puzzled look crossed his face. His eyes bore into Sarah as he awaited an answer.

"It's a long story," Sarah replied as she averted her eyes away from his.

"If we have time later," he said with a smile popping out from beneath his thick, brushy mustache. "Maybe you'll indulge me and fill me in on the details."

John looked at Stephanie with an ingratiating smile and Sarah took the opportunity to appraise his physical bearing with her professional eye.

He only looks short and chubby but that's all muscle under his khaki shirt and he has huge gnarly hands like a steelworker. They must take a lot of daily abuse.

He stands with such ease as though he fears nothing. I'll bet this is J.T.'s old boss from the CIA he talks about. At least now I know his name.

"Make yourselves at home," Stephanie said. "I'm going to put a few finishing touches on dinner then I'll call when it's ready."

"I'll help," Sarah offered.

"No thanks, I've got it. It's only one or two small things," Stephanie replied cheerfully. "You better stay here and keep an eye on these three."

"OK," Sarah said as she shared a smile with the three men before turning to John.

"I'm afraid J.T. hasn't had time to fill us in on you as well as he has obviously done about us," Sarah said coyly with a polite smile. "What is it you do?"

"I'm a businessman dealing in the Middle East," he replied quickly. "I dabble in any number of adventures but always in that area of the world. They're the ones with money these days, you know."

"So I've heard," Chauncey said. "I've been studying the Middle East a little since that region of the world is in the news so often."

"Yes, it's an intriguing area," John added. "What in particular interests you about the Middle East?"

"Nothing in particular," Chauncey replied. "The fact that it's in the news so often, as I've mentioned, keeps my interest piqued."

"And what have you learned about the Middle East that continues to pique your interest?" John asked innocently as his mustache twitched back and forth.

"I've learned there are many mysteries and few concrete truths to be learned other than geography."

"And how is that?"

"Take the culture for instance," Chauncey said. "As far as I can figure out, it's not a homogenous culture even within each country."

"That's true to a certain extent I imagine," John confirmed with a small nod of his head. "And what else have you discovered?"

"The main thread that binds the Middle East together is their religion," Chauncey replied. "And curiously, it's also the thing that seems to cause the most strife among different factions."

"Very true," John confirmed once again. "Historically, the jihadists have been fighting and following in the footsteps of their warrior Prophet since the seventh century."

"And that attitude continues on today?" Chauncey asked inquisitively.

"Absolutely," John said as he warmed to one of his favorite subjects. "The radical Islamic movement is dedicated to converting the entire world to Islam at the point of a sword."

"Go on," Chauncey said simply, making an effort to maintain a low, calm voice while listening intently.

"To comprehend the situation you have to know and understand the teachings under which the radicals are operating," John said unemotionally.

"And those teachings are?" Chauncey asked quizzically.

"For example let's look at Osama Bin Laden. He didn't refer to his organization as al Qaeda," he went on in a learned manner. "Rather, he called it, 'World Islamic Front for Jihad Against Jews and Crusaders.'"

"That's a mouthful," Chauncey said. "But why do they single out Jews and the so-called Crusaders?"

"It is a mouthful," John agreed. "But in Middle Eastern terminology, Jews and Christians - Christians are the crusaders - are described as 'the vilest of creatures' because they reject Islam. At least according to Qur'an 98:6."

"You seem to have committed certain pertinent information to memory."

"Yes I have," he said. "When the command found in Qur'an 47:4 is to 'smite the necks' of 'unbelievers' you'd better start paying attention especially if you're one of the unbelievers because the radical Islamists may take it upon themselves to behead you and feel quite righteous about it."

"Surely that's a misinterpretation of the Qur'an."

"Not really," he replied. "These affirmations are rampant within the Qur'an but since it's written in classical Arabic, and must be read and recited during prayer in that language only, most Muslims really don't understand what principles they're pledging allegiance to."

"So if all Jews and 'Crusaders' as they're referred to are considered to be unbelievers, why don't the Muslims just start killing us all by cutting off our heads?" Chauncey asked unbelievingly.

"If they followed the last passage to be revealed to Muhammad, that's sura nine, they most assuredly would," John explained calmly. "Sura nine states that Muslims should wage war against the People of the Book- that's the Jews and Christians who follow the teachings found in the Bible or 'Book'- until they either convert to Islam or are subdued as second-class citizens called dhimmis."

"And that's why you say Muslims want to convert the world to Islam at the point of a sword?"

"That's why."

"And is this attitude what's behind the unrest in the Middle East?" Chauncey asked seriously.

"It's a large part of it."

"Then why don't we hear more about these teachings?" Chauncey asked with a hint of desperation in his voice. "Are we being lied to?"

"That's a distinct possibility," John said gravely. "Religious deception, as long as it's practiced on unbelievers, is taught by the Qur'an."

"What do you mean?" Sarah asked sharply.

"I mean that Qur'an 3:28 tells Muslims to not make friends with unbelievers except to guard themselves against them," John said as he stared directly at Sarah to emphasize his point. "Islamic spokesmen may be downplaying or even denying aspects of their religion that unbelievers, that's folks like you and Chauncey, may find unpalatable, disgusting, or repulsive."

"Oh my God!" she said when the reality of John's words had sunk in. "They do that all the time! I remember thinking how much the Muslim representatives lie when they give interviews on the news. They don't even seem ashamed when they're caught in an obvious untruth."

"So you've noticed that, have you?"

He remained silent for a moment, leaving a pregnant pause to allow his words to settle like a veil of truth upon everyone's mind before attempting to make his next statement. Before he could continue Sarah interrupted in an agitated manner.

"So the Muslims consider those of us who are unbelievers to be second-class citizens unworthy of respect or the truth, and Muslim women are not much better off than us unbelievers?"

"That pretty well sums it up," he said simply. "One cleric puts unbelievers into the same category as urine, feces, dogs, pigs, and dead bodies. Nice company to find yourself lumped in with, eh?"

"John, be realistic, you can always find some crackpot in any group who makes stupid statements," Chauncey said defensively.

"But this isn't some crackpot," he said calmly as he looked directly into Chauncey's eyes. "This list of unclean things is from the Iraqi Shi'ite leader Grand Ayatollah Sayyid Ali Husayni Sistani, a man considered by many in the West as a reformer and moderate thinker."

"Oh brother!" Sarah said. "What do the radicals think about us if this guy lumps us in with pigs and shit?"

A stunned silence fell over the room followed by an avalanche of laughter that left Chauncey and Sarah gasping for breath.

"OK, so why hasn't the huge number of Muslims around the world risen up and wiped us infidels off the face of the earth?" Sarah asked when she was finally able to breathe without laughing.

"Like I said," John replied. "The vast majority of Muslims only have a glancing knowledge of what Islam really teaches."

"That's why you differentiate by speaking of the radical Islamists."

"That's right," he said. "There are groups around the world who believe it's their responsibility to wage war against non-Muslims and impose Islamic law upon all the lands. Those are the guys we have to be concerned about."

"But you've been saying that the passages the radical Islamists are basing their perverted, distorted vision of their religion on are actually in the Qur'an," Sarah said as she sifted through the information in her mind. "Which means that it really isn't perverted or distorted; it's the way Islam is."

"If you don't believe me maybe you'll believe Omar Ahmad, the board chairman of the Council on American-Islamic Relations who said that Islam is in America to become the dominant religion and the Qur'an should be the highest authority in America. He finished by saying that Islam should be the only accepted religion on earth."

"Isn't that the group that likes to call themselves CAIR so it sounds like the well-known humanitarian group?"

"That's them."

"It sure sounds like world domination to me," Chauncey said in agreement as he nodded his head solemnly.

"Surely the media would be all over this if it were true," Sarah said with fear beginning to creep into her eyes. "They wouldn't stand by and see us conquered from within."

"Don't hold your breath on that one," Chauncey said as he interrupted. "Even the FBI can't seem to admit that this threat exists within our borders."

"What do you mean?" she asked.

"I'm referring to an explosion that occurred in Texas City, Texas," Chauncey replied as he warmed to the topic. "The FBI immediately ruled out terrorism even though they didn't visit the site to investigate until eight days after the explosions occurred."

254 · D. E. HEIL

"But it was terrorism," John said quietly. "Wasn't it?"

"So it would seem," Chauncey replied. "From what I can remember from the magazine article, it was discovered there were five different explosions at the refinery. That's definitely suspicious since a group calling itself Qaeda al-Jihad claimed responsibility."

"That's a situation where Americans have invited millions of Muslims to live amongst them, assuming they could live as equals," John said. "Unfortunately we're now finding that Islam must struggle to make itself supreme to all other religions and political systems."

"That's scary," Sarah said with a tremor in her voice.

"And that's only one instance of Muslim involvement in violence within the United States that may be religion-motivated," John said. "You can keep your head firmly buried in the sand, Sarah, or you can begin preparing for when they come for you and your loved ones."

A cloud of fury immediately exploded on Sarah's face at the same instant Stephanie bounded into the living room with a flourish.

"OK y'all, it's time for dinner," she announced. "The girls are putting the finishing touches on the table so it's time for everyone to wash their hands."

"That's one of the sweetest sounds in the world," Chauncey mused.

"The call to dinner," John said in finishing Chauncey's sentence with a chuckle. "J.T. and I'll catch up to you two in a minute if that's alright with you."

"Any time I get first dibs on the bathroom it's alright with me," Sarah said as she headed toward the door while still obviously deep in thought.

"Chauncey, there's a bathroom down the hall and Sarah can use the one upstairs in our bedroom," J.T. said as he verbally guided his guests to the restrooms.

After everyone except John left the room, J.T. said quietly, "That was quite a lesson for those two."

"Yes it was," John replied seriously. "Every word I uttered was the truth. And you better take some major precautions for you and your family. You've had one run-in with these bastards, your name was in the media for days for Chrissake after that Hallelujah Gathering affair, and the jihadists don't forgive or forget."

"I've taken some precautions," J.T. said as he carefully picked his words. "Sarah brought a Bushmaster with her; it even has a CompM4 sight, and she made me borrow it indefinitely. Though I may be too embarrassed to take it to the range and practice with it."

"And why is that?"

"Sarah had a hot pink paint applied to it. It looks like something Barbie would own."

"You don't have a rifle?" John asked as he stifled a chuckle.

"I didn't have a need for one until recently," he said evenly. "Stephanie and I both carry pistols and that seemed to be sufficient until the Hallelujah Gathering."

His voice trailed off as he fell into deep thought.

"J.T.!" Stephanie called from the kitchen. "Would you and John please come to the table so we can say Grace?"

"Uh-oh!" John said boyishly. "We'd better hurry or we'll be in deep trouble with the boss!"

"You got that right," J.T. said, his face beaming with a large smile.

CHAPTER 37

AFTER DINNER CONVERSATION

"J.T., will you please clean the meat from the bones so I can boil them down in the stock pot?" Stephanie asked politely. "I want turkey broth for soup this week."

"Yes dear," he intoned in a slavish, downtrodden voice meant to poke fun at his lovely wife.

"Chauncey and I'll begin washing the dishes," Sarah volunteered. "If that's OK with you, Chauncey."

"It's fine with me if I can still move. Thank you all for such a wonderful dinner."

"I'll second that," John added sleepily. "And I'll begin wiping down the table and counters."

"Y'all don't have to work," Stephanie said. "You're guests."

"And you're a very gracious host," John replied. "But many hands make light work."

"Mom, are you sure you don't want us to help clean up?" Mary asked solemnly. "We still have five minutes before Maria's mom picks us up for the movie."

"You'd better get going so you're not late," Stephanie replied as she snuck a quick glance at the kitchen clock.

"Besides," John added in a teasing manner. "How are we supposed to eat your share of the pies if you're still here?"

"You better not eat my pie, Uncle John," Joan cried with glee at being teased by her favorite visitor before running upstairs to brush her teeth.

"The girls really enjoy spending time with all of you," Stephanie said.

"And we enjoy them," Chauncey replied.

The clean-up went quickly.

"Why doesn't everyone go into the living room and I'll bring the coffee in as soon as it's finished brewing," Stephanie said as she began removing heavy ceramic coffee mugs from the cupboard and arranged them on a silver serving tray.

"Coffee sure sounds like a good idea," John said with a satisfied sigh as he turned to follow the others into the living room.

Stephanie had just finished serving coffee to her guests and taken a seat when Sarah sat back with a weary look on her face.

"All that turkey is making you sleepy, I see," Stephanie said as she smiled at Sarah.

"Maybe a little. I just realized this is the second Thanksgiving since Josh's murder," Sarah replied. "But thanks to y'all I'm not having as bad of a time with it as I thought I would."

A pall fell over the room.

"But I don't want to dwell on that," she said with a breezy air of enthusiasm as she physically roused herself out of her funk by sitting up straighter. "Today is a day to give thanks for the gifts we've been granted over the last year. There's a lot for me to be thankful for and you're a large part of it."

A beaming smile spread across Stephanie's face showing she was gladdened by Sarah's recovery.

"John, you've really piqued my interest," Sarah said as she spun in his direction so quickly that it startled him as he sat entranced in his feast-induced stupor. "What impact will a Muslim jihad have on us directly?"

"It can affect you in many ways," he began. "To fully appreciate the impact jihad may have on you and your country, you have to understand their mindset."

J.T. cringed noticeably at the turn this conversation was taking and looked sheepishly at his wife.

"You see," John said as he warmed to the subject. "Jihad does not recognize universal human rights; therefore, they're very brutal in their ways. It's because they view infidels as inferior to Muslims."

"That's understandable," Chauncey said. "Considering they lump infidel unbelievers in with pigs and excrement."

"Exactly," John replied. "You have to understand their point of view is vastly different from those of us raised in a culture of Judeo-Christian values."

"How do their values differ from ours?" Chauncey asked innocently.

"War is despised and hated while peace is praised in the Judeo-Christian cultures," John explained cordially. "But under jihadist ideology, it is war that is praised and the killing of infidels is held in high esteem."

"So the traditional sentiments we feel about war are not valid when the outlook of the jihadist is taken into consideration."

"You're so very correct, Chauncey," John replied. "Jihad warriors do not accept the tenets of the Geneva Convention or the conventional rules of war. All that matters to them is the death of infidels by any means."

"That's scary," Sarah added intuitively. "Coyotes play by the same lack of rules. No emotion or feelings- only the death of their prey counts to them."

"That's a good analogy," John said with a nod of satisfaction. "But at least with coyotes you know they're predators designed by nature to kill. With jihadists, the media has repeated misinformation over and over again about Islam being a religion of peace. So people are confused and aren't prepared to defend themselves like they would against a known threat."

"For crying out loud!" Sarah interjected as she sat upright in her seat. "President Bush called Islam a religion of peace within a few days of 9-11."

"And the result of this disinformation," John continued, "is that citizens have their concept of reality clouded and any chance of developing a clear, honest understanding of who their enemies are and why they're coming to kill them is lost."

Sarah stared intently at the floor as though seeing a movie reveal itself in the woven golden threads of the carpet.

"Are you still with us Sarah?" John asked in a kidding manner. "Maybe the turkey is finally getting to you and you need a nap, eh?"

"No," she said with a smile. "It just settled in is all."

"What settled in?" Stephanie asked with concern.

"The fact that jihadists are just like coyotes," she said evenly. "We're told they're cute and cuddly but in reality they'll rip your throat out just for the fun of it."

Silence descended upon the occupants of the room like a fog bank as the truth of Sarah's words sunk into their psyches.

"If the jihadists try to kill us," Sarah asked with a slight hitch in her voice. "How do you think they'll attack?"

"WorldNet Daily reported that captured al-Qaeda leaders and documents revealed a plan for an 'American Hiroshima,'" John said, making sure J.T. knew it was information that had been released to the general public. "Their plan is to use nuclear devices in major U.S. cities simultaneously. New York, Boston, Washington, Las Vegas, Chicago, Los Angeles and others would be hit at the same time if the reports are to be believed."

"They can't do that!" Sarah cried with anguish in her voice. "They don't have the missiles to hit that many cities at the same time!"

"They don't need missiles," John said deliberately to allow his next statement to sink in. "Al-Qaeda has obtained over 40 nuclear devices.

Suitcase nukes, artillery shells, missile warheads, and nuclear mines from the former Soviet Union. Then there's always the possibility of them making their own bombs from fissile material they purchase on the black market."

"But they can't smuggle those into the United States!" Sarah wailed. "We have Customs stopping---"

"Oh God!" she wailed, interrupting herself. "They can't even keep bales of pot out of the country!"

"There may already be nuclear bombs here," Chauncey said solemnly. "I remember reading about it. Retired Spetznaz agents, the former Soviet Special Forces, are helping al-Qaeda find nuclear weapons they hid in the United States during the Cold War. I remember that article."

"Bin Laden's goal is to kill four million Americans with the 'American Hiroshima' attack," John said with resignation in his voice. "And he wants two million of those to be children in order to 'avenge the Arab and Muslim world'; whatever that means."

"How would they hope to get so many nukes into the U.S.?" Sarah asked while Stephanie remained strangely silent. "That's a lot of nukes."

"It's surmised they used the MS-13 street gang and other organized crime groups to smuggle them over the southern border of the United States."

"What?"

"You heard me," John said evenly. "The entire furor you hear about illegal immigrants coming across the border with Mexico is not about Mexicans seeking honest work. It's about our sworn enemies coming into our county to kill us where we live."

John allowed his last statement to lie upon the air like a cold, wet blanket.

"You didn't know that Islam is making major gains in converting the native populations of Mexico and Latin America, did you?" John asked snappily. "And our Pentagon has confirmed that Latin

American smuggling rings are attempting to sneak al-Qaeda operatives over the southern border of the United States?

"All Central and South American countries have become springboards for smuggling extremists into the United States. The most common route involves Middle Easterners wending their way to Brazil where a false identity is assumed before entering Mexico.

"U.S. officials have long known about the growing Muslim influence in what has become known as the Muslim Triangle: Brazil, Argentina, and Paraguay. Even Islamic "charities" moved their bases of operations to Central and South America since international pressure coerced them into cutting their traditional ties with terrorists and other allied Islamic organizations such as al-Qaida. It was released in the news but no one paid it any attention."

"That's scary," Chauncey said as he began searching his memory for information related to the news John had just dropped upon them. "Now I remember!"

Everyone looked at him with open mouths and wonderment in their expressions.

"You have your memory back?" Sarah squealed with glee.

"No! No! I don't remember everything!" he said as he chuckled at their misunderstanding. "I remember reading that the FBI director, I can't remember his name, informed congress that al-Qaeda supporters had crossed into the U.S. after adopting Hispanic names while in Brazil and Mexico."

"I seem to remember reading something like that myself," John confirmed with a nodding of his head. "And I was surprised to read that tens of millions of Muslims of Arab descent are living in Latin America."

"But they're not all al-Qaeda or terrorists," Sarah said.

"You may be right," Chauncey replied. "But there may already be terrorists here who crossed over that porous border and our government doesn't seem interested in doing anything to stop them."

"And on that high note of setting our minds at ease," Stephanie said airily as she stood up. "Does anyone want a refill of coffee or some pie?"

CHAPTER 38

DRIVING HOME TO THE FARM

"That was a nice visit," Chauncey said as he and Sarah pulled out of the Tobin's driveway, a cache of leftovers securely stashed in the trunk of Sarah's new Mercedes C-300 Luxury Sedan.

They gave an enthusiastic good-bye wave toward the Tobins standing on their front porch as Sarah turned the 4-spoke steering wheel.

"It certainly was," Sarah agreed emphatically. "It's always nice to get together with family; especially on Thanksgiving."

Out of the corner of her eye she saw Chauncey's head drift slowly to his chest and his eyes drop dejectedly downward.

"I'm sorry, Chauncey," Sarah said sympathetically. "I didn't think about your circumstances before I said that."

"That's OK," Chauncey replied with a twinge of regret in his voice and a faint smile dimly cast upon his lips. "You and the Tobins treat me like family, and y'all seem like family to me."

"Thank you," she said. "You don't know how happy it makes me to hear you say that."

"So, are you planning on going to the Christmas Youth Ministry mass at St. Boniface?" he asked, trying to change the subject.

"I don't think Joan and Mary will let us miss it," she said with a smile, allowing herself a quick glance away from the road toward Chauncey. "They're both part of the ceremony."

"You're probably right," he said with a chuckle.

"And they expect you to be there too," she said. "Did you see how their faces lit up when you said you'd come?"

"Yeah, it's great to see such fine young people being involved in their church," he said. "This bunch of kids has really come together since the Hallelujah Gathering tragedy."

"It's great seeing adults volunteering their time to guide the kids in their ministry with the church," she replied. "A lot of adults wouldn't want to be bothered with someone else's kids, especially during the teenage years."

"I think it's nice how the young people provide everything from the music to the entertainment for the mass," he said. "If I'm not mistaken, Joan is even doing sign language while the youth choir sings *Silent Night*."

"No, it's Mary who's signing. Joan is a candle lighter," she corrected him.

"I think you're wrong," he said standing his ground.

"Well, we're either going to argue about it or put our money where our mouths are," she said with a teasing lilt to her voice.

"Are you so sure of your memory that you're willing to bet the maximum bet allowed by law?" he asked.

"There is no bet allowed by law," she said with a laugh. "So you're willing to bet an entire five bucks on your memory?"

"That's not funny, Sarah," he said returning her laugh with a hearty chuckle. "And yes, I'm willing to bet five bucks because I know it's an easy win; and I always like winning money from you!"

"Oh, is that so? Well, let me tell you---"

And so it went for the rest of the ride to the farm.

CHAPTER 39

UNWELCOME VISITORS

"Are you OK?" Chauncey inquired after a long period of silence. "If you're too tired I can help drive."

"I'm fine, just thinking a little and enjoying the silence," Sarah replied hoping he would take the hint. "Besides, you don't have a driver's license."

"The chances of getting pulled over out here are remote to say the least," he said with a tiny bit of irritation evident in his fatigued voice.

They were almost to Predator's Bane when Chauncey sat straight up in his seat and said, "Your lane is coming up soon."

Sarah ignored him.

"Do you have all the electricity hooked up in the old machine shed the way you want it?" Sarah asked inquisitively. "Is it ready for the inside to be finished?"

"I prefer to refer to it as my cottage now that it's been converted into living quarters," Chauncey replied playfully. "I don't want people getting the impression I live in a shed."

"You know what I mean."

"Yes I do," Chauncey said. "I even have that old computer hooked up so I can do work from either office, even when I'm here at the farm. Maybe someday I can telecommute and work from here and not have to go back to the city."

"That way you can be closer to Annie all week long. Right?"

"Well, yeah," Chauncey replied with a slight blush reddening his face. "That and I can be here to keep an eye on the place. Besides, Nadine needs some help doing the heavier work at her place during the week."

"How can you telecommute from way out here?" Sarah asked as she carefully steered her vehicle from the paved road onto the gravel of her farm's lane.

"I can use an internet service that allows me to access the computers at both offices," Chauncey said.

"How much does the service cost?" Sarah asked seriously.

"Don't worry, it's less than thirty dollars per month," he replied solemnly. "That's less than it costs me to commute to and from both offices on the Metro every month. I keep an eye on the office overhead just as much as you do."

"I know you do," she said feeling a bit guilty for doubting his decision. "And I appreciate that."

Chauncey's eyes abruptly riveted on the farmhouse, his searching gaze scanning rapidly for the anomaly that caught his attention.

"Stop!"

"What's wrong?" Sarah asked as she applied the brakes and brought the Mercedes to a sliding halt as a billowing cloud of grayish dust overwhelmed it, momentarily obliterating their view of the buildings.

"I thought I saw lights on in the upstairs bedroom," he said breathlessly. "Now I can't be sure with all this dust."

"I never leave those lights on," she said with a hint of fear creeping into her voice. "The kitchen and living room lights are on timers."

"Pull up a little so we can see the house better, that tree is in our way," Chauncey instructed as the dust began to settle. "Try and stay over toward the fence so it helps block the headlights."

"OK," Sarah replied as she began moving the Mercedes forward at a snail's pace. "I can definitely see the upstairs bedroom light is on from here."

"Oh shit!" Chauncey swore in an uncharacteristic utterance of profanity. "It just went out. Back out of here. Don't get excited. Just be careful you don't run off the lane because the grass may be soggy from the rain we got yesterday."

Sarah did not reply but began backing the Mercedes toward the road. When she reached the macadam road she stopped to look for traffic. Seeing no headlights she backed onto it.

"What do we do now?"

"We call the state police," he said unemotionally.

"Shit!" she said as she took her turn muttering a profanity. "The cell phones don't pick up any signals until we almost get to Thompsonville."

"Well, let's get moving then," Chauncey replied solemnly. "Hurry but watch for deer crossing the road. We don't need an accident on top of everything else."

CHAPTER 40

BREAK-IN

Tom Mahoney, a thirty-five year old with fair skin and even features quickly swung his long legs out of his police cruiser and rose to his full six feet in a matter of seconds. His lithe form carried a compact 170 pounds and was topped by a smattering of closely cropped light brown hair. He was a thirteen-year veteran of the Virginia State Police having applied to the organization before finishing his stint with the United States Marine Corps.

His eyes rapidly perused the scene with a single glance as his mind processed all the visual information his gaze could glean.

He took a brief moment to smooth the front of his uniform and glanced rapidly from top to bottom to make sure he was presentable to maintain the honor and dignity of his job.

He angled toward the two occupants of the metallic gray Mercedes. His eight-hour shift was to have ended an hour and a half ago but a recent outbreak of the flu demanded mandatory overtime from the officers not yet affected by the virus.

A light misting rain had begun to fall adding to his dreary mood.

"Ma'am, it's OK to return to your home now," the tall, lean officer said as he approached Sarah and Chauncey as they walked across the convenience store parking lot to meet him. "I'm Officer Mahoney and I'll escort you back. Follow me please."

"Was there a break-in?" she asked with a barely perceptible tremor in her voice.

The lightly falling rain made the grayish-black macadam surface of the parking lot appear slippery but it was just an optical illusion. Tom Mahoney turned slowly to face them and said, "There does seem to have been a break-in but the perpetrators are gone."

"Was anything stolen?" she asked shakily as the earthworm-like smell of newly moistened soil reached her nostrils. She absent-mindedly tried straightening her now ruffled hair as it blew in the gusting wind.

"We don't know," the officer said evenly. "That's why I need you to follow me back to your house so you can tell us if anything is missing." His unchanging expression did not add any further clues as to what the situation was at the farm.

Without another word, Officer Mahoney turned and walked back to his cruiser.

"It looks like we better hurry," Chauncey said as he took Sarah by her arm. Normally she would have been offended at his motherly attitude but tonight she felt violated and agreeably followed his lead.

The familiar landmarks flew by as the State Police cruiser motored down the wet, deserted two-lane road well above the posted speed limit. Only a smattering of Holstein cows watched their journey back the exact way they had sped only forty-five minutes earlier.

In a short period of time they arrived back at the farm, and when she turned into the lane, Sarah's stomach lurched at the scene that met her eyes. Eerie, flashing lights glinting from the light bars of three police cars shimmered off the white painted outbuildings and gave the familiar landscape a surreal appearance.

"Please don't touch anything until the fingerprint team has completed their work," Officer Mahoney said unemotionally when he met Sarah at her car door. "If you can just walk through the house and tell me if anything is missing it will help us."

"Oh! They smashed the front door!" she said as her shaking fist flew to her mouth. Previously stifled tears threatened to begin coursing down her cheeks. She started to run toward the door as though she were somehow able to rescue the shattered remnants.

"Yes Ma'am," he said as he trailed behind her with long, even strides. "There's a clear print of a tennis shoe on the door near the lock. It appears they just kicked it in."

"God knows how strong that door was," she said as she surveyed the devastated door lying cock-eyed off its hinges. "It was pretty old."

"It wasn't very strong," he observed. "Before I leave, I'll give you a brochure on what to look for when you buy a new one. A more secure door may deter them in the future."

"Do you think they'll come back?" she asked with fear in her eyes.

"It's been known to happen," he said solemnly. "Where's the man who was with you?"

"He went to his cabin," she said as she pointed toward Chauncey's vanishing form in the strobe-pulsing blue lights. "He's been rehabbing the old machine shed into living quarters."

Sarah slowly surveyed the entire house room by room with Officer Mahoney following her closely. She was careful to not touch anything that may hold fingerprints from the perpetrators.

"Sorry, I can't see anything that's missing other than my laptop," she said after walking through the entire house. "My desk was rifled through, and papers are scattered all over the floor, but it looks like everything is there."

"Are you sure?"

"The best I can tell," she replied. "I don't have a list of all the bills and other paperwork I was working on."

"That's strange," the officer said with a troubled look on his face. "Even the gun safe didn't show signs of attempted forced entry, and there're other items worth more than the laptop computer that haven't been stolen, but your papers have been disturbed."

"Maybe they didn't have time to steal anything else before we showed up."

"Maybe," he said absently with his mind trying to sort out the situation. "But I doubt it. Burglars usually stack the items they want beside the door or window they used to enter the building so they can easily carry it all out when they leave. There's a Bose stereo and flat screen television in the living room on the first floor that are untouched yet they took your laptop from upstairs."

"Was anything stolen?" Chauncey asked Sarah as he walked up.

"Only my laptop and they searched through my desk," she replied with a shiver. "Anything stolen from your cottage?"

"Just that old computer I told you about," he replied.

Tom Mahoney's eyes narrowed noticeably.

"They were after information," he said evenly. "What data did you have that was valuable enough to commit a felony?"

"I don't know," she replied with a look of puzzlement on her face.

"Neither do I," Chauncey added. "We don't have anything to hide and the information we have wouldn't be worth anything to anyone. It's only bills for the farm and chiropractic offices."

"Yeah," Tom Mahoney said as he looked at the two with suspicion.

CHAPTER 41

MUHAMMED'S CHRISTMAS PLAN

A single table lamp with a stained yellow shade sat precariously on a rickety card table, giving off an anemic glow in the corner of the dimly lit room. It was enough illumination for the six men seated in middle of the floor to conduct their nefarious business.

Muhammed Shah was the only man who knew the identity of all the jihadists under his command. They had been implanted into American society and waited for his arrival to gather them together and lead them to glory.

"Bishr and Haady have done well," Muhammed said expansively. "They have been able to supply us with information that will give us success in accomplishing our next mission. The infidels who interfered with our operation at the Hallelujah Gathering will pay for their impudence."

"They have found valuable information that makes our next undertaking possible," Muhammed continued. "Obviously Allah is guiding us."

"With your leadership and Allah's blessing we will succeed in any endeavor, Commander," Bishr said.

Not to be outdone, Haady asked, "Commander, what was of such value in the trash the Americans discarded that will be helpful to us?"

"A very good question, Haady," Muhammed said as Bishr flashed an angry glance in Haady's direction. "The discarded papers contained a permission slip for Jeremy Tobin's daughters to attend the Children's Mass at the St. Boniface Roman Catholic Church."

"And what does that mean, Commander?"

"It means that there will be a large number of infidels gathering at one place," he informed them. "And the man whom we seek to annihilate will be there with his family."

"But Commander, if I may be so bold in asking, doesn't the fact that the permission slip was discarded mean they will not be attending?"

"Very good, Zayd," Muhammad said proudly. "But there is information you do not have that shows this permission slip was likely discarded by mistake."

Zayd was obviously of Middle Eastern extract with very dark walnut hued skin peeking out from beneath a shockingly black head of hair and a full beard. At six-foot two and 170 pounds he often towered over any crowd he was standing in. He had entered the United States on a student visa ten years previously and had stayed after the visa expired. He worked as an auto mechanic in a service center owned by one of the group's supporters.

"And what is that information, Commander?" Zayd asked respectfully.

"There was a weekly bulletin from St. Boniface's Church that had a large red circle around the Children's Mass," Muhammed replied. "And the bulletin went so far as to give the number of people expected to attend the celebration.

"We also have an e-mail he printed out then discarded that discusses family members who will be attending. And more importantly, the e-mail is from the man named Chauncey whom we also seek."

Tortured thoughts of retribution and his hatred for Jeremy Tobin and Chauncey twisted Muhammed's mind. The vengeance he would wreak upon them had occupied his thoughts every day and night since his defeat at the Hallelujah Gathering.

"We will annihilate the meddlers at the same instant we unleash Allah's wrath upon the infidels," he shrieked hysterically as flecks of spittle flew from the edges of his mouth. "The Americans will see the devastation resulting from their ill-chosen ways on their television sets and hear about it on their radios. They will understand that a greater power is not happy with them and their decadent ways."

"Praise be to Allah," the men said in unison.

"What is your plan, Commander?" Najeeb asked after quiet fell once again upon the men.

"I want you and Haady to go to the St. Boniface Church during their worship times and reconnoiter," Muhammed replied immediately. "You will determine the physical layout of the church, note where the worshippers congregate at different times, determine if there are any armed security people present, and see if there are any areas of the structure that may present problems for our attack."

"Why have you chosen Najeeb and Haady, Commander?" Mahdy asked. "What tasks will Bishr, Zayd, and I perform?"

"It is not your place to question my decisions, Mahdy!" Muhammed screamed as his face reddened with rage. "It is because they look more like the lily white Europeans who make up the majority of worshippers at the St. Boniface Church."

Mahdy was obviously not able to blend into a crowd comprised mainly of people hailing from European backgrounds. At five-foot ten inches tall and two hundred pounds he looked much like every other earth-toned Egyptian in Cairo. Even in the three-piece suits he wore in his profession as an economics professor, he was identifiable as a Middle Easterner.

"You have been to the church, Commander?"

"Yes I have been there," Muhammed said irritably. "I cannot wait for you. It is my responsibility to complete this task and I will do so whether you are ready or not!"

A silence fell over the room as the men looked toward the floor in shame.

"Najeeb and Haady are both fair skinned and clean shaven," Muhammed continued. "They have been in this cursed country for most of their lives so speak without accents. They will not only blend in with the worshippers, but will be welcomed as one of their own."

Najeeb and Haady looked discretely at each other to confirm this was true, and it was. Each was as Muhammed described them.

Najeeb was tall at six-foot two inches and had a shock of jet-black hair closely trimmed to his head. His elongated face was highlighted by an oversized nose that gave him a comic, open look, an impression that was further enhanced by his ever-present smile showing narrow but even teeth.

Haady was almost a total opposite of Najeeb. He looked short at five-foot four inches tall and dumpy with a rounded head and belly to match. His fleshy lips and puffy cheeks hid a mouth full of crooked, discolored teeth. While he rarely smiled, his overall appearance led anyone meeting him to regard him as being a harmless, jolly fellow. There was nothing about either man that would raise suspicions about them. Neither would stand out in a crowd, especially an assembly in a church where people rarely noticed or acknowledged other attendees.

"Commander, if you have been to the church, why is it important for Najeeb and Haady to get the same information you must already have?"

"Because, you fool," Muhammed said maliciously. "I want their input without me influencing their observations. The more independent each observance is, the more opportunities we will have of formulating an effective plan of attack."

"While you are there," Muhammed continued as he thought of other angles to his plan. "Make sure you obtain a copy of the weekly bulletin and read all the messages on the various bulletin boards scattered throughout the building. All information is important to us regardless of how inconsequential it may seem."

"What type of information should we specifically be looking for, Commander?" Najeeb asked respectfully.

"The bulletin I took when I visited the St. Boniface Church revealed when the worship times are to be held, which services are most crowded, which aisles are to be kept open for emergencies, and where the children will be seated during the special Children's Mass being held for their Christmas celebration.

"The infidels do not realize how their unguarded gibberish reveals information that makes our tasks more profitable," Muhammed boasted as he warmed to the topic. "They even mention that the Fire Marshall has warned them to keep the crowds below 1,500 people and not to allow more than 300 to stand along the side walls of the church.

"It is very convenient that they will herd the children into a small area where we can kill many of them in one fell swoop," Muhammed said. "This is the seed of the next generation. Their deaths will impact the future of this decadent land and break the morale of the survivors."

"Have you formulated a plan yet, Commander?"

"Yes, I have."

"We are willing to follow you and lay down our lives for Allah. He will reward us for our sacrifice in satisfying his will."

"That is correct, Zayd," Muhammed said. "Allah will reward his true believers but I do not want you to sacrifice yourself unless it is absolutely necessary. There are other tasks needing your skills before you can collect your reward. My plan will allow us all to live more days and continue doing Allah's work."

"Is it too soon to tell us of your plan, Commander?"

"I will tell you my intentions because I want Najeeb and Haady to understand what I have planned when they attend the St. Boniface Church," Muhammed said. "It may help them to understand what may be important during their reconnoitering visit."

Muhammed began speaking in an expansive voice, "A plan must be kept simple to be successful. If it is complicated there are more things that can go wrong. This project is so elementary that it should be foolproof."

"Prior to Christmas Eve on December 24 when the Children's Mass will be held at St. Boniface's Church, we will procure three vans with sliding side doors. The vans must be stolen so they are untraceable and should be work vans that do not have windows on the sides," Muhammed lectured to an audience whose attention he held with every word. "Two will be parked at a Park-and-Ride located three miles from the church. We will ride in the third to launch our attack."

"Commander, if I may interrupt," Bishr said. "Won't we be observed by others at the Park-and-Ride lot?"

"No, you fool!" Muhammed roared, incensed for being interrupted. "The Park-and-Ride lots are located along major thoroughfares so commuters can share rides. Their purpose is to save gasoline and reduce traffic congestion into the major cities. Do you suspect there will be many commuters in the lots on Christmas Eve? A major holiday when few people work?"

Undeterred, Muhammed continued, "The Park-and-Ride lots are perfect for filling our needs. There will be few people, if anyone, there at that time of night."

He stopped to glare menacingly at Bishr then continued.

"Even if anyone is there, the lots are where strangers are not uncommon so new faces are not noticed nor remembered. It is also common for commuters to be leaving one vehicle and get into others," he said with an air of finality. "It is where we will return to make our getaway after our work at the church is done."

"By abandoning the van we use at the church it will throw the authorities off our trail for a short time. When we transfer to the other two vans to make our escape, we will dispose of our firearms by discretely throwing them in the pine trees surrounding the Park-and-Ride."

"Commander, will separating the group into two vans be enough of a deception to confuse the authorities?" Mahdy asked respectfully.

"No it will not, Mahdy," Muhammed explained patiently. "That is why each van will proceed to various small towns in the immediate area surrounding the interstate highways. There, you will each find a discharge man at their privately owned vehicles which have been parked there earlier in the day. The driver of both vans will abandon them when they arrive at their own automobile."

"So we will have men driving their own vehicles in six different directions to various locations within a few short minutes of leaving the church. Since we will have disposed of our rifles the authorities cannot easily connect us to the church raid," Zayd said admiringly. "It is a good plan, Commander."

"Thank you, Zayd," Muhammed replied before scowling perilously at the other men for not acknowledging what he considered a brilliant plan. "If anyone is stopped by the authorities he can claim to be driving to a friend's home in a distant city for the Christmas holiday; a visit each of you should arrange as soon as possible."

"You have planned well, Commander," Haady said in an attempt to redeem himself in his leader's eyes. "Can you tell us about how we will kill the infidels?"

"Yes, Haady," Muhammed said. "The plan is simplicity itself. Now pay close attention."

"I will be attending the Children's Mass on Christmas Eve seated on the right side of the church near the door leading to the outside exit. It is upon my command, given over a disposable cellular telephone that will only be used for this project, that the attack will begin," Muhammed continued. "Just so there is no confusion, when I refer to the right or left side of the church, I am referring to the view from the rear of the building. This is the direction you will be attacking from so it is the perspective which offers the most clarity to avoid misunderstanding."

"Thank be to Allah that you have the gift of planning with great detail," Haady stated emphatically.

"Praise Allah," Muhammed said in an obligatory manner before continuing. "I have discovered that these Catholics are very obedient and rigid in their rituals. Any disruption is disdained and will not elicit an immediate reaction from those attending the service."

"And you were able to discover this just by observing them?" Zayd asked seriously.

"Yes, Zayd," Muhammed replied patiently. "On the one occasion I was there, an old lady fell unconscious. Unlike other settings where Americans will rush without thinking to help the fallen person, these Catholics stood in place without moving and just stared at the old lady's body lying on the floor. Apparently, their training forbids them from immediately leaving their places during a mass even when a fellow worshipper is obviously in need of their assistance. They will not act but will only observe any disturbance as long as it is not immediately apparent they are personally in any danger."

"And we will use this defect in their training against them?" Najeeb asked, not wanting to be outdone by his fellow jihadists.

"Yes," Muhammed replied. "It is the key to my plan. Now let me continue.

"I will wait until the priest begins preparing for the Communion time of the service before giving the signal to attack; it seems to be the time when they are most reluctant to act outside of their worship rituals. The aisles will not yet be filled with worshippers waiting for their turn to get their piece of bread.

"During that time they all seemed to be waiting quietly in their seats. The communion ritual started in earnest approximately forty-five minutes after the mass began. That is when they leave their seats and stand in the aisles.

"This may be different during the Christmas worship, I do not know, just wait for my signal and be ready to go at any moment. We must attack before they jam the aisles and make it impossible for you to maneuver. We only have a small window of time in which to act. Do not allow yourselves to be lulled into complacency while waiting."

"How will we assure that we are close enough to act immediately when we receive your signal, Commander?"

"The weekly bulletin speaks of automobiles parking on the grassy areas because it is such a crowded gathering," Muhammed said with a glowing sense of satisfaction in his voice. "That is why the bulletin is such an important source of intelligence for us. You will park among the hordes then sit quietly in the back of the van to wait for my signal."

"That is why it is important that the vans do not have windows in the rear area," Mahdy mused.

"Very perceptive, Mahdy," Muhammed said approvingly.

"What will we do when we get your signal?" Haady asked, his physical appearance mistakenly giving the accomplished computer programmer the appearance of suffering from low intelligence. The people he worked with at the Union Bank knew he was a very bright and educated man but even they often looked into his black, beady eyes poking out from beneath brushy jet-black eyebrows and spoke to him as if he were brain damaged.

Muhammed laid out three poster-sized photographs showing the front entrance of the church. "I had these photos enlarged at Wal-Mart when I bought the disposable cellular telephones," he said. "These Americans offer anything for mere money even if it will lead to their own destruction."

"Upon my signal you five men will drive the van up to the front of the church," he said as he pointed to heavy wood framed glass-fronted doors situated under a large portico built to protect church-goers exiting their vehicles during inclement weather. "In this next photo you can see the driveway leading up to the front entrance."

"Najeeb, you will be driving the van so one of your duties will be to get a close-up view of this entranceway. It is a foyer approximately twelve meters wide and three meters deep," Muhammed said. "I want the driver to be intimately familiar with the building by actually seeing it in person. Haady, you also will pay attention to these details, especially the escape route, just in case something happens to Najeeb - you will be our back-up driver."

Haady nodded his large, round head in acknowledgement then asked, "Commander, is it possible to see through the foyer into the lobby?"

"Yes," Muhammed said patiently. "The glass fronts of the doors are full-length top to bottom and almost the entire width of the door except for the wood frame. There are eight doors side by side so you can see into the lobby very well. Now let me continue."

"This third picture is from across the street and shows a larger view of the entire building," Muhammed pointed out. "While Najeeb and Haady are in the church, they will discretely use their cell phones to take many pictures of the interior so the rest of you will know how the facility is laid out."

"And after we all arrive at the front doors of the church?" Bishr asked anxiously, concerned about Haady's observation of the glass doors.

"Then you will exit the side door of the van, with Najeeb staying in the vehicle," Muhammed said as he gestured toward the four men. "Each will have an AK-47 that has been smuggled into this country from our friends in Pakistan hidden under a long coat. Each of you will carry a backpack on your back."

 Picking up a blank piece of white photocopier paper Muhammed drew a crude map of the inside of the church.

"Najeeb will park the van here," he said as he pointed with a dirty fingernail in need of a trimming. "The four of you will proceed through these doors into the lobby."

"Bishr, you will veer to the left to go down this long hallway," he said as he continued tracing with his filthy finger on the map. "It leads to an entrance near the front of the church where the altar is located.

You will place your backpack half-way between this door and the altar."

"Haady, you will proceed straight through the lobby and enter this door then walk with long strides up the aisle that's situated slightly to the left of center," Muhammed said as he took a quick glance at Haady's face to make sure he was comprehending the instructions. "You want to walk rapidly but smoothly. Do not run. Such movements will not raise an alarm with the worship participants. Then you will place your backpack about halfway down the aisle."

"Mahdy, you will go down this aisle that is slightly right of center of the church's main hall and do exactly as I have already instructed Haady."

"Zayd, you will veer to the far right and go down this long hallway mirroring the one Bishr is going down on the left side," Muhammed said expansively. "You will place your backpack halfway between the door you enter and the altar. We are targeting the churchgoers, not the priest. We want to maximize the injuries and death among the worshippers, especially the children."

"Commander, how do you know that the children will be sitting toward the front near the altar?"

"The weekly bulletin given out by the St. Boniface Church instructs the parents of the younger children to sit in the front of the main hall so it will be easy for the children to find them when they are finished performing their songs at the altar," Muhammed replied. "I told you the bulletin was a treasure trove of information."

"And where will you be sitting, Commander?" Haady asked in his slow, wandering voice while his pig-like eyes bored intensely into Muhammed's.

"I will be here," he said as he pointed to a spot near where he had showed Zayd to place his backpack. "I will leave just before you arrive, pass Zayd in the hallway on my way to the van, and there I will wait for you to finish your work."

"How much time do you think we will need to place our backpacks?" Bishr asked seriously.

"I estimate fifteens seconds from the time you enter the doors until you place your backpacks."

"And what is in the backpacks, Commander?"

"High explosives with small pieces of metal to wound and maim," Muhammed answered unemotionally. "You each will activate the timers on your explosives at the same instant just before exiting the van. The timers will be set for one hundred forty-five seconds. That will give you sixty seconds to place the backpacks then return to the rear of the church, and thirty more seconds to shoot three magazines from your AK-47 into the seated crowd. Each magazine holds thirty cartridges so many infidels will be killed or wounded. The AK-47s are fully automatic like the ones you trained with in Afghanistan and Somalia."

"Commander," Mahdy asked politely. "Will we have an opportunity to shoot these rifles before we use them at the church?"

"There is no need," Muhammed replied in a snobbish tone. "They have been tested for reliable functioning before they were shipped and I have been assured they are 'mechanically perfect' for a mission such as this. Besides, at the close range you will be deploying them, sights will not be necessary. Killing unarmed infidels is not difficult."

"Why should we shoot the infidels if they will be killed by the explosions?" Bishr asked impatiently while fidgeting.

"You are too stupid and impudent for your own good, Bishr!" Muhammed growled angrily. "If you were paying attention you would have noticed that all the backpacks are toward the front of the church; that is by design. By shooting from the back of the church you will not only be killing infidels in that area of the building but you will also terrify those sitting in the front. When they panic they will begin running from their seats toward the backpacks when the explosives detonate."

"And there will be a greater number of casualties because they will be closer to the explosives," Zayd said admiringly.

"As well as having dispersed the infidels," Muhammed added. "If they are tightly packed into the pews, that is what they call the rows of seats they sit on, the flying metal from the explosion will be absorbed by the bodies closest to it. By spreading the infidels out, the explosion will have greater destructive effect against more people."

"Are there any other ways to increase the destructive effects of the explosion?" Mahdy asked.

"Yes, there is, and it has already been discussed," Muhammed said impatiently. "By having the bombs coordinated to explode at the same time the combined effect from the concussion will amplify the destructive effects."

"Who is this bomb maker?" Bishr asked suddenly. "And where is he located? Can we be sure he is competent in his craft?"

"Why do you ask, Bishr?" Muhammed asked suspiciously as his internal warning alarms began sounding in his mind.

"I ask because this is a wonderful plan and I want to be sure the bomb maker constructs explosives that will wreak massive amounts of destruction upon the infidels," Bishr answered meekly, knowing he had overstepped his bounds.

"I will take you to the bomb maker so you can observe his work firsthand, Bishr," Muhammed answered slyly. "It is time that you meet more of the people in the organization."

"Thank you, Commander," Bishr answered gleefully as his spirits soared for having his talents recognized.

"So the terrified infidels will be exterminated by the explosions after we have left the building?" Mahdy asked quizzically.

"Yes, we will maximize the destruction by spraying the infidels with automatic weapons fire directed from side-to-side," Muhammed instructed them as he mimed with his hands as though he held an AK-47 in front of him. "Kill as many as you can by shooting into the crowd. Do not pick out single targets unless they resist and threaten you. If that occurs then you must deal with them individually. Then immediately return your attention to again shooting into the crowd in the way I have described."

"Commander, how will we know when our time is up and the explosions occur?"

"Each of you will carry a common digital kitchen timer which you will coordinate and set for one hundred twenty-five seconds. That will give you twenty seconds to return to the van before the explosives detonate," Muhammed explained patiently as if he were speaking to a child. "When the kitchen timer sounds you must leave immediately even if you have not expended all your ammunition."

"Won't survivors be able to identify us?"

"No, you fool," Muhammed snapped. "Everyone except me will be wearing a face mask as the infidel children do when sled riding. I will not be associated with the attack because I will be observing the worship service from the crowd."

"What will I be doing while the others are performing their tasks?" Najeeb asked.

"You will be guarding the van: it is our only means of escape," Muhammed replied. "Then you will cover the others as they leave the main worshipping area of the church. If any of the infidels interfere with them, you are to intervene. Each man will carry four thirty-round magazines when they enter the church. Shoot three into the crowd and save the fourth to fight your way out if necessary."

"When the shooting starts, won't the infidels just want to escape?" Najeeb asked.

"There will always be the possibility that some of the infidels standing in the back of the church or in the lobby will attempt to stop you even though they only have bare hands against your rifles," Muhammed replied. "Do not forget the attempt to stop our brothers from destroying the U.S. Capitol Building on 9-11. All perished in the fields of Pennsylvania, but the people in the Capitol Building were spared. The American fighting spirit is not to be underestimated, Najeeb."

"Will there be infidels standing in the rear of the church instead of sitting in the, what did you call them? Pews?" Mahdy asked respectfully.

"The weekly bulletin from the St. Boniface Church spoke of this phenomenon," Muhammed replied sagely. "It told of the Fire Marshall warning the church elders to keep the aisles clear and restrict the number of worshippers standing toward the rear of the main hall and in the lobby. That is how I know you should have unrestricted access up the aisles but returning to the van may bring problems."

"How large is this lobby in the rear of the church?" Mahdy asked with concern in his voice.

"It is large," Muhammed replied. "I estimate it is forty feet from the front doors where the van will be parked under the portico to the doors leading into the main worship hall and sixty feet wide. It will hold a large number of people. There are many infidels who worship at St. Boniface's church and the Children's Mass is a special event so many of their out-of-town relatives will be attending."

"Commander, what if the authorities intervene before we escape or interfere before the attack can begin?" Zayd asked.

"They will not," Muhammed replied simply. "I have another group of men, men you will probably never meet, placing stolen cars packed with explosives at three other churches. The worshipping services at those churches are starting at 8:00 p.m. That is one hour after the Children's Mass begins at St. Boniface's. The timers on the car bombs will be set to detonate at 7:40 p.m. precisely when most of the worshippers will be arriving at those churches. That is approximately five minutes before the attack will begin at St. Boniface's."

"The authorities will be too busy with those incidents to be concerned about St. Boniface's," Zayd said admiringly.

"Yes, Zayd, but you have to understand the large impact this will have on the infidels because it is more than just a diversion,"

Muhammed replied as he smiled smugly. "The media will report this as four churches being attacked simultaneously with hundreds killed or injured."

"And the simultaneous attacks will shake the faith of the non-believers, forcing them to convert to Islam," Zayd said admiringly. "It is a brilliant plan, Commander. Allah has blessed you."

"Yes he has, Zayd," Muhammed said. "Yes he has. Praise be to Allah."

"Praise be to Allah," they chanted in unison.

CHAPTER 42

THE BOMB MAKER

Muhammed Shah's flint black eyes flashed incessantly across the table filled with chemistry equipment. The thirty-four year old native of Saudi Arabia had trained ten years for this event and he did not want to risk failure when he was so close to achieving his objective.

"Be careful," Muhammad reiterated unnecessarily to Idries Iqbal, the master bomb-maker of the terrorist cell he commanded. "We don't want to have to explain to our Almighty Allah how we blew ourselves up without killing any infidels."

"What is it?" Bishr asked inquisitively.

"It is hexamethylene triperoxide diamine. HMTD is easier for you to remember, I'm sure." Idries said with contempt and disdain clearly evident in his voice as he spoke to Bishr.

"Do you have enough of the explosives to meet our needs?" Muhammad asked, trying to assuage his curiosity and fears.

"Do not be so nervous," Idries consoled. "There are one and a half times more explosives than we need. I made sure to add extra."

"Do you think we will need extra?" Bishr asked and was greeted by a steely stare from Idries.

"I want the destruction of the building to be extensive," Idries explained calmly as he fiddled with the glass beakers containing clear liquid being gently heated over the bluish-orange flame of a Bunsen burner. "The American television news crews will fly over the remains of the church taking pictures and video from a helicopter. I want them to have a strong visual image of utter destruction to show the people watching at home."

"That is true," Muhammad said with a faraway look in his eyes and wonder in his voice. "The infidels will not be touched by the death of hundreds of children and their parents if they are strangers, but one picture of a destroyed building will remain in their minds."

"The pictures of the destroyed Murrah Federal Building in Oklahoma City and the piles of rubble from the World Trade Center still haunt the Americans."

"How will these bombs be constructed?" Bishr asked innocently.

"Each of the men running into the church will carry a 100 pound backpack filled with HMTD and many shiny, steel ball bearings," Muhammed replied. "The HMTD will be stuffed into a section of small-diameter metal stove-pipe that has small holes drilled into it to hold the ball bearings in place. This will then be slid into a larger diameter pipe that also has ball bearings imbedded in it. More HMTD will be placed between the two ball bearing laden stove-pipe sections in a shaped charge configuration to maximize the outward thrust of the explosive's blast."

"Will it be placed into the backpacks like that?" Bishr asked.

"Of course not," Idries replied. "If the device is not held upright, the ball bearings will fly into the ceiling and floor instead of into infidels."

"How will you keep the device in the proper position?" Bishr asked while feeling important for having input into the details of the plan.

"The entire assembly with the pipes and ball bearings will be secured to a plywood base that has been cut to perfectly fit the bottom of the backpacks," Idries replied unemotionally. "This will assure that when the backpack is set on the floor it will remain upright which is very important to guarantee that the maximum amount of damage will be inflicted upon detonation of the bombs."

"Is that all that is needed to direct the flying ball bearings into the crowd of Christmas Eve worshippers?" Bishr asked expansively as he puffed out his chest, realizing he was being given information the others were not. He was quite proud of the elevated level of trust he had ascended to.

"No," Idries answered dryly. "A steel plate on the top and bottom of the assembly with a threaded steel rod running between them and secured with a washer and nut will securely hold it together. Such a sturdy apparatus is necessary to direct the ball bearings laterally instead of allowing the blast to dissipate skyward."

Bishr tried to slide his chair back from the scarred kitchen table the three men were huddled around, but the chair legs became entangled in the thick, shiny plastic drop cloth spread over the floor.

"Why do you have plastic on the floor?" he asked.

"It is because the chemicals in the explosives can bleach the color out of anything it touches and this is a rented apartment," Idries answered with irritation in his voice. "And to catch other messes I do not want on my floor."

Bishr smiled and settled back into his chair when Muhammed walked behind him and placed his left hand on his shoulder in a fatherly gesture.

"Do not be aggravated, Idries," Muhammed said. "Bishr is the inquisitive one of my group."

The smile that spread on Bishr's face when he heard his Commander brag about him was like a child's after hearing his father boasting of his good grades. This elated emotional state lulled Bishr into a false sense of security and complacency that allowed Muhammed to slip a ten-inch butcher knife under his chin and slice his throat from ear to ear.

Blood poured freely from the severed ends of the carotid arteries on both sides of his neck while his last breath spewed a spray of thick, red blood across the length of the kitchen table. His lungs instantly began shrinking in size as the pressure difference between them and the surrounding atmospheric pressure equalized.

Muhammed pushed the panicked man firmly into the chair with his left hand then used his right to plunge the butcher knife into Bashir's chest in order to pierce his aorta where it exited the top of his heart. The additional wound served to speed the loss of blood while offering Muhammed a handhold to control his victim's thrashing body.

Idries leaned toward the dying man and looked directly into his terrified eyes and asked, "Which of the accursed American intelligence agencies do you work for Bishr? Who has paid you to ask all these questions? Why did you want to know who I am and where I live?"

Not expecting to get an answer from a man whose throat had been cut, Idries continued harassing him in his last moments on earth, "To answer your question before you die, this plastic drop cloth was placed here to catch your blood and wrap you in to make it easier to dispose of your cursed body."

When Bishr ceased thrashing, Muhammed allowed his body to drop gently to the floor.

"Idries, you will take care of this?"

"Yes, Commander," he said simply.

"You will take Bishr's place carrying the backpack of explosives down the left side of the church on Christmas Eve."

"Yes, Commander," Idries replied. "I am honored."

"Are the car bombs ready?"

"Yes, commander," he replied respectfully. "My men are prepared to perform the tasks Allah has ordained for them. Creating the three diversions at the other churches was very intuitive of you."

"Thank you, Idries."

CHAPTER 43

CHRISTMAS EVE
AT ST. BONIFACE

Sarah usually scheduled patients until three o'clock on Christmas Eve and New Year's Eve to assure they have the care they need to help them through the holiday. Two emergency cases had called for appointments shortly after two o'clock, causing her whole afternoon to be delayed. She was late getting out of the office because she never turned down a person in need.

"Why do people wait until the last minute before coming for treatment?" Chauncey asked as he placed gifts for the Tobins into the trunk of her Mercedes C-300 Sedan.

"Oh, it's because they're busy shopping, or baking cookies, or decorating, or any of the hundreds of things people do to prepare for the holidays," she said noncommittally. "Everything but their health is on their minds until the last minute, then it's a crisis because they realize they can't enjoy the holiday when they're in screaming agony."

"It's rude and inconsiderate to ruin your holiday because of their lack of foresight," he said irritably. "They both had pain for weeks but suddenly this afternoon it became a top priority. Why didn't they get it taken care of weeks ago?"

"I've learned to expect it and not get upset by discourteous behavior," she said whimsically. "Don't let their lack of consideration ruin your holiday."

"I won't," he replied as he mentally admonished himself to calm down. "I called J.T. and told him we'd be late. They're going ahead to the church because it begins filling up at five-thirty for the 7 o'clock mass."

"The Children's Mass is really big," she said. "The entire family from Grandma and Grandpa all the way out to aunts and uncles want to see the kids do their thing. It's more of a circus than a serious religious service."

"And that's probably OK with God," he replied seriously. "I'm sure He's happy when the children have fun going to His House for worship. Religious services don't always have to be solemn and boring."

"Are you saying that going to the Baptist church with Annie is livelier than attending the stodgy, formal masses at the Catholic church?"

"Something like that," he said with a huge smile breaking over his face and a glimmer of vivaciousness twinkling in his eyes.

It was only a twenty-five minute drive from Sarah's office to St. Boniface's Roman Catholic Church but traffic was light and the trip went smoothly. The parking lot at St. Boniface's was a different story.

"Look at those idiots!" she said heatedly. "They're parking on the grass and in the little spaces with the yellow lines painted on them!"

"Calm down, there's no reason getting all worked up over other people's inconsiderateness," he said teasingly. "Isn't that what you told me just a little while ago?"

"Yeah, well--" she sputtered. "Damned! Who do these people think they are? Seeing their grandkids can't be that important! Get out of my way you moron!"

"Calm down, calm down," he said with a chuckle. "Let's get away from here a few blocks and see if we can find parking on the street."

It took Sarah over five minutes of impatient waiting to work her way out of the church's parking lot.

"I'll be glad when you have a license and can drive," she said as they sped down a side street. "Then we'll see how patient you are with these imbeciles."

"If I ever get a driver's license you'll see the quintessential example of coolness under pressure," he said chidingly. "If you look in the dictionary under 'cool' you'll see my picture."

Sarah laughed until she had to wipe tears from her eyes.

"OK, OK, you win. I'll calm down. Assuming I don't run over a few of these halfwits first!"

"How about parking in that supermarket lot?"

"That will work. They're closing soon so they probably won't mind."

"It's only a few blocks to walk," he said. "We'll be able to get there on time if you can walk that far in those heels."

"I'll manage," she replied determinedly. "Just as long as there're any seats left by the time we get there."

The walk to St. Boniface's went quickly. Upon entering the church, Chauncey was shocked to see how many children were in attendance.

"This is a real zoo!" he gasped. "There are kids everywhere! Where are those kids' parents?" he asked incredulously as he pointed wide-eyed at a pair of boys wildly having a jumping contest.

"A real children's zoo you might say, eh?" she said with a kidding tone in her voice.

"Very funny," he said as he guided her by her elbow toward the main hall. "Let's go over here to the right and see if we can find any seats."

"Some of those little kids may have never seen a crowd this large. It's really exciting for them," she said. "Try not to step on any kids."

"What do you think?" she asked with exasperation in her voice as she tried to see around the main hall of the church.

Chauncey, being much taller than Sarah, saw there were ushers cruising up and down the aisles seating people in available seats.

"Let's go over this way," Chauncey said, indicating they should go farther to the right side of the church. "This is the side J.T. usually sits on."

"Lead the way," she said.

The teenage usher was standing halfway up the aisle. When he made eye contact with Chauncey, his inquisitive eyes asked "How many?" without a word having to be said.

Chauncey held up two fingers and the usher took three steps forward and motioned for the people sitting in the pew to move toward the middle. The grumpy glances from the people in the pew clearly conveyed they were not happy with having to slide closer to their neighbor.

"There are some seats," he said as he again took her arm. "Let's go."

"You sit on the aisle so you have room for your long legs," Sarah said considerately.

After settling themselves and offering a smile of gratitude to the disgruntled people in the pew Sarah asked, "Do you see them anywhere?"

"No, I can't see them," he replied after standing and looking around.

"Stay standing," she instructed him. "They'll see you if you don't find them first."

"There they are way over there," Chauncey said as he waved his right hand high above his head.

"I'm going over to say hello. Save my seat," she said as she prepared to slide past him and into the crowd once again. He stepped into the aisle and let her pass.

"Leave your coat here to save your place," he said helpfully. "I'll stay here."

In the lobby of the church, Sarah saw children beginning to take their places for the beginning of mass. This left a multitude of grandparents, aunts, uncles, and cousins scrambling to find the best seats or places to stand beside the walls to get a good view of the children.

"Why did you sit all the way over here? Don't you always sit on the other side?" she asked in way of a greeting. She hugged them tightly as though she hadn't seen them for years.

"This side will give us a better view of the children as they perform," Stephanie explained.

"Why are you wearing that raincoat?" Sarah asked J.T. "Are you cold?"

"No, I'm comfortable, thank you."

"I must admit, J.T., that light tan raincoat makes quite the fashion statement but you'll roast in here with all these people giving off body heat," she said chidingly. "At least open it up before you pass out from the heat if you're not going to take it off."

"I'm fine, thanks," he replied.

They enjoyed small talk but the specter of the Hallelujah Gathering debacle still hung heavily over the parishioners of St. Boniface's.

"It's a little scary that this is the first Christmas since the Hallelujah Gathering massacre," Stephanie remarked.

"Did they ever find out why they attacked the Gathering?"

"The terrorist Jason Hagen captured said it was because they took offense at the Pope's comments about the views held by a twelfth century cleric regarding the Islamic faith," Stephanie replied with trepidation in her voice. "It was the words of a guy who died centuries ago for crying out loud! But it was enough for those crazies to attack a bunch of churches around the world and the Hallelujah Gathering. I wonder if they're still mad at us."

"It's a concern," Sarah replied. "That's why I'm a little better prepared than usual. And I'm sure a number of others are also."

Confessing to anyone, even Stephanie, that I'm armed is something I never do, something the trainers at ARI warned us not to do, but I had to say something to help assuage her fears.

Stephanie smiled as her eyes made an unconscious sweep of Sarah's body.

She says she's armed but I can't see where she would hide it. How does she conceal something as big as a pistol on that slim figure she has?

Maybe I should have worn my pistol but it's such a burden. Besides, this is a church.

"I'd better get back to Chauncey before he gives away my seat. I'll see you at your house tomorrow," Sarah said then turned and began wading back through the crowd.

"Thanks for saving my seat," she said breathlessly as she popped out of the crowd at Chauncey's side. "I think this show is about to begin."

The beginning of the Children's Mass was signaled by the sounds of the organ reverberating around the cavernous hall. A massive jumble of bodies began scattering in every direction as everyone scrambled to take his or her seat.

Children of differing age groups performed each presentation and the time passed quickly. Before long the presiding priest began preparing for the communion offering and Muhammed made a discrete cellular telephone call from the last pew on the right side of the church.

I shouldn't have drunk that decaf coffee on the way over here. This mass has gone on way too long. I can't wait.

"I'll be back in a few minutes," she whispered into Chauncey's ear as she made her way out of the pew.

Look at how all these people are crammed in here. If there was a fire they'd never all get out safely. The Fire Marshall must be having a bird

The bathrooms are on the other side of the lobby. I hope there's not a long line because of all these people overloading the facilities.

When she pushed her way through the glass front doors leading from the main hall of the church into the spacious lobby, she was aghast at how many children and parents were moving about. Barely audible over the din was a broadcast of the events from the mass so people in the spacious lobby could follow the proceedings.

J.T. told me this building won an architectural award for its innovative design when it was built ten or so years ago. It does have some nice features.

As she looked beyond the swarms of people, she took greater notice of the unique architectural aspects of the building itself.

Those large ceiling-to-floor windows forming the outside walls of the lobby give a commanding view of the front yard and really make it pleasant to sit out here on sunny days. I never realized how peaceful I am when I sit out here in the mornings before attending mass. I'm glad I started attending services here those few mornings during the week.

She began to wend her way through the throng of bodies.

A lot of these people probably couldn't fit into the main hall of the church. I wonder how far over the maximum allowed capacity we are tonight?

When she was halfway through the lobby she had to make a decision.

The large three-by-six foot carved natural Pennsylvania stone baptismal fountain sat ten feet away from the wall. Its round-bottomed basin sat grandly on a laid stone foundation four feet tall. The entire structure formed a narrow alleyway between it and the wall.

Thirty feet of open space lay between the fountain and the front doors. Both the area in front of and behind the fountain was jammed with a seething, multitude of smiling, chattering people of all ages.

J.T. says that baptismal fountain is a full sixteen inches deep and was designed to perform full-body infant immersion baptisms if the parents opt for that type of ceremony.

I better go toward the outside doors to avoid the congestion behind the baptismal fountain. I'll never get through that mess.

She excused herself over and over again as she crossed the lobby, dodging left then right as she sidestepped around individuals and groups. She was forced closer and closer toward the glass-fronted doors leading to the portico. When she was standing ten feet from the doors, she detoured around a group of children dressed as shepherds and happened to glance through the foyer toward the portico outside and saw a very strange sight.

What is a van doing discharging passengers now? The mass is almost over.

I hope these kids get out of my way. I'm really getting desperate.

She was pushing past a group standing in her way when she noticed a pair of men wearing long trench coats and black facemasks jump out of the van's side door.

The gravity of the situation hit her like a slap in the face.

In a flash, a ball of fear and dread settled in the pit of her stomach and her legs buckled slightly when the shock of reality struck her.

"What the hell's going on here?" she heard herself say without conscious thought.

Then the dumpily built Haady jumped from the van and allowed his trench coat to fall open revealing an AK-47 swinging wildly on a black nylon sling.

Oh my God! she thought as her right hand dove into the confining bowels of her Coronado Leather Classic concealment handbag.

The Velcro closures sealing the hidden compartment holding her holstered pistol parted with a loud ripping sound. Her groping hand gripped the polymer stock of the Glock in an adrenaline-vitalized fist and yanked it from its moorings.

I hope this isn't just a bunch of kids playing an elaborate prank, she thought as time seemed to slow precipitously.

In a spasm of fear and surprise, she began backpedaling away from the glass-front doors as the heart-stopping scenario began playing out in front of her eyes. Just as she brought the Glock up to eye level, her back slammed into a harried mother chatting amicably with a woman in a coyote fur coat. The collision jostled them all.

"What the hell are you doing?" the woman growled angrily as she spun around to give Sarah a piece of her mind.

Sarah did not hear her. Her attention was glued on the armed man rocketing directly toward her.

Haady had already passed the first set of glass-front doors with Mahdy directly behind him by the time she recovered from the rear-ender. Just as his sweat drenched hand grasped the brass handle of the inner door Sarah placed the XS System's 24/7 Big Dot front sight on his upper chest and pressed the Glock's safe-action trigger.

BAM!

The woman Sarah had collided with screamed, grabbed her golden-haired daughter, and blindly fled as the panicking hordes surged forward in mass confusion, desperately trying to escape the violence erupting behind them.

The look of shocked horror and surprise on Haady's face as the glass in front of his eyes disintegrated into a shower of glittering shards was clearly etched into Sarah's mind. Because of his adrenaline-charged nervous system, he did not feel the 115-grain CorBon DPX bullet smash into his chest at 1,250 feet-per-second then release its 399 foot pounds of energy into his lungs and heart.

The solid copper DPX, laboriously heat-treated for toughness with a deep cavity in the front end peeling back in six razor-edged petals, retained 100% of its weight as it bore a straight path of destruction along the entire length of its travel.

Suddenly Sarah was acutely aware she was suffering from tunnel vision and auditory exclusion. Her instructors at ARI had warned her about the reduction of sight and hearing when involved in a gunfight, which is understandable when someone is trying to kill you. She ignored both phenomena and concentrated on the threat staring her in the face.

Create distance between you and the threat. Distance is your friend.

Shuffle your feet backward. Never cross them to avoid tripping.

Concentrate on the front sight.

Press the trigger. Don't jerk it.

BAM!

Shuffle backward. Front sight. Press trigger.

BAM!

Shuffle backward---

Training and repetition had engrained the lessons into her subconscious actions.

Move! Move! Move! Keep moving. Don't give them a stationary target!

Deadly slugs slammed into Haady's upper chest with sickening regularity. The terrorized crowd assumed Sarah was the perpetrator and parted like the Red Sea under command of Moses's staff clearing a path between her and the baptismal fountain. Their only concern was to save themselves and their children.

She continued to step backward toward the fountain because it offered the only cover within the immediate area capable of stopping incoming bullets. At the same instant her buttocks met the chilling, wet torrent of water flowing over the side of the cold, stone fountain, Haady tried to take a step over the lower portion of the wood doorframe.

His oxygen-starved, befuddled brain would not allow him to pick his foot up high enough to clear the frame. When his toe caught, the 100-pound mass of explosive material on his back plunged his body forward. His mind registered the six-inch by six-inch Georgia Red Clay tiles of the lobby's floor just before his forehead made contact.

He did not hear the abysmally loud cracking noise that accompanied the shattering of his cranium.

Sarah did not waste time staring at Haady's crumpling body.

Her eyes scanned for other threats while her feet felt blindly around the raised stone rim surrounding the fountain. Before she could maneuver to the backside of the fountain, Mahdy and Idries bolted through the doors on either side of Haady's limp body. They hurtled toward the main hall of the church, their eyes locked on the doors they must breach to deliver their payload of death.

Before the crash of the first gunshot faded away, Muhammed pushed himself to his feet from the kneeling position he had assumed to imitate the other worshippers and launched himself from the end of the pew where he had strategically situated himself.

What is wrong?

What has gone wrong with my perfect plan?

A legally armed citizen had not been calculated into Muhammed's scheme.

A spasm of fear clawed at his guts as he propelled himself through the side door to the small hallway leading toward the lobby. Ninety feet away, in the same lobby Muhammed was running toward, Sarah was battling a similar spasm of fear gnawing at her.

Now! You have to shoot now! If those two get too far into the lobby you're toast because they'll outmaneuver you. Keep them contained as best you can.

Mahdy was running to his right while Idries maneuvered to his left. Their respective positions would indeed allow them to outflank Sarah if they were allowed to continue unimpeded in their headlong rush. Both terrorists had begun clawing at their trench coats in a struggle to free the AK-47s hidden beneath.

This is not supposed to be happening! Mahdy's terrorized mind screamed. Swinging the Big Dot sight on her Glock toward him, Sarah loosed a round.

BAM!

A miss! Damn it! Slow down and concentrate. Speed only slows you down. Concentrate!

Settling the front Big Dot sight into the 'V' cradle of the rear, Sarah carefully caressed the trigger. Six pounds of pressure on her finger tripped the safe-action trigger mechanism sending a 115-grain pill into Mahdy's humerus.

SNAP!

The unbelievably loud noise when the bullet blasted the bone of his upper left arm into innumerable shards startled him even before the pain began searing into his brain. The hardened warrior had experienced pain many times in his young life, and it was not unfamiliar to him, but the flaming agony he now experienced sent his fevered mind to the brink of consciousness.

The fact that his arm now moved where it had never moved before, in an area four inches below his shoulder, overwhelmed his increasingly confused thoughts.

After demolishing the arm bone, the DPX disintegrated the lateral aspect of his sixth rib before lodging in his lung when its momentum was finally spent. He tried unsuccessfully to ignore his useless arm swinging lazily at his side then began staggering like a drunk.

Ignore him. He'll wait. Deal with the one to your right.

Before Sarah's body could respond to her mind's commands, Idries managed to rip open the restraining buttons on his trench coat and was frantically tearing at the interfering cloth to bring his AK-47 into play. Sarah planted the Big Dot squarely on the center of his upper chest.

WHOCK! WHOCK! WHOCK! WHOCK! WHOCK!

A swarm of 123-grain, full-metal jacketed bullets began slamming into the polished wood covering the concrete block wall behind her. Najeeb the driver was assuring that the men with backpacks were not hindered by anyone while at the church.

He was positioned in the center of the van's side doorway with his AK-47 held tightly to his shoulder. His right eye sighted down the barrel as he had been taught to do in the training camp situated in the relative safety of the Somalia desert.

But one fact had escaped him and his comrades. Their rifles were not sighted in for them and were not shooting to point of aim.

Najeeb's rounds were impacting a full three feet high at twenty-five yards. Such carelessness did not matter when the goal was to mow down unarmed victims at point blank range with automatic rifle fire, but became crucial in a firefight against an armed and capable opponent.

Shifting her attention from Idries, who was still struggling with his overcoat, to Najeeb, she established a flash sight picture on the silhouette in the van and loosed a double-tapped flurry of bullets.

BAM! BAM!

Through a shimmering starburst of shattering glass she saw him flinch but not fall. Sarah would have shot Najeeb again because he was still standing, and was therefore still a threat, but a specter of movement caught her attention as Zayd made his move. In a blur of motion, Zayd erupted from the far right glass door between the foyer and the portico.

He had flattened himself against the wall when Sarah began shooting, and now that he had sorted out the situation unfolding before his eyes, he was ready to act. His headlong sprint for the main hall of the church was hindered by the staggering bulk of Mahdy who continued wandering aimlessly in tight circles holding his drooping arm with his uninjured right hand, his AK-47 and mission forgotten.

Seeing him dashing by out of the corner of her eye, Sarah swung her nine-millimeter ahead of the running man and loosed a single round.

BAM!

She instantly knew it hit low because a puff of shredded cloth and bloody tissue burst from the side of Zayd's hip just above the joint. He fell face first onto the unforgiving surface of the tile floor sprawling helter-skelter beside the prancing feet of Mahdy. The weighty mass of the backpack and its contents pinned him to the floor, crushing the breath from his lungs.

Before Zayd had stopped bouncing from his impact with the unyielding floor, Sarah shifted her sights slightly upward and centered them on Mahdy's upper chest, sending a pellet of destruction into the boiler room of his body. It tore into the area where his lungs joined the bronchial tubes shredding the once vital tissue into useless flaps of gelatinous goop.

Mahdy stopped his nonsensical movements and stared dumbfounded at her before his eyes rolled back into his head. He fell onto his haunches and sat for a second on his ankles then tottered gracefully to his right before sprawling ungraciously across the cold floor, the pain in his broken arm forgotten.

PPTTING! PPTTING! PPTTING!

The splattering of bullets on the rounded underside of the baptismal fountain's stony side did not register at first. It was only after Sarah saw the deflected rounds smashing into the floor tiles and tossing up a cloud of debris did it register that she was under attack from behind.

Pieces of broken terra cotta became injurious secondary projectiles springing from the traumatized floor.

Just as Najeeb's shots had been high, Idrie's rounds were striking low. Sarah ducked behind the craggy basin and stooped low. She didn't want to expose herself by moving from behind the protective bulk of the stone, but she had to in order to see what Idries was up to.

Staying as low to the ground as she could, she peeked around the side of the basin with the Glock thrust forward on straightened arms, her elbows locked in place to stabilize the wavering pistol. What she saw made her blood run cold.

There stood Idries, half hidden behind a massive laminated wood structural support, aiming his AK-47 directly at her. Her trigger finger tightened instinctively at the same instant Idries squeezed off a long burst from the thirty-round magazine of his rifle. The thunderous roar of full automatic fire blasting from Idries's barrel drowned out the crashing sound of her solitary pistol shot.

The flurry of rifle bullets chewed a huge chunk of stone from the lip of the basin. Chunks of granite the size of tennis balls flew from the mangled rock with terrific force. One exceptionally large piece of the jagged ore flew like a well-thrown baseball and smashed into Sarah's left temple.

She crumpled to the ground in an untidy heap not knowing what hit her. Her left hand flew to her head in a natural reaction to touch the injured area and came away drenched with bright, red blood.

Get up!

You can't lie there and let them run up on you.

Get up and fight! Fight for your life!

Now!

With almost supernatural strength she caught the edge of the fountain's stone base and heaved herself to a seated position then tugged until her feet were beneath her. She raised her eyes cautiously above the jagged edge of the destroyed fountain as water cascaded down its side growing into a puddle on the tile floor. What she saw made her breath catch in her throat.

Oh shit! He's coming for me! He's only two car lengths away!

Idries was slinking toward her and was taking great care to carefully place each step. His AK-47 was held at the ready with the pistol grip of the butt end held close to his armpit. Sarah saw the whitening of his left hand as it forcefully grasped the fore end of the sinister looking rifle as though he were afraid it would escape if given the chance. With a sense of relief flooding over her, she also noticed the rapidly spreading splotch of bright red blood flowing freely from an incredibly small hole in his upper chest.

The nine-millimeter DPX had found its mark. On its deadly path through Idries's body, it had shredded the left atrium, pulmonary artery, and ascending aorta at the top of his heart. Before she could command her fear-frozen legs to flee, Idries pitched forward never to move again.

Jerking herself to her full height she again raised her hand to her bleeding temple.

Where's my gun? What happened?

In her semi-conscious state she could not locate the Glock lying only three feet behind her. She had also forgotten that her assailants might not all be incapable of carrying on the fight.

Zayd shrugged off his unbelievably heavy backpack and forced himself to ignore the pain screaming at him from his masticated butt muscles and the pulverized hole in his pelvis as he struggled to right himself. In an effort only known to desperate men, he compelled himself to sit on his injured hip before pulling himself up to kneel on his right knee.

He did not believe what his eyes were showing him.

It was a woman who did this!

There stood his opponent: an unworthy, disrespecting infidel woman with her back toward him. The left side of her baby blue sweater was quickly becoming saturated with blood from a wound to the side of her head.

With extremely deliberate movements, Zayd raised his AK-47 to eye level and sighted on her upper back between the shoulder blades. Wavering vision shimmering like a mirage in front of his eyes made him unsteady. Timing the swaying of his body he tugged heartily on the gritty trigger of the AK.

BRRRP! BRRRP! BRRRP!

The fully automatic fire spewing from Zayd's rifle ripped into Sarah's delicate body, scattering chunks of bloody debris from her left shoulder.

She crumpled to the ground so quickly her upper body bounced from the waist up when her buttocks hit the floor. Almost immediately, she toppled backward with her legs curled beneath her. The back of her unprotected head cracked off the rock-solid ground.

Ever so slowly her twisted legs relaxed and straightened, allowing her to lie flat on her back. Holy water splattered over her from the shattered remains of the fountain.

His swaying body and pain racked brain resulted in his shots flying far wide of the middle of Sarah's back. Only one of Zayd's bullets found a mark, totally destroying the integrity of her shoulder joint; its once solid bony components now lying shattered in miniscule shards.

She lay semi-conscious, not quite sure what had happened. She did not attempt moving her useless left shoulder.

Zayd fought his way to an unsteady standing position.

"You infidel bitch! You killed my comrades and tried to kill me!"

He took one faltering step after the other while holding the AK-47 at port arms across his chest.

"You deserve to die in the worst way, but I do not have time to cut off your head," he said maliciously. "I have your fellow infidels to deal with before I die."

He staggered drunkenly toward her, his undivided attention glued to the area behind the fountain where she fell.

When he rounded the corner of the sprawling pool with the fountain in its midst he saw Sarah lying on her back, her left arm uselessly flung to the side at an odd angle. She was pawing at the front of her navy blue, pleated, mid-calf length skirt. The creamy smooth skin of her bare thighs was exposed as she pulled the skirt ever higher toward her waist.

"Infidel bitch. You cannot save yourself by offering me sexual pleasure in order to spare your life," he said cruelly. "Even with your decadent garter belt you will not be able to tempt me enough to spare your---"

The hateful words Zayd uttered were the last he ever spoke.

Time seemed to stand still when he realized the garter belt had a holster attached to it and the Smith and Wesson Centennial .38 Special revolver it once held was now in Sarah's clenched right fist and swinging deliberately toward his face.

312 · D. E. HEIL

The luminous red dot from the Crimson Trace Laser settled a half-inch above Zayd's voice box as he spoke his last words.

BAM!

The Centennial's one and seven-eighths inch barrel propelled the Winchester 158-grain lead semi-wadcutter bullet to hit exactly where the red dot lay superimposed on his throat.

When the soft lead projectile entered Zayd's throat, it soared easily through the cartilage rings of his trachea then punched effortlessly through the fleshy, flaccid esophagus. It began expanding with the lead mushrooming on the front portion of the bullet, which slowed its forward momentum but certainly did not stop it. Continuing its deadly trek through his neck, the slug angled steeply skyward to smash into the forward, lower edge of the first cervical vertebra where it pulverized the anterior arch on its way to destroying the dens of the second cervical vertebra before severing his spinal cord at the brainstem.

Zayd died instantly. His body unceremoniously crashed to the ground as Sarah's right hand fell limp, allowing the Centennial to clatter noisily to the floor. Her mind slipped effortlessly into the comforting silkiness of unconsciousness.

CHAPTER 44

MUHAMMED'S REWARD

The entire firefight in the lobby of St. Boniface's had taken less than twenty-four seconds.

Muhammed burst into the lobby from the side hallway just as Zayd's body crumpled to the ground in a disorderly heap. He cast his eyes around the devastation of his terrorist cell with a veil of dread falling over him like a death shroud. The emotional stress was so overwhelming he almost fell unconscious.

Regaining his composure, he swore to carry out the operation on his own.

The infidels will be afraid to run toward the sound of gunfire. They will be huddled in fear asking their impotent God for mercy that will not arrive. It is I, Muhammed Shah, who will avenge the deaths of my men.

He ran wildly to where Zayd lay unmoving and yanked the AK-47 from his dead hands. Bolting to where Zayd's discarded backpack lay, Muhammed shimmied into the straps and hefted the pack onto his own back with a mighty grunt issuing from his pursed lips.

Turning on his heels he sprinted spryly toward the main hall of the church.

CHAPTER 45

CHAUNCEY THE HERO

Before the first gunshot finished echoing throughout the main hall of the church, Chauncey was on his feet.

Sarah just left and that's the direction she headed, he thought as panic gripped his guts.

He sprinted toward the rear doors of the main hall and had almost reached them when a crush of panicked people poured through the doorway and overwhelmed him, sweeping him back the way he had come. Even Chauncey's strong desire to aid his beloved friend could not overcome the fear driving the hordes of people streaming side-by-side through the narrow entryway.

Screaming children, hysterical mothers with tears streaming down their terror etched faces, and wide-eyed men flooded into the main hall as a frenzied mob.

This is lunacy!

Oh my God! More gunshots! What's going on?

Chauncey began clawing his way into the crowd, forcing his way upstream like a lovesick salmon in the springtime. He powered himself past one or two hurtling bodies only to be pressed backward three steps by the unrelenting onslaught of wild-eyed people driven past their mortal capacity for calm, deliberate and orderly action.

In an attempt to gain an advantage over the blitzing crowd, he sidestepped the smothering throng to place himself beside the pews hoping he could use the wooden seats to pull himself forward.

Valuable time is being wasted. How can I get past these people? She needs me!

Chauncey looked to the other side of the church in a vain attempt to find J.T. but the pandemonium between them prevented him from locating his friend.

Just as it looked as though the crowd was beginning to thin and may give him a chance to get through, a small girl tripped and fell flat on her belly six feet in front of him. He couldn't ignore the child's plight regardless of how pressing his desire to rush to Sarah's side.

"Hey! Stop! There's a kid on the floor here!" he screamed at the top of his voice as he rushed toward her. He used his elbows to bowl people out of the way in his mad dash to save her.

"Get back! Stop!" he shrieked as he savagely elbowed a fat woman to the side, preventing her from stepping on the hapless youngster. She bounced off him and continued fleeing toward the front of the church without breaking stride.

Chauncey's actions prompted an older man in a black three-piece suit with a red and gray striped silk tie to step out of his pew, scoop the child up, and shove her into the pew to his wife before being swept away by the surging crowd.

Throwing caution and gentlemanly decorum to the wind, Chauncey began plowing his way through the multitude of people rushing toward him. Those he could not shoulder aside he flung violently out of his way.

Where are all these people coming from?

He used his height to look around and determined that the hundreds of people who had crammed themselves into the rear of the church, the choir loft, and along the sides of the rows of pews were joining the mass exodus toward the perceived safety at the front of the church like a frenzied herd of migrating lemmings.

Churchgoers in the pews began streaming into the aisles to join the mob fleeing the conflagration occurring in the lobby.

The pews are emptying out!

They're empty enough that I can jump from one seat to the next until I get to the back of the church!

Stepping into the nearest pew, Chauncey vaulted onto the seat and began jumping from pew to pew by slinging one of his long legs over the back of the bench and firmly planting his foot on the seat of the next.

The crowds began to dissipate. The rear of the main hall of the church near the doors was almost devoid of people. Since he was making good time, Chauncey continued jumping from pew seat to pew seat.

When he finally reached the end, he jumped to the ground and began sprinting across the twelve foot space separating the last pew from the door. He was so intent on reaching Sarah that he ran headlong into the door when Muhammed smashed it open from the lobby side.

Chauncey was stunned and his nose bloodied in the collision but he remained upright.

The men stood face-to-face staring at each other for a bizarre moment. Time seemed to stand still and the pandemonium surrounding them was temporarily forgotten.

Stunned and gazing dimly through watery eyes, Chauncey did not immediately recognize the swarthy man with a backpack slung over his shoulder and an AK-47 held at port arms. But Muhammed immediately recognized him. The features of Chauncey's face would forever be seared on his warped mind.

This is one of the men from the Hallelujah Gathering, Muhammed thought.

He was standing over Samir as he lay on the ground after making him crash his van. This is one of the infidels we are seeking to wreak vengeance upon!

A split second later, terror gripped Chauncey's heart when in a flash of recollection he remembered where he had seen this man.

Before Chauncey could react, Muhammed swung the AK-47's steel butt plate into the side of Chauncey's face, just below the left cheekbone. He crashed to the ground, his mind momentarily blank.

When his sight began to clear he was appalled to see the glaring Muhammed standing menacingly over him in an obvious posture of dominance. The sinister eye of the rifle's muzzle was staring directly at the center of his forehead. A wicked grin spread across Muhammed's face as he scowled down at Chauncey.

So this is how it's going to end.

Dear Lord, I have sinned. Please forgive my transgressions and take me into your Home---

A very strange sight interrupted Chauncey's final prayer.

The man whose name Chauncey did not know suddenly had a bewildered look appear on his face at the same instant a starburst of brilliant red mist spewed from a tiny hole in the center of his chest.

A .22 caliber 55-grain hollow point bullet from Black Hills Ammunition Company traveling at 3,300 feet-per-second had just blown a grapefruit-sized crater in the Muhammed's left lung.

What the hell?

Then Chauncey heard the answer as if it came out of a muffling fog. The crash of a rifle being fired from the other side of the church rumbled through the cavernous hall.

The report of the shot was accompanied by the instantaneous appearance of a second spurting rouge starburst erupting adjacent to the first on Muhammed's chest. Before the splatter from the second bullet's impact dissipated, Muhammed crumpled beneath the crushing weight of the explosive-filled backpack. He landed heavily beside Chauncey's outstretched body.

Chauncey slowly rose to his feet. His head swam in a kaleidoscope of swirling images. He laboriously tried to recalibrate his senses and regain his balance.

Looking around the church as if he were seeing it for the first time, he saw a ridiculous sight. J.T. was standing on the seat of a pew with Sarah's hot pink Bushmaster AR-15 held to his shoulder, the CompM4 sight in line with his eye, and pointing in his direction.

As soon as J.T. saw Chauncey he began waving his right hand wildly above his head while using his left to keep the Bushmaster in a ready position against his shoulder. His long tan raincoat hung open revealing the black nylon sling that had held the rifle with its collapsible stock folded to its shortest length.

"Chauncey! Get that backpack out of here! It's probably a bomb!"

Chauncey looked numbly around the floor in front of him and finally located the pack still strapped to Muhammed's dead body.

"Get it out of here!" J.T. continued to yell. "I'll get Sarah!"

As if in a parallel world, Chauncey stooped and began sliding Muhammed's flaccid arms out of the straps of the backpack.

Holy Hell! This thing is heavy!

Slinging the right strap over his shoulder, Chauncey heaved himself to his feet then staggered toward the door leading out the back of the church into the lobby.

It had been one minute and ten seconds since the terrorists had set the timers on their bombs and exited the van.

CHAPTER 46

GRAND FINALE

"Stephanie!" J.T. yelled above the din of mass confusion that had gripped everyone in the church. "You and the girls run up front and lay behind that small brick wall beside the altar. Run as fast as you can then stay put and stay still. Play dead!"

Knowing he would be delayed in reaching Sarah if he tried to run toward the back of the church via the aisles, he began leaping from pew seat to pew seat like Chauncey had.

If Chauncey hadn't stood up on the pew I would have never seen him in trouble. It's good for him he's so tall.

Thank God Sarah insisted I keep her rifle when she brought it for me to borrow at Thanksgiving.

He managed to vault over each seat with ease, and arrived at the rear door of the church in less than ten seconds.

I hope Sarah's all right and this isn't just a body recovery exercise. That had to be her shooting because I saw her leave the main hall of the church just before the shooting started. There were definitely at least two different guns being fired.

He cautiously approached the glass-fronted door and saw Idries lying face down and motionless in a pool of blood. Sliding smoothly to his left in order to place himself behind the protective shield of a brick wall, he began 'slicing the pie' with the AR-15 held to his shoulder and ready to bring into action with the flick of his trigger finger.

He continued to 'slice" the room into visual pieces until the prostrate form of Haady came into view. His feet were still suspended above the floor by the wood doorframe.

Holy shit! They all have identical backpacks!

What the hell happened here?

He had seen as much of the lobby as he could from inside the main hall of the church so he cautiously pushed the door open with his left foot making sure he shuffled to never allow his feet to cross and trip him. His eyes continually scanned back and forth as he warily trundled forward.

Only after moving ten feet into the lobby was he able to see Sarah's feet sticking out from behind the baptismal fountain.

Oh no! Oh God NO!

With his goal in sight, he hastened his advance until he had the entire lobby under visual observation. Only then did he allow himself to rush to Sarah's side.

Crouching beside her he laid his fingers along her neck to feel for her carotid pulse.

There it is! At least she's alive.

He glanced around to make sure of his surroundings and saw the backpack on Mahdy's body.

I better not waste any more time.

If those backpacks are bombs they're probably on timers or a remote detonator. Either way they may blow at any moment.

At that instant, kitchen timers on the bodies of Haady, Mahdy, Zayd, and Idries began chirping in unison.

Holy shit! Time's up! I've got to get her out of here.

He allowed the Bushmaster to slide under his tan raincoat where it dangled idly on its nylon sling. With both hands free he scooped Sarah into his arms.

I better take her to the church office. It's sheltered and has telephones to call 9-1-1.

He ran across the lobby with her dangling limply in his arms. He was ready to duck into the long hallway leading to the office when Chauncey burst back into the building from outside.

"Chauncey! This way! Come on!" he yelled as he bolted past him. "Did you get rid of that backpack?"

"Yeah, I dumped it off the side of the handicapped ramp into the Blessed Virgin's grotto," he yelled back, matching J.T.'s pace. "I figure if it is a bomb that brick wall will deflect the blast away from the building."

"Good!" J.T. said breathlessly as they reached the end of the hallway and burst into the priest's office.

"Get under that desk, curl up and cover your head!" he screamed loudly as he gently laid Sarah under a desk on the opposite side of the room. He had no sooner covered her body with his own than all the bombs detonated simultaneously.

The results were spectacular.

CHAUNCEY MEETS HIS WIFE

J.T. and Chauncey rode in silence from Washington, D.C. to Baltimore. Neither had much to say because they were lost in their own thoughts and the uncertainty of events that had enveloped them.

"I hate these parking garages," J.T. said as he spun around beside Sarah's Mercedes C-300 Luxury Sedan and shinnied sideways between it and the powder gray Buick LeSabre parked beside it.

"I guess they're a necessary evil in a city as crowded as Baltimore," Chauncey opined as he slid sideways on the passenger side of the car. "At least Sarah was nice enough to loan us her car. It's not as wide as your van."

"You're still always looking for the one bright angle aren't you?"

"It'll make your life go a little smoother if you try it," Chauncey replied chuckling.

They walked very slowly through the parking garage, not willing to rush into an unknown stage of Chauncey's life.

"How did you reserve the Baltimore Courthouse to meet your wife in?" J.T. asked.

"I didn't reserve it," Chauncey replied. "Apparently I knew some important people, at least they knew me, and they arranged it. Some politician probably thinks this reunion will be good for his career and wants to be front and center of the attention."

A relaxed silence fell between them as each man was lost in his own thoughts.

"Did you see a doctor about your memory loss?" J.T. inquired tentatively.

"I saw a neurologist, a man I used to be quite friendly with, I am told," Chauncey replied as he rapidly glanced up and down the street they were about to cross. "He doesn't know how or why I lost most of my memory but says I almost have a totally barren mind. They call it Tabla Rosa in new born babies, a blank slate."

"You mean that a baby has no memory at all because they were just born?" J.T. asked quizzically.

"Exactly, except I kept the ability to speak and other mental faculties that allowed me to function," Chauncey replied with a grin. "It's all pretty strange."

"It is strange," J.T. said with a gently nodding of his head. "What did they say your name is?"

"Robert Fogler," Chauncey replied absently. "Apparently I'm an obstetrician and have a family."

"That's a doctor that delivers babies, isn't it?"

"Yes it is."

"I'm having a hard time imagining you as an obstetrician," J.T. said as he eyed him. "Especially since I can only envision you swinging a sledgehammer at the farm."

"Yeah, it's a difficult concept to get your arms around, isn't it?"

They both laughed heartily as only good friends can.

When they finished laughing, a somber mood befell them.

"The priest says it'll take over a year to rebuild the damage at the church," J.T. said.

"I heard it was heavily damaged."

"The roof in the atrium, that's what the priest likes to call the lobby, was trashed," J.T. continued. "The blast totally blew it off; at least between the big laminated wood supports. The supports themselves were still intact but have to be replaced because they're structurally unsound."

"That means they'll have to tear the whole front off the church and rebuild it."

"I think that's what it means," he agreed. "The portico was ripped off the front of the building. I saw one of the terrorists lying in the doorway right underneath where it attached to the church. His bomb must have cleaved it right off at its attachment point. The whole thing ended upside down on the lawn."

"To top everything off, I heard they wanted to charge you and Sarah with illegally carrying firearms into a church," Chauncey said as he raised his eyebrows.

"They sure did," J.T. replied with a chuckle. "It was just the chief of police trying to get his name into the newspapers along with his boss, the mayor."

"What happened there?"

"He was referencing the law forbidding carrying a firearm into a place of worship without a good cause as being a class four misdemeanor in Virginia. He looked very foolish when it was pointed out that the parishioners of St. Boniface's did have a very good reason for carrying firearms since the Hallelujah Gathering scenario happened only a few months prior," J.T. stated flatly.

"He didn't look nearly as foolish as the senator who called for more restrictive gun control measures," Chauncey replied. "When a commentator pointed out that the terrorists broke over a dozen laws that were already on the books, and used bombs as well, he really didn't have an answer why more gun control laws would have made a difference."

"The fact that fully automatic firearms are already heavily regulated under the 1934 federal gun laws doesn't seem to deter the freedom haters from wanting to curtail the rights of law abiding American citizens every chance they get," J.T. stated emphatically. "You'd think the voters would get rid of morons like that."

"What was the final determination with the dead guy they found in the ditch?" Chauncey asked.

"The word I get is he was the driver," he replied. "Sarah remembers shooting twice at a man in the van but doesn't know what happened to him. They found one of her bullets in his left lung and one in his guts that nicked the abdominal aorta. Both wounds would have been fatal without immediate medical attention."

"So they figure he died trying to get away?"

"That's the theory."

"Have you heard any news from your friends whether this was an organized gang?" Chauncey asked.

"Yeah, I can't say much but this was an organized terrorist cell living in the United States; apparently for years," he replied evenly. "When the authorities searched their cars and houses they found information, mostly on computers, that will help deter a lot of attacks."

"What about the guy you shot in the church?"

"He was a heavy hitter. A real bad guy the authorities have been watching for almost a decade. They lost track of him last year and didn't know he was in the United States," J.T. replied.

Their conversation lapsed into a serene quiet while they walked side-by-side until J.T. broke the silence.

"Chauncey?"

"Yeah?"

"They found Sarah's laptop and your work computer in one of the apartments along with a few bags of garbage from my house. They'll be released to the Virginia State Police and you'll get them back after they process them as stolen property."

Chauncey was silent while his mind digested the significance of this information.

"So they were stalking us?"

"That's the way I see it. It's probably some fallout from our involvement at the Hallelujah Gathering. The police won't be able to answer any questions about where they found your computers so don't bother asking, and I can't say any more either."

An uncomfortable silence hung in the air like a toxic fog. To break the awkward silence Chauncey said the first thing that came into his mind.

"I hear the grotto was destroyed but the statue of the Blessed Virgin was untouched."

"Yeah, they're calling it a miracle."

They left the cool, dank darkness of the parking garage and stepped onto the sun-drenched sidewalk.

"It's another miracle you found out who you are."

"Yeah, it is a miracle," Chauncey agreed. "When my picture appeared in newspapers across the country, folks who saw it and knew me as Robert Fogler called my wife to tell her they found me."

"You're a hero," J.T. said solemnly. "It's only natural the media would pick up the story."

"I guess so," Chauncey said with discouragement in his voice. "I don't think I'm a hero."

"Our country needs heroes," J.T. said. "You have to live up to that role for the kids whether you want it or not."

"Thanks for keeping Sarah's name out of the newspapers," he said to change the subject.

"No problem," J.T. replied. "I gave a friend a fake name and that's what the media picked up on. She didn't need to have her real name plastered all over the world. Islamic radicals would surely declare a fatwah against her."

"I wish I could say the same thing for myself, but my story is attracting way too much media attention to not have my name, names I should say, and picture picked up by media around the world."

"You can always legally change your name now that you know who you are," J.T. offered sincerely. "But I don't think you'll have any problems. You just carried a bomb out of the church. Sarah actually stopped their plan by killing four of them."

330 · D. E. HEIL

"I'll take your point of view under consideration," he said solemnly. "But what about you? You killed the terrorist to save me. Won't they be coming after you?"

"My friend got my name wrong also," J.T. said with a smile.

Chauncey weakly returned his smile.

They stood on the curb across the street from the courthouse waiting for the light to change.

"That was pretty strange having all the electricity go out yesterday in the entire eastern part of the country wasn't it?" Chauncey asked.

"Yeah, they say it was human error and it made the computers shut down."

Chauncey looked at J.T. who refused to acknowledge his gaze. He returned his eyes to the crossing light across the street.

"So it wasn't human error," Chauncey said softly. "They're here and they're out to kill us all, aren't they?"

The silence between the two men was suffocating even amongst the din of street noise.

"Yes, they're here," was all he said.

Chauncey allowed his eyes to wander and take in his surroundings.

"What's your opinion of how Sarah's holding up?" J.T. asked to change the subject.

"As well as can be expected," Chauncey replied with despair in his voice. "The orthopedic surgeon says that since she needed a complete shoulder replacement, her career as a chiropractor is over."

"That's not going to sit well with her."

"Actually, she's accepted the news pretty well," he replied. "She's already making plans."

"That's a good sign," J.T. said solemnly. "What types of plans is she making?"

"Well, it'll depend on how much range of motion she gets back in her shoulder and that won't be known for a few months," he replied. "But if she can, she wants to train to become a defensive shooting instructor."

J.T. was silent for a moment.

"Well, she'll be a good one if she can handle it physically," he said slowly. "She did one hell of a job at the church. Only God knows how many lives she saved and how much misery she prevented."

"More importantly, she's been empowered," Chauncey explained slowly. "Now she knows she can defend herself and her loved ones unlike when your brother was murdered. I think it's a turning point in her life."

They walked on in silence, each lost in his thoughts.

Without saying a word, they stopped at the front steps of the courthouse and stood silently while staring up at the huge, ornate doors. The television vans lining the street in front of the courthouse made it obvious the media were out in full force to cover the biggest human interest story of the century.

"Are you OK?"

"Yes I am," Chauncey replied resolutely as he continued staring at the front doors of the courthouse. "You don't know what it's like not knowing who you are, what you've done, or what your future may hold. It'll be good to have a documented life again."

"You still don't have any idea what made you lose your memory?" J.T. asked without taking his eyes from the doors of the courthouse.

"I don't have a clue," Chauncey replied noncommittally.

Suddenly Chauncey turned to J.T., startling him, and said, "I'm really excited about meeting my wife and children. It sounds like I have a wonderful life."

"I'm sure you do and I'd like to stay in touch," J.T. said before quickly looking away.

"That we will definitely do," Chauncey replied with a faraway look in his eyes.

"Well, you ready?" J.T. asked as he looked at his friend.

"As ready as I'm going to be," Chauncey answered wearily. "Let's go."

Chauncey and J.T. barely had enough time for their eyes to accommodate to the dim interior of the courthouse when the media spotted them. The naked glare of television lights swung in their direction and blinded them while reporters shoved microphones into Chauncey's face. The bombardment of questions instantly turned his homecoming into a circus.

J.T. faded unnoticed into the crowd.

Chauncey answered each question with a short, courteous reply and a smile. He continued walking and refused to allow the reporters to impede his progress toward the small office where his family awaited him.

Irene Fogler, Robert's wife, had been nervously rehearsing what she would say to her husband after not seeing him for almost three years. It had been a mentally draining ordeal. Many different thoughts had run through her mind when he vanished. Had he abandoned his family because of the pressures of his job? Had he found another woman and run away with her?

Those scenarios did not make any sense and baffled her as well as the police. The stress of the unknown had driven her to the brink of a nervous breakdown. Robbery was ruled out because his wallet was found in his abandoned vehicle with cash and credit cards intact. During his absence, none of his bank accounts were touched so a romantic dalliance was determined to be unlikely.

These facts offered some solace to Irene but the uncertainty of not knowing the truth was mentally devastating.

She had asked their minister, Marvin Jones, and his wife Sonya, to accompany her to the reunion. They had been a great help to the Fogler family throughout the ordeal. Marvin was the same age as Robert and the two couples had been close friends for decades.

Chauncey courteously forced his way through the swarming mob of obnoxious reporters in the courthouse lobby. The mayor appeared out of the crowd and shook his hand briskly as the heat of camera lights beat down upon them, then personally led him toward the office where the reunion was to take place.

Irene heard the rumble from the crowd growing in volume and knew Robert was coming.

"Marvin, I feel faint," she whispered with a shaking voice while unsteadily grasping his arm.

"Here's a seat. Sit in this chair before you keel over," he said, as he led her gently to a gray steel desk. The mottled gray cloth covering the back of the chair showed signs of wearing through from being backed against the wall, but it offered her a place to recover.

He pulled the secretary's chair out and held it steady while maintaining a firm grasp of her arm. She slid onto the chair using the wall to steady herself.

"Watch yourself," Marvin warned. "There's not much room to scoot in between the desk and wall; it's pretty close."

The brass nameplate on the desk faced toward the door and informed the world this was the workstation of Mary McCutcheon.

"I'm so nervous," Irene said with a quivering voice. She was on the verge of tears.

"Calm down," Marvin said in a deep, soothing voice. "You've been married to this man for thirty-one years and have known him since you were both five years old so there's no reason to be nervous."

"I'm shaking like a leaf," she replied. "I don't want a bunch of reporters seeing me like this."

"Cross your hands and place them on the desk," Marvin instructed. "Sit up straight and keep your feet flat on the floor. Breathe deeply and evenly. You'll be fine."

Irene pursed her lips tightly together and held herself rigidly erect as her firmly clenched fingers blanched to a pale tan. She fought to keep anxiety from overwhelming her.

The unrelenting barrage of questions from the reporters was beginning to take its toll on Chauncey and showed in the strained expression on his face.

Keep your head about you.

Don't let the camera lights disorient you. Just look at the floor and keep your balance.

The clamor of the crowd was reaching a crescendo. Irene was startled when the mayor suddenly popped into the room with his hand on Chauncey's arm. With a flourish, he released his grip and gently said, "Welcome home, Robert."

The room fell silent. Even the reporters lining the path to Mary McCutcheon's desk held their breath in anticipation.

Chauncey slowly and deliberately raised his eyes from the floor and saw Irene sitting stiffly behind the intimidating steel desk. A broad smile spread across his face but his feet were unwilling to move.

A heavy veil of stillness held the room in a stony grip as seconds agonizingly clicked by while Chauncey unwaveringly stared at Irene. She could only smile weakly as tears of relief began cascading down her face leaving rivulets of saturated rouge marring the smooth lines of her cheeks.

With halting steps Chauncey forced one foot in front of the other until he was standing with the front of his thighs lightly touching the cold steel rimming the top of the desk.

Irene had readied herself for this moment but was totally taken aback when he extended his hand and said, "Hello Mary, I'm supposed to meet my wife here today. Has she arrived yet?"

The End

Want even more? Sign up for my mailing list and receive a FREE copy of DELAYED JUSTICE, a novella related to the True Justice series!

One of the best things about writing is building a relationship with my readers. I love sending information to you: newsletters with details on new releases, special offers, and other bits of news relating to the True Justice series that my readers report finding very interesting.

If you sign up for the mailing list I will immediately send you a copy of Delayed Justice for your reading pleasure.

Your email listing will NEVER be sold or used for anything other than an occasional announcement pertaining to this series of novels. Naturally, you can unsubscribe at any time.

To get your FREE copy simply sign up at https://dl.bookfunnel.com/bhnevz7rhh and your book will be sent to you in the blink of an eye!

A preview from your FREE copy of
DELAYED JUSTICE
Novella of the True Justice Series

Neighbors at odds.
Predators on the hunt.
A quiet neighborhood.
A mother who just wants to defend her child.

The urges of human predators overcome their fear of discovery, and the prospect of thrills beyond their wildest dreams goads them into undertaking a bold plan.

Delayed Justice delivers heart-pounding action and an astonishing ending that will change lives forever!

If you enjoy reading works books that balance the dark psychological musings of evil with the uncertainty of good triumphing over it, be sure to get your immediate copy of this True Justice Novella! I only need to know where you want it sent.

To get your FREE copy simply sign up at https://dl.bookfunnel.com/bhnevz7rhh and your book will be sent to you in the blink of an eye!

If you enjoyed this book…

I would truly appreciate it if you would help others to enjoy it also. Reviews of books are a vital part of helping readers find series they will love. Reviews are often what make the difference between passing over a book or finding a series that will keep you on the edge of your seat and demanding the next installment.

Your review will mean a lot to both me and to future readers. You can leave a review at Amazon by visiting:
http://www.amazon.com/review/create-review?&asin= B07KFF9829

Or you can leave a review on Goodreads.com. Creating an account at Goodreads is very simple and you will discover a new home there with other readers who have reading interests very similar to yours. Check them out.

Thank you very much in advance for taking the time to post a review and your opinion of this book. It is greatly appreciated, and I look forward to reading your review!

Be A Beta Reader Team Member

I am recruiting willing volunteers to be members of my beta reader team.

What's all involved in being a beta reader? Well, you'll be helping me flesh out my manuscripts for each book before it is published. Many authors use beta readers because you are very astute at reading and any errors will jump off the page and strike your eye as being incorrect.

What types of things might you find?

One author likes to tell the story (OK, he reluctantly tells it) of the time he had his main character flicking the safety off a pistol that does not have a safety. Whoops!

But these are the types of things I need your help with.

If you are willing to help, I will make the un-edited manuscript available for a few days on BookFunnel. You can download it, read it, email me with anything you find that is not right within the following two weeks, and I'll look over your suggestions.

This will be a tremendous help to me and will give you insights into the processes of how the books you love to read are put together.

I have a standalone chapter that is just a small gift to you for joining the team.

You can get a free chapter for becoming a beta reader by visiting https://dl.bookfunnel.com/q1z60hf7io.

ABOUT THE AUTHOR

D.E. Heil was born on a wintry day in Pittsburgh in 1956. His mother was perpetually late for important appointments, and in keeping with her tardy nature, never spent more than twenty minutes in a hospital before birthing any of her four babies.

He received an undergraduate degree in Psychology from Slippery Rock University, spent an adventurous winter in Aspen, CO as a ski bum, then attended the National University of Health Sciences in Lombard, IL where he received a BS in Human Biology and a Doctorate in Chiropractic. In a tremendous stroke of good luck, the best luck he has ever had, he met his wife, Maria, who lived nearby.

Heil has supported his wife's activism for the Second Amendment since the year 2000. Currently, she is a Member of the Board of Directors of the National Rifle Association. It is through his close association with Second Amendment issues that he has gained great insight into the world of ordinary Americans willingly accepting the responsibility of providing protection for themselves, their family, and their communities.

Because of his fellowship with typical yet remarkable Americans, the True Justice series of novels was born. In addition to writing fiction as well as non-fiction books, Dr. Heil recently obtained a Master's degree in Industrial and Organizational Psychology.

He and his wife live in Pennsylvania where they raised their four children.

CONTENTS

RIGHTEOUS JUSTICE

Book Two of the True Justice Series

D. E. Heil

Get an exclusive book related to the True Justice series!

One of the best things about writing is building a relationship with my readers. I love sending information to you: newsletters with details on new releases, special offers, and other bits of news relating to the True Justice series that my readers report finding very interesting.

If you sign up for the mailing list I'll send you a book related to the True Justice series entitled DELAYED JUSTICE. My books normally sell for $12.99, but this one can be yours for free.

Simply go to the back of this book to learn how to get your FREE book.

JOHN MCGUIRE

John McGuire was a tall, burly hellion. A mop of flaming red hair flew across his shoulders as he viciously swung a sledgehammer to smash Harry Zalone's knee into bloody pulp.

He winced when a spray of gore mixed with cement fragments splashed his eyes.

Zalone momentarily froze as he lay helplessly on his garage floor. A look of disbelief crossed his face and was instantly replaced with a mask of terror and a blood-curdling howl, revealing the hole where his front teeth used to be.

Wiping his face with the grubby sleeve of a red plaid flannel shirt, McGuire stared approvingly at his handiwork.

He wasn't concerned about anyone hearing Zalone's demented screams in this desolate area; otherwise he would have silenced him with the same duct tape he had used to bind his prisoner's wrists and ankles.

McGuire preferred simple solutions to problems, and sadistic torment was an uncomplicated technique he used often and with unfettered enthusiasm.

He glared into Zalone's grief-stricken eyes before stooping to grab hold of the man's boot. A ferocious twist didn't elicit the expected reaction, because a merciful blanket of unconsciousness had silenced Zalone.

Irritated at this turn of events, McGuire slammed the foot to the floor and yelled, "Hey asshole! Where you put my stuff?"

"Should we throw water on his face or somethin' to wake him up?" Bill Fenne, known since childhood as Squeaky, asked in a faltering, high-pitched nasally tone.

"The only thing we gonna throw on this bastard is gasoline," McGuire replied as he gave Zalone's disfigured leg a swift kick. "Wake up, you cock-sucker, before I burn you up!"

"He ain't gonna wake up enough to tell you anything, the shape he in."

"He damned well better before I get mad."

"Let me throw some water on him."

"Go ahead and be quick about it. I'm gonna look through the house and see what I can find."

Squeaky grabbed a garden hose from outside the garage and turned a torrent of frigid water on Zalone, who began tossing and groaning, although he was far from being fully conscious and capable of answering questions.

"Listen man," Squeaky wheezed as he leaned over Zalone. "You gotta wake up or he's gonna really hurt you. Come on, man."

He began squirting water on Zalone's ruddy cheeks, then down his body and onto the mangled leg. Shards of white bone protruded through the skin above and below the flattened knee.

Squeaky marveled at the macabre beauty of the bloodstained water meandering lazily toward a drain in the center of the floor.

"Come on, man," he pleaded over and over again. "This is gonna get ugly if you don't cooperate."

McGuire reappeared in the doorway leading from the garage to the kitchen, a triumphant look brightening his face.

"Looky what I found in back of his kitchen cabinets," he said as he held a zip-lock plastic bag aloft. It contained numerous smaller bags; each sealed and filled with methamphetamine. He turned his attention back to Zalone.

"You shit! You try stealing from *me*! You don't do that, shithead!"

"That's not good, asshole," Squeaky said to Zalone in a defeated voice as the crippled man lay groaning pitifully on the wet floor.

Dejectedly, as though he had failed his once trusted accomplice, Squeaky allowed his hand to slowly fall dolefully to his side. The streaming torrent of water splashed uselessly off the concrete beside Zalone's prostrate form.

Zalone's situation was beyond any help Squeaky could offer him.

This boy is screwed, he thought disgustedly.

"Get rid of that water," McGuire growled through clenched teeth as he grabbed one of two gasoline containers from beside a battered lawnmower.

Squeaky immediately threw the hose aside and looked expectantly at McGuire.

"Here, take this," McGuire said impatiently, tossing the methamphetamine-stuffed bag to Squeaky. "Just stay in the car."

Without saying another word, McGuire spun on his heels and disappeared into the house with a gas can dangling from his hand.

He reappeared in the garage a few minutes later, empty-handed.

Without speaking a word to Zalone, and with a pleased grin, he took the second container and began splashing its contents around the garage. After he was satisfied, he drenched the condemned man's face until he began to cough and sputter, which seemed to heighten McGuire's ghoulish pleasure.

McGuire trailed a steady stream of gasoline behind him and out the double doorway. With a flick of his wrist he nonchalantly tossed the container back into the garage where it bounced off Zalone's chest, spun toward a workbench, and came to rest with the remaining gas trickling out.

With a theatrical flourish, McGuire jabbed a button on the wall of the garage.

A satisfied, demonic grin plastered his sweaty face when he lit the gas with a disposable lighter. The flame shot into the house just before the garage door slapped the ground with a resounding thud.

His eyes twinkled as he strode away from the seemingly tranquil scene of a middle class house surrounded by the forested Tennessee hills. The horses that had gathered to curiously peer over the slats of white board fencing surrounding the pasture scattered in terror when they sensed the evil of the scene unfolding in front of them.

An emotionless Squeaky sat silently, watching pensively as a smirking McGuire approached the car.

Zalone's screams began escalating to an incomprehensible cacophony of agony, and McGuire's step took on a childlike, springing gait.

"What the hell we gonna do now?" Squeaky whined through the open car window as the entire house burst into flames with a resounding whoosh, blowing out the windows.

Resting his hand on top of the car, McGuire bent down and stared wickedly at Squeaky. Then he spun around to take a long, admiring look at the flames.

"What we gonna do now?" he repeated as he shielded his face from the blistering heat. "We goin' to Virginia and set up shop there, 'cause Tennessee's gettin' too hot. Besides, I got some unfinished business with my ex and that's where she's livin' these days."

CHAPTER 1

MEDICAL EMERGENCY

"How much junk was Minnie able to jam into this old chicken coop?" Nadine Brand asked, throwing a rusty watering can into the bed of Sarah's new cherry-red Chevy pick-up truck.

"I don't know," Sarah said, surveying the last of the outbuildings to be cleaned and renovated on the farm she'd recently acquired following the death of her husband. "And we'll never know until we get all this trash out of here, so just keep working."

Sarah Collins, D.C., was an athletic thirty-five year-old with a shock of short auburn hair that threatened to go its own way regardless of the amount of hair spray she applied.

She had been the director of the District Spinal Care Clinic in Washington, D.C. when her husband Josh, a promising orthopedic surgeon, was viciously murdered in the parking lot of her chiropractic office during a botched carjacking. Escaping the confines of Washington had allowed her to salvage the tattered remains of her sanity as she established a new life in the Virginia countryside.

Her flight to Nadine's horse farm in western Virginia had been a last-ditch effort to make sense of the unfathomable situation in which she found herself.

Nadine Brand, Sarah's former college roommate, had been a loner since her husband left her for another man. Her middle school teaching experience, and understanding of how to rebuild a shattered life, made her well-qualified to mentor friends in need.

Her bitter experience salvaging the ruins of her own shattered life by raising and training Rocky Mountain horses was instrumental in helping Sarah through her ordeal.

And now Sarah had her own farm she had purchased from Minnie Schneider, who'd used the proceeds of the sale to retire to Florida with her daughter.

The money Sarah received from the sale of her chiropractic practice, along with her husband's estate, left her independently wealthy and she could treat the farm more as a hobby without the pressure of making a living from the land, which was a good thing. She was much too competitive to run the farm as a business and enjoy its beauty at the same time.

"It's a good thing you got that bed liner when you ordered your truck," Nadine said, as Sarah continued to pull at the piles of trash, too tired to answer. "Otherwise all the nice new shine would be scratched off it by now."

"Having all the shine scratched off me is more of my concern at the moment," Sarah replied wearily, a stray piece of baling wire tugging at her sleeve.

"One of the smartest things you ever did was bringing Chauncey to the farm with you on the weekends," Nadine said. Chauncey was formerly a homeless man Sarah had employed over a year earlier as the bookkeeper for her chiropractic practice. Since that time Sarah and Chauncey had become nearly inseparable friends, rebuilding their devastated lives together.

Nadine threw a bucket into the back of the pick-up. "He's not only handy around the farm, but I feel a lot better knowing you're not here alone."

"Listen to you talking," Sarah said. "You live alone all the time!"

"Yeah, well, I'm used to it," Nadine said. "But you're new to this area and people notice when someone new moves in; the good as well as the bad."

"I'm sure they've noticed a new person in the neighborhood," Sarah said solemnly. "But I'm armed twenty-four-seven now that my concealed carry license came through. I really don't expect any problems from the local riff-raff ... all one or two of them."

"It's not funny. There are bad people everywhere, even out here in the country," Nadine said seriously.

Both of their minds flashed back to the terrorist attack on St. Boniface's church during the Christmas Children's Mass. The memory caused Sarah to unconsciously rub her arm where a prosthetic shoulder was a stark reminder of the injuries she suffered in that confrontation.

"So, how's Chauncey's house coming?" Nadine said to change the subject before an argument began.

"It's coming along fine," Sarah replied. "He's really doing a nice job converting the old workshop into a cabin. It's almost finished, and I've been getting my house upgraded too. When Chauncey had electricians wire his place, I had them put floodlights on the outside of my house. I don't want to have a mercury-vapor light on a pole burning all night long like a lot of farms around her do because I sleep better in total darkness, but I'm still a little spooked about living in the country."

"That's a good idea," Nadine said. "It will put your mind at ease, a little at least."

"It took longer than expected to get that job done because I had them put in extra light switches, including one in my bedroom. That way I can flick one switch and illuminate all around the house."

"That's another good idea. What's he working on today that's so important he can't help us here?" Nadine said as she mopped a flood of sweat from her forehead with the sleeve of her shirt.

"He's putting in a composting toilet. We decided it would be the smartest way to go since a new sand mound and septic system would cost more than twenty thousand dollars to have installed."

"That's a major expense, for sure," Nadine said. "Then he can spread the composted waste around the trees for fertilizer, I assume."

"Yeah, it's just another way we can reduce, reuse, and recycle to be good conservationists, and it saves me money."

"You're starting to settle into this country life pretty well," Nadine said.

"Here, help me with this," Sarah said as she tugged at a cultivator stuck under a mound of broken gardening instruments.

"Damn!" she cried, grabbing her left wrist.

"What happened?" Nadine asked, running to her side and trying to see in the dim light filtering through the filthy windows.

Sarah moaned, "My hand slipped and that sharp hook-looking thing ripped across my palm. It's bleeding pretty badly."

"Let's get outside where we can see it better," Nadine said, taking Sarah's elbow and leading her.

"Shit! That's tendons you can see there," Sarah said. "I have to get some stitches and a tetanus shot."

"Dan Lewis is the closest doctor," Nadine said. "His office is in Spinale, that little tourist town we went to when we ate at D'Amato's restaurant. Remember it?"

"Yeah, I remember it," Sarah said. "I have to wash this with soap and water, and then put some hydrogen peroxide on it to help ward off infection. That'll hurt like hell. Then I'll be able to drive to Spinale."

"I'll call to make sure they're still there," Nadine said breathlessly as adrenaline took hold of her. "Then I'll drive you."

"I can drive myself."

"No, you can't, and don't give me any guff," Nadine said, a toothy grin on her dirt-smudged face. "I can whip your ass with no problem now."

"Bitch!" Sarah joked in return.

CHAPTER 2

DANIEL LEWIS, M.D.

"They'll only be there until noon so we better hurry," Nadine told Sarah as she disconnected the phone call.

"I hate going to the doctor," Sarah said childishly.

"*You're* a doctor," Nadine said, grabbing her purse and pawing through it in a feverish search for car keys. "So quit whining and let's go."

"I am not whining. It's just that I don't make a very good patient," Sarah said.

"And stop trying to make light of your injury," Nadine said. "Or I'll just chop off your hand with one of those old axes and save the gas we would waste taking the trip to Dr. Lewis's office."

Chauncey looked on with concern as the two women bantered back and forth. "I will never be able to understand how you two can make fun of such a dire situation," he said seriously. "It's just not right."

Chauncey was fifty-four, but looked like an athletic 40 year old. His tall frame carried sinewy muscle with only a hint of paunch around his midsection. With close-cropped hair showing a slight smattering of gray and creamy ebony skin, the affable African-American could easily have been featured on the cover of GQ magazine.

He'd once been known as Dr. Robert Fogler, whose idyllic existence was ripped asunder when he suffered a series of head injuries while helping a young woman who was being assaulted by two hoodlums. His life as a prominent obstetrician in Baltimore ended and his existence as a homeless man began when he awoke with injury-induced amnesia in a rundown neighborhood of Washington, D.C.

In a stroke of luck, he was found sleeping on the street by William Collonem from the Bethlehem Mission for Homeless Men. Because he couldn't remember his name or any other facts about his life, he was simply called Chauncey and the name stuck.

"You have to go to the doctor's office and have your hand attended to," Chauncey said. "Don't worry, I'll keep an eye on Rex. As a matter of fact, after lunch he and I will probably take a nap, so don't be overly concerned about us."

Rex, a rambunctious Golden Retriever, was adopted by Sarah when she found him wandering the rural roads of Virginia. Now he spent his days between naps guarding the farm.

"I never worry about you two," Sarah said with a chuckle, then winced as a searing bolt of pain flew from her injured hand.

"Well, let's go then," Nadine said brusquely, heading toward her battered Ford pick-up.

Sarah accepted her fate and trailed behind her.

The twenty-mile ride to Spinale was uneventful with Sarah cradling her injured hand swaddled in white gauze bandages. Jerking to a stop in front of the doctor's office, Nadine turned toward Sarah.

"You'll like Dan. He's patched me back together every time I've hurt myself."

"I don't like doctors," Sarah reminded her, yanking the door handle with her uninjured hand and sliding out of the truck.

The doctor's office was located in an old but well-kept Victorian house on Main Street. The meticulously maintained sidewalk was swept clean and had no weeds growing in the cracks, unlike the neighbors. A discrete, gold-lettered sign designed to look like an antique hung on a lamp post. It slightly overhung the black cast-iron fence and announced that this was the office of Daniel Lewis, M.D.

The cavernous reception room was empty except for a receptionist in the corner. It had once been the parlor of the house, but now boasted every imaginable modern amenity to make it inviting. A large, walnut coffee table was littered with dog-eared magazines.

An enclosed area was obviously designated for children, because it seemed to hold more Fisher-Price toys than the local Wal-Mart. A wall-mounted television quietly played a DVD, reminding everyone of the benefits of getting their annual flu shots early.

"Hi, Mary."

"Hi, Nadine," Mary Moore, the receptionist, crooned with a wide smile and dazzling red lipstick much too eye-catching for a professional to be wearing.

She was hunched behind a computer set in the middle of an ancient office desk. A corkboard on the wall behind her was plastered with hand-scrawled notes stuck in place with brilliantly tinted pushpins.

"Thanks for getting here quickly. Dr. Lewis has plans for a bicycle ride with his daughters this afternoon."

"Well, we don't want to hold him up," Nadine said. "This is Sarah Collins. She's a doctor also, a chiropractor, but she really needs Dr. Lewis's help this morning."

"I can see that," Mary said, casting a suspicious look toward Sarah and the blood that was beginning to peek through the homespun bandages. "If you can help her fill out this paperwork, I'll get her back as soon as possible."

Mary furtively glanced at Sarah before disappearing into the back office.

They sat down with a pen and stack of paper attached to a clipboard. Sarah whispered to Nadine, "My, she's a real peach, isn't she?"

"I noticed she didn't say a single word to you, if that's what you mean."

"Not to mention those daggers she sent my way."

"Oh, you noticed that look, did you?" Nadine asked with a crooked smile, as she handed the clipboard to Sarah. "Put this in your lap and fill it out the best you can. I'll help if you can't do it."

After Sarah completed the paperwork, Mary escorted them into the treatment room.

"You can have a seat and Dr. Lewis will be with you shortly," Mary said coolly, waving nonchalantly toward two wooden chairs facing a huge desk.

The furniture looked ancient, but Sarah noticed the medical equipment was state-of-the-art technology as she warily took in her surroundings.

Dr. Lewis entered the room three minutes later under the close scrutiny of Sarah's unwavering glare.

He was forty years old and tall, but his full head of slightly graying hair added to the illusion of additional height. He was clean-shaven and wore an immaculately ironed and heavily starched white shirt under his pressed laboratory coat. A stethoscope was draped over his broad shoulders highlighting his well-muscled chest, which overshadowed a slightly paunchy belly.

Nice timing, Sarah thought cynically. *The delay provided the right theatrical effect for maximum impact on a new patient. And the brilliantly white smock with your name embroidered on it really adds a nice touch to establish the doctor/patient relationship.*

"Hello, I'm Dr. Lewis," Daniel said, taking care to extend his right hand toward Sarah as he glanced at her bandage-shrouded left hand.

He hesitated for a split second as their eyes met.

"Hello, I'm Dr. Collins," Sarah said haughtily. "May I call you Daniel, and you can call me Sarah?"

What in the hell is the matter with you? Nadine thought, aghast at the way Sarah was acting.

Daniel quickly recovered from Sarah's affront.

"It's nice to meet you, Sarah," he said with a sudden, unmistakable air of professionalism. "Now, what can I help you with?"

"I cut my hand on a rusty hook while cleaning out a shed," Sarah said. "The tendons are showing, but appear to be undamaged. I don't detect any nerve damage, but it needs a few stitches, and a tetanus shot may be a good idea."

"Well, let's have a look at it," he said, reaching for her hand.

"I'll unwrap it," Sarah snapped.

Nadine sat silently with her mouth slightly agape.

"Yep, it's a mess alright," Daniel said, after observing her mangled hand for a long time.

"Very professional assessment," Sarah said flatly. "Can you fix it or do I have to go to the hospital?"

Nadine seemed to begin saying something, but couldn't form the words before Daniel replied.

"I can take care of it," Daniel said, mimicking Sarah's manner. "If you want me to."

"Of course I want you to," Sarah shot back. "That's why I'm here."

"Well, let's get to it then," he said.

He chatted amicably with Nadine as he worked on Sarah's wound.

"There you go," he said. "That should do for a few days. Stop back on Wednesday or Thursday so I can have another look at it."

"I'm not back in this area until Friday," Sarah said, as though he should have known.

"Then get in here Friday or see another doctor," he said, with an air of finality.

"Thanks, Dan," Nadine said sweetly, forcing an extra-large smile. "Sarah and I are planning on having lunch at D'Amato's now, while we're over this way. Would you like to join us?"

"Thanks anyway," he said with a pleasant smile directed toward Nadine. "But I have a date to go bike riding with my daughters. It helps get me out in the fresh air for a little exercise."

"Maybe some other time," Nadine said. "Be careful on those country roads."

"That's for sure," Daniel replied. "It would be nice to be able to enjoy a little fresh air without having to worry about being run over."

"Sarah and I are going to start shooting sporting clays at the Millvale Sportsman's Club on Saturday nights to get away for a little while and relax," Nadine said, hoping she had remembered correctly that Millvale was a course he visited regularly.

"Really? I shoot at Millvale just about every Saturday night," he said, warming to the topic. "It's my night out. My mother watches the girls and I get a little time to myself away from everything."

Sarah listened intently, but didn't join in the conversation.

"Maybe we'll see you there some day," Nadine said. "Thanks for all your help."

"Yes, thank you," Sarah added woodenly.

"You're welcome," Daniel said as he turned to leave. "Just see Mary on your way out and she'll take care of you."

As soon as they got back into the pick-up truck and pulled out of the parking space, Nadine snapped, "What the hell's the matter with you?"

"What the hell are you talking about?"

"You know damned well what I'm talking about," Nadine said. "You were decidedly rude to him, and for no good reason."

"He was an uppity pain in the ass," Sarah said defiantly. "What's it to you?"

"He was not a pain in the ass and you know it. He was rather smitten with you and acted like the perfect gentleman. You were the eminent pain in the ass!"

"I was not," Sarah fired back. "We just passed D'Amato's. Aren't we going to eat?"

"A pain in the ass like you doesn't deserve to eat," Nadine said, concentrating on the road to avoid looking at Sarah.

After a short period of silence she added in a calmer voice, "I think you're attracted to him and it scares you."

"Go to hell," Sarah said.

Nadine allowed the deathly silence to sit heavily, knowing Sarah needed time to sort her thoughts.

"Okay, for the last few weeks I've been thinking about resuming a romantic life," Sarah said suddenly. "I knew this day would come, but I didn't expect it this early and I'm uncomfortable now that it's here."

"It's okay. You have a void in your life and nature abhors a void," Nadine said. "Nature has to fill every void and this may be the time you get your void filled."

Both women looked at each other surprised, and then broke into a fit of laughter. The hilarity only subsided when they were forced to stop and suck in gasping breaths of air.

"You better keep your eyes on the road before we wreck," Sarah said.

"And you better wipe the tears out of your eyes," Nadine replied.

"So tell me about Dan Lewis. I heard about his daughters twice, but no mention of his wife."

"She died five years ago from ovarian cancer," Nadine said sadly. "They were a very close couple and he took her death extremely hard, as you can imagine."

"And he was left with two daughters."

"Amy was six and Kathy was eight years old when their mother died. Dan has made them the focus of his life."

"Amy must be eleven now and Kathy thirteen," Sarah figured out. "Teenage girls," she added, an icy sense of trepidation slithering down her spine.

"Teenage girls aren't the worst thing in the world," Nadine said. "Near the top of the list maybe, but not the worst."

Both women giggled knowing there was more than a grain of truth in it. A comfortable silence fell between them and they enjoyed a few minutes of quiet.

"So you're going to teach me how to shoot sporting clays?" Sarah asked tentatively.

"Yeah," Nadine said simply. "I guess I have to now that I've opened my big mouth to Dan."

CHAPTER 3

METH DEALING

"Okay, this is what we gonna do," John McGuire said, standing at the head of the decrepit kitchen table while his eyes darted menacingly at his three men slouched around it.

He moved a few of the empty beer bottles to avoid knocking them over and diverting the limited attention of his cohorts.

"I rented this farmhouse for a year and paid half up front from the money we're makin' in Tennessee. That'll keep the landlord from gettin' too nosey and give me time to figure out what we're doin' and get you lazy bastards organized."

"Nacco, you and Twister have to get the lab set up on Jacob's Mountain behind this place. I want it over on the other side up near the top."

"You mean we have to lug all that shit up and over that mountain?" Twister complained. "Why don't we just keep everything on this side so we can get to it easier?"

"Because, you dumb shit, if the lab is busted we don't want it obvious we're operatin' it out of here. We'll have more labs scattered around this whole area and we don't want the place we're livin' in bein' discovered."

"Fine," Twister said disgustedly. "We'll do it your way."

"Damned right we'll do it my way. The only way we do things is my way, you understand that?" McGuire said, looming menacingly above them.

"Yeah, that's the way we've always done it, and things have turned out okay," Nacco said in an attempt to avoid violence.

"And things will turn out good here too. Just do what yer told."

"Are we gonna make enough meth to keep Tennessee supplied and be able to start new operations in Richmond and D.C.?" Nacco asked.

"We'll be able to make plenty once we get all the labs set up," McGuire said, glaring at Twister to keep him from saying anything, then his eyes shifted back to Nacco. "We supply Tennessee, and then use the money from there to get the Richmond and D.C. networks up and running."

"We gonna be gettin' into some trouble with them Mexican boys, eh?" Squeaky asked with more nasally twang than usual. "What we gonna do about them and the boys they already supplyin'?"

"We gonna take what's ours," McGuire said with a steady gaze. "We doin' real good in Tennessee and now we're growin'. If we stop growin' then we'll start shrinkin', and you don't want us to be on the run from them boys, do you?"

"Hell no! We got a right to be here, they don't," Squeaky said, looking at his two partners for approval. "We gonna get rich and live like millionaires."

"Yeah, that we gonna do," McGuire added. "Now let's get down to business. Nacco, you buy the stuff we need?"

"Yeah, I got everything on the list you give me. It's in the truck. I'll get more when we set up the other labs."

"Twister, you get the chemicals?"

"Yeah, I got antifreeze, Drano, lantern fuel, coffee filters, coolers, and all those other gadgets you said we need."

"Good, then all we'll need is the narcotic shit we make the stuff out of."

"And I'm workin' on that," Squeaky said. "I have to find some new suppliers 'cause of the volume we're workin' at now. We're growin' so fast it's gettin' hard to keep up with demand."

"You better make sure we able to keep up with demand, 'cause we start losing ground to them Mexican boys it'll be your ass," McGuire said. "I want to keep pushin' this shit, so you find any way you can to keep supplies up."

"You know I'm on it," Squeaky said with a wicked grin.

"Okay, we set for now," McGuire said with a sigh of relief. "Now all I need is for you three to stay out of trouble."

CHAPTER 4

SPORTING CLAYS

"Not too bad," Nadine said, as the clay target disappeared in a puff of black dust. "I think you're finally starting to get the hang of this after four trips to different sporting clays ranges."

"Thanks," Sarah said, skillfully lowering her shotgun and flipping open the action with a deft flick of her thumb. The empty shell flew past her shoulder to land on the grass. "What's the name of this sporting clays game again?"

"It's a form of sporting clays called Five Stand. On Saturday mornings this shooting facility offers a much larger course through the woods, and then towards the evening they shoot this condensed course of Five Stand here by the clubhouse under the lights."

"It's fun. Kind of like golf with a shotgun."

"That's how I've heard it described."

"When do you think he'll get here?" Sarah asked with a tinge of concern.

"He arrived when you were shooting stand three," Nadine said. "He's in the clubhouse."

"Then I need a soda. I'm feeling a little parched."

"Yeah, it's all the exertion walking fifty feet between stands we've been doing," Nadine said sarcastically. "It will definitely parch you."

Not many words were exchanged as they trudged up the slight rise toward the clubhouse.

It was an austere structure with concrete block walls painted an off-white color. The history of its members was exhibited in faded pictures and ratty-looking taxidermy from decades past.

One end of the clubhouse had a four-foot high stage with sound equipment for presentations, while the other end held a cafeteria-style snack bar. Coffee, hot chocolate, and soda were served alongside juicy-looking hamburgers and fat, grilled hot dogs. Bags of potato chips and pretzels rounded out the fare. Alcohol was prohibited.

The middle of the clubhouse was filled with trestle tables and folding chairs. Homemade wooden gun racks lined the walls to accommodate firearms while shooters enjoyed their food and refreshments.

Daniel was seated alone at a table in middle of the room. He was reading a tattered and finger-smudged American Rifleman magazine and waiting for his squad to be called to the shooting line. He curiously glanced up to see who was entering the clubhouse and his face brightened when he recognized the two women.

Acting surprised and happy to see him, Nadine waved emphatically above her head then strode toward him. Sarah made an effort to keep a friendly smile plastered on her immaculately lipstick-painted lips. Daniel laid his magazine aside, stood up without taking his eyes off them, and moved smoothly to the end of the table to greet them.

"Dan, it's good to see you," Nadine said. "You remember Sarah, don't you?"

"I most certainly do," he said as he took Nadine's hand. "How have you been?"

Not bothering to wait for an answer from Nadine he turned toward Sarah.

"It's nice to see you again, Sarah," he said cautiously.

She accepted his gently offered handshake in a friendly manner while maintaining steady eye contact.

"You'll have to excuse my cold hands," Sarah said, while her rosy cheeks appeared to blush a deeper shade. "It's getting a little chilly out there."

"No problem," Daniel said, continuing to gaze directly into the depths of her large, brown eyes. "It gets nippy up here in the mountains at this time of year, as soon as the sun goes down."

They exchanged smiles as a tongue-tied silence enveloped them. In a fit of recognition they realized they were still holding hands, and embarrassed, broke their grip.

"I'm going to get some soda," Nadine said to break the awkward moment. "Would you like anything?"

"No thanks," Daniel said. "I'm waiting for my squad to be called. I have to be ready to go on a second's notice."

Nadine said, "I'm going to park Sarah with you for a minute while I get the sodas, if that's okay with you."

"Of course," he said, with a sparkle in his eye.

Sarah pulled out a chair directly across the table from where Daniel had been seated, settled herself gracefully, and patiently waited for Daniel to maneuver back around the table and sit.

"Before you get called out to shoot," Sarah said clumsily. "I want to apologize."

"You have nothing to apologize for," he lied unconvincingly.

"Yes I do. The way I acted in your office was boorish and totally out of character for me. I'm sorry for getting off on the wrong foot with you."

He looked at the tabletop as if the words he was searching for were written there.

"You were hurting and out of sorts," he said slowly. "I'm sure you see it in your patients all the time."

"My behavior was inexcusable and you know it," she said as his lower jaw dropped ever so slightly. Before he could say anything she went on, "I'd like to start over as if we never met, if that's okay with you."

He sat staring at her dumbfounded as Sarah extended her hand toward him.

"Hello, I'm Sarah Collins," she said with a large, friendly smile. "What's your name?"

"My name is Dan. Dan Lewis," he said hesitantly as a huge smile burst from his lips and he took her hand in his. "It's nice to make your acquaintance."

Again their hands lingered together for a second too long and they both abandoned their handshake with an uncomfortable shifting of their gaze away from each other.

After a second of self-conscious silence, Sarah gathered her composure.

"So, do you come here often?" she asked with a flirtatious curl to her smile.

"Yes I do," Daniel said through a boyish grin. "Do you?"

"No, I don't," she replied, carrying on the game. "This is my first time here. It's rather, uh, quaint."

They both giggled in a gushing release of tension.

"How's your hand?" he asked with genuine concern in his voice.

"It's healed perfectly. At least that's what my internist friend said. He even commented on how good of a job the attending physician did."

He blushed at hearing the comment.

"So what are you doing cleaning up rusty old tools?" he asked.

"I'm making my new farm my own and clearing out decades of accumulated junk," she said simply. "I hear you also live on a farm."

"Yes, it's been in my family for four generations. And I'm afraid that any clutter is of my own making."

A trap boy called, "Squad seven! Squad seven is ready to line up on the shooting line at the number one station. Squad number seven is now forming at the shooting line."

"Excuse me," Daniel said to Sarah before turning away. "John?" he called to the trap boy.

"Yes, sir?" John asked courteously as he walked toward them.

"John, is the squad full?"

"No sir, there are still two spots open."

Turning his attention back to Sarah, he asked eagerly, "Would you and Nadine like to join me in a round?"

She glanced toward the snack bar. "Nadine seems to be tied up in a conversation. But I'd love to shoot another round."

"Good, but we'll have to hurry."

"Oh! I'm out of shells. I have to get some more."

"I'll take care of it," he said, clumsily standing up and almost knocking his chair over. "Do you need twelve or twenty gauge?"

"I shoot twenty gauge."

While Daniel went to the pro shop for the shotgun shells and to register Sarah for squad seven, she cast a tentative glance toward Nadine. Their eyes met and the knowing smiles they exchanged said it all.

Sarah casually began gathering her gear.

Stay cool, she reminded herself. *Don't hurry. Stay cool. It'll be just fine.*

Daniel returned and handed her two boxes of Winchester AA shells. "I got you an additional box just in case you need some extras. I hope seven-and-a-half shot is okay?"

"It'll be fine," she answered calmly as she accepted the shells. "Thank you."

Sarah breathed a sigh of relief that he seemed to be just a bit flustered.

CHAPTER 5

NADINE'S LEMONADE

"Thank you, gentlemen, for coming over to help me move all those fence posts down the pasture," Nadine said, flicking a wisp of hair from her brow after an afternoon of hard labor on her farm, The Shire.

"No problem," Chauncey replied. "Saturday is a good day for me, and William arrived at noon so the hottest part of the day was over by the time we started."

"It was still plenty hot out there," she said. "How about some lemonade? It's freshly squeezed."

"That sounds like a great idea," William replied with a tired smile crossing his dirt-streaked face. "Doing a little honest labor sure makes me thirsty."

"Go sit in the shade under the sugar maple in the front yard and I'll be with you in a minute."

Nadine turned and walked toward her house while Chauncey and William forced their leaden feet to move toward the shade of the maple. Chauncey flopped into an aluminum chair. William wisely lowered himself gingerly onto a wooden Adirondack chair that would better support his three hundred and twenty pounds. Aged thirty-three and standing well over six feet tall, in the past William's size served him well at the Bethlehem Mission on the occasions when he had to convince the mission's unruly guests to obey the rules.

It was only natural that when Chauncey began spending his weekends at Sarah's farm that his friend William would eventually become an occasional guest at the cabin he was converting from a long-unused workshop.

William appreciated the much too infrequent opportunities to escape the dismal slums of Washington, D. C.

As soon as William saw Nadine appear at the inner door to the Florida Room marking the entrance to her home, he sprang from his chair. It only took a few steps to clumsily work the kinks out of his stiff joints before he was able to nimbly glide up to the screen door and hold it open for her.

"Thank you, William," she said sweetly. She looked directly into his eyes for a split second before moving toward the umbrella covered glass-topped table sitting under the tree.

Lively conversation made the time go quickly as they enjoyed their refreshments.

Suddenly Chauncey said, "Well, I have to go. I want to finish some house cleaning before leaving to shoot sporting clays tonight."

"So you're making it a regular routine to go shooting at Millvale on Saturdays?" Nadine said with a teasing tone in her voice.

"Yeah, Sarah still doesn't want to go by herself even though she spends the entire evening talking with Dr. Lewis."

"Have you met other people, so you're not burdened with those two lovebirds?"

"I wouldn't exactly describe them as lovebirds, but I'm getting to know some of the folks at Millvale rather well. There are quite a few very nice people there and they're more than willing to share their knowledge and experience with me to help improve my shooting game."

"Chauncey ..." Nadine said slyly. "Some of those 'folks' wouldn't happen to be the ladies who shoot there, would they?"

"Well, some of them are women," Chauncey said, blushing slightly and glancing sheepishly toward the ground. "But I'm only interested in how much they can teach me about the sport."

They all looked at each other, and then laughed out loud.

"Yeah, sure," she said between gasps. "You better get going so your cleaning doesn't get neglected on the way to your shooting lessons."

"Thanks for the lemonade, Nadine," he said cheerfully, as he grunted softly then rose stiffly from his chair. "William, I'll see you tomorrow and we'll knock off a few more of the finishing touches on my cottage."

"I'll see you then."

Nadine and William watched silently as Chauncey stiffly clambered into his Mercedes SUV. It was one of the things he retained in the divorce settlement from his wife, Irene.

"You've got a good friend there," she said appraisingly.

"Yes, I do," William said in agreement. "I've been blessed to have met him."

"How did you two meet?"

"Believe it or not, I picked him up off the street."

"Really? Tell me about it."

"I was working at the Bethlehem Mission for Homeless Men in Washington as a social worker," he explained. "One of my duties was to drive a van around to the areas men congregate in the wintertime, like steam grates and under bridges and overpasses, to get out of the cold and wet weather."

"It's not my idea of a good time, but go ahead," she said with a mixed tone of interest and trepidation tinging her voice.

"Well, someone has to do it or these guys will die when the temperatures plunge below freezing," he said. "It was on one of those runs that I picked up Chauncey."

"I never heard this story," she fibbed, as she leaned forward in her chair.

"Chauncey probably doesn't remember most of it because he was beat up badly and wasn't too coherent."

"How'd he get beat up?"

"No one knows," William replied solemnly. "When Doc Reynolds checked him out in the morning he had gashes on his head, face, back, and thigh. Some of the gashes were pretty deep and overall he was a mess."

"It sounds like he was a wreck."

"That's not the worst of it. He had shards of glass in his hands and knees. What Doc Reynolds couldn't find and remove with tweezers took weeks to work out on their own."

"Is that how he lost his memory?"

"No one knows."

"Didn't he have an MRI or anything to see if he had brain damage?"

"Nadine, these were homeless people, men that society has forgotten and would rather have just go away and not bother anyone. There isn't money for things like MRIs unless it's obviously a life-threatening situation—then by law the emergency room has to take them. That's the only way they'll be able to afford medical care."

"What about that doctor's fees?"

"Doc Reynolds does it for free. He says it's his way to repay his debt to society. That's his private joke, because he has a nice practice in an upscale neighborhood," he said with the tinge of a smile.

"Then how'd Chauncey meet Sarah?" she asked, feigning ignorance of the way they met.

"Doc Reynolds arranged that. Chauncey had really severe migraine headaches, and pain in his back and down his arms, so he thought chiropractic care would help. He arranged for Sarah, Dr. Collins I mean, to take him on as a charity patient. She made a huge difference in him, but he still has a lot of stiffness and pain, especially in the mornings."

"She was able to help a lot of people when she was working as a doctor," she said. "But those days are gone forever with her shoulder having been replaced and all."

"Yeah. It's a shame."

"So, what about you? Do you have any family?"

William's eyes dropped and his shoulders slumped.

She said, "Wrong question. I'm sorry for asking."

"No, it's okay. It's just really difficult for me to think about them. Talking about it always causes me to break down and that's embarrassing."

"Crying for a good reason is nothing to be embarrassed about," she said, stifling the urge to reach out and comfort him. It was heart-rending to see such a large and strong man weakened by his emotions.

"Then I guess crying is okay, because it's a good reason. You see, it all started when I was in college. There was this really great girl named Christie and I fell madly in love with her," he said, a mask of pain clouding his features.

Straightening his shoulders as if to steel himself for what was coming, he continued, "To make a long story short, she ended up pregnant and we couldn't afford for both of us to continue with school." His eyes remained fixed on the ground. "Then the second one came along. The babies were named Jessie and Jamie. Jessie was the oldest. They were such a beautiful bunch."

Tears began streaming down his dirt-streaked face, leaving rivulets in the dust. He wiped the tears away with the back of his hand, smearing the muddy mess.

"William, it's okay. You don't have to go into it."

"Yes, I do. I have to learn to get over this somehow and telling the tale, regardless of how difficult that is, may be the answer. At least that's what my psychology professor said a long time ago."

"Well, if you have to, go on. But stop anytime you need to," she said, a tiny tear forming in the corner of her eye.

"I switched my major from accounting to psychology and sociology because I wanted to save the world. Christie agreed. We were so young and foolhardy."

"That's what being young is all about."

"We were living in a three-room rundown boarding house because we couldn't afford anything better. The heat didn't work too well so we had a kerosene heater to keep the pipes in the kitchen from freezing. I came home one day and found them all snuggled together in bed. They were trying to stay warm, and they were dead from carbon monoxide poisoning. The damned heater killed my family."

He broke down in gut-wrenching sobs, his fists crammed into the sides of his head.

"Oh, William, I'm so sorry," she said, tears flowing freely. "I'm so sorry."

"I should have just crawled in bed with them and let the gas kill me too, but I was too stupid. All the fresh air from the windows I threw open, and the breaths I tried blowing into them were useless. It was all useless …" he said. "The EMTs said I did everything I could, but it was too late."

"Such a tragedy."

"Yeah, so I finished my last semester with an internship at the mission and just stayed on until Reverend Yates left. I guess I was hiding out from the world. I really didn't know what else to do or where to go."

Happy for a reason to change the subject, Nadine asked, "Why did he leave?"

"The stress was really beginning to get to him. It's difficult working in that environment," he said after loudly clearing his throat. "He managed to land a nice but temporary position with a large church in Shreveport, Louisiana. He said the area and people are really nice."

"I hope it works out for him."

"You and I both."

"So you quit when he did."

William chuckled, and then said, "You can say that."

"What do you mean?"

"The new guy came in like gangbusters. He didn't like the way anything was being run and wasn't afraid to voice his opinion. He was especially livid about Reverend Yates faxing invoices for the mission up here so Chauncey could do the mission's bookkeeping."

"Chauncey was doing the mission's bookkeeping?"

"Ever since he lived there," William said. "That's how he got the job being Sarah's bookkeeper. He's pretty good with numbers."

"Was he working at Sarah's office when her husband was killed?"

"Yep, he was with her when she ran into the parking lot where her husband was murdered. Then he rode to the hospital in the ambulance with her after she fell and hurt herself."

"Sarah never told me all that."

"I was talking with her brother-in-law before he and his family moved to Omaha. Apparently, he and Chauncey kept a silent vigil beside Sarah's bedside the entire time she was in the hospital."

"Wow. I never knew. So you ended up here because you knew Chauncey?"

"Yeah, I used to have lunch a couple times a week with him at his apartment in D.C. when he was working at Sarah's office. It was a nice chance to escape from the mission and have some peace and quiet. Reverend Yates joined us sometimes. I guess it was the first sign he was burning out on his job at the mission."

"Did you live at the mission?"

"Yeah, I had my own little apartment there. It wasn't much, just two rooms, but it was all I needed."

"So when you quit your job, you lost your home too."

"Yeah," he said with a short laugh. "That's when I called Chauncey and he found me a room to rent on a monthly basis until I could figure out what to do."

"And now you're working at the County Turf and Tractor store."

"Yeah, I landed that job as soon as I got here," he said, slightly embarrassed. "I'm working their front desk and taking care of customer's paperwork and such."

"You sound like you're ashamed of your job."

"Oh no, don't get the wrong idea. It's a good, honest job, but I'm used to being in charge and only having Reverend Yates to answer to. Now I'm low man on the totem pole and everyone tells me what to do, when to do it, and how to do it."

"So you're used to being your own boss, for the most part, and this job isn't sitting too well with you."

"Something like that," he said with a chuckle. "So how about you? I've been running off at the mouth for way too long."

Nadine laughed.

"My life hasn't been nearly as interesting as… as everything you just told me," she said, careful to avoid the subject of William's loss. "Well, I went to the same college as Sarah and we ended up rooming together for three years. That relationship is obviously still going on. Then I got married and began this horse farm with my husband, but we got divorced."

William said, "I don't want to get too personal, but it doesn't make sense why a man would leave a great woman like you and give up living on such a wonderful farm."

"Well, he didn't leave me exactly," Nadine said, looking into William's eyes. "You see, I came back from a visit to my mother's unexpectedly. It's not every day you find your husband being mounted like a horse by another man. Come to think of it, his boyfriend was even hung like a horse."

William looked at her in silence for a stunned moment before breaking into a fit of laughter.

"And you said your life wasn't as—what term did you use? As 'interesting' as mine? I wonder what you'd consider a very interesting life?"

"Well, when you put it that way," she said between giggles. "I guess a few moments of it were rather different."

"So what did you do?"

"I didn't know what to do other than scream. If I remember correctly I screamed all the way from the bedroom to my car, and then drove like a maniac to a lawyer's office in town. I didn't know what else to do."

"That must have been an attention-grabbing story to make the lawyer's day."

"Yes, it was," Nadine said, suddenly very serious. "He told me to go home since he didn't want it to look like I had abandoned the household. He thought it would strengthen my case, and legally at least, he was right. But by the time I got back home my husband—my ex-husband I should say—and his boyfriend were gone."

"Lawyers think differently than the rest of us."

"You're damned right about that!" Nadine said. "My ex didn't want the story to become public knowledge, so the divorce was handled discretely and quickly with the settlement being very much in my favor."

"And that's why you got the farm, I suppose?"

"That's the way I got the whole farm in my name only."

"I'm sorry you had to go through so much torment to get such a nice farm."

"It was hell for a while, but I got through it," she said with a forlorn look. Then she brightened. "But life goes on and I adopted a new attitude. As soon as a person accepts reality, the past slowly recedes into the murky depths of time. I think that's one of the mechanisms God gives us to cope and not lose our mind over the shit that happens to us as we go through life."

"Yeah, I guess that's true," William said, his demeanor taking on an ominous hue.

Not wanting to see him sink into the doldrums of his memory, Nadine changed the subject.

"So what are your plans now that you've moved up this way?"

"I'm not really sure," he said, raising his eyes. "This is really a nice, peaceful area especially compared to D.C., but I've only been here three weeks and haven't looked beyond getting settled into my room."

"You keep saying 'room'," she said. "Is it really just a room, or do you have a small apartment?"

"No, it's just a bedroom. A nice old guy in town has to rent out one of the rooms in his house to help make ends meet. It was available, I needed a place to stay right away, and it was near Chauncey, so I took it. It's really important that I can rent it month-to-month. By not being committed to a lease I can figure out where I'm going and what I'm going to do, then act upon it without being tied down by a piece of paper."

"Do you have a private entrance?"

"Kind of," he said. "I use the back door that leads into the kitchen. My bedroom and a small bath are off the kitchen."

"At least you have a place to cook."

"No, not really. The old man is a bit apprehensive about letting anyone use his kitchen and utensils, not to mention being near his food, so I just keep a small refrigerator in my room."

"What do you eat?" she asked, alarmed.

"Anything that's small enough to fit in the mini fridge and doesn't have to be cooked."

"Which is?"

"Sandwiches and cold cereal with milk mostly. I'm able to use paper plates and bowls so I don't have anything other than a few dirty utensils, because I have to wash them in the bathroom sink. It's easy to wash a plastic spoon or fork, but dishes and pots would be too difficult."

"Oh my God!" Nadine's mouth flew open in amazement. "When's the last time you had a hot meal?"

"At the mission," he said simply.

"That was over three weeks ago! We're going to change that tonight," she said firmly. "I have a nice venison stew in the crock pot and a good cabernet to wash it down with, or do you have other plans?"

"Nadine, I couldn't impose on you. You've been more than hospitable already with the lemonade and everything."

"Baloney. You did more work out there in one afternoon than I could have done in a week," she said, before a coquettish expression spread across her face. "And it's only fair I feed you."

"But I'm all dirty and sweaty. I'm not really presentable for ..."

"No problem," she interrupted him. "We'll both take care of the horses and put them to bed, then we'll get cleaned up. I can throw your clothes in the washer and by the time you're done in the shower they'll be clean and dry."

"That's kind of the way we did things at the mission when we brought the men in for the night," he said.

"You never had food this good at the mission," she said, standing up with only a slightly stiff posture. "That I can promise you."

MADELYN LEWIS

"Hello Dan," Sarah said coyly as she walked up behind Daniel. He stood at the snack counter of the Millvale Sportsman's Club, talking with a vivacious redhead.

Daniel spun around with a look of surprise.

"Oh, hello Sarah," he said absently, before remembering his manners. "Sarah, I would like you to meet my sister, Madelyn."

Madelyn looked Sarah directly in the eyes. "Hello, it's nice to meet you. Dan has told me so much about you."

Her smile was genuine, and her emerald green eyes shimmered under heavily mascaraed eyelashes, but they seemed to have lost the vigor of life.

She has such terribly dark circles under her eyes and her hair is a bit disheveled for such a well-dressed woman, Sarah thought as she tried to determine how to handle this unexpected meeting.

Deciding against making a hasty judgment, Sarah returned her smile and said, "Hello Madelyn, it's nice to meet you."

"Madelyn has recently decided to move back into this area and is staying at our farm for a few days—not more than three days," he added much too quickly. "Until she can find an apartment."

The flustered tone of his voice is a sure sign that all is not right with this situation, Sarah guessed. *And the fact he specified such a short period of time for her to find an apartment is really odd.*

"Well, welcome back," Sarah said. The furtive glance between Daniel and his sister made it obvious there was tension between them. "Are you moving back permanently?"

"I'm not sure right now," she said with a nervous glance in Daniel's direction. "I have to make some decisions that'll determine where I go from here."

Not sure what else to say, Sarah said, "Do you shoot sporting clays, or are you here to learn?"

"I've never shot a gun before," she said nervously. "Even though I was raised on the farm, shooting and hunting was always left to Dad and the boys."

Madelyn appeared to be only slightly younger than Sarah, and was taller. She was much more stocky and muscular, with a decided weight advantage. Mousy-brown roots with a smattering of gray confirmed that the soft, flowing curls of brassy red hair wasn't her natural color.

"Would you like to join us to learn the game or would you rather watch a few rounds before jumping in?" Sarah asked.

"I better just watch," Madelyn replied uneasily, wiggling a dazzling set of long, acrylic fingernails painted hot pink with floral decals. "I don't think these would make it easy to shoot a shotgun."

"You may be right."

"We were just waiting for our hamburgers," Daniel said. "Madelyn hasn't eaten today and is famished. Would you like anything?"

"No thanks, I've had dinner. I'll just have a caffeine-free soda."

"I'll get it," he said eagerly, glad to have a task to keep him occupied. "Why don't you two grab us a few seats?"

"That sounds like a plan."

As the two women wound their way around scattered folding chairs to an unoccupied table, Madelyn said, "Dan has been telling me about you. He seems impressed."

"Well, thank you," Sarah said pleasantly as she pulled out a chair for Madelyn then chose one for herself across the table. "I'm sorry to say we've been spending most of our time learning about each other and haven't gotten around to exchanging much about our families yet."

"It wouldn't surprise me if he didn't want to talk about me much," she said as she cast her eyes shamefully toward the ground. "There's not much to tell about me that he would be proud of."

"I'm sure that's not true."

"Actually, it's very true and unfortunate," she said with a tremor in her voice. "I left ten years ago and moved to Tennessee with my boyfriend. Things didn't go well. Dan knew how things would turn out. He was vehemently against me going, but he couldn't stop me. Dan knew my boyfriend wasn't any good, but I wouldn't listen. You know, little miss know-it-all." She shook her head with embarrassment.

Straightening to her full height and raising her head to show she still had pride, Madelyn looked straight at Sarah and said, "Naturally, I didn't listen to my big brother, and now I'm crawling back home begging for his help."

"Madelyn, you really don't have to tell me any of this," Sarah said uncomfortably. "I'm not family and you don't have to explain anything to me."

"Please, call me Maddy," she said with a wan smile. "Everyone else does."

"Thanks, Maddy," Sarah said, uncertain as to what else to say. She was thankful to see Daniel weaving his way towards them.

"Here's Dan with the food," Sarah said with a twinge of relief.

After Daniel distributed the hamburgers and sodas, he sat beside Sarah and glanced around as if lost for anything to say. An uncomfortable hush enveloped them until Maddy broke the thorny silence.

"I was just telling Sarah why I've come back."

"Oh …" Daniel muttered.

"Actually, she hadn't gotten into anything other than telling me that she lived in Tennessee for ten years," Sarah said, in an effort to bridge the communication gap between the siblings.

"Maddy, maybe you better explain your situation," Daniel said hesitantly.

Sarah's eyes flitted uneasily back and forth between the two.

"Well, to take up where I left off," Maddy said in a quavering voice. "I lived with my boyfriend, John McGuire, for ten years. Things weren't too bad until about two years ago, and then he started changing. First it was just little things, and then he began getting real possessive. He would follow me to work and be waiting for me when I finished. I really didn't think too much about it until he began following me shopping. Shopping! For crying out loud!"

Sarah didn't know what to say or do. She was expecting to shoot a few rounds of sporting clays with her boyfriend, and now she was embroiled in the middle of affairs that didn't concern her. She stared at Daniel with irritation evident in her gaze.

In a hollow attempt to be polite, Sarah asked without looking at Maddy, "He started this strange behavior all of a sudden?"

Her gaze remained frozen on Daniel, who dropped his head in resignation.

Feeling sorry for the situation Daniel was in, Sarah softened her scowl. After all, this mess wasn't of his making. But being a responsible person, he would shoulder the burden of helping his sister.

"Yeah, it was like day and night," Maddy said, oblivious to the discord between her brother and Sarah. "Of course, he began hanging around with a bunch of losers about the time he began getting strange."

"That can make people change," Sarah said.

"But this was different," Maddy replied. "I didn't know it until only recently, but these guys were meth-heads. They not only use the stuff, but they make and sell it too."

"Methamphetamine?"

"Yeah, that's it. I don't know if he started using it and that made him strange, or if he just started getting paranoid because he sells it."

Sarah sat in stunned disbelief.

With a deep sigh, Daniel explained, "Recently John began pressuring Maddy into setting him up with places around here to manufacture methamphetamine. He knew she had relatives with farms here, and he wanted her to help him set up meth labs on them. She refused, of course."

"Then what happened?"

"Then he began beating her," Daniel said, getting angry. "The bastard put her in the hospital. After she was released, she hid out at a friend's house in Memphis for a few weeks to recuperate, then ran here with only the clothes on her back when she realized some of his buddies were asking around the neighborhood about her."

"Did the police arrest him?"

"There's a warrant out for his arrest, but they couldn't find him, so he's still on the loose," Maddy said, her hands and voice shaking. "And he's going to come after me sooner or later. He promised."

With trepidation, Sarah asked, "So what can I do to help?"

"Dan says that you have experience defending yourself with guns. I was hoping that you can teach me to shoot. That way I'll be able to protect myself when he comes to kill me."

"Are you sure he'll come after you?" Sarah asked.

"Definitely," Maddy confirmed.

CHAPTER 7

SARAH IS MAD

"What the hell's the matter with you?" Sarah demanded as they walked to the first station on the five-stand sporting clays course. "You know damned well that I can't ignore someone in need and you made sure that Maddy and I met, which is like dumping her and her psycho boyfriend in my lap."

"Sarah, I didn't know what else to do," Daniel pleaded. "When she showed up on my doorstep the only thing I could think of was to ask you and Nadine to help her learn how to shoot in a tactical situation so she can defend herself. She's okay; it's her boyfriend that's the problem."

"And I don't want it to be my problem. I have enough of my own, thank you!"

"I know, and I don't want you to get into the middle of this. You're right. I shouldn't have asked you to become involved. It could be dangerous and it's not your concern. I'm sorry."

His pitiful tone flushed the anger out of Sarah.

"Look, let me think this through while we shoot this round, then we'll talk afterward."

"Okay."

"Can you find her a safe apartment?"

"I guess," he said. "But they'll all want at least a year's lease and I don't know if she'll be able to stay here that long."

"It figures," she said grumpily, stuffing hearing protectors into her ears and snapping muff protectors over top, effectively shutting out all noise, which included Daniel's conversation.

Thirty minutes later, the squad had finished the round and Daniel was handing the trap boy four dollar bills and thanked him.

After he rejoined Sarah for the walk back to the clubhouse, she said, "Here's what you may consider doing. You have relatives all up and down this valley. Arrange for Maddy to stay for three days at each of their houses. Keep her on the move and out of sight. Tell the relatives not to reveal her whereabouts to anyone. You know how everyone around here talks to everyone else."

"Okay," Daniel said calmly. "But how is that going to solve her long-term problem?"

"It won't, but it'll buy you some time to see if he really does follow her up here."

"And if he does?"

"Then she better have a protection from abuse order and a gun handy. Not necessarily in that order."

CHAPTER 8

CHAUNCEY'S NEW SHOTGUN

"Let me get this straight," Nadine asked over a steaming cup of coffee as Saturday morning was ending at her farm. "Chauncey went to New York to take a sporting clays class, ordered a shotgun, and now has to pick it up at The Conestoga Trading Post?"

"That's it in a nut shell," Sarah said with a grin. "And he wants us to go with him so we can help pick out all the accessories he'll need."

"I'll like that," Nadine said. "I always enjoy helping other people spend their money."

"They'll be picking us up here a few minutes after noon. I told them we had to swing by your church to hit the craft show, and they agreed as long as there's good home-cooked food there."

"They?"

"Yeah, William's coming along."

"Well, I better hit the restroom and put on a bit of make-up to make myself presentable," Nadine said. "I can't go out in public like this."

When Chauncey's SUV crept down the lane to avoid raising a cloud of dust, the two women abandoned their chairs under the sugar maple where they had been waiting for a short while.

The vista of The Shire spreading toward the mountains offered a breathtaking view of the western Virginia countryside.

William jumped out of the vehicle as soon as it stopped to hold the rear doors open for them. They climbed in like schoolgirls going out on the town.

"Where are we going first?" Sarah asked excitedly.

Nadine said, "First, let's go to The Conestoga Trading Post to pick up Chauncey's new shotgun, and then we'll drop by my church's craft show and see if they have any bargains at the tail end of the day. The women from the congregation usually have quite a large spread of food so if we hurry we may be able to pick up something from the baked goods table at a reduced price. They'd rather sell the leftover pies and cakes cheaply than be stuck with them."

William shifted in his seat so he could make eye contact with the women.

"Thanks for waiting until I got off work this afternoon. I appreciate any opportunity I can get to see more of the area. It helps me learn my way around."

"No problem," Nadine said. "It's a pleasure to have you along. Just hang onto your sanity with this bunch, because you're never sure what we'll get into."

"I'll keep that in mind," he said. "It's getting used to Chauncey's driving that may make me lose my mind."

"Don't give me that baloney," Chauncey said with a laugh. "The way you drive, anything short of the Indy 500 seems like a ride in the park."

"Seriously, Chauncey," Nadine asked. "Were you able to remember the rules of driving or did you have to take a course?"

"I just kind of picked up the rules from watching everyone else drive," Chauncey confessed. "After I found out I was Robert Fogler, my driver's license and record were still intact, so I just began driving. Apparently, I've always been a good driver. My record is spotless."

"And he picked it up again like he never missed a day behind the wheel," Sarah said. "Just to be sure, we both went up to West Virginia and took an accident avoidance course."

"What was that all about?"

"It was really neat. They hold it at a race track up there and have a water-covered skid area with everything all set up to mimic potential accident causing scenarios."

"Who teaches it?"

"It's the people who teach the police how to drive. The police courses are offered five days during the week, and then they throw in this one-day course on Saturday for civilians to round out their week."

"It was worthwhile then?"

"I thought it was," Sarah said solemnly. "Especially when you consider they teach you not only how to avoid accidents, but also how to minimize the risk of personal injury or death when an accident is unavoidable."

"So you've been busy going back to school, eh Chauncey?" Nadine teased him. "Didn't you go to a course, and that's how you bought this shotgun?"

"Yes, I went to the Clay Buster School weekend sporting clays course in New York, and part of the program included a gunstock fitting."

"Cool! What was it like? Hey! Weren't the lessons I gave you enough?"

"Nadine, the lessons you gave me were wonderful," Chauncey said. "Your instructions helped me realize I needed a professional shooting instructor if I ever hope to compete with you and Sarah on the clays course."

"You're pretty good at clays," she said. "Tell me about the classes."

"Well, it begins with shotgun safety," he replied. "The students are grouped together according to their ability and experience. Since my class was all beginners they spent a little extra time on the safety aspects of shooting."

"All good classes begin with a review of gun safety regardless of how much experience the shooters have. That's what I always do," Nadine said.

"Since they teach the English Churchill method of instinctive shooting, the first technique they teach is the gun mount," Chauncey said as he enthusiastically continued his story. "With a proper mount the shotgun is positioned so you'll shoot exactly where you're looking."

"How was your mount?" William asked. "Were you doing it correctly?"

"It was pretty sad according to the instructor, but it only took them half a dozen shots to teach me the correct way. My instructor said Nadine probably wanted to teach me incorrectly so I'd never have a chance of winning against her."

"I did not!" she gasped.

"He thought you may have sabotaged my gun mount so you could rake me over the coals and win any bets we made."

"He did not, you rat."

Chauncey laughed and everyone joined in.

"Actually, he said my first instructor, that's you Nadine, did a great job in teaching me the fundamentals and that I only needed a few minor adjustments to my technique," he said as he wiped a tear from the corner of his eye from laughing so hard. "That, and a shotgun that fit me. Apparently, the gun you lent me doesn't fit and I wasn't breaking as many targets as I should have been."

"You're at least six or eight inches taller than I am," Nadine said. "And your neck is much longer and thicker because you have more muscle than I have. Come to think of it, I've never shot that gun particularly well myself."

"Maybe you and I should take the course and get a proper gun fitting," Sarah said to Nadine. "It may be nice to hit more clay targets when I go shooting, because I definitely have lots of room for improvement."

"It's something to consider," she said. "What type of shotgun are you getting, Chauncey?"

"It's a twelve-gauge and has a Prince of Wales-style butt stock," he replied. "That's the one with a rounded knob on the end."

"Those are nice, because they're a compromise between the straight stock and the heavily curved pistol style grip."

"I liked the feel of the shotgun they had in stock, so I had them put upgraded wood with some figure in it on mine," he said, half-expecting them to kid him about paying more just for a fancier grade of wood. Vanity was not an attribute he wanted to be known for.

"You'll be happier with the better grade of wood," Sarah said. "A properly fit shotgun will last your entire life and give you pleasure every time you see or handle it."

"Does it have fixed chokes or choke tubes?"

"It's the sporting clays model, so it has five flush-fitting choke tubes," he said. "They've become the standard on the clays ranges."

Just as he was finishing his sentence, they arrived at The Conestoga Trading Post. He tried to enter the parking lot slowly, but a huge gray cloud of gravel dust still billowed behind his vehicle and enveloped it when he ground to a halt. Chauncey cringed knowing the dust would dull the sheen he had painstakingly buffed into the Mercedes.

"I ordered it while I was at the school, then called Nadine to get the address of the store where she buys most of her guns," he said. "The gun-makers sent it here and all I have to do is complete the paperwork."

"And it should fit you like a glove since it's made to your dimensions," Sarah said. "Cool."

"Life does get good at times, doesn't it?"

"Wow! This is something," William said, staring out the windshield in amazement.

"It sure is," Nadine said. "It's an everything-for-the-outdoors store. They even have indoor shooting ranges so you can try out any guns you want to buy, as long as you pay for the ammunition and range time."

"Nadine knows a lot about this place, because a long-time friend of hers owns it."

Nadine looked sharply at Sarah, who shrugged her shoulders with her extended palms upward then silently mouthed, "What?"

"Scott and I have gone out on a few dates and I don't want William to know," Nadine whispered into Sarah's ear.

"Oh," Sarah murmured back.

Nadine looked away quickly and spoke to William in a very sweet tone. "It's built to resemble a hunting lodge. That's why the mahogany front doors you see there have engraved scenes of rutting bull elk fighting for the right to breed cows. Even the brass kick-plates have engravings of flying geese."

"The ornate brass door handles are cast in the shape of whitetail deer antlers," Sarah added. "I love it here."

Nadine once again looked sharply toward Sarah, who took the hint and sullenly remained quiet.

"Most of the building materials come from local sources," Nadine told William. "The taxidermy specimens inside are world-class."

"Maybe we should go inside and see it firsthand instead of waiting until they begin closing the doors on us," Chauncey said anxiously. "It's getting late in the day and we have to visit the church before they run out of goodies."

"Well, let's go then," William said, getting out of the vehicle with unexpected grace. "Let me get the doors for you ladies." He rushed to hold Sarah's door then helped her step down from the high running boards. He then ran around the rear of the Mercedes to assist Nadine.

After Nadine and Sarah fell in step behind the men they looked slyly at each other, and then stifled giggles with the back of their hands held to their mouths like schoolgirls sharing an unspoken joke.

After entering the huge building, William's eyes glistened with a look of child-like wonderment as he scanned the interior of the building from top to bottom.

"This is really something," he said, as his eyes flitted from one mounted trophy animal to another. "I think I'm going to like this place."

"Just remember to look down occasionally so you don't trip," Sarah teased.

Nadine led the way to the rear of the store where shotguns of every type stood side-by-side along the walls in mahogany gun racks lined with protective forest green felt to prevent the delicate bluing of their barrels from contacting the hard surface of the wooden racks. Their muzzles pointed safely skyward in the traditional manner of displaying guns, while glass-fronted counters containing handguns of every imaginable type separated the shopping area from the storage space.

"How many guns did you say they have here?" Sarah asked Nadine.

"Scott says there're usually between three hundred to seven hundred long guns in here depending on the season."

"There're almost five hundred there today according to this morning's inventory report," Scott Maurier, the owner, said from the end of the counter.

"Hello, Scott," Sarah said cheerfully.

"Hello Sarah," he replied carefully.

Scott was tall and built like a college linebacker. His dark blue L.L. Bean chamois shirt displayed white silhouettes of moose and hung loosely from his bulging chest muscles to his thin waistline. Blue jeans and cowboy boots completed his outfit. Except for a smattering of gray speckling his hair and full beard, he could have been mistaken for a football player in his prime.

"Scott, this is Robert Fogler. His nickname is 'Chauncey' and this is his friend William," Nadine said. "Gentlemen, this is Scott Maurier, the developer and owner of this fine establishment."

"Hello Scott, it's a pleasure to meet you," Chauncey said, going to where Scott was standing and extended his hand.

"Yeah," Scott said, giving Chauncey's hand a non-committal shake. "We got your shotgun in and Tom has the paperwork ready for you to fill out. He's right there waiting for you," he said, gesturing toward a man standing farther down the counter. Scott and William coldly nodded their acknowledgement of each other.

"I'll keep Chauncey company, if that's okay with you ladies?" William asked, as he continued to stare belligerently at Scott.

"That's a good idea. We'll just be shopping around," Sarah said.

Nadine and Sarah exchanged a wary glance. The display of hostility between the men was unexpected and unsettling.

"Is there anything I can help you with, Nadine?" Scott asked hopefully.

"No," she answered. "Sarah and I are going to look at the Muck Boots while Chauncey fills out his paperwork. Now that she's raising cattle on her farm she needs a decent field boot."

"What type of cattle are you keeping?" Scott asked, shifting his attention to Sarah.

"I have Belted Galloway," she answered pleasantly, but offered no further discussion.

"Is there a particular reason you picked that breed?" he asked, glancing toward Chauncey and William. "It's not one of the more common types raised around here."

"I chose that breed because I like the way they look, and the potential for making a profit by selling calves is much greater than with other breeds."

"They're the ones that look like Oreo cookies, aren't they?"

"That's them. They have a white band around their middle, but the front and back end can be either black like mine or red," Sarah said. "They even have a dun-colored version."

"Muck Boots will work well around cattle," he said thoughtfully. "Do you need any help finding your size?"

"Thanks, but it's not necessary," she said. "Nadine knows where they're at."

"Well, if you need anything, just yell."

Sarah and Nadine looked at each other as they made their way upstairs to the outdoor clothing section.

"What do you think that was all about?"

"I don't know, but I think we better hurry up and get back down there."

"Good idea."

They wasted no time in getting Sarah her boots, and then returned to the gun counter where William and Chauncey were perusing the latest models of handguns. Chauncey had a long cardboard box leaning against the counter.

"Do you see anything you like?" Nadine asked, as they came up behind them.

"I've never shot a gun before, so I don't even know what to look for," William admitted.

"We'll have to remedy that."

"It's a lost cause with these two, Nadine," Scott said, as he walked up beside them.

"And what's that supposed to mean?" William said, as he slowly turned to face him. It was obvious both big men were standing as straight as they could to accentuate their stature in a masculine effort to achieve a height advantage.

"What it means is that he depends on the charity of these nice ladies for everything from his job to his house. Everyone is talking about it, and yet he has the audacity to buy a premium grade shotgun for himself. That isn't right," Scott said, gesturing at Chauncey without removing his eyes from William's. "And you're not much better. Are you going to start mooching off women all the time too?"

"Scott!" Nadine said with a look of horror and astonishment. "That's untrue and downright mean to say!"

"It's true enough," he said, still staring at William. "And everyone knows it."

"Look mister, I don't know what your problem is ..." William began.

"You're my problem, pal," Scott said. "Maybe you want to step outside so I can rectify that problem?"

"I haven't had an offer like that since third grade," William said with a wicked grin. "So I'm going to assume you have the mind of an eight-year-old and let you slide. If you want to press your luck some day when there aren't ladies present, I'll be happy to fix any problem you have. Chauncey, why don't you and I leave like two adults and the ladies can join us when they're done with their shopping?"

His eyes never wavered as he stared directly into Scott's.

During the entire exchange, Chauncey had only stared unemotionally at Scott. With no expression he slowly picked up the box holding his new shotgun. With a shuffling gait, his shoulders slumped, his eyes downcast, he left without saying a word.

Nadine watched the two men as they walked out the doors. Sarah stared in disbelief at the side of Scott's head. An evil smile and look of triumph spread across Scott's face as the doors swung shut behind them.

With fury in her eyes, Nadine turned toward Scott and said, "You are a real ass! What's the matter with you? You had no right to say those things, because you know they aren't true!"

"Nadine, you know every word is true," Scott said, pleading. "He lives for free in that shack at Sarah's place and depends on her for any job he's ever had."

"For your information, Scott," Sarah said haughtily. "He's the bookkeeper for two chiropractic practices, neither of which I own, and until recently did the book work for a mission for homeless men. That 'shack' you referred to is a refurbished home with all the modern amenities. And not that it's any of your business, but he pays me rent every month because he's a tenant, not a freeloader."

She lifted her chin high, turned on her heels, and proudly walked toward the door, abandoning the Muck Boots on the counter.

"Really Scott, you are such a boor," Nadine said, before following on Sarah's heels.

"He's trouble, Nadine," Scott yelled after her as customers paused in their shopping to stare at the scene. "They're both no-good troublemakers. Mark my words!"

Scott then stood perfectly still and stared at Nadine's back as she disappeared. After a moment's hesitation, he turned toward Tom who stood with an amused expression and asked, "Why did she call me a wild boar?"

Stifling a snicker, Tom answered, "I don't think she called you a wild boar. She called you a boor, spelled B-O-O-R. Look it up in a dictionary."

Scott just looked at him disgustedly for a moment, and then stalked to his office, clumping the heels of his burnished cowboy boots on the floor.

CHAPTER 9

CHAUNCEY'S PLAN

The ride from The Conestoga Trading Post to Nadine's church was quiet in the front seat, but a lively conversation raged in back.

When they arrived at the church, the two women wasted no time and immediately began to feverishly peruse the craft section to seek out last-minute bargains before the bazaar came to a close. The sullen men went directly to the food court where scores of hungry patrons had left the dining area looking somewhat disheveled.

After getting their food, Chauncey and William sat side-by-side at a folding table covered by a condiment-splattered plastic tablecloth and ate in silence for a moment.

"Sorry for getting you involved in that situation," Chauncey said, after swallowing some hot sausage that was almost hidden by steaming mounds of greasy hot peppers and onion.

"There's no need for you to apologize," William said quietly, looking curiously at Chauncey. "The guy's an asshole and you didn't have anything to do with making him that way."

"He was trying to pick a fight with me and you just happened to be there."

"You're wrong. He was pissed because there were four of us together, two men and two women. Like the other local yokels around here, he probably thinks you and Sarah are having an affair. That left me and Nadine as the other couple."

Chauncey paused and carefully swallowed a mouthful of the spicy sausage before asking, "So you think he was jealous of you?"

"I'll bet that was it," William said. After wiping his mouth with the remains of a paper napkin that was already blemished with yellow globs of mustard, he continued, "Didn't you see the way he was staring at me when we first walked into the place? He was definitely pissed before we ever met."

"I'm going to have to pay more attention," Chauncey said.

"I guess he and Nadine may have had something going on," William said. "If so, she may have learned something about him today she didn't know before."

"Maybe so," Chauncey said.

"What's wrong?"

"What do you mean?"

"There's something that's still bugging you, I can tell."

"Besides the fact he's an asshole of the first degree," Chauncey said. "He was still right."

"What? About us being freeloaders? We don't mooch off those two, no way, no how. He doesn't know what he's talking about."

"Yes and no," Chauncey said deliberately. "He's wrong about us mooching off them, because I pay rent for my house and I have two paying jobs. I had three, but the new reverend at the mission put a halt to that one."

Chauncey paused to smile slyly at William who returned his smile with a knowing one of his own, then continued, "Still, I don't have a real job, at least not in the sense that people think of jobs being."

"Bookkeeping is a real job," William stated defiantly. "If I could have gotten even ten percent of the guys from the mission to get and hold a responsible position like being a bookkeeper, I would have been beside myself."

"Exactly."

"Huh?"

"A job like bookkeeping is an entry-level position. Yes, it requires accuracy and responsibility, but it's still an entry-level position. It's not what people expect of more mature and worldly gentlemen like us."

William concentrated as he meticulously took another bite of his hotdog and chewed it thoughtfully before saying, "So what you're saying is that we need more respectable jobs. Something more suited to our highly held stations in life."

"Exactly," Chauncey said. "Even your job at the County Turf and Tractor store is an entry-level position that you'd just as soon move above. At least, that's what you said the other day."

"Yeah, I say it every day. That place gets on my nerves. So what do you suggest?"

"Well, ever since you mentioned it the other day, I've been thinking on it. The scene with Scott Maurier only brought it to the forefront today," Chauncey said. "I think we should try our hands at accounting."

William stared at the bitten end of his hotdog. He asked tentatively, "Why accounting?"

"Three reasons. I'm already doing bookkeeping, and I enjoy it," Chauncey said. "And you have some experience in accounting from college."

"Yeah, I had a year or two of it, but then I switched to Psychology. Besides, that was a long time ago, so I'd probably have to start over."

"If you can get me up to speed with the math, to make sure I can do it, we can go through the courses together."

"What do you mean, get you up to speed?"

"I mean that I can't remember how to do mathematics," Chauncey explained. "I must have known that stuff once upon a time to be a doctor, but it's all a mystery to me now."

"Oh brother, this will be the blind leading the blind," William said as he laughed gently. "You said there were three reasons to pursue accounting."

"There's actually more than three, but these are the big ones in my mind. The other reason is that accountants aren't really tied into a single locale."

"Well, I'm not too sure about that …" William said.

"Think about it. Federal tax laws are the same throughout the entire United States. The state tax codes are the same throughout each state, which encompasses a large geographic area. So, I figure we can live in a nice, rural area like this, yet have clients from a number of different states. Of course, we would have to learn the tax laws in each of the states we'll be marketing in, but we can concentrate on a small number of contiguous states in this region to keep it all manageable," Chauncey said. "That way, we can have a nice income, have relatively close proximity to our clients, and yet not have to live in a city."

"That sounds nice," William agreed. "But I'm not too keen on sitting in a classroom with a bunch of snot-nosed kids."

"We don't have to. The internet courses through accredited universities are accepted the same as if we were sitting in a desk beside those snot-nosed kids."

"So you think we can take courses from here, keeping the jobs we currently have, and still get accounting degrees?"

"Yep, and then we can take our C.P.A. test and be respected members of society."

"It sounds too easy."

"It won't be," Chauncey said. "We have to be sure I can do math first before wasting time on any internet courses. Then we have to be very conscientious about our study habits. If we can take the courses together, using the computer in my cottage, we may get through this more easily."

William stared across the hubbub of the craft show with unseeing eyes as he thought Chauncey's proposal through.

"You only have one computer, so we'll need another one if I'm to take the course simultaneously," he said. "But before we go to the expense of installing another computer, we should make sure you like accounting as much as you think you might."

"Good point."

"I think we should start out with free math lessons and accounting tutorials on the internet to see how you do with them and get me up to speed. It's been over thirteen years since I took any accounting courses," William said.

"A good plan."

"Only then should we consider putting a second computer in your cottage," William continued. "We have to get Sarah's okay before we start any of this, because it will mean I'm hanging around her farm every day and that may be too much to ask of her to put up with."

"Another good point."

"So when do we get started?"

"How about tonight? We can cook dinner at my cottage while we're going over the introductory information to see if I can do the work. Sarah can go shoot sporting clays with Dr. Lewis. Their relationship has been a bit strained since his sister showed up last Saturday, and it will do them good to spend some time alone."

"A grand idea," William said with a large, satisfied grin.

CHAPTER 10

CHAUNCEY'S WINDFALL

"Chauncey, I think you're not only going to do okay with accounting, but you're going to be way ahead of me in no time flat," William said. "You're so intelligent it's scary. Even the concepts you can't remember, and I know you had to know this stuff long ago to be a doctor, you pick up so fast I can hardly keep up."

"Thanks for the compliment," Chauncey said somberly. "But we'll stay on the same lesson so we can help each other. I'm sure we'll each have our difficult moments as we go through the accounting courses."

"That's a safe bet," William agreed wholeheartedly. "But there is one problem. I don't know if I can afford all the courses it'll take me to get a degree. I was able to save almost all I earned working at the mission because I didn't have any living expenses, but I never made much to begin with. I don't make much at the tractor shop either, so I'm not sure if anyone will give me educational loans."

"If you can't get a loan I'll co-sign for you," Chauncey said simply. "It's not a problem."

"You make enough to do that? And you can do that?"

"Of course I can do it, or I wouldn't have offered," Chauncey replied quietly.

"I'm sorry, Chauncey, I shouldn't ask about your income, but I still think of you as having been a homeless person only a short time ago. I know you work like crazy for the chiropractic practices and all but ..."

"William, don't worry about it," he said with a laugh as he spun his chair to face his friend. "I was a homeless person, but then I found out I had been Dr. Robert Fogler, remember? I apparently did well as a doctor and got half of everything we owned jointly when my wife divorced me."

"Wow," William said. "I didn't consider your divorce settlement. I'm sorry you couldn't return to your old life as a doctor and husband, especially since you said your wife was a real nice lady."

"Well, it wasn't meant to be," Chauncey said with a forlorn look. "But life must go on. Besides, I have other sources of income. You see, I had to have a hearing before the Board of Medical Examiners. Those are the people who give you your license to practice in one of the health care professions, and they determined I wasn't competent to practice medicine anymore."

"What?"

"Yeah, I was examined by one of their doctors. Apparently I knew the man quite well before I lost my memory, and it was determined I couldn't remember more than a few scattered medical terms. It's almost like I never went to medical school, so it's dangerous for me to try practicing medicine. They pulled my medical license immediately."

"That must have been a terrible blow to your ego and prospects for any type of future, I'm sure," William said gloomily. "I'm sorry that things worked out that way for you."

"Don't be sorry, it's going to be alright." Chauncey said. "The Board of Examiners was only doing their job, which is good because people should expect to have a competent doctor caring for them and their families. Besides, I had own-occupation disability insurance that kicked in when I was unable to practice. Luckily, my wife Irene kept up the premium payments even after I disappeared. She had faith that she'd find me alive …"

Chauncey looked away with misting eyes and wiped away a small tear. "So, I get a nice check every month from the insurance company."

"Don't they take your bookkeeping income into account and reduce the amount they pay you?"

"No, it was an own-occupation policy, so as long as I can't work as an obstetrician, I get the full amount from them every month regardless of any other income I have coming in."

"Cool!"

"Very cool," Chauncey agreed. "This brings up another aspect of our studies I'd like to pursue."

"What's that?"

"I have the proceeds from the sale of my house, a vacation home on Fenwick Island, and half of my pension plan that I received in my divorce settlement. It's all invested in stock and bond funds, and I'd like to be able to determine whether I'm getting the best return I can on those investments."

"That's being smart."

"My wife, or maybe I should say ex-wife, told me I used to play the stock market as a hobby. Apparently, I used to be a very astute investor because I made a lot of money in the markets. She gave me all the books I had read to learn how to invest in the stock market, and I've read them all again since I couldn't remember anything from the first time. I'd like to see if I'm still good at it without risking any real money, at least in the beginning."

"So what do you have in mind?"

"If you're interested in helping, I'd like to pretend we have a certain amount of money to invest, and then see how much we would gain or lose with our fictitious funds. I figure it will be a good exercise to sharpen our accounting skills. If we're any good at it, we might begin putting real money into the stock market."

"We can start that right away since we're only using pretend money."

"Actually, I've already started," Chauncey said, his conspiratorial grin growing. "My salary from my bookkeeping jobs covers my living expenses, so I've been saving my monthly occupational disability checks then investing them in the market when I have enough to buy a block of a hundred stock shares."

"Do you make that much from your disability checks?" William asked, and then quickly added, "I'm sorry, that didn't sound right. I don't want to know how much you make."

"No problem," Chauncey replied earnestly. "So far I've been restricting myself to the lower-priced stocks. If I find a more attractive stock that looks exceptionally good, but is much higher-priced, I'll keep an eye on it then save up until I can buy it. I may even sell off some of the lower-priced stocks if they're not performing as expected."

"It may be a good strategy to decide if higher-priced stocks are worth it. If they are, then it may be worthwhile to save a larger amount in an easily liquidated investment vehicle so you can jump on a good deal if it crops up."

"That's one of the strategies I want to explore as we go through our little exercise with fake money," Chauncey said.

"Well, why don't you catch me up to speed and we'll put our heads together to see how we do?"

"What I think may be a wise move is to discuss the virtues of certain stocks, then invest our fake money on those we can agree on. In addition to the fake money we invest as partners, we can each have our own fake money to invest, say fifty thousand to start with, and see who has the most gains after six months. That way we can see who the shrewdest investor is."

"A little competition never hurts to keep the mind sharp, and it makes sense to start with a significant amount of fake money so limited funds don't hinder our learning experience," William said. "It will help us determine if we're better making investment decisions together or separately."

"Competition is what capitalism is based upon," Chauncey said, grinning again. "And that seems to work just fine."

"If this is going to be a competition, are we going to make a small wager to keep it interesting?"

"The highest bet allowed by law!"

"Five bucks it is," William said. "Though I think Sarah is right when she says there are no bets allowed by law."

"If we start getting out of line with the law, I'll let you know."

"Chauncey, you can't remember what the law is or isn't," William said with a laugh.

"That's just a minor detail."

CHAPTER 11

METH LABS IN VIRGINIA

"Whoa, Shawnee," Nadine crooned gently to her favorite horse as they crested the last bench before Jacob's Mountain began a precipitous rise to the top. "It's been a nice morning, but there's no need to push the horses beyond their limits," she said over her shoulder to Sarah.

"I didn't realize how sure-footed Rocky Mountain horses were," Sarah said, as she ducked to avoid getting hit in the face by a sapling branch that sprang back after Nadine let go of it.

"This is why they became popular with the mountain people of Kentucky where this breed is from," Nadine replied. "Riding up and down steep trails demands different techniques from the rider. You learned the ins and outs of mountain riding quickly. You have a lot of natural ability."

"I'm glad you slowly broke me into this type of riding. I would have freaked out if I hadn't had you as an instructor. You're really a great teacher."

"Thank you," Nadine replied. "It's advanced riding techniques but once they're mastered you can ride just about anywhere it's reasonable to go with a horse."

"Where do we go from here? It looks pretty steep from here on up."

"It is, and it's definitely much too steep and rocky to take a horse up or down. We'll just ride on this bench until it begins descending then begin taking switchbacks down until we get back to the pasture."

"What are those doing up here?"

"What's what doing up here?"

"Those coolers off to your right," Sarah said, pointing to the brightly colored coolers aligned a few yards off the trail.

Nadine looked where Sarah was pointing and saw five large plastic coolers hidden under the limbs of a dead, fallen tree.

"Oh shit!" she said, pulling her Smith and Wesson model 60 in .357 magnum from the floral carved holster belted around her waist. "Let's get out of here. Turn around the best you can and go back the way we came."

"Why? What's the matter?"

"I'll explain later! Just turn around and get your ass moving!"

Sarah gingerly pulled on the reins and allowed her horse, Tonka, plenty of room to make a wide turn until he was facing the opposite way. Not sure why Nadine had pulled her revolver, but not wanting to be caught unprepared, she flicked the safety strap off her holster.

"Don't try shooting while mounted, because he hasn't been trained for that the way Shawnee has and he'll buck you right off," Nadine warned Sarah. "Just get moving because the next bench is wide enough for me to sneak past you, then I'll lead the way back down."

BA-WOOM!

"That's a rifle!" Nadine yelled in terror. "Move! Move! Move!"

BA-WOOM! BA-WOOM! BA-WOOM!

The crash of rifle shots rang up and down the mountainside. Sarah spurred Tonka onward, but the mountain-wise gelding picked his way carefully to keep his feet on the rock-strewn trail. Stepping gingerly but quickly over fallen tree branches, he steadily put more ground between them and the hidden shooter.

"There's a wider bench coming up where I can pass you," Nadine said, breathing heavily. "You pull to the left and let me by. I know these trails better than you and I can get us out of here faster."

"What the hell's going on?" Sarah asked, her heart beating like a bass drum. "Who's shooting? Are they shooting at us?"

"No time to explain. Get ready, here's the wide part of the bench coming up. Just let him have his head and he'll get you down the mountain safely. He can handle this mountain better than you can, so let him do what he wants. You just hang on and remember how to position your body for going downhill like I taught you."

Without hesitation, Sarah nudged Tonka to the left, allowing Shawnee with Nadine to move smoothly by. As soon as Nadine was in the lead, she picked up the pace. Tonka stayed right on Shawnee's tail the entire way down the mountain. The women didn't speak until they were safely into the pasture.

"Slow down, but keep moving," Nadine said. "Let them have a breather, but let's get back to the house."

Sarah noticed that Nadine had slid her revolver back into its holster. She had been riding with it and the reins in her hands all the way down the mountain.

"What the hell just happened?" Sarah asked, pulling Tonka alongside Shawnee.

"That, my dear, was a clandestine meth lab you just discovered. They have warnings every so often on the radio and in the local newspapers about them," Nadine said without looking at her. "Those shots were from the drug dealers who operate the lab, protecting their investment."

"They were making drugs up there? In those coolers?"

"Yep, didn't you smell the acetone? It's a dangerous, but very profitable business."

"Why did we turn around? Wouldn't it have been faster to just keep going the way we were heading?"

"We knew what was behind us," Nadine said. "Only God knows what may have been in front of us."

"Like what?"

"Booby traps, for one thing. These bastards have been known to rig trip wires to explosives to blow up anyone trying to raid their lab. They don't care if it's other drug dealers or law enforcement, they'll blow them all up."

"Oh shit," Sarah said, and began to shake. "You mean we could have been killed?"

"That's exactly what I'm saying. Whoever was up there was either a terribly bad marksman or those were just warning shots. We weren't hit that we know of, and I didn't hear or see any of the bullets hitting the trees around us."

"What do you mean, 'not that we know of?'"

"I don't see any blood on any of us but we won't know for sure until we stop and do a thorough search of us and the horses. Bullets can punch holes through a big muscle and not be felt right away. It's not like in the movies."

"Those *bastards*!" Sarah cried. "They're willing to kill or maim us and the horses just to protect their drugs? What *assholes*!"

"You're right," Nadine said with a nervous laugh. "But to these assholes, as you so eloquently refer to them, this is their life. They don't want to lose their stash and they most certainly don't want to go to jail for a long, long time."

"Speaking of which," Sarah said. "You have your cell phone, don't you? You better call the police."

"There's no coverage out here. We'll have to wait until we get back to the house and use the land line."

"Son of a bitch!" Sarah said, resigning herself to the fact she could do nothing except get to the barn as quickly as possible. "I hate not having cell phone coverage around here. I'm going to get a satellite phone and be done with this nonsense."

Beside the barn, Nadine pulled the saddle off her sweat-drenched horse and instructed Sarah to do the same. "We'll brush them down later. Let's just put them in the small pasture so they can cool down and get some water. Make sure you check for bullet holes in Tonka, they can be hard to see."

After turning the horses out to pasture, they went to the house and Nadine called the State Police.

"What did they say?"

"They said to sit tight and someone would get back to us."

"That's all? That's all they said?" Sarah sputtered in astonishment.

"Let them do their job," Nadine said. "You know how long it took us to get up there. What do you expect the police to do? Run out here with guns drawn and charge up the mountain with no idea where they're going?"

"You're right," Sarah admitted. "There's an armed drug dealer up there who's obviously willing to shoot at, if not kill, anyone who gets near their stuff."

"They're going to send an officer around to take our statements, but they said it may be awhile. Apparently there are more important things for them to do right now."

"More important than catching a potential murderer who shoots at women?"

"Honey, you have to realize what they're up against," Nadine said. "What can they do now that we're out of danger? Nothing. They'll start the paperwork then proceed with their investigation as best they can."

"I guess you're right, but it's infuriating that someone actually shoots at us and they may get away with it!"

"Of course it's upsetting, but look at the logistics of the situation," Nadine said. "The police are equipped to handle situations on the road and in settled areas. In these wilderness areas, they have to have specially trained personnel and equipment to get up there to see what's going on. That's difficult terrain."

Sarah looked up the mountain. "So what do we do now?"

"We brush down the horses, make sure they have everything they need, and then we get us some lunch. The State Police will be by when they can to take our statements."

"Bastards," Sarah said again, as she took one last look up the mountain before turning toward the barn.

CHAPTER 12

OFFICER TOM MAHONEY

"That's all I need," Officer Tom Mahoney of the Virginia State Police said to Sarah and Nadine as he neared the end of their interview. "Is there anything you have to add?"

"No," Nadine said. "I think that about covers it all. When will we know if the police find anything up there?"

"It will be a while before we get any word about what the investigation turns up," he said. "If you see or hear anything else, please give us a call immediately."

"So that's it?" Sarah asked.

"Yes ma'am, for now that's all we can do."

"What's the story behind this meth stuff?"

"Ma'am?"

"Why are they up on a mountain making this stuff? Is it that lucrative?"

"Yes ma'am, it is. The number of clandestine meth labs being uncovered by law enforcement is increasing tremendously. That means it's on the rise and it's all money-driven."

"Is it that easy to learn how to make this poison?"

"Yes, ma'am," Officer Mahoney replied. "There are literally thousands of websites on the internet with recipes and information about making it, but if you do a search you may have to look for crystal meth. That's a more common name for it."

"Thank you, Officer, we appreciate your help," Nadine said, trying to end the conversation quickly because she saw Sarah working up to launch into a tirade.

"Dr. Collins," Officer Mahoney said as he turned to address Sarah, "I don't know if you remember me, but I investigated the break-in at your home last Thanksgiving when your computers were stolen."

"I thought I recognized you," Sarah said coolly. "Thank you for being so professional and helping when things hit the fan."

"Yes ma'am, thank you. I was wondering if you allow anyone to access the mountain behind your farm to hunt."

"You mean, you want to hunt on the mountain behind my farm?"

"Yes, ma'am. That area seems to have a good crop of deer and turkey this year. I see more there than I do in other places when I'm driving by on patrol."

"That may be because we've been harassing the coyotes. I haven't killed many because I can't shoot too well at longer distances with my prosthetic shoulder, but they're not coming around as much as they used to."

"That would explain why there are more deer and turkeys around there. More survive if they're not being preyed upon as heavily."

"Do you hunt a lot?"

"Not as much as I'd like to, ma'am," he said with a smile revealing boyish features that were usually masked behind an unemotional, professional demeanor.

"That's the first time I've seen you smile," Sarah said, as she allowed herself to smile back. "And you can call me Sarah."

"Yes, ma'am, or I mean Sarah. I guess I don't get much chance to smile with my job and all."

"That's understandable. You can park your car on the other side of the barn. That should keep it out of the way of any work we'll be doing. Will you be driving your cruiser?"

"No, I'll probably have my old green Chevy pick-up. I'll stop by in the daylight someday so you get to recognize it."

"That's a good idea," she said. "When you stop by, we can talk and go over when you'll be there and where you'll be. After today you'll want to be careful in the woods. They aren't safe with these drug dealers running around shooting at people."

"I'm well aware of the danger of those people," he said gravely. "I'm glad to see y'all weren't injured this morning."

"Thank you," Nadine said pleasantly, glad that Sarah's anger had dissipated.

"One other thing, Tom," Sarah added. "If you see any predators like coyotes, you have to promise to shoot them on sight. I don't like predators, whether they're on two legs or four, waiting to prey on my animals or good folks like you and me. That's why I named by farm Predator's Bane."

"Agreed," he said with a grim, knowing expression. "Keeping predators at bay is what I've devoted my life to, though I usually deal with the two-legged variety in my line of work."

"Well, keep up the good work," Sarah said, and then she turned and walked back toward the house.

CHAPTER 13

SUPERMARKET CONFLICT

"Did you remember your shopping list?"

"I have mine and yours," Chauncey said stolidly. "You would have forgotten it on the kitchen table again."

"I would not have."

"Yes, you would have."

"Would *not* have."

"*Would* have."

"There's a parking spot over there," she said, pointing. "Pull through so you're pointing outward and don't have to back out later."

"You're being a little bossy, don't you think?" he chided her as he expertly slid the truck between two cars. "And I really pulled through those two tiny spaces with quite a bit of flair, wouldn't you agree?"

"You're getting pretty good at driving," she admitted.

"Driving skills must be like riding a bicycle, once you do it a while you never forget how. The rules of the road I had to relearn, though."

They exited the truck and managed to shimmy between the huge pick-up and the compact cars parked on either side before walking side-by-side to the door of the supermarket. Inside, they shopped together but used separate carts.

The ritual of paying for their items and allowing the teenage clerks to bag their purchases was uneventful. Just as they reached the doors, Sarah exclaimed in a near panic, "Oh! I forgot my lottery tickets!"

"I told you you'd forget something."

"You did not."

"Did *too*."

"Did not."

"Well, you'll have to go back for them otherwise you won't be happy all week. Your gambling addiction has to be fed, otherwise there's hell to pay."

"I don't have a gambling addiction. I only buy ten dollars' worth of tickets each week."

"Whether it's an addiction or not, you need your lottery tickets. I'll take your groceries to the truck while you go back and get them."

"There's probably a long line of people waiting for lottery tickets. It'll take too long."

"The Big Game is up to seventy-eight million dollars. If you miss that drawing you'll be intolerable. Go get your tickets."

"Thanks, Chauncey."

"No problem."

He pulled the two carts over to the side so he did not inconvenience other shoppers then loaded Sarah's purchases into his cart. After pushing Sarah's empty cart into the line of others parked in front of the store he meandered lazily through the parking lot, making sure to keep an eye on traffic.

It'd be my luck to get run over in the parking lot just as I'm beginning to rebuild my life. Why is life such an irony? God must have one heck of a sense of humor, he thought.

Parking the cart so it gently touched the rear bumper of the truck, he loaded the grocery bags into the back seat of the crew cab. When he was finished, he pushed the cart into a corral and sat in the driver's seat to patiently wait for Sarah. His eyes slowly closed and his breathing became regular as he drifted off to sleep.

CHAPTER 14

DAMNED LOTTERY TICKETS!

Waiting patiently in long lines at the grocery store was difficult for an active person like Sarah. Her intolerance of listlessly wasting time combined with the innate stupidity of many people almost always surpassed her mental ability to remain calm and subdued while waiting for her turn at the register.

What's taking so long? What's the matter with these people? Can't these idiots read? The sign clearly says this line is for fewer than eight items and lottery tickets. What's that moron doing with ten items? Now he has to pay with a credit card! And he wants lottery tickets also and he has to find the cash for them because they won't accept credit card payments for lottery tickets! AAAARRRRRGGGHH!

She managed to get her lottery tickets without having a stroke, and then headed for the door. What she didn't know was that destiny had ordained she meet Bill Fenne, Kenny Nacono, and Sammy Yadamski in the worst way.

Bill "Squeaky" Fenne was the number one flunky of John McGuire. His nickname came from the noise emanating from his nose when he spoke. The scarring caused by surgical cleft palate repair when he was a small child had been the center of ridicule from his classmates but was now invisible under a bushy Fu-Manchu mustache. A very tall man, he demanded respect and had a habit of pummeling those who made mention of his affliction. Even in prison, he was respected for his violent temper, which only came to the surface when the tone of his voice was ridiculed.

Surprisingly, he was proud of his nickname.

Squeaky had moved from Tennessee to Virginia with Kenny "Nacco" Nacono and Sammy "Twister" Yadamski. They were adapting well to their new surroundings.

Squeaky, Nacco, and Twister were not enthused about food shopping, but knew it was a necessary chore. Just because they were working didn't mean they would pass up an opportunity to have some fun to help relieve their boredom. Unfortunately, the prospect for entertainment went by the name of Sarah Collins.

"Look what's comin' out the store," Nacco said through the side of his mouth as he peered through the huge glass windows toward the checkout counters. "She lookin' like my kind of woman."

"That nice stuff, for sure, man," Twister said. "But she not gonna' want your scrawny hillbilly ass. She got class."

"She may have class, but you sure as hell don't," Nacco said. His greater height was more than enough to intimidate the smaller Twister. While the three men differed greatly in height, their facial features were similar enough to make them passable as cousins.

Their closely set, beady eyes peered out darkly from beneath black, brushy eyebrows atop the bridges of their hawkish noses. Disheveled hair, the same murky color as their eyebrows, protruded wildly from atop their heads and laid askance in short, oily strings high on their sloping foreheads.

"She need a man big enough to satisfy her and that me. What you think, Squeaky? Twister the needle-dick bug-humper gonna be able to satisfy a fine woman like that?" Nacco said.

"Piss off, man," Squeaky said. "She need a handsome devil of a man and that only leave me. You boys sit back and watch how a real man operates and learn somethin'."

Sarah noticed the rough-looking men enter the foyer leading into the store, but her concentration was focused on stuffing lottery tickets into her purse. The purse strap was slipping from her shoulder, further distracting her.

The inner door leading toward the parking lot automatically swung open with a gentle whirling noise and she walked briskly through. She was not paying any attention to the men until Squeaky vaulted the waist high aluminum railing separating the entryway from the exit.

"How you doin' pretty lady?" he asked from two steps behind her.

Immediately, Nacco and Twister jumped the barrier to follow Squeaky. It was the classic game of cat and mouse; the scenario played out millions of times daily around the globe between predators and their prey.

"Calm down, baby," Nacco called. "We just want to say hello."

Getting her purse under control, Sarah jammed her hand into the hidden slot sewn into the lining of her handbag and spun to face them. Her fingers tightened around the grip of the pistol secured there with Velcro straps.

This was the same pistol Sarah had used to defend her Golden Retriever, Rex, from being eaten alive by a pack of coyotes. It didn't seem to matter whether predators walked on two legs or four; their intention was always the same—the domination and potential demise of their prey.

Don't pull your pistol until they prove they're a threat, she reminded herself as her mind reeled frantically in a vain attempt to find an escape route. *You can't shoot them just because they're obnoxious louts.*

Damned! I knew I should have carried a revolver. That way I could shoot right through the purse if I have to. The slide will jam after the first shot if I try that with this semi-auto. And equipment failure is not an option when there are three of them and only one of me.

"Back off!" she snapped. She tugged the pistol loose from the Velcro, but kept it concealed inside the purse while she carefully stepped backward to create distance between herself and the intimidating men.

Her rebuff merely made the game more interesting to the menacing men and their demeanor took on a much more sinister tone.

Sarah calmly looked side to side, moving her eyes more than her head, and was able to rapidly ascertain these were the only threats to her at the moment.

Because her assailants were male, that fact alone immediately established there was a discrepancy of force, which would legally support the need to use a gun in self-defense if she felt threatened. The fact there were three of them further justified the use of lethal force on Sarah's part.

Where the hell is Chauncey? she wondered while she cast a furtive glance toward the parking lot.

"What the matter, baby? You lookin' for someone?" Nacco asked. "You not wantin' to talk to us?"

Sarah continued walking backwards, but they matched her step for step.

Once they were past the railing, they spread out with Nacco on her left, Twister on her right, and Squeaky boring directly down on her from the front.

Sarah's hands began to sweat profusely making the grip of the .45 slick beneath her fingers.

"What say we party a little, baby? You got somethin' better to do?"

Just as she stepped backward off the curb, Chauncey's head bounced onto his chest rousing him from slumber. He snorted a deep breath into his lungs then groggily opened his eyes and looked toward the front of the store.

What's keeping her? Oh shit! She's in trouble!

He bolted upright, and in one fluid motion gave the ignition key a vicious twist while deftly flicking the electric door lock to the open position.

The powerful engine instantly jumped to life a split second before he threw the gearshift into drive. Mashing the gas pedal to the floor, he wheeled out of the parking spot, barely missing the cart corral railing.

Those bastards are trying to outmaneuver her, he thought as he focused with laser-like intensity on the four people directly in front of him.

Nacco picked up his pace as he attempted to slither behind Sarah, but she countered his move by taking faster strides backward.

I have to back up against a car or else these guys will surround me, she thought, as she shuffled backward, never lifting her feet completely off the cracked macadam of the parking lot to avoid tripping. She snapped her head around to determine the safest route to a more secure location and just as rapidly returned her eyes to fix her tormentors with an unwavering gaze.

It'll be better if I can get between cars. Then I'll only have them coming from two restricted directions, she thought as adrenaline continued to flood her veins.

In a surprise maneuver, Nacco dashed in a long loop behind her, effectively cutting off any hope of her reaching the line of parked automobiles. His only mistake was keeping a significant distance between them in a sadistic attempt to prolong the game.

Sarah was surrounded.

In the split second before her muscles contracted to pull her .45 out, she saw Squeaky's eyes widen in amazement and his mouth drop open in astonishment.

Chauncey swung the huge vehicle toward the throng of bodies in middle of the driveway in front of the grocery store. Aiming carefully, he guided the truck directly at Nacco. At the last minute he swerved to the right, barely missing him. With tremendous effort, he heaved with all his might to swing the driver's door wide open.

Nacco barely had time to raise his arm in a futile attempt to shield himself against the impact as the door slammed into him and sent him spinning out of control. He sprawled face-first onto the grimy macadam in a futile effort to break his fall.

Squeaky and Twister's drug-dulled mental functions didn't allow them to decide if Chauncey intended to run them over, so both placed discretions far ahead of valor by backpedaling until they flipped backward over the curb.

Even Sarah was taken aback by Chauncey's daring maneuver and stared unbelievingly at the chrome bumper that had stopped only a few feet from her.

"Get in!" Chauncey yelled at Sarah as he again shoved the driver's door open as far as it would go.

Without a moment's hesitation, she ran around the swinging door and hopped up on the running board, grabbing hold of Chauncey's shoulder harness. She yelled, "Go! Go! Go!"

Chauncey flung his left arm around Sarah's slender waist and pulled her to him, hit the gas, and wheeled away from the three men. Only when they were at the far end of the parking lot did Chauncey stop and give Sarah an opportunity to run around to the passenger side and jump in.

"Did you see that? Did you see that? That nigger tried to kill us!" Nacco cried as he scrambled on his hands and knees to avoid being run over by an elderly lady driving a Buick. "Crotchety old bitch! Watch where yer goin'!"

"Son of a bitch! That bitch has a nigger boyfriend!" Squeaky whistled through his nose.

"And the asshole just about killed us all!" Twister added in an awe-tinged voice.

"Son of a bitch! He gonna pay for that. That asshole definitely gonna pay for that!" Nacco exclaimed loudly as he stood up to his full height then bent from the waist to brush dirt and stones off the knees of his tattered jeans.

All three men stood transfixed as they watched the Chevy disappear out an exit and speed down the street.

"We gonna get them and make them pay!" Squeaky bellowed. He abruptly bolted toward their battered Ford pick-up and roared angrily over his shoulder, "Let's follow and see if we can find them!"

"Just get us out of here," Sarah pleaded to Chauncey in the cab of the truck as she looked fearfully over her shoulder and back toward the parking lot. "I'm going to call the police and let them know what happened. The first person to report an incident is usually considered to be the victim. We don't want those bastards to call first and tell lies about you trying to run them down for no good reason."

"Good idea," Chauncey said, checking the rearview mirror. "I'm going to go a little faster just to put as much distance between them and us as I can."

Sarah fished her cell phone out of the depths of her purse and quickly punched 9-1-1. It took almost an entire ten seconds for the call to be connected.

"Emergency dispatch, what is your emergency?"

"This is Doctor Collins, I was just accosted by three men in front of Harper's Supermarket in Florentine."

"Were you injured, ma'am?"

"No, my friend drove toward them with my pick-up and caused them to scatter before they could hurt me."

"Did he hit them with the vehicle, ma'am?"

"No."

"Would you like me to dispatch police to your location?"

"No, we're on the road and safe for the moment, but I don't know what to do."

"Are they following you?"

"Not that I know of, but they may be."

"Well, you can either pull over in a safe area and I will have a police officer come by to take your statement, or you can drive to the State Police office and give them your statement there."

"Where is the police office from Florentine?"

"It's approximately three miles outside of town if you go south on Route 24."

"We're heading in that direction," Sarah said uneasily. "We'll just go to the police office."

"Do you want me to stay on the line, ma'am?"

"No, thank you. Thank you for your help."

"Goodbye and if there's anything else you need please don't hesitate to call back, okay?"

"Yes, thank you."

Sarah flipped the phone shut just as Chauncey said, "There's a pickup truck coming after us. And he's going pretty fast."

"Where?" Sarah asked as her head whipped around to peer out the rear window.

"About a quarter mile back."

"Hit the gas," Sarah said. "We have to get to the police office before they catch up to us."

Just then, the pursuers caught sight of their prey.

"There the sons a bitches."

"Yeah, I see 'em."

"What we gonna do when we catch 'em?"

"We gonna teach that nigger some hard lessons and let that white bitch make things up to us. She gonna be real nice to us," Squeaky said. "Go faster. You drivin' like my granny."

"I don't know these roads," Nacco said. "You want me to go in the ditch like your granny too?"

"Quit cryin', you asshole. Just ketch 'em."

Chauncey had to slow down for a tight right-hand turn.

"Don't slow down! They'll catch us!" Sarah cried.

"They'll catch us for sure if I end up wrecking!"

"Just hurry!" Sarah said with a quivering voice. "I'm going to call 9-1-1 again."

"Good idea," Chauncey replied. "This could get rough."

"Emergency dispatch, what is your emergency?"

"This is Doctor Collins again. I just called you about an altercation we had in the parking lot at Harper's Supermarket in Florentine."

"Yes ma'am. I spoke with you. Is everything alright?"

"No, it's not," Sarah said shakily. "We're on our way to the State Police office outside of Florentine on Route 24, but the men are chasing us in a pick-up truck and we're about a mile away from the office."

"You're proceeding south on 24 like you said you were going to do?"

"Yes, and they're gaining on us," Sarah said impatiently, looking nervously out the back window.

"Ma'am, just stay on the route you're on and I'll alert the State Police of your predicament. Please stay on the line. Don't hang up."

"Thank you. I won't hang up."

"There's the sign for the State Police," Chauncey said, pointing out the windshield. "It says one mile."

"Then step on it."

Chauncey gently nudged the gas pedal with the tip of his toe and the big Chevy responded immediately. He was careful to smoothly steer into the curves avoiding any quick jerking motions. He stayed close to the middle line of the road on each curve to minimize the distance the vehicle had to travel. Each of these efforts contributed only a small bit to their attempt to escape their pursuers, but every second gained helped to speed them closer to safety.

"There's the office on the right!" Sarah said breathlessly. "Drive straight up to the front door."

Chauncey hit the brakes only enough to allow him to safely guide the careening truck into the almost deserted visitor's parking lot. A grayish plume of gravel dust from the shoulder of the road followed them as they sped toward the front of the building.

As soon as he entered the visitor's lot Chauncey steered into an empty spot by the front door just as two officers were leaving the building.

One of the officers ran to the driver's side door with his hand on his pistol and said, "Okay, keep your hands where I can see them."

"What are you doing?" Sarah demanded hotly. "We're being chased and you're getting tough with us?"

The other officer, the taller of the two, slid around to the passenger side of the truck and replied, "Calm down, ma'am, and keep your hands where I can see them."

The officers simultaneously pulled the heavy truck doors open with one hand while keeping the other on their pistols. The shorter one said to Chauncey, "License and registration, please."

"But officer ..."

"License and registration, now!"

As Chauncey stared at him in disbelief, the trio following them briefly tapped their brakes then continued driving past the parking lot, going the speed limit while trying to look straight ahead and disinterested.

"That was close," Nacco breathed heavily.

"We better learn where the cops are around here if we want to stay out of jail, man," Twister said. "Where that .30-30 rifle at?"

"Shit! It behind the seat," Twister said.

"Nacco is allowed to have a rifle because he never been in jail. Just calm down," Squeaky said.

"He ain't allowed to have a stolen one," Twister said tersely. "McGuire wanted a gun that can't be traced to us, so he scratched the serial number off it the same day I snatched it from that old dude's house. That's two federal felonies I don't want no part of."

"Shit!" Squeaky swore. "As soon as we out of sight you best haul ass outta here. Start takin' a lot of turns."

"Twister, get that map out and see if you can get us back to the farmhouse."

"Ain't we gonna get us some food?"

"Not now, you dumb shit. Later."

"What we gonna do about that nigger and his bitch?"

"We gonna find where they live. That truck's easy enough to spot," Squeaky said through a crooked sneer. "And payback's a bitch!"

CHAPTER 15

LET DOWN

"You're kidding me," Nadine said, astonished. "While the 9-1-1 dispatcher is talking to the cops inside the building telling them to hurry out to the parking lot to protect you from those three yahoos, two others are coming out the door and almost arrest you for driving recklessly in their parking lot?"

"No, I'm not kidding you," Chauncey said, reaching for his drink. "It scared the dickens out of me. I'm still shaking."

"I'm still shaking a little too," Sarah added unsteadily. "I'm not used to being treated like a criminal."

"They're just doing what they have to do when they're not sure about the situation," Chauncey said. "They don't know what's happening and they have to take control before bad things happen."

"That's very nice of you to say, considering they wanted to take your driver's license away from you for reckless driving," Nadine said.

"Yes it is," Chauncey replied with a chuckle. "But when the officers who got the information from the 9-1-1 dispatcher showed up, we got things sorted out and they were much nicer to us after that."

"But the confusion allowed those bastards to escape," Sarah said bitterly.

"Really Sarah, there wasn't much they could do at that point," Chauncey said. "It's just the way things worked out."

"Yeah, I know. But it still pisses me off."

"Can I have another of these?" he asked, holding his empty glass aloft and tinkling the ice cubes.

"Help yourself. You know where everything is. Besides, Sarah's having lemonade so she can drive," Nadine said.

Sarah looked at her but didn't say anything. Suddenly her shoulders sagged and she began sobbing softly.

"What the hell would cause people to act like this?" Sarah asked incredulously. "What kind of upbringing did they have that allows them to act like this and expect they'll get away with it?"

"You know the answer," William said solemnly. "You have a psychology degree just like I do."

"Yeah, I know," Sarah admitted. "It's the old sociopathic behavioral model, but it can't all be hereditary. There has to be a huge environmental influence."

"And there is," William said. "Sociopathic behaviors spring from heredity and lack of emotional development."

"And what's that mean in English?" Chauncey asked, as he headed toward the kitchen where Nadine kept the liquor.

"It means that sociopaths like the jokers who assaulted Sarah in the grocery store parking lot lack any understanding of other people's feelings. They don't care if they hurt or scare someone. They have no conscience to speak of," William said. "It's almost like the world revolves around them and to hell with everyone else."

"So they're a bunch of psychopaths," Nadine said emphatically.

"Not really," William corrected her gently. "Psychopaths are different than sociopaths."

"What's the difference?" Chauncey yelled from the kitchen.

"Psychopaths are really mean and nasty people. They have a true mental disorder that makes them aggressively antisocial. Sociopaths are more likely to manipulate people around them for personal gain."

"Kind of like what we saw a lot of at the mission?" Chauncey asked.

"Exactly," William said. "In that type of job you have to know what you're working with, or you're going to get hurt."

"Manipulating people for personal gain like sociopaths do is a technique taught to salespeople," Sarah said, shocked. "They're trained to mimic the speech patterns and personality types of their customers to ingratiate themselves to them. It creates a bonding that they then use to sell their wares. I've taken those classes."

"As you're beginning to see, the sociopathic behavior of those goons in the parking lot isn't much different than what society teaches us to revere."

"So the public loves a good sociopath who can channel their mental illness into a semi-acceptable endeavor because they become the innovator, the free spirit, and the one who takes the path less traveled," Nadine said. "Exactly the person we all strive to be."

"But we don't all attack victims in parking lots," Sarah said bitterly.

"No, but people use it every day in dating behavior," William replied solemnly.

"This is getting juicy," Nadine said, leaning forward. "Go on."

William chuckled. "Think about a smitten young man trying to gain the attention of the young lady he's amorously interested in, at least the sociopath who is good at dating. The rest of us are just bumbling idiots who stick our foot on our mouth every chance we get."

"So the best men are the bumbling incompetents?" Sarah asked as she tried to stifle her smoldering anger with humor.

"Maybe," William said. "I never thought of it that way."

"Come on," Nadine prodded. "I want to hear about dating."

William looked at her. "The sociopath is good at dating because they have a smooth, engaging personality. They're not shy, self-conscious, or the least bit afraid of anything. Conversely, they tend to be self-assured, exciting, and take chances to prove they're superior to others."

"That sounds like the type of guy most girls would go for," Sarah agreed.

"But the down side is that the sociopathic male tends to be a pathological liar, cunning, and manipulative. Not to mention being shallow, callous, irritable, as well as impatient, which may lead to threats, aggression, and verbal abuse if he doesn't get his way."

"That's a fair description of a lot of men I've known over the years," Nadine said, and Sarah also nodded. "Most of the men who seem to be the perfect guy end up being an exploiter, a parasite, or irresponsible. In other words, he ends up being a royal pain in the ass."

"That's because the ingratiating characteristics that are so attractive to women in the early stages of courting are not conducive to long-term, stable relationships."

"That explains a lot," Sarah said, reflecting on the poisoned relationships she had helped her girlfriends through over the years.

"That's why it's easy to categorize and identify the traits those Neanderthals in the parking lot used on you," William said, not sure how Sarah would take what he was about to say.

"What do you mean? They were trying to date me?"

"It may have not seemed like it to you, but they have no conscience, cannot love or be loved, and are unable to abide by accepted social norms. So, yes, it may have been their form of dating."

"That's a little off-base, I think," Chauncey said, standing up and shaking the ice in his glass again. "Anyone want another while I'm up?"

"Yes," Sarah said, handing him her near-empty glass of lemonade. "Don't put as much ice in it this time, if you would please."

Nadine glanced at William.

"No thanks," William told Chauncey, then continued the conversation. "That type of guy can be very dangerous, especially if he shows a sadistic streak as evidenced by chasing you in the truck.

No one knows what would have happened if they had caught up to you. They probably don't even know what they would have done."

"That's pretty scary, if what you say is true, and I'm sure it is," Nadine said seriously. "If everyone who lies, is impulsive, irritable, or is consistently irresponsible has sociopathic tendencies, then most people have shades of mental illness."

"It adds support to my idea that we're all nuts," Sarah said with a nervous laugh.

"You may be right," Nadine nodded.

"I think it's the lack of remorse that sets the sociopath aside from the rest of us, more than any other characteristic," William said as Chauncey gingerly wove his way back into the room and carefully handed Sarah her drink.

"So, they could have easily hurt us and not given a damn," Chauncey said, flopping onto his seat.

"That may explain why so much crime can occur over and over again without the criminals feeling the slightest bit of remorse or guilt," Sarah said, then looked at Nadine.

"What?" Nadine asked, surprised.

"What do you mean, 'What?'"

"That look you gave me. What's the matter?"

"There's nothing wrong," Sarah said as she slumped into her chair. "Chauncey did a great job driving the truck and using it to chase those guys away. The door wasn't even dented where it hit that one bastard. Man! You should have seen him go flying!"

"I wish I could have seen it," Nadine said. "It would have made a great show now that I know the good guys win."

"That's what I'm talking about."

"What are you talking about? Really, Sarah, you confuse the hell out me at times."

"She's talking about me getting a concealed carry permit," Chauncey said glumly. "She's concerned that things could have gone terribly wrong if they hadn't scattered at the sight of a truck almost running them over. I must admit, while a truck is a very effective fight-stopper, it has its drawbacks."

"I was armed and ready to defend myself if it got to that point, but he wasn't equipped to help me or to defend himself, really," Sarah said. "The truck worked this time, but a handgun is much more versatile for personal defense."

"Well, things turned out okay," Chauncey said as he settled deeper into his chair.

"But they may not have," Nadine said flatly. "I can see her point."

Chauncey let the conversation drop while he concentrated on taking a long swallow of his drink. "These Kahlua and cream drinks are pretty good. I could get used to this tradition of having sundowners at the end of the day."

"They are addictive," Nadine said, then turned to Sarah. "So what do you think you should do?"

"It's not what I should do," Sarah replied evenly. "It's what Chauncey should do. Besides trying to change the subject, I mean."

He said, "Oh brother! What do you want me to do now? I'm relaxing after a harrowing day."

"Not today, you pain in the ass," she said kindly. "But first thing tomorrow morning I think you should call the Armed Response Institute and sign up for their intro course."

"What?"

"The Armed Response Institute," Nadine said. "Their ARI-1 course is the one I sent Sarah to last year. They teach you when, how, and when not to shoot in self-defense."

"So you think I should take a course and begin carrying a gun like Sarah?"

"It wouldn't be a bad idea," Nadine said.

"It would have been nice for you to have more options than just using the truck. What would have happened if your stunt hadn't worked out as well as it did?" Sarah said quietly. Her hand holding the glass of lemonade began to shake slightly.

"She's right, Chauncey."

"I already took a course at a place in Texas," he replied. "I found the certificate in the boxes of papers and documents my wife, my ex-wife I should say, gave me after the divorce."

"But you've forgotten the lessons," Sarah pointed out. "You couldn't even remember you took the course."

"That's true," he said. "But they may offer a discount for repeat customers."

"Even if they do offer a discount, it may be a better idea going to an ARI-1 course," Nadine said. "It would be advantageous if you and Sarah, and that includes me since I took the course also, to have the same background. When the shit hits that famous fan, it's good if everyone has the same training. That way each one knows what to expect from the others."

"Good point," Sarah said.

"It does make sense," he conceded.

"Well, it's settled then," Sarah said. "Tomorrow you register for the ARI-1 course."

"But tonight I'm going to get a little giddy by having another one of these," he said, holding up his empty glass again for everyone to see.

CHAPTER 16

THE NEIGHBORHOOD'S CHANGING

"How much of the space in your barn will a flatbed full of hay take up?" Chauncey asked as he surveyed the dark, cavernous hollow of the feed shed.

"It'll take up the entire back half if we stack it tight to the ceiling, and that's after the hay loft is jam-packed full up top," Nadine said without looking up from the block and tackle she was working on.

"It's no wonder you get as many helpers as you can for this job," Sarah said. "Getting the hay off the tractor trailer and up this little slope leading into the barn will be hard enough, but then it has to be stacked all the way up to the underside of the loft?"

"Yep, and as soon as I get this block and tackle rigged up, I'll show you the easiest way to get this done. There's a secret to it that'll make it go as quickly as possible while expending as little effort as we can get away with. I've done this before by myself, but helpers sure make it a whole lot easier."

"And we have to remember to do the job as fast as possible, because the truck driver charges for the time his rig is sitting here," William reminded them.

"That hardly seems fair considering how much he's charging to haul the hay here," Sarah said huffily.

"It is fair, because we have use of his rig while he's sitting here waiting for us to unload it. He can't be on the road with it earning a living if it's sitting here while we waste time. Time is money, especially when equipment is involved," Nadine said. "Doug's told me horror stories of customers wanting him to just leave his flatbed sit while they finished another job before getting around to unloading their hay. He had to put an hourly charge in place to avoid losing money because of a few inconsiderate idiots."

"With this many helpers and the proper equipment we should be able to get this truck offloaded with a minimum of muss and fuss," William said.

"That's the way I have it figured," Nadine replied. "That's why I bought those used steel rollers from the beer distributor when they replaced their old ones. They're still serviceable for this job."

"How do you plan on using them?" Sarah asked. "Chauncey's back can't take too much abuse from really heavy labor."

"I'll use them the same way the beer distributor used them," Nadine said with a sly grin. "They shoved beer cases down the roller ramps from the delivery truck into their warehouse. We'll set them up on carpenter's wooden horses then slide the hay bales up them and into the barn."

"That'll take some effort going uphill won't it?" Chauncey asked.

"It's much easier than it looks at first glance. Doug usually helps by slinging the hay bales onto the rollers. If you and Sarah can roll them up into the barn, then William can slip this hook under the baling twine. William, since you're the strongest, it's your job to pull the rope and heave these bad boys up to me in the loft. Don't use your arms because you'll get too tired. Just throw the rope over your shoulder and walk toward the door to use your leg muscles."

"That makes sense, but won't they be able to off-load the bales faster than I can pull them up to you?" he said, as he eyed the hayloft.

"That's almost a certainty," Sarah said. "Chauncey and I will be able to stack some bales underneath the loft until the pile gets too high. I just can't reach very high with my shoulder."

"That should work," William said as he cast a glance toward the inside of the barn. Just as they finalized their plan, Doug McCarron appeared at the end of Nadine's long lane with a flatbed loaded high with freshly baled hay. The four friends paused to marvel at how easily the huge truck maneuvered down the narrow track. Rex perked his ears and barked a warning.

"It's okay, Rex," Nadine said, reaching down to scratch his ear. "Good dog."

The rumbling road monster pulled in front of the barn so its load was centered at the doors. A plume of dust from the gravel lane enveloped the rig as it slid to a halt.

"Hello, Nadine!" Doug yelled cheerfully from the cab. "You ready to get some exercise?"

"As ready as I'll ever be!" she replied, waving.

When Doug jumped from the tractor, it was easy to see that this short, wiry man had plenty of energy. The spring in his step reminded Sarah of a young boy gearing up to jump into puddles after a spring rain.

"Hello, I'm Doug McCarron," he said as he extended his hand toward William. His shaved and polished head glinted in the early morning sunlight.

"Hello, Doug, I'm William."

"It's a pleasure to meet you, William," he said with a beaming smile crinkling his cheeks with deep wrinkles. He then turned toward Sarah. "And you must be Sarah and Chauncey. Nadine has told me a lot about you, and your trials and tribulations with that farm you bought."

Sarah enthusiastically took the hand he thrust at her. "Hello Doug, it's nice to meet you."

"Have you been able to get Minnie's old place up and running? I was afraid she may have let it go downhill in the last few years. She was pretty old to be running a farm that size by herself all those years, you know."

"I've got it running pretty smoothly these days, thanks to Chauncey, William, and Nadine."

"It's a pleasure to meet you, Chauncey," Doug said as he shifted his hand toward the tall, quiet man standing patiently beside Sarah. "I saw your picture in the paper when you saved all those people in that church. I never dreamed I'd have the pleasure of meeting you in person. It's good knowing there are still men like you around."

"Thank you for your kind words," Chauncey replied as he took his hand and gave it a firm shake while blushing slightly at the complement.

"Y'all ready to get this job done before the sun gets to heating things up too much?"

"We're ready when you are, Doug," Nadine said.

The morning went rapidly as one bale of hay after the other slapped onto the steel rollers and was instantly moved away from the flatbed toward the barn. It didn't take long for the team to fall into a rhythm like a well-oiled machine. The stack of hay on the truck dwindled steadily as the mounds in the barn grew taller and taller.

In a little more than an hour and a half, Nadine declared, "That's all that'll fit into the loft. Let me get down out of here and we'll move this last set of rollers out of the way. That way all three of us can roll the bales into the barn and someone can jump up on the truck and help Doug."

"I'll help Doug," Sarah called. "It may be easier on my shoulder since I can't reach the upper levels of the stacks."

"That'll work," Nadine said as she descended the rickety ladder. "Is everyone holding up okay or do you need a break?"

"I'm doing fine," Chauncey said. "Having that old wash tub filled with ice and bottled water was a great idea, Nadine."

"Anything to keep you guys hydrated and working." She jumped down the last three feet from off the stack of hay and her feet hit the dusty floorboards of the ancient barn with a resounding thud. "Doug, you doing okay?"

"I'm fine, you ready to get back to work?"

"Let's do it," William said with wilting enthusiasm.

The remainder of the hay seemed to disappear from the flatbed more quickly with the new manpower arrangement. Many factories could only wish for an assembly line as efficient as the crew at The Shire worked that morning.

Nadine had nicknamed her farm The Shire after the region where hobbits lived in J.R.R. Tolkien's novels. Hobbits, little hairy human-like individuals with a very formal social structure, have seven named meals during the day and take on life's challenges with a smile and a congenial attitude. Nadine decided that she wanted to live her life in the same manner, with plenty of meals and a great attitude.

As a regular reminder to herself of how she wanted her life to be, she placed the name of the farm in prominent letters on the sign over the entrance of the lane leading into The Shire.

In a very short time, the last of the hay bales clattered down the steel rollers and were whisked away to join the rest.

Giving a huge sigh of relief, Nadine said, "Okay, well done. Is everyone ready for something to eat? I have a pulled pork barbeque in the crockpot that's been slow-cooking since last night, and burgers and hot dogs for on the grill."

"I'm so hungry I could eat one of your horses if he fit on the grill," Doug said, looking at his watch to note the time so he could stop charging Nadine. "But since he won't, a few burgers and some of that barbeque will fill the hole in my belly just fine. I really appreciate you feeding me every time I deliver here, Nadine. You really don't have to do that."

"I most certainly do," she said. "You put a lot of work in helping to unload hay that you're not being paid for. You're paid to haul it, not unload it, and I really appreciate your help and your friendship, Doug."

He said, "Just like those signs displayed by guys on median strips at busy intersections saying, 'Will work for food,' I work for food too. Sometimes people feed me for the work I do, and other times they pay me so I can buy food for my family. Regardless, we all work for food, so let's eat!"

They all laughed and headed for the welcoming shade under the sugar maple. After cleaning up, they enjoyed a fine meal and good conversation. A sluggish mood befell them as their full bellies lulled them into a peaceful respite that could only be improved upon by a nap.

"That was excellent, Nadine," Chauncey said, wiping his face with a white paper napkin. "You are the best slow-cooker chef I know."

"I'll second that," Doug piped in, covering his mouth with his fist to silence a belch.

"You're all welcome." Nadine said as she tossed her paper plate into the trash can. "I really appreciate all your help."

"Manual labor is good for us," Sarah said contentedly. "But I think I've had as much healthy work activity as I can stand today."

"That's for sure," William added tiredly.

"So what's new in your world, Doug?" Nadine asked to avoid having the conversation lag as everyone's eyelids became heavy.

"Well, everything is just fine with me and my family," he said. "But there're some strange things happening around."

"What do you mean?"

"I mean that there're some strange things happening in the area that don't make much sense," he replied hesitantly. "Nothing anyone can put their finger on, but I been hearing things. Just folks talking, you know."

"No, I don't know," Nadine said. The other three listened more intently to hear what the mysterious whisperings amongst the local people all were about. "What have you been hearing? I haven't heard anything too far out of the ordinary."

"Well," he began "There're some rumors that strangers are moving in, and it's making some people a little nervous."

"Doug! You're being evasive and it's driving me crazy. Now what's going on that I don't know about?" Nadine demanded.

"Well ..."

"Doug!"

"Okay, it may be nothing, but I don't really know. Have you ever been down to the Hunter's Lodge near Thompsonville?"

"The place with the really good chicken wings?"

"That's the place. I have a weakness for their Cajun seasoned wings and like to dip them in ranch-style dressing. I seem to need a plate every few weeks to keep my cravings at bay."

"Where is this Hunter's Lodge?" Sarah asked. "I live over near Thompsonville and I don't remember seeing it."

"It's a local hangout down past Thompsonville near Renovo. Renovo's only a wide spot in the road and most folks don't know it's even a town, but most everyone knows where Thompsonville is," Doug explained. "It's owned by a guy who's a scorer for the Boone and Crockett Club. When someone shoots a big deer or bear he scores it, and the biggest taxidermy mount in each category gets hung up in the restaurant side of the business with a little brass plaque with the owner's name, where it was taken, and date of kill engraved on it. It's a big thing to have your mount hung on those walls. One of them has been hanging there for over thirty years."

"What's the Boone and Crockett Club?" Sarah asked.

"I read about it in the outdoors magazines at the barbershop," Chauncey said, his curiosity having overcome his fatigue. "They maintain the records of North American big game animals to assess the success of wildlife conservation and management programs."

"So it's just so everyone knows who shot the biggest buck?" Sarah asked, surprised.

"Far from it," Chauncey said. "The data they've collected has shown the conservation practices in the United States are working. If they hadn't been keeping records, no one would know for sure if there has been a dramatic increase in the amount of game and other wildlife, which there apparently has been."

"Do you hunt?" Doug asked as the conversation was swinging toward his favorite sport.

"No, I don't," Chauncey replied. "Maybe someday I'll look into it a little more, because the sport does intrigue me, but for now I'm too busy to put much effort into it."

"Well, if you do take up hunting just let me know and I'll be happy to show you the right way of doing things," Doug offered.

"Thank you. It's always good to have a mentor and proper instruction when beginning to participate in a new sport. Thanks to Nadine, I had a great start into sporting clays and that's given me many hours of enjoyment."

"Not to mention many hours of meeting and talking to a lot of women who hang out at the sporting clays clubs in this area," Sarah said with a sly smile.

Chauncey didn't take the bait.

"Let's get back onto topic here," Nadine said impatiently. "You can hunt up on Jacob's Mountain behind my farm anytime you want to, you know that. What's going on down at the Hunter's Lodge that's got everyone concerned?"

"Well, it's what's happening on the bar side of the Hunter's Lodge that's got some folks concerned," Doug said, searching for the right words. "The restaurant side is family-oriented so the kids can come in and see the taxidermy mounts and look at all the pictures on the wall of the trophies that aren't big enough to get the privilege of being displayed."

"The bar side serves liquor and that's where the strangers have been hanging out. They're not making trouble or anything, but they won't say where they work or tell anyone anything about themselves. They pretty much just stick to themselves and shoot pool."

"That doesn't seem to be much to worry anyone," Sarah said. "As long as they're not causing any trouble why should it bother anyone else? Everyone around here is too nosy for their own good."

"That's a reasonable question, Doug," Nadine said, trying to soften the impact of Sarah's harsh statement. "What's everyone so worked up about?"

"Well, they say they're up here doing construction, and they have southern accents that are much stronger than you normally hear around here, but they won't say where they work and no one knows of any new construction around here that may have workers from out of state."

"What do these guys look like?" Sarah asked, her suspicions and fear rising.

"There's a bunch of them," Doug said. "You see different ones together on different nights. And they don't always come in regular. At least that's what Bonnie, the waitress there, told me the last time I took my wife over there for a plate of wings. The whole dining room was talking about them. Why do you want to know what they look like?"

"Chauncey and I had a run-in with three guys over at the supermarket in Florentine. They had strong southern accents and it struck me at the time they might not be from around here," Sarah said shakily.

"You think it may be them?"

"I don't know, and I don't want to find out, so maybe I'll pass on the Hunter's Lodge wings for a while."

"So what else is new other than gossip about a few strangers?" Nadine asked to change the subject.

"Well, the Holder boy was killed down in Richmond the other week," Doug replied lazily as sleep began creeping back into his voice.

"An auto accident?"

"No, his body was found lying in an alley. They say he had his knees smashed before being shot."

He shook his head slowly back and forth.

"It's such a shame. He was a good boy. My son used to play football with him up at the high school. They were on the same team, but he was two years ahead of my Sammy. Sammy was pretty big for his age and did real good at football until he messed up his shoulder."

"What was he doing in an alley in Richmond?"

"They say it was drug-related," he said somberly. "I asked Sammy about it when I called him at college last weekend, and he says he never knew him to be involved with drugs. I guess you just never know anymore."

"Was he down there buying drugs?" Chauncey asked.

"No, they say he was down there *selling* them," Doug said. "That's another thing that's bothersome and has everyone talking. Where did he get drugs all the way up here to take down there to sell? He had to get them around here because he was still living on his family's farm."

"Did they say what kind of drugs he was selling?" Nadine asked.

"Something called crystal. I never heard of it."

"Crystal meth," Nadine said, as she looked far off into the sky, trying to remember where she'd heard that name. "I've heard about it."

"Yes, we have," Sarah added. "That's one of the street names Officer Mahoney said methamphetamine was sold under."

"What are you talking about?" Doug asked, suddenly wide awake and attentive.

"A few weeks ago, Sarah and I were taking the horses up Jacob's Mountain back there," Nadine said as she motioned toward the mountain visible above the peak of the barn. "And we ran onto a clandestine meth lab, you know, like the ones they're always warning us about on the local news. The bastards shot at us with a rifle."

"Was anyone hurt?" he asked.

"Luckily, no, no one was hurt though we could have been killed either from being shot or if our horses stumbled down the hill," Nadine said gravely.

"What came of it?" Doug asked, eager to add to the gossip the next time he visited the Hunter's Lodge.

"Nothing came of it," she answered wearily. "The police investigated, but by the time they could organize a team to go all the way up there, the scumbags were gone. It really pisses me off. Who do these assholes think they are to just move in and take over? Excuse my French."

Doug ignored her cussing. "I don't know what's happening with this world we live in, but it sure is changing."

"Times are surely changing, and fast," Nadine agreed.

Not knowing what to say, William and Chauncey could only sit and stare blankly at them.

"Things are getting bad on the road also," Doug added. "There're a lot of robberies at the truck stops now. The bastards either jump drivers when they're on their way back from taking a shower with their hands full of personal gear, or they just attack them while they're sleeping."

"Don't the police watch the truck stops?" Sarah asked in astonishment.

"They sure do, but that doesn't stop the bad guys from taking advantage of folks being alone out there. Lots of times those places are out in the middle of nowhere and the cops are spread pretty thin. You know what it's like in the country."

"Yes, I do," Sarah said. "My farm was burglarized last year and they were long gone by the time the police arrived. Of course, that's not uncommon in the cities either."

"No, it's not," he agreed. "That's why a lot of drivers are risking their jobs just to be able to defend themselves."

"What's that about?" William asked, reaching for the half-full lemonade pitcher, its glass sides dripping with condensation.

"What do you mean?"

"I mean, why are they risking their jobs just to keep themselves safe?"

"Oh, the companies they drive for won't let them carry a gun to defend themselves. Too much liability, they say. I guess they're worried about a driver having to shoot someone breaking into their cab while they're sleeping in the back, and then the company will get sued."

"So, they can't even carry a handgun to defend themselves?" Sarah said.

"Even if they could, they wouldn't carry a handgun. It's too much trouble trying to get concealed carry permits for all the states if they're running cross-country. Each state has its own laws and requirements for a concealed handgun permit. The drivers have too damned many permits and licenses and fees to pay now without having to worry about more. And that's not even taking the paperwork into account. They don't need any more, if they're to have any time left to do their job," Doug said.

"It's a shame we can't get a national concealed carry permit law passed that would allow law-abiding citizens to travel from one state to another and still be able to keep their gun handy for an emergency," Nadine said disgustedly. "Shouldn't all states have to respect that license, like they do driver's licenses?"

"Well, they don't," Doug spat the words out like he couldn't wait to get the taste of them out of his mouth.

"So, truck drivers don't have any way to defend themselves?" Sarah asked, accepting a refill of lemonade from William as he refreshed everyone's drink.

"They're finding ways," he said with a sly grin. "One guy I know pretty well told me he slings one of those black nylon cargo nets from the trunk of his car across the seats in his cab so if someone tries breaking in and rushing him they'll get tangled up in it."

"Then what's he supposed to do? Scream like a princess until someone calls the police and they show up whenever they're able to?"

"Not that old boy," Doug said. "He carries a double barrel shotgun. It breaks down into two pieces in a few seconds for storage and transport, but when he needs it he pops it back together and loads it in less than ten seconds. That way it's not inconvenient to assemble and he can have it ready to go every night without any troubles. In the close confines of the cab he can easily swing those twenty-inch barrels and it will blow big holes in anything or anybody at that range. He sleeps much better now, or so he tells me."

"By carrying a shotgun he doesn't have to worry about crossing state lines and running afoul of their concealed carry laws like he would if he carried a handgun," Nadine said. "That's pretty smart."

"It's only smart if his company doesn't catch him with it," Doug said. "If they do, then he gets fired immediately."

"I think I'd rather run the chance of losing my job than losing my life," Sarah said firmly.

"That's his take on it," Doug said. "He can always get another job, but he only has one life and he doesn't want to risk losing it to some thug trying to rob him of a few dollars."

"Do you take precautions while you're on the road?" Nadine asked hesitantly, not wanting to get too personal.

"Yeah, Nadine, I do. As a matter of fact, I was hoping you'd let me bust a few clays with my new double barrel shotgun on the range you have behind your barn. Knowing where a new gun shoots is important if a person's going to trust their life to it, you know."

"Yeah, Doug, I know," Nadine said.

CHAPTER 17

THE FUTURE

"So what do you want to be when you grow up?" Sarah asked her three companions. Then, looking at Nadine, she asked, "And what are we drinking tonight?"

"It's a peach brandy fizz. You may not find it in any book on mixology, because I made it up myself one day when I was in an experimenting mood," she replied, rubbing her aching back. "What do you mean, 'what do I want to be when I grow up?' I have enough to do already with these horses and keeping you three on the straight and narrow. Besides, putting up all that hay today almost killed me, so I may never get to grow up."

Chauncey and William laughed. "You don't have to keep us on the straight and narrow, Nadine," Chauncey said. "We don't have enough energy to stray after helping you keep these horses fed. As a matter of fact, I need a nap."

William said, "Since meeting you three I haven't had enough energy to get into trouble if I wanted to. I love staying busy and my days have been blissfully filled to the max ever since I moved up here. I'm having such a good time I don't know why I'd want to grow up."

"William and I have our plans set to become Certified Public Accountants and Wall Street tycoons," Chauncey told them. "Between our studies and working on the farm, not to mention William working at the County Turf and Tractor store and my bookkeeping chores, we really don't have time to think about much more to accomplish in the near future. Don't you agree, William?"

"I wholeheartedly agree," he said. "These peach brandy fizzes really sneak up on a person! What about you, Sarah, what do you want to be when you grow up?"

"Well, ever since the terrorist attack on St. Boniface's church last Christmas, I've been thinking about taking the classes to become an NRA certified firearms instructor," she replied seriously. A somber mood fell over the room at the mention of the shootout that left her handicapped. "I think I've regained sufficient range of motion in my shoulder to be able to shoot well enough to demonstrate to a class, if I have to."

"You have been shooting pretty well," Nadine agreed. "You've been able to work your way back up to the .357 magnum range of handguns without too much pain, either during or after a range session, and that's the heaviest recoiling handgun you'll probably ever shoot in a self-defense class."

"I'm still handicapped while shooting sporting clays, but I can shoot my AR-15s pretty well," she replied.

"As the local coyote population can attest to," Chauncey said.

"Well, my coyote hunting isn't very good, because I can't seem to call them in very well, but Tom Mahoney has been doing a pretty good job of getting their numbers down. He's obsessed with thinning out the predators so the deer and turkey populations rebound. He really likes his venison."

"Have you looked into what it all takes for you to become an NRA certified instructor?" Nadine asked.

"I've looked into it for us to become instructors, yes."

"What's this 'we' stuff?"

"You and I," Sarah said hastily. "You're the one who not only taught me how to shoot, but you've taught everyone else, and that's soon to include Maddy Lewis. You're an excellent teacher. I think you miss teaching. Maybe not the classroom stuff you studied for in college, but the excitement is still there when you're instructing a pupil."

"Good luck getting me into an instructor's training course," Nadine said with a nervous laugh. "I have so much to do around here I barely have time to breathe."

"You can get William and Chauncey to watch the horses for a few days while we attend the classes."

"We'd be happy to look after your farm," William said.

"You've taught us everything we need to know to take care of the horses' daily requirements," Chauncey added.

"I know you guys are quite capable of running this place, but why do I need a course to teach me what I already know?" she replied half-heartedly.

"Because you need the credentials, so your students take your lessons seriously," Sarah said. "If they know you take your responsibilities as a teacher to heart, and you completed the certification courses to be the best instructor you can be, then they'll be more attentive at the lessons. You know I'm right."

Nadine sighed heavily. "Yeah, you're right. I spent four years in college and another three with continuing education just to get my teaching degree so I could be qualified enough to be a school teacher. I guess I should get the credentials to be a shooting instructor also."

"It's settled then," Sarah beamed. "You and I will attend the courses to become firearms instructors, and Chauncey will attend an ARI-1 course to learn all he'll need when he gets his concealed carry permit."

"You make it all sound so easy," Chauncey said. "Why do I think this is going to be a much more involved undertaking than you're making it sound?"

CHAPTER 18

A.R.I. SHOPPING

"Are you sure I need all this stuff?" Chauncey asked as he scanned the list of gear. "This will take forever to get and I don't know if I can afford all this."

"You can afford it," Sarah said. "You just don't like to go shopping, even if it's for yourself."

"Oh! You noticed that, did you?"

"How could I not notice? You whine and cry the entire time we're at a store. You sound like a little kid. 'Are we done yet? Can we go home now? I'm tired. I'm hungry. I have to go to the bathroom. Can we stop for ice cream?'"

Chauncey broke out in a deep, resonating laugh. "Okay, you're right. I didn't know I was such a pain, but that all sounds mighty familiar."

"Well, you have to have this stuff to attend the ARI-1 course. They say it's rain or shine, and they mean it. You'll be glad you have all this. Believe me, I've been there. It's grueling."

"Luckily Nadine took you shopping to get all this stuff when you attended the course. So now we know where to get what I need, and that saves us from having to run around trying to figure out where to find it all."

"Most of it we can get at The Outdoors Connection," she said. "It's almost a one-stop shopping trip."

"And for that I'm grateful," he said.

The rest of the journey was uneventful and their shopping carts filled quickly. If they hadn't been having so much fun and laughing like children at their silly antics, they may have noticed Twister lurking amidst the aisles keeping a close watch on them.

"Are you sure we have everything?"

"We have everything on the list we printed off the A.R.I. website," Sarah replied. "When I took the course the only thing I would have added was more bottled water than they suggested. You'll get very thirsty since you're outside most of the day."

"We'll get that at the supermarket, which is our next stop, unless you want to get lunch. Are you sure you're not comfortable going back to Harper's Supermarket in Florentine? They have a much nicer produce section than the store here in Spinale."

"I'm not going back there for a long time, just in case those assholes shop there all the time. I don't want another run-in with that bunch. And I do want lunch before we go to the supermarket, otherwise we'll be hungry and buy much more than we need."

That's them! And that bitch called us assholes! I'll teach her for calling us assholes ...Twister thought as he eavesdropped on their conversation from two aisles over.

"I still want Klondikes whether we have lunch or not," Chauncey said. "Maybe you can live without ice cream, but I think it's uncivilized."

"You're going to get fat and that stuff will clog your arteries."

"With all the work I do around the farm, I burn up enough calories to eat an entire box every day and still not get fat. Besides, I eat enough green leafy vegetables to stop any artery plaquing before it starts."

"You do not eat enough raw vegetables."

"I do too."

"You do *not*."

"Do too."

And so it went throughout their entire shopping excursion.

CHAPTER 19

FOLLOWED

"You won't believe what I seen."

"What you see?"

"I was down to The Outdoors Connection buyin' some new coolers and such to replace the ones we lost up on the mountain when the po'lice come," Twister said with glee. "And I saw that black bastard and his snowy white bitch. Them ones that almost run us over?"

"Yeah?" Nacco said. "Where they go?"

"They went food shoppin' then home after buying a whole bunch of stuff. They had sun lotion, hats, raincoats, bullets, all kinds of stuff."

"Did you follow them?" Squeaky asked, leaning forward on the bed rail of the battered pick-up. "Where they go?"

"They went to the supermarket over in Spinale down the street from The Outdoors Connection after they had lunch, then they went to a farm named Predator's Bane. At least that's what the sign said out at the road."

"You remember where it's at?"

"Yep, I even got mileage back to a small town called Thompsonville," Twister said with pride. "We gonna get that bitch and her nigger boyfriend back for messin' with us!"

"Here what we gonna do," Squeaky said, his eyes flicking back and forth feverishly. "We gonna scout out that place and see what they do and when they do it. Then we figure out how we want to get 'em. We gonna have us some fun."

"What you thinkin' about?"

"I thinkin' we need to show that bitch what real men like," Squeaky said. "Then we burn their place just to let them know we mean business."

"What about the nigger?"

"He's a dead man walkin'," Squeaky said with a look of hatred.

CHAPTER 20

MADDY SETTLES IN

"Nadine, this is Maddy, Dan Lewis's sister," Sarah said, making introductions as Nadine strode up to meet them at Sarah's truck. "Maddy, this is Nadine Brand."

"Hello Maddy," Nadine said.

"It's nice to meet you," Maddy said in reply.

"Maddy is having a problem with her old boyfriend stalking her and she needs to learn how to shoot defensively as soon as possible," Sarah said.

"Dan has helped me out of some pretty difficult situations when I got sick, so I'll be happy to see if I can help," Nadine said. "But you do know that Sarah and I haven't gone to the firearms instructor courses yet, so we don't have our certifications. Is that alright with you?"

"Of course," Maddy said. "My brother says you've gotten a lot of the local folks on the right track to shooting, and if he places his full trust in your abilities, then so do I."

"Did you get a protective order from the courts?"

"Yes I did," Maddy hesitated. "They issued a temporary order and I'll have a hearing in two weeks to see if they'll issue a permanent one."

"Good, that's the first step," Nadine said. "Just remember that the protective order is not to protect you against any aggressive actions he may take against you. It's only a piece of paper that'll give you a little legal protection to help verify you thought your life was in danger."

"In other words, I'm laying a paper trail so if I have to shoot him I can more easily prove it was self-defense?"

"That's it in a nutshell," Nadine said. "Now, let's go down behind the barn and see if we can give you a few skills to help you in the most extreme circumstances."

"To save my life?"

"That's right. Are you ready?"

"Let's go."

As always, the lessons began with the rules of shooting and range safety. To give Maddy added confidence, Nadine had Sarah and Maddy shoot side-by-side as if they both were pupils. By doing so, Maddy was able to see how Sarah handled a firearm and was better able to mimic her actions. The morning went quickly with Maddy acquiring the skills to manipulate and fire a revolver with smooth and proficient movements.

"How am I doing?" Maddy asked.

"You're doing quite well," Nadine said.

"You have to understand, Maddy," Sarah said. "Nadine was a schoolteacher for a number of years. Her teaching skills really come in handy during any lesson she's giving."

"Thank you so very much for your help," Maddy said. "I hope I never have to use what I just learned, but I'm much more at ease knowing I have the power to stop him, if he comes to hurt me again."

"We've only gone over the actions of shooting," Nadine said. "Let's go up and sit in the shade and get into the difficult part."

Nadine saw the questioning look in Maddy's eyes, but chose to ignore it.

The women cleaned up the range area and retired to the sugar maple. After everyone was settled in the shade, Nadine excused herself and returned with a glass pitcher brimming with iced tea and three tall glass tumblers.

"I have the lemon wedges and sugar in separate bowls because Sarah can never make up her mind whether she wants her tea sweetened or not," Nadine said.

"I like to be difficult just to make Nadine's life miserable," Sarah said wryly.

"This is very nice," Maddy said, looking around the farm. "You've obviously put a lot of work into this place."

"Yes I have," Nadine replied. "I really appreciate you noticing. That means a lot to me, especially since you know what running a farm is like. Why did you ever leave your family's farm in the first place?"

Sarah looked quickly at Maddy, not sure how she would take Nadine's question. Sarah need not have worried, because Maddy took it in stride and didn't seem to mind answering.

"I was in love," she said whimsically. "Young, stupid, and in love."

"Been there and done that," Nadine said.

"John was handsome and full of energy. He was going to build an ideal life for us, but his troubled past always seemed to taint his future plans," Maddy said, wiping a small tear from the corner of her eye. "Obviously, the world had different plans for us."

"What happened?"

"He couldn't seem to get any of his plans to bear fruit," Maddy said. "God knows he tried, but something always seemed to sink his best efforts. Looking back on it, it may have been John's wretched upbringing that kept him from being able to get his feet under him financially. We ended up in bankruptcy. If it hadn't been for me working full time, plus having a second job at the convenience store on weekends, we wouldn't have survived."

"That's a tough thing for a man to have to endure."

"Yes, it is," Maddy said, as she took a long swig of her iced tea then decided it needed more sugar. As she stirred her drink, she continued, "When we had to file bankruptcy it took the life out of him. I could see the changes in him as it was happening."

They sat in silence for a few moments, then Maddy said, "But that's all in the past. What do I have to do to deal with my current situation?"

"You have to develop a proper mindset," Nadine said. "Everything you learned this morning will be for naught if you can't pull the trigger when and if the time comes."

"So you're saying I have to be absolutely positive I can pull that trigger, and possibly kill the man who was my lover for eleven years, before I even consider carrying a gun?"

"That's right."

"The answer is yes," Maddy said, her hands shaking badly enough that she had to set her glass down. "John McGuire is not the man I knew. He's a stranger who almost killed me once, and who will never lay a hand on me again."

She broke down in gut-wrenching sobs, sending Nadine in search of a box of tissues while Sarah placed a comforting arm around her shoulders. She wiped her nose on her wrist just as Nadine thrust the tissues toward her.

"Thank you," she said, pulling a handful from the box. "Sorry about that. So, how do I develop the proper mindset?"

"The easiest and most effective way is to visualize or imagine a number of different scenarios. This may not be easy and you'll have to force yourself to imagine the most horrific events in great detail."

"Such as?"

"Think of likely situations you may be in when attacked," Nadine said. "If you're driving down a lonely country road and he tries to run you into the ditch, how will you react? In that instance, you should have a cell phone to call police, tell them where you are, and then ask where you should try driving to meet them. Give them a description of the car he's driving and explain you have a protective order."

"So, I have to think of how I would react in different situations, and be ready to defend myself if I have to, but contact the police if at all possible?"

"Yes, and in this case it would be documented because all 9-1-1 calls are recorded. That's why it's important to give them as many details as possible. That can work to your advantage, so keep the phone lines open."

"Unfortunately, the cell phone coverage in this area is spotty."

"Put that into your scenario," Nadine said. "How will you react and what will you do if you're not able to get phone reception?"

"Wow! That's a good question. What would I do?"

"It's up to you to answer that question. You have to imagine the most likely scenarios and then visualize how you will handle it over and over again in your mind."

"That way, it will be like I've been in that situation before," Maddy said. "I'll have done it before in my mind, or at least a mental scenario close enough to not be totally caught off-guard."

"That's the idea," Nadine said. "By using visualization, you can develop a mindset so you'll do what's necessary without hesitation. Indecision can get you killed, sometimes by your own gun if he gets close enough to take it away from you. Then there's paying attention to your surroundings."

"That seems obvious," Maddy said.

"Yes, it does, but you'd be surprised how many people are busy rooting in their purse in the parking lot of the supermarket and forget to keep vigilant about who's around them," she said, looking at Sarah.

"I'll bet I do that without thinking about it."

"I'll bet you do, most of us are guilty of it," Nadine said.

"So how do you train yourself to overcome habits you may have had all your life?"

"You work on it. It sounds trite, but it's the only way to begin learning new behaviors."

"So I'm supposed to be paranoid all the time?"

"I didn't say paranoid," Nadine said. "Being vigilant means knowing who is around you at all times and if they belong there."

"I should look for things out of the ordinary then?"

"Yes," Nadine said. "If something looks suspicious, then it's probably out of the ordinary and demands a higher level of scrutiny."

"Luckily, if I can use that term, Maddy knows who the most likely person is to harm her," Sarah said.

"Maybe, maybe not," Nadine replied. "This guy could hire someone to harm her. You just never know."

"What other tips do you have for visualization?" Maddy asked, trying to change the subject to a less scary one.

"Well, you'll want to imagine a confrontation occurring in a place you would never expect it to," Nadine said. "What about church? Can you imagine having to shoot someone during a church service?"

"Well, actually, I can," Sarah said. "That stuff happens."

"That's true," Nadine said. "There are actually more shootings in churches than you'd imagine, because they're considered to be gun-free zones where a killer can murder at will and without interference, just like universities and high schools."

Sarah asked, "Since you know John so well, how do you think he may come after you?"

After careful consideration, Maddy finally replied, "I think I can assume John will act like a stalker in some manner or the other. It's his style. What are some of the traits of a stalker I should be aware of?"

"From what little I know, a stalker usually hangs around your home or work," Nadine said. "Those are places they know you'll show up and it's easier for them to formulate a plan."

"During one of the breaks at ARI-1—that's where Chauncey is right now—a bunch of us were talking with one of the instructors and he said some interesting things that may be helpful to you," Sarah said. "One thing that stuck in my mind is that the majority of women who are assaulted by their stalker are attacked while sleeping in bed."

"From the stalker's point of view, that makes sense," Nadine nodded.

"It does," Sarah said. "According to the instructor, the attacker usually jumps on their victim while they're in bed, pinning them beneath the blankets. Just the thought of that will keep you awake all night long."

"So how are you supposed to defend yourself while in bed, especially if you're asleep?" Maddy asked. "Should I keep a gun in my nightstand? A lot of people do that. John did."

"That isn't a good plan because you may not be able to get to your nightstand drawer," Sarah said. "An attacker will expect you have a weapon in the drawer and can easily prevent you from getting your hands on the gun. You don't want your firearm just out of reach."

"The same goes for putting your handgun under your pillow," Nadine added. "In a scuffle you may push the gun from under your pillow and lose it off the bed, or worse, it will pop out right in front of your attacker and now he's armed and you're defenseless."

"That's scary."

"It is, but you'll have to figure something out that will keep the gun where you can find it in middle of the night and not get lost if you need it. Has there been any word of him being in this area, looking for you?"

"None yet, and I hope it stays that way. I'm beginning to look for a job and an apartment. If he shows up, then I'll deal with it. I can't keep my life on hold by living in fear."

"That's wise," Nadine said. "But you have to take a few more things into consideration, because a gun isn't a magic talisman that'll protect you from evil. It's just a tool that you hope you'll never have to use."

"What are you talking about?"

"I'm talking about taking precautions to avoid a violent confrontation," Nadine said, reaching for the pitcher. "Let's look at the problems with getting an apartment."

"I have to live somewhere. I can't be mooching off my relatives forever."

"That's true, but you have to realize the limitations an apartment puts on your ability to avoid being attacked."

"You mean besides living alone?"

"Exactly. You should try to have early warning of an intruder getting into your apartment, but most apartment complexes don't allow you to keep a dog, and having an alarm system installed in a building you don't own may not be an option."

"So what should I do?"

"I'm going to suggest you begin reading up on the subject and then attend a Refuse to be a Victim course offered by the National Rifle Association."

"But you've already taught me how to shoot."

"The course doesn't teach shooting," Nadine said. "It teaches how to pay attention to your surroundings and other techniques to avoid being attacked."

"Where can I find out about where the course is offered?"

"I'm a member, so I'll call and get you the information."

"You're sure hell-bent on sending people to various self-defense courses, aren't you?" Sarah teased.

"Somebody has to keep you girls safe."

CHAPTER 21

AMY AND KATHY LEWIS

"I don't know why I let you talk me into these situations."

"Oh, quit griping," Sarah said. "You'll love being in the front row to see Dan introduce me to his daughters, and you know it."

"I guess it's much better than hearing about it secondhand," Nadine said. "And I must admit that I love riding in this car."

"Yeah, I thought I deserved a nice luxury sedan so I'm not driving around the city in my pickup truck," Sarah said. "Seriously though, I really appreciate you coming along."

"No problem. How is this whole thing supposed to work?"

"Dan and I came up with a plan to meet accidentally at the mall while he's shopping with his daughters. Having you along will hopefully make our initial meeting a little less stressful, and ease them into the idea of their dad beginning to date again."

"Are you going to tell them you're dating their father when you meet today?"

"No way! The idea is to meet them on neutral ground with you and I being introduced as acquaintances of Dan's. The goal is to allow them to get to know me in a non-threatening situation."

"Then you're going to be introduced as the wicked step-mother at a later date?"

"Avoiding the wicked step-mother gig is why we're going through all these charades," Sarah said, nervously biting her lower lip.

"Hopefully they'll get used to me as a friend and I can slowly work on gaining their trust."

"It sounds like a well thought-out plan. I hope it works half as well as it sounds."

"You and I both."

Sarah wheeled into a spot toward the end of the parking lot, well away from the crush of chubby couch potatoes jockeying for the spaces closest to the door.

"You would still rather walk across the entire parking lot instead of fighting those folks for a closer parking place?" Nadine said, knowing Sarah's habit of getting physical activity every chance she had.

"A little exercise will do us both good," Sarah said, her mind fixed on her upcoming get-together with Daniel and his daughters. "I have enough stress in my life and the last thing I need is to be fighting someone for a parking space when perfectly good ones are available out here with plenty of room around them."

"So where are we supposed to accidentally run into them and at what time?"

"We're supposed to meet in the dead center of the mall, at the jewelry store."

"Let me see," Nadine said. "It's almost eleven-thirty now, so the meet must be scheduled for high noon."

"So right you are, Oh Sage One," Sarah said. "When else would you arrange the meeting of this well-orchestrated plan other than high noon?"

"Am I going to get lunch out of this?"

"Yes, you are. The plan is to bring up lunch in conversation, then go to the food court for an impromptu meal together. Eating off plastic trays has a nice homey quality about it for our get-acquainted meeting, don't you think?"

"Oh yeah," Nadine said. "It's the New Americana alright. Norman Rockwell would be beside himself painting that scene."

"Oh, by the way," Sarah said. "It would look better if we have some packages with us. Do you have anything you have to buy before noon?"

"I need a new pair of jeans, but that may take longer than we have. How about you?"

"I need some lingerie, but carrying a Victoria's Secret bag may not be such a good idea when I first meet the girls."

"How about birthdays? Do you need any birthday cards?"

"No, but I may be able to pick up a new shirt or something for Chauncey."

"Do you know his size?"

"It doesn't matter," Sarah replied. "I can return it if he doesn't like it."

"Good point. Let's hurry or we'll be late for the big moment."

Sarah had a plastic bag containing Chauncey's new striped shirt looped over her wrist so she could handle the gold necklaces she and Nadine were ogling when Daniel and his daughters, Amy and Kathy, stopped to look at the aquamarine jewelry exhibited in the secured display case. The brilliantly intense light from strategically placed halogen lamps bearing down on the gems made them sparkle seductively. The young girls pointed excitedly as their eyes grew wide with wonder.

They're such happy young ladies, Sarah thought as she observed them through the glass.

Nadine gave Sarah a nod, signaling her to give the necklace back to the clerk, so they could leave the store. As planned, they walked out just as Daniel and his daughters were still in the midst of being enthralled by the beauty of the jewels.

"Well, hello Dan!" Nadine said, as she came abreast of the trio. "Are you three out supporting the economy today?"

"Why, hello Nadine," Daniel replied with an overdose of surprise in his voice. "How are you?"

"I'm doing fine, thank you for asking. You remember Sarah, don't you?"

"Yes I do. How's your hand doing?"

"It's healed up wonderfully, thank you," Sarah said. "Thank you for treating it so well."

"Oh, excuse me for not making introductions," he said, stepping aside. "These are my daughters, Amy and Kathy. Girls, this is Nadine Brand and her friend, Sarah."

The girls looked suspiciously at the two women before remembering their manners. "It's nice to meet you," Kathy said, shaking hands with Nadine. After a momentary pause, she took Sarah's.

Amy stood still for a long moment before following her sister's lead.

"Well, have you found all you were shopping for?" Daniel asked as he looked at Sarah's bag.

"I have a good start," she said. "So far I've bought a shirt for a friend's birthday gift, but I have more shopping to do."

"We were going to get some lunch, then continue our shopping after we're refreshed," Nadine said.

"We were going to get lunch, then jump into our shopping list," he said. "Would you like to join us at the food court?"

"That sounds nice," Nadine said. "It will be nice having a chance to chat. Are there any suggestions you girls have for lunch? I don't shop here much and don't know which restaurants have the best food."

"The pizza is good," Amy offered.

"That sounds like a good idea. Is everyone ready?"

"I am!" Amy said.

"Let's get some lunch then," Daniel said.

The food court was like a zoo at feeding time with frazzled parents and gibbering children hurrying to and fro in a frenzied rush. Wisely, Daniel chose a table on the outskirts of the hubbub.

After getting their food from various vendors, they all sat down to eat and talk in a jumbled mixture of conversation and adolescent silliness. The girls and Nadine were happily munching on pizza and soda, while Sarah and Daniel enjoyed specialty salads and bottled spring water.

"Do you girls come here often?" Sarah asked.

"Only when we need clothes," Kathy said. "Dad doesn't get off work on Saturdays until late in the afternoon, and Sunday is too busy to go shopping."

"Have you ever tried going shopping during the week?"

"Dad works too late," Amy said. "The stores are all ready to close by the time we can get here."

"Your father is busy," Sarah said. "There are a lot of people who depend on him to take care of them."

"That's what Aunt Maddy says," Amy added emphatically.

"What do you do?" Kathy asked Sarah warily.

"I was a Doctor of Chiropractic practicing in Washington, and then Northern Virginia, but I got hurt and had to stop. Now I spend time on my farm and consulting with other doctors on how to operate their chiropractic practices. What school do you attend?"

"How did you get hurt?" Amy asked.

"I got shot in my shoulder and had to stop practicing," Sarah explained.

"You got shot?" Kathy asked incredulously.

"Yes, terrorists attacked a church I was attending, and I was injured."

"I heard about that on the news," Kathy said. "It was at Christmas time, wasn't it?"

"Yes, it was," Sarah said, and then quickly asked, "What grade are you in?"

"Were there other people hurt at the church?" Amy asked, not willing to give up the topic.

"Yes, there were," Sarah said, desperately looking at Daniel and Nadine for help to get out of explaining a distressing tale that renewed painful memories. "Does anyone else need more soda?"

"I could use some more," Nadine said, seeing Sarah was becoming exasperated. "Would you girls like to come with me to get more?"

"Yes, I'd like more," Amy said. "Can I have more soda, Daddy?"

"Only half a glass," Daniel said sternly. "Kathy, would you like more soda?"

"No thanks, I'm fine," she replied coolly.

These kids are so well mannered and mature. What am I trying to do, getting in the middle of all this? Sarah thought. "So, you live on a farm?" she asked Kathy.

"Yes, it's been in our family for generations."

"You've lived on the farm all your life then," Sarah said. "That's a nice place to grow up. I was raised in the city."

"The city is okay to visit, but I wouldn't want to live there."

"I agree. I didn't know how nice a farm was until I came to visit Nadine for a few weeks, and then I learned how much I had been missing all the years I lived in cities."

"Are you finished?" Daniel asked, pointing to Sarah's plate. "If you are, I'll take it to the trash can to make more room on the table."

"Yes, thank you." Their eyes lingered on each other for a brief moment. As she handed him her plastic tray their hands brushed against each other.

This is going well. Maybe this will work out okay, Sarah thought as Kathy, with thoughtful nibbles, returned to eating her pizza. The conversation lagged and a peaceful quiet descended upon them. Enjoying the sense of belonging and peacefulness of being with a family, Sarah wrapped herself in the tranquility of the moment. With a small smile beginning to curl at the corner of her mouth, Sarah thought, *Yeah, this may work out just fine.*

When Nadine returned with Amy, Sarah gave her a confident smile.

Nadine thought, *Sarah certainly looks happy, so things must be going well with Kathy.*

Daniel, Amy, and Nadine sat down and had just gotten settled when Kathy organized the trash on her tray, then abruptly stood up. She stood with her spine straight and rigid as a board while her expression was austere and business-like.

"Come on, Amy, we're going shopping," she declared brashly as she lifted her tray and stepped away from the table.

"But I just got back."

"Come *on*," she insisted. "We're going shopping."

Amy was dumbfounded, but obeyed her older sister without further comment and stood up.

"Why don't you just sit here for a little longer and we can all go shopping together when everyone is done with their drinks?" Daniel said evenly.

"Because I don't want to go shopping with *her*!" she yelled, tossing her head in Sarah's direction.

Sarah's mouth dropped open and her head snapped toward Nadine, looking for guidance. Nadine could only shrug her shoulders and silently shake her head in confusion.

"Kathy! What's the matter with you?" Daniel cried in exasperation and embarrassment. "Where are your manners?"

"I'll tell you what the matter is. You're dating *her*! You think we wouldn't notice? I'm out of here. I'll meet you later at Sears when you're done visiting with *her*!" She spun on her heels and began walking away. "Amy! Come *now*!"

Amy stared at Sarah, and then at her father, with a look of horror. She was obviously shaken and distressed. Without a word, she bolted after her sister, tossing her unfinished soda into the trashcan as she sped by it.

"I'm sorry," Daniel said as he stood. "You'll have to excuse me. I'm truly sorry," he stammered, and then he stumbled after his distraught teens.

Sarah continued to sit with her mouth hanging open in stunned silence as she watched them disappear into the crowd.

Nadine said, "Well, that went well, don't you think?"

CHAPTER 22

FATHER AND DAUGHTER HEART-TO-HEART

"Daddy, you haven't said much, and you seemed mad while we were shopping," Amy tentatively said.

Daniel stopped walking and looked at his youngest daughter as they climbed the front steps of their house after arriving home from the disastrous shopping trip.

He looked down at the sagging wooden planks of the front steps and took a moment to organize his thoughts. His mind wandered from fatigue, and he began thinking, *I have to have those steps replaced before someone gets hurt, but first I have to get this mess straightened out with my daughters.*

Why does everything always have to be done immediately? Why in the hell can't I ever have time to think things out and handle them in an orderly manner instead of always fighting off the latest crisis?

He pulled his mind out of his reverie and admonished himself. *Don't let yourself wallow in self-pity; this is entirely of your own making. It just didn't turn out like you had hoped it would and now you have a mess to clean up.*

"I'm not mad, honey," he replied sweetly, taking her hand. "I'm just a bit disappointed in how you girls acted today. Let's all go to the kitchen table and talk about how things should have been handled in a more appropriate manner."

"We didn't do anything wrong," Kathy snapped.

"Let's get settled, then I'll meet you both at the kitchen table in five minutes and we'll discuss it," Daniel said firmly, heading upstairs to change his clothes.

After dressing in what he considered to be his "weekend suit" consisting of a well-worn pair of blue jeans, a long-sleeved plaid cotton shirt, and ragged sneakers, he tossed the clothes he had worn to the mall into a laundry hamper. He sat down heavily on the edge of his bed, and hung his head in exhaustion. Slowly raising his eyes, he looked across the room at the silver-framed picture from his wedding day so many years ago.

Honey, I need your help, he thought as hot tears began coursing down his cheeks. *I know this is a hell of a thing to be asking your help with, but you're the only one I have to turn to. You've always been my best friend and always will be, even if I'm asking you how I'm going to get another woman into my life.*

You know I've always been faithful to you, but the girls need a woman in their life. Hell, I need a woman in my life. This isn't easy for me to talk to you about, but you know it's true. Without you here I'm just wasting away from the inside out; I'm getting like a prune inside and I can't do my job or raise our children correctly if I lose my humanity.

I've met this really nice woman, Sarah Collins. She lost her husband over a year ago in a carjacking. He was a doctor too, an orthopedist, and criminal animals executed him just for thrills. His death doesn't make any more sense than yours does. Good people shouldn't have to die so young and leave a grieving spouse behind. It's just not fair.

I don't know which is worse; watching your loved one slowly die like I watched you wither away, or have a spouse murdered just when life seems to be going so well. That's what happened to Sarah, but she seems to have adapted pretty well to being single again; much better than I have, it seems.

I've wondered if it would be easier to see you lying in a pool of blood in a parking lot like Sarah found her husband, or having time to face the reality of being alone like I did. At least I had time to try and be brave. She didn't.

Anyway, she's a good woman and I think you two would have liked each other. You may have even been the best of friends, if you'd have had a chance.

I need your help, honey. You have to give me a sign of some type and lend a hand so I say the right things to the girls. They need your assistance in getting through this more than I do.

He wiped the tears from his face with the back of his sleeve, and then went into the bathroom to wash his face with cold water. He stared blankly at his reflection in the mirror.

He wagged his head back and forth in disgust thinking that he looked like hell warmed over, but knew he had to do his best to get this situation straightened out.

He flipped the light off and with a determined stride headed downstairs, focusing on the upcoming conversation he was about to have with his daughters. When he entered the kitchen, Amy and Kathy were busy baking a batch of brownies from a box.

"I'll clean up the mess, Daddy," Amy said, before her father could comment on the flecks of brownie mix that splattered the sink board. "I pulled the mixer out of the bowl before it was finished spinning."

"As long as you clean it all up," he said. *My God! They're so cute working together. Can I risk ruining the life they've known by bringing someone else into our lives?*

"We can talk after the brownies are in the oven," Kathy said matter-of-factly, not bothering to look at her father. "It will just take a minute."

Kathy scraped the mix into a glass pan and gingerly placed it into the oven while Amy held the door open.

Being careful not to burn her bare hands, Kathy gingerly slid the glass pan toward the back of the middle rack of the oven. Satisfied it was perfectly centered, she then stepped back and watched as Amy gently closed the oven door.

"Set the timer for twenty minutes, then we'll check the brownies with a toothpick when it goes off," she told Amy, before taking a seat directly across the table from her father. Her reflection bounced off the polished surface and she lovingly glided her hand across it.

"I like it when the light shines off the table instead of using a tablecloth," she said, in an attempt to postpone the discussion.

Daniel didn't reply.

"I like the pretty white embroidered tablecloth," Amy said, as she slid into the chair beside her sister. "It gets stained easily, but it's prettier than just wood."

Daniel remained silent, waiting for Amy to settle herself. Only after she was happy with her seat and looking expectantly at him did he begin.

"I want to discuss your behavior at the food court this afternoon. I understand you were upset with meeting new people and we will discuss that situation also, but first I want you to understand that the type of behavior you displayed will not be tolerated. It was childish and not what is expected of young ladies your age."

"What did you expect?" Kathy answered. "You think we wouldn't notice you making goo-goo eyes at her? It was disgusting."

Daniel was shocked. He fought to keep the fury in his gut from showing on his face.

"Let me explain something to you. It has been over five years since your mother passed away. I miss her so much I thought I would never want to date anyone else again. Then I met Sarah and I realized how lonely I had been all those years."

"You have us to keep you company," Amy cried in a quivering voice.

"I know, honey," he replied as his eyes began filling with tears. He fought to keep the churning in his gut from erupting in an emotional breakdown. "But this is different, and you know it. I need adult companionship. It's not normal to go through life without someone your own age to share it with."

"How did you meet her?" Kathy demanded. Her gaze didn't waver.

"She came to my office with a wound on her hand," he said calmly. "She and Nadine were cleaning out a shed and an old garden tool cut across the palm of her hand. It was dirty and would have gotten infected without proper care."

Kathy's rage seemed to melt when she visualized the pain involved. "So you fixed her hand and then asked her for a date? Isn't that against the rules of being a doctor?" she asked, after remembering she was supposed to be the injured party in this discussion.

"No, I didn't ask her for a date, and you know it. We met again at the Millvale Sportsman's Club a few weeks later when she was shooting sporting clays. We shot a round together and then ate cheeseburgers and drank an orange soda. It wasn't anything clandestine or illegal. We found out that we enjoyed spending time together. When things like that occur unexpectedly, it's as though God just wanted it to happen."

"Did you have sex with her? That's what they always do in the movies," Amy asked innocently.

Taken aback, Daniel stammered, "No, I have not had sex with her. That's always kept for after people are married. Remember that. Sex is only after marriage and never before. What movies are you watching that have that in them, anyway? Nothing I allow you to watch."

"Becky's mom allows her to watch movies with sex in them. Remember? I go over there on Thursdays to play, and sometimes we watch movies if it's raining."

"I'll have to speak with Becky's mother," he said, gruffly.

"So what did you think we would do when you faked not knowing her at the mall?" Kathy asked. "Do you think we're so stupid that we'd just fall in love with her like you did?"

"I never said I was in love with her," Daniel said. "She's a nice woman I enjoy talking to and doing things with, like shooting sporting clays. And her name is Sarah, so why don't you try using it when referring to her? It's a common courtesy to use people's names when speaking of them."

"*Okay.* So this Sarah is fun to be with. What do you want us to say? That we like her and we're glad you're dating her? Well, I'm not happy about it and I *don't* like her."

"And why don't you like her?"

Kathy had no immediate answer.

Realizing her silence was speaking volumes about her being caught in a lie, Kathy began talking in a flurry of words so rapid that she couldn't put a full sentence together. "She's bossy, and mean, and—and doesn't like kids, that's why she wouldn't say anything to us and—and she looked mean!"

Daniel couldn't help smiling and knew it was a mistake as soon as he felt it curl the corners of his mouth, but he couldn't stop himself.

"It's not funny! You don't care about us! You just want a new wife!" Kathy began to turn away with the intention of running from the room. Daniel gently grabbed her arm.

"Stay here. We're still discussing this and you running away won't end the conversation. But you will remain calm and civil as we continue. It's something we have to talk about. This is a family matter and it won't go away by itself."

"So talk!" Kathy said, dramatically crossing her arms.

Daniel asked, "Amy, what do you think about me starting to date again?"

"Date again?"

"That's the way they say it when a person starts seeing other people after their spouse dies or divorces them," he said carefully.

"You see, I dated your mother, and then we stopped dating when we were married. Now that, er, now that, uh, I'm single again, I would begin dating again."

"People don't date when they're married?

"Technically, no. They may go on a date to a movie, or out to dinner, but they're not really dating. I think dating is considered to be only for single people."

"Well," she said, glancing toward Kathy to see her reaction. "I like Sarah—at least, as much as I know her. We only talked a little bit over lunch."

Daniel heaved a silent sigh of relief. "So it would be okay with you if Sarah and I went to the movies or out to dinner occasionally?"

"Yeah, I guess it would be okay. But you'll still take us places, won't you?"

"I won't be abandoning you, if that's what you mean," he said with a kindhearted chuckle. "I love you two more than anything in the world and would never give up my time with you for anyone."

Kathy's shoulders slumped in defeat. "So you really want to date this woman—Sarah, I mean. This is something you really have to do?"

"I don't have to, but I want to," he said. "Adults need the companionship of other adults. Just like you wouldn't want to only have adults to play with, we need to interact with someone other than children."

"So it's an age thing, right?"

"Yes, it's an age thing." Their eyes locked in an unsteady truce. "Can you understand and accept that?"

"I don't know." Kathy was unsure of whether she should remain obstinate or not. Looking for a way to save face, she said, "I'll have to ask Aunt Maddy."

Maddy! Of course!

"Asking Aunt Maddy is an excellent idea," he said. "Aunt Maddy may be able to help clear this up."

And you better, Maddy, he thought hopefully. *You owe me.*

CHAPTER 23

THE LEWIS GIRLS

"Thanks for taking us shopping, Aunt Maddy," Amy said, smiling lovingly up at her favorite relative.

"You're welcome, honey," Maddy said. "I hear you weren't able to find any jeans you liked on your last shopping trip to the mall."

"We had an absolutely horrible time," Kathy said. "We didn't have time to shop at hardly any of the stores."

"Really? And why was that?" Maddy asked innocently, knowing exactly what had happened.

"Dad's girlfriend was here," Amy said. "Kathy got really upset when she found out she and Dad were dating."

"I did not," Kathy snapped. "She ruined the whole day by lying to us."

"She lied to you?"

"Not really," Kathy had to admit, knowing she had been caught in an exaggeration. "But she pretended to not know Dad until I called her on it. Then you should have seen her face."

"Kathy, honey, this isn't a game of 'gotcha.' This is a chance for your father to have some friends his own age."

"What do you mean?" Amy asked. "We keep Daddy company."

"I know you do, honey, but what I mean is that your father loves you both dearly and would do anything for you, but he needs adult company. You have your friends, and he needs to have friends his own age."

"But he's dating that woman, and that's different than just being friends," Kathy said defiantly.

"That woman's name is Sarah, and it's true that dating a person is different than just being friends with them," Maddy said calmly. "But it's not that much different."

"What do you mean?" Amy asked, frowning in confusion.

"I mean that being friends is the most important part of dating. Can you imagine how lonely you would be if you didn't have any friends?"

"I have lots of friends," Amy said gleefully. "And so does Kathy. Most of them are from school, but we have friends from church and from gymnastics and dance class."

"That's nice," Maddy said.

"So you know how good it is to have friends your own age. How would you feel if all your friends went away and you were all alone?"

"Dad has all his brothers, and you, and all the rest of our relatives," Kathy said insolently. "He knows all kinds of people in town and from his office too."

"Relatives don't count as friends," Maddy said, struggling to hold her temper. "Does he spend time with the people from town having fun? No, he doesn't. And he doesn't with his patients, either. That's a different kind of relationship than you have with friends."

"So you mean he wants to have sex with her?" Amy asked.

Kathy said, "Amy! That's gross. Dad wouldn't have sex with that woman."

Stifling a smile, Maddy said, "Adults do have sex after they're married, but dating means they just go places to have fun and get to know each other."

"Dad *has* friends," Kathy said hotly. "He goes golfing every once in a while with Mr. Hollobaugh."

"Kathy, you know that's not what we're talking about. The relationship between a man and woman is different than golfing with your buddies. Though a lot of women do like golfing and to spend time on the course with their boyfriends or husbands, it's different. Do you like any of the boys at school?"

"Mary Jane McDougall likes John Baines," Amy said with a giggle.

"Is that a girl from school?" Maddy asked.

"Yeah. And Kathy likes Tommy Wright."

"I do *not!*"

"You do too! You look at him funny and act goofy when you're around him."

Kathy looked meanly at her little sister, but before she could say anything nasty, Maddy interrupted.

"It's natural to start liking boys when you're teenagers. It's the way things are supposed to be. It's the way things are with your father."

Kathy looked away as a tear trickled from the corner of her eye.

"I want to go over here and look at bras," she said, pointing toward the lingerie department. "Dad doesn't know much about shopping for bras."

"Most men don't, honey," Maddy said. "It's something they just don't have any experience in buying."

They walked into the lingerie department and the three were silent for a few minutes while Kathy rifled through the racks of training bras. She said, "So you think Mom would think it's okay for Dad to date that woman?"

"You have to stop referring to her as 'that woman,'" Maddy told her sternly. "It's not going to help matters if you can't use her name and discuss this like a young adult."

"Why not? What difference will it make what I call her? I don't like her and I never will. Amy doesn't like her either."

"I like her," Amy said. "I like her as a person, at least. I don't like her dating Daddy."

Maddy took a moment to gather her composure and allowed her anger to dissipate before speaking.

"If you two are going to be selfish and ask your father not to date, he will feel obligated to deny himself the pleasure of having adult companionship," she said. "Do you know what that means?"

"No," Amy said with a tremor in her voice. Kathy looked at Maddy with veiled hatred in her eyes.

"It means your father will live a very unhappy life just to keep you happy, and he'll do that for you. You know he will," she said, emotion dripping off every word. "If you deny your father the chance to date, he'll become old before his time and wither away from the inside out. It's what happens to people and it'll all be because you're being selfish."

"We're not being selfish!" Kathy exploded as tears began streaming down her face. If she wasn't at the mall and needed Maddy to drive her home, she would have run away. Unsure what to do, she just stood staring at her aunt.

"I'm not going to argue with you," Maddy said. "Just think about what is best for your father."

Tears began coursing down Amy's face, too. Her lips quivered but she didn't speak.

"Come on, let's go get something to drink at the food court," Maddy said with a wan smile. "I think we can all use a little pick-me-up."

They followed her through the store and into the mall without saying a word. Not once did either of the girls try to walk beside Maddy or hold her hand. Finally, Kathy said, "So what should we do?"

"That's up to you," Maddy said. "But if you want to support your father in all this, you can at least not make it any more difficult for him than it already is."

"What do you mean?"

"Your father loved your mother and always will. He feels like he's betraying the memory of your mother by starting to date again. It's been five years since she died, and he's never dated anyone since she passed away. That's a long time to be alone without someone to love."

"He has us to love him!" Amy cried.

"Amy, you know it's different."

"I know, but she's not Mommy!"

Maddy stopped, turned, and faced the girls. "No, honey, she's not your mommy and no one can ever take your mommy's place. Your mother's gone and there's no bringing her back. It's a sad fact of life and I'm sorry to see you and your father having to live without her, but it's the way things are. Now there're only two choices."

"What are those choices?" Kathy asked, on the verge of tears again.

"You two and your father can either move forward into the future together, or you can force him to spend some of the best years of his life without adult companionship. The choice is really yours. Whether you'll make him miserable or allow him to move on with his life is a decision you'll have to make."

Amy and Kathy stood stunned. With a faltering voice Kathy asked, "What should we do?"

"I think you should meet with Sarah and learn a little about her, before you pass judgment on her."

"We already met her."

"But you haven't gotten to know her. There's a big difference."

"So, how are we supposed to get to know her?"

"You have next Friday off for a teacher in-service day, don't you?"

"Yeah."

"Well, how about I set up a nice luncheon at her farm for the four of us?"

"I may have plans."

"No, you don't!" Amy said, disgusted at her sister. "Friday lunch will be a good idea. Does she have horses?"

"I think she has cattle on the farm, but I'm not sure about horses."

"It doesn't matter."

"Is that okay with you, Kathy?"

"Fine," she said tightly. "We'll go to her farm for lunch on Friday, but I'm not promising I'll like her."

"Just give it a fair try, and I do mean an honestly fair try, then we'll see what happens."

"Okay."

"Let's go get those drinks now, I'm parched."

CHAPTER 24

TWO BULLS

"I love the Old Tyme Days fair," Nadine said to no one in particular as she sauntered down the grassy midway with the gentle warmth of the sun lulling her into a contemplative mood. "I love the exhibits showing the peacefulness and slower pace of farm life years ago and the implements they used back then. It takes my mind back to times when life wasn't as complicated or fast-paced as our world is now. At least that's my perception of what simpler times were like. I don't really know for sure because I've always lived in the hustle and bustle of modern times. But I do know this is a great way to spend a Saturday afternoon."

"That's for sure," Sarah agreed in an equally contented voice. "I often try to imagine what life was like back in the late 1800s or early 1900s. No computers, no airplanes, and a more genteel lifestyle. What happened to us, and how did we get to the hectic days we have now?"

"I don't know what happened. I guess the machines went faster than we could, which is why they were developed in the first place, and we have to keep up the best we can."

"I've often thought about whether the human mind is designed to handle all the information we have to retain these days," Chauncey said. He and William trailed behind the two women as they meandered down the grassy but well-manicured thoroughfare. "Sometimes it seems we have so many bits and pieces of data to process and remember that our brains just shut down and refuse to accept any more."

"That's what computers were meant to do, process and retain bits and pieces of data. We only get in over our heads when we try to remember as much as computers do," William said. He lazily munched on a huge ball of pink cotton candy.

"Just look at these old tractors and imagine what life must have been like when this was cutting-edge technology," Nadine said. "All the farmers had to remember back then were to plant seeds in springtime and harvest crops in the fall."

"That's a fair bit different than today, when the farmers have to know how to use computer and satellite technology to track the growth rate of their crops, or monitor how much of which fertilizer a particular section of their acreage needs to maximize production," Chauncey said. "I read an article about the changing technology used in agriculture and it certainly seems that the peaceful aspect of farming is a thing of the past."

"Just look at the difference between the huge combines and modern tractors we saw working the fields on our way over here. Compare that to the leather belts on these steam engine tractors those farmers in the past used to plow fields and do heavy work," Sarah said in wonderment. "It's night and day on the technology spectrum."

"It's so nice seeing all these volunteers working together to get this entire event together," William said. "It must take a lot of effort to organize all this and then actually get it done."

"All the work is performed by supporters of the volunteer fire company here in Spinale," Nadine said. "As soon as everything's cleaned up from this weekend's activities, they'll begin planning next year's show."

"It's a wonderful tradition," William said. "It fosters a real sense of community that you don't see in many places these days."

"What's really great is that a man who was a volunteer fireman most of his life donated all this land to the town to use as a recreation park and fairgrounds. Otherwise, they wouldn't have any place to hold an event this big," Nadine said. "His family farmed this property for four generations and when he didn't have any heirs to leave it to, he decided to leave it to the community."

"Wow! It would be great to be able to do something like that for other people to enjoy."

"Yeah, it would."

"He may have used equipment like the old implements on display here to work this land back then," Sarah said as she looked over the hundreds of acres of donated land and gestured toward the old-fashioned equipment. "I guess he had some peaceful times living here, and wanted to leave a small taste of that tranquility for others to experience."

"Speaking of more peaceful times, when is the sheep shearing, wool spinning, and weaving demonstration you wanted to see, Nadine?"

"We have about a half-hour before it begins. That's a popular show, so we may want to begin heading over that way."

"How long does the spinning and weaving display go on?" Chauncey asked.

"The entire sheep to shawl contest goes on for about five hours," Sarah said. "I don't want to stay for the entire time. I'd go crazy with boredom."

"Good!" William said. "Maybe we'll still have some time to visit the shingle-making exhibit. I'm interested in seeing how they make wooden shake shingles."

"And I want to see the threshing and baling demonstrations," Chauncey added. "Can we fit all that in?"

"They've organized the demonstrations so that one begins only after another has ended, except for the spinning and weaving demonstrations because it's such a long event," Nadine said. "I can keep checking back with the weaving demonstration to see how it's progressing, that way we can see all the rest."

"Thanks Nadine," Chauncey said.

"Anything to keep y'all from getting bored," she said with a laugh. "Although we may have to take some time to get all that cotton candy out of William's beard."

"I am making a mess of things," William admitted. "Maybe I shouldn't have let it grow this long, but a lot of the farmers I work with at the County Turf and Tractor store seem more at ease with a guy who wears a full beard."

"There's something calming about a bearded man," Nadine said.

The day passed quickly as the foursome moved from one event to the next. After dark descended upon the fairgrounds, a country music band began serenading in the middle of the food vendors.

"This is really nice," William said. "They have a bunch of different stands set up with each offering a different type of food."

"Each community association or church rents a stand from the firemen, and then they can sell any foods they want to raise money for their organization," Nadine explained.

"That way the firemen make money for buying new equipment, and the community groups raise funds for their organization's activities," Sarah said, marveling at the simplicity of the arrangement.

"And we get to enjoy a large selection of ethnic and regional foods that just isn't available anywhere else," Nadine added.

"That sounds like a great idea to me." Chauncey cast his eyes over as many food stands as he could see. "Do you have any suggestions?"

"Do you want to be a responsible adult and have good solid food first, or do you want to act like a kid and get dessert first?"

"I'm hungry enough to jump back and forth between solid food and dessert until I've had my fill."

"Why don't we each share whatever we get so we have room to taste a bunch of different things, instead of filling up on just one or two?" Sarah suggested.

William said eagerly. "How about starting with a funnel cake?"

"You are incorrigible," Nadine said with a glint in her eye. "But starting off with funnel cake does seem like a great idea. It's my favorite."

Listening to the country music, they enjoyed sweet Italian sausage with grilled onions and peppers, French fries, deep fried ice cream, and Philadelphia cheesesteak sandwiches.

"I'm stuffed," Chauncey said, swallowing the last bite of his cheeseburger and washing it down with a hefty swig of sweet iced tea.

"So am I," William said.

"And I'm ready to burst," Sarah said. "I drank too much lemonade."

"That is wonderful lemonade the ladies from the Methodist church make, isn't it?" Nadine said.

"It certainly is. But I better find a restroom soon. Where are they?"

"They're right over there behind the food stands." Nadine pointed to the other side of the grandstand where the band was playing. "I'll go with you. The gentlemen's is to the left and the ladies port-a-potties are all grouped to the right."

"We'll meet you outside the lady's area when you're finished," William said.

"If we're not there when you're ready, just wait a few minutes and we'll show up," Chauncey told them. "The potato donut stand is over that way and I want to get a half dozen to take with us."

"You have got to be kidding me," Nadine said. "How can you even think of food as full as we are?"

"I'm a growing boy," Chauncey said with a glint of devilishness in his eyes.

"But at your age you're growing out instead of up! Make sure you get me a sugar and cinnamon coated donut," she called over her shoulder.

"We'll see you in a bit," William said, and headed toward the crowd gathered in front of the donut stand. Chauncey followed him.

The line at the potato donut stand was always long. The delightful globs of potato dough boiled in hot lard were one of the most popular foods served at the fair. It was not unusual to wait fifteen minutes to place an order.

While Chauncey and William were waiting in line, the two women met outside the port-a-potties.

"That's the only problem with fairs," Sarah said. "The restroom facilities get really gross."

"That's for sure," Nadine said. "A little common courtesy would go a long way in making everyone's visit a lot more pleasant."

As they sauntered through the dimly lit area behind the food stands, making their way back toward the multi-colored lights of the midway, they occasionally glanced around to locate their companions.

"Uh-oh. Don't look now, but here comes Scott Maurier," Sarah said out of the corner of her mouth.

"Oh shit! I don't want to see him."

"Nadine!" Scott yelled in his booming voice as he waved wildly and smiled from ear to ear. "It's nice to see you."

"Hello, Scott."

"It's been a long time since I've seen you," he said with resentment in his eyes, though his smile never wavered. "Where have you been keeping yourself? I've left messages on your answering machine, but haven't received any calls back."

"I don't want to call you, Scott," Nadine said angrily. "Can't you take a hint? I'm ashamed for you the way you treated Chauncey the last time we were at your store."

"Aww, Nadine! I didn't mean nothin' by it, but you have to admit I was right."

"You were *not* right! You don't know what you're talking about, and you still don't have a clue how boorish you were."

"Listen, Nadine. I don't have to take that from you or anyone else. You're in the wrong on this and I am not a boor, I looked it up in the dictionary."

"You most certainly are, and I want nothing to do with you or your Neanderthal ways."

"Well, I …"

Sarah's eyes widened and Scott's words trailed off when William suddenly appeared out of the shadows.

"I think the lady has made herself clear," William said in a low growl. "She doesn't want anything to do with you."

"This is between Nadine and me, and has nothing to do with you, pal," Scott said, roughly grabbing Nadine's arm and pulling her toward him. "And we're going to continue our conversation in private …"

William's fist smashed into Scott's nose so fast it was impossible for anyone to comprehend what was occurring. Only when Scott's head whipped violently backward and blood splattered did anyone realize what had happened.

Scott toppled backward and landed heavily on his back, then rolled over onto his belly as if struggling to regain his feet. He shakily tried to gather his limbs beneath himself as he made a futile effort to get to his hands and knees, and then fell clumsily onto his face. He didn't move again.

William looked down at him and said, "He's okay, just knocked out." Then he turned to Nadine and stammered apologetically, "I'm sorry, Nadine, but no one should be allowed to manhandle a woman like that. I know I shouldn't have hit him, but he deserved it. I'm sorry."

He stiffly turned and began walking away with his head hanging.

"You're right, he deserved it," Nadine said slowly and deliberately. "I know you're not a man of violence, and it's nice knowing you're not afraid to take decisive action when it's warranted."

William slowly turned back and looked at her with no expression on his face. Slowly, a small smile began to crease the corners of his mouth, and then he gently extended his hand toward her. Without a word, she took it and smiled up at him. Then they unhurriedly walked hand-in-hand toward the parking lot.

Chauncey and Sarah stood in wide-eyed amazement, dumbfounded by the scene. They then looked down at the prostrate form of Scott lying on the dew-dampened ground with his eyes closed and his mouth open.

Chauncey calmly said, "William's different when he's mad."

Without another word, they followed William and Nadine, Chauncey protectively clutching the grease-saturated bag of donuts to his chest with both hands.

CHAPTER 25

SARAH AND THE GIRLS

Maddy wheeled her brother's Ford Explorer into the yard of Predator's Bane.

Without waiting for the dust cloud to settle, she jumped out and left the still-rocking vehicle in middle of the drive as she strode toward the house. Amy and Kathy reluctantly followed her a moment later.

"Hello!" Sarah hollered from the front door as she waved.

Keep a smile on your face and don't seem too eager, Sarah old girl, she thought.

"Hello Sarah!" Maddy yelled back as she returned her wave.

"Hello girls," Sarah said. She exchanged a nervous glance with Maddy.

"Hello," Amy replied.

"Hello," Kathy said reluctantly, only after everyone looked at her.

"How is everyone doing today?" Sarah asked nervously.

"I'm doing fine, thank you," Amy said, then gazed toward the pasture. "What kind of cattle are those? They look like Oreo cookies!"

"They're called Belted Galloways," Sarah said, relieved to have something to talk about. "They're a beef breed that's pretty hardy, so they do well being outside in the winter weather. I like them *because* they look like Oreo cookies. I love Oreos."

"Me too!" Amy cried.

"Do you like to twist the two halves apart to lick the cream out of the center, or do you prefer to dunk them whole into a glass of milk?"

"Both."

"Good answer," Sarah said with a chuckle. "How about you, Kathy?"

"I don't eat many cookies, because I don't want to get fat."

"You're a growing girl," Sarah said carefully, looking again at Maddy. "And you're not at all overweight."

"And I don't want to be, so I don't eat cookies."

Sarah allowed the uncomfortable topic to die of its own weight and cast a desperate peek toward Maddy, her eyes pleading for help.

"Do you make the cattle into beef?" Maddy asked quickly to keep the conversation from lagging.

"No, the breed is growing in popularity so I'm raising these to sell to other breeders," Sarah said. "In about three years I'll have my herd to a size where I can begin selling a few. Until then, they're like big pets living the good life."

Everyone smiled except Kathy.

"How did you get into raising cattle?" Amy asked. "I thought you were a doctor like my daddy."

"I was a doctor, but not like your daddy," Sarah explained. "He's a medical doctor and I was—am—a Doctor of Chiropractic."

"What's the difference?"

"The main difference is that medical doctors use drugs or surgery to help people. Chiropractors use just about everything else that is available except drugs or surgery."

"Like what?"

"Like spinal manipulation where they move the bones in your back, so the nerve flow from your brain can get to your organs and systems and then back again without being interfered with," Sarah explained this in gentle tones to Amy without noticing Kathy paying close attention to what she was saying. "They may also use nutritional supplements, acupuncture, physical therapy, and exercise.

Chiropractors believe in keeping the body healthy so it doesn't get sick, instead of waiting until people are in deep trouble and need emergency medical help."

"That makes sense. But you're not a chiropractor anymore?"

"No," Sarah said sadly. "I got hurt and had to give it up."

"How did you get hurt?"

Sarah looked at Maddy, who nodded her approval.

"I was shot by bad men who attacked the church I was attending, but we talked about this already when we were at the food court in the mall," Sarah replied, and was immediately sorry for bringing up their first disastrous meeting.

"The church in Northern Virginia?" Kathy asked with increasing interest.

"Yes, that church. My left shoulder was destroyed and had to be replaced by a very nice bunch of orthopedic surgeons who did a very good job."

"If they did such a good job, why can't you work as a chiropractor anymore?"

"Because the fake joint they use doesn't have the range of motion a real shoulder joint has, and it's not strong enough to take the pounding a chiropractor would put it through every day."

"You know a lot about this stuff," Amy said.

"Yes, my husband was an orthopedic surgeon, and we used to talk about this type of stuff a lot."

"You have a husband?" Kathy asked sharply.

"Had."

"What happened to him?"

Maddy said, "Sarah, why don't you three go sit around the table out there in the yard and get into the shade, while I get us some refreshments?"

"Good idea, it's getting hot out here. There's lemonade and iced tea in the refrigerator. The sugar is on the kitchen counter. I didn't sweeten the tea."

After they were around the table, Kathy pointedly asked, "So what happened to your husband?"

"He was killed when three men stole his car," Sarah said hesitantly. "He was waiting for me to finish with patients so we could go to a special dinner with other doctors from his practice, and the carjackers shot him while he waited in my parking lot. After that I came to visit my friend Nadine, because I couldn't make myself return to our house or to my practice."

She paused to wipe a tear from her eye then smiled wanly at both girls.

"I'm sorry you lost your husband," Amy said sincerely. "My mommy died and my daddy isn't married anymore either."

Kathy looked angrily at her little sister but didn't say anything.

"I'm sorry you lost your mother," Sarah said. "That must have been very difficult for young girls."

"It's getting easier," Amy said frankly. "I'm learning to live without her being there all the time."

"You must be a very strong young lady."

"Not really, it's just what you get used to."

"I guess so."

"So you liked living here and moved?"

"Something like that," Sarah said. "I found this farm while living with Nadine, but I didn't move here to live full-time until after I was hurt at the church."

"What do you mean, you didn't live here full-time?"

"Before I was hurt, I was working as a chiropractor at a friend's practice in Northern Virginia so I could spend a long weekend here at the farm. So I was only living here three days a week."

"Where did you live the rest of the time?"

"I had a nice apartment near where I worked."

These really are pleasant young ladies, she thought.

Maddy appeared at the door with a tray full of ice-filled glass pitchers and plastic glasses.

"Let me help you with that, Aunt Maddy," Kathy said, bolting toward her.

"Just make sure I have a clear path to the table," Maddy said. "It's better if you let me set it down on the table. There's less chance of having a disaster that way."

"Okay," Kathy said dejectedly.

As Sarah was pouring the drinks, Chauncey appeared at the door of his cabin and waved on his way to the barn.

"Who's that?" Kathy demanded.

"That's Chauncey," Sarah said. "He was the bookkeeper for my practice. He still does the books for the farm for me, as well as for my friend's practice."

"What's his last name?"

"Fogler. Chauncey is his nickname. His real name is Robert Fogler and he's a doctor also. He's an obstetrician. That's a doctor who delivers babies."

"If he's a doctor, why is he working as a bookkeeper?"

"Because he lost his memory and can't work as a doctor anymore. He only remembers things from a few years ago."

"So if he can't remember anything, how does he know his name?"

"He saved the lives of many people at the church where I got hurt by carrying a bomb outside before it exploded. His picture was in the newspapers and his friends and family recognized him."

"If he has a family, why does he live in that little cabin?"

"He couldn't remember anything about his family, not even his wife. So they got divorced and now he lives here on the farm."

"It's better to get divorced than it is to have your husband or wife die," Amy said, looking Sarah in the eyes.

"I'm not sure about that," Sarah said shakily. "But you may be right. I'll have to think about it."

"Are you going to live here for a while?" Kathy asked.

Her terse and unexpected question took Sarah aback for a split second. After a brief pause, she slowly answered, "I think so."

After a short period of uneasy silence, Sarah added, "Why do you ask?"

"I was just wondering," Kathy replied in a more pleasant and thoughtful tone as her eyes wandered toward the pasture. "If we have enough time today, can we get a closer look at your Oreo cookie cows?"

"Yes, we can," Sarah said. Unnoticed, she gave Maddy a huge smile. "We most certainly can."

CHAPTER 26

A NEW RELATIONSHIP

"There's William's truck," Chauncey said as he and Sarah turned into The Shire on Sunday morning. "I wonder what he could be helping Nadine with at this time of the morning?"

"Maybe it broke down and Nadine had to drive him home last night," Sarah replied. "That poor old truck has seen better days."

"Regardless, it'll be good having someone else to help us load the straw bales she wants taken down to her church for the building fund bazaar. It's always nice being able to help out with charitable events."

Stopping in middle of the gravel lane, Sarah put her truck into park. Just as they looked toward the front of Nadine's house, a flash of red twirled in the Florida Room. A blanket rocketed skyward and two people scurried toward the kitchen.

"Did you see what I saw?" Chauncey asked.

"It depends on what you think you saw."

"I thought I saw two large white asses running into the kitchen," he said. "One was very hairy."

"And the other was very, well, it was very jiggly," Sarah said. "I think Nadine has to lose a few pounds."

"What do we do now? This could be embarrassing."

"Well, Nadine obviously forgot she asked us to be here at seven o'clock this morning, and they surely saw us, so we can't just leave."

"How about we mosey over to the corral and take a look at the horses and you point a lot like you're explaining something to me. That way we'll give them a few minutes to get themselves together."

"Good idea. That way we can deny seeing any hairy, jiggling white asses bouncing around."

"It's the best plan we have. Let's go look at the horses."

Nadine's horses were very cooperative and came to the fence to be petted. Their original plan was to spend only a few moments with the horses, but before they knew it, fifteen minutes had gone by.

"I think we better go see Nadine, otherwise those bales of straw will never get to the church," Chauncey said.

"I guess you're right," Sarah said. "Remember to smile."

"And try not to laugh," Chauncey added.

"Great, now I have an irresistible urge to laugh. You did this to me on purpose."

"I did not."

"You did too."

"Did *not*."

"Oh, quit bickering you two and get in here," Nadine called from the front door. "We have coffee on, but breakfast won't be ready for a while."

"It's good to ... *see* you, Nadine," Chauncey said innocently.

Sarah abruptly snorted as an unexpected burst of laughter exploded from behind the hands cupped over her mouth.

"Okay, very funny," Nadine said, blushing. "Do you want some orange juice until the coffee's ready?"

"I'm sorry," Sarah said, as she tried to get herself under control and wiped tears from her eyes with her sleeve. "Yes, I'd like some juice. A small glass, please."

"How about you, Chauncey?" William called from the kitchen.

"Yes, I'd like some juice also," he replied. "Are you cooking breakfast?"

"Yep, we're having bacon, eggs, and my special oatmeal pancakes."

"Do you need any help?"

"No, I always cook alone. You know that."

"William is a great cook," Chauncey told Sarah and Nadine. "He makes the best pecan sticky buns in the world."

"I guess I forgot to call you and cancel," Nadine said. "Instead of us having to do it, Harry Stitt said he'd take a few straw bales down to the church."

"So we're off the hook and this can actually be a day of rest?" Chauncey asked.

"Yes, you're off the hook. You can all stay for breakfast then get on with your day of rest. Grab a seat and I'll get the juice."

After they settled in with juice and coffee, Sarah said, "I'm glad I have a chance to talk with you all, I need your opinion."

"Uh-oh. This sounds serious."

"It is to me," Sarah said more snippily than she intended. "What am I supposed to do about Amy and Kathy? As you know, they really had a bad reaction when they met me and figured out I'm dating their father. Things seem to be a little better since Maddy had them over to my place the other day, but it's still a very sticky situation. Which is understandable, I guess."

"I hope you don't mind," Nadine said. "But I was discussing this with William this morning. I thought his background in psychology and working with psychotic people may give us some insights into the minds of teenage girls."

"I'm not sure if having worked with psychotics is enough to be able to begin understanding teenage girls," Sarah said, wryly. "They're starting to come around a little, but our relationship still needs a lot of work."

"This will all take time, as you well know," William mused. "Do you mind if I make a suggestion?"

"Fire away."

"Have you ever heard of Dr. Laura?"

"Yeah, she has a radio show."

"She also writes books. I would advise you get a few of them and read up on how to handle this type of situation. That will probably get you a lot further than any advice we can give you."

"That's the best idea anyone's had yet. Do you have anything to munch on until breakfast is ready? I'm starving."

CHAPTER 27

SURVEILLANCE

"What am I supposed to be lookin' for?" Twister whined as he peered through the binoculars up the lane at Predator's Bane.

"Look for where the house is and the barn," Nacco replied testily. "We need to know where the main buildings are so we can draw a map and get our plan together. That what Squeaky says to do."

"Well, I can't see shit from here with you buzzin' down this road so damned fast," Twister said as he took the binoculars from his eyes and settled into the passenger seat of Nacco's battered pick-up. "There gotta be a better way."

"Look around then and see if there's a hill or somethin' we can get up on to look down on them."

"How about the mountain behind the farm?" Twister said, looking at the steep incline bordering the back of Sarah's property. "That's all forest land up there, so we have a right to be there. All we need is a way to get to it."

"Let's go down here," Nacco said, turning down a seemingly deserted road. It was paved, but narrow and had many bumps. "Maybe we can find how to get onto that mountain without anyone seein' us."

They drove almost a mile before the road began climbing up a gently sloping grade that got steeper the closer they got to the mountain.

"There!" Twister said, pointing to a small pull-off. "That looks like an old logging road."

"Damned if it ain't," Nacco said. "This may be just what we're lookin' for."

"Be careful when you pull in there," Twister said. "Some of these damned hillbillies love to throw beer bottles in places like this and we don't need no flat tire."

"Let me do the drivin', asshole. You look for beer bottles or anything else that can cause us trouble."

The pick-up bounced over the uneven ground and slid to a stop at the edge of the woods.

"We can't hide the truck, so we better have a good story why we're here," Nacco said.

"I don't know about you, but I'm scouting for deer and turkey," Twister said, holding up the binoculars. "Can't start trying to find the big ones too soon, you know."

Nacco returned his grin. "Let's go, we only got about an hour before McGuire is expectin' us. He gettin' all antsy anymore and I don't want to piss him off none. He's having trouble finding Maddy and that ain't good for none of us."

"Having that Holder kid not telling him where she's hiding was a mess," Twister said, as he swung his legs out the door and jumped to the weed-choked ground. "I'm glad McGuire did all that in Richmond and not up here. I don't need that kinda trouble no way, no how."

"Let's head straight out the benches that run along the side of the hill and we'll angle up if we need to," Nacco said. "No use in climbin' this damned mountain if we don't have to. I'm so damned tired of luggin' shit up these God-forsaken mountains I could puke."

"I damned near did puke after luggin' those propane tanks up to the new lab yesterday. Those bitches are heavy."

"Yeah, but those pack frames we was allowed to buy make it a hell of a lot easier than tryin' to get 'em up there just holdin' onto 'em."

"All this work better be worth all the hassle is all I gotta say," Twister said, stepping over a fallen tree. "I ain't up here pissin' around for nothin'. We best start puttin' some big money in our pockets real soon. I'm tired of livin' like a damned hermit."

Twister had to duck to avoid getting hit in the face by a sapling as it rocketed toward him. "Hey! Watch what the hell you're doin'! Hold onto those branches and don't let 'em just fly back at me like that. You damned near took my eye out."

"You just followin' too close. You anxious to get these two or what?"

"Yeah, I am," Twister admitted, puffing for breath. "Ain't you?"

"Yeah," Nacco said, breathing more heavily from the fast-paced hike through the woods. "I need some time with the ladies. It been a long time we been holdin' back and layin' low."

"That's fer sure," Twister said as he broke a branch to get it out of his way. "McGuire wants us to stay out of trouble. Shit! We got no choice when we don't have no money."

"But we don't need money to jump this bitch's bones."

"Yeah. You horny bastard," Twister said. "You just want to get into this bitch's pants!"

"She's nice, man. Don't try tellin' me you don't think she's a fine lookin' woman."

"She's been getting laid by that nigger," Twister replied. "You want sloppy seconds after a nigger?"

"What the hell the difference, man? I get what I want. She gets what she needs. And the nigger will get what's comin' to him."

"We gotta get a plan together first," Twister said, stopping and looking down the slope with the buildings of Predator's Bane laid out before him. "We don't want to be goin' off half-cocked."

"Can you see good enough from here or do we have to climb higher up this damned mountain?"

"I can see just fine," Twister replied testily as he focused the binoculars.

"What you see, man?"

"I see the main house, but nobody outside. Wait a minute! There's the tall nigger! He just came out of that little building. It looks like an outbuilding, but now I see it has flower beds in front of it."

"Let me see!" Nacco demanded, groping for the binoculars.

"Hold on a minute!" Twister said, elbowing him away. "I can't see if you be pawin' at me."

"Piss off, you son of a bitch, and give me the glasses," Nacco insisted.

"There! The nigger knockin' on the door to the big house. There she is! I bet she lives in the big house and he has that little building made up into a nice little house for hisself."

"Let me see!"

"Oh, here! You worse than a little piss ant kid!" Twister said angrily, shoving the binoculars into Nacco's chest.

"It about time, you hog." Nacco put the binoculars to his eyes and leaned against a tree with his shoulder to steady himself. "They're just talking."

"Just wait a minute and see what they do."

"Now she goin' back in the house," Nacco said. "He's just lookin' around. There she is agin! She givin' him a half-gallon of milk."

"What the hell she doing givin' him milk?" Twister said, reaching for the binoculars. "Give me those."

"Piss off," Nacco said, pushing Twister away with an open hand on his chest while keeping the binoculars to his eyes. "He goin' back to his little house now. You right! He must live in that little place."

"Let me see."

"Well, now ain't that interesting," Nacco said with a wicked smile as he handed the binoculars back. "They live in different houses. That means we can get rid of him and not hurt her till we done with her."

"You got some sick thing goin' for that woman?" Twister said scornfully. "You don't even know her and you act like you love her."

"I told you she one fine woman," Nacco said. "Now let's hurry back to McGuire before he gets all bent outta shape."

CHAPTER 28

OBSESSION

The remainder of the week went quickly for the Tennesseans.

In addition to attending to their burgeoning business, their minds were consumed with personal projects. Each man's obsessive thoughts drove him to push himself and his co-workers to work harder than they had since arriving in Virginia.

Each day, McGuire would drive by the Lewis farm in his unquenchable quest to find Maddy while the three stooges, as he had begun calling them, made sure to alter their travels to pass Predator's Bane.

Every day as they sped by Sarah's farm one of them would ask, "What you think Predator's Bane mean?" And every day he would get the same response from his cronies, "I don't have no freakin' damned idea."

All of the men had spent considerable time in their sordid pasts stalking victims for a variety of reasons, and they knew not to make more than one glimpsing contact with their target each day to avoid detection. Their victims were almost always unaware they were being observed, but nosy neighbors seeing strangers lurking around the neighborhood was always a potential problem.

Witnesses of any type were unacceptable liabilities and had to be avoided at all costs.

The week also passed quickly for their intended victims as they tended to the mundane matters of everyday life.

CHAPTER 29

CHAUNCEY IMPROVES

"How'd you do?" Daniel asked Chauncey as they finished a round of five-stand.

"I got twenty-two," Chauncey replied. "This new shotgun has helped me improve my scores tremendously. If I wouldn't have missed those three on the high teal station I would have had a perfect twenty-five for the round."

"A little more practice and you'll get them," Sarah said, slinging a shotgun borrowed from Nadine over her arm. "Maybe I'll attend that course Chauncey took and get my measurements taken so I can get a shotgun fit for me. Nadine's gun is close to what I need to shoot effectively, but I don't think it's quite right."

"I'm convinced that having a professional fit you is the only way to go," Chauncey said. "If my experience is any indication, it makes all the difference in the world on how well you shoot."

"It only makes sense," Daniel said. "With a shotgun, your eye acts as the rear sight. If it doesn't consistently look straight down the barrel for each shot you'll be shooting all over the place. You have to be hitting where you're looking."

"Especially on a moving target," Chauncey said. "Everything has to fit perfectly so when you're tracking your target, you can concentrate on it and nothing else."

"I think that's one of my problems," Sarah said, taking care on the concrete stairs leading into the clubhouse. "Every once in a while, when I mount the shotgun, I know I don't have it in the pocket of my shoulder and it's almost always a miss."

"I'll look into taking the course you took," she said tiredly. "You'll get me the contact information, won't you?"

"First thing tomorrow morning. What does everyone want to drink?"

"I'm buying," Daniel said, fishing in his pants pocket. "You bought last time."

"I'd like a hamburger, though," Sarah called over her shoulder, gently closing the action of her shotgun so it could be placed in the gun rack. "I'm famished."

"I'll go," Chauncey said. "You two look tired and I want to ask old John about a shotshell reloading machine he may be selling. I swear, that man not only makes the best hamburgers around, but he comes up with some great used shooting equipment also."

"That he does," Daniel said, handing Chauncey a twenty-dollar bill. "If you don't mind, I could use a hamburger myself."

"Well, I better get one also so I'm not staring at you two eating," he said, shoving the bill into his shirt pocket. "Iced tea all around?"

"That would be fine," Daniel said.

"It sounds delightful," Sarah said. "Make sure mine is unsweetened, if you would please."

"When the burgers are ready, just give me a sign and I'll come up to help carry it back to the table," Daniel said, before adding, "Don't let old John sell you any junk."

"Don't worry, he's always been fair with me," Chauncey said, and then he turned away to give them some quiet time alone.

"Chauncey is really one of the nicest guys I've ever met," Daniel said after he had walked away. "He seems to get along with everyone and never says a nasty thing about anyone that I know of."

"He's been that way ever since I first met him," Sarah said. "Even when he was in great pain he was very calm and considerate of others."

"It's a shame you had to give up practice," Daniel said with a twinge of sadness. "Do you miss it?"

"Sometimes," Sarah said. "To be quite truthful, my heart hasn't been into it since Josh was murdered. Every time I see a chiropractic office I think about that horrible evening."

"The images of our worst nightmares will always haunt us," he said sadly. "Especially when our nightmares really happened."

"How about you?" Sarah asked to avoid their conversation from degenerating into the doldrums. "Are you still as excited about medicine as you were as a bright-eyed intern?"

"Yes, I am," he admitted. "I really enjoy getting into the office each and every day. If I ever stop enjoying it, I'll quit."

"That's a pretty serious statement." She flicked a wisp of hair from her forehead.

Daniel looked directly into her eyes and said, "Life is too short to waste time doing anything that doesn't make you happy."

"That's rather philosophical."

"I'm in a philosophical mood. I remember a quote by Anna Quindlen that I got out of *Reader's Digest*. It went something like this, 'Think of life as a terminal illness, because if you do, you will live it with joy and passion, as it ought to be lived.'"

"Did it go 'something' like that or was that an exact quote?" Sarah asked, smiling.

"It was an exact quote. I bought her book, *A Short Guide to a Happy Life*, and was so impressed I used my computer to make a poster of the quote. Then I memorized it. It's hanging in my office. Didn't you see it when you were there?"

"My hand was sliced open the last time I was in your office. Do you really think I was interested in looking around just to see what you have hanging on the walls? I didn't even care if you had a diploma hanging on the wall. You looked like a doctor and had the equipment to sew me up, and that was all that concerned me."

"I guess that's true."

"So, you *really* read *Reader's Digest*?"

"Doesn't everyone?"

"When do you have time?"

"I do take a few moments every day for myself, you know," he said.

"I always felt that the publishers made the articles the perfect size for Throne Room reading material."

"Smart publishers," he laughed.

Sarah was looking at the table and not laughing along with him.

"What's the matter?" he asked.

"We get along so well together."

"And that's a bad thing?" he asked, taking her hands into his.

"You and I get along great together, but we don't live in a world by ourselves."

"Oh," he said dejectedly. "My daughters."

"What are we going to do? I don't know what to do to make teenage girls like me."

"It's not that they don't like you," he said. "It's just that ..."

"I know, it's because I'm horning in on their territory," she said, exasperated. "Nadine explained it to me."

"They're just feeling confused. They don't know what to do either. They want their mother, but that can't be, so they just lash out. They don't know what to do any more than you or I do."

"This is new territory for all of us," Sarah said with a sigh. "I know that, but it doesn't make it any easier. Should we just forge ahead and ignore their attitudes, or do we give up and go our separate ways like nothing ever happened?"

"I don't think either of those makes any sense," he said. "I don't want to give up so easily, because I think we're beginning to have a nice relationship. You said so yourself. Then on the other hand, if we force our relationship on the girls, then they'll just dig in their heels and make things more difficult."

"So we're back to square one," she said angrily. "And we have to take their delicate teenage sensibilities into account or else they'll be scarred for life?"

"It's what you have to do with teenagers, damn it!" he hissed under his breath. "Exactly what in the hell do you expect me to do?"

"I don't know what to do, and I don't know what I want *you* to do. It doesn't matter which way we turn, we're still back in the same position of indecisiveness."

"I've been raising these kids all by myself for over five years, and I've done the best I could," he said. "I knew I couldn't ever make up for the mother they lost, but I had to try and fill that gap the best I could."

"So you devoted your life to them, which is commendable," she said in a strained tone. "But now they think you should be totally devoted to them and they won't give you a chance to live a life of your own."

"Maybe Dr. Laura's right," he said, his face reddened. "Maybe single parents should devote themselves to their kids and not try to find another mate, because it only causes problems."

"Who in the hell is this Dr. Laura I keep hearing about?" Sarah asked in a confused tone as she held her hands out in front of her with palms skyward in a sign of submission. "William suggested I read her books to find the answer to our dilemma. Why does she know everything and we know nothing?"

"Maybe because she has compassion for kids and understands they need a parent's undivided attention to be raised correctly," he said hotly. He stood up, picked up his shooting bag, and turned to leave. "I'll call you early next week after we've had a chance to think things out, assuming you put any thought into this at all!"

"Fine!" she growled. "Don't forget your shotgun!"

"Don't worry! I won't!"

Everyone within earshot looked on with amusement.

Without looking at her, he spun on his heels, picked up his cased shotgun, and slammed through the door on his way to the parking lot.

Just at that moment Chauncey appeared with a tray full of food and drinks.

"Does this mean we get to split his hamburger?" he asked with a straight face.

CHAPTER 30

CHAUNCEY'S ANGUISH

"How was your training session?" Chauncey asked the three women as he sauntered up to them sitting under the sugar maple, and then he flopped tiredly into a chair.

"It went well," Nadine replied cheerfully. "Maddy is a natural. I wish I had her hand-eye coordination. She could easily move into competitive shooting if she ever takes up the sport."

"That's a bit of an exaggeration," Maddy said, blushing. "It's easy to do well when I have some of the best teachers available, showing me step-by-step what to do and how to do it."

"You're much too modest," Sarah said. "You shoot like you've been at it for years."

"Thank you, not just for your kind words, but for helping me get off on the right foot. It's not everyone who will help when the chips are down."

"Have you heard anything about your ex?" Nadine asked, not sure if she should broach the subject. "Where he is, what he's up to, that kind of thing?"

"No, no I haven't. I've called a few of my friends in Tennessee and asked about John, but no one has seen him for quite a while. That's good in one way, but rather unsettling in another."

"You didn't tell them where you were, did you?" Sarah asked with a tinge of horror in her voice.

"No, I made sure I didn't make any mention of where I am. The ones who asked, I told them I was in Vermont with my aunt. Luckily, I don't have any relatives in Vermont," she said with a sly but weak smile. "I trust the friends I contacted, but I can't take any chance he'll be able to find me. He could have threatened them, and I can understand if they'd fink on me to save themselves or their families. John can be ruthless in getting what he wants."

"That was a good idea," Sarah said to reassure her. "It's best to not trust anyone at this point."

"Excuse me for interrupting, but I just remembered something I have to ask Chauncey and have to say it before I forget again," Nadine said, in an attempt to change the subject to avoid inflicting any further anguish on Maddy. "Is there any hope for that old lawnmower you've been working on, Chauncey?"

"I'm afraid it's just too old and worn out," Chauncey replied hastily, happy to avoid having Maddy dwell on her dilemma. "You can buy a newer and much more efficient model for less than it would cost to fix that one."

"I think I'll get a self-propelled model," Nadine said. "Even though I only use it to trim around the bushes, it's getting a little bit tiring to push that old thing around this large of a yard."

"Yeah, things do get old," Chauncey said tiredly.

"Are you feeling a little old these days, Chauncey?" Nadine asked playfully. "You seem a little depressed. If you're sad because that old lawnmower is getting replaced by a younger model, don't worry, we won't be replacing you any time soon."

"That's awfully nice of you. But no, my age isn't an issue today. At least I don't think so."

"What's wrong?"

"Oh, it's nothing for you to worry about. I'm just not sure what to do about Annie, is all."

Nadine told Maddy, "Annie is a woman from his church that Chauncey has been seeing socially. She seems to be a more frequent worry of his lately."

"What's the problem?" Sarah asked. "You've got three females here who are all well-versed in the types of problems women can have. Fill us in on the details and let's see if we can offer any tips on how to handle the situation."

"I don't know," he said. "The best I can explain it is that I can't remember my past, and Annie can't seem to forget hers."

"That sounds rather philosophical, but we'll need more information to go off of, if you want us to be able to help," Nadine said.

"She's so wrapped up in the bad marriages she's had, and the problems her grown children are having, that she can't seem to concentrate on having a life of her own," he said despairingly. "It seems as though she allows herself to be dragged into everyone else's mess, then gets depressed because she doesn't have a magic wand to wave and make their problems, which are usually of their own making, just disappear."

"So everyone else's foibles are foisted upon her and she takes it upon herself to try and help them out of the situation they created," Nadine said.

"That sounds about right."

"Chauncey, this is a woman who has a big heart but no common sense," Sarah said firmly. "Sorry to put it in so blunt of terms, but it's true. If what you say is true, and I'm sure it is, she seems to be trying to make amends for not instilling discipline in her children when they were young. Now that they're grown she feels guilty and is trying to clean up the turmoil they're creating."

"That's the way I've been seeing it," he said. "It would help explain why she's been married three times. She's just a nice lady who's a lightning rod for misfortune to strike."

"That's too deep for me," Nadine said. "It looks like you're going to have to make a few decisions about what you want your future to look like."

"I know," he said. "So, on to a happier topic, does anyone have anything exciting planned for the weekend?"

"I'm spending the weekend with my nieces," Maddy said, glad to change the subject. "Friday night we're going to get pizza and watch movies at home. On Saturday we're going to the mall, then a movie at the theater, and Sunday we'll go out to brunch after church."

"That's right," Chauncey said. "Daniel is going to that medical conference in Virginia Beach this weekend. He said he wouldn't be shooting sporting clays this week. That means Sarah won't be shooting clays, so I don't have to either."

"Are you getting tired of the game now that you've taken lessons and gotten a new shotgun?" Sarah asked.

"Not at all. William and I have been struggling with this one section of our accounting course, and we've also hit a rough spot with the economics course, if the truth be known, so we could use the extra time to go over it until we understand it. Would it be okay if he comes over to study on Friday night, then comes back again on Saturday after he's done with work?"

"You don't have to ask permission to have someone over," Sarah said. "You live there and pay rent, so you can have anyone over any time you want. Besides, it's always nice to see William."

"Don't keep him too late, Chauncey," Nadine scolded. "I have a late dinner planned for us on Saturday and I don't want to have my roast dry out waiting for him to show up."

"No problem, Nadine," he said with a smile. "What time do you want him there?"

"About an hour and a half after it gets dark. That should give me time to finish up with the horses and get dinner ready. Just make sure he isn't any later than that."

"Well, this should be a nice weekend for everyone."

CHAPTER 31

MADDY IS LOCATED

"Tell me what you got," McGuire said to Allen Murphy, a resident of Thompsonville who wore most of his extra weight in his belly.

"I was over in Spinale at Doc Lewis's place gettin' this cough checked out. I think that shit we been cookin' up is gettin' to me," he said.

"I asked you what you got about Maddy," McGuire said gruffly. "Not how you're feelin'."

"I was sittin' in the waiting room forever, you know how it is, and the receptionist was talkin' to a lady waiting with me. She says Doc Lewis is going to a medical conference in Virginia Beach this weekend and he's having his sister Maddy babysit his little girls."

"That so?"

"That's what I heard," Allen said. "Hey! Can that shit give me bronchitis? That's what I got. Bronchitis."

"No, it won't do that," McGuire said dismissively. "Forget about it and take your medicine. You'll be okay. What else she say?"

"She just said Doc Lewis was leavin' early Thursday afternoon so he could get down there and get a decent night's sleep before classes and meetings begin on Friday."

"So Maddy's gonna be babysitting, eh?" McGuire mused, rubbing his whiskered chin thoughtfully. "I've been in that house before when Maddy and I was dating. It's a big, fancy place."

"I remember when you and Maddy were dating," Allen said. "You guys made a nice couple. What ever happened between you two?"

"It ain't none of your business," McGuire growled. "What else she say?"

"She was just goin' on about how the girls was planning to have a sleepover and play cards and watch movies and such. They're plannin' on going to the mall on Saturday to do some shopping. You know how women are."

"How old are those girls now?"

"They're in their early teens, best I can recollect."

"That means their bedtime should be about ten o'clock or so, don't ya' think?"

"My sister's kids stay up a lot later than that on the weekends. Of course, they're a little bit older than the Lewis girls. About two or three years older, I'd guess."

"So they should be in bed by midnight," McGuire murmured.

"I guess, but I don't really know for sure. Why don't you call Maddy and ask, if it's so damned important to you?"

"You getting smart with me, asshole?" McGuire exploded. He thrust his face into Allen's and grabbed him by his shirt lapels. "You wanna be a smart-ass and see if I can kick your ass all over this county, you whiny cock-sucker?"

"I didn't mean nothin' by it," Allen said. "I swear it. You was askin' questions I don't have no answers to, is all."

"Don't you tell no one about this little talk, you understand me?" McGuire said, shoving him backward.

"It's just between us, I promise," Allen said shakily, after regaining his footing. "I'm goin' now unless you need somethin' else."

"You just get back to your place and keep cookin' that shit up," McGuire snarled. "If I need anything else I'll tell ya'."

Allen quickly turned and left the house without looking back.

"Yeah," McGuire said to himself. "I got everything I need."

CHAPTER 32

DATE NIGHT

The haunting revelation of Maddy being so close totally consumed his thoughts and forced McGuire to put his business dealings on hold and out of his mind.

It been a long time, Maddy, he thought as he drove toward the Lewis farm. *I wanna get a better look at what that place lookin' like today. If that pain in the ass brother of yours hasn't made too many changes to the place I shouldn't have any trouble at all getting around there in the dark.*

He didn't slow his truck on his first pass past the farm, but his eyes were riveted on the well-kept farmhouse.

He still takes good care of the place, he thought as his anger seethed unrelentingly. *The rich bastard must have paid someone to put that nice bright white vinyl siding and black shutters on the place. He sure as hell wouldn't get his delicate, little hands dirty doin' real work. The lazy son of a bitch probably put the vinyl on to avoid having to keep it painted.*

Instead of turning around and cruising past the house again, he made a left turn onto a gravel road and drove over a mile around a long country block. The maneuver took five minutes and brought him back to the hard-topped road.

192 · D. E. HEIL

Hell, I remember these roads like I drove them yesterday. One more pass then you're done for today. You don't wanna be spotted or seen hangin' around the place.

Just as he was approaching the lane for the farm, a battered Toyota Corolla slowed in the oncoming lane and made the turn onto the driveway.

Shit! That's Maddy! he thought as he ducked his head to his chest, allowing his shoulder-length hair to partially cover his face until she had completed her turn. *So you're drivin' a little Toyota, ain't that nice.*

A depraved smile ominously curled the edges of his mouth as he straightened himself in his seat and hit the accelerator.

"It's good to see you again, Maddy," he murmured. "We got us a date Friday night, baby."

CHAPTER 33

BAD BOYS

"I need you boys to make the rounds on Friday night late," McGuire said as he addressed Squeaky, Nacco, and Twister in the dilapidated farmhouse. "You know how it's done. Don't go to nobody's place to collect the shit before ten o'clock. We don't need no nosey hayseed askin' questions 'bout why you there."

"What you want us to do before ten o'clock then?" Squeaky asked.

"That's up to you," McGuire grumbled. "Just don't be gettin' in no trouble 'cause I'm sure as hell not comin' to bail you out. I don't know you guys, you get thrown in jail."

The three men looked slyly at each other then Squeaky replied, "We won't get in no trouble. We promise."

"I gotta get some personal business taken care of," McGuire said. "I'll see you guys later."

They waited until McGuire's pick-up rumbled out of the farmyard and down the dusty farm lane toward the paved road.

"We got to get this done early so we can get McGuire's work done after ten o'clock," Squeaky said to the others. "We gotta get us some gas and big glass jugs."

"I seen vinegar in gallon jugs at the store when we was there," Nacco said. "That big enough?"

"That should do fine. And vinegar cheap enough it won't hurt to pour it out just to get the jug."

"We gotta get the gas separate 'cause they won't let you put it into glass jugs at the gas station," Twister said. "And we'll need some rags, but that won't be no problem. I'll cut them just the right size after we get the jugs so they fit. That's important."

"Well, let's get off our lazy asses and go shoppin' then. We got a long night ahead of us."

CHAPTER 34

SCOUTING FOR DEER

"It's okay," Officer Tom Mahoney said to Ron Davis, a fellow Virginia State Police trooper. "I checked with Dr. Collins yesterday and she said it would be fine if you want to come scouting for deer with me, but if you decide you want to hunt on her property, she'd like to meet you."

"We won't have enough time before it's too dark to see anything up there," Ron said. "We only get off an hour before it gets dark."

"It's the only time we have to scout," Tom said. "Besides, I prefer to be in the woods as it's getting dark. The deer are moving from bedding areas to feeding areas, and it's a great time to map out their movement patterns."

"That's true. Have you been able to pattern them at all?"

"I know where there are a few hanging out," Tom said. "Though I haven't seen the big buck Bill said he saw crossing the road down there last month. He may be hanging out along the creek across the road, but we'll never know unless we get up on that mountain and see if we can find sign of him."

"Okay," Ron said. "As long as we can get up on the mountain before it starts getting really dark."

"Don't worry," Tom said. "I got permission to park my truck at the end of a lane on the farm next door. That will save us at least fifteen minutes of walking to get where I've been seeing most of the deer activity."

"Why don't we just hunt that property?"

"Because the owner wouldn't give me permission to hunt," Tom said. "I busted him for DUI about three years ago when I first joined the force and he hasn't forgiven me."

"He can't forgive and forget, eh?"

"Not this guy. He was really smashed when his wife left him for another man and moved to Arizona or New Mexico, I can't remember which state it was. He was weaving all over the road when I turned the lights on him. I felt sorry for the guy, losing his wife and all."

"You can't be concerned why a person's drunk," Ron said. "The important thing is you got him off the road before he killed a bunch of kids or a family. The less of that we have to attend to the better."

"I agree," Tom said somberly. "But at least he'll let us park there, that's the important thing right now. Do you have your gear ready for when we get off?"

"I'm ready to go. Can I get my car in that field without ripping the bottom out?"

"We'll leave your car out by the road, and then I'll drive you back with my truck."

"That sounds good. I'll meet you there when our shifts end. Don't dawdle."

"You either!"

Luckily, the troopers were able to leave at their scheduled time that evening, which wasn't often the case. Too many unforeseen emergencies cropped up for the men to routinely plan activities for after work.

The evening was pleasantly mild with no rain. Their scouting was fruitful with many deer seen ghosting through the dense underbrush, but the large buck they sought remained elusive.

"There are definitely some deer up there," Ron whispered, when he and Tom arrived back at Tom's truck.

"I told you this area has more deer than most places around here," Tom said. "Sarah has been trying to keep the coyote population down and it's evidently allowing more fawns to survive."

"It's amazing how fast the deer population will rebound if some of the predatory pressure can be taken off them."

"If you figure that each mature coyote has to eat its own weight in meat each week, that adds up to a lot of deer."

"And turkey, and rabbits, and everything else that walks, runs, or flies," Ron added.

"Especially when you take into consideration that coyotes live in packs. That's each coyote in the pack that has to eat that much each week."

"No wonder the deer herd has taken such a nose dive with the predator population growing steadily."

"Are you ready?" Tom asked impatiently.

"Yeah, let's go."

"I'm going to keep the lights off until we're out at the road. I don't want to alert any deer that may be down here in the fields feeding. The harder it is for them to pattern us, the better."

"Good idea."

The men rode in silence as they bounced slowly down the rutted tractor lane between a fencerow of heavy brush and high stalks of corn in the field. Only after they arrived at Ron's car parked by the road did they speak in hushed tones to avoid alerting any deer feeding in the fields to their presence.

"That was a good night," Tom said.

"Yeah, it sure was."

"So, do you think you may want to meet Dr. Collins and see if she'll let you hunt her property?"

"Yeah, I'm going to ask. I kind of liked a few of those areas we saw up on the mountain, especially those little areas of ferns. The deer seem to be concentrating on those."

"Well, it won't hurt to have permission, even if you never hunt her woods," Tom said. "You never know when – "

He stopped abruptly and stared towards Predator's Bane, his attention riveted. Ron froze in quick response and focused his gaze across the pasture in the direction Tom was looking.

"What the hell are those guys doing?"

"What guys?"

"Over there at the end of Sarah's lane," Tom said, pointing as he reached behind his seat to find his binoculars. "The driver of that old pick-up shut their lights off before turning off the hard road onto her lane, and then parked real close to the fence."

"Can you see anything with the binoculars?"

"No, it's too dark. I think we better cut across this pasture real quiet-like and see what they're up to. Do you have your cell phone?"

"My cell phone, flashlight, and pistol are always with me. You know that."

"Good, let's go."

CHAPTER 35

HOT TIME

"Be careful! I don't want gas all over my truck!" Nacco grumbled under his breath as Twister accidentally bumped the gasoline-filled glass jug against the side of the pick-up bed.

"Why'd ya have to get these big-assed gallon jugs that're so damned hard to lift with only these little tiny loops at the top of 'em? Besides this is an awkward angle to be pickin' 'em up," Twister said. "Why the hell don't you help a little instead of just complaining all the time?"

"It was a great idea of mine to get these glass gallon jugs, so quit yer bitchin'," Nacco snarled. "Alls we had to do was pour out the vinegar and fill 'em with gas. Bingo! Instant big-assed firebomb."

"We still have to take the screw caps off and stuff a rag in the spout for a wick," Twister said, concentrating on the task at hand. "Make sure you bring the rags. I cut 'em all just the right size."

"You just make sure ya get all six of those jugs out of the truck without breakin' any," Nacco said. "I don't know why we each need two of these damned things. Three should be enough to get the job done."

"You know Squeaky," Twister said. "He always likes to be makin' sure to get the job done right. Besides, it's better to have too much than not enough gas burnin' up a house."

"Both of you just shut the hell up, will ya?" Squeaky wheezed, his affliction becoming more evident when he whispered. "You want to let 'em know we're here?"

"They don't know shit," Nacco spat. "I watched them the last three nights from up on the hill there. They always do the same thing. As soon as the sun goes down they go inside and stay there."

"Where's that big son-of-a-bitch you say always visits the nigger about six o'clock?" Squeaky asked. "Where's he?"

"He's probably in the nigger's little cabin with him already," Nacco said. "They always go in there, and then he leaves sometime long after I'm gone."

"So what the hell we gonna do about him?"

"The same as we do with the nigger," Twister said with a demonic smile twisting his upper lip. "They probably doin' faggot things in there I don't even want to know about, so let's just take care of 'em all."

"I thought you said the nigger was screwin' the white bitch?" Squeaky said.

"He probably doin' them all, but it don't matter none, because we gonna get him for almost killin' us," Twister replied. "We teach a lesson to his big-assed boyfriend too. What the difference?"

"The difference is that we only got one pistol and if it takes more than six bullets to get that big bastard killed then we in trouble," Nacco said, as he checked the revolver stuck in his waistband. His finger subconsciously ran over the smooth groove where he had ground off the serial number shortly after he stole it in a burglary three weeks prior.

"The nigger and fat dude may just burn up," Squeaky said with an ominous tone in his voice. "That cabin's pretty small. If we can get some gas on 'em maybe we don't need no gun."

"So how you wanna do this?" Nacco asked excitedly.

"You sneak up real close to get a good look in the nigger's cabin and make sure they both in there," Squeaky said. "Then cut the phone lines on both places while you up there. No use chancing the damned po-lice screwin' us up. You got your cutters?"

"Yeah, I got 'em."

"And what'll you and me be doin'?" Twister asked, suddenly nervous.

"You and me will wait till Nacco reports back, then we'll all tiptoe up the lane and light up the nigger's place before goin' get the bitch," Squeaky wheezed. "We want the men out of the picture as soon as possible, so trap 'em in there with fire. If they do get out it'll be easier to kill 'em if they already fried a little."

"That sounds about right," Nacco said. "Everybody got their lighters?"

"Shit! I lost mine," Twister said, frantically searching his pockets. "Squeaky, you got yours?"

"Yeah, I got it. Nacco! Hurry up down there then back here so we can get this done."

Without another word, Nacco disappeared into the night.

CHAPTER 36

RIGHT TIME AND PLACE

"What the hell are they doing?" Tom asked Ron in a barely audible whisper.

"They unloaded what looks like glass jugs out of the truck and now they're talking," Ron said.

"I see three of them."

"I can only see three too."

"Do you want to get closer to try and hear what they're saying, or what?"

"We should probably stay here and see what happens," Ron said. "We've been pretty lucky so far and there's not much cover out in this pasture."

"Hey! One of them is going up toward the house."

"Shit! That complicates things."

"Let's stay with these two and see what happens."

"I don't think we have a choice."

***

In less than five minutes Nacco returned from his reconnoitering trip.

"What you see?" Squeaky asked.

"The big guy and the nigger are in the front room of his lil' cabin," Nacco gasped, catching his breath after sprinting back. "They each workin' on a computer. Can you believe that? They each have their own computer in there! What a bunch of freakin' damned nerds! I'm not goin' to bother cuttin' the phone lines, because that'll just alert 'em that somethin's up if their computers shut off. I can put both my firebombs into that small room and it'll probably kill 'em both lickety split before they have time to call anyone. Y'all can throw yours into the other windows out back."

"Did ya cut the lines to the big house?"

"Yeah, I don't know what she doin' though. The only lights on are upstairs, so maybe she takin' a bath or somethin'."

"I hope so. I like nice-smellin' women," Twister said, grinning wickedly.

"Okay," Squeaky said impatiently. "Everybody grab your jugs and let's go. We'll stuff the rags into 'em when we get up near the cabin. No use spillin' gas all over ourselves tryin' to carry them all the way up there."

"That only about two-hundred yards up to the house," Twister said. "Why the hell you still huffin' and puffin' so damned much?"

"I think it's those damned chemicals we usin' to cook that meth," Nacco said. "That shit startin' to get to me."

"Catch your breath, and then we get this job done," Squeaky said. "It's time to have some fun."

CHAPTER 37

MYSTERY SOLVED

"What the hell was that?" William asked, peering intently out the window of Chauncey's cabin. "It's so dark I can't see much, but it looked like someone was out there."

"There shouldn't be," Chauncey said, calmly making his way to the front door. "Maybe you're just paranoid after working at the Mission all these years."

"I ain't paranoid," William said in a low growl. "When I stood up to go to the bathroom, I caught a glimpse of something out of the corner of my eye. Be careful."

William followed silently behind Chauncey as they crept stealthily toward the door, then he whispered, "Only crack the door open a little bit, just enough to slip outside. Allow a few minutes for your eyes to adjust to the dark. Move slowly and quietly."

They softly closed the door behind them and stood still, making sure they stayed in the shadows of the cabin. Small rhododendron bushes broke up their outlines.

"Can you see anything?"

"I'm not sure if I saw someone running up the lane toward the road or not," Chauncey whispered into William's ear. "This little sliver of a moon doesn't cast much light."

"Stay quiet and listen," William told him. "Your ears are sometimes more useful than your eyes in the dark."

"We won't be able to hear much with this wind blowing. There must be a storm brewing."

"Sssshh!"

"What do you hear?" Chauncey asked.

"I think I hear voices," William said. "Luckily, the wind is blowing this way so it'll blow the sounds our way if there is anything. Now be quiet."

They listened intently, trying to strain out the normal night sounds of the country from any unusual noises.

"There! Did you hear it? It is voices," Chauncey said breathlessly.

"Yeah, I hear it," William said. "I can't tell how many of them there are, but the voices seem to definitely be coming from up the lane by the road."

"I better tell Sarah," Chauncey said.

"You don't have time," William said. "It looks like there are three of them walking side-by-side down the lane right toward us. Maybe you better get your shotgun in case there's trouble."

"Right," Chauncey replied, slipping back into his cabin, being careful to open the door only enough to slip in sideways.

Inside, he turned the lights off and tossed a blanket over each computer monitor to mute their flickering blue illumination and reduce the likelihood of his silhouette being seen from the outside darkness. He hurriedly dropped to his knees, slid the aluminum gun case from under his bed, flicked open the latches and snatched up a box of shells along with the shotgun.

With a grunt, he used one hand on the bed to help himself up from the floor when his arthritic knees protested, and then he bolted in a loping, pain-induced gait toward the door to join William outside.

Chauncey nearly bumped into William's silent form beside the wall of the cabin.

"What's going on?" he hissed into William's ear.

"They're still walking this way," William said. "They seem to be carrying glass jugs. I can see the moonlight glinting off them."

Chauncey had heard enough. He expertly plunked two shotshells into the gaping chambers of the shotgun. His hands were shaking, but his eyes never wavered from the trio plodding toward them in a shuffling gait.

"William, go back inside and call the police. Tell them we don't know what's going on, but we have trespassers, and then stay on the line to keep them up to date on what's happening."

"You going to be okay out here?"

"I'm going to be fine. Go now."

Chauncey watched the men move closer.

His sweating hands slipped on the shotgun's stock, so he dried each on his pants in a methodical manner. This was the routine he performed prior to calling for a clay bird on the sporting clays course at Millvale. It helped calm his nerves.

I can't run across the lane to alert Sarah or they'll see me. My best bet is to stay hidden until I can see what they're up to, or until the police arrive. If I have to, I'll fire into the ground to alert her so she isn't taken by surprise. What could they possibly want?

***

"See there," Nacco whispered as they subconsciously huddled closer together as they neared their destination. "The upstairs lights are on in the big house, just like I said."

"The nigger's cabin looks pretty dark," Twister said, uncertain. "Ya sure they're in there?"

"Yeah, they in there. I saw 'em. They had most of the lights out, prob'ly so they could see their computers better."

"Would you two shut the hell up?" Squeaky said. "As soon as we get up to that little bush on the side of the lane, we gonna stop there and light these things up."

***

"What do you think?" Ron asked, as the two troopers snuck from shadow to shadow, tailing the three hunched figures down the lane.

"I think we're on our own since there's no cell phone reception out here," Tom said. "Can you smell the gasoline? Those bastards may have Molotov cocktails. Really big ones."

"If they're planning on setting fire to the buildings, we'll have to stop them before they get a chance to throw them."

"Keep up. We may not have much time once we can confirm what the hell they're up to."

***

Dear Lord. Please watch over us tonight and offer me guidance, Chauncey prayed silently as he expectantly watched the situation unfold before him.

***

The trespassers clustered together beside an overgrown spirea bush as if being close to the concealing shrub offered them comfort. After gently setting their glass jugs on the gravel, each man stooped and began unscrewing the caps.

They worked wordlessly until, in a fit of nervous chatter, Twister muttered, "After you stuff the rags into the top of the jug, hold it in place and turn it upside down so the gas soaks it real good."

"We know that, ya' asshole," Squeaky said.

"This damned wind gonna make it real hard to get these lit," Nacco said. "Maybe we better get close and make a windbreak with our bodies so we each have one lit. When we're in place and ready to throw 'em, we can light the other one from it."

"Yeah, That'll give us a big flame from the wick, not like the itty-bitty one from the lighter," Twister said.

Shifting their bodies to block the wind, they stood side-by-side with their shoulders touching, each man with one gasoline bomb in his hands, and his second nestled between his feet.

Squeaky pulled a butane lighter from his shirt pocket. Each man held the wick of their firebomb toward the lighter as Squeaky flicked the flint wheel creating a shower of sparks.

***

"What the hell are they up to?" Ron asked.

"They're all huddled up for some reason," Tom said.

"Should we try getting closer?"

"Yeah, let's stay on the right side of the lane. There are more shadows from trees over here. Try to stay in line with a tree trunk, if possible, when you move."

***

"Keep the damned thing still!" Squeaky hissed. His patience with the others was wearing thin.

"Just light the damned thing!" Nacco said.

"Here, let me have the lighter," Twister said, lunging for Squeaky's hand.

"Asshole!" Squeaky snapped, pulling the lighter away. "Stay back or I'll bust yer freakin' damned head, dipshit."

"Then light the damned thing!"

***

"They *do* have Molotov cocktails!" Tom told Ron. "And they're lighting them."

"We better put a stop to this right now. We have more than enough cause to justify it."

"Okay, let's move in. You take the left and I'll go right."

"Ready?"

"Ready."

***

Chauncey saw the flare of a lighter as its flame flicked back and forth in the bucking wind.

A flash of flame burst from the top of Squeaky's jug then jumped immediately to the other two wicks.

Dear Lord! They have firebombs!

Without hesitation Chauncey raised his shotgun to his shoulder, making a perfect gun mount as though he were pulling down on a pair of clay targets.

William, filled with adrenaline at seeing what was happening, burst from the front door behind Chauncey and yelled, "They have firebombs! Shoot! Shoot!"

The shouting from the doorway made the surprised trespassers jerk their heads in unison toward the cabin. Almost simultaneously two bellowing male voices began shouting, "Police! Drop your weapons and get your hands where we can see them!"

A disoriented and confused Twister continued to turn toward the cabin, while Nacco jerked his head behind him to face the unknown threat coming from that direction. The bewildering and disorienting shouting in front of and behind them caused Nacco to spin his body in the direction he was looking. In the ensuing confusion, he unwittingly smashed his jug into Squeaky's.

In the blink of an eye a flaming torrent of liquid engulfed their legs in a conflagration of heat and flame.

"What the hell!" Squeaky screamed hysterically, ignoring everything but the inferno overwhelming his lower half.

Twister flung his arms into the air to shield his face from the blazing heat, dropping his jug squarely onto two sitting on the ground.

The sound of smashing glass was lost amidst the anguished cries of the men.

Recoiling from pain and fear, they gulped air deeply into their lungs with each agonizing scream as adrenaline surged throughout their tortured bodies. Searing hot gases scorched delicate lung tissue like seared sirloins, hastening their body's desire for oxygen.

Chauncey and William stood transfixed, too horrified to move except to throw their hands up to block the blazing light.

Despite the pain and being blinded by the flames, Nacco's hatred of police combined with his fear of returning to prison gave him the strength to rip the handgun from his waistband.

He raised the .38 to eye level and pointed it in the direction of the officers.

"Gun!" Tom Mahoney screamed, his combat-honed instincts taking control of his actions the instant he saw the .38 in Nacco's clenched fist.

BAM!

BAM!

Two bullets raked Nacco's chest from one side to the other, shredding scorched lung tissue on their deadly path to freedom out the opposite side.

The Smith and Wesson flipped through the air and landed in the middle of some bushes. His legs collapsed and he crumpled to the ground, smashing the remaining jug and releasing its contents.

In terror, Squeaky and Twister beat at the inferno engulfing them with their feet rooted firmly to the ground. Then, as a pair, they wheeled and ran in a panicked and futile attempt to escape the flames consuming their clothing. Their manic antics only forced them to breathe more heavily and inhale greater amounts of superheated air into their lungs.

"Oh shit!" Tom muttered, swinging his pistol toward Chauncey and William. "You! Drop your weapon! Now!"

Chauncey blinked and looked dumbfounded at the trooper shouting orders at him.

"Drop your weapon, now!"

William raised his hands, and then slowly looked at Chauncey, who dropped his shotgun and did the same.

"Do you have blankets inside your cabin?"

Chauncey looked at him dumbly, unable to comprehend his question.

"Do you have *blankets* inside your cabin?" Tom shouted again.

"Yes," he answered slowly. "Yes, I do."

"Both of you get on the ground," Tom yelled in a booming, authoritative voice as he closed the distance between them.

Chauncey and William obeyed immediately by dropping to their knees and using their hands to lower themselves onto their bellies. Each tried to stay as far away from the shotgun lying between them as they could.

Tom moved swiftly to secure the shotgun.

"Stay there!" he shouted, shoving the cabin door open and slapping at the light switch. "Keep your arms spread so we can see your hands!"

Moving smoothly, he went inside, flicked the shotgun's lever to eject the shells, and dropped the gun and shells on the kitchen table. Then he snatched the blankets off the computer monitors and rushed back outside.

"You two stay there and don't move!" he yelled. "Ron, watch these two!"

"Got them!"

Tom ran to Twister who was slowly walking in circles. Flames were still blazing below his armpits when Tom threw one of the blankets over him and gently wrestled him to the ground. After smothering the flames, he sprang to his feet and grabbed the second blanket.

Squeaky had collapsed to his knees and was numbly staring at his singed arms while flames blazed unabated on his trousers. With a pitiful shake of his head, Tom threw the blanket over him and calmly helped him to the ground.

He threw a glance over his shoulder and saw Twister rolling back and forth beneath the blanket.

An array of floodlights mounted under the eaves on Sarah's house suddenly illuminated the yard.

"Tom!"

The frightened female voice that came from out of the darkness behind the lights startled him and he jumped.

"Sarah! Is that you?" Tom asked, squinting into the darkness. "Where are you?"

"I'm upstairs in my bedroom," Sarah said. "Do you need help? I have my gun."

"Are you safe where you're at?"

"Yes, I'm upstairs in my bedroom," she replied. "Let me turn a light on so you can see me."

"No!" Tom said. "Keep your lights off! We don't know if these are the only guys. If there is someone else, don't make it easy for them to see you! Lock your bedroom door and stay where you're at! I'll come get you after we secure this scene."

"I'm on my satellite phone to the police dispatcher," Sarah said. "She says there's help on the way."

As she was speaking, flashing lights appeared at the end of the lane.

"The cavalry has arrived!" he shouted to Ron who looked up and smiled when he saw the cruiser approaching rapidly from the paved highway.

Both officers holstered their firearms and pulled their badges out. Holding them high, they raised their other hand to show the responding officer they were unarmed.

"You two just stay where you are and don't move," Ron said to Chauncey and William when they raised their heads to watch the flashing lights approach.

The cruiser pulled into the center of the yard and an officer warily got out, speaking into his radio.

"Police officers!" Ron and Tom called, waving their badges.

"Ron? Tom? Is that you?" he asked as his head continually pivoted from side-to-side keeping the area under surveillance until he could thoroughly evaluate the situation.

"Bill? Yes, it's us," Ron said. "Do you have extra handcuffs? I have two men over here on the deck."

"What happened here?" Bill demanded as he cautiously began walking toward Ron, keeping an eye on as much of the scene as he could. Try as he might, his eyes were continually drawn to the flickering mounds of flame scattered about the yard.

He handed Ron a pair of cuffs.

"Three men had firebombs that backfired and lit them up over there," Ron said, gesturing toward the still-burning trio. "That one pulled a gun and was shot, and the other two are probably badly burned. You better call for the Life Flight helicopter, or two ambulances, if it's not available. And alert the coroner that she'll probably be needed here tonight."

Tom knelt and gingerly pulled the blanket off Twister, who still rolled back and forth groaning pitifully. Rising, he moved cautiously toward Nacco's unmoving body, dragging the smoldering blanket behind him.

Shielding his eyes with his forearm, he moved toward Nacco in an attempt to smother the flames consuming the remains of his lifeless body, but the heat kept him at bay. He involuntarily cringed when Nacco's arms began contorting at grotesque angles as his muscles contracted spasmodically in the intense heat.

Tom gestured toward Twister and Squeaky and said, "Just keep an eye on those two. It'll be safer to search them after back-up arrives."

"You got here quickly," Ron said to Bill. "Were you in the neighborhood?"

"Yeah," Bill said, still looking at the carnage. "I was taking care of a wreck about a mile from here. A Volkswagen hit that huge buck I told you about, and it went through the windshield. It's not good."

Ron looked over at Tom with a sick look on his face and asked, "How big was the buck?"

"An eleven point with one small sticker tine," Bill said. "The bases were as thick around as your wrist and the main tines were from seven to nine inches long."

"This night just keeps getting better and better," Ron said disgustedly.

CHAPTER 38

PARTY CRASHER

McGuire strained to see through the murky darkness outside the Lewis home. The late hour was beginning to take its toll on him and his red-rimmed eyes burned as they tried to focus.

To make things more difficult, dancing shadows from wind-swept maple trees dotting the front yard camouflaged the house and partially obscured the windows that showed the flickering blue glow from a television.

I ain't gonna see shit from here, he thought. *I may as well leave the truck and get a closer look.*

Sliding slowly from the cab, he eased the door closed. The lonely call of bullfrogs from the swamp signaled the end of summer.

I may as well take the duct tape and rope with me in case I need it. No use runnin' back and forth and chance being seen.

Gliding noiselessly from one shadow to the next, McGuire wove his way down the gravel drive aided by the ghostly-pale light from the sliver of a waning moon.

Approaching from the side of the house, he stepped gingerly over coils of a haphazardly tossed hose leading from a faucet on the side of the house to an oscillating sprinkler in the yard. Peering through a window and a tiny opening between the curtains, it appeared that no one was in the kitchen, at least not the portion he could see.

I can't see a damned thing from here. I gotta get onto the front porch.

Slipping towards the front of the house, he flattened himself against a side wall until an automobile on the road sped past, then he snuck up the wooden steps on the porch. He made sure to keep his feet over the support of the stair stringers instead of risking making the ancient steps squeak.

That damned brother-in-law of mine better get off his lazy ass and fix these steps 'fore someone gets hurt on 'em.

Stretching his neck, McGuire peered into the lower edge of the large bay window. He spied a big-screen TV across the room playing a movie, and the high back of a couch facing the television.

I don't know where the kids are, but that's the back of Maddy's head for sure.

As he craned his neck back and forth trying to get a better view, Amy stood from where she had been lying with her head on her aunt's lap.

"I'm going to the bathroom," she said, running from the room. "Just keep the movie playing. I saw this part when I was over at my friend Cindy's house. I'll be back in just a minute."

"She always does this," Kathy said disdainfully, leaning on Maddy's other side. "If I don't stop it, she'll be asking so many questions about what happened when she gets back that it'll ruin it for us."

She picked up the remote control and hit the pause button. "Is that okay with you, Aunt Maddy?"

"It's fine," Maddy said, stretching with clenched fists and yawning widely. "I think I have to go to bed, you girls wear me out."

"Can't you stay up just a little bit longer?"

"Not if you want me to be any good tomorrow," she laughed. "We have a busy day planned and I want to be able to keep up with you two without having to take a nap."

"I'm a little tired myself," Kathy said. "But I want to stay up and see the end of the movie."

Amy skipped back into the living room and stopped short when she saw Maddy picking up the remnants of pizza crusts, paper plates, and empty plastic soda bottles.

"Aren't we going to watch the end of the movie?" she asked, with a pitiful look of disappointment on her face.

"Honey, I'm worn out and there's at least an hour left to the movie. I can't keep my eyes open."

"Can I stay up and finish watching it? I do it all the time when Daddy's here."

"If Kathy stays up with you," Maddy said with a tired smile.

"I'll stay up with her if she doesn't fall asleep," Kathy said. "But I'm not going to wake her up and chase her to bed. She gets grumpy."

"Well, if she falls asleep, you wake me up and I'll come down and take care of her," Maddy said as her fatigued smile widened slightly.

Shit! Those damned kids will be up half the night! McGuire thought as he steadied himself on the handrail. *But it will make it easier for me to find which bedroom she'll be sleepin' in. She'll have to turn the light on, and then I'll know for sure. No use flounderin' around in the dark tryin' to find her if I can know exactly where she's sacked out.*

After throwing the paper plates into the kitchen trashcan and placing the glasses into the dishwasher, Maddy checked the back door to make sure one of the girls hadn't unlocked it. She'd made a thorough inspection of the house earlier to make sure all doors and windows were secured. When she was satisfied, she trudged upstairs while calling to the girls, "I'll wake you at eight o'clock sharp, so don't stay up too late."

"We won't, Aunt Maddy," they replied in unison from the couch.

It took her a few minutes to get ready for bed. It was enough time for McGuire to slink around the perimeter of the house and locate her room. It was the only room with a light on upstairs.

Other than damned-near breaking my neck tripping over that freakin' garden hose my lazy assed brother-in-law left layin' in the yard, that was easy, he thought bitterly. The fact he had once loved Maddy didn't mean anything to him. Plotting revenge upon her for leaving him consumed his every thought and emotion.

Sitting quietly with his back against the side of the house, he watched the serene fields surrounding the Lewis home, occasionally checking his watch until one hour had passed.

In a slow and deliberate manner, McGuire made his move.

He crept to the back door, which had a small foyer as a mudroom where coats, hats, and muddy shoes could be left to dry. Carefully placing duct tape over the small pane of glass closest to the door lock, he broke the glass with his elbow, reached through and flicked the lock open.

A satisfied, wicked grin spread slowly over his face in the gloomy darkness of the still night.

Pushing the outer door open, he let himself into the mudroom and stood perfectly still, listening intently.

He could hear no sounds coming from the rest of the house.

After two minutes of silent vigilance he gave the knob of the inner door a twist and nudged it open.

It swung open on well-oiled hinges.

He froze in place, his ears tuned for any sounds that would mean he'd been discovered. His heart beat feverishly in his chest, the rushing blood echoing in his ears. After another two minutes of near-breathless listening, he slithered past the door. Moving silently past the entrance to the cellar, he verified that its door was slightly ajar and not locked.

Breathing a sigh of relief, he moved towards the sound of the television while keeping in the shadows at the edges of the room, his shoes landing noiseless on the linoleum. He nervously fingered the roll of duct tape he had slipped over his wrist, and then began stripping a piece of tape from the roll, making sure it didn't make a sound.

Take your time, he reminded himself. *You ain't in no hurry. Ya have all night.*

After freeing a ten-inch strip, he ripped it free one strand at a time. He smiled to himself for having performed the job in total silence.

Repeating this, he soon had two pieces of the tape stuck lightly to the flannel of his shirtsleeve. Just as he finished, he heard one of the girls speaking to the other.

"Get up!" Kathy said. "Don't make Aunt Maddy come down here and have to carry you up to bed."

Amy groaned tiredly without waking up.

"Come on! Wake up!" Kathy said a little louder.

Kathy threw a pillow at her sister, who stirred, but didn't awaken.

"You're a real pain!" she said, stalking out of the living room toward the kitchen. McGuire flattened himself against the wall beside the doorway.

Kathy marched briskly into the kitchen, and McGuire pounced.

He brutally clasped one grubby hand over her tiny mouth and nose, and grabbed Kathy around her waist to lift her off the ground.

His meaty, filthy fingers smothered her terrified scream.

"Don't yell or I'll kill you," he growled into her ear. "If I have to kill you, then I'll have to kill your sister and Aunt Maddy. It's your choice."

She suddenly went limp in his arms and a heart-rending whimpering noise came from deep within her chest.

Carrying the hysterically sobbing child into the mudroom, and with his hand still savagely clenching her mouth, he was able to close the inner door.

"I'm not going to hurt you or anyone else," he lied as he plucked a piece of duct tape from his forearm and slapped it over her mouth. "Just cooperate and everything will be okay."

Surprised, she wriggled to free herself and sucked in a huge gulp of air through her tear-swollen nose, but the tape stifled her horrified shriek before it could pass her swollen lips.

Reaching into his back pocket, McGuire produced a piece of laundry line and expertly bound her wrists. The thin cotton rope cruelly cut her tender flesh, drawing blood.

She gasped in agony, but the tape still held tightly against her soft skin and muffled her squeal of torment.

When she was securely bound, McGuire used the second piece of tape to cover her eyes. Roughly yanking her to her feet, he pushed her blindly back through the kitchen toward the cellar door.

Kathy was powerless in his grasp.

"I'm gonna take you down the cellar. Don't you try anything or you know what'll happen," he snarled gruffly into her ear.

After opening the cellar door he groped toward the ceiling for the pull cord, and gave it a gentle tug. A bare bulb burst into brilliance, blinding him momentarily.

Pulling the door shut behind them, he guided her down the steps with one hand on the nape of her neck, using the other to steady himself along the handrail. The rickety steps groaned under his weight.

I hate the way musty basements smell, he thought. *But it'll keep her scared and hopefully too afraid to try and escape.*

He stood her beside a support pole in middle of the basement then kicked her legs out from beneath her. Her buttocks bounced off the damp, chilly dirt floor and snot blew from her nose when she tried to scream in muffled agony and surprise.

Wasting no time to see if she was injured, McGuire ripped more tape from the roll and crudely trussed her ankles together.

Viciously grabbing her face, he forced her head back, and then fastened it to the pole with a generous amount of tape, making sure to cover her eyes but not her nose with each loop. He reveled in feeling the rapid, gasping snorts of moist air expelled from her nose onto his sweaty forearm as he held her head in place.

As an afterthought, he looped tape around her slender neck and wound it around the pole taking care not to cinch it too tightly and prevent her from breathing.

That'll keep her sittin' up straight and stop her from scootin' down and gettin' loose. Now to take care of her sister, then it's time to reacquaint myself with Maddy.

Before leaving the basement, McGuire pulled three long strips of duct tape from the roll and lightly stuck them to his sleeve.

Amy was sleeping peacefully on the couch, curled up at one end with her head on a pillow. Most people would look upon the sleeping child and marvel at the peace and serenity on her cherubic face.

McGuire, however, only saw an easy-to-dominate victim.

He clamped his hand over her mouth and crushed her with his body. Amy's wild, terror-filled eyes flew open.

After plastering the tape over her mouth, he heaved Amy over his shoulder and easily carried her into the basement. Tying both sisters to the same support was the closest he came to committing a compassionate act that evening.

That'll keep 'em both quieter if they know each other is okay.

Without a second thought about the girls, he turned on his heels and clambered up the steps two at a time as his mind focused on his anticipated carnal delights.

Giving the light cord a gentle tug, he left the girls in the darkness. He only hesitated long enough to close the cellar door.

He made his way up the well-worn stairs to the second floor, being careful to place his feet close to the wall to avoid making noise. Like a specter of doom he ghosted silently upward.

At the top of the stairs he stood in silence to get his bearings.

He identified Maddy's room and crept forward, placing his weight on the outsides of his feet to minimize the sounds from his footfalls. Hugging the wall, he stopped beside the door leading into the corner bedroom where he had seen Maddy flick off the lights when she went to bed.

Hot Damn! She left the door open. Probably so the girls could look in and see she was here. The bitch always was thoughtful that way.

A sudden weakness overcame him and he leaned heavily against the wall.

Why in the hell didn't you support me, Maddy? Why couldn't you see I was doing the best I could?

Why'd you leave me? We coulda worked things out.

He straightened himself and thought bitterly, *because it didn't matter what I did, it was never enough. That dickhead of a brother of yours was always sayin' what a bum I was and that I wouldn't amount to nothin'. Well, he can kiss my hairy Irish ass! I got you, his kids, and his big-assed house. And he ain't got shit!*

He poked his head past the doorframe and scanned the room with laser-like intensity. The waning moon cast barely enough light for him to see Maddy lying peacefully under the covers on a huge, ornately framed brass bed. Her gentle breathing lifted the quilt in a deep, regular rhythm.

He smiled warmly at memories of the times they had shared a bed.

But a split second later his smile and happy memories were displaced by a smirking grin and malice-laden heart.

Now we'll have a bit of fun my way. You're going to be mine forever. It's only over my dead body you'll ever be with another man.

He stood beside the bed looking down on her.

Her breathing maintained a steady cadence in her dream-filled slumber. His hand crept towards her as if to caress Maddy, and then hung motionless as he savored the moment of being near her again. He momentarily hovered over her to admire the serene curves of her face, an attractive face he had once adored and loved.

Then his eyes squinted as his mood swung to the polar opposite of love and tender adoration.

Don't worry about her screams. There's no one here to hear them.

He lingered over her, his body aligning with hers.

The familiar aphrodisiac-like effects of predatory power surged within him, as it always did when he was in total control.

In a blinding flash he pounced upon his prey.

It took Maddy a moment to realize she was not on a white sand beach in Tahiti, and something was terribly wrong. The dream that had engrossed her seconds ago disappeared.

Intuitively, she knew what was happening. In a fit of panic she realized McGuire was lying on top of her, trapping her beneath his crushing weight. This was no nightmare, but reality.

She had dreaded this moment, but had expected it.

She knew he would come seeking revenge, and it would be of a time and place of his choosing, because that was the way of predators. And if John McGuire was nothing else, he was definitely a predator.

A scream escaped her lips and she began squirming under the covers.

"It's me, Maddy," he growled. "You knew I'd be comin' for ya."

She said nothing. Her writhing continued. She grunted.

"You think I'd let you just run away?" he said, as his breathing started coming in short, choppy gasps. "You're my woman. No one else's. Ever."

She thrust her elbow into his chest in a futile attempt to pry him off her.

Pushing off the bed, she strove for leverage, her clenched teeth pressing into the sheets.

"Look at me!" he snapped.

She burrowed her face into the bed.

Her incessant twisting and bending continued wordlessly.

"Look at me!"

She curled into a ball and went still.

"Look at me, you bitch!" he bellowed, foamy spittle erupting from his lips.

Slowly her face turned toward him.

"Up yours, John," she said quietly. "Go to hell, but don't bother waiting for me."

"Why you prissy-assed bitch!" he roared, rearing up and cocking his fist back behind his head, his contorted face a mask of fury.

BAM!

The muzzle blast from the 2 1/2-inch barreled Smith and Wesson handgun blew a storm of fluff and shredded cloth from the heirloom quilt as the 135 grain Speer Gold Dot sliced through flimsy cloth and entered John McGuire's pelvis.

The rapidly expanding bullet blasted its way through his pubic symphysis, macerating it in a splatter of splintering bone and connective tissue.

With its remaining energy, the bullet expanded and ripped violently through his anal sphincter, dashing any chance of him ever again having a normal bowel movement.

The instant the forward anchorage of his pelvis burst into shards of useless minerals, his legs splayed pathetically, devoid of strength or value.

Maddy spun beneath the covers, jammed her elbow to his chest, and pushed.

BAM!

The slug raked through his body, bursting his abdominal aorta in a spectacular splash of hydrostatic mayhem. Tatters of the one-inch thick artery began fluttering wildly as wisps of gory tissue churned haphazardly on a torrent of cascading blood.

McGuire involuntarily sucked debris-filled air into his oxygen-starved lungs as he stared blankly and uncomprehendingly at her rage-darkened face.

Maddy saw his eyes begin to dim, but she knew he was still a life-threatening menace due to his close proximity to her and his tremendously greater strength, so she had to continue the fight until he was no longer a menace.

In a fit of renewed strength, she viciously grabbed a fistful of his matted red hair with one hand then twisted her body as she violently rolled him over.

He was helpless to resist.

BAM!

Her third and final shot entered three inches above the second, angling sharply upward to demolish the great vessels at the top of his heart, which beat wildly in a futile attempt to keep life-giving blood flowing to his brain. Instead, it only hastened the pooling of blood in his chest.

Maddy heaved mightily, twisting his head and neck as far as she could reach, and then violently kicked at him in a hysterical fit to be rid of his presence.

John McGuire's lifeless body crumpled in an untidy heap beside Maddy's bed at the same moment Squeaky and Twister were being loaded into ambulances at Predator's Bane.

It had been a wild Friday night.

CHAPTER 39

CALL THE CAVALRY

Maddy rolled over and fumbled in the dark for her cell phone and flashlight lying on the bedside table, doing her best to keep her revolver pointing at McGuire's unmoving body.

His unfocused eyes stared vacantly into space, indicating that he was likely dead.

When she was satisfied he was no longer a threat, she aimed the gun at the door and slid shakily out of bed. Kneeling at the foot of the bed and steadfastly keeping the revolver pointed at the bedroom door, she feverishly dialed 9-1-1.

"Emergency dispatch," the bored voice droned. "What is your emergency?"

"This is Madelyn Lewis," she cried hysterically. "I need the police immediately!"

"What is your address, ma'am?"

"A man broke into my house at 79346 Thompsonville Pike and attacked me while I was in bed. I need the police *now*! My nieces were downstairs and I don't know where they are."

"Are you injured, ma'am?"

"No."

"Are there more intruders in the house?"

"I don't know," she cried as tears rolled down her face. "Send the police, please! I don't know where my nieces are!"

"Where is the man who attacked you?"

"He's been shot and needs an ambulance. Send the police! I need the police!"

"Stay calm, ma'am," the female voice was more animated. "I've dispatched the police to your location. I need you to stay calm and help me. Where were your nieces the last time you saw them?"

"They were watching TV downstairs and I went to bed," she wailed. "I should have stayed with them! Oh my God! I have to go find them!"

"Ma'am, stay where you're at until the police get there."

"I have to get them!" Maddy repeated hysterically.

"Are you armed, ma'am?"

"Yes, I have two shots left. I'm going downstairs. Tell the police to just kick the door in if I can't get there to meet them."

"Ma'am, is the door kicked in already?"

"I don't know. Why?"

"Ma'am, the police will not kick in the door. You'll have to meet them there."

"They won't kick the door in?" Maddy gasped incredulously. "We're in trouble here!"

"At least open the door, ma'am."

"Holy hell! Son-of-a-bitch!"

"Ma'am?"

"I'm going downstairs to find my nieces," Maddy said with resolve. "I'll open the door if I can. The cops can catch up to me when they get here."

Maddy left the phone connection open and slipped it into the breast pocket of her flannel pajamas to maintain contact with the dispatcher but free her hands for whatever she still had to deal with. Almost as an afterthought, she put on her slippers so her feet would be protected as she explored the darkened house.

"Ma'am?" the dispatcher asked, the voice muffled from her pocket. "Ma'am?"

Maddy pulled the phone out and said hurriedly, "Tell the police not to shoot me. I'm five-foot seven and one hundred and fifty pounds with shoulder-length red hair. I'm wearing red plaid flannel pajamas and brown corduroy slippers. I'll be armed with a black snub-nosed revolver until they get here in case there are more assailants in my house. Hurry!"

She slipped the phone back into her pocket.

"Ma'am?" the muffled female voice of the dispatcher continued.

Maddy snatched the flashlight from her nightstand with her left hand while she clenched the Smith and Wesson in her trembling right. The ankle holster where the revolver had rode snugly and unnoticed against the inside of her left ankle was forgotten as she cautiously rose to her full height, then strode toward the open door before flattening herself against the wall.

She stood listening for any sounds as her heart pattered wildly against the inside of her chest for what seemed an eternity, but in reality was only ten seconds.

"Ma'am?" the muffled female voice continued. "Ma'am? Are you still there?"

Calm down, she admonished herself sternly.

You must go slow or you'll screw up. Clearing bad guys from a house is for professionals and Nadine warned me never to move through a house where assailants are suspected of being, but I have to find the girls.

If there's anyone else in this house they could be anywhere. They may be hiding and waiting for you to come to them, so they'll have the element of surprise. You're at a disadvantage, so take it slow and easy. Listen closely, and then move silently.

Maddy peered around the doorframe and down the hallway.

It was empty.

She moved silently out of the room and into the hall, feeling the wallpaper glide beneath her back with each step, painstakingly making her way to the head of the stairs. Her eyes scanned every nook and cranny of the darkened hallway. Stopping halfway down the hall, she forced herself to take a deep breath and listened intently.

Calm down.

You'll be useless to the girls if some bastard jumps you before you can get to them. If they're still alive, she thought as hot tears began coursing down her puffy cheeks.

Satisfied that she heard nothing, she began descending the stairs one step at a time.

SQUEAK!

The third step from the top squealed loudly when she placed her weight on it. She froze in place, afraid to move.

You knew that stair step was squeaky! Think! You have to use your head or you'll screw up royally.

After forcing herself to slowly count to one hundred, she again began her stealthy descent down the steps.

Placing her feet next to the wall, she managed to reach the bottom without mishap or making any undue noise. When both her feet were firmly on the floor, her legs almost collapsed as the strain of tension overcame her.

Breathe. You have to breathe slowly and deeply to stay calm. Keep your mouth wide open to remain silent, but breathe. Keep your gun in front of you, but close to your chest so no one can grab it.

Oh my God! You can't do this! Trying to find the girls in this huge, dark house is insanity!

She didn't have to.

The flicker of multicolored lights from the approaching State Police cruiser flashed across the front window.

With a flood of emotions Maddy rushed to the door and tore it open with almost superhuman strength.

Shit! You can't run out there with a gun in your hand! You'll get shot.

Unsure what to do, she turned to set her revolver on a shelf next to the front door.

Bad idea. You may need it.

With a sudden flash of inspiration, she shoved the gun inside the sports bra she wore with her pajama set.

Damned! That's cold!

She flicked on the front lights, and then marched onto the porch with her hands held high and in front of her. She barely noticed the ancient boards squeaking as she moved into the deluge of flashing lights from the police cruiser as it slid to a shuddering halt.

Headlights centered on the shapely figure clad in red plaid flannel pajamas standing erect on the front porch with her hands stretched to the sky while a muffled female voice asked incessantly from her breast pocket, "Ma'am? Ma'am? Are you there?"

CHAPTER 40

THE CAVALRY ARRIVES

The responding officers ran from their vehicles.

A uniformed officer emerged from the passenger side of the cruiser with a short-barreled pump shotgun held firmly across his chest. The driver pulled his service pistol from its holster as soon as he cleared the swinging car door.

Maddy yelled, "I don't know where my nieces are! They were watching TV when I went to bed! I don't know where they're at!" She broke down in hysterical paroxysms of anguished tears as the last of her adrenaline-charged energy drained from her.

"How many intruders are in the house?" the officer demanded as he covered the front doorway with his shotgun.

"I don't know," Maddy blubbered. "One is upstairs on the floor. I think he's dead."

"Did you see anyone else?"

"No," was all Maddy could say.

"Ma'am, we have back-up on the way. Please sit here on the front steps and do not re-enter the house. We're going to check it out and we don't want you in there. Do you understand?"

Maddy dumbly stared at him as he helped her to sit down.

"Do you understand?" he asked again, giving her shoulder a gentle shake. "Sit on the steps and stay out of the house!"

"Yes." Maddy slumped forward and her arms crossed her chest as if to protect herself, and then great sobs began racking her body in horrific spasms of grief.

Before the officers could leave her to begin their search of the house, more lights began flashing on Thompsonville Pike.

"We're going to wait until our back-up arrives. That's them coming now," one officer said calmly. "Why don't you come with me and you can sit in my vehicle. You'll be more comfortable."

Maddy stared at him dumbfounded until he took her by the arm and gently guided her toward his cruiser.

A police cruiser turned into the farm lane and rocketed toward the house. It veered toward the rear of the yard and parked between the house and the barn.

Another cruiser pulled in front of McGuire's truck parked alongside the lane near the road, illuminating it with its headlights. Satisfied that the pick-up truck was unoccupied, he joined his fellow officers in front of the house.

Before long, four Virginia State Police troopers were milling at the front of the house and preparing to enter. In a hurried conference, the senior officer on scene formulated a plan to clear the house.

As the officers swarmed throughout the home, a steady cadence of troopers loudly calling "Clear" was heard as each room was searched.

In less than ten minutes, the job was done. Amy and Kathy were led out of the house by an officer who smiled broadly as they ran to their aunt with outstretched arms. After giving them a few seconds to kiss and hug, the officers continued with their jobs.

"Ma'am," one asked her. "We have to ask you some questions."

"Okay," Maddy said, straightening her shoulders and pulling the girls closer.

"Ma'am, we found the man upstairs on the floor." He looked apprehensively at the girls out of the corner of his eyes. "Where is the gun?"

"It's in my bra," she said. "I didn't want to have it in my hand when I ran out of the house."

"Can I have it, please?"

"Of course." Maddy shoved her hand into the front of her shirt and fished around before producing it with a flourish. "It's still loaded with two rounds, so be careful."

He expertly unloaded the revolver and placed it, the empty cartridge casings, and the two loaded rounds on the hood of his car. The other three officers drifted over and began congregating within earshot.

"Now tell me what happened," he said solemnly.

VULNERABILITY

"I want to thank you gentlemen for helping me with this," Sarah said sincerely. "My shoulder doesn't allow me to do heavy manual labor like this anymore."

Chauncey lifted the facemask from in front of his nose and mouth before saying, "It has to be done. This is terrible, but I live here and have to do this. It's William who deserves all the thanks."

William didn't bother moving his facemask, but just spoke through it. "I wish I could say it was my pleasure, but it's not. If you don't mind, I'd rather just keep shoveling and get this finished. I'll chit-chat later when the job's done."

"Sorry for interrupting," Sarah said, shifting her position to keep herself upwind. "I'll go make lunch while you two finish."

"Please don't be offended if I can't eat much," William said.

"I may be able to eat, so don't be too chintzy with the chow. All this shoveling is making me hungry," Chauncey said.

"You're a sick puppy," William said, leaning into his shovel. "How can you even think about food with this horrendous stench?"

"The living needs food to survive. The stench of the dead shouldn't take precedence over maintaining life."

"Just keep shoveling and let's make sure to get all this contaminated gravel out of here. We may have to remove some of the soil beneath also. Keep shoveling."

The two men put their backs into their work and finished as quickly as possible. William was motivated by a need to distance himself from the stench of burned human flesh. A growling belly goaded Chauncey to labor more furiously.

After they were satisfied all the contaminated gravel from the driveway had been hauled back to the woods and heaped in a pile, the exhausted men ambled to rejoin Sarah as she sat contentedly at a table in middle of the yard. She had two large pitchers filled with freshly squeezed lemonade and murky brown iced tea sitting beside three tumblers. A cooler sat a few feet from the table holding ice cubes.

"Maybe we should shower before we sit down," William said. Chauncey shuffled a few steps behind him.

"That may be a good idea," Chauncey said.

"Nonsense," Sarah said. "Just sit downwind."

"I made the offer," he said, as he gingerly lowered his bulk into a chair. "Don't say I didn't warn you."

"You guys aren't very dirty, and the smell really didn't get on you," she said. "The tools may take a few days to lose the odor, but you're okay."

"When are you having more gravel delivered?" William asked.

"I have them delivering tomorrow morning," Chauncey said. "They said they could just open the back of their dump truck and lay the gravel down where we need it to minimize the amount of shoveling. I'll only have to flatten it out a little with a garden rake."

"Everything considered, we got through that debacle fairly easily."

"Things could have gone much worse, that's for sure."

"Yeah, it could have been the stench of our burned bodies and buildings stinking up the place, instead of the bad guy's remains."

"Thankfully, they died without us having to get involved," William mused. "Not to be cruel, but the reality of the situation is that if we had to defend ourselves, the judicial system would have put us on trial. That doesn't always work out the way we think it will in some self-defense situations. There are way too many good people in jail who had to defend themselves against a criminal threat, but the system worked against them."

"That's very true," Sarah said. "If Chauncey had fired his shotgun and broken those firebombs, it would have been up to a jury to decide if he had a right to shoot those men since they weren't in his house."

"It's also a good thing that you stayed locked up in your bedroom with your AR-15 to keep yourself safe," William said. "If you had come out here with a gun in your hand after the police arrived, they wouldn't have understood what an armed person was doing in middle of that mess. They may have shot you."

"Sometimes it's better to just wait instead of starting to shoot right away, especially if the situation isn't crystal clear as to whether you're legally allowed to shoot in self-defense or not," Sarah said. "And this was definitely one of those times."

"From what I learned at the Armed Response Institute class," Chauncey said, "It can cost over a hundred thousand dollars to defend yourself in a self-defense shooting. Lawyer fees, not to mention the mental anguish involved, can be horrendous."

"That's what they taught me too," Sarah said soberly.

"Unfortunately, when the situation is unraveling, there isn't time to consider all the possible ramifications," William said. "You're so focused on saving your life you can't think of how a jury, sitting in the safety of a courtroom with all the time in the world to calmly consider the facts, will rule on your actions. It's not fair in many ways."

"God was looking after us that night, that's for sure," Chauncey said. "I'm happy I didn't have to be responsible for their deaths. On the other hand, dying from pneumonia because your lungs were burned can't be a good way to go."

"The guy who pulled a gun on Tom may have been lucky," William said. "A bullet was much quicker than lingering in a hospital for days not able to breathe on your own, like his partners had to endure."

"Whoever says a cop is never around when you need one?" Sarah said to lighten the mood. "Thank God those two saw what was happening and investigated."

"So, I assume you're going to let them keep hunting on your property?"

"It's a safe bet. I like having cops around. They're the good guys."

"Actually, I read an interesting article about how various misconceptions began and one of the items they reported on was why police began hanging around donut shops," Chauncey said.

"Yeah, to eat donuts and drink coffee instead of being out protecting the public like they're paid to do," William said with a snort.

"On the contrary," Chauncey said. "As the story goes, the owner of a donut shop offered free coffee and restroom use to the local police so there would always be a strong police presence around his business. That kept the robbers at bay. It was a mutually beneficial arrangement."

"Cool," Sarah replied. "That's thinking ahead."

"Thinking ahead was you getting a satellite phone because your cell phone can't get reception out here," William said. "When they cut your phone lines you would have had no way to contact 9-1-1."

"That's why I spend a tremendous amount of money for that thing," Sarah said. "When my house was broken into last year we had to drive ten minutes into Thompsonville before we could get any cell phone reception. Preparation is vital to being able to handle an emergency when it happens. If you don't have smoke alarms or fire extinguishers in your house before a fire starts, you're going to lose your house, and maybe your life and the lives of your family. The same applies to other emergencies."

"Unfortunately, all too many people don't think ahead," Chauncey said. "They're under the mistaken assumption that because something terrible hasn't yet happened to them, it never will. When they realize they were wrong, it's too late, and good people get hurt when it could have been avoided."

"The 9-1-1 dispatcher verified what I was saying over the satellite phone with what William was reporting from the landline phone in the cabin," Sarah said. "That spurred them to action, knowing such a bizarre event was truly unraveling."

"Why they cut the phone lines to the house but not to the cabin is perplexing," Chauncey said. "It's obvious the electric and phone lines come from the pole into the cabin, so they must have known we were in there."

"Actually, it's very lucky they did cut the lines to the house, because it was valuable evidence that allowed the police to determine those three really were dangerous and a threat to us," William said. "It was pretty scary when they began questioning us like we were the perpetrators."

"The police have to gather information so they have a good idea what happened," Sarah said. "They have to treat everyone like a suspect until they get enough facts established to form a reasonable scenario of how and why various events transpired."

"Have you heard anything more about who they were and why they were willing to commit murder?" William asked.

"All they'll tell me is that the three were all from Tennessee and had extensive criminal records dating from their teen years, including many violent crimes. One of them was wanted for questioning in a murder. These were bad actors, according to Tom Mahoney," Sarah said. "They have no address in this area and nobody from around here came to claim the bodies. Their relatives from Tennessee reluctantly performed that task. Apparently, they weren't much liked even by their kin."

"Maddy's attacker had lived in Tennessee also," William added. "Maybe there's a connection between all these guys."

"Everything is just speculation at this point until more information becomes available," Sarah said. "Maybe the cops know more than they're saying at this point. We may never know the whole story."

"So they were here, but no one knows why?"

"It's suspected they may be involved with the recent increase in methamphetamine labs cropping up around here. There were substances used to cook meth found in their truck, but it's only an assumption at this point without more evidence. Tom told me not to pass that information around, but he felt we deserved an explanation on what was going on."

"How are Maddy and the Lewis girls doing?" Chauncey asked.

"As well as can be expected. They're visiting with relatives and Dan is arranging for the entire family to attend counseling."

"Unfortunately, those young girls will need all the counseling they can get after going through what they did," William said bitterly. The dark cloud of anger on his face gave mute testimony to how infuriated he was at the thought of such sweet children being traumatized in such a horrendous manner.

To change the subject and avoid the tsunami of anger he felt welling up inside him, William swept his arm in the direction of the gravel driveway and added, "And this all began with those guys terrorizing you at the supermarket?"

"It's the only thing we and the police can figure," Sarah said. "It's a good thing Chauncey and I left a paper trail by filing a complaint after the supermarket escapade. It helps fill in a few of the gaps in this mystery."

"We'll probably never know the whole story behind this," Chauncey said. "But I know I'll never feel safe regardless of where I am. Home is supposed to be a secure place away from the horrors of the world. That security has been violated and I doubt I'll ever feel totally safe again. If I can't feel safe at home, where can I?"

"So what are you getting at?" William asked. "You think you need counseling too?"

"Counseling may be a consideration, but I really think I better buy a handgun like Sarah wants me to," Chauncey said. "My shotgun was close because I was in my cabin. What would have happened if those three showed up when I was in the barn? Whether I'm here on the farm, or in town, I should have the means to protect my loved ones and myself. Hell, I should have learned that lesson and began carrying to church after St. Boniface. I can be so damned stupid at times."

"You're not stupid," Sarah said quietly. "Many folks need to have a traumatic event touch their lives before they understand that bad things can happen out of nowhere and at any time. Did you like the pistol I lent you to take the ARI-1 course?"

"It's a nice firearm, but I think I like revolvers better."

William remained silent.

"William, are you okay?" Sarah asked.

"I wasn't even involved in the supermarket situation," he said. "I was just in the wrong place at the wrong time, visiting with a friend like we always do, when shit hit the fan."

"Shit can hit the fan at any time, regardless of who you're with or what you're doing," Sarah said gravely.

"I think I just had an epiphany," he said.

"How so?"

"I just realized that even a man as big as I am was almost useless, because I wasn't armed. If a guy my size can be defeated by a few punks on a spree, how do women like you survive?"

Sarah smiled wanly and softly replied, "Welcome to my world. Would you like a large dollop of bourbon in that lemonade? You look like you need it."

The End

If you enjoyed this book…

I would truly appreciate it if you would help others to enjoy it also. Reviews of books are a vital part of helping readers find series they will love. Reviews are often what make the difference between passing over a book or finding a series that will keep you on the edge of your seat and demanding the next installment.

Your review will mean a lot to both me and to future readers. You can leave a review at Amazon by visiting:
http://www.amazon.com/review/create-review?&asin=B07LDZ92ZW

Or you can leave a review on Goodreads.com. Creating an account at Goodreads is very simple and you will discover a new home there with other readers who have reading interests very similar to yours. Check them out.

Thank you very much in advance for taking the time to post a review and your opinion of this book. It is greatly appreciated, and I look forward to reading your review!

Be A Beta Reader Team Member

I am recruiting willing volunteers to be members of my beta reader team.

What's all involved in being a beta reader? Well, you'll be helping me flesh out my manuscripts for each book before it is published. Many authors use beta readers because you are very astute at reading and any errors will jump off the page and strike your eye as being incorrect.

What types of things might you find?

One author likes to tell the story (OK, he reluctantly tells it) of the time he had his main character flicking the safety off a pistol that does not have a safety. Whoops!

But these are the types of things I need your help with.

If you are willing to help, I will make the un-edited manuscript available for a few days on BookFunnel. You can download it, read it, email me with anything you find that is not right within the following two weeks, and I'll look over your suggestions.

This will be a tremendous help to me and will give you insights into the processes of how the books you love to read are put together.

I have a standalone chapter that is just a small gift to you for joining the team.

You can get a free chapter for becoming a beta reader by visiting https://dl.bookfunnel.com/q1z60hf7io.

Want even more? Sign up for my mailing list and receive a FREE copy of DELAYED JUSTICE, a novella related to the True Justice series!

One of the best things about writing is building a relationship with my readers. I love sending information to you: newsletters with details on new releases, special offers, and other bits of news relating to the True Justice series that my readers report finding very interesting.

If you sign up for the mailing list, I will immediately send you an eBook of Delayed Justice for your reading pleasure.

Your email listing will NEVER be sold or used for anything other than an occasional announcement pertaining to this series of novels. Naturally, you can unsubscribe at any time.

To get your FREE copy simply sign up at https://dl.bookfunnel.com/bhnevz7rhh and your book will be sent to you in the blink of an eye!

A preview from your FREE copy of
DELAYED JUSTICE
Novella of the True Justice Series

Neighbors at odds.
Predators on the hunt.
A quiet neighborhood.
A mother who just wants to defend her child.

The urges of human predators overcome their fear of discovery, and the prospect of thrills beyond their wildest dreams goads them into undertaking a bold plan.

Delayed Justice delivers heart-pounding action and an astonishing ending that will change lives forever!

If you enjoy reading works books that balance the dark psychological musings of evil with the uncertainty of good triumphing over it, be sure to get your immediate copy of this True Justice Novella! I only need to know where you want it sent.

To get your FREE copy simply sign up at https://dl.bookfunnel.com/bhnevz7rhh and your book will be sent to you in the blink of an eye!

CONTENTS

EDUCATED JUSTICE

Book Three of the True Justice Series

D. E. Heil

Receive a FREE Gift!

Building a relationship with my readers is the very best thing about writing. I love to send newsletters with details on new releases, special offers, and other bits related to the True Justice Series so we can build that relationship.

Look for information on how to sign up for my mailing list and immediately receive your FREE gift at the end of this book.

Chapter 1

PROMISING LIFE WASTED

"Gwen, do you work tomorrow?" Dawn Simpson asked Gwendolyn Dowling as she slipped on her pink down-filled nylon jacket.

"No," Gwen replied courteously, tugging at the right sleeve of her grey cotton watch coat. It was twisted at a funny angle and steadfastly denied her burrowing hand and arm entry. "I have a huge final I have to study for. This is the big one for my major, so it's super important I do well on it."

"Is that because you're graduating this spring?"

"Yep, this is the test that can make me or break me," Gwen said.

"You have a really good job waiting for you when you graduate, don't you?"

"I do," Gwen replied. "The internship I had last year turned into an offer for full-time employment and I took it. It truly is a God-send because there are still students who graduated last year who are trying to find a decent job."

"You really think you'll like that job? Does it pay enough to have made all the time, money, and effort you put into college worth it?" Dawn asked. She was continually trying to gain some understanding of how the people she considered more fortunate than herself viewed their lives.

"Yeah, I really do like it," Gwen replied. "The people there were super nice, and they made me feel right at home. It was as if they were one big family working toward a common goal, except without the bickering a family would have. I genuinely liked being a part of that."

"I'm glad it works for you, I really am."

Gwen was now excited thinking about her future, and she was motivated to talk more about it.

"Working there made me feel good about myself. I think liking where you work is more important than how much money you make. Of course, the money is a big part of what makes that job so appealing. It pays well and has great benefits."

"It must be great to have a bright future waiting for you," Dawn said. "I should have gone to college or maybe even to a technical school. That way I could have learned something that would have made me qualified for a good job. But I didn't. Now I'll have to work in this place for the rest of my life." She glanced around with a disgusted look on her face.

"This is a good company with lots of opportunity for advancement," Gwen fibbed. "If you apply yourself, work hard, and let management know you want to move up in the company they can put you into their management training program."

"I'm not smart enough to learn all the stuff I'd need to be a manager," Dawn said. "I don't have the brains like you do."

"You're plenty smart," Gwen said. "All you need is the desire to complete what you start and be willing to put in the time to learn the things they want you to know."

"I guess I just don't have the patience to stick with anything," Dawn said. "I never could finish anything I ever started, and that includes high school. I just don't have the motivation and my mind always seems to wander."

"Getting a good education does require motivation and concentration so you can stay focused on your goals," Gwen said. She continued struggling with her recalcitrant right sleeve and it finally let her slip her slender hand and arm down its length.

She smoothed both coat sleeves until she was satisfied.

She had outgrown the coat two years previously, but she was always mindful of the financial burden she was placing on her parents. They supplemented her educational costs, putting off buying many things for themselves that they desperately needed, so she refused to buy a new coat until she could afford it on her own.

"There are plenty of things that can draw you off task or be discouraging enough to make you want to quit. You just have to keep going if you want to reap the rewards. You can do it if you want to," Gwen said, hoping she sounded encouraging and not patronizing.

"You better get yourself a new coat when you begin making some money at your new job. That one is way too small for you."

"I'm going to take your advice on that. I promise to get a new one for next winter," Gwen replied, chuckling because the same thought had been going through her mind. "By then I'll have been able to get a few bills paid off. Maybe I'll even be settled into an apartment of my own."

"You have such a good future," Dawn said, selfishly wishing it was her and not Gwen. "I wish I were you."

The tone of Dawn's voice made Gwen believe she hadn't heard a single encouraging word she said.

"Well, you keep trying. I'm sure things will work out just fine for you," Gwen said, giving Dawn a feeble, flipping wave of her hand. She then headed out of the employee lounge. Turning the corner without glancing left or right, she strode toward the weather-beaten rear door of the discount store.

The second shift had worked well for Gwen because she was able to schedule her classes in the morning and early afternoon. That way she could work the late afternoon shift, getting off late at night. Retail stores often had need of additional employees on that shift since most of their customers did their shopping in the evening hours.

Gwen barely had enough time after her classes ended to hurry to the congested student parking lot where she would retrieve her aged Toyota Corolla. It was always easy to find her car in the expansive lot because its dinged front fender made it easily identifiable among the mishmash of other vehicles.

After throwing her backpack stuffed with books and the detritus of student life into the back seat, she'd wheel through the rows upon rows of student vehicles to weave her way out of the lot.

Luckily, most of the cars parked in the lot were owned by travel-weary students who lived within commuting distance of the college. Usually, they were still finishing up their day in class when Gwen left for work. She appreciated having fewer students wandering around the lot and getting in her way, which was in stark contrast to the nerve-racking crowds she encountered each morning when everyone was scurrying to their first class of the day.

After exiting the college's parking lot, she'd drive furiously for two miles through crowded residential streets to the store where she would unhappily labor for the next eight hours. Grinding away the seemingly unending hours at the front check-out as a cashier was not high on her list of fun things to do, but she was willing to put up with it to achieve her career dreams.

Starting at three o'clock in the afternoon and ending at eleven o'clock at night allowed her to get back to her college dormitory room by midnight. This schedule helped her maintain good relations with her roommate.

Doreen, her congenial roommate for the last two semesters, was a late-night person and rarely went to bed before one o'clock in the morning. Gwen was happy she could get settled into her dorm room at such a late hour without being concerned about waking Doreen.

The discount store management only allowed employees to park in the rear parking lot to reserve the cherished parking spots in front for paying customers.

Gwen hated leaving the store by the rear exit because the door wobbled precariously on deformed hinges. The fact that it emptied out into the broad expanse of a creepy parking lot, which was almost always devoid of life late at night, did not help soothe her mind.

She placed her shoulder against the thick steel door and gave it a mighty shove to unstick it from its buckling frame. As soon as it screeched open, a biting blast of frigid late winter wind grabbed hold of it and almost ripped it from her feeble grasp.

She stepped out into the tempest. The chill seemed to drive straight through her aged coat as it callously whipped her face.

A shiver gripped her muscles and took her breath away.

Spinning in a semi-circle on the balls of her dainty feet until she was facing the door's exterior, she again placed her shoulder against it and labored mightily as buffeting blasts of wind made it almost impossible for her to slam it shut.

Mustering all her strength, she doggedly struggled against the incessant force of the undulating wind by throwing her diminutive body against the door's scarred exterior before it finally slammed shut with a deep, resonating clang.

A quick glance across the parking lot showed a few scraggly tufts of winter-dried grass precariously clinging to tiny dirt-filled cracks scattered throughout the wasteland of battered macadam. Gusts of bone-chilling wind ruthlessly battered them helter-skelter causing them to flutter erratically back and forth. It seemed they were dancing to a haunted tune only they could hear.

The walk across the secluded parking lot behind the store was always scary. It was dimly illuminated by an anemic yellow-tinged glow that seemed to dribble from ancient mercury vapor lamps. Intermittent flashes from car headlights on the highway two blocks away gave the shadow-blotched parking lot an eerie, ghostly quality.

Gwen felt ill at ease every time she took that walk to her car.

She imagined that the gut-tightening feeling she'd suffer through was the same sensation any rational person walking through a derelict graveyard would experience. It frequently flittered across her mind that this forbidding stretch of real estate was like a haunted cemetery in many ways.

A particularly gusty blast of wind flung her long, straight blonde hair over her head and whipped it into her watering eyes. With a purposeful tug, she pulled her fluffy maroon and white knit cap tightly down onto her head, over her wind-reddened ears, and then she snugged it closely about her eyes in a feeble attempt to keep the slicing wind at bay.

She hunched her scrawny shoulders forward and leaned into the wind in a pathetic attempt to minimize her exposure to winter's frosty pall.

With her attention riveted on each halfhearted step she took, she reminded herself to avoid the black ice that was almost impossible to see in the murky shadows dwelling in the buckled macadam.

With her head down, and her attention captivated by where her icy-cold feet would be placed, she did not see nor hear the door slide open on the side of a dirty panel van as she squeezed between it and an equally rundown Ford Taurus. But when a ragged pair of men's tennis shoes hit the macadam directly in front of her, she knew she was in trouble.

Startled, she sucked in a frosty breath at the same instant her head bolted upward to see who was wearing the shoes that inexplicably appeared before her.

Before she could react, an iron hard fist smashed into her spongy abdomen six inches above her belly button. The half-breath she had in her lungs gushed out in a single billowing jet of vaporous steam.

The blow forced her to bend forward at the waist, and in a smooth, practiced move, her assailant added to the momentum of her twelve-pound head dipping toward the macadam by roughly placing his hand onto the nape of her neck. He followed through with a vicious push on her skull, forcing her head downward and sideways.

In this position, her mind was confused as to where her head and body were oriented in time and space, and her feet slipped chaotically from beneath her.

With a resounding thud, she fell clumsily into the open side door of the van.

It was only a short fall inside the vehicle, but the momentum of her tumbling body combined with her inability to understand that she was about to crash into an immovable object, produced enough energy to cause serious harm to her young body. When the point of her shoulder forcefully impacted the dust-covered corrugated steel floor of the van, it snapped with a loud and horrifying sound that seemed to resonate throughout her entire skeleton.

She felt a paralyzing jolt of sharp pain shoot caustically from the joint of her shoulder as it separated. The delicate ligaments that had held it together only a few seconds before violently ripped and tore as the two bones went their separate ways.

Before her reeling mind could register that her arm had gone numb, her attacker pounced upon her prostrate body, and pinned her to the cold, uneven decking. His steel-hard hands showed no mercy as the unforgiving metal of the van's flooring bore into her flesh.

Mommy, help me, she pleaded in her befuddled mind as the realization of what was happening to her flashed through her brain at warp speed.

Maybe he'll just rape me then let me go, she thought as an insuppressible whimper escaped her fear-constricted throat. *I may be able to live with that, and it'll be okay. I may still be able to have a husband and children if I don't get HIV and die of AIDS.*

She had almost convinced herself that she may survive this savage attack when, in a fit of rage and euphoric domination, her attacker snatched a handful of hair on back of her head. With a mighty yank he viciously wrenched her face around so she could see his smirking face.

When her tear-filled eyes fell upon the scarred and deformed face of Joey Valentino, she knew she wouldn't see the dawn of another day.

Chapter 2

ROUGH MORNING

Sarah Collins awoke with a start, bolted out of bed, and was standing upright in a fighter's stance in the middle of her bedroom ready to fight for her life before it dawned on her she was simply having a nightmare. She relaxed and took a deep breath when she realized the terror she felt was not the result of a real and life-threatening scenario.

She gulped refreshing and revitalizing air into her lungs while her pulse beat a rhythm that sounded like a bass drum in her head.

Standing with her feet shoulder-width apart and her hands held loosely in front of her in the defensive posture of a martial artist, she tried to rationally think through her situation. Eventually, she was able to convince herself that all was well with the world. But in her heart, she knew that was not true.

Not true at all.

Her mind sluggishly began recognizing the familiar country motif of the bedroom she'd painstakingly decorated in a style that was totally different than the one she'd shared with her late husband, Josh Tobin.

Bright sunshine of late morning beamed around the sides of heavy, dark blue curtains that were dotted with golden brown silhouettes of moose and fringed with a tasteful tassel of forest green designs that gave the illusion of evergreen branches.

She desperately struggled to calm her jangling nerves, but her shaking hands were verification of the futility of her efforts.

A moment later, she felt the familiar softness of her golden retriever's fur brush against the flannel of her sleeping gown, and she instinctively relaxed her arm so she could reach down to pet him. She ran her trembling hand down the entire length of his broad, muscular back, and they both began to relax.

When Sarah flew from her bed in a panic, Rex, the wayward golden retriever she and her friend Nadine Brand had rescued, also sprang from his bed to come to his master's assistance. His unbridled loyalty to the two women was not diminished by the callous way his previous owners dumped him on a lonely country road.

Sensing that Sarah was distraught, he looked up at her with large, deep chestnut brown eyes. It was easy to see the love in those eyes. His solid, burly head was covered with wavy golden locks. He cocked it to one side, looking sideways at her out of the corner of his eyes.

Realizing that Sarah was not in danger, Rex began wagging his massive tail. The golden plumes extending from the underside waved gently like the fabled amber waves of grain immortalized in the patriotic song "America the Beautiful."

Sarah drew in another deep, cleansing breath of relief when she realized she was safely standing in the secure confines of her bedroom. She was equally relieved that the horrors of a few nights previously were merely a blip in history with no malevolent relevance to the present.

On that fateful night, her best friend Chauncey, and his pal, William Collonem, had been working together at their computers in the small cabin Chauncey had converted from a workshop on her farm. The two men were taking online accounting courses and were engrossed in their studies when methamphetamine-abusing troublemakers who had sworn to kill Chauncey arrived with firebombs and a revolver.

Based upon reports of the men stalking Sarah, the police investigating the crime speculated that the men had planned to kill Chauncey and William, and then rape and murder Sarah.

Sarah shuffled over to her recently vacated bed. Her leaden feet seemed almost too heavy to lift. She flopped down on the edge of her bed as an exhalation of air burst from her lungs.

Rex gently placed his huge head in her lap so she could pet him. She obliged him by gently and lovingly stroking the velvety hair behind his ears with long, easy strokes.

"You've come a long way from the gangly, stinking mess of a puppy you were when Nadine and I found you," she murmured in a husky sleep-laden voice. "I thought for sure you were going to be run over by a car or truck out on that road. Now look at you! You're a sleek, well-mannered member of the canine world, aren't your Rex?"

Rex responded by stamping his front feet gleefully as his thick tail swished excitedly from side-to-side in paroxysms of joy at being close to his human. He snuggled closer to her warm thigh, raised his head so his eyes met hers, and beamed a doggie version of a broad smile at her.

"You're such a wonderful dog. I wish you had a chance to meet Josh. He would have loved you," she said with lilting admiration in her voice.

Josh Tobin, Sarah's deceased husband, had been a promising orthopedic surgeon with a bright future ahead of him when he was murdered as he was waited for Sarah in the parking lot of her chiropractic office. The botched carjacking was the first crime of a short spree the murderers would embark upon that fateful evening.

"Josh was a great guy," Sarah said mournfully, her voice cracking with lingering grief.

A tiny tear glistened in the filtered morning light beaming through her bedroom window. She swiped it away with the back of her free hand.

She continued speaking confidentially to Rex and he began bumping into her knee with his brawny chest in an attempt to goad her into continuing to pet him.

"But he's gone now, and I have to move on," she whispered hoarsely.

The shrill ringing of her cell phone as it rested on the night table took her by surprise. Once again, she jumped to her feet ready to do battle.

Rex also sprang to his feet, stood with his front feet held apart, his ears upright and alert, as he turned to face the door leading into the hallway. He was ready to pounce on any enemy that threatened his master, but he relaxed immediately when he saw her take control of her emotions and grab the brashly pealing phone.

"I'm going to have to change that ringtone to something more genteel before the damned thing gives me a heart attack," she mumbled under her breath.

Composing herself as well as she could, she answered the phone with an adrenaline-charged but distressingly disjointed voice. "Hello," she croaked. She then held the phone away from her face, covered her mouth, and forcefully cleared her throat of phlegm that had accumulated after a fitful night of sleep.

"Aren't you up yet?" Nadine Brand asked in a cheerful but chiding voice. "Lately you seem to be reverting back to your sleeping habits from when we were roommates in college. Do you remember how grumpy you were back then or has time clouded your memory and given you rosy, cheerful recollections of how grouchy you can be when you wake up before you're ready?"

Nadine Brand, Sarah's former college roommate, had been a loner since her husband left her for another man. Her middle school teaching experience and understanding of how to rebuild a shattered life made her an exquisitely qualified mentor to friends in need, and in this case, that friend was Sarah.

"That's a bunch of baloney and you darned well know it," Sarah retorted good-humoredly. She began relaxing and embraced the feeling of wellbeing the sound of her long-time friend's voice gave her. "You're probably not aware of the fact that I'm usually up well before dawn to begin my morning run. I'm up even earlier on the days I go to church services during the week with the ladies' group from my church."

"Yeah, so you're always telling me, but I never see you huffing and puffing up and down the road before noon," Nadine replied.

"Well, today you won't see me 'huffing and puffing up and down the road' as you so tactfully put it," Sarah stated, a serious tone in her voice. "I'm still having some depression, well, it's not really depression, yet it is, of some sort. I don't really know how I feel. It may be fear, sadness, insecurity, anger, and only God knows what all combined to make me feel like crap. Even though I shouldn't, I mean, I am alive after all. And so are Chauncey and William. I'm glad of that, for sure, but yet I'm sad and kind of depressed. Well, it's not really depression …"

"Stop!" Nadine said. "I know you're having a hard time mentally by the way you're babbling in circles."

"So what can I do about it?" Sarah whined.

"You can be at my house for lunch at noon, that's what you can do," Nadine quipped. She was happy to have a snappy answer to give Sarah before she could go off on another meandering tirade. "Just bring yourself and Rex. I'll have plenty of hot comfort food and good company."

"Who's the company?" Sarah inquired. She was not in the mood to socialize.

"Reverend Yates is coming to counsel William and Chauncey," Nadine replied.

"Who in the hell is Reverend Yates?" Sarah asked. "And why should I care?"

"You've at least heard his name before," Nadine said. "Reverend Yates ran the Bethesda Mission for Homeless Men in Washington, D.C. where William used to work as a counselor. Chauncey also worked for him as a bookkeeper, which is where he learned that trade so he could then work for you at your chiropractic office."

"Oh, THAT Reverend Gates," Sarah said. "My mind is really foggy today because a nightmare woke me in the middle of a dream cycle. His name didn't ring a bell. He's the one who gave Chauncey the bookkeeping job because Chauncey was able to figure out that one of the mission's suppliers were cheating them by not actually delivering all of the goods that were listed on the invoice."

"That's him," Nadine confirmed. "Except his name is Yates with a 'Y' and not Gates with a 'G' like you called him."

"It's amazing that Reverend Gates managed to train Chauncey as well as he did. Especially considering that Chauncey had absolutely no memory of anything that happened before William picked him up off the street in the mission's van."

"Reverend Yates," Nadine corrected her calmly. She began to understand that Sarah was not intellectually firing on all her mental cylinders. "You called him Gates again."

"Yates, yeah, OK," Sarah replied absentmindedly.

Nadine continued talking in an attempt to better assess Sarah's mental state to rule out stroke as a possible organic reason for her scatter-brained meanderings.

"If you remember the story of how William and Chauncey met," she continued, ready to listen for clues so she could monitor Sarah's ability to remember a story she was familiar with hearing, "William was driving the van when he saw Chauncey lying on the sidewalk beside the steps of an abandoned house. He woke him up to get him into the van so he could take him to the mission to avoid freezing to death. The temperatures were predicted to drop way below freezing that night and the mission was trying to get the homeless people under shelter."

"And he thought Chauncey was drunk out of his mind because he couldn't remember his own name," Sarah said, finishing Nadine's sentence. "I remember that story. It was total amnesia that caused Chauncey to forget everything about his previous life and no booze or drugs were involved."

"As a matter of fact," Nadine said, realizing that Sarah was beginning to get her thoughts back together, "It was William who named him Chauncey because there was no way to know that he had, in reality, been Dr. Robert Fogler, a prominent OB/GYN from Baltimore."

"Yep, that's the way I heard the story," Sarah said, confirming the details were correct. "And then Chauncey began working for me using the bookkeeping skills he learned at the mission."

"Exactly. Now that your mind and memory is working again, get ready and be over here by noon," Nadine said. She ended the call before Sarah could protest.

CHAPTER 3

DARK NIGHT OF THE SOUL

Sarah eased her cherry-red pick-up truck along the lane at Nadine's farm, making sure to go slowly to avoid kicking up dust from the gravel driveway. She glided her truck into a space beside William's ancient Dodge pick-up truck. It was an indescribable color that may have once been a shade of tan.

The Dodge sported rusty fenders on all four corners, a crushed rear bumper that hung dangerously low on the driver's side, and a gaping hole where a tailgate used to be. The bed was so dented and rusted that it was unwise to carry any cargo in it as it could fall through to scatter on the roadway.

Rex's thick tail began beating a rapid, steady rhythm against the tinny side of Sarah's truck bed. He was gazing intently out the rear window of the fiberglass truck cap that perfectly matched the color of her pick-up.

He recognized Nadine, Chauncey, and William, all of whom he considered part of his "pack" and therefore were his friends.

Canines defined their relationships by grouping people and other canines they were familiar with as being in their pack and deserving respect and consideration. Anyone outside of their pack warranted closer scrutiny, and possibly a show of hostility.

Reverend Yates fell into this second group.

He would be given Rex's undivided attention until he was clearly identified as being acceptable and granted permission by the golden retriever to mingle freely with the members of his pack.

Rex was observing the farmyard through the dusty window of the truck cap, and he noted that the newcomer was being accepted by the people in his pack. In his mind, it seemed likely he could welcome him as a guest.

Reverend Yates was sitting peacefully under the spreading limbs of the sugar maple tree situated in the middle of Nadine's yard. The maple was the focal point of outdoors entertaining at the farm because of its central location, proximity to Nadine's front door, and the welcome shade and protection it offered from the blazing sun or drizzling rain.

Sarah dropped the tailgate of the truck with a resounding metallic clang. She always worried it would startle Rex, but he'd become accustomed to riding in the bed of various pick-up trucks and he was used to the noise.

She stretched her arm to its full length, reaching inside to unsnap the restraining harness that kept Rex securely held in place in case of an auto collision. With a practiced move based upon experience, she stepped quickly out of the way so the burly Golden Retriever could have a clear path to the tailgate.

Once, she had been struck by the muscular dog and knocked to the ground when he enthusiastically fled the confines of the truck bed. She'd learned that painful lesson quickly, and now gave him ample room to scoot by her.

Because of that experience, Sarah taught Rex to sit on the tailgate waiting for her hand signal accompanied by a verbal command to "Go" before he could stand and leave the truck bed.

As Rex sat impatiently, Sarah placed a ramp on the lip of the tailgate so he could walk down it instead of jumping out of the truck and possibly damaging his delicate leg joints. She didn't want him developing an early onset of arthritis, and she did everything she could to prevent that from happening.

She positioned herself beside the tailgate out of harm's way, and then gave Rex the hand signal and verbal command to "Go."

In the manner of excited dogs, Rex ignored the carefully placed ramp and leaped to the ground. He landed heavily on the cushiony mat of closely shorn grass of Nadine's front yard and ran straight to his pack mates without as much as a glance back at Sarah.

Sarah watched him as he gracefully flew through the air, and observed with wonderment the way his soft, fluffy fur floated on the gentle breeze. It gave him the appearance of a well-paid model making a shampoo commercial.

But even in her admiration for her ward she still managed to sternly admonish him for his indiscretion. "Rex! You know you're supposed to use the ramp!"

Her reprimand fell on deaf ears because Rex was already weaving his way between his seated friends, shimmying uncontrollably in his joyful passion, and was much too engrossed to bother paying any attention to Sarah's admonitions.

"We'll have to work on that," she muttered to herself, removing the ramps. She slid them into the bed of the truck, and slammed the tailgate closed. She was careful to not injure her prosthetic shoulder as she reached up and pulled the flipped-up rear window into place before twisting the handle to secure it.

When she finished organizing her truck, she glanced toward the gathering and saw that everyone was giving Rex a good rub as he ran from one to the next. They rose in unison to greet her as she sauntered lazily toward them.

"How was the ride over?" Nadine asked. Before waiting for Sarah to answer, she took the opportunity to glance around and assure herself that everyone had a full glass of refreshments.

"Uneventful," Sarah replied in a monotone voice. "Just the way I like it. And I see everyone else made it here just fine." She visually scanned the festive assemblage with a feigned smile on her ashen face.

"Yes, I left home a little early to help Nadine and William prepare for our distinguished guest," Chauncey said. "I was so excited to have Reverend Yates visit us that I barely slept at all last night."

"Hello Reverend Yates. I'm Sarah," she said in a consistently monotone voice. She offered him a limp hand to shake. "It's nice to finally have the opportunity to meet you. I've heard so many nice things about you."

"It's nice to meet you also," he said. He had a cautious look in his eyes as he took her fragile hand in his. He had a bony but sturdy hand that showed dark, bulging blue veins demonstrating that he was accustomed to performing hard work. "And please, call me John."

"John," she repeated, her eyes dropping despondently to the ground.

An awkward silence followed and hung in the still air like rancid flatulence in a crowded church pew. Gnats buzzed happily around the perimeter of the gathering in ignorant bliss of the emotional drama unfolding before their uncaring eyes.

"Well!" Nadine said, trying to interject some positive energy into the stifling void of uncomfortable silence. "What can I get you to drink, Sarah? The food will be ready in about a half hour."

"An Arnold Palmer would be great with your homemade lemonade and iced tea," Sarah replied. Then, as if she didn't know Nadine's penchant to have an abundance of food available any time there were guests at her house, she said, "If you have any."

"You know I do," Nadine said with a sly grin. "William loves my iced tea and Chauncey is wild about my lemonade, so I always have some on hand for them."

"And since they seem to be inseparable, you have to have some of each to satisfy both of them," Sarah said without much enthusiasm. Then, she slowly lowered her eyes again and fell silent.

"That's right," Nadine said. With a look of trepidation, she shot a furtive glance at John Yates. "John, do you need more iced tea?"

"No, I'm fine, thank you," he replied, gazing intently at Sarah, gauging her mental state and posture.

"Well, I'm going into the house to refill these pitchers," Nadine said, picking up the tray holding the refreshments. She then turned toward her front door and said, "If anyone needs anything, speak up."

No one said anything, but everyone watched her walk away.

With a practiced eye, John noted that Sarah's body movements appeared listless. Now that she was standing still, her hands hung limply to her sides in an unspoken sign of defeat.

With swift, deft movements reminiscent of a much younger man, he stood, slid smoothly behind an empty chair situated beside his, and moved it forward in a welcoming gesture, offering it to Sarah.

"Please sit here, Sarah," he said, presenting the sturdy, green plastic lawn chair to her. "This is a nice level spot and you look like you're tired."

"Why thank you," she replied, hesitant. "I didn't think I looked that bad."

"You look great, just a little fatigued is all. I imagine keeping as busy as you are demands a lot of energy," John said with a large, authentic smile that showed small but even teeth with a generous amount of gum surrounding them. His kind and benevolent face exuded trust and confidence in a way that few people possessed. It was a trait that was very handy in his chosen profession of being a preacher.

It was a compassionate face etched with longitudinal creases caused by a complex, emotionally draining life. Horizontal wrinkles at the corners of his eyes had been caused by his habit of always smiling.

Closer and more intense inspection beyond the obvious signs of friendliness revealed that his penetrating, brown eyes were as hard as ebony. They seemed to possess the ability to infiltrate people's souls and could scrutinize a person's true nature regardless of how well they were attempting to conceal their intentions.

He was an unassuming man in middle age with thinning salt-and-pepper hair combed straight back. He liberally applied a greasy gel to keep it from becoming unruly throughout his often active days. This archaic hairstyle accentuated his high, strong cheekbones, which showed a patina of sun-kissed tan faint enough to pass as his normal skin pigmentation.

The checkered western-style shirt with faux pearl buttons he often wore gave him an air of being a cowboy from the American West though he had never ventured beyond the eastern front of the Allegheny Mountains.

He continued speaking without missing a beat. "I could be wrong about you being tired at this early hour in the day. Are you tired, Sarah?"

"Actually, I'm exhausted," Sarah admitted in an unsettled, fatigued tone. "Which I find really strange because I slept for almost nine hours last night. That's much more than I normally get, even when I've had a busy week of work."

"Did you sleep deeply during that entire time or did you wake up frequently?" John inquired in a calm and compassionate voice. "And have you been avoiding situations that may bring back memories of the traumatic events from last week?"

"Actually, I didn't sleep that well," Sarah admitted, her suspicions rising about John's intense questioning. "I did have a few nightmares last night about the event from last week though I never really woke up enough to be able to identify them as nightmares. I wasn't able to fully disregard them, and then the unsettling doubts about whether they were nightmares or not kept waking me up."

"But it did involve the shooting and flames that led to the deaths of those men?" John inquired. The intensity of his inquiry was reflected in his eyes.

"Actually, it was more about the aftermath. All the questioning from police really upset me. The stench from their burned bodies and the fluids that leaked from them into the gravel of my driveway seems to be stuck in my nose," she replied, hesitant to reveal such personal information to a man she had just met. "Of course, the smell was much worse until Chauncey and William dug up the contaminated stones from the driveway and hauled them back to the woods. The hole it left has been filled in with fresh gravel, so there's really no visual sign left of what happened there."

"Out of all the scary things that happened that night, is it the smells in your driveway that really stand out in your mind?"

"They apparently do, now that you mention it. Thinking about it, I've even been avoiding looking at that area of my driveway."

"Why?"

"It causes me to become anxious and depressed, so I don't do it. I guess that's to be expected after the realization hit me as to how close I'd come to probably being raped by those three horrible men. It doesn't ease my mind any that the police suspect they would have likely murdered me after they were finished."

"And you started your day with a nightmare and being scared by what you imagine could have happened that night? At least that's what Nadine told me," John said. He was purposefully inquiring as delicately as he could with such pointed and probing questions.

Sarah didn't reply.

He then asked, "Have you lost interest in doing things you'd normally do? And do you want to isolate yourself from other people?"

"Am I being interrogated for a reason or is it that you're just being exceedingly nosy?" Sarah snapped angrily.

"I'm sorry, Sarah," John said in a low, calm and soothing voice, and then he was cut off by Chauncey.

"Sarah, we haven't had time to talk with you because of all the craziness going on in the last few days with the shootout at your farm and all. I'm sorry about that. Reverend Yates, sorry, John, I mean,"

Chauncey stammered. "I'm afraid I'll never get used to calling you by your first name. John travelled all the way here to help William and me. He's just trying to be helpful, so please don't be upset."

He made a contrite gesture with his hands, and then he continued in a low tone, "William and I were having emotional difficulties dealing with everything that happened. William called John to discuss it. As it turned out, John only lives a few hours south of here because he's accepted a pastor position at a small church in North Carolina. He was able to take some time to visit and help us deal with what we're going through."

"So you're actually here to help all three of us?" Sarah asked John. She didn't bother hiding the anger in her voice, and then she added, "Whether we asked for your help or not."

"John is kind of an expert in counseling people with PTSD," William said. He hoped to avoid Sarah working herself into a frenzied state of indignation. He leaned forward to continue his explanation, but was cut off when John waved a hand in his direction.

"Well, William, that's a bit of a stretch to call me an expert, especially with a syndrome as complex as PTSD," John said. He leaned forward and looked directly at William as he spoke, but cautiously kept Sarah in view out of the corner of his eye.

"But you saw a lot of men who were suffering from PTSD at the mission when we both worked there, and we discussed the signs and symptoms, not to mention the high prevalence of this syndrome in the population we served," William replied, defending his comment. "You were able to help a lot of them, at least the best they could be helped," he added in a dispirited tone.

"I did what I could," John said. He became somber as his mind flashed back to his work at the mission.

"And you were definitely able to help me with my PTSD," William added, sitting up straighter in his chair and looking adamantly at John.

"You suffered from PTSD?" Nadine asked, walking up to the gathering. She paused a moment to set a tray of fresh drinks on a glass topped table, and then added, "I didn't know that."

"I told you what happened to my family," William said.

"Yes, you did," Nadine said. "I just didn't realize that PTSD could occur from a tragedy like that. I thought it was only from war and such."

"They weren't calling it PTSD at that time," William said. He cleared his throat and paused a moment to compose himself. "But it was definitely something I was suffering from."

"And how did you know that?" Sarah asked. Her interest was always aroused by anything medically oriented.

"I had nightmares and social isolation. Those are both signs of PTSD."

"You mentioned that to me and I must have forgotten," Nadine said.

"I was agitated all the time and hostile to everyone I came in contact with," he said. "But I think the worst part was when I began exhibiting self-destructive behaviors. I really didn't care about anything anymore. It was strange how I lost interest in everything, and I mean everything."

He glanced furtively at Nadine to see if she fully understood his meaning.

"You don't have to go into all that," Nadine said quietly. She began to regret having begun the conversation.

"Well, I didn't want all that to begin again. I don't think I could live through it a second time, so I called John. He helped me get through it once, and he may be able to help me bypass it this time."

"And you started to have all those symptoms of PTSD again?" Nadine asked. She didn't bother trying to hide the apprehension she was experiencing.

"Maybe," William said, flipping his hand dismissively. "I feel bad that I didn't confide in you but I haven't been sleeping very well the last few nights. That may be a normal reaction after having a few assholes trying to kill us. I'm still pissed about it, and a little bit afraid, I guess."

"That's not an unusual reaction, I imagine, to the horrendous events of the other night," Sarah said. "But what's been happening to me goes a bit beyond, way beyond actually, the symptoms you describe as being PTSD."

"And what would that be, Sarah?" John asked, quickly leaning forward until he was sitting on the edge of his seat.

His sudden movement frightened Sarah, causing her to snap her head toward him so quickly that he jumped. Simultaneously, he slid back in his chair to give her more personal space. Then he stammered, "I'm sorry. I didn't mean to intrude again or to frighten you."

"I'm sorry, John," Sarah said. She stumbled over the words and a tremendous wave of embarrassment overcame her.

Her cheeks reddened, and she sputtered, "I didn't mean to be nasty or anything, but I've really been on edge lately. I even jump at the slightest sound these days. It's embarrassing." She chuckled, trying to hide the fact that tears began to build up in her eyes and hastily wiping her nose with the back of her hand.

"It's nothing to be embarrassed about," John said. He made sure his sweat-dampened back was firmly pressed against his chair so he appeared as non-threatening as possible.

"I don't know what my problem is or why I'm acting this way. Please forgive me." Mentally shaking herself, she boldly looked at him straight in the eyes, taking a deep breath to gain her composure.

"Having heightened reactions to normal occurrences, such as having an exaggerated startle reflex like you just exhibited, is another well-known manifestation of PTSD," he said. He kept his eyes looking at the ground to appear as nonthreatening as possible.

"It's not just things like that," Sarah said.

She sat unmoving for a moment, and everyone started thinking they had to say something to fill the silence. They didn't get the chance.

She began speaking again and her emotions gushed out of her in an unstoppable torrent. "I've been questioning a lot of things lately. Everything from my goals in life to my faith in God. Nothing is beyond my pathological scrutiny."

She fell silent again, but this time everyone knew not to say anything. They simply sat looking expectantly at her and gave her time to work her way through whatever it was that had her struggling.

"I'm not even sure I can discuss these types of things with my closest friends let alone a relative stranger, no offense to you," she said, looking at John. She then flopped back, looking defeated and resigned to her fate.

"No offense taken," John said. He offered a large, friendly smile to console her as she hesitantly looked at him. "I totally understand, and it's OK."

"Do you really understand? Or are you just saying that?" Sarah asked. She took another quick swipe at her snotty nose with the back of her hand.

Before continuing, John made sure his posture was still conveying the message that he was nonthreatening, and then, in a meek tone, he said, "I have to apologize about how excited I got. You see, a fellow pastor in Baltimore is doing his doctoral dissertation on a situation that's very similar to what you just described. He refers to the phenomenon as the Dark Night of the Soul."

"That doesn't sound good," Nadine said, chiming in as she handed Sarah her drink. Then, she plopped heavily onto her own chair with an exaggerated sigh.

"It's not a pleasant thing, but it is a good thing," John said. He was thankful for the opportunity to speak directly to Nadine because it removed Sarah from being the center of attention.

"That's a rather confusing statement, John," Nadine said, scrunching up her face. "Would you mind explaining it a little bit better so we mere humans can understand what the hell you're talking about?"

John chuckled delightedly and continued, "The concept was first aired in about the 16th century by St. John of the Cross, a Carmelite friar and priest, who was renowned for his reformation of the Carmelite order. He wrote numerous works of poetry and seemed to have a focused interest on the growth of the soul. A rather interesting fellow if my friend's research into his background is any indication."

"But aren't the Carmelites a Catholic bunch? You're protestant, aren't you?" Nadine asked.

"That's true," John affirmed. "The Catholics discuss these concepts in seminary but the Protestants seem to be largely unaware of its existence. Soon, that may all change because of my colleague's work."

"So, what's this all about? What did you call it?" Nadine inquired, a quizzical expression on her face. Her nose again scrunched up like a puzzled teenager. "Dark Soul in the Night?"

"Dark Night of the Soul," he corrected her kindly. "It's a crisis of faith where God places us in situations that involve troubles, trials, and tribulations. These difficult times are usually misinterpreted by good people as God having abandoned them. When people are going through this process, they often comment that God is simply not listening to their cries for help. It causes a lot of despair, to say the least."

Sarah sat quietly and didn't comment, though he held her undivided attention. John purposefully didn't look in her direction.

Chauncey chimed in. "You mean it's kind of like when Jesus Christ cried out while he was on the Cross, 'My God, My God, why hast Thou forsaken Me?' You mean that folks feel forsaken like that?"

"Exactly like that, but not as severe as the torment Christ had to suffer on the cross," John confirmed. "And the feeling of abandonment is what leads to a crisis of faith. That's why my pastor friend has such an acute interest in this phenomenon. He wants his fellow pastors to understand what is happening so they don't fall into depression if they're ever called to suffer through it."

"Huh," Nadine huffed noncommittally.

"If people of faith enter an episode of the dark night of the soul without any warning or understanding about what's happening, they may easily come to the incorrect conclusion that this is a personal mental problem. It's easy to confuse it with depression, and a lot of people do. They may even think it's a spiritual blunder on their part that's being punished by God for some reason. They get all kinds of crazy ideas about what's happening to them because they can't explain it. They just don't understand why a bunch of bad things are happening to them. It can throw them into a crisis of faith where they begin doubting everything, especially the things they hold dear."

"Wow!" Sarah said. "That must be what I'm going through!"

"It may be," John said, giving a silent prayer of thanks that Sarah was warming up to the subject. He hoped it was enough to make her stop being hostile toward him, if nothing else.

"So, this Dark Night of the Soul situation may help explain why bad things happen to good people?" William asked. His face scrunched up like Nadine's had a few minutes earlier.

"Maybe," John replied dismissively. "The biblical theology presented by Saint John of the Cross does answer that question to a certain degree, assuming he's correct. His explanation at least provides a somewhat sufficient and satisfying understanding of why troubles appear in everyone's life. It's the best description we have to rationalize the dark moments in life that we all experience."

"But those moments may last for a very long time," Chauncey said, mulling this information over in his mind. He was comparing it to the life-changing events that ripped him from his nearly ideal former life to thrust him into being homeless. He could understand how the trials and tribulations that now tested him every day in his new life could fit into the scenario John was describing. "I'll have to think about this one for a while, and then do some reading on the subject."

"But why would God put us through bad stuff when he's supposed to be a loving and kind deity? He's supposed to shepherd us. He even calls us his 'children' for crying out loud! All of this Dark Night of the Soul stuff seems to go against that concept, and I don't like it," Nadine said.

"That's a very similar question I asked my colleague as we were discussing this subject over a hot cup of tea at a recent conference we both attended," John stated, his mind searching for the correct words to better describe the machinations of this theory. "My friend explained that it's actually a gracious work of God. He's merely toughening up folks for the next and potentially much more difficult stage of their life."

"Holy shit!" Sarah exclaimed. She flopped back into her chair and let her arms hang limply over the armrests as a stunned expression settled upon her face. "Are you trying to tell me that my calm, peaceful, beautiful life was ripped from me by a merciful act of God? Just to toughen me up? How's that supposed to prepare me for the next disaster in my life?"

"It could be exactly that," John said. He made sure he was using a cautious tone when addressing Sarah. "Give me a moment to flip through my pocket Bible and find a certain passage I marked so I could easily find it. Please bear with me. I thought this may help me understand this concept a little more clearly. It's a bit difficult to get your head around, for sure, and I'm obviously still struggling with it myself."

Everyone fell silent and stared at the man as he fished into the scuffed leather briefcase sitting beside his chair. He triumphantly raised a small book aloft and exclaimed, "Here it is. I knew it was in there somewhere!"

He took a moment to leaf through a tattered Bible that had dirt-smudged grey duct tape holding it's binding together. It appeared to be considerably more worn than his ancient and well-travelled briefcase.

With a flourish, he tugged his reading glasses from his breast pocket. With a flick of his wrist he opened them one handedly, carefully guided them over his ears, and carefully set them on the bridge of his sun-burned nose. He took an unusually long time adjusting them so they were the correct distance in front of his eyes.

It was obvious to everyone in attendance that he was in dire need of a new pair of eyeglasses with an updated prescription.

"John, when was the last time you had your eyes examined?" William inquired.

"Oh, I guess I'm due for a check-up soon," John replied, concentrating on finding the correct bookmark, which was one of many he'd placed in his Bible.

With painstaking care, he selected the appropriate page, pulled a bookmark from its resting place where it had marked the page in question, and took another moment adjusting his reading glasses again. He wiggled them back and forth to sit more sturdily on his nose, scooched them up and down a time or two, and then triumphantly declared, "Ah, here it is!"

"Here's what?" Sarah asked. Her voice had a cynical tone to it as though she was not enthused about what he was about to read to them.

"This is a passage from Luke," he said. "It says that much will be required of the person entrusted with much, and still more will be demanded of the person entrusted with more."

"So you think that God has entrusted me with a lot and now that I've reached a higher plane, so to speak, that more will still be demanded of me?" she growled. "I don't want more. I've had enough stuff happen to me already. This can't be right."

"Does anything about your life seem to fit this scenario?" John asked, peering over the top of the Bible he still held in front of his face. He tried to say it quietly so he didn't sound belligerent. Eliciting a harsh reaction from Sarah that could thrust her back into a defensive attitude was a situation he wanted to avoid. He was particularly interested in doing what he could to keep her congenial and talking about her situation.

"Only everything from a few years ago to now," Sarah said, her mind playing over the tragedies that had occurred to her. "Everything was going so well, my husband and I had a great life planned and everything was coming together so nicely, and then he was murdered in the parking lot of my office while I was busy working inside. And that was just the beginning of my personal dark night of the soul adventure."

"Just the beginning?" John asked. His eyebrows rose in surprise and he slowly lowered his Bible to his lap. He sat still, and just looked at her, nonverbally inviting her to continue talking.

"Yes," Sarah said. She fought to keep the rapidly rising exasperation and anger she was feeling from showing in her voice. "Because of Josh being murdered I couldn't return to the house we shared. I had to sell it and everything in it, including my personal belongings. I also had to sell my chiropractic practice, which was a bit more heart-rending. I'm ashamed to admit that but it's true. I built that practice from scratch and couldn't face going back into the parking lot where I'd seen my husband lying in a pool of his own blood. In the twinkle of an eye I was basically homeless and without a job."

"You were not homeless," Chauncey said gravely. The memories of his homeless experience came flooding back to him, which seemed to mentally and physically deflate his spirit, causing him to slump dejectedly. "Trust me."

"OK, so that was a poor choice of words," Sarah admitted. "But I had very difficult, or to use the proper term as it pertains to our current discussion, very dark times in my life that included me having to move from the house Josh and I shared, even though that's been a blessing in disguise, having my house at the farm burglarized, and now this most recent episode involving three hillbilly assholes trying to kill Chauncey, William, and me. Is that a strange series of events, or what?" she asked incredulously.

"Were you injured when your husband was killed?" John inquired calmly, but with concern strongly evident in his voice.

"Yes, no, I mean, well, I was but I wasn't shot like he was," she stammered. "When I saw him lying there on the ground and realized he was dead I passed out, fell backward over a gurney the EMTs had parked behind me, and smashed the back of my head onto the asphalt parking lot. I was in a coma at the hospital for days. I even missed Josh's funeral, which didn't help my mental state at all, I guess."

"And it was during your recuperation here at my farm that you started to rebuild your spiritual life," Nadine said, thinking back.

"Just for the sake of discussion," John said to Sarah, directing his attention toward her. "If all of that were an episode in your life where God was toughening you up for a more difficult period in your life, was there a more difficult episode that occurred?"

"Holy shit," Sarah murmured softly. She had a profoundly stunned expression on her face as the significance of events in her life settled upon her embattled psyche like a thick, grey fog rolling across the tepid waters of a brackish back bay.

"The church," Chauncey gasped in disbelief. His voice was strangled and barely audible.

"The church," Sarah repeated as if in a daze. "Josh's murder toughened me up for the shootout at the church. I forgot all about the church when I was listing all the crap that happened to me over the last few years."

"The church," Chauncey indistinctly whispered a second time. His blank, unmoving eyes stared vacuously into space as though he were in a deep trance.

"It may even be why Chauncey went through all he went through," Sarah said, her mind churning. "If he hadn't been spiritually and emotionally toughened up to carry that bomb out of the church hundreds of people may have been killed or seriously injured."

"This is crazy and really spooky," William snapped irritably. "It's way too much to fathom."

"That's because we need food," Nadine chimed in with faux cheer in her voice in an attempt to lighten the mood of the gathering. "Let's eat!"

"That's the best suggestion I've heard today," Chauncey said enthusiastically. He shook his head to rouse himself from his reverie. Then, with a mighty heave, he hauled himself out of his chair.

Taking a moment to gather his feet beneath him, and without as much as a glance toward the others, he headed toward the kitchen with a pained, gimping gait. It took a half-dozen steps, but his cramped legs slowly began loosening with each determined stride.

With concerted effort, he managed to ponderously push the significance of their discussion into the recesses of his reeling mind and purposefully focused on the food that Nadine, his favorite cook, had lovingly prepared for them.

CHAPTER 4

SOULFUL DISCUSSION

Everyone, including Sarah, ate with gusto.

"Nadine, your barbeque is out of this world," John stated appraisingly, mopping sauce from his mouth with a heavy-duty napkin.

"I'm addicted to her potato salad," Chauncey chimed in, wiping vigorously at his lips. With a flourish, he set his napkin down on his lap, and then extended his hands out in front of him in a receiving gesture. "Can you please pass the bowl over this way?"

"Chauncey! That's your third helping!" Sarah admonished him harshly. "Someday you're going to wake up fat if you keep eating like that."

"Let him eat," Nadine said in his defense. "He's going to need his energy because he's helping me dig more dirt to shore up the backstop on my new shooting range. That'll burn any extra fat he has on him in no time flat."

"Well, in that case, I guess it's OK," Sarah said, a devilish grin appearing on her face. "I have to take care of him, you know. He's like the little brother I never had."

"Little brother?" Chauncey protested. "I'm many years your senior, I will remind you."

"But you act like a little kid sometimes," she teased him.

"Do not."

"Do too."

"Do not."

"That's enough, children," Nadine scolded jokingly. Both Sarah and Chauncey began snickering softly at her jesting.

"This is the best I've felt in days," Sarah confided to no one in particular.

"Good food will do that," William said.

"It's not just the food," Sarah said. Her tone was much more serious. "I'm relieved to learn that I may just be experiencing the Dark Night of the Soul syndrome instead of God abandoning me."

"In what way?" John inquired, and then quickly added, "Assuming you want to discuss it."

"I don't want to discuss it," Sarah replied, uneasy, "Now I realize that Josh being murdered may only have been toughening me up for what happened in the church and what occurred last week at Predator's Bane."

"Predator's Bane?" John questioned, a dumfounded expression furrowing his brushy brow.

"That's the name I gave my farm," Sarah replied. "It's a constant reminder that there are predators in this world, evil if you will, that'll prey upon the innocent and unprepared. I want to always be prepared so I'm the bane of any predator stupid enough to try preying upon me, innocents, or my loved ones."

"Loved ones like Chauncey and William at your farm the other night?" Nadine asked tentatively. She was trying to grasp which direction this conversation was heading.

"Yes," Sarah replied. Looking evenly at Nadine. "But before that it was the incident at the church."

"In what way?" Nadine asked. She was pressing her for more information in an attempt to continue the conversation so Sarah could get out what was on her mind.

"In that me simply going to church on Christmas Eve, a ritual the majority of people in this country observe, led to a gunfight with terrorists and my chiropractic career coming to an unexpected end, and an unwanted end I might add, because my shoulder was injured so badly it had to be replaced with plastic and titanium parts. How strange is that?" Sarah asked. Her shoulders slumped from fatigue caused by the tremendous effort needed to simply utter those few but emotion-draining words.

Everyone sat in silence with downcast eyes knowing there was no real answer for the question she'd asked, and none was expected.

With a grief-stricken voice, she added, "And I've been asking God ever since why he'd forsaken me instead of simply delivering me from the evil that took my husband away from me. Now I have a potential reason for my situation that seems to make sense, even though it's still not very comforting. At least it makes sense for now and gives me something to be hopeful about."

"So, you think it's this Dark Night of the Soul stuff that screwed you up?" William inquired.

"It's the only thing I've heard yet that makes even a little bit of sense," Sarah replied gravely. "And that episode at the church led me to be motivated enough to continue preparing myself for when evil came to cause harm. In turn, I helped Chauncey prepare for his role in this whole scenario by encouraging him to get proper self-defensive training. It got him prepared so he was able to competently deal with what occurred last week. It's all very strange but the pieces fit when the Dark Night of the Soul is taken into consideration."

"Holy Moly," Chauncey said, slumping heavily back into his chair. He let his head dangle backward. "I didn't want to go to the firearms training course, but you shamed me into going. It probably saved my life."

"And mine too," William added soberly. "If it hadn't been for you, I'd be dead instead of sitting here enjoying good food, the company of good friends, and a beautiful day."

"So, if I understand you correctly, Sarah," John inquired in a scholarly fashion. "If you hadn't gone through the Dark Night of the

Soul experience, then you, and Chauncey by proxy, wouldn't have been ready to meet the next challenge in your lives, which occurred at your farm last week?"

"I think that's a fair assumption," Sarah said. "But does that mean I have more of this crap coming my way and even greater challenges ahead in my life?"

"If I understood what my colleague from Baltimore was trying to teach me, and what Luke tells us in the Bible, then yes, that's exactly what's in store for you," John replied humorlessly.

"Oh great," Sarah whined flippantly. "More tragedies to look forward to. Pass the potato salad."

CHAPTER 5

DEBT REPAYMENT

"That was excellent," Chauncey said, politely shaking John's hand. "Your biblical insights on good and evil helped me understand what happened last week. It put things into a vastly different context for me. I really appreciate your help."

"It was a great help to me, too," William added. "But then again, all of the counseling you've provided to me over the years has always helped keep me centered. Thanks again, John."

"You're both welcome," John replied with a large gratified smile. "I'm extremely thankful for Nadine's hospitality, and for allowing us to meet in her home."

"It's my pleasure having you here," Nadine said. "I've heard so much about you from both William and Chauncey. It seems your reputation grew to mythical proportions, and deservedly so. It's a true pleasure to learn firsthand that you're as kind and giving as these two described you."

"Sarah, are you okay with everything we went over today?" John asked. His eyes searched her face for clues as to her true sense of wellbeing.

"I'm a little concerned to learn that the Dark Night of the Soul stuff may get worse," Sarah added, her eyes flicking back and forth apprehensively. "I don't know if I can handle much more 'toughening up' as you put it."

"Don't let that worry you," John replied. "Just place your faith in God, even though it may seem like He's abandoned you during these periods of struggling with your difficulties. He'll give you the strength to get through the tough times if you ask for it."

"That's about all anyone can do," Sarah said.

Then in a much lower and softer tone, in what was almost conspiratorial, John said, "And you'll be a much better person after you come out of the challenging times."

"You're absolutely sure that God will never give us more than we can handle?" Sarah asked.

"That's right," John said. "Don't worry, Sarah. You'll be fine."

"I know I will be," Sarah said. "It's just that I'm used to being the one to help other people. I'm not very good at accepting help when I need it, I guess."

After taking a deep, cleansing breath, she added, "I don't know how I can ever repay you for all the advice and guidance you've given all of us here today."

"You don't owe me a thing," John replied humbly. "But you can help me by guiding me in the right direction, if you don't mind."

"In a skinny minute, John," Sarah said. She was glad for the opportunity to offer him something in return for his kindness. "But how can I possibly be of assistance to you?"

"It's only for me indirectly," he said, loudly clearing his throat. "But I could really use some good advice, particularly from a woman who's had unique life experiences like you've had."

He'd captured Sarah's undivided attention. She carefully placed her glass of lemonade closer to the middle of the table to avoid knocking it over. Then, very slowly, she slid closer to the edge of her seat and scowled at him.

"John, that sounds almost ominous," she said. "Maybe you should start with some background information so I can get a good understanding of your predicament. What exactly do you mean when you say, 'a woman who's had unique life experiences as you've had?'"

"Well," John began, hesitating. A distressed grimace caused by conflicting emotions clouding his face. "I meant, and I don't want this to sound ghoulish, especially after our discussion about your Dark Night of the Soul situation, but you've had experience as a woman who's had to use lethal force to defend yourself and others. And now you're a female firearms instructor. So, you're the best person I know who can offer advice to my niece, Adrien. Or at least you may be able to get me up to speed so I can offer her informed guidance in the concealed carry and use of firearms."

"Why don't you start at the beginning so I can understand what Adrien needs," Sarah suggested.

She sat back in her lawn chair, reached for her glass, swept the water droplets from its side with a deft downward sweep of her hand so they wouldn't drop onto her shirt, and took a long, slow sip. As she drank, her eyes peered over her glass and settled unwaveringly upon John. He squirmed in his seat.

"Adrien is my niece, my sister Amy's child," John said, regaining his composure. "Her father died a few years ago and my sister, as a single mother, has had a tough time raising Adrien even though she's a very intelligent and well-behaved young lady."

"And?" Sarah asked, prompting him to continue.

"I need advice because Adrien is going to college on a full scholarship based upon her superior academic achievements. That scholarship may be in danger of being lost, at least according to my sister, who tends to be a little emotional about anything that may affect Adrien."

"John, what exactly are you trying to say?" Sarah asked.

"Adrien is getting involved in gun rights activism by being an outspoken proponent of the concealed carry of firearms on her college campus. That worries my sister."

"Well!" Sarah exclaimed, straightening up in her chair. "Now that's something I may be able to help her with!"

"Great!" John said.

"Adrien has to realize that she's putting herself into dangerous waters because universities are notoriously political," Nadine said. She had been content to sit and listen to the conversation, but now she was becoming more interested in participating. "Administrators in those organizations are not strong supporters of our Second Amendment rights."

"Your sister may also be concerned that there's more crime occurring at Adrien's college than she knows about," Sarah said. "There has to be some reason that has Adrien so concerned that she's willing to take on this political hot potato."

"I think you may be right. The idea of Adrien being in an environment where she fears for her safety, as well as being willing to injure another person to protect herself, must be part of my sister's worries," John said. "She may be as worried about what she doesn't know than what she does, if that makes any sense."

"It does make sense, to me at least, but I think every parent has worries about their child's safety when they're away from home," William said. "Don't they?"

"I'm sure that's true," John said. "But I think this situation goes far beyond that. My sister is certainly concerned that Adrien feels she has a need to carry a concealed weapon to defend herself, but it's also worrisome to her that her little girl, as she still looks upon Adrien, is willing to fight for that right. All of this is a very heavy emotional burden that's affecting my sister in more ways than she's letting on, I fear."

"I can understand your sister's concern for her daughter's views, especially when it involves a subject like self-defense," Nadine said. "Your sister may have never had to think about these types of things, but she has to realize that not all crime occurs on campus."

"What do you mean?" John asked.

"Adrien's concerns may encompass a much greater geographical and societal realm than your sister is accustomed to dealing with," Nadine said. "In the larger scheme of things, crime also occurs where students are living or working off campus. It may not be crime on the campus itself that's the main concern."

"Which is why they should have their firearms with them at all times whether they're going to campus, after they leave campus, or are going about town on the other business of their daily lives. I understand that now," John said. "I hadn't thought of it that way."

"I thought college campuses had a low rate of crime because everyone there is a student, not criminals," Chauncey said. His eyebrows furrowed as he strove to understand what was being said.

"My sister says the college has a low rate of reported crime. It's something she checked into before allowing Adrien to go there. So, she ends up arguing with Adrien that she shouldn't need to carry a gun. Naturally, Adrien sees things differently," John said.

"But many colleges and universities are located in high crime areas so students may need to be armed any time they're leaving campus grounds," Nadine said. "Then you have to consider that there were horrendous mass shootings that took place on some college campuses. They had high rates of injury to innocents because no one was armed and able to stop the maniac from committing murder."

"Police, whether they're on or off campus, cameras, text alerts, or anything else - they try can't protect students all the time, but being armed will. A thug bent on taking a student's possessions or dignity can show up at any time," Sarah said. "So I can see why your niece is concerned. But what can I do to help her?"

"If you don't mind, can you include her in your next training class?" John inquired. "At least that way she can have a good understanding of what's all involved in carrying a concealed firearm. That way she can make informed decisions as she pursues her political agenda on campus."

"I can do that," Sarah said, nodding toward Nadine to see if she agreed.

"Does she have a friend she works with on her quest to secure concealed carry on her campus?" Nadine inquired.

"I'm not sure," John said. "Why?"

"Because college-aged women like to travel with a close friend," Nadine explained as she smiled and tilted her head towards Sarah. "She may be more inclined to attend one of our classes if she has a friend to accompany her."

"That's how Nadine and I became so close in college," Sarah added. "As roommates, we went on a number of adventures together, which we may have never considered doing by ourselves."

"I'll ask about that," John said. "The other thing I have to ask about is the cost. My sister doesn't have much money to spend, and I certainly can't speak for the financial situation of any friend Adrien may bring with her."

"The only class cost to Adrien or her friend will be the cost of ammunition," Nadine said. "Sarah and I will gladly donate our time to helping these young ladies out. Naturally, the cost of transportation, a few nights in a hotel, food on the road and other incidentals can add up quickly. It can get expensive, and while I'll gladly donate my time, I'm unable to help them with the other expenses."

"That shouldn't be too much of a problem," John said, grinning with relief. "She's a local girl who was born and raised in Thompsonville, just down the road."

"Well, I'll write down Sarah's and my contact information for you. She can call us, and we'll get them set up with some training!"

"You don't know how much I appreciate this," John said, his voice cracking with emotion.

"Anything to help young people get a proper education," Sarah said, smiling.

CHAPTER 6

ADRIEN

Rachael Fiorenza strode purposefully into The Underground, the college's premiere cafeteria and meeting place for students, holding the hand of her preppy boyfriend, Cole Hockings.

Rachael was a tall beauty with long, shapely, and darkly tanned legs. She knew her legs were a great asset and liked to show them off by wearing brightly colored dresses and skirts that barely stretched below mid-thigh. Her long, flowing chestnut brown hair hung slightly below her shoulders and had a gentle wave that most models could only dream about possessing without the aid of computer enhancement.

The allure of her stunning emerald green eyes masked her mediocre intelligence enough that she was able to muddle her way through the political administration classes she continuously struggled with in hopes of landing a mid-level government job upon graduation in the spring.

Cole, on the other hand, was highly intelligent but had an unquestionable lack of common sense in any and all matters beyond the gridiron where he'd excelled as his high school's star quarterback. His studies in pre-law were positively influenced by his stately presence, which was enhanced by a muscular but slender physique. His majestic manner was augmented by broad shoulders and slim waistline.

A mop of unruly blonde hair framed the rugged features of his face. All in all, he was a fine specimen of masculine beauty and highly sought after by most of the women on campus.

The couple were very close and had become much closer in the last three months since the unexpected passing of Rachael's father. Their discussions over living together had become serious deliberations in the last few weeks.

They zigzagged their way through the clutter of backpacks that had been dumped and were now scattered about the floor and clogging the aisles between closely spaced tables. The tables always started each day arranged in long rows but ended up being knocked askew by the multitude of students constantly jostling in and out of The Underground between classes.

"Keep your crap out of the aisles," Cole said, staring contemptuously at a scrawny student who peered meekly up at him with owl-like eyes outlined by large, thick eyeglasses. With a vicious kick, Cole shoved the student's backpack under the cowed man's chair with the tip of his highly polished loafer. "You don't own this place so be considerate of other people."

When Rachael looked sideways at him with a disapproving glare, he quickly added in a mocking tone, "Please."

"Oh! There's Adrien!" Rachael said, frantically waving her hand high above her head. Her brightly painted fire engine red nails glittered as she tried catching her friend's eye. Adrien remained unaware of Rachael's presence and continued reading the book laid in front of her as she sat in a corner booth. "She doesn't see me! Let's go over there and say hello. I have to ask her a few things about the campus concealed carry meeting on Thursday night."

"Oh no, not that crap again," Cole groaned. He purposefully slowed her forward progress by clinging tightly to her hand and slowing his pace. "I was hoping to never hear anything about that nonsense ever again."

"It's not nonsense," she snapped, her face clouding over with anger. "There are real dangers on college campuses. The same evil people that plague society are on campus legally as students or faculty. Then there are the maniacs or criminals who can easily wander into our midst. You know darned well that anyone can come onto campus anytime they want to, and no one questions why they're here."

Cole momentarily let go of her hand to push a gaudy plastic chair out of his way, and then he brusquely shoved it under a nearby table.

"I hate it when these slobs just leave chairs scattered around instead of being considerate enough to slide them back under the table when they're finished using them," he grumbled.

A fulminating fit of anger fizzed up her spine and into her brain like a fast burning cannon fuse when Rachael noticed Cole didn't immediately return to her side. Instead, he chose to weave his own path through the minefield of backpacks that were looked upon as being a required piece of equipment to keep a student's mobile lifestyle organized.

To avoid a confrontation in a public place, Rachael chose to ignore his indiscretion and childish behavior, which was the way she usually handled most issues involving Cole.

Putting Cole temporarily out of her mind, Rachael deftly skirted around a group of three male students discussing the prospect of getting a date for the upcoming weekend. She then dodged a pair of female students focused on securing the last two seats together at a table packed with engineering students. The women's minds were focused on not spilling any of the steaming hot caramel lattes they balanced in their outstretched hands and not on being courteous to their fellow students.

Finally, with graceful athletic maneuvering, Rachael managed to weave her way to Adrien's booth without tripping over anything or anyone. Adrien drowsily lifted her eyes from the thick book lying open in front of her and took a moment to gather her bearings. After her eyes refocused and her mind shifted from reading, she recognized Rachael.

Adrien flashed her friend a dazzlingly brilliant smile of welcoming, which then faded quickly into a frown of contempt when Cole popped out of the crowd and slid up beside Rachael. He possessively took Rachael's delicate hand in his meaty mitt and stared directly at Adrien.

"And how is my favorite friend of a friend doing today?" he asked insincerely, addressing Adrien with thinly veiled disdain.

"As well as can be expected," Adrien murmured. She wondered if he was astute enough to catch her meaning that things had been much better before he showed up, but she doubted it.

"Hello Adrien," Rachael said. She carefully tucked her skirt under her to avoid wrinkling it and sat on the booth seat opposite her friend and fellow grassroots Second Amendment activist. "Are you studying for that big calculus test you were telling me about? Are we bothering you?"

She scooched over to make room for Cole, and he slid into the booth beside her.

"Of course we aren't bothering her," Cole said in a bold and artificially friendly manner. "Adrien already knows all that stuff and doesn't have to study. That's why she's always on the Dean's List for Outstanding Academic Achievement."

"It's because I study a lot that I 'know all that stuff' as you so succinctly put it," Adrien said. She carefully closed her notebooks and slid them toward the wall to be out of Cole's reach.

"And you have enough time to study even though you waste tons of time on that campus concealed carry crap."

Cole's chin rose higher as he arrogantly looked down his nose at her.

He continued to berate her. "If this were the 1960s you could be labeled as a radical and booted off campus. As a matter of fact, I wouldn't be surprised if they did boot you off campus. The only reason they haven't done it yet is because they want to have smart kids like you getting good grades and landing stellar jobs after graduation. That way the administration can use you as an example to improve their ability to market this school to prospective students. That keeps the money flowing into the college, and that's the most important thing they care about."

"Is that so?" Adrien asked. Her voice took on a mocking tone. "Tell me more about all this very important stuff you seem to know all about but no one else is privy to."

"The administration will put up with a bunch of nonsense from the likes of you two spouting Second Amendment garbage just to keep the big bucks coming into this school. That way they can keep their cushy jobs. Otherwise, they'd get rid you in a heartbeat, I'm sure."

"And you know that's how the administration works, do you?"

Rachael was so outraged that she was on the verge of sputtering her words.

"You never know what or when something bad will happen. Immediate action by an armed person with a legally concealed firearm, if one is there, is the best course of action in that type of situation. The armed citizen will be ready to lend assistance while the stuff is hitting the fan, and not five minutes afterward, which is about the time campus security or the local police will arrive."

"Bullshit!" Cole countered. It was a vulgar and less than intelligent response, but he didn't care. His face reddened and he blurted, "That's craziness and you know it. Security is ready and willing to be anywhere on campus if anything did happen, and that's highly unlikely except in the fantasies rattling around in your overly active mind."

"Local law enforcement may not even be asked to intervene until things get totally out of hand. Campus security looks at the entire college as their territory. They don't want to share the glory, whatever that may be, with any other law enforcement agency," Adrien countered, seeing that Rachael was seething. She struggled to maintain her composure and take control of the conversation to give Rachael time to calm down.

"But nothing has happened here, and probably never will," Cole exclaimed. "No terrorists have tried to take over the student union, no buildings have ever been the target of a mass murderer or even a suicide bomber. Unless you count when they're serving baked beans and franks in the cafeteria," he said, laughing contemptuously at what he knew was in poor taste and likely to offend the women.

"That's not funny," Rachael said, scrunching her nose up in disapproval.

"You can joke all you want," Adrien said, admonishing him. "But the fact remains that the most effective deterrent to crime is an armed citizen who's on the scene when stuff happens. And it's especially vital for women to have the ability to fight back against a much larger and stronger attacker. It's well-known that a woman is a potential victim every day of her life since we're smaller and weaker on average than most men."

"And that's what you wake up every morning thinking about?" Cole asked. He overemphasized the disdain in his boisterous, booming voice to make his point that Adrien was a hysterical crackpot. "Do you really wake up imagining yourself as being a victim of some horrible crime? Don't you have anything better to be thinking about? What about the lack of healthcare for millions of Americans? Or racial or LGBT discrimination issues? Those are being perpetuated by the rich, white majority in this country whose only concerns are about their ability to accumulate more wealth!"

"That stuff is important and deserves everyone's attention, of course, but no one wakes up thinking, 'Oh, maybe I'll be a victim of a violent crime today,'" Adrien replied, purposefully calming herself so she didn't sound irrational. "But bad things do happen to good people every day and in all different types of situations."

Rachael couldn't curb her anger any longer and rejoined the conversation. Cole knew she was angry, so he refused to look at her. Instead, he opted to glare contemptuously at Adrien.

"Responsible people think ahead by having smoke alarms and fire extinguishers in their homes and businesses because they don't know when a fire may break out. If it does, they want to be able to put out the flames or at least contain them until help arrives. Those same people often plan for unforeseen emergencies when they're on the road. They carry tools and flares in their car in case it breaks down," Rachael said. "They do these things even if they've never been stranded on the side of the road by a tire blowing out or their engine having mechanical failure. They know it's the smart thing to do so they do it even though it costs money and is inconvenient."

"They may even go as far as having a gun with them. That'll come in handy if today is the day they become a victim of a violent crime," Adrien added, finishing Rachael's line of reasoning. "Being prepared is what sensible people do, and experience has shown them it's the best policy.

"And a lot of college students are the type of people who plan ahead for unexpected catastrophes," Rachael said. "If they can't avoid a violent encounter, and aren't allowed to have a gun with them, what else would you have them do?"

"They can dial 9-1-1," Cole responded. A triumphant and condescending smirk beamed across his shiny face.

"And what do they do while they wait for the cops to arrive? Bleed? Lay back and enjoy being raped? What?" Rachael shot back heatedly. She was thoroughly disgusted with Cole's attitude.

Adrien's ire rose to a fever pitch and she said, "The only first responders that'll arrive fast enough to be of any help to a victim of a crime is the victim themselves, so they better be ready to take care of things."

Rachael was getting into the swing of debating in tandem with Adrien. She said, "Remember, when seconds count the cops are only minutes away. That isn't the fault of the cops, it's reality because they can't be everywhere all the time. It's unrealistic to think that they could be. They're only humans trying to do the best they can with tight budgets and limited resources."

"The cops are trained to work on tight budgets," Cole said. "They're used to it, so your argument has big holes in it."

Rachael's face reddened to almost a purple hue, and she was getting close to saying things to Cole she would later regret. Her mind flashed over the other points she wanted to make, but before she could say anything, Adrien interjected, "It's not just violent crime happening on campus."

Adrien knew she had to defuse Rachael's anger if they were to keep the moral high ground in this discussion with Cole.

"That's my point," Cole said. "Crime doesn't happen on campus. This is a safe place!"

"Students also have to go off campus, and dangerous situations can confront them there," Adrien said.

"Really?" Cole said, dragging out the syllables of the word. "Give me one instance of that happening."

"It wasn't on this campus, but a Utah Valley State College student with a license to legally carry a concealed weapon shot a pit bull that was attacking him," Adrien replied. "If it weren't for him having a gun, he could have been badly mauled or even killed."

"A dog attack?" Cole sneered, condescension dripping from his words. "That's the best example you can give for having maniacs running amok around campus with guns?"

"College students are not maniacs!" Rachael said. "If they have a concealed carry permit, they've been vetted by law enforcement as being responsible citizens."

Adrien was still trying to distance Rachael from the discussion to avoid having her become too aggravated with Cole's asinine assumptions. So, she continued, "If having a dog tearing at a person's flesh with their teeth is not enough of a threat to convince you that responsible citizens, like college students with concealed carry permits, should be allowed to be armed, then how about the Virginia Commonwealth University student who was confronted by an armed gang member outside a laundromat? He had to use his concealed handgun to save his own life."

Rachael's voice was surprisingly calm and composed when she asked Cole, "So, is an armed gang member enough of a threat to convince you that a college or university student needs the means to protect themselves, whether they're on campus or not?"

She allowed a smirking smile to project the attitude she was feeling inside. The look angered Cole and caused him to become defensive. Cole didn't like that feeling. To get back on the offensive, his usual tact was to say something outlandish to irritate the people he was verbally sparring with and cause them to lose their train of thought.

"Women probably can't bring themselves to shoot anyone anyhow, even if it's a violent criminal because, well, because they're women" Cole said, arrogantly mocking the two women.

Rachael took a moment to calm herself. It was obvious by the look in her eyes that she was on the verge of losing her composure. "Maybe they'll just have to forget about how awful it'd be to have to shoot someone, and it would be terrible, no doubt. But maybe, just maybe, they should focus on what the violent attacker is planning to do to them instead of worrying so much about their attacker's wellbeing."

"Then she'll forever blame herself for causing someone's death," he shot back. The look on Rachael's face told him he was on the losing side of an argument with a woman who could make his life miserable in many ways.

"If the predator gets shot because of their socially abhorrent behavior then it's their own fault. It's what they deserve. After all, it was their decision to be a predator," Rachael said. "Victims don't choose to be victims except by choosing not to be trained in the use of force and by not accepting the responsibility to be armed at all times."

Rachael's anger began to wane, and fatigue triggered by emotional stress caused her body to visibly slump. Cole saw this and decided to take advantage of what he considered a weakness.

"That's just nuts." He said it snootily and was beginning to regain his confidence. He leaned back in his seat and glared at them with unfettered disdain.

"So, you don't think that a violent criminal who's in the business, and yes, it is a business, doesn't deserve to be challenged by their intended victim? They make a conscious decision to act aggressively to achieve some goal, so shouldn't they assume the risk of being shot or injured?" Rachael asked.

"That's right," Adrien said, taking up Rachael's argument. "After all, if it's a business decision, and Rachael's already established it is, then there are risks associated with it. These risks must be expected, and the consequences of those decisions must be accepted. It doesn't matter if they're advantageous or not. It's all part of any business transaction."

It was now Rachael's turn to lean forward aggressively as the tide of victory shifted in her direction. She felt her resolve strengthening.

"It's just nuts," he repeated. His confidence in being able to win this argument on an intellectual, or even on an emotional level, began fading rapidly.

Rachael took his subdued attitude as being an indication that she was making an impression on him. With renewed energy, she forged ahead.

"Don't you think that if the life of a thug is wrought with the danger of being seriously injured, that most of those cowards would choose to not be a thug? I think it's about time that timid college and university students, and everyone else who's righteously living in society for that matter, should make thuggery a very hazardous business to be in."

"So, you think it's your job to make all of the thugs in this world choose a new career?" he asked. His unpleasant and snippy attitude caused the blood pressure of both women to rise. "That's pretty ruthless of you, don't you think?"

"If someone is in the business of violently attacking innocent people, then yes, getting seriously injured or killed should be an occupational hazard for them," Rachael stated, her resolve unwavering. "To paraphrase a great philosopher who said, "If not I, then whom'?"

"What great philosopher?" Cole asked.

"I can't remember who it was. You'll have to look it up if you want to know that badly." She refused to allow herself to be drawn off topic by thinly veiled attempts to distract her.

"Exactly why are you so against women being armed and having the ability to protect themselves?" Adrien asked. The look on her face was accusatory.

"Why do you ask? What are you insinuating? And what does that have to do with anything we're discussing?" he asked. His anger was rising, and his patience began to wane. He was tiring of verbally sparring with a woman like Adrien, especially when he didn't particularly like her, and wouldn't talk to her at all if she and Rachael weren't friends.

He knew he didn't have an intellectual argument to make, and he had no substantive rationale to add to the discussion other than making an emotional plea based upon unfounded sentiment. He didn't want to lose face and have to admit his beliefs were unfounded and unsupportable.

All his life he'd steadfastly refused to admit when he was mistaken, even when he was obviously in the wrong, because it was a matter involving the inflated pride and ego that dwelled at the core of his being.

"I've always been suspicious of any man's motives when he wants to deny a woman the opportunity to defend herself from violent criminal attack. Why should a capable woman be threatening to you?

Huh? Why?" Adrien asked. She leaned forward aggressively the same as Rachael had done a moment previously.

"Are you a closet predator?" she chided him. She purposefully placed a tone of sarcasm in her voice.

"Yeah," Rachael said, her eyebrows rising mockingly in jest. "Is there something I don't know about you? Why don't you want me to be able to take care of myself?"

"Don't be absurd," he said defensively. His eyes darted about nervously to see who in the crowded cafeteria may be eavesdropping.

After assuring himself that no one else was listening to their conversation, he blurted, "There's no reason for anyone, male or female," he said, emphasizing the genders to be dramatic, "to be armed on a college campus. Only campus police should have guns."

"And they don't!" Adrien said. She triumphantly poked her forefinger into the air. "That's why legally permitted citizens that have been fully vetted by law enforcement should be allowed to carry their concealed weapons just like they do everywhere else."

"What do you mean, 'they don't?'" Cole demanded, indignant.

"What I mean is, you dolt, is that campus police do not carry firearms at this college. They have Tasers and pepper spray, but no guns to counter a serious attack if one would occur," she said. Her eyes bore directly into his with a steady, defiant gaze. "And they're only able to use those tools if they can reach over their big bellies to grab them from their belt!"

"And you can do better?" Cole asked. "You'll be lucky some big, bad guy doesn't take your gun away from you then shoot you with it!"

"A well-trained woman can keep a violent criminal from taking her gun away simply by drawing her firearm and shooting. It's the type of thing they teach you. That's why Rachael and I are going to take a training class my uncle has arranged for us. It's near my hometown of Thompsonville."

"Both of us are taking a training class?" Rachael asked, surprised and excited. Then, with a disheartened tone she said, "I can't afford that."

"During mid-term break you'll stay with me and my mom. We have a comfy little guest room ready for you, and we'll take the class together," Adrien said. She was beaming as she popped her surprise on an unsuspecting Rachael. "She'll be glad to have us visit. My uncle has arranged for us to take the class for free, except for the cost of ammunition."

"That's that then!" Rachael exclaimed. The corners of her mouth rose in in an ecstatic grin. She looked directly at Cole, and stated in a calm, matter-of-fact voice, "I have to hurry, or I'll be late for my next class."

"I can see it's impossible to talk any sense into you two so I'm going to class too," he said. Cole stood up, turned toward Rachael, fixed her with an intolerant stare, and then gruffly grumbled, "Are you going to walk with me or should I just go ahead alone?"

"I may as well walk with you since we're going the same way," she replied, nonchalantly flicking a wisp of hair from her face. With an air of aloofness, she slowly stood, got her clothing situated to her liking, and glanced toward Adrien. With a jubilant lilt in her voice, she said, "See you later, Adrien."

Then, without looking at Cole again, she strode purposefully toward the door with him trailing dutifully a few steps behind her like a faithful Labrador retriever.

Adrien watched them walk away, and muttered under her breath, "That boy surely has a really cute butt, which makes it all that much more of a shame that he's such an arrogant dumbass."

She picked up her calculus book and notebooks, put Cole Hockings out of her mind, and began studying in earnest.

CHAPTER 7

WOMEN AND GUNS

The morning had been mentally grueling as Sarah and Nadine pored over classroom material they'd painstakingly prepared to present to their students. Topics ranged from the non-shooting information of basic knowledge and skills for the safe handling, storage, cleaning, and use of firearms, to the extremely important range safety rules.

The weather had been relatively cooperative with a chilly morning rain falling gently but persistently as the four students sat snugly in the pleasurable confines of Nadine's living room. An infrared quartz fireplace radiated comforting warmth to ward off the dampness permeating the early portion of the day.

Sarah and Nadine conducted class from in front of a natural stone fireplace that hadn't held a fire since 1979 when the former owner of the farm sealed it with cement to avoid bats and other unwelcomed creatures from descending the chimney and getting into the house.

The students sat on a sectional sofa covered by heavy velour blankets depicting wildlife scenes and various other outdoor motifs.

Nadine had purposefully placed the sofa in the middle of the room facing the fireplace. This made a cozy, intimate learning environment. She hoped it would make the women feel more at ease since they would be studying topics which they had very little if any background in, exposure to, or familiarity with.

Temporarily converting her living room into a classroom had been a spur-of-the-moment decision when the rain appeared unexpectedly. The weather report had totally missed predicting it, but so far, everything was working out well.

An updated weather report predicted clearing skies and bright sunshine in the upcoming afternoon when the students would be shooting the live ammunition portion of the class on the range behind the barn. Nadine hoped the weather service had it correct this time.

The morning classes conducted in the living room had gone quickly with lively discussions and pertinent questions being asked by the students. Nadine preferred a learning environment that encouraged students to take an active role in the learning process, and she had achieved that goal with the arrangement of her living room furniture.

At noon, weary and hungry with their heads swimming with newly gained knowledge, the class retired to Nadine's spacious country-style kitchen for a nourishing lunch.

Sarah, Nadine, and the four students sat at a weather-stained picnic table Nadine had moved inside in anticipation of feeding the members of her class.

The heavy, massive oak picnic table had sat largely ignored by a stainless-steel gas grill situated on a flagstone patio at the side of her house. It had mainly been used as an outside food preparation table instead of seating people at mealtime but was again being used for its originally intended purpose.

The rectangular table had been strategically arranged in the corner of her large kitchen. She paid attention in its placement to avoid having anyone sitting directly under the half-round wrought iron pot rack accidentally injure themselves in case they hurriedly stood up. It would be unacceptable to have anyone bang their head on the unforgiving appliance. Thinking ahead, Nadine removed the array of well-used but tenderly cared for cast iron cookware that usually hung from the rack in an interesting jumble of chaotic order.

She found that serving lunch to her students gave them an opportunity to discuss subjects of concern that may not be presented in the classroom setting. The give-and-take of discussing various topics gave students a more wide-ranging learning experience. Offering a well-rounded understanding of all facets of handling firearms was the main goal Nadine had set for herself when she outlined her courses.

Two students sat on each of the sturdy bench-style seats arranged on both the sides of the table. The table itself had been draped with a thick red and white checkered cotton tablecloth to hide the deeply ingrained food stains that were a permanent blemish from years of hard use as an outdoor prep table.

Captain's chairs made from heavy, walnut-stained pine with thick, flat arms and high backs sat at either end of the table. These were reserved for Sarah and Nadine to give their aching backs the comforting support bench seats couldn't offer. Thick, quilted seat and back cushions, each cream colored and embroidered with an Amish hex sign pattern, helped to soften the unforgiving wooden seats of the captain's chairs, allowing prolonged periods of relatively comfortable sitting.

Two small, white wicker baskets lined with eye-catching blue and white checkered cloth napkins sat in the middle of the table and held condiments, sugar, salt, pepper, paper napkins, and plastic utensils. A small, white insulated ice bucket sat between the wicker baskets and nearly overflowed with ice cubes. A set of silver colored tongs sat on small red plastic plates in front of the ice bucket so everyone could serve themselves without having to use their hands. Neat stacks of sturdy white Styrofoam cups sat like solitary sentinels on either side of the cooler.

A large translucent blue pitcher of unsweetened iced tea sat at one end of the table while an identically shaped opaque red pitcher of lemonade sat at the other. A thick glazed ceramic bowl with a fat bladed stainless-steel butter knife stuck vertically into huge square globs of not-yet-soft yellow butter sat beside each pitcher.

Savory aromas permeated the kitchen.

The sink board had been arranged in a buffet line boasting sturdy foam plates and bowls. A large wooden salad bowl containing arugula, assorted baby greens, spinach, sliced radishes, diced onions, cubed zucchini, and tomato chunks was the centerpiece. Farther along the buffet, a large crock pot decorated with a yellow and red floral design was brimming with gently simmering venison chili.

Beside the crock pot, a scarred pine wood cutting board laden with two loaves of thickly sliced golden-brown crusty bread sat precariously on the edge of the heavily loaded sink board.

In addition to Adrien and Rachael, two other women were in attendance. Mary Tulsworth and Susan Eckley had shown themselves to be affable classmates during the brief periods of time the students had to chat.

After the women had consumed enough food to take the edge off their hunger, they began to talk, and their eating took on a more leisurely pace.

"So, Mary, what exactly is it that brought you to this training class?" Nadine asked to begin stimulating conversation.

Mary carefully placed a thickly buttered piece of bread onto the side of her nearly empty salad bowl, carefully wiped both hands on her napkin, took a tiny sip of lemonade, and replied with a very succinct and well enunciated tone. "Well, I'm a schoolteacher, and have the summers off. That's the time of year my husband begins going to the shooting range more frequently to 'burn up' some of the ammunition he's spent most of the winter reloading. For years he's wanted me to join him since I'm not working. I think he misses me at times."

"That's so cute!" Adrien cooed.

Mary smiled coyly at her, and then continued in a prim voice. "We rarely do much together because he's on the road most of the time in his sales job. I thought shooting would be a nice opportunity to spend some time together, but I wanted to get an education on how to use firearms before I joined him on the range. Formal instruction is important in anything we want to do so we can get a firm understanding of the discipline. Since I'm a teacher, I know the value of receiving a proper education."

"But this is a self-defense course," Rachael interjected. "Aren't there other, less involved courses available that'd teach you how to shoot paper targets with your husband?"

"I'm sure there are," Mary, a mousy brunette with her hair cut in a pixie style, replied. "But since my husband is on the road so frequently, I wanted to learn about self-defense. I'm usually alone for at least two nights a week, and sometimes more if he's attending a trade show or convention."

"That makes sense then," Rachael said, nodding her head in understanding. "I'm attending with my friend Adrien."

Rachael nodded her head toward Adrien, who bobbed hers in return because her mouth was full of salad, acknowledging her agreement with Rachael's statement.

Rachael continued speaking to give Adrien time to swallow her food. "We're both involved in the movement to allow concealed carry on our college campus. It's imperative that we have as much information and understanding about the issues involved so we can speak from experience instead of relying only on academic sources of information to wage this type of political battle."

"It's great that you young people are becoming politically involved while in college," Susan Eckley said. "You'll gain familiarity with the politics governing our everyday lives, and that's very useful. It may have long lasting effects on your careers and may even impact other aspects of your life, you never know."

"It could be very handy if I get a job in political administration, which is what I'm studying in school. It'll also look good on my resume, otherwise I'll only have an academic background from college. Practical experience is what most employers seem to be looking for, and at least some student activism will show I'm dedicated enough to become involved in something," Rachael said. "Why are you attending this course?"

"I'm interested in learning about self-defense because of my job as a real estate agent," Susan explained candidly. "My business takes me into a lot of high-crime neighborhoods. I always go into homes or commercial properties with strangers, and that can be scary. If something were to happen indoors, all the screaming I'd do inside those tightly closed buildings wouldn't attract any attention from anyone outside."

"That's a very scary thought," Adrien said, a wide-eyed expression on her face. She was speaking carefully so she didn't spew partially chewed food across the table. Swallowing most of the masticated salad still in her mouth with one huge gulp, she said, "I never spent much time thinking about the predicament real estate agents are placed in every day they work." She struggled to swallow the last scraps of salad remaining hidden beside her tongue.

"The real estate field is rife with stories of agents being robbed, sexually assaulted, tortured, or killed. Sometimes it's all four. In most of those cases it's criminals posing as clients," Susan said. Her hands and voice both began quivering slightly, her mind poring over what she imagined had occurred in those assaults.

After placing her utensils on her plate so she could use her hands to add emphasis to her words, she continued in a tremulous voice. "The family of a murdered real estate agent is suing the agency where she worked for not supplying proper safety training. They claim it may have saved the woman's life."

"It may have," Adrien said, trying to sound sympathetic.

"I'm not going to wait for my agency to get around to giving me training. It's not one of their top priorities so I'm getting it on my own. My life is more important to me than it is to them, so I consider it my personal responsibility to take care of myself."

"Really? They don't care enough about you to pay for something that may keep you alive?" Mary said. The look of disbelief on her face was profound. "Don't they do anything to help you avoid situations like that?"

"Yes, some do, but mine doesn't," Susan said. She began getting slightly out of breath, becoming more emotional thinking about what occurred to people in her profession. "Some agencies supply background checks and conduct preliminary meetings to try and identify dangerous troublemakers. They may also arrange for agents to travel in groups when showing rural homes or businesses to unknown strangers. But you just don't know who may be dangerous, and no one will know until it's too late."

"Don't the agents all have cell phones? That should help," Mary asked. Adrien and Rachael looked at her with wonder, shocked at her lack of knowledge about personal security and the foolishness of relying solely on a cell phone for such matters.

"A lot of agents are encouraged to use GPS to alert authorities if they get into trouble, but it's still not enough. They can be terribly injured even while help is on the way. There simply isn't enough time for the police to get there and be of any help in preventing something bad from happening."

"Not enough time?" Mary asked. "Why wouldn't there be enough time for police to get there? I thought they sent someone as soon as you told them you were in trouble."

"Think about it for a moment," Susan said, reminding herself to be patient. She took on the role of teacher as everyone seated at the table looked at her. Sarah and Nadine kept eating and allowed her to continue talking because she was correct in all she said so far.

"It only takes a second or two for an assailant to overpower a female, or even a small male for that matter, so it's imperative that they, or in this case, I, have the means to stop an attack immediately."

"I never thought of it that way," Mary said. "I really didn't."

"You don't have to apologize for not thinking about this type of situation and what you should do to prepare yourself," Susan said. "Few people do."

"But you certainly do," Mary said.

"You're right. I have to think about things like that because it's happening to my fellow agents, and it could easily happen to me," Susan said, striving to control a small, fearful tremor in her voice.

Susan took a deep breath, exhaled loudly, then took another deep breath. Everyone gave her time to compose herself. They were so engrossed in what she was saying that they temporarily stopped eating.

When she was ready, Susan said with a shaky voice, "I can't afford to wait for help to arrive. It'll be too late to do me any good."

"By that you mean?" Mary asked. She allowed her words to trail off into a question.

"I mean that any harm they want to inflict on me will already be done by the time help arrives. And that's assuming it arrives at all. Any injuries they inflict on me could be permanent. Whether it's physical or mental damage or both, it doesn't matter. It's too horrible to contemplate what could happen."

Susan's eyes began to redden and swell with tears that popped up at the corners of her eyes and threatened to escape just above her lower eyelid. She cleared her throat as she fell into an awkward, self-aware silence.

"You definitely don't want to be killed just because you're trying to do your job," Mary said reassuringly. She was sorry she'd brought up the subject.

"Realistically, I'm more fearful of being permanently incapacitated with brain injuries or having my face disfigured by scars than I am of dying," Susan murmured softly. Her lower lip continued to tremor as if she were going to burst into tears at any second.

"Oh," Mary said. She subconsciously cast her eyes onto her plate to avoid staring at Susan's face. She'd lost her appetite and laid her fork aside.

"As horrible as having my life cut short by some deviate lowlife looking to get his jollies would be, permanent injuries would be far worse," Susan said. "Scars last forever as a constant reminder of the Hell I would probably be going through if something like that happened. They would plague me for the rest of my life."

Rachael had a sudden urge to add to the conversation and said, "I recently tried to explain to my boneheaded boyfriend that the only first responders that'll arrive fast enough to be of any assistance to a victim of violent crime is the victim themselves. Violence happens quickly, and the victim is truly the first responder. Of course, the police are likely to be the first professional responders on scene."

Boneheaded is much too nice of a term for that asshole, Adrien thought bitterly, but kept her feelings and thoughts to herself.

"I like that term," Sarah said. "The first professional responders; it really puts a fine point on the fact that the true first responder is someone already at the scene of an attack."

"That's true," Nadine said, and returned to chasing a chunk of tomato around her nearly empty bowl with her plastic fork. She had not lost her appetite like Mary had.

"It's the same reason why it's important for everyone to have first aid and CPR skills. You may be the only person available to provide life-saving procedures in an emergency," Sarah added. "Since it may take the professionals a while to get there, having a trained individual capable of lending immediate assistance may mean the difference between life and death if a serious injury occurs."

"And the death you prevent could be your own," Nadine confirmed, her tone grave.

"One of the things Rachael and I discuss at times is whether a woman can actually shoot someone, even if her life is in grave danger. We tend to be nurturing and all that as opposed to men who are not, at least not to any great degree," Adrien said. Her voice was halting, coming in spurts, because she was still uncomfortable with what she was about to say. "We finally decided that, yes, we could intentionally harm an attacker."

"But you still aren't sure?" Sarah asked with an understanding smile.

"That's true," Adrien admitted. "I'm really not sure I could, even though I've told myself I'd definitely do it. I really don't want to kill someone."

"You're not shooting to kill someone. Don't ever say that!" Nadine said. Her tone was stern but coaching. "If you ever have to shoot in self-defense, it's only to stop their aggressive actions. They may die because of getting shot but that's the risk they take by attacking you in the first place."

"Adrien, you're not alone in feeling that way, and it's not just a female thing," Sarah said. "Men also have a difficult time coming to grips with that very question. We've all been raised in a society that teaches us not to hurt others. It's just more common for men to find themselves going to war or being placed in some other life-threatening situation where they have to kill or be killed."

"So, how do men overcome that type of inhibition? They have to, especially if they're in the military where they may have to face life-or-death situations day after day," Rachael said. She noticed that the other women had stopped eating again and were anxiously leaning forward to hear Sarah's reply.

"I can't answer that question because it's a very involved subject, but I do have a book on the subject I can lend you, if you're interested," Sarah replied. "The military has psychologists studying ways to teach their recruits to kill. They have to answer the very same question you're asking, and it has to be answered for them if they're going to be able to do their job. The book I'm referring to is written by one of those psychologists."

"That's interesting," Adrien said. "I hadn't thought about needing anything like that to desensitize people to killing."

"What's even more interesting is that the author equates the violence on video games with the techniques they teach in the military," Nadine said. "He makes the point that violent video games remove the societal inhibition to killing. He feels this may be a huge factor in mass shootings."

"I've heard that mentioned before," Rachael said, her interest piquing. "I just never thought about how it might apply to self-defense and our ability to kill – I mean, to stop some else's aggressive actions."

"It's just another glaring example of how politicians are ignoring the root cause of mass shootings and such. They disregard the actual cause of the mayhem these desensitized lunatics are wreaking upon innocent people. Then they'll hurry to get in front of television cameras when they begin calling for more restrictions on the God-given constitutional rights of law-abiding citizens to bear arms," Nadine said. The disdain she felt for ignorant politicians was obvious.

"Politicians wonder why people get angry. They're wasting valuable time, money, and effort on something that's not going to help," Sarah said. "The misguided and ill-informed information they spew in sound bites that show well on the news simply muddies the issues. Then the true cause of problems never gets fixed! Their misleading rhetoric doesn't remedy the predicament. It only infuriates people who are educated on these issues and understand what's going on."

"Unfortunately, most people are too lazy or disinterested to educate themselves on important matters. Then they choose to put their head in the sand because they don't believe that something as simple and innocent looking as video games can be so deadly. In the end, society suffers," Nadine said, disgusted.

"I'll be reading that book," Adrien said. The look of sincerity on her face gave credibility to her words.

"It's interesting but very involved reading. I'll write down the specifics for you before we're done today. You may take away a different message from the book than I did. Read up on the subject then make your own decision," Sarah said, an air of finality in her voice.

"After studying up on the subject, and spending some time thinking about it, you may want to try visualizing yourself in a self-defensive situation. Then ask yourself if you can pull the trigger if you must," Nadine said.

"Visualization is a wonderful tool to use for preparing yourself," Sarah said. She thought that was the end of this conversation and took a big bite of salad, but Nadine was not finished.

"The greatest lesson you learn this weekend may be to not carry a gun if you can't answer the question of whether you can shoot if your life is in danger," Nadine said. "If you're not mentally prepared to use a firearm to defend yourself or others, then you shouldn't carry one. Period."

"That's kind of weird since you're teaching us how to use a gun in self-defense," Mary said pointedly in an accusing tone. "It seems very contradictory, and that makes me uncomfortable."

Nadine was ready to say that she didn't give a damn if she was uncomfortable or not, it was the truth. Sarah quickly intervened before she could say anything nasty and ruin the rapport they'd worked so hard to build with their students.

"Not at all," Sarah interjected, quickly swallowing her half-chewed bite of salad. She knew her good friend well enough that she recognized when Nadine's anger was beginning to flare, and she didn't want her to lash out at a naïve student. "You can be taught how to safely handle a firearm, but to answer the question of whether you should shoot is something only you can decide. Try not to wait until you're in a bad situation. That's a bad time to hesitate and try figuring things out."

"Besides reading, which you already suggested, how are we supposed to do that?" Mary said rudely. Her attitude had obviously taken a turn for the worse.

"Visualization, which we just mentioned, is a tremendous help. If you can picture yourself in various scenarios you may encounter, and you continue to practice what you learn here this weekend, it'll help. But the final decision to pull that trigger or not will be totally up to you," Sarah said, struggling to remain pleasant.

"I guess it would depend on the situation, for sure," Mary said, sullenly mulling the intriguing question over in her mind.

"In many encounters with criminals, actually shooting is not necessary, but you can't ever expect that just pointing a gun at a bad guy will make him stop his demented actions," Sarah said, warning her with a very serious tone.

"Such as?" Mary asked cynically.

"For instance," Sarah said, continuing without pause. "In a recent incident I read about, a mentally troubled man went to his church armed with a shotgun, intent on causing harm. A man inside the church had a concealed-carry license, had his firearm on his person, drew his gun, and pointed it at the man with the shotgun. The assailant hesitated and abandoned his plans because he had met armed resistance. He hadn't planned on that. That gave other parishioners an opportunity to disarm the bad guy and hold him for police."

"So, bloodshed was prevented by the actions of the armed church-goer," Adrien stated matter-of-factly. "And the true first responder, the armed citizen, was able to stop the attack until the professional responders, the police, were able to get there to arrest the assailant."

"That's for sure. In that case, the bad guy gave up when he was confronted by an armed citizen – all without anybody physically pulling a trigger," Sarah said. "But if he'd been determined to cause harm, the armed citizen would have had to make a split-second decision to shoot him or not. That's not a decision you want to make without having a definite plan already in mind. There's no time to ponder philosophical and moral questions when split seconds between life and death hang in the balance."

"It's the ongoing battle between good and evil," Nadine said, moving her glass of iced tea back and forth on the table in a distracted manner, thinking about what she was about to say. "As Edmund Burke once said, 'The only thing necessary for the triumph of evil is for good men to do nothing.' You, and only you, have to decide if evil deserves to be shot."

"So, what you're saying, if I understand you correctly, is that I may not have to pull the trigger in a self-defense situation, but I had better be ready to if it's warranted?" Rachael asked.

"Pretty much," Sarah said. "And you have to have committed to that decision long before the proverbial stuff hits the fan. Bad things happen in the blink of an eye, and you have to be ready to act immediately."

"What types of guns do you think are best for women to carry?" Mary blurted out, more because she wanted to change the subject than for any other reason. This discussion was beginning to make her uncomfortable. "My husband wants to buy me a small revolver because he thinks it'll fit my hand better. I told him I want to pick out my own gun. He doesn't buy my bras for me and he shouldn't consider buying me the gun he thinks I should carry."

"Good point," Nadine said. Her round, jelly-like belly began jiggling from laughing. "I've never heard it put exactly that way, but I'm certainly going to remember it. It'll come in handy to explain why men shouldn't insist on which gun they think their wife or girlfriend should have."

"We'll be shooting both revolvers and semi-autos this afternoon when we get to the live fire portion of the training," Sarah said, her demeanor suddenly very serious. "The decision of which one of them you like will be up to you. Maybe you'll like both and shoot one as well as the other."

"Why would I like one more than the other? What's the difference?" Mary asked, warming to the subject.

"You may find that the semi-auto requires more practice to master, but they usually offer greater firepower because they can hold more rounds of ammunition. They're also much easier to reload, especially when you're under stress," Sarah replied.

"So you both prefer a semi-auto over a revolver?" Adrien inquired.

"Not at all," Nadine said. "I personally prefer a good revolver because it's simple to use. Just pull the trigger, and it fires a shot. Simple. And simple is the way I like things."

"And I prefer a semi-auto," Sarah added quickly. "The handgun seems to absorb more of the recoil because of the mechanism and that's a big deal for me because of my prosthetic shoulder. A person with arthritis in her hands, or someone who is just naturally weak, may prefer one over the other for a variety of reasons. It's all very personal depending on your needs and preferences, just like choosing the right bra if I can continue with your analogy!"

"There are some really cute semi-auto handguns on the market these days. Some even come in really cool colors instead of just black or silver," Rachael said. "Though I'll bet they each have their good points and bad regardless of how cute they are."

"That's for sure," Nadine agreed. "Not too many years ago it was a whole different story. Now we have so many choices in handgun sizes and chamberings that it's sometimes difficult to choose which one you want."

"So, my husband may be right. A really small handgun is probably the best choice for me," Mary said, glad to have the decision made for her.

With a crumpled brow Nadine stated, "Small handguns have become an increasingly popular choice for folks because they're lightweight and easy to conceal. Naturally, they sell well to the consuming public for these reasons, which is why there are so many of them on the market right now. But there's a tradeoff. They're much more difficult to shoot accurately than a larger handgun."

"Why is that?" Susan inquired.

"It's because they're small and lightweight, the very reason why people buy them in the first place. It takes a steadier hand and greater grip strength to shoot them accurately," Nadine informed her. She was speaking to Susan, but everyone was listening intently. "They typically have small, almost miniscule sights. When combined with a very long and heavy trigger pull like most of these types of handguns have, it makes it much more difficult to keep the sights aligned on target. It's a real battle to complete a smooth trigger squeeze without pulling the gun off target."

"Will we be shooting some of these smaller type pistols this weekend?"

"For sure," Nadine replied. "I have large pistols, small pistols, and various sizes of revolvers for you ladies to try out this weekend, and they come in a wide range of cartridges. It's an opportunity for you to compare one firearm to the other. A side-by-side test, if you will."

"It may not really matter to me," Mary stated. "I'll usually only keep my gun at home, or transport it to the shooting range, and only occasionally carry it outside to go shopping in a bad neighborhood or something like that."

"That's a bad plan," Nadine quickly interjected. "You should either never carry a gun or always carry a gun."

"Why is that?" Susan queried, her eyebrows furling into a puzzled scowl. "That seems like a very strange statement. We may not always need a gun with us."

"I say that because you project yourself differently when you're carrying a concealed firearm," Nadine explained, making sure to keep her voice calm and reassuring. "If you never carry a gun then you'll probably exude a please-leave-me-alone attitude that predatory criminals can easily pick up on. That may actually attract them to you and result in them purposefully choosing you as a victim. You don't want that."

"That's for sure," Rachael said, giggling nervously.

Nadine ignored her.

"However, when you're carrying a concealed weapon that you've trained with and are confident in using, you subconsciously radiate an aura of confidence. You naturally become more aware of your surroundings and are in a different frame of mind," Nadine said.

"And predatory criminals can pick up on that the same as they will on you being afraid? Will that make them leave you alone?"

"They'll definitely pick up on that. It's the same way they're able to easily identify the wimp in a crowd," Nadine said. "That's how career criminals make their living. They've done it all their lives, and they're good at it."

"Making a mistake in the victim selection process can be a fatal mistake for them," Sarah quietly confirmed in a flat, matter-of-fact tone. "Criminals work very hard to avoid the consequences of choosing the wrong victim."

"Can't you just bounce back and forth between the two?" Rachael asked. The look of doubt on her face and her tone of voice reflected her uncertainty about what Nadine had said. "After all, we project numerous body language messages all day long. It's impossible to do otherwise considering all the people and situations we have to deal with every day."

"This is subconscious posturing," Nadine said, clarifying her statement. "And it's not anything like what you go through in normal social situations."

"And it becomes a bad habit to not have your gun on you at all times. Evil can attack at the most unexpected moment," Sarah said. A tiny shiver shuddered throughout her body as a fear-fueled sensation slithered down her spine. It was caused by a sudden, vivid memory of the events of a few weeks prior when three sociopaths come onto her farm to commit murder and other heinous crimes. Then she added with a trembling voice, "It can even show up at your home when you're least expecting it."

"So, we should carry our gun on us even when we're at home?" Susan asked. She tried to imagine herself trying to relax at home with a firearm strapped to her side.

"It's a good idea," Nadine replied quickly, trying to steer the subject away from Sarah's ordeal. She didn't want Sarah to develop a glum mood and become depressed.

"I think I'd have a hard time being armed all the time I'm at home," Mary said.

"Think about how many times you run down to the corner store for a loaf of bread or jug of milk on the spur of the moment. If you don't have your gun on you, it's plausible that you could walk into the convenience store in the middle of a robbery or be in the back getting your milk when an armed robber walks in to rob the place. In either scenario, you're unarmed and at the mercy of an armed robber. They've already determined they're ready and willing to exchange your life for a few dollars, otherwise they wouldn't be armed."

"And that's only at the store," Adrien said, thinking of other scenarios. "There've been instances where college students were accosted in laundromats, on the street near where they live, or experienced road rage incidents while commuting. All of those situations confirm our need to have a firearm carried on our person to defend themselves."

"That's why we advocate campus concealed carry. Students may get into dangerous situations on their way to or from campus," Rachael added. "But it's really difficult to get those realities through the thick skulls of university administrators. They seem to be living in ivory towers, have their head in the sand, or somewhere else for that matter, as far as the safety of students is concerned."

"It can be a difficult topic for a lot of people to get their heads around," Nadine said, agreeing with Rachael.

"If you're permitted to carry a firearm and don't, then you're part of the problem with criminals having no reason to fear their victims. If you're one of the people who want to pass laws making it more difficult for law-abiding citizens to own or carry a gun, then you're also part of the problem," Sarah said. "In either scenario, the bad guys get a free pass. They only fear an armed opponent and simply look at an unarmed person as another victim waiting to be taken advantage of."

"I can see how being a person who wants to pass laws making it more difficult for law-abiding citizens to own or carry a gun is a problem, especially for folks like me who want to protect ourselves, but how can someone who's permitted to carry a firearm and doesn't carry regularly become a problem also?" Susan inquired.

"They're part of the problem by not teaching the predators in society there are potential consequences to attacking innocent people," Sarah said evenly. "Because when predators can get away with their nefarious acts without repercussions, they'll continue to do so until they're stopped."

"It's the way predators operate," Nadine said, nodding her head in affirmation.

"If all people who're legally allowed to carry a concealed weapon did so, the number of times a predator could safely prey upon innocents would drop precipitously," Sarah said. She began nodding her head up and down for emphasis. With Sarah and Nadine both nodding in agreement, it sent the message to their students that this was a highly valid point.

"And the predators would learn to leave innocent people alone," Susan replied, the concept sinking into her mind.

"It's the same as when a rape victim goes through the legal system and has to go to court to testify, isn't it?" Adrien asked, her voice quavering.

"In what way? How can carrying a gun be in any way similar to someone being raped?" Mary asked. Her quarrelsomeness was becoming evident to everyone, and Nadine was tiring of it.

"The end results are the same," Rachael explained patiently. "If a societal predator can successfully steal from or hurt an innocent person their behavior won't change. That's the same as a rapist not being convicted and sent to jail. They'll continue to rape until they're caught or otherwise forced to stop."

"It's difficult for a rape victim to go through all the court proceedings, but I guess it should be done," Adrien said, her shoulders slumping. "Otherwise, the rapist will just go on to rape others."

"Societal predators will continue to prey on innocent victims until they're stopped either by being sent to jail or confronting an armed citizen," Nadine said.

"So, you're saying that everyone who carries a concealed handgun should even carry it in their own home?" Mary asked, sounding as though she hadn't heard any of the things being said.

"Do you know when someone will break into your house, or accost you while you're putting trash at the curb for weekly pick-up?" Sarah asked. Her patience was wearing thin. "Bad things happen when you least expect them and in places you can't possibly anticipate them occurring."

"That's probably true, because I've often thought about situations where an assailant could gain control over their victim by grabbing a child or grandchild in order to force the adult to comply with their demands," Adrien said.

"I can see that happening," Susan said, realization showing on her face.

Adrien looked at Susan and nodded her agreement.

"It'd be easy for the assailant, possibly attacking in a mall parking lot or large store where other people are not near enough to see or hear what's happening. The victim, it'd probably be the mother but could be a grandparent, may be occupied putting groceries into the car, getting one child into their car seat or handling a temper tantrum while another one or two are standing around waiting their turn to be taken care of."

"I see that happening all the time," Mary said, thinking about her own experiences in large parking lots.

"We all have. The adults aren't paying attention to what's going on around them, and the bad guy grabs a kid," Adrien said, continuing her thought. Her face scrunched up in thought, and she continued, "At that moment the mom would probably trade all her worldly possessions for the gun she left at home. I guess it's important to always carry a gun if you can."

"Or they left it locked in the glove box," Rachael said, her mind flitting to the times she'd done exactly that so she could attend class unarmed or go into the post office to mail a package. In a guilty, sheepish voice she added, "That's not a good thing to do, I guess."

"Plus, a gun can be easily stolen when it's left unattended in a car," Sarah said.

"That's true," Nadine confirmed. "Even police, and worse yet, chiefs of police, have lost their firearms when they were stolen from their unattended vehicles. They don't like those types of stories to get out and become public knowledge, but they do happen."

"The only thing worse than being murdered by a thug would be having to watch a loved one being murdered or brutalized because you were a fool for not carrying a gun," Susan said. "Or so it seems to me."

"I agree," Rachael said, and then went back to eating, not interested in pursuing the topic further.

"Ok, I understand what you're saying now," Mary said. It was almost as though she was surrendering and admitting her argument had been based on faulty logic. "I certainly wouldn't want to watch my husband die because I didn't have a gun on me when I needed one most."

Nadine cast a quick glance at Sarah to see her reaction since her husband had been murdered in very similar circumstances, but the comment didn't seem to affect her at all. *Maybe she's beginning to come to grips with losing Josh since having that discussion with Reverend Yates about that Dark Night of the Soul stuff,* Nadine thought to herself.

"But how are we supposed to carry a gun all the time?" Mary continued, not ready to concede her point entirely. "I wear different types of clothes depending on the weather, the time of year it is, or where I'm travelling. That all makes it more difficult, I'm sure."

"I have a bunch of assorted holsters for different types of carry," Sarah said. She was a bit embarrassed to admit how many holsters she owned. "I'm a holster junkie and buying them more often than I do shoes these days. That's kind of sad, but true, I guess."

"Many of Sarah's holsters fit my guns so you can try different ones," Nadine said, trying to be helpful. "That way you can try different gun/holster combinations to see what suits your needs."

"So, it's simply a good idea to try as many guns, holsters, and carry methods as possible then make your decision?" Susan asked.

"That's what I always suggest," Nadine said. "Everyone has different needs and desires. It's why Sarah and I keep a variety of handguns available for our students to try. Holsters are as personal as your choice in lingerie."

"I don't know how some women can wear those thong things," Mary said, wrinkling her nose in disgust. "It must be like they have a string up their butt all day long."

Everyone else at the table simply ignored her comment or hid their smiles behind napkins.

"There are many reasons people have for carrying a concealed weapon," Sarah said, trying to keep the conversation from straying off onto lingerie. "What's important is that you identify why you want to carry. That'll give you a solid frame of reference to help you make determinations about whether a particular gun and holster combination is suitable for your needs."

Nadine paused to wipe a dribble of chili from the side of her chin, being careful to avoid snagging a small mole with a single, black hair growing from it. Then she said, "For instance, I carry because I don't want other people, such as the police, to be responsible for my personal safety when I'm perfectly capable of taking care of myself."

"That's an interesting way of looking at things," Adrien said, perking up to rejoin the conversation. "It shows you like your independence."

"I believe it's my responsibility to protect myself. It's not someone else's task to watch out for me. I don't want to live by having to depend on someone else to protect me," Nadine said.

"That's a very individualistic frame of mind," Adrien said, beaming with admiration.

"If, God forbid, something happened to the person tasked with protecting me, I wouldn't be able to forgive myself. I can't place that burden on someone else. It's a decision I made long ago, and I'm sticking to it," Nadine said.

"It appears to be the same decision Sarah made long ago if what she told us about her life is any indication," Adrien said. "I respect that."

"It's nothing to be admired for or have anyone else approve of," Sarah said in a flat tone. "It's a decision you have to make for yourself. It's very personal, so don't ever allow anyone else, like a boyfriend or husband," she paused as she glanced around the table then settled her eyes on Mary, "to influence your decision or the preparations you have to make to stand by that decision."

"It's good that we'll have an opportunity to try some guns here today but there are all types of handguns on the market," Susan said, thinking about the huge number of choices she had before her. "If we don't try anything here today that we like, how can we sort through all the different choices out there? I think it's important that we make a good decision on which gun to carry."

"Hit the Internet," Nadine said with a deep, chuffing laugh. Her full belly gently shook up and down. "There's a lot of information available to help you make a decision. It's always a good idea to spend some time on the video sites like Ugetube.com. That's a pro-gun site where you can not only get a person's opinion about a certain firearm, but you can also see how the handgun recoils. That's a nice thing about seeing a video instead of just reading about a gun. And best of all, it's free, and free is good!"

Nadine laughed a little bit more at her little joke even though no one else seemed to think it was as funny as she did.

"I just hate to make the wrong decision because guns are expensive," Susan said.

"Pinching pennies when buying a gun that's to be used for self-defense is the wrong place to try and save a few bucks," Sarah said. "If you're going to splurge on anything this year, make sure you spend enough on the gun and holster you may have to use to protect your life. You absolutely must have a gun that's not only a quality, reliable firearm but must function 100% of the time. It's also very important that you're intimately comfortable handling it, and that can only come from practice and regularly handling your handgun."

"This is one of those instances where being cheap is way too expensive," Nadine said, no longer laughing. "Spend a couple hundred dollars more to get the gun you want. You don't want it letting you down at the worst time. You really don't want to put your life in the hands of a psychopathic creep. If that happens, all the money you have in this world isn't any use to you."

"In that case, maybe I should just buy two guns!" Susan quipped, trying to be cheerful and lighten the gravity of their discussion.

"Maybe you should," Sarah said, her tone serious. Then she lightened the character of her voice and forced a friendly smile to make the words she was about to utter sound less ominous.

"There're good reasons why professionals like police officers often carry more than one gun. If one runs dry, runs out of cartridges," she clarified for the students, "or you lose your gun because your assailant took it from you, or you dropped it for some reason, it happens you know, you can simply grab your other gun and continue the fight."

"Having a second gun ready to go is also much faster than trying to reload, I would imagine," Adrien said, thinking through the advantages of carrying a second gun.

"It's much faster," Sarah agreed, nodding.

"Having two guns is a good idea for anyone wanting to carry their primary firearm in one of the purses specially designed for concealed carry," Nadine added. She was beginning to assume the role of the trained teacher she was. Then she added, "If a someone grabs your purse, and it could simply be a crook wanting to steal your purse and not necessarily hurt you, but then you still have a second gun on your person to defend yourself with since the bad guy now has possession of your first gun."

"And purse snatchings are epidemic, especially in crowded cities," Susan said, allowing the magnitude of Nadine's comment to sink into her mind. "It's almost to be expected in some areas."

"So a purse may not be a good idea to use to conceal a handgun?" Adrien asked, scrapping her plan of using her backpack.

"It's fine if you use one of the purses specifically made for that purpose, except for the potential for your purse being snatched," Sarah said, clarifying her previous statement. "You should never just throw your gun into a regular purse. There are way too many dangers involved with that practice."

"Such as?" Adrien asked, now sure she'd have to rethink using her backpack to carry a gun.

"Such as you not being able to find it quickly in an emergency. Think about having to dredge through all the junk you probably carry in there," Sarah said, raising one eyebrow to signal she was probably right.

Adrien smiled, acknowledging Sarah was correct, and then she returned to eating without commenting further.

"You're right," Mary agreed, her mind wandering to the unruly jumbled mess that always lurks inside the bowels of her purse.

"Your husband will totally understand and may even encourage you to go shopping if it involves you carrying a gun for personal protection," Nadine said. "It may be the only time he'll encourage you to spend money."

"That'd be the first time he'd be encouraging me to go shopping!" Mary said, beginning to enjoy the conversation.

"Just tell him you have to accessorize your wardrobe to carry a concealed handgun. That's the truth because you'll have to rethink the clothing you wear," Nadine said. "A lot depends on where and how you want to carry your gun. The size of the firearm you carry, your body's build, and the different weather conditions throughout the year will dictate how you carry. In turn, that will determine what clothing, or handbag you need."

"So, now we have a good excuse to go shopping?" Susan chuckled. "That's great!"

"You better believe it!" Sarah said. "What you'll find out very quickly is that women need multiple holsters for various social environments, not to mention the different clothes we wear to social functions. That can range from a formal evening gown to shorts at a picnic."

"Really?" Rachael whined. "I was hoping to make do with one holster. College students don't have much money, and I imagine they're expensive."

"Don't be afraid of trying a bunch of different holsters to explore what works for you. There's no single way to carry a concealed firearm that works for all women and is appropriate for all social environments. You may even find you'll opt to have a custom holster built for your specific needs."

"Oh yeah!" Nadine agreed as her belly began to jiggle hysterically as another deep chortling sound emanated from deep within her chest. "It's easy to form a real close relationship with your custom holster maker. It's a whole lot of fun ordering a new one from them!"

"This sounds like a long, drawn out process," Mary stated dryly, again falling into her usual cynical attitude.

"It's a never-ending process," Sarah said, her tone as dry as Mary's. She was rapidly forming a dislike for Mary but knew she couldn't let it show. "Your needs will change, and you'll have to change with them. Get used to the idea and the entire process goes much more smoothly."

"These types of processes are nothing new in life," Nadine said, continuing to explain for everyone's benefit. "People have to buy new clothes because they gained or lost weight, they have to learn to use a cane because their arthritic knees demand some help, or they're forced to use crutches due to recent surgery. We learn to adapt, and luckily, there are various options and tools available to make our lives easier or safer."

"Sorry to interrupt, but can I have more chili?" Adrien asked politely. "It's so good I want to fill up before I have to face cafeteria food again."

"Certainly, Honey," Nadine said, beaming. She liked it when people enjoyed her cooking. "Can you please hand me another slice of bread while you're up? I used William's recipe and I think it turned out better than when he makes it, but don't tell him that." She smiled at her little joke, and this time, others joined her.

While Adrien was helping herself to more chili, Mary leaned forward with a serious look on her face, paused for a split second to collect her thoughts, and with a tiny twinge of trepidation in her voice nervously asked, "What about recoil? I'm afraid of it. My husband has even had to sell some of his guns because he can't handle it the way he did when he was younger."

"That's an excellent question. It used to be said that you should only carry a handgun for self-defense if the caliber starts with a '4' as in the popular .45, .44, or .41 caliber cartridges. That's not as true today as it used to be," Nadine said. She straightened herself in her chair. "Progress in bullet technology has made smaller calibers as effective as the larger ones."

"But, it's also interesting to note that many women prefer a cartridge such as the .45 ACP, which is what I shoot, because it recoils with a slow, gentle 'shove' instead of the 'snap' that a higher pressure round such as the 9mm, and especially a cartridge like the .40 S&W, generates," Sarah added, trying to be helpful.

"Smaller calibers with new styles of bullets can be effective against even a large, aggressive attacker?" Susan inquired. Her eyes were wide with astonishment. "Little guns will be easier for me to conceal under the business suits I wear on the job."

"It still may be a good idea to use the largest caliber and cartridge you can shoot comfortably," Nadine said, better clarifying her statement.

"Assuming it comes in a handgun you're comfortable with," Sarah added.

"Of course," Nadine said. "As always, it may be more important for a woman to decide which firearm fits her best and then determine if that particular firearm comes in a caliber that can be reasonably expected to be effective in a wide range of circumstances."

"So, you suggest we buy a gun we can shoot well, and only then look at the cartridge it shoots?" Adrien asked, struggling to clarify what Nadine was trying to say.

"Exactly," Nadine said. "That way you're sure you're shooting a gun you can shoot accurately, which is the number one consideration. That'll give you greater confidence in your choice. Having confidence in how well you can shoot your chosen firearm is extremely important. That confidence will make it more likely you'll regularly practice with it. In turn, that usually leads to greater enjoyment from practicing. More practice will lead to you being more proficient with your chosen tool for self-defense, and that's the goal, isn't it?"

"That's the goal," Rachael said, nodding her head in agreement.

"It's interesting that many handguns come in a wide variety of cartridges," Sarah said. "You have a lot to choose from."

"We live in a wonderful time right now because there are so many great handguns on the market," Nadine said. "It's almost too difficult to make a choice, but that's the wonderful thing about shopping, isn't it?"

Adrien and Rachael giggled at Nadine's little joke.

"With that many choices, how am I supposed to figure out what'll work best for me?" Mary whined pathetically.

Sarah and Nadine looked at each other, frustrated with Mary's incessant whining and complaining.

"A great way to decide if a cartridge/gun combination works for you is to attend as many training classes as you have time for and can afford. Learning and maintaining your shooting skills is a constant process," Sarah explained. "In the process of training you'll learn what works for you and what doesn't."

"Good point," Nadine said. "Just like Sarah and I offer a large number of handguns and holsters for our students to try, other instructors do the same, so by attending additional training classes you'll be exposed to different combinations of firearms and accessories."

"Some folks take one week every year and use their training experience as a vacation," Sarah said, acknowledging Nadine's contribution to the conversation with a slight bob of her head. "That way they can get away to a different location, allowing their mind to focus on a program of their choosing."

"An added benefit is that since each course is usually planned around a specific agenda, you'll be learning the skills you're truly interested in learning. That allows your mind to be completely off work, so you'll truly be rested when you're finished. That's vastly different than worrying about what's going on back at the office instead of relaxing."

"That's a good idea," Susan mused, thinking about what Nadine said. "It'd allow me to genuinely get some rest without thinking about work, or returning to work for that matter, because that's what usually happens while I'm on vacation. I really never get any rest because my mind is always on work one way or the other."

"Your mind will stay off work, for sure, at least for the duration of your training," Sarah said amicably.

"So this is just the start, eh?" Adrien asked.

"This is just the beginning," Sarah said.

CHAPTER 8

CERTIFICATION CLASSES

"Look at this," Nadine said to Sarah after their students had departed, pointing toward the computer screen. "This says the National Rifle Association has been providing education and training in the safe and proper use of firearms since 1871. That's plenty of time to have formed a good track record."

"Not only that," Sarah said, interrupting Nadine's train of thought. "Since 1960 they've been offering courses specifically designed to provide law enforcement officers a way to get certified."

"That's impressive," Nadine said. "Training cops is a major undertaking."

"And look here," Sarah said, reaching over Nadine's shoulder to point out a specific section on the web page. "They want classes to have a minimum of four students with the ideal class size being ten to twelve students."

"So far, we've usually tried to keep our classes to four students maximum thinking that smaller class sizes would make a better learning experience," Nadine said. "I guess we were wrong."

"It may have not been ideal according to NRA protocol but for us stumbling around on our own and trying to teach ourselves how to conduct training classes, keeping class size smaller has helped smooth our way into becoming certified trainers," Sarah said. "Either way, it only shows how much we didn't know."

"Yeah, I guess you're right," Nadine replied. "You definitely got us on the right track by insisting we get our NRA instructor certifications."

"I knew you'd agree," Sarah said. "So, we should take the six-hour Basic Instructor Training course, which is a prerequisite for the Pistol Instructor Course?"

"Does that certify us to become defensive pistol instructors?"

"No," Sarah said, clarifying her statement. "Those two courses are the prerequisites for the fifteen-hour NRA Instructor Basic Personal Protection in The Home Course."

"Then we can teach people how to carry a concealed firearm legally?"

"No, again," Sarah said. "That's only a prerequisite for the twenty-two-hour NRA Instructor Basics of Personal Protection Outside the Home Course. It seems that every course builds on the other. They become more complex from one to the next and they have to be taken in a specific order."

"I guess that's important. At least it's the way we taught in school when I was a teacher, so I'm familiar with the process."

"It's important that we foster the skills our students will need to competently and confidently carry a gun for self-protection. They'll need at least that much to help them develop a defensive mindset."

"Well, let's quit jabbering about it and see when our schedules allow us to attend a course," Nadine said.

"There are a lot of courses offered in every state so it shouldn't be too difficult finding a time we're both able to make it," Sarah said.

"We'll have to coordinate with Chauncey and William to make sure they can take care of the livestock on both our farms so we can get away and concentrate on our coursework," Nadine said, thinking through the details.

"Let's set some tentative dates, and then check to make sure they're available to babysit the farms before committing to a specific course."

"We should have done this a long time ago," Nadine said, ashamed at herself.

"To do things out of order or otherwise backwards only makes us human," Sarah mumbled, concentrating on the courses, their location, and the dates they were being offered.

CHAPTER 9

BAD BOYS

"So, what're you thinking?" Joey Valentino asked his two cohorts.

"I was thinking we need what those old people have," Marty Noorey said, a wicked grin spreading across his face. "What did you think I was thinking?"

"I don't even want to be guessing what you're thinking," Alex Doyle said, thinking he'd made a clever joke. His buddies missed it if there had been anything resembling humor in his statement.

The three were all in their early twenties and had been friends since they were high school age. They shared a long list of crimes they'd been arrested for, and a much longer list of crimes they'd committed for which they were never caught.

"You sure about them having tons of money and dope in that apartment?" Joey asked.

"I'm telling you, they've been dealing out of that place for years," Marty replied. "Who would ever suspect nice old people like that dealing dope out of an apartment complex set up specially for old folks? They got a really sweet deal going there."

"So, what are you thinking?" Joey asked again.

"I figure we can just hit the place the way we usually do," Marty said with authority. He'd tacitly become the planner for the trio because of his superior brainpower.

"Fast and hard," Alex stated, a sly grin spreading over his chubby face. Alex thought of himself as the most intelligent one in the trio, but he was the only one with that viewpoint.

"Fast and hard," Joey agreed, holding up a five-inch screwdriver that materialized like magic out of his cavernous coat pocket. "And if they give me any crap, they'll get taught a lesson."

"Why don't we just shoot them in the head and be done with it?" Alex asked. He had bluster in his voice as he pulled a small, silver colored .380 handgun with black plastic grips from his coat pocket. "If there's that much stuff in there they're going to be armed to the teeth. We can go in fast and pop them in their grey old heads. It'll all be over with no problems and everything of theirs will be ours with no muss and no fuss."

"No guns," Marty stated sternly. "We have to do this real quiet. All those old people living in that old-folks-only apartment complex have nothing better to do than worry about what's going on with their neighbors, and they all have the police on speed dial."

"Yeah," Alex agreed, dejected. "You may be right."

"Are we just going to smash their heads in with something like this?" Joey asked, holding a silvery eight-inch crescent wrench aloft. He always carried it in the coat pocket opposite the one where he carried the screwdriver.

"That's right," Marty said with a wicked, smirking smile. "Real nice and quiet."

"We can't screw around at all," Joey said, looking sideways at Alex. "They've been dealing dope for a long time, so they probably have guns. We don't need the noise of us getting shot, right?"

"That's right," Alex agreed, chuckling with a rumbling sound that came more from his nose than his chest. "I don't want to get shot. Ain't there something easier and less risky we can do to get some money? Besides working, I mean."

Alex grinned, but didn't laugh after seeing the grave look on his friends' faces.

"Well," Marty said, rubbing his chin. "There's that old fart bastard and his bitchy old lady down on Vilsack Avenue. You remember me telling you about them and all the money they're supposed to keep in that big, old house of theirs?"

"You're talking about that mean old bitch and her uppity old man who were always yelling at us kids to stay off their shitty looking lawn?"

"That's them," Marty said, grinning at the fond memories from his childhood. "You remember me telling you about them and their money?"

"Yeah," Alex said. "I remember them always driving that big old Lincoln Town Car! It was a boat!"

"And that old guy drove it like a boat," Joey confirmed. The pleasant memories of his misspent childhood came flooding back to him. "Do you remember that time he ran over Steve Perkovich's bike with that little prick Stevie sitting on it? Then the old bastard yelled at him like a crazy man because it scratched his fender?"

"Yeah, I remember," Alex chuckled. Then he broke out in a deep, belly shaking laugh, conjuring up more graphic images of the old man in his lackluster mind. He rarely delved deeply into faded memories from his bleak childhood years.

"What do you say to us hitting them first? Just for practice, you know," Marty said, his eyebrows scrunching up as he thought about it. "That'll give us some practice before we hit the old folks dealing drugs."

"Especially if the old fart dopers have guns," Alex added seriously. "Some practice may do us good."

"It'll put some big money into our pockets too," Joey said in anticipation. He immediately began thinking about what he could do with the easy money they'd make from this one simple job.

"Yeah," Alex said, his feeble mind beginning to align along the same lines as Joey's. "That's a good plan. Make some money while having a little payback with those nasty old folks will make it all a little more like fun and less like work."

CHAPTER 10

LIES, DAMNED LIES,
AND STATISTICS

Rachael and Adrien sat huddled closely together in a relatively secluded booth tucked away in the farthest back corner of The Underground, laboriously poring over stacks of reports from various governmental sources. They were looking for pertinent statistics and facts they could use to convince the college administrators that allowing, if not encouraging, concealed carry of firearms on campus by legally licensed individuals was good policy.

"Where's Brian?" Rachael complained bitterly. "He's the one who wanted to get together to do this and he's not even here."

"He said he'd be a little late because practice for the college jazz band would be running a little over," Adrien replied dismissively. "Apparently they're trying to perform some of Wynton Marsalis' jazz arrangements and it's giving them a fit."

"Who's Wynton what's-his-name?" Rachael inquired. She asked just to have something to talk about even though she wasn't really interested. It was as good of an excuse as she could come up with to avoid having to delve further into campus crime statistics. Mathematics and statistical analysis were not high on her list of fun things to do so she avoided them when possible. She also had a difficult time understanding these academic disciplines and didn't want to look stupid in front of intellectuals like Adrien and Brian.

"He's only one of the best-known jazz trumpeters around for the last few decades. He composes and teaches it as the Artistic Director of Jazz at Lincoln Center in New York City."

"Oh," Rachael replied, sheepish. "He sounds old then."

"He's only in his fifties, I think," Adrien replied. "It's funny you haven't heard of him because his music appeals to younger audiences. I'll bet you've heard his music and didn't even know it was him playing it."

"I really never listen to jazz," Rachael admitted. "I occasionally listen to classical music because my dad really liked it. He often had some playing in the background while he worked in the garage reloading shotgun shells so he could go trap shooting."

"Well, Wynton Marsalis is also a respected classical trumpet player so your dad may have heard of him," Adrien said. "He's the only musical artist ever to win Grammy Awards for both jazz and classical records. He's one of Brian's heroes and he tries to imitate him when he plays jazz trumpet."

"Wow! That's saying something," Rachael said. The sincere tone of her voice conveyed that she truly was impressed. Then she began tapping maniacally at her phone. "I'll look up some of his stuff later while I'm studying. It may be good music to help me memorize all those statistics I need to know for the final in my administrative justice course. Statistics drive me nuts and make my life miserable."

"Oh, there's Brian now," Adrien said, her gaze shifting across the expanse of long tables.

Rachael looked, but it was difficult to see him because of the constantly shifting throng of students bustling about the room. Finally, her eyes fixed on the wide doorway as a tall, thin young man entered. He began systematically searching for the pair of women. When his and Adrien's eyes met, he nodded his acknowledgement of having seen her and began laboriously weaving his way toward them.

Brian Breen was the epitome of a band geek with his pale, smooth complexion, oversized shiny black wayfarer prescription glasses, and maroon V-neck sweater that sported accenting white stripes at the neck and cuffs. He dressed and projected a clean, natural look that made him appear to be imitating the look that Buddy Holly, the late, great pioneer of rock-and-roll music had cultivated as his own unique and distinctive look before perishing in a tragic airplane crash in 1959.

Brian's naturally thick dark brown curly hair was cut short and worn above his ears. It was shorn so the back never touched his collar, but he let it grow longer on top. The height of his hairstyle accentuated the appearance of fullness and allowed his topknot to cascade down his forehead in an untidy mass that persuasively contributed to his retro 1950s appearance.

He unceremoniously slid his fake alligator skin trumpet case with the gold-toned coating chipping off the cheap metal clasps onto the floor beside the banquette's bench seat. Then he dumped his tattered and dirt smudged backpack that was grossly overstuffed with textbooks beside the trumpet case. With an awkward, shuffling gait he unpretentiously plopped his slender, six-foot frame onto the cool plastic of the seat opposite Adrien and Rachael.

"Sorry I'm late," he stammered, mopping a rivulet of sweat from his forehead and desperately trying to catch his breath. "I ran all the way here hoping we'd still have time to get a few things done before my next class. I don't want to hold you up."

"You didn't have to run," Adrien said. "We don't have any classes beginning for at least forty-five minutes, the same as you."

"Well, let's get started then," he panted, bending sideways and shoving his hand deeply into the bowels of his backpack. He pulled out a raggedy, lime green composition notebook with its binding in shreds.

With a deft flick of his wrist he tore the stained rubber band holding it closed from around its periphery. He flipped it open, revealing that most of its ruled white paper and ink smudged pages contained a hodge-podge of barely decipherable scribbled notes, hand-drawn charts, graphs, and random diagrams.

Flipping to a page he'd recently worked on, his callused index finger slid down the page and ended at a diagram he'd made.

"This is the most recent information available from the Department of Education showing annual crime statistics for college campuses," he said without fanfare. "As you can clearly see, a little over one-third of crimes occurring on college campuses are assaults of one type or another. Another third or so are robberies."

"What percentage of the crimes are rapes?" Adrien asked. There was obviously concern in her voice.

"Rapes make up about a fourth of crimes occurring on college campuses," he replied matter-of-factly without looking up from his notes. "That's a full quarter of all crimes on campus involve rape."

"That fits with the generally accepted statistics of rape or sexual assault," Rachael said.

"That's a lot of rapes happening on campuses, regardless of how you look at it," Adrien said.

"Don't get confused when you look at these statistics," Brian cautioned them. "While it's hard to get your head around all these figures, the fact remains that over eleven percent of all college students experience rape or sexual assault."

"That's over one in every ten students getting assaulted," Rachael gasped. "That's a much easier statistic to understand."

"Yeah," Adrien said, an angry edge as sharp as broken glass in her voice. "College aged women are a very vulnerable group."

"And they should be able to defend themselves whether they're college students or not," Rachael said. Her shoulders slumped, and she looked forlornly at the top of the table, allowing the helplessness she felt inside to show on her face.

"It isn't just the women who are under attack," Brian said, feverishly flipping through the dog-eared pages of his notebook. "Look here."

He pointed to a non-descript sentence of the report with a nail-bitten forefinger. "It says male college students have over a seventy-five percent greater chance of becoming a victim of rape or sexual assault than non-students of the same age. That's a difficult statistic to get your head around."

Brian had a pained look on his face as he continued scanning the page.

"Which only highlights the need for all college students to be allowed to carry a concealed weapon on campus if they so choose," Adrien said, a look of triumph on her face. "If physically fit young men can't defend themselves from violent sexual assault, how are weaker and more vulnerable women supposed to defend themselves without a gun?"

"Good point," Rachael agreed.

"That's scary enough, but look at this," Brian said, excited. His gnarly index finger rapidly traced further down the page. "Some college students were stalked while attending college. That's something you don't think about."

"That's definitely creepy," Adrien said. A shiver slithered down her spine and she involuntarily shuddered.

"Most of these crimes are grossly underreported. Only about one in five female college student victims of assault report it to law enforcement," Brian said. "That gives the impression college campuses are much safer than they probably are."

Rachael shook her head back and forth in disbelief.

"I can understand why they don't report it," Adrien said without thinking. She was glad they didn't question her further about why she thought that way.

Brian straightened himself in his seat. A puzzled look settled upon his face.

"Why do you think only such a small percentage of victims ever report crimes committed against them?" Brian wondered aloud. He really didn't expect an answer.

"The best information I could find says that many women felt it was a personal matter and not anything the police should be involved with," Rachael said.

"Women have a very real fear of reprisal from their attacker. That can keep someone from reporting any crime committed against them," Adrien said, her eyes narrowing. "The potential for reprisal by an assailant is another good reason to be armed and properly trained."

"It's horrible to think that someone can be assaulted and then be forced to continue living in fear of their assailant, possibly for the rest of their lives," Rachael said. "Just because they reported the crime committed against them, their life may never be the same."

"It sounds like that training you two had last weekend really made an impression on you," Brian said, laying his notebook down and leaning forward. He was obviously tired of reviewing statistics and wanted to talk about something less depressing.

"It was really a good time," Rachael said. She leaned forward and became more animated. "The experience was tremendously uplifting. I think I gained a huge amount of confidence to carry, and God forbid, use a firearm in self-defense if things ever came to that."

"It really opened my eyes," Adrien added. "Having women instructing the course really made the whole process go much more smoothly for me. I think I was able to begin feeling more comfortable in the class much faster than if I'd been in a class with men."

"I wholeheartedly agree with that," Rachael said, her mind playing back to the class.

"Is it that much different than being in a class with men?" Brian asked. Both women looked at him like he was totally clueless, which he obviously was.

"You bet it is," Adrien said, steadfastly affirming her previous statement. "Shooting has traditionally been looked upon as being an activity men participate in, but women traditionally do not. That makes a difference in the way both men and women view being in the same firearms training class together."

"How's that?" Brian asked. He was genuinely interested.

"Men have to be better than women in what they look upon as an athletic event, which it is not, but that's their problem," Rachael said, flashing a coquettish smile and locking eyes with Brian.

Brian promptly lost his train of thought as he gazed into the depths of Rachael's gorgeous eyes. His mind went momentarily blank, hypnotically entranced with tiny golden flecks that danced seductively within the glimmering sea of her emerald green irises. The dazzling colors seemed to shimmer like tiny faceted diamonds in the flickering glare of the fluorescent lights illuminating The Underground.

"And women can be intimidated in a mixed gender environment, so they may not freely ask questions for fear the men will think they're stupid or something," Adrien said. She haltingly shifted her eyes from Brian to Rachael and then back again. They continued gazing at each other.

Adrien began feeling like she was intruding. Brian and Rachael continued ignoring her.

Then she quietly added, "Or they begin to flirt with their fellow students and forget about concentrating on the reason why they're in the training class to begin with."

Her voice trailed off. She began silently gathering her belongings to go to class earlier than planned.

CHAPTER 11

EASY MONEY

Martha and John Pinquette had been following the teachings of financial guru Dave Ramsey for over twenty years and had amassed a considerable amount of money in that time. They enjoyed being wealthy and generously gave to a large array of charities, which gave them a tremendous sense of wellbeing and pleasure knowing their lifetime of hard work was helping to benefit those in need.

John had been an insurance salesman all his life. His wife of fifty-three years, Martha, was a high school mathematics teacher at the local high school until she retired. They'd always been savers and had never gone into debt the way most Americans did as they competed to see who could accumulate the most useless items over their lifetimes.

Early in their lives together, they'd decided to avoid using credit to buy anything. Subsequently, they never applied for any credit cards, only borrowed enough on a mortgage to purchase their house on Vilsack Avenue, and paid cash for all other purchases.

By paying extra each month, they were able to pay off their fifteen-year fixed mortgage in eleven years. They'd owned their own home without any mortgage payments since John was age 33 and Martha was 30. This plan allowed them to put the money they would have spent on their mortgage into savings, which grew nicely over the years due to compounding interest.

When they needed to make a large purchase like buying a car, they saved the money and used a cash deal as leverage to get the best price possible on the automobile of their choice.

Their two children, Amy and Amanda, had been raised with these values. Ever since each of the girls were born, the Pinquettes put money aside for them specifically earmarked as an educational fund. This financial tactic allowed their daughters to attend college and graduate debt free.

Amy worked for ten years as a C.P.A. before marrying and becoming a full-time stay-at-home mother. Straight out of college, Amanda went to work as an actuary for the same insurance company her father had worked at his entire career. She married, divorced, and remained childless to enjoy the independent lifestyle of a single adult.

This Friday evening had started out as quietly and as boring as most for the Pinquettes. John and Martha were listening to classical music on the stereo they'd purchased in 1976. They'd been forced to add Bose speakers to it in 1986 to replace the damaged pair that succumbed to Amy blasting heavy metal music on them. Amy's teenaged ear-splitting shenanigans caused the original speakers to crack and vibrate annoyingly. But new, high grade Bose speakers allowed the Pinquettes to continue marveling at how well the old stereo sounded year after year.

John was in his study poring over the monthly household bills and reconciling their financial statements. He took periodic sips out of a crystal rocks glass half-full of Knob Creek Kentucky Straight Rye Whiskey as a reward to himself for finishing each goal he set for himself while doing the finances.

Martha puttered industriously around their spacious country style kitchen baking a cream cheese pound cake with almond glaze in anticipation of celebrating Amanda's birthday at an afternoon brunch in their home the next day. Late Saturday mornings were a convenient time for family gatherings because no one worked over the weekends. This gave everyone an opportunity to sleep in late then congregate for a meal together. This schedule gave Martha time to clean up after everyone left and still take her customary late afternoon nap.

It was hectic having all their children and grandchildren in their home, but they enjoyed every minute of it, though they both agreed it was getting more difficult to host family gatherings due to their advancing age. Growing older slowed their ability to make their home ready for guests, but Martha and John didn't mind spending additional time preparing if it meant spending a few joyous hours with their grandchildren.

Amy and Amanda's birthdays were a few months apart and had become annual events. On those days, the entire family was expected to be sitting around the large, highly polished cherry table sitting in the middle of Martha's immaculately appointed dining room. Martha kept the pristinely polished table draped with a Lenox French embroidered blended linen tablecloth, even though her grandchildren frequently spilled their milk on it. It was a small detail that made her happy, so she put up with scrubbing food stains from the fine linen.

Family gatherings always started at noon sharp on the planned day and were expected to be completed by three. This time-honored schedule was just another example of the meticulous way the Pinquettes lived their lives.

But today was winding down, and it was getting late in the evening for the elderly couple to be this active. They were weary from frenzied housecleaning, anticipating the arrival of their guests the next day. Unexpectedly, the solid brass doorbell chimes at the front door sounded, and it caused both Martha and John to startle in surprise.

"John," Martha called in a questioning, irritated voice from the kitchen. "Who could that be at this hour?"

"I don't know but I'm going to find out," he called back, heaving his lanky, tall frame from the black leather-covered executives chair. He took a moment to get his balance, oriented his alcohol-befuddled mind, and then meandered in an irregular weaving pattern down the hallway. He paused briefly to push himself off the wall when he staggered a bit too far to one side.

Reaching the end of the hallway without stumbling too noticeably, he flipped the light switch that peeked out from the polished brass switch plate conveniently situated on the side of the darkly varnished walnut front door.

But no porch lights came on.

The doorbell ding-donged again in a resonating three-toned cadence and was followed immediately by a frantic pounding on the heavily constructed door.

"Help me," a stifled voice called from outside. "I have to use your phone to call an ambulance."

"What?" John called out, shouting into the small diamond-shaped leaded glass window embedded in the door at eye-level. Not hearing anything, he ducked his head lower to get a better view out of the window and bellowed again, "What?"

"What is it, John?" Martha called from the kitchen.

"Some guy is yelling out there and this damned light is out," he roared angrily.

"What does he want?" Martha asked, concern tinging her voice.

"Help me. I have to use your phone to call an ambulance," the desperate voice called from the porch.

"What?" John hollered again, fumbling with the lock. "What's happening?"

"My friend was changing a flat tire and the jack slipped," the frenzied voice explained. "His foot got caught under the tire and I heard his ankle break. Please! Please! Let me use your phone to call an ambulance! He needs help!"

John gave the lock a final twist and began swinging the heavy wooden door open as its worn hinges creaked in protest. He only pulled it halfway open before Joey's heavily muscled shoulder hit the outside of it, flinging it forcefully into John's forehead.

The solid edge of the door smashed into the frontal bone of John's forehead, splitting the skin in a nearly vertical but ragged gash from his hairline to his eyebrows. Stunned, John fell backward and tripped over his own feet. His bony arms flailed wildly and flew helter-skelter as he unsuccessfully tried to break his fall, but it was inevitable he'd end up sprawled on his buttocks in the middle of the hallway.

He didn't have time to assess his situation or even mutter a few confused syllables before Joey's silvery eight-inch crescent wrench snaked forward in a high, wide arching swing and landed directly over the gash in his forehead.

John dropped like a rock and lay still except for an incessant quivering movement that took control of his hands.

"John?" Martha called from the kitchen. Marty and Alex rushed past Joey, homing in on her quavering voice. They swiftly stepped around the unconscious John, and without hesitating, bolted toward the kitchen.

Joey slowly closed the front door. When there was just a crack left open, Joey peeked out, scanned the deserted street, and then with uncharacteristic care, gingerly finished closing the door with rock-steady rubber-gloved hands until he heard the tiny clicking sound of the bolt settling into its mortise.

HUNGRY BAD BOYS

"What the hell?" Marty Noory groaned, still lamenting the fact that he and his cohorts didn't reap the monetary rewards they anticipated by invading the home of John and Martha Pinquette three nights previously. "I know those old farts had a ton of money stashed somewhere, but where is it?"

"It's right here," Joey Valentino stated flatly, pointing to the pile of papers he'd snatched on a whim while rifling through John Pinquette's oak roll-topped desk. "I knew these papers were worth boosting, but I didn't know why at the time."

"What you are talking about?" Alex Doyle inquired, lazily dragging his filth-encrusted fingers through the detritus at the bottom of an empty tin of Planter's salted peanuts. His futile search for pieces of broken nuts hiding in the pile of brittle red skins littering the silvery interior of the can kept him occupied for much more time than a person of average intelligence would have dedicated to such a fruitless pursuit.

"They have a ton of money, probably a ton and half of money, but we can't get to it," Joey said. Without further comment, he handed the now-crumpled document across the grimy surface of the ancient kitchen table to Marty. The wobbly legs of the table were scrunched up against a grungy handprint-smudged wall in Marty's squalid three-room apartment to keep it from rocking back and forth as much as it would if left to stand on its own.

The crudely painted tabletop was currently bright maroon but showed at least three different colors beneath where it chipped from countless dings that had been inflicted upon its once shiny surface. The color of the table clashed with the dingy yellow of the crooked wallpaper in an eye-irritating splash of colors, but it didn't seem to bother Marty or any of his friends. He reached across the table to warily take the proffered paper from Joey's two-fingered grasp.

"What the hell are you talking about?"

"It's all there in black and white," Joey crooned knowingly. "Those old farts had over three hundred thousand dollars in what that paper calls a growth stock mutual fund."

"Three hundred thousand dollars!" Alex cried out, allowing the peanut can to slip from his pudgy fingers and crash to the table. He was totally unconcerned that the tin crazily spun in erratic circles, randomly scattering plumes of feathery red skins across the battered tabletop. Nor was he worried that the mess would lay for days waiting for Marty to eventually shoo them onto the floor. "How we supposed to get our hands on that?"

"We don't," Joey replied evenly. "It's all on paper. We can't get to it unless we have all the passwords and proper identification. Then it would all have to be transferred electronically to a bank account, and that would have to have our names on it. And you don't want your ugly face or name being anywhere near this stuff after what happened to them old folks."

"You mean all their money is in these grow funds and we can't get to it?" Alex asked, confusion showing on his scrunched-up face. His whirling mind futilely tried to understand why they couldn't get the money after all the effort they'd put into trying to obtain it.

There was a brief pause while Alex churned the information around in his mind. A smile brightened his face. "And who you callin' ugly, you prick!" he added, trying to bolster masculine camaraderie with his long-time friend.

Ignoring Alex's lame attempt at being friendly, and with unfettered patience for him, Joey slowly mouthed his words. "Growth stock mutual funds."

He took great care in annunciating each word distinctly so the dimwitted Alex could better understand, an exercise he'd grown accustomed to over the years he'd known him. "They probably had a bunch more money in other mutual funds if those piles of paper on his desk and in his files are any indication."

"That's why they didn't have hardly no money in the house," Marty mused. "They had it all put away in mutual funds."

"Earning a bunch of interest," Joey stated flatly. "And we can't get at any of it."

"None of it?" Alex asked forlornly. He picked up the paper Marty had let drift from his fingertips to land in midst of the peanut skins.

"None of it," Marty confirmed. "And we're going to burn these papers right now before anybody catches us with them. That'd tie us to that house and them old people for sure."

"But we used all the money we got from them for pizza and wings and beer," Alex whined. "I'm hungry."

"Well boys," Joey said, snatching the papers from Alex's hand with a grand flourish. He stood and walked to the dirt-stained sink with the financial papers in his one hand and a butane lighter the other. "After I burn these we better go out and see who's going to give us some money for food. We'll need our strength for hitting those dope dealers at the old folk apartments Saturday night."

"Willingly or not," Marty said with a grin.

"Probably not willingly," Alex chimed in, grinning broadly. He thought he'd uttered another witty and hilarious joke, but once again, he was the only one who thought so. His belly growled and he stood up. "Why are we waiting until Saturday night? We need more money now. I'm hungry!"

"Because Saturday night will give them old dopers a chance to sell most of their dope on Friday and Saturday, two big party days over the weekend, and they'll have mostly money by then."

"And we only want the money? Dope isn't any good?" Alex asked, still a little confused.

"Selling the dope to get money is a hassle and has a long jail term if we get caught with it. Let them do all the work of selling it, and we'll just take the money," Joey explained slowly and distinctly so Alex could more easily follow his logic to understand why they had to wait until Saturday night.

"Yeah," Alex said, licking his chapped lips in anticipation of a large payoff. "Money is better," he muttered as the idea laboriously seeped into the deep recesses of his sluggish mind.

CHAPTER 13

COLLEGE DISCUSSION

Rachael bustled through the door of The Underground in an anxious rush. She frantically looked around the perimeter of the huge room, quickly scanned the long lines at the burger counter, and then began a systemic visual search of each individual booth lining the walls until she spied Adrien and Brian waving her over.

"I didn't think I'd make it," she gasped after slogging her way through the crowd to reach them. With a look of exhaustion, she unceremoniously dumped her backpack on the floor beside the plastic seat of the banquette and collapsed into the booth beside Brian. She slid toward him until the outsides of their thighs were touching.

"I missed the cross-campus bus because my economics professor decided to pop a quiz on us at the last moment. It was pulling away just as I was getting out of the building, and I panicked. I ran to catch it waving my arms like a maniac, but it didn't stop," she blurted. Her heart and mind were still racing from the exertion. Then, continuing without seeming to take a breath, she said, "It took me longer to complete the essay question than it should have. My mind was torn between what I wanted to say to you and what I was supposed to be concentrating on for the essay. To make matters worse, the next bus was late. Isn't that the way things usually go when you're in a hurry?"

"They're supposed to run every fifteen minutes," Adrien said, trying to be sympathetic. She said it while scowling at how close they were sitting. When she realized her brow was furrowed, she relaxed it, and to soften the effects of her harsh glare, she said, "but you really can't count on them being on time."

Neither Rachael nor Brian noticed her disapproval and wouldn't have cared if they had.

"I usually end up walking across campus even though it may take longer. I hate standing and waiting for a bus that may or may not come," Brian added. He was trying to show forgiveness for Rachael being late without saying it outright.

"It's a problem," Adrien said, a weary tone in her voice. "Brian was just explaining about the material this seat is made from."

"Really?" Rachael cooed, looking sideways at Brian.

"I was just learning about this stuff in my chemistry class," Brian said, excited. He continued in a professorial tone as though he were teaching a class on the material, "ABS, or Acrylonitrile Butadiene Styrene, is the perfect substance for upholstering college furniture because it has a waterproof surface that's tough like rubber while being hardwearing. These properties make it ideal for fast-paced environments where it'll be subjected to bumps and scrapes that would destroy less resilient coverings. It's very durable and that's why it's used in a lot of products from kitchen appliances to children's toys, including the famous Lego brick."

"That's interesting," Adrien said, sarcastic. She exaggerated rolling her eyes to let Brian know she was mocking him in a friendly way. "But we're here to organize an empty holster march across campus and not discuss the finer points of furniture coverings."

"Right," Brian said, suddenly realizing he was boring Adrien half to death. He straightened himself in his seat and said, "Let's get to it then."

"Rachael, have you contacted the dean's office to see what hoops we have to jump through to keep this all legitimate and not run afoul of any obscure campus ordinances?" Adrien asked, being very business-like.

"Of course," she said, glancing sideways at Brian. "We just have to apply for a permit at the administration office. Then, once it's approved, we take a copy of it to the security office. That way they'll know what's going on, especially since we'll be wearing empty holsters. We don't want the security officers taken by surprise because they don't know what to expect."

"It seems a shame that we have to go through all this when it's obvious the campus security, or even the police off-campus for that matter, can't protect us. It's not right that the powers-that-be on campus still want to deny us our God-given right to protect ourselves and loved ones," Brian said, dismayed.

"It seems out of character for you to be speaking so meanly about anybody, let alone the police," Rachael said, looking at him skeptically. "And what's up with this protecting our loved ones? None of us has any family here with us so we couldn't protect them even if we had the means."

"Oh, Brian's upset because a girl he knows from the college jazz band is a local who commutes from home and the neighbors down the street from her parent's house were found this morning all beat up in their house," Adrien said. His tone was succinct and factual, with little emotion.

"She's a really nice girl. A really cute little blond that plays trombone like a pro. I mean, she's really good, especially with the improvisational parts. I admire her ability, and it's a shame those old people got beat up," Brian said, jumbling and stumbling over his words. Anxiety bubbled up inside him.

Adrien and Rachael merely stared at him, not sure what to say.

Brian looked back and forth at the two young women, and a look of despair clouded his face.

"They're in the hospital. It's all over the news. The old guy is in critical care, and he may not make it. At least that's the way the lady on the noon news made it sound. She was talking about the police filing murder charges against whoever did this if he dies."

Rachael was struggling to think of something to say when she realized she was jealous of the emotions Brian felt for this trombone-playing blonde.

She immediately got her emotions under control and made sure her facial features remained expressionless. As calmly as she could, said, "Can you possibly add one more 'really' into a sentence when you're talking about that girl? Besides, since when do you watch the noon news? Don't you have enough important things to do instead of sitting around watching TV?"

"I only watched the news because I wanted to see what happened that made Jennifer, that's the girl's name, so upset," Brian replied, defensive. "They think it was a home invasion. Now Jennifer is concerned about what may happen at her house since those poor people lived just down the street from her parents."

"Well, did you learn anything?" Rachael asked, her anger barely held in check.

Adrien sat back and looked at them with an amused look on her face as they began to verbally spar back and forth. She didn't say a word and let them get it out of their systems.

"Yes, I did, as a matter of fact," Brian said, oblivious to Rachael's emotional involvement in this conversation. "As you know, I'm a researcher at heart, and it's what I'm studying so I examined the topic from a statistical point of view."

"I didn't know you were studying to be a researcher," Rachael said, suddenly embarrassed. "I only knew you were a musician. I thought you were studying music and only got into all these statistics because you're researching what we need to get concealed carry on campus."

"Musician by avocation, researcher by vocation," he replied by way of explanation. "I thought you knew that about me."

"Sorry," Rachael apologized. "I'll have to spend more time with you so I can make sure I know who I'm hanging around with."

"That's a great idea," he replied, leaning a little closer to her.

"Can we stay on topic here, please?" Adrien pleaded. Then her curiosity got the best of her. "What did you find out about home invasions?"

"Well," Brian began, warming to the topic. "Surprisingly, an aggravated assault occurs every forty-five seconds in the United States."

"That sounds like a lot of people getting beat up," Adrien said.

"It is a lot," Brian agreed. "But what's even scarier is that a rape occurs every five minutes in this country."

"What does that have to do with home invasions?" Adrien said, suddenly defensive. Then, in an exasperated tone, she added, "Are we off topic again and wandering farther away from discussing the empty holster demonstration?"

"No, we're not off topic again," Brian said gently. "It's scary because over half of rapes occur during home invasions."

"That must be a lot of home invasions," Rachael said. Her mind reeled to put the figures into a context she could easily grasp.

"It is a lot of home invasions," Brian replied, agreeing. "These are all statistics from the FBI and the U.S. Department of Justice so they're probably fairly accurate. There are well over a million home invasions every year in this country. Those stats were garnered over a six-year period, and they're fairly consistent."

"What?" Adrien exclaimed. "That's absurd! How many houses are there in the United States? There can't be that many."

"There are a little over 126 million households in the U.S. according to the U.S. Census Bureau. That makes it roughly a one in 126 chance your house will be invaded every year. Those don't sound like very good odds to me of not having this type of thing happening."

"OK, wait a minute here," Rachael stammered. She was struggling to comprehend the vast amount of information Brian was spewing at a rapid rate. "How many burglaries did you say there were?"

"I didn't say anything about burglaries," Brian replied calmly. "Burglaries and home invasions are two almost totally different things."

"What?" Adrien asked. Her mouth dropped open in surprise.

"Burglaries and home invasions are two different things," Brian repeated.

"So, what's the difference?" Rachael asked. She was obviously confused and struggling to understand it all.

"A burglary is when a criminal enters an unoccupied but protected structure like a locked home or business with the intent of committing a crime once inside. Typically, a burglar is only interested in simply stealing something of value like money, which is why they enter an unoccupied building. They really don't have any intention of committing a crime that goes beyond stealing something," Brian explained, his tone scholarly.

"And a home invasion?" Rachael said, pressing him for more information.

"That's a whole different story," Brian replied. His head dipped and his shoulders drooped with concern. The seriousness of such situations weighed heavily upon his psyche and elicited a visceral response as though such a crime was a physical burden on his shoulders.

"A home invasion is when an individual, or most likely, a group of people, use force to enter a home that's occupied. They can break down a door, smash a window, or they may even use physical violence against the occupants of the home to gain entry. That's what the police think happened to that older couple in Jennifer's neighborhood."

"Someone beat them senseless instead of just simply breaking a window when nobody was home? That's what makes it a home invasion?" Rachael asked.

"That's what they think happened," Brian replied. "Usually, a home invasion occurs when the criminal wants to commit a violent crime. It can get out of control easily, I guess. A lot end up in a murder, rape, or kidnapping."

"That's why home invasions are so dangerous," Adrien said dully, staring at the table and not looking at them. She appeared to be in deep thought or mild shock. "The home invaders are purposefully coming to hurt people."

"That's right," Brian said. He hastily added, "That's what's bothering Jennifer. Those old people were hurt on purpose. What kind of animals would purposefully hurt someone, especially an older person? I wish I could help them somehow."

"We can't help them now," Adrien said, a stern look in her eye. "So, we should just concentrate on what we can do for the students on this campus, and that's get this empty holster protest organized and under way."

"I hope that if I'm ever in a situation like a home invasion that I have more than an empty holster to use in protecting myself," Rachael said, her voice trembling with fear.

CHAPTER 14

POOR PLANNING

Joey Valentino and Alex Doyle anxiously sat in a white panel van parked amongst a long line of cars on a busy street. The street was well illuminated by both streetlights and the stores lining both sides.

Alex was nervously chattering while Joey ignored him, lost in his thoughts, but on alert.

Joey sat in the driver's seat watching the side mirror intently. He knew their prey was expected shortly. He also knew she drove fast but not recklessly, and he didn't want to miss seeing her.

An hour earlier Alex had dropped Joey off near the van as it sat in a crowded mall parking lot. They'd visited two other malls before locating a non-descript van with a sliding side door that met their needs.

Alex was driving his mother's car, and after dropping Joey off, he went in search of a similar van he could steal the plates from. After securing the plates, they met to put them on the van Joey had stolen. This was a system they'd used successfully in the past because it greatly reduced the potential for unwanted interference from police.

Later, after committing their felonies, they'd drive the van to where Alex's mother's car was parked in a deserted area near the river. There, they'd set the van on fire using a delayed timer. By the time the vehicle ignited, they'd be far away with no evidence remaining for the police to trace to them.

They'd always gotten away with other crimes by following this system, and there didn't seem to be any reason they shouldn't expect it to be successful again. It was a proven way to destroy all traces of DNA, whether it was theirs or their victim's.

They sat in silence for a while, each man lost in his private thoughts.

"What do you think Marty would say if he knew were doing this?" Alex asked.

"What the hell kind of question is that?" Joey said, demanding.

"I don't know. I was just wondering, is all," Alex said, apologetic.

"You know damned well what he'd say. He's never had to worry about getting a woman to pay attention to him."

"You really think he'd be that upset, huh?"

"He'd probably never talk to either one of us again. He can be pretty funny when it comes to moral things like raping women."

"Yeah, I knew that was what you'd probably say. We better make sure he never finds out."

They allowed the topic to fade away and returned to their private musings.

"You sure this bitch is going to come this way?" Alex inquired, the tension causing his voice to quaver. "She's late."

"She is not late," Joey replied, never taking his eyes off the side mirror. "I've followed her from her night class at the college to her apartment three times. She always comes this way. Sometimes she stops off someplace for a few minutes to pick up fast food, but she always comes this way."

"That's what you said," Alex replied. "I don't like the waiting part."

"It's something you'll have to learn to live with," Joey said without emotion. He'd learned long ago to not allow himself to get distraught over any of Alex's inane comments.

"How we going to do this?" Alex asked. "The last time when we got that girl from behind the department store, I was driving. You want me to drive again?"

"We already went over this," Joey said, trying to be patient with his partner. "I'm driving because I know exactly where she's going. Last time we knew exactly what time that girl would be getting out of work. I don't want you following this one too close and make her suspicious. I can stay back in traffic."

"You sure I'll be able to catch her before she gets to her door?"

"That shouldn't be a problem. She lives in a loft above a garage. The driveway is short and slopes up only a little bit. You should be able to jump out as soon as I stop and grab her. Just make sure you keep her mouth covered with your hand until we can get some duct tape on her. We don't need her screaming and waking up the whole neighborhood."

They sat silently for a few minutes without speaking. Suddenly, Alex whipped his head around and said, "I really hate that we have to do things this way. If I wasn't so damned ugly, I'd be able to get a girl like everyone else does."

"You're not ugly," Joey said. "And don't ever talk about being ugly, especially to me."

"Sorry," Alex said, realizing he had just offended his friend. It was a fact that Joey would never be able to improve the scarred image he presented. Alex thought he had to say something to help assuage the affront he'd made to Joey, so he said, "I had a girlfriend, but she dumped me. I guess I've never really gotten over that."

"She dumped you because you were a bastard and mistreated her," Joey said. "You can't treat women like that. They'll leave you every time."

"Yeah, well ..."

"There she is!" Joey said, sitting up in his seat. He fiddled with the bare ends of the wires sticking out of the steering column and the van's engine roared to life.

Alex sat up straight, suddenly excited, and craned his neck over his shoulder trying to see the woman they'd targeted.

"Don't be looking around like that! It's suspicious. Just stare straight ahead and I'll let you know when it's her car passing us," Joey said. The tension in his voice reflected his eagerness. "This'll be her passing us right now."

A compact red car sped past them and continued without slowing.

"OK, we're on her," Joey said, easing out of the parking spot and slowly trailing her. "I told you she drives like a bat out of Hell."

"Don't lose her!" Alex said. "She's going pretty damned fast!"

"I won't," Joey said. "I know exactly where she's headed, and it takes her a minute to get all her books and other crap together. That'll give you the chance you'll need to get out and grab her."

"I'm ready," Alex said, trying to boost his confidence.

Joey didn't answer. His concentration was focused on timing his speed to that of her car. He knew he couldn't arrive at her apartment too late because it'd make it impossible for Alex to snatch the woman before she was safely inside.

Timing was critical to the success of their mission, and they both knew it.

"She'll be making a right up here and then two blocks down, she'll make a left. Her apartment is three houses up the street on the left," Joey said.

"And you're sure she parks on the street and walks up the driveway?"

"Yeah, there are other cars parked in the driveway sometimes. I guess they rent her the apartment over the garage but don't have enough space for her to park close to it."

"That's good for us!" Alex said, licking his lips nervously.

"There! She just put her right turn signal on. Just like I said."

"I never doubted you for a moment, you know that!" Alex said.

"Bullshit," Joey said. "Just be ready to jump out when I tell you to. I'll be beside the side door to slide it open when you get her close to the van."

"You don't think she has a gun or pepper spray, do you?" Alex asked.

"Pepper spray, maybe," Joe said, smoothly steering the van to make the same right hand turn she'd made a few seconds before. "They're not allowed to have guns on campus, so she probably doesn't. I don't think they even let students keep a gun in their cars because they're parking on school property, so you don't have to worry about that."

Alex was silent. His mind was focused on the task at hand, and the time for conversation was past.

"If she does have something like pepper spray, she'll never have time to get to it if you grab her fast. Hit her if you need to, but keep her mouth shut. Don't let her scream. Not even a little one!"

"We went over this already. I know what I'm doing."

Joey made the left-hand turn onto the street where the woman lived and saw the rear lights of her car flicker out.

"Get ready!" Joey said, slowing the van to time their attack so she was well away from her car and in the open.

The woman slid long, thin legs out of the car and without looking around, gracefully slid out of it. She poked her head back into the car, reached across the console, and grabbed her backpack off the passenger seat.

Straightening up, and without looking around, she slammed her car door. She hit the lock button on her key fob and slung the backpack over her shoulder before heading toward the driveway.

"It's nice and dark here," Alex said, looking around. "You picked another good one. You're really good at this!"

"Just grab her and get the bitch into the van without her screaming. I don't want all my work being wasted," Joey said. "I'll stop at the bottom of the driveway. You jump out as soon as we stop moving."

Alex turned in his seat and loosely grabbed the door handle in his trembling hand. His hand was not shaking from fear but from anticipation of what the rest of the night would bring.

"Easy now, just wait," Joey hissed. The van slowly glided closer and closer to the entrance of the driveway. "She's just starting up the driveway. Now!"

He stopped the van and Alex jumped out. His attention was focused on the woman's swaying hips as they seemed to float up the dimly-lit drive.

Alex began pumping his legs like pistons to gain the momentum he'd need to smash into the woman and take her by surprise. He sensed Joey moving the van forward ever so slightly, so the side panel doors were aligned with the center of the bottom of the driveway.

Alex was still twenty feet from the woman when porch lights attached to either side of the door to the house suddenly illuminated the area. Alex slid to a halt and foolishly stared at the lights, wondering what it all meant.

"Josie! I'm glad I caught you. Your rent is due today, and I know you don't like being late," a burly man in a sleeveless tee shirt said as he pushed the screen door open.

"I know. I'll get you a check as ..."

The woman stopped in midsentence when she saw her landlord staring at something behind her.

"Hey! What the hell are you doing here? This is private property!" The landlord pushed the screen door all the way open and stepped out with a menacing scowl on his rugged face.

Alex had seen everything he needed to see to know their carefully laid plan had just failed. His street-honed survival instincts goaded him into action.

Spinning on the balls of his feet, he turned and ran back toward the van. He could see the ghostly outline of Joey's panicked, wild-eyed face staring out the side window at him. Joey's hands were beating the air, frantically waving Alex toward him, urging him to run faster.

Joey leaned across the passenger seat, pulled the door handle, and threw the door open for Alex.

Without pausing or looking behind him, Alex rocketed into the van, and Joey hit the gas before his buttocks hit the seat.

"What the hell happened?" Alex gasped. "I thought she lived alone."

"She does," Joey said. "I didn't know her landlord would be waiting for her to get home so he could collect the rent. That sucks! I had it all planned out!"

Joey struck the steering wheel with the flat palm of his hand in frustration.

They drove in silence for a few minutes. Joey concentrated on zigging and zagging down side streets to avoid having anyone follow them. He made sure to never go over the posted speed limit to avoid attracting unwanted attention from police.

Finally, Alex broke the tension by saying, "What the hell! That didn't turn out as we planned."

They looked at each other and broke out in laughter. Slowly, their heartrates began returning to normal and excess adrenaline slowly dissipated from their bloodstream.

"That was close!" Joey said, grinning and shaking his head in disgust.

"What do we do now?" Alex asked.

"We burn this van, just like we planned in case they got a good look at it. They definitely got a good look at you, and we don't want the police to be able to tie you to this van."

"If they tie either of us to this van, they may make the connection between us and that last girl we took from behind that store," Alex said. He nervously stroked his chin with a trembling hand and anxiously glanced back and forth as though the police were already watching them.

"A good gasoline fire will destroy any DNA and fingerprints we left behind in here," Joey said. "Even though we didn't leave the type of DNA we wanted to."

They grinned at each other in the darkness.

"After we torch it, what're you going to do?"

"I have to get my mom's car back to her," Alex said. "Then I have to feed and walk her dog."

"You and that damned dog. You'd think it was the most important thing in your life."

"In some ways it is," Alex admitted. "He treats me better than most people do. He's always glad to see me and is sad when I leave. Nobody else acts like that."

"Yeah, I guess that would be worth a little time and effort to keep him fed," Joey said noncommittally.

"Besides, my mom isn't able to walk him around the neighborhood since her knees got so bad. Taking care of her dog just gives me an excuse to visit with her and help her out a little around the house," Alex said. "What you going to do for the rest of the night?"

"You can drop me off at the bar before going to your mom's place," Joey said. "Maybe there'll be something going on there."

They drove the rest of the way in silence.

CHAPTER 15

RACHAEL'S DEBATE

Professor Michael Schumer was an unassuming man of average height, build, and outwardly exhibited a calm demeanor. However, mentally he was a jumbled mess of raging pathological emotions. He incorrectly viewed himself as being the persecuted subject of cruel disrespect and disdain by almost everyone he came in contact with in his daily life.

He rabidly desired to be highly respected and revered by his peers and held in high esteem by the university's administration. He felt strongly underappreciated by his peers and the administration, thinking his academic work was held in utter contempt by everyone at the college. These feelings of inadequacy festered in his mind day and night, fostering an intense resentment within him.

He had spent the first ten of his thirty-five years on this earth trying to find his place in society but gave up after a group of bullies menacingly hovered over him as he sat alone in his school's cafeteria. To make themselves feel superior, and to force him to experience the humiliation of being inferior to them, they slowly poured chocolate milk over his plate of food while they laughed uproariously at his emotional discomfort.

Their mocking laughter echoed loudly in the back of his mind for months afterward.

Then one day, his tumultuous and continually questioning mind figured out that if he single-mindedly immersed himself in his studies so he was always at the top of his class, he may be able to position himself in a lofty enough profession so bullies wouldn't dare belittle him again. Daily harassment by them gave him the motivation to keep his goal foremost in his mind.

It was the only way he could think of to seek revenge on his tormenters. The fact that these toughs were always at the bottom of class rankings and usually in dire fear of being held back a grade made his sacrifices to achieve academic superiority more palatable. Each notch up the ladder to higher scholastic achievement gave him strength and fortitude to continue at a feverish pace. It made him feel good about himself.

His monk-like study habits and deeply ingrained habit of dictatorially wielding his academic mastery over classmates unintentionally hurled him headlong onto a scholarly career path that led to his acquiring a Ph.D. by age twenty-five and eventually to full academic tenure.

It was from this lofty academic mindset that he coolly called to Rachael Fiorenza and politely requested a minute of her time as her class was adjourning. The other students filed out of the classroom in what would best be described as organized chaos.

With a tremendous amount of difficulty Rachael extricated herself from the hectic mass of jostling young adults as they staggered under the heavy weight of overloaded backpacks in a mad rush to get to their next class. It was not unusual for everyone to hurry from a classroom when the class ended because their next one may be on the other side of campus.

Rachael obediently reported to Professor Schumer with the expectation of being praised for her exemplary performance in the public policy debate she'd just finished presenting to her class.

Standing with her backpack slung over her sagging shoulder, she thrust her shapely hips far to the other side to offset its weight. She peered inquiringly at her professor while he needlessly busied himself with a stack of papers. He incessantly shuffled through them without truly reading any of them, stacked, and then reshuffled through them again.

She sensed he was merely making her wait for him as a childish display of his superiority. She knew this was a ploy often used by petty bureaucrats to set the stage by sending subordinates an unmistakable signal they were in charge and all others were inferior to them.

Finally, he set the stack of papers to the side, rudely cleared his throat, and stared directly at her for an inordinately long time before speaking.

"Rachael, you did a wonderful job of debating Maryanne in front of the entire class today," he said with a flat, unemotional attitude and furrowed brow.

Not knowing how to take the mixed message of an obvious compliment that was accompanied by such a stern look, she took a moment to gather her thoughts. Her whirling mind desperately sought to sort out this baffling situation. His demeanor had taken her aback, and she needed extra time to ponder the perplexing quandary before replying.

After taking a moment to try to process his mixed message, she respectfully answered with what she perceived as being a safe reply, "Thank you, professor."

"You offered what you thought was well-documented information, used the same for rebuttal, and seemed pleased with yourself that you were doing a wonderful job of convincing the class that your views on gun control and self-defense in your pretend role as an administrator setting public policy were on the cutting edge of innovation," he offered in a scholarly manner. He readjusted his round, rimless glasses on the bridge of his long, beak-like nose and stared at her with unblinking but faded greyish blue eyes that seemed to have long ago lost all luster and joy of life.

Rachael didn't know how to respond to his comments, so decided to take them as a compliment, flashed a brilliant smile, and cheerfully said, "Thank you again."

He didn't smile, but simply replied in the same flat, emotionless tone, "Because you delivered the information in such an efficient, well organized, and sincere manner I will be able to give you a middle grade for your debate, but no more."

He sat unmoving and continued staring at her with an unwavering gaze as he waited for his statement to sink into Rachael's mind. It took a few seconds to do so, and in a state of near shock, she was only able to stammer a stunned monosyllable reply.

"What?" she croaked from a dry, emotion-constricted throat.

"I said that I'm being charitable and will give you a middle grade today instead of failing you for taking the stance you took on gun control and self-defense," he replied with no emotion evident on his face. He went back to mindlessly shuffling his papers.

"But I don't understand," Rachael sputtered, emotional. "I put a lot of time and effort into preparing the debate material, double checked all my references to make sure they were from referenced journals and other trusted sources in academia and research, and then presented them in what I thought was a very convincing manner. You said so yourself!"

Her lower lip began trembling and her eyes welled up with tears. She struggled to maintain her composure and waited for what seemed like an eternity for his answer.

"I'm sure that is all true," he replied, trying his best to be haughty. "But you're on the wrong side of this discussion. Therefore, you are wrong, will always be wrong, and you will never again take this stance in my class. If you do, I'll give you a failing grade regardless of how well prepared you think you are or how well you present your ill-mannered ideas."

He continued staring at her with unblinking eyes that were void of compassion. After a moment, he continued, "You can take that to the bank. So, get with the program, my program, or you'll definitely be flunking my course and any other course I teach." His statement was made with finality. Then he again looked at his papers, spun around in his chair, and faced the opposite direction signaling the discussion was finished.

Rachael stared at the back of his head for a long time trying to fathom exactly what he'd said.

In a stupor of disbelief at the reprimand she'd just been given, she stumbled toward the door. As she was exiting the room he called after her without taking his eyes off the papers, "And if I ever hear about you participating in those idiotic empty holster protests again, or any pro-killing or pro-gun demonstration at all, I'll definitely fail you and ruin your career in any way I can. That is a promise."

Numbly, she staggered slightly as she maneuvered down the crowded hallway, and then in a frenzied rush hurried as quickly as she could down the linoleum covered steps at the far end of the building. The staccato noise of her frantically paced footsteps echoed and mingled with those of other students in the impersonal confines of the concrete and steel stairwell.

She hit the panic bar and burst through the heavy double steel doors in a faulty run, dashing into a centrally located sunlit area known by everyone on campus as The Quad. She threw her head about looking at the four austere classroom buildings surrounding the commons. She desperately tried to figure out her next move, but her mind was a blank.

Then a thought struck her like a runaway truck.

Adrien will know what to do, she thought to herself. She began rushing recklessly through the surging mass of students bustling this way and that in a chaotic mix of humanity.

Looking around frantically for an escape route to the street, she fled in the most familiar direction leading to a bus route she was used to taking every day.

When she arrived at the bus stop, she was taken aback by the huge throng of students milling about waiting for a bus that was obviously running behind schedule. Desperately scanning the street, her eyes filled with tears of anger as the professor's words reverberated in her skull. She gave up on the idea of waiting for the bus. She began walking briskly toward The Underground.

Rachael half-walked and half-ran down the street. She blundered across professionally maintained grassy areas around classroom buildings, and through clean, well-maintained service alleys between dormitories. The only thing she could think about was finding Adrien to seek her advice and solace.

Her breathing became more panic stricken and rapid, causing her to slow her pace. She couldn't afford to fail a single class, especially when she was doing everything the was supposed to be doing. When her eyes betrayed her again with tears and a sob threatened to break free from her constricted chest, she began running faster again.

She slowed from a frenzied run to a hasty walk, wiping the blinding tears from her eyes with the back of a trembling hand so she could see. Tears continued to to trickle down her ruddy cheeks unchecked as she navigated her way across campus in a stumbling gait.

During the last few blocks of her journey, she slowed to a lurching, surging walk that didn't seem to carry her very far because of the short, choppy steps she was taking. Finally, her shuffling gait took her through the gaping doorway of The Underground. She began searching hysterically for Adrien or Brian.

Thankfully, she spied them both sitting in a booth halfway down the side wall. They were oblivious to her presence as they pored over papers laid out on the table between them. She could see them bickering back and forth like two old cronies arguing over politics.

Rachael stumbled up to the banquette, flung her burdensome book-stuffed backpack onto the floor, and cried in an anguished voice,

"That son-of-a-bitch!" She continued to repeat her mantra. "That son-of-a-bitch! That son-of-a-bitch! That son-of-a-bitch!"

When she was too fatigued to continue standing, she fell silent and collapsed onto the seat beside Brian.

Adrien and Brian simply stared at her. They were at a loss for words.

Finally, Brian asked in a low, meek voice, "What's the matter?"

"That son-of-a-bitch public policy teacher of mine is the matter," she said. The words flowed out of her in a garbled mishmash that flowed together in a seemingly uninterrupted stream of syllables.

Not knowing what to do, Brian offered her a sip of his soda, which Rachael accepted without comment.

Taking the condensation streaked waxed paper cup in both hands, Rachael slurped mightily at the end of the straw until she began to get nothing but air bubbles. A rude gurgling sound emanating from the bottom of the ice-filled glass, so she stopped drinking.

"Sorry," she said. "I'll get you another one." She began standing up, but Brian gently grabbed her upper arm and held her to him the best he could in the cramped confines of the booth's seat.

"Don't worry about it," he said in low, even tones. "Eat the ice if you want. It may help. I'll get you more if you want it."

"Thanks," she croaked. Her throat still felt parched from crying.

"What the hell happened?" Adrien inquired. "If it was that damned Cole again, I'll ..."

"It wasn't Cole, it was my public policy teacher, like I just said," Rachael said in a strangled voice that seemed to refuse to clear up. "He threatened to fail me for the entire course if I ever discussed any self-defense subjects in class. He even told me that I can't participate in any demonstrations like the empty holster campaigns ever again. He doesn't care if it's in the classroom or outside it."

"What?" Adrien said, astonished.

"You heard me," Rachael said. Her voice was finally beginning to return closer to normal and her breathing slowed. "The bastard threatened to fail me because he doesn't like the stance I take on Second Amendment and personal freedom issues."

"He can't do that!" Adrien huffed. Her face reddening and she fidgeted in her seat. Her agitation was evident, and it made Brian slightly afraid to speak, but he did.

"He can and I don't doubt he would," Brian said, a sad look on his face. "The administration will always back the professors unless it involves something like sexual misconduct, then they'll drag their feet investigating. That's just the way things are in the real world."

"But what about college being a time of having frank discussions and learning about debate and compromise and all that type of stuff? I thought that was what it was supposed to be about, so students can enter the real world after having explored and questioned everything under the sun."

"That's what it's supposed to be, but it's not anymore," Brian replied evenly. "You know that. Universities have become close-minded institutions that circle the wagons to protect their points of view, which are almost always liberal or progressive in most institutions of higher education these days."

"That's why organizations like Turning Point USA are growing rapidly on college campuses across the U.S.," Adrien said, beginning to calm down.

"Who are they? And what do they do?" Rachael asked. She was confused, but her inquisitiveness was returning now that she was beginning to quiet down.

"Turning Point USA is a conservative organization whose mission is to organize students to promote the principles of freedom and limited government," Adrien replied.

"I imagine having an organization like that on campus would really aggravate administrators. They may even be more disliked than we are," Rachael mused.

"We have them on campus. You've never heard of them?" Adrien asked.

"I've heard of them. That's the group the sophomore saxophone player from the jazz band formed on campus last year. She told me about it, but I really don't have the time to get involved in two groups at the same time. I do have to have time to study, you know," Brian said, smiling. "She says that even though the organization has a presence on well over a thousand campuses across the country, they're still not being taken seriously by the administration. Just like us."

Adrien's shoulders slumped and her head dipped slightly as the weight of the truth in Brian's words settled upon her. "It's what we've always been up against trying to get concealed carry on campus. The conservative groups on campus will run into the same opposition we do. That's just the way it is and most likely will be for many years to come, I'm afraid."

"It seems the administration, and that includes most of the professors, only want students exposed to their point of view and no others. They'll forcefully quash any opposing views using any and all means they have available to them," Rachael said. "I've only heard about it before but haven't experienced it firsthand until now. It's scary."

"What did you present in your debate that got this professor so fired up?" Adrien asked. She was very interested in getting the particulars of what had happened to Rachael.

"Well, I presented the fact that Brian pointed out last week about the University of Kansas experiencing a thirteen percent drop in criminal offenses being committed on campus in the first year concealed carry was allowed there. All without the apocalyptic effects of blood running in the hallways and shootouts in the cafeteria that the anti-gun critics had promised would occur."

"And the reported thefts on campus were down to about one-quarter as many as the previous year, if I remember correctly," Brian added, diving into his backpack in search of the magazine article where the information was reported.

"Then I presented the work by Dr. John Lott from the second edition of his book More Guns Less Crime. I used a lot of his research because he's used documented research that's withstood academic scrutiny," Rachael said. "I thought it'd be good to use the findings of scientific research for my arguments since this is a college class. You'd think that would be important. But no, the only thing that matters is the professor's personal opinions."

Rachael wiped a tear of anger and frustration from her eye.

"That's pretty heady reading," Brian said, giving up the search for the magazine article about the University of Kansas. "Even with my background in research it took me a long time to review and evaluate all of the information Lott presented. It's all good stuff."

"It's well worth the effort it takes to read. It shows, based upon available research and not emotions, that arming law-abiding citizens not only reduces crime but also has a staggering impact on the economy," Rachael said, straightening herself. "Dr. Lott is an economist, after all."

"The economic impact is staggering," Brian said, warming to the topic. "The amount of money that can be saved when citizens are allowed to repel criminals is absolutely mindboggling."

"In what way?" Adrien asked, scooching further forward in her seat.

"Well," Rachael said, taking on a professorial air, "The evidence presented in Lott's work implies that the most cost-effective method of reducing crime, at least when studied and analyzed from an economist's point of view, is the carrying of concealed firearms."

"Get out of here!" Adrien said, her eyes widening in surprise. She was happy to see Rachael focusing on something other than the professor.

"No, really," Rachael said. "The research shows that carrying concealed handguns reduces crime more than increases in law enforcement, incarceration, or even implementing social programs.

And all of those are more expensive. Economists pay attention anytime money is being spent. It's what they do."

"Really?" Adrien said.

"Really," Brian said. "The research is very clear and powerful. That's why it's so mindboggling to me that some folks push so hard for gun control when just the opposite has tremendously greater benefits to reducing crime and benefitting society."

"And economists can figure all this out?" Adrien asked, thinking of ways she could use this information to sway gun control arguments in her favor.

"You bet," Rachael said, gaining confidence. "Lott has even been able to show that for each additional handgun permit that's granted, it reduces the losses to victims of crime by between three and five thousand dollars. That's how much money it saves for each permit issued. I wonder if it's too late to switch my major to Economics? I kind of like this stuff."

"No!" Adrien gasped in disbelief. "You've got to be kidding."

"No, I'm not kidding," Rachael said. "I really like this stuff."

"Not about you," Adrien said, grinning. "Is it true that concealed carry has that big of an economic impact?"

"Absolutely," Rachael continued. "In the State of Pennsylvania, for example, the potential cost to victims is reduced by over five thousand dollars for each additional concealed handgun carry permit issued."

"That's only one state," Adrien said, astonished. "And he can prove this with readily available statistics?"

"Yes. In Oregon, that drops to only a bit over three thousand dollars per permit issued, but that's still a huge amount of money. And it's all being saved by simply allowing people to carry concealed firearms," Rachael assured her.

"Then why are misguided people still pushing for more gun control instead of advocating for more people being armed?" Adrien asked. The incredulity in her voice was unmistakable.

"Because they're stupid," Brian added flatly.

"Brian!" Rachael said, admonishing him. "That's not nice to say about anyone, regardless of how irresponsible they are."

"OK, let's be nice and call them irresponsible then," he said, trying to be agreeable. "But I'll bet your opponent in the debate didn't have any hard research to bolster her arguments like you did. Usually, people arguing for more gun control rely on emotional pleas for disarming law-abiding citizens."

"That's true," Rachael said, ruminating in a low tone. Her mind was replaying the details of her recent debate. "Every time I'd bring up a piece of research, she'd counter with an emotional statement. Most of the time, no, all the time, her statements weren't based on anything substantive. They seemed to be more of a passionate knee-jerk reaction."

"That's why we have such a hard time convincing people using a rational, scientific approach," Brian said, confirming his previous statement. "The people who advocate gun control are not rational. They'll almost always resort to name calling when their arguments are shown to be lacking any standing. Their arguments are based solely on what feels good and right to them in the moment."

"They are passionate," Adrien said. "I'll give them that."

"But their emotions and feelings are getting people killed," Rachael said, tears welling up in her eyes. "Especially children."

"How's that?" Adrien asked, her brow furrowing in confusion.

"Well, another one of my arguments, and I think this one was what really got Professor Schumer riled, was that in the states that adopted shall-issue concealed carry laws, meaning that everyone who applied for a concealed carry permit had to be issued one as long as no evidence was found that barred them from legally possessing firearms, had a major impact. This one simple action significantly reduced mass public shootings in those states after four or five years of the law going into effect."

"You're kidding!" Adrien exclaimed, bouncing excitedly in her seat. "It had that great of an effect?"

"Yes, it did," Rachael confirmed, raising her chin proudly. "Even if a person is deranged and wants to kill innocent people, they don't want to risk being shot by a concealed carry holder."

"Well, I'll be damned," Adrien said.

"I don't think we want that, but it's been demonstrated over and over again that the freedom haters refuse to give the research and experiences from other countries any credence or consideration," Rachael said. "They keep repeating their emotional mantra of disarming everyone who's innocent. Apparently, they want to punish all the law-abiding citizens for the criminal acts of a single, deranged person. It's not right."

"School shootings fall into that category," Brian said.

"That's definitely the discussion taking place right now on whether or not to allow teachers and other school staff members to be armed so they can protect children. In the event of a deranged person, or a terrorist for that matter, trying to kill and maim innocent children the first person there will most likely be someone who works at the school."

Rachael began to relax as she discussed familiar topics with like-minded people like Brian and Adrien. The occasional tear still streamed down her face, but she quickly swiped at it with the back of her hand. Only after she realized she was wiping her mascara across her face in large, wide streaks did she snatch up a paper napkin from the chrome dispenser and begin dabbing more delicately at the corner of her eyes.

"Remember, this is a public policy class, so when I pointed out that studies showed that most of the murders occurring in the United States are all concentrated in only two percent of the counties, it should have been a big deal," Rachael said.

Her voice was gaining strength and vigor.

"A few public policy changes to address the root cause of the problems in those few counties may possibly reduce the overall murder rate. That should have gotten me a great grade for suggesting such a simple solution to a huge public policy problem, but that didn't happen."

"Since you proposed something other than gun control in your debate, the all-high-and-mighty Professor Schumer merely ignored the research and your suggestions. It certainly sounds reasonable that changing public policy could possibly alter the underlying cause of an out-of-control murder rate in those areas. That would save lives, but he obviously doesn't care about that," Adrien said.

"Exactly!" Rachael exclaimed. "Since murder is such a huge problem in a very small area within the United States, then it stands to reason that there may be something unique to those areas that public policy could have a hand in helping. Reducing the murder rate and saving lives has to be something good, doesn't it?"

"It should be a good thing, but crazy people like your professor don't always see things that way. You're way too good at this public policy stuff to start thinking about switching to economics," Adrien said. "Besides, it's too late to change now. You're too close to graduation. On the other hand, a minor in economics should make you more valuable in the job market."

Rachael became distracted thinking about the viability of having a political administration degree with a minor in economics. She was jolted back from her private thoughts when Brian continued the discussion.

"I'll bet that a high legal gun ownership rate is not a factor in the high murder rate in those counties," Brian stated.

"It's not, which is why I don't understand why he'd threaten me with failing his course if I'd be able to use that research to help people," Rachael said, tears welling up in her eyes again.

"Here, eat some ice," Brian said, offering her the remnants of his soda.

"Thanks," Rachael said, taking the cup from him. She deftly flicked the plastic lid off, raised it to her lips, and carefully shook a few ice cubes into her mouth.

"If you did your research, and you obviously have, then you probably mentioned the problems with gun-free zones," Adrien said, raising her eyebrows in expectation.

"That's another thing that really set him off, now that I think back on it," Rachael said. "I distinctly remember glancing over at him and seeing him frowning with a loathsome look on his face as he shook his head in revulsion. That's why I was trying to just duck my head and get out the door after class ended, but he called me back."

"What exactly did you say about gun-free zones?" Brian inquired. He hesitated for a moment while his mind sorted through the research he'd read about them.

"Well," Rachael replied, searching her memory of what she'd said in the debate. "I pointed out that since 1950 all of the public mass shootings except four have occurred in places where the general public can't carry guns for protection."

"Well, that'd certainly get his ban-all-guns dander up in a fluff!" Adrien said. A broad smile creased her face.

"I guess it did," Rachael said, her wan smile framed on either side by tear-streaked cheeks.

"Gun-free zones are dreams come true for any deranged person or terrorist because it's easy to find a place that doesn't allow law-abiding people with carry permits to be armed. That gives the bad guy a relatively safe place, for them at least, to kill anyone they want with only a minimal chance of anyone offering resistance," Brian paused to take a breath. "It's not right, and it's a really poor example of public policy, to put it into terms Rachael is familiar with."

He smiled at Rachael. She looked at him with admiring eyes, and they shared a private moment between them. Adrien helplessly looked on hoping this wouldn't lead to another embarrassing display of public affection.

"Of course it's not right," Adrien huffed, trying to get them reengaged in the conversation to avoid an embarrassing scene. "But the mass media virtually never reports that gun-free zones are the problem. They'd rather blame an inanimate object like a gun for the mayhem instead of the person committing the crime, or fault gun-free zones for that matter."

"As far as public policy is concerned, and that's what my class is about, don't forget," Rachael added, wiping the last remaining tear from her cheeks, "We could prevent or at least reduce the incidence of mass killings by abolishing gun-free zones."

She fell silent for a moment. Without saying another word, she put her face in her hands and began crying again.

"If Professor Schumer fails me, I'll have to stay for another whole semester because I need this course to complete my degree," Rachael wailed into her cupped hands, struggling to catch her breath in small gasps.

Adrien and Brian remained silent. They didn't have any advice to offer her.

"Oh no!" Rachael blurted out, raising her face to stare at them with a surprised look, which only highlighted her red, teary eyes. "He's the only professor who teaches that course! If he fails me, I'll have to take his public policy course over again. I'll never be able to graduate if he keeps failing me! I'll have to switch majors and that'll put me back two whole years!"

Rachael broke down into uncontrollable sobs, grieving for her wasted time and money in trying to obtain the degree that had been her dream since middle school.

"Listen," Brian said. He was compassionate but hesitant, wrapping his arm over her shoulder and pulling her toward him. "This is your last semester. You only have to get through with a passing grade then you'll graduate. Why don't you just lie low and not do anything to aggravate this guy enough to fail you?"

"Yeah, cooperate and graduate," Adrien added, a look of disgust on her face. "I hate to admit it, but that's the best plan of action. It's probably why so many of these whack-job professors can keep their teaching positions. No one complains because they want to graduate."

"If students had a decent way to file a grievance and still get their degree without being punished for expressing their views, little tyrants like Schumer would be bounced from their ivory towers. Decent professors who don't squash viewpoints that are different from their own may be able to take their place," Brian said, continuing to hold Rachael. Her sobs began to wane. "As it is, the institutions of higher learning are havens for these bullies. That only gives them a pulpit to continue foisting their beliefs onto students who in turn accept the professor's garbage as the truth. The bad part is, they begin to accept those potentially narrow-minded opinions as their own."

"So you agree that I'm in the right here?" Rachael said, sniveling while looking at Brian.

"Of course I agree with you," Brian replied, looking directly into her eyes. "And I'll always back you up on things like this. You have to learn how to pick your fights or you'll wear yourself too thin if you try to do battle all the time. This fight is just not worth it. Please cooperate and graduate. Once you're secure in a good job, then you can write a letter of complaint to the college and tell them about this situation."

"I'll do that," Rachael said, returning his stare. Their eyes locked. "I'll send a letter to the office of alumni affairs and tell them about it. I'll also mention that I won't send money back to my dear old alma mater until they get rid of despots like Schumer."

"Withholding money is a great way to draw attention to these intolerable situations," Brian replied. They continued staring at each other.

"Geez, you two!" Adrien said, kidding them with an exaggerated tone of disgust in her voice and an insincere look of revulsion on her face. "Why don't you just get a room?"

Brian and Rachael slowly shifted their eyes toward her and gave her an embellished look of shock for having made such a crude comment. Without further comment, they sheepishly untwined their arms, and as inconspicuously as possible, moved a few inches away from each other.

Of course, in the back of his mind where he kept all of his unfulfilled dreams, wants, and desires, Brian silently thought that acting upon Adrien's teasing suggestion would be a grand idea.

Fat chance of a beautiful woman like Rachael ever wanting to get romantic with someone like me, he thought to himself. He sat silently for an awkward moment trying to remember what they'd been talking about.

CHAPTER 16

TWO BOYS AND ONE GIRL

"You're doing what?" Cole demanded, looming over Rachael and glowering at her. She sat calmly on a couch with a pattern of loopy interlacing multicolored bubbles designed to hide the stains students always seemed to make on furniture in the student lounge. She didn't say anything or respond immediately in any way to his rude comment.

She kept her eyes cast toward the drab carpeting and carefully sipped at the salted caramel latte she held protectively in both hands. She was struggling to keep her anger and blood pressure from rising to dangerously high levels.

"We're organizing a demonstration so those of us who support concealed carry of legally owned and licensed firearms can someday carry them on campus. The empty holster signifies that currently our rights are not being recognized by the college administration," Rachael said in reply to his question. She knew Cole was simply trying to start another pointless fight over her political activism, and she didn't want to expend the energy it would take to become embroiled in another tiff with him. She was tiring of his insensitivity to her.

"That's the stupidest thing I've ever heard," he bellowed.

"It's not stupid but it is an attention getter," she replied. She was practicing holding her temper but was afraid she may not be able to hold it much longer. "We want to raise awareness of this issue. It's important to educate everyone that this is potentially a life or death situation."

"What is such a stupid protest supposed to prove?" he demanded. His unruly blonde hair made his flustered face appear a much deeper shade of red than it truly was.

"It's the students protesting against college policies, though it may even involve the law in some states. These arcane policies force students to be disarmed even if they're law-abiding citizens who're legally permitted to carry a concealed firearm. They can carry their firearm everywhere the law allows except on the campus where they're enrolled as a student. Just because you choose to be a student at a college or university doesn't mean you should have to give up your God-given right to self-protection as soon as you place a foot on campus property."

"Sure it does," Cole muttered. His face remained a bright red. "What are you going to do? Rush the administration building and burn it like they did during the Vietnam war?"

"Absolutely not," Rachael replied. She took a few deep breaths to calm her rapidly rising anger. "It's a peaceful demonstration that involves students wearing empty holsters to class, distributing literature, and holding debates on concealed carry issues. Some of us may sponsor a speaking event. It's good experience."

"So what is all that supposed to prove?"

"It doesn't prove anything, but it does demonstrate that criminals don't honor rules against firearms, and that leaves the law-abiding college students at a serious disadvantage," she said, explaining it with as much restraint as she could muster. "The empty holster is simply a token symbolizing that disarming citizens creates gun-free zones, which are sometimes called defense-free zones because an unarmed student is easy prey for criminals. Those make attractive targets for bad guys to hit."

"The next thing you're going to tell me is that schools create a gun-free zone that attract crazies and that's why we're having so many school shootings," Cole huffed.

"That's exactly right," she replied coolly. "Arming college students or teachers would give the legally armed citizen caught in those situations a chance to stop the crazy from hurting as many people as they are able to currently. As it stands now, the crazy person is acting without the threat of death or grave bodily injury, which could be inflicted by a legally armed citizen who, by pure chance, finds themselves at the scene of the attack."

"Bullshit!" he exclaimed loudly. "You're trying to get concealed carry on campus, which is a stupid idea in the first place, but you're going to wear an empty holster in plain view? That's idiotic."

"Yes, our goal is to get concealed carry on campus for law-abiding citizens. Until that goal becomes reality, we want to raise awareness of the situation. That can't be done with a concealed holster or any other hidden object. Since we can legally wear an empty holster without a gun in it, that's what we're doing to make a visible statement on this issue," she said, emphatically poking her finger in his direction to help make her point.

"And you're going to take pictures of each other wearing empty holsters so you can plaster it all over the Internet and let everyone around the world know you're being idiots?"

"We'll take video also. If it's not recorded and broadcast it loses most of its impact," she replied frostily. "And don't call me an idiot."

"I didn't call you an idiot," he said quickly, knowing he was on the verge of getting in trouble with her if he resorted to calling her names. "It's this whole idea that's idiotic. Now everyone on Facebook and Instagram will know about this lunacy also."

"That's the idea," she quipped triumphantly.

"I need a coffee," Cole said, abruptly turning away in disgust before walking briskly toward the coffee counter.

Rachael sat and stewed, her anger simmering. Then melancholy took hold of her emotions.

He can be such an asshole at times, she thought. She sat with her latte in her hand but didn't sip from the cup. Instead, she sat still and stared at it as her preoccupied mind flitted from one thought to the next.

She was still staring absently into space when Brian unexpectedly appeared with his trumpet case swinging nonchalantly from one hand and his tattered and dirt-smudged backpack slung precariously over his opposite shoulder.

"Well, you sure look glum," he said, cheerfully beaming a smile as he stopped directly in front of her. He looked down at her with trusting, puppy dog eyes.

"Hello there," Rachael replied, a grateful smile appearing from beneath her furrowed brow. Then her smile disappeared and she asked, "What are you doing here?"

"Oh, I had to meet Jack Higgins, the bass player from the jazz band, to give him some guitar picks the band director received as promotional items from some company that wants our input on their new design," he replied. "I'm glad I met you here. May I sit down?"

"Sure," she replied demurely, scooching over to make room for him on the couch.

He shrugged off his backpack and let it fall heavily to the floor beside the couch, set his trumpet case gently beside it, and gingerly lowered himself onto the couch. He made sure to keep a respectable distance between Rachael and himself.

While he was still situating himself, she leaned forward, and in a conspiratorial voice, said, "Cole and I were just discussing the empty holster demonstration."

"I'll bet he was thrilled to hear about you being involved in that!" he said, chuckling at the thought.

"Yeah, well," she replied hesitantly. "Cole is Cole. You know."

"I guess," he said. Then, he tried to change the subject. Brian really didn't want to think about Cole being Rachael's boyfriend.

"What do you know about Adrien's boyfriend, Lance?" he asked. He wasn't really interested in the relationship between Adrien and Lance, but it was the only thing he could think of to change the subject away from Cole.

"He's really nice," Rachael said, becoming more animated, visualizing Lance in her mind. "He really treats her well and they seem to be getting very close these days."

"They didn't used to be?" he asked.

"Adrien really didn't pay any serious attention to him at first," Rachael replied. "She was rather cool to his advances for quite a while. Eventually, she began to think of him and her as a couple, and then things began moving more quickly after that."

"I didn't know that."

"Yep, he tried to get her to go out with him for over a year. She kept putting him off and then he joined the Students for Concealed Carry group on campus. That gave them some common ground and they started talking. Of course, Adrien still has her doubts. She thinks Lance isn't a real strong supporter of the Second Amendment and only joined the group to be close to her. She's always a skeptic," she said. "The next thing you know they're going out and soon thereafter they began dating each other exclusively."

"Cool," he said. "It's a real love story."

"It is," Rachael replied. "Hey, listen, I've been meaning to ask you ..."

"What the hell are you doing here?" Cole demanded, striding up to them. He was antagonistically posturing and waving his hand to intimidate Brian. "Shouldn't you be off tooting your horn or something?"

"Cole! Don't be so ignorant!" Rachael admonished him. She tersely set her a salted caramel latte on the sturdy laminate end table, taking great care to not spill the hot liquid.

"I turn my back for a minute and he sneaks right in here and takes my seat."

"You weren't even sitting here, and he did not sneak!" she snapped. Without saying a word, Brian stood up meekly.

"I'm going to class," he said, moving to pick up his battered trumpet case and frayed backpack. "I just had to ask Rachael a question."

"Well, you asked it, and now you can be on your way," Cole growled. He puffed out his chest and moved in closer, placing his flushed, scowling face within a foot of Brian's. "And don't bother us again."

"Cole!" Rachael scolded him. She stood and faced him the best she could with the arm of the couch in her way. "There's no reason for you to be acting like this!"

"See you later," Brian mumbled, turning away. He sauntered slowly away without saying another word or further acknowledging either of them.

"Dweeb," Cole sneered derisively under his breath. For a moment, he watched Brian walk away. He had a smirking grin of triumph on his face. With a start, he remembered Rachael was standing beside him. She was glaring at him with hate-filled eyes.

He turned to face her, his face softened in apology, and he stammered, "Hey, listen ..."

"NO! You listen," Rachael snarled under her breath. She didn't want everyone in the student lounge to hear her though most of them were trying to listen intently. "You're out of line and really skating on thin ice with me. Straighten up your act or else."

"Listen," he pleaded. He knew he had to try to assuage her anger and not let it fester.

"Not now Cole, not now," Rachael said sternly, holding her palm toward him in the universal sign to back off. She gathered her belongings and stormed off, abandoning Cole.

"Aw shit!" he muttered. Then he sheepishly looked around to see who'd witnessed his humiliating display of childishness.

CHAPTER SEVENTEEN

MUGGING OF INNOCENTS

"Thanks for walking with me down to the laundromat," Alexandra Thomas said to Brian. They were walking side by side down the grime coated street. Swirling clouds of putrid red dust spun in tiny tornadoes of airborne crud as persistent wind battered them mercilessly.

They were trying to be good-humored and gracious, but flying debris made it difficult.

"It's my pleasure," Brian replied, shifting his tattered backpack into a better position over his left shoulder, which placed it on the street side opposite from Alexandra. His mother had taught him at an early age that any time he was walking with a woman, he should always be on the street side of the sidewalk. The theory was to protect her from traffic, as well as the wind and grit thrown up by cars speeding by. Dust devils stirred by the chilly wind funneling down the street made it a moot gesture.

But it was the gentlemanly thing to do, so Brian did it.

He also carried his trumpet case on his left so he could place his body a little closer to Alexandra's. His motive could not be viewed as a gentlemanly thing to do, but he didn't care. Alexandra didn't care either. She liked being close to Brian. Neither of them seemed to care that the uneven weight distribution gave him a decided list to his port side.

They sauntered lazily down the uneven sidewalk, deviating only slightly from their path to avoid stepping on scruffy tufts of yellowish-brown grass that grew out of almost every crack in the crumbling concrete. There were few people left on the streets after dark due to the economic decline that plagued the once-prosperous working-class neighborhood abutting their college campus.

The unearthly yellow glow of solitary streetlights strategically situated at the intersection of cross streets lent a surreal quality to the scene surrounding the young man and woman as they verbally sparred in the timeless practices that defined the dating rituals of humans.

"I like spending time with you even if all you're doing is going to the laundromat," he said, gazing upon her like a love-sick beagle. "I'd rather spend time with you than do anything else I can think of."

"That's so sweet," she crooned, bashfully casting her radiant blue eyes downward. She wasn't looking at the depressing grime of the neglected sidewalk because her mind and attention was riveted on Brian. The joy she felt at that moment made her blind to the depressing landscape they were meandering through.

"Here, let me take that sack of laundry from you, it looks pretty heavy," he said. He raised his free hand to remove the straps of the laundry bag from her slender but shapely shoulder. His hand lingered longer than necessary, but Alexandra didn't mind.

"You can't carry all that," she said, shrugging out from beneath the crushing weight of the overstuffed bag. "Let me carry your trumpet case, at least."

"Thanks," he said, handing the case to her. With a mighty heave, he slung the heavy laundry bag onto his scrawny shoulder with a not-so-subtle grunting noise. "Carry the trumpet on the opposite side from your backpack to better distribute the weight so your load won't be off balance."

"The laundry bag is heavier than usual because I have a bunch of quarters my mom gave me. It's a lot less of a hassle to feed the washing machines and dryers at the laundromat if I don't have to fight that dollar-changing machine they have hanging on the wall."

"I hate using those machines," Brian said. "They don't work half the time and then I not only lose my dollar, but I don't have change to wash my clothes. The whole trip ends up being just a huge waste of time."

"That's true!" Alexandra said. "My mom tries to think of everything I'll need to make things as easy as possible for me. She says she does it because she loves me. I think that's so cute! She really does miss me though, I can tell, and she hates that I'm so far away from home."

Brian grinned at her, admiring the curves of her face.

"And there's never an attendant on duty who can help you get your money back," she said with a smile that showed wide even teeth gleaming from behind full, luscious red lips. "Especially after five o'clock."

"Everyone wants to get home to relax after a hard day of work," he replied absentmindedly. His attention was fixed on three men who'd moved like mythical wraiths mysteriously materializing out of the mottled stygian shadows in the middle of the block. They were only ten feet away from them and closing quickly.

Without warning, Brian rudely grasped her biceps then pulled her closer to him. His adrenaline-charged grip made his vise-like hold of her slender arm much stronger and far cruder than the gentlemanly caressing touch he usually used when guiding women through a door or toward a chair in a restaurant.

"What the ..." she yelped in surprise. Her head whipped around to look up at him. The scowl on her face seemed to ask, "What's the matter with you?"

"Good evening, folks," Marty Noorey said. He quickly veered in front of Brian, blocking his path. He knew the tall, skinny young man wouldn't turn and flee leaving his girlfriend behind.

Alexandra's head whipped around to stare at the man speaking to them. She'd been totally unaware of him moving toward them.

"What do you guys want?" Brian asked, a tremor betraying his voice as he struggled to sound nonchalant. Without replying, Alex Doyle and Joey Valentino skirted to their flanks. Joey came in on Brian's burdened left side while Alex slickly swooped in on Alexandra's right.

Brian and Alexandra crowded closer together in a desperate attempt to assume a defensive position. Brian was still firmly holding Alexandra's upper arm trying to guide her backward. He knew they had to create distance between them and the rough men.

It was a desperate attempt to gain a few precious steps of a head start in what he hoped would be a mad dash back the way they'd come. He knew it was the safest route to take out of this increasingly dangerous situation.

He thought he'd have to try holding the three men off with his bare hands, and knew it'd be a losing battle. He didn't have a chance to be valiant.

Joey and Alex each took a premeditated sideways step that placed them slightly behind their prey. The streetwise career criminals anticipated Brian's next move, but still paused, waiting to be sure of what Brian's reaction would be.

They ignored Alexandra for the moment. The look of abject fear radiating from her pallid face like a beacon told them she couldn't formulate a plan of action. She was obviously too frozen by fear to move.

She'd never considered having to use violence, or the best way to retreat from a threat. This was her first exposure to the sad, brutal realities of life.

Realizing the situation called for the use of physical force and there was no way to avoid confrontation, Brian slid his backpack off his shoulder and held Alexandra's laundry bag in front of him as an impromptu shield. It was a reasonable plan, but one he'd never have an opportunity to use.

Before Brian could realize what was happening, Joey stepped forward, shifted all his weight from his trailing foot to the other, and threw a sucker punch that drove his knobby, ebony-hard and fight-scarred knuckles into Brian's temple.

Brian's entire body sagged, his knees buckled, and his head lolled listlessly forward. Before he could fall to the ground, Marty hit him square in the mouth with a roundhouse punch that almost mimicked the one Joey had flung into side of Brian's head a split second previously.

Brian's head snapped backward on his limp neck, jamming the facet joints of his cervical spine together with such tremendous force that it assured he would suffer periodic and debilitating neck pain for the rest of his life.

In that same irretrievable instant, Brian's lips split in a shower of splattered blood and shattered teeth. He continued plummeting to the ground where he landed in an unresponsive heap. He'd lie in this exact spot without moving until paramedics scooped up his limp body thirty-five minutes later to rush him to the hospital. By that time, his brain would be swelling from the devastating trauma it had just endured.

Later in the evening of the attack, when the emergency room personnel at the hospital questioned him, Brian wouldn't be able to remember the events leading up to his injury or anything that transpired over the three hours following his unscheduled trip to the hospital.

Brian lost consciousness the instant Joey's rock-hard fist contacted the vulnerable side of his head. As he lay unconscious, he was unaware that the damage wreaked by the savage blow resulted in his brain suffering a concussion, which immediately and unceremoniously caused an alteration in his normal brain function.

Due to parietal lobe damage, Brian would always suffer a reduction in his ability to process sensory information, which altered his ability to know where parts of his body were in time and space.

The second injury to his brain occurred when Marty's massive fist smashed his lips and front teeth to bloody pulp. This blow added significantly to the total amount of brain damage Brian suffered that night. Damage to the frontal lobe of his brain from Marty bashing his face would eventually affect Brian's ability to move his body smoothly and remember important details of his life.

Thirty years later, the incident wouldn't be recognized as the cause of him beginning to experience early signs of dementia due to the debilitating later-stage consequences of concussion.

Brian would never realize the connection between the injuries he received that evening and eventual onset of dementia, but over the next few weeks, he did lament the tragic loss of the embouchure he'd spent the previous twelve years developing. He'd sat for hours playing musical scales on his trumpet to build up the facial muscles, lips, tongue, and teeth into a harmonious team of body parts that allowed him to play his beloved instrument in an accomplished and melodious manner.

He'd never be able to play the trumpet again following the events of that fateful night with anything more than a raspy, irritating blare that spewed sluggishly from an instrument's shiny depths. Trying different mouthpieces, and a slew of different trumpets borrowed from friends, wouldn't make a difference. The dismal results would forever be the same.

Before Brian's flaccid body hit the dust covered pavement like a cloth sack stuffed full of wet oatmeal, Alex had taken control of the situation by clamping his hand over Alexandra's mouth. When Alex's hand sealed her mouth, she had been sucking in a lungful of air to scream. His hand effectively kept her silent and assured she had enough oxygen to survive the encounter.

Swiping his leg viciously into the back of Alexandra's knees, and wrenching her head back and downward, Alex was able to drop his prey to the ground in one swift, smooth motion. He didn't waste energy or compassion trying to make sure she landed gently, and she landed heavily on her buttocks.

When her coccyx contacted the unforgiving concrete, a blinding lightning bolt of incapacitating pain shot from her tailbone to her brain as the row of tiny bones separated and shifted in separate directions. The dislocated bones would never again regain their natural positions, and life-long low back pain would plague her till death.

To Alex's delight, she was immediately disoriented and temporarily paralyzed with pain. He liked his victims being defenseless and at his mercy.

Roughly throwing her sideways to the ground, and in the same fluid motion, twirling acrobatically around like a whirling dervish, he spun her onto her belly before crashing the weight of his entire body on top of hers. His knees and legs splayed on either side of her hips. He wisely maintained a stifling, compressive gag over her mouth with his cupped hand. His abnormally strong fingers bit deeply into her baby soft cheeks.

"Check her pockets for money and only money, no jewelry or anything else that can link us to her, and then let's get the hell out of here," Marty growled in a low, gravelly voice. He knelt beside Brian's unmoving body. "I'll check this guy's pockets."

"I got the backpacks and that suitcase thing he was carrying. I left that big bag. It looks like it's just dirty laundry," Joey said, snatching up the pieces of luggage. The heavy, awkward backpacks swung wildly and banged into his knees as he tried to rapidly shuffle away from the carnage littering the desolate sidewalk. "We can check these better for any money they stashed inside once we're away from here," he called over his shoulder. He hunched his head to his chest and lengthened his stride length to hasten his getaway.

"Hey asshole!" Marty admonished Alex who lay on top of Alexandra with a hand jammed between the sidewalk and her chest. "I told you to look for money! Quit groping her boobs and do what you're supposed to do if you want to eat tonight!"

"Aw, what the hell! You don't know how to have no fun is all," Alex whined, pulling his hand out from beneath her inert body. Then, with a smirking sneer on his face, he grabbed the largest fistful of her buttocks that he could grasp. He looked up at Marty while keeping a vise-like grip on her curvaceous derriere. "You mean search her pockets like this? You sure you don't want to search them a little yourself?"

"You really are an asshole," Marty chuckled, smiling. Then, in a snarling tone, he added, "Hurry up, check her pockets and let's get out of here, we ain't got all night."

Alex gave her pockets a quick, one-handed frisking, and pulled a pair of folded, sweat-worn dollar bills from the front pocket of her skin-tight blue jeans.

Alex leaned down with his lips lightly brushing Alexandra's ear, and whispered, "You keep quiet. Stay here lying on your belly and your eyes to the ground until you count to five hundred. Slowly! Then you can stand up. If I hear anything from you before that, any scream, any yelling, anything at all, I will come back here and rape your sweet ass until your eyeballs fall out!"

With a final and unnecessarily rough shove on Alexandra's back, he yanked his hand from her mouth, heaved himself into the standing position, and began leisurely swaggering away. With an ominous growl, he muttered, "Let's get the hell out of here."

Alexandra lay still. The only sounds to be heard were rasping breaths that caused her chest to heave with each gasping mouthful of air she gulped. Her tear-soaked cheek pressed painfully against the cold concrete. She whimpered pitifully, much too afraid to move.

CHAPTER 18

COLE'S NEW APARTMENT

"You're what?" Eric Enoch asked in amazement. "How'd you manage that? Then again, you've always been one lucky son-of-a-bitch," he said as if answering his own question.

Eric had always been a big boy ever since he and Cole Hockings had started first grade together. His very tall frame was surprisingly wide with over three-hundred pounds of bone and hard muscle serving him well in his football career. He and Cole had progressed from one level of football to the next as they grew up together. Each helped the other because they weren't direct competitors for the same position on the teams they played on. It was an arrangement that worked out well for them both.

Their friendship had never wavered and when they had the opportunity to attend the same college, they sat down to fill out their applications together.

Cole was not selected to receive a football scholarship, but Eric received a full athletic scholarship because he had played in the Offense-Defense All-American Bowl, an annual high school football all-star game organized to spotlight the top high-school seniors. Cole hadn't been good enough to be chosen to play in that prestigious event but was not jealous that Eric had. They each had a realistic idea of what they were and were not capable of achieving.

Cole and Eric lived in the same freshman dormitory their first year at college, but not as roommates. They would have preferred rooming together because each of them was apprehensive about beginning their academic studies in a new and daunting environment. The first semester they were both unaccustomed to and somewhat inhibited by their unfamiliar collegial surroundings, though neither would admit it to the other.

They eventually became acclimated to college life, and by the second semester, Eric began drifting away from his life-long friend. It was natural for him to begin spending more time chumming around with other members of the college's football team and spending considerably less time with Cole.

Their friendship had remained strong, but they were not nearly as close as they'd been prior to their sophomore year.

Eric moved to the off-campus fraternity house where most of his newly-found friends from the football team were members. Cole remained on campus in a dormitory where he could be close to all the extra-curricular activities the college had to offer. He partook of intra-mural co-ed flag football, volleyball, and soccer as much as he could with his academic achievement a secondary consideration to his social life.

His father didn't like paying for an entire dorm room so his son could have a room to himself, but Cole's freshman year had been a disaster. His roommates kept moving out because of his selfish and slovenly ways.

Cole loved that his on-campus dormitory was a mere three-minute walk to the college's cutting-edge gymnasium facility geared toward helping students and faculty feel and look better. Physical fitness was also encouraged to bolster student's self-esteem. The administration had long ago learned that a happy, active, and psychologically secure student body resulted in an ever-increasing number of new students applying for admittance.

Sport facilities such as an indoor Olympic style pool, basketball courts, volleyball courts, and squash courts were dwarfed by a climbing wall equipped with safety harnesses. The gym facility was open every day of the week and was busy from the time it opened to when it closed.

The library was only another two-minute walk from the gym. This was where Cole spent the remainder of his free time that was not spent in class or at the gym. He seemed to spend more time socializing and flirting with girls at the library than he did actually studying. The main and most desirable cafeteria, The Underground, was a leisurely walk from either the library or the gym. Cole's life seemed to be ideal for him until the first semester of his senior year when he became bored with the Spartan confines of his dormitory room.

Cole took a swipe at his dripping brow with a white hand towel he clutched loosely in his hand. Then he flopped tiredly onto the bright red rubber-coated steel bench seat bolted to the wall outside the squash courts.

A split second later, Eric flopped his wide buttocks onto the bench beside Cole.

Both young men looked straight ahead and continued gulping air as fast as they could to try and recuperate after a particularly fast and rousing game of squash. Each of them was sweating profusely and didn't seem to care that the moisture dripping from their faces splattered into small pools on the floor in front of them, creating a potentially slippery and dangerous situation for anyone walking by.

"How'd you manage that?" Eric asked again.

"Yeah, well," Cole panted noisily, and then he paused because he was too out of breath to answer.

Before trying to continue answering Eric's question, Cole gulped a lung full of air. He collapsed back against the painted cement block wall, and blew out a long, forceful breath that spewed sweat across the hallway. He tossed his racket onto the bench beside him, paused for a second, and finally said, "My dad asked around. One of his business associates has an apartment with five months left on the lease, and he'll rent it to my dad for almost nothing compared to how much he's paying for my dorm room."

"How'd your dad find an apartment that'll lease for only five months?" Eric wondered aloud. "I thought they always rented for twelve months minimum because they're on an annual rental cycle."

"Well," Eric said, unsure if he should continue, but he did, with puffs of breath punctuating each sentence. "It's cheap, and my dad really likes things that don't cost him much. The only problem is, the apartment's in a community for senior citizens. That'll cramp my lifestyle a little."

"You're kidding!" Eric howled raucously, an unrestrained laugh rushing from his aching lungs. "And that makes it cheaper? Why in the hell would they let a college student of all people into a senior citizen apartment complex? Don't they know what college students do to apartments?"

"Yeah, well," Cole continued, grinning. "This deal came through a lawyer friend of my dad's. His clients got kicked out of the apartment for dealing drugs."

"They were dealing dope out of an apartment complex for old folks? I don't believe it!" Eric bawled, amused. He collapsed back against the wall in a fit of laughter.

"Yeah," Cole said, a deep, guttural belly laugh shaking his wide shoulders. "My dad's lawyer friend is representing them. They must be old hippies or something, I guess. They can only pay his retainer if they're able to sublet their apartment. That motivates everyone in this deal to get the place rented as soon as possible."

"And nobody cares you're a college student?" Eric asked, skeptical.

"They don't care who they rent it to as long as the apartment complex approves it. My dad's friend represents them too, so he'll cut them a deal if they approve me renting the place. See how that works?

It's how business is done. It all depends on who you know and how much everyone is willing to give up to make the deal work."

"They're going to rent it to a college student," Eric said, chuckling and shaking his head in disbelief.

"You bet. No self-respecting senior citizen wants to rent an apartment dope was being dealt out of. It damages their social image, you know," Cole said, poorly imitating a high society Bostonian accent. Then he continued in his normal voice, "So my dad was able to get it for next to nothing, which makes him happy, and it gives me the freedom I want. Everyone wins."

"You'll have to walk quite a way to get to the gym and library where you always hang out," Eric said, thinking about the logistics. Then, with a sideways glare, he added, "Do you think you can handle that?"

"Don't worry, I can handle it," Cole replied. "I already have a parking permit for the library and the gym is right next door. I try to think of everything. Being prepared is very important if you're going to get ahead in this world. Don't you agree?"

Eric did not reply for a moment. He was deep in thought.

"You can have all kinds of parties, you lucky S.O.B.," Eric said. He continued breathing heavily and gulping air from their recent athletic contest. He mulled the possibilities around in his mind of having his close friend having an off-campus apartment. He liked thinking about the possibilities and how he could fit into the various scenarios he was imagining.

"Not really," Cole said, his voice dispirited. "I had to promise to not have more than four people in the apartment at one time, and definitely no loud music or yelling. Those old people will call the cops on me in a skinny minute, then the owners will throw me out immediately. It's a promise I plan on keeping. They were nice enough to allow the former tenants to sublet the place and I don't want to screw up this sweet deal."

"So when are you having me and my girlfriend over?" Eric replied huskily, his mind wandering to the opportunity of spending some private time with her without all his fraternity brothers knowing about it. "We can make a nice dinner date with you and Rachael. How many bedrooms does this apartment have?"

"It's a two bedroom, you horny bastard," Cole said, chuckling deviously. "I already thought about having you two over. You just have to keep it quiet. Remember the old folks! They like their quiet time and don't want you grunting and groaning all night long."

"Aw, they'll probably have their hearing aids out and be heading to an early bedtime," Eric joked disrespectfully. "If they're not sleeping all the time, they have the volume on their television sets turned way up so they can hear it. Then they fall asleep in front of the television! That's what old folks do. They won't hear us, don't you worry."

"I do have to worry," Cole said. "No loud noises or yelling. I promised."

Eric ignored what Cole said.

"Do you need help moving your stuff from your dorm to the apartment?"

"I was hoping you'd ask," Cole replied with a snicker. "Are you available Saturday morning?"

"I'll meet you in The Underground, we'll have breakfast, and then we'll get you moved."

"Well, how about dinner at eight on Saturday night?" Cole asked.

"That's a great idea!" Eric replied. "What do you think the girls will want to eat?"

"I'll make my famous spaghetti sauce with angel hair pasta. You bring the wine."

"What else do you need?"

"Nothing. It'll be fine."

"That'll be great," Eric replied. He smiled, imagining the private time he was anticipating having with his girlfriend. "It should be a memorable evening."

CHAPTER 19

LOVER'S QUARREL

The Underground was not usually crowded at three o'clock in the afternoon because it was between lunch and dinner and most students were in class. Because of its central location, it gave Rachael and Cole an opportunity to meet there on Fridays during a break they each had between classes.

Hamburgers are indigenous to college campuses throughout the United States, but The Underground was known far and wide for the superior burgers they served.

Most of the alumni, who usually visited campus during Homecoming weekend, made a stopover at The Underground for a burger a mandatory part of their visit. Homecoming was always held in the beautiful autumnal weather of October. That way alums could ogle the kaleidoscope of colors radiating from the changing leaves of the deciduous trees that adorned the steep mountainsides surrounding the college.

These intrepid guests descended upon The Underground in such great numbers that the cafeteria administration had to hire, orient, and train extra staff just for this one occasion. They'd also order triple their usual amount of supplies just for that special weekend. This ensured no one would be denied the exquisitely prepared burgers they so warmheartedly remembered from their halcyon college days.

It was with the expectation of a leisurely meal consisting of one of The Underground's famous burgers that Rachael and Cole found themselves sitting across from each other at one of the communal tables lined up in straight rows across the cavernous room.

Rachael stacked her burger with a modest amount of smoked gouda cheese, baby greens, dill pickles, and slathered a light coating of mayonnaise over the bottom of the challah bun. A spritz of yellow mustard graced the top and added a dash of color to the menagerie. Overall, it made a neat package she could consume while keeping her dignity intact.

Cole, on the other hand, piled yellow American, Swiss, and cheddar cheeses in an untidy mound atop his burger before smothering it all with a huge mound of Asian coleslaw.

Most people would have been more moderate with the amount of slaw heaped on their sandwich, but not Cole. He didn't seem to care that it refused to be confined by the boundaries of the ciabatta roll his burger was precariously perched upon.

The mess he made while consuming an Underground burger was legendary.

A colossal heap of perfectly fried sweet potato fries vied for space on his crowded plate. There always seemed to be either a few fries or a glob of coleslaw squirting off the sides of his plate, but Cole simply ignored the mess. Eventually, he'd get around to spearing the escapees with an industrial grade fork then ferociously shove them into his gaping maw of a mouth.

Rachael sat nibbling absentmindedly at the edges of her burger after having gracefully pushed up the sleeves of her canary yellow shirt. It was one of her favorites because it was made of a stretchy, spandex fabric that resisted wrinkles and was soothingly comfortable in a wide range of temperatures. She took extraordinary care to not allow it to be stained with burger juice or drippy condiments.

In between nibbles, she watched Cole with wonderment. She never tired of watching him savagely shovel the scattered remnants of food from his plate into his mouth. It reminded her of feeding time at the zoo when her parents took her there when she was a young child. The comparison made her smile.

With a satisfied burp, Cole sat back, cast a quick, covetous glance at Rachael's uneaten burger, and with all of the couth of a Cossack asked, "What's the matter with you? Don't like your burger?"

"The burger is great, as usual," she replied softly. "I just don't have much of an appetite."

"Are you still upset about what happened to that wimp you and Adrien always hang around with?" he asked gruffly.

Adrien slowly and carefully set her burger down, and then she looked directly into Cole's eyes. "His name is Brian, Brian Breen."

"Yeah, him," Cole said, brusquely wiping his hands clean of sticky burger residue with the tattered remains of a paper napkin. "He gets the shit kicked out of him because he was chasing tail in a bad part of town and that's got you too upset to eat? He's not worth it."

"Really, Cole? That's the most sympathy you can show for someone who was seriously injured?"

"He was in a bad place and got what he deserved. Nothing more, nothing less. It was his fault, as far as I'm concerned. He was asking for it."

"It was not his fault! Brian's a student who was unable to defend himself against violent attackers because this damned college won't allow concealed carry on campus," Rachael said. Tears of fear, rage, and concern began streaming down her face.

"He couldn't have been hurt that bad. He was just punched a few times from what I heard," Cole said, looking longingly at the remnants of Rachael's burger. Rachael moved her plate closer to her.

"His parents had to take him home. The doctors at the hospital didn't want him to be alone for the next week or so. His mother says they have to keep him under observation to be sure he's not having any problems that pop up unexpectedly."

Not wanting to get into a fight over Brian, a man he really didn't care much for or about, Cole made the decision to show some concern for him. He knew it'd be disingenuous, but that didn't bother him, and he wanted to stay in Rachael's good graces.

"You talked to his mother?" he asked, trying to inject a sympathetic tone into his voice. He failed.

"Yes," she replied. "I didn't know about him getting mugged until Adrien told me about it. Neither one of us had his home address or phone number so we searched the Internet. It only took a minute to find his parent's phone number at their home. She was a very nice person and we spoke for almost an hour."

"Did you talk to him?"

"No, just to his mother," she replied. For some reason she was wary with her reply, and she wondered why. "He wasn't able to speak much because of the injury to his mouth. His mom said it took him a few days to get even a few words out, and they were almost unintelligible. His missing front teeth and smashed lips make it really painful to speak."

"Yeah, well," Cole stammered. He had no sympathy for Brian and couldn't figure out what to say to continue this charade.

"It's all horrible, just horrible," she sobbed.

"How's he doing overall?" he asked, furtively glancing at his cell phone to see how much time they had left before having to leave for class. "Besides his busted up chops, I mean."

"He's coherent, and knows who he is, but that's about all," she said, then began sobbing with increasing anguish. She snatched a paper napkin from the ever-present dispenser placed on each table in The Underground and blew her runny nose. "He can barely talk because his mouth is all busted up, but other than that, there aren't any outward signs of him being hurt too badly, at least nothing his mother mentioned."

"That's not too bad," Cole said, hoping to end this conversation.

"He sleeps a lot," Rachael said. "His mother says the doctor thinks it's from a concussion."

"Getting hit in the mouth may help his pitiful wailing on that horn he's always carrying around," Cole said, forgetting his charade for a moment.

"Cole! That's a mean thing to say!" she admonished him. "They stole his trumpet, and when the police found it in a dumpster later that night it had been smashed beyond repair."

"Huh!" was all Cole said, glancing again at the time on his cell phone.

"He loved that trumpet," she sniffed, and then a disheartened keening sound escaped her grief-constricted throat.

"You going to eat the rest of your burger?" he asked, hungrily eyeing her food.

"Yes, I am," she replied irritably. "Can't you have any feelings at all for someone who was savagely attacked? They were only walking to a laundromat for crying out loud! It was such a simple, innocent thing to be doing. They probably didn't think something like this would ever happen so close to campus."

"Not really," Cole replied coolly. "It was his girlfriend who was doing her laundry. He was probably just along so he could peek at her undies coming out of the dryer."

He thought he had been witty, so he finished with a sly smile.

"Cole! That's rude!"

Her face began to redden to a deeper hue that bordered on becoming purple. She calmed herself before trying to say anything else. "You think you're being funny, but you're really not."

"So, what time do you think you'll be getting to my new apartment tomorrow night?" he asked, trying to change the subject. "Eric and I should have everything set up by five o'clock with the kitchen ready to go."

"It depends on what time you're planning on serving dinner," Rachael replied curtly, allowing him to change the subject but not forgetting his demeanor only a moment ago. She inconspicuously moved her plate a few more inches closer to her chest and draped her forearms on either side of it to protect it from Cole's predatory grasp.

"Eric and his girlfriend, whatever her name is, are supposed to be there at seven," he replied. "Do you think you could be there about five to help me get the food ready?"

"Her name is Elena, Elena Spacek," Rachael replied. "I can be there about six. I'm studying at the library with some friends all afternoon to get ready for a big test we have coming up and I want to stop by my dorm room to get freshened up a bit before coming over."

"Six?" he snorted. "I'll need some help getting dinner ready. I thought I could count on you."

"It's only spaghetti and canned sauce with Italian bread on the side, for crying out loud," she said. She didn't try to hide the irritation in her voice or the look of contempt on her face. "It'll take you less than five minutes to plop the dry spaghetti into a pot of boiling water then start warming the sauce in a small pan. Even you can do that."

"We're having a salad also," he replied defensively.

"You bought the mixed spring salad greens in a bag from the supermarket. They're already washed and ready to go," she said, knowing he just wanted her to do all the cooking while he drank beer. "How hard is it to throw that into a big bowl, give it a toss or two, and then lay some chopped tomato and onion slices on top?"

"I was counting on you to do that," he shot back angrily. "I thought you'd be happy for me getting an apartment of my own."

"I'm happy for you," she said, feeling obligated to reply to his comment. "I just don't want you to think I'm going to be over there all the time, especially doing what you have on your horny little mind."

"Darned," he muttered under his breath, trying to make a joke. Rachael ignored him.

"Really, Cole, I have some really challenging courses this semester that I have to study really hard for just to pass with a halfway decent grade. Then there're all my other activities on campus that keep me busy. It's almost impossible to find enough time to keep up with it all. You know that."

"By saying 'other activities on campus,' do you mean that concealed carry crap you and Adrien are endlessly harping on?" he sniffed, a look of disgust on his face. "You better not yap all night about that garbage tonight. I don't want Eric and what's-her-name to have to put up with you yammering on and on about that drivel. It'll ruin the entire celebration."

"Elena, her name is Elena. You better remember that for tomorrow," she shot back at him angrily.

"And you better not bring up that self-defense bullshit. Especially don't be going on about how Brandon got his ass kicked because he couldn't carry a gun. The wimp should go to the gym and put some muscle on himself so he can be man enough not to need a gun."

He glared at her, stood up, and without another word, grabbed his backpack.

"I have to get to class. See you tomorrow five, if you can make it." Then, with a mighty heave, he shouldered his pack and began sauntering away.

"I said I'd be there at six!" Rachael called after him. "Not five!"

Then she sat for a moment and mulled over the other things he'd said. Suddenly she remembered what had been bugging her.

"Brian!" she yelled after him so forcefully that her voice cracked and a few of the sparse diners stared. "His name is Brian!"

Rachael sat staring after him. Tears of anger and frustration welled in her eyes, but this time there were not enough of them to begin spilling down her cheeks.

Before she was able to do anything other than flex her fists into tighter balls, a tall, shapely young lady with flawless creamy brown skin that seemed to glow with the lusciousness of a Hershey chocolate bar slid out of the booth beside the table Rachael was sitting at. Rachael looked up at her classmate Nika who said, "Rachael honey, if I were you, I'd dump that asshole. It doesn't matter how good looking he is. There're plenty of good guys out there, you just have to open your eyes to see them. See you in class, it starts in five minutes."

Without another word, the statuesque woman straightened herself to her full height and strode away on long, smoothly swinging legs. Her swaying hips slid seductively from side-to-side while she absentmindedly straightened the large, glittering bangles that hung limply from both earlobes. She put a lot of effort into keeping them from tangling in the loopy collar of her form-fitting sweater.

"I can't just dump Cole," Rachael growled to herself in a low mechanical tone. She stood up and took a moment to steady her wobbly legs.

Standing beside the table littered with the remains of the lunch she and Cole had just shared, she mulled over what was already seeping into her thoughts, *I really should dump him, I guess, but he's been so supportive of me since Daddy passed away. I can't just dump him without a good reason. He doesn't deserve that. Well, yes he does. I don't know what to do. I hate him but I love him. That's stupid.*

With her mind reeling with confusion, she stooped and grabbed the strap of her backpack. Using all her strength, she gave the bag a robust tug, snatching it from the floor. With one fluid motion she slung it over her shoulder. It bounced off her back, throwing her slightly off balance.

Then, in a flash of lucidity, she made a definitive decision regarding her relationship with Cole. Clarity returned to her thoughts and her future with him became crystal clear in her mind.

Taking a moment to compose herself both mentally and physically, she stood to her full height, and raised her chin. It was confirmation of her newly formulated commitment to be her own woman.

Then, with deliberate and smooth movements, she shook her long, flowing chestnut brown hair free from her shoulders so it hung loosely down her back, and began following Nika to class.

CHAPTER 20

BAD BOYS BIG NIGHT OUT

"Why you figure those old folks still have lights on at eleven o'clock at night?" Alex asked, a puzzled tone in his voice. "Don't those old folks go to bed early?"

"They're dealing dope, you asshole," Joey said callously. Adrenaline was coursing through his veins due to anticipation, putting him on edge. "They're staying up for junkies who need what they have. Most of them sleep late because they're up most of the night getting high. They're only starting to come out to play about now."

"Yeah, they're out all night then they can't get they asses out of bed in the morning," Marty said, gruffly confirming what Joey had said. "They only wake up in midafternoon or so then they'll be ready to stay up all night again. It must be a bitch to live that way. There ain't nothin' good about dope the best I can tell."

Marty Noorey was not only the most intelligent of the trio but also the most handsome. He had a dark complexion, hawkish nose, large green eyes, and slender eyebrows that peeked out from beneath a tussled mop of curly bangs that cascaded across his forehead. He was tall, muscular, and slender at the waist. He usually turned the heads of most women when entering a room.

Alex Doyle, on the other hand, had missed out on both intellect as well as good looks. His round face and double chin seemed to engulf his small pouty mouth that sported small, yellowed teeth with wide uneven gaps between them. When the boys in his second and third grade classes had likened him to a hideous jack-o'-lantern at Halloween time, they were not completely incorrect.

His chaotic mess of unruly red hair rarely felt the cruel uniformity of a comb's teeth. Deep, dirt saturated creases etched the flushed, ruddy skin of his cheeks from just below his bulging bloodshot eyes to skirt unevenly around his pig-like nose. A forest of wild, shiny black hairs erupted from both inside its gaping, stygian depths as well as from the center of a misshapen dark brown mole growing on its blunted tip. Small, almost black, emotionless eyes and a squat ill-defined frame only added to the heartless but truthful Halloween analogy of his youthful classmates.

Joey Valentino had fared much better, having had rugged good looks since the third grade, but they disappeared in a flash late one night.

A drunk who had lost a fist fight with Joey in a bar on a snow-swept January night waited for him to exit the building. He had jumped from the shadows of an adjacent alley, swinging a clenched fist that held a broken red clay brick.

The sharp, ragged edge of the brick traced its destructive path from just below the inside corner Joey's eye, smashing the zygomatic arch where the not-so-delicate cheekbone nestled tightly beside the nose. As it continued along its path, it pulverized the thin nasal bones that form the bridge of the nose and ripped the cartilaginous tip from its moorings. Only a small scrap of skin kept what was left of this nose attached to his face.

Joey fell to his knees from the unexpected blow to his face, and then, true to his nature, he grabbed his assailant's testicles, and gave them a mighty twist. He picked up the half brick when it fell from the man's grasp and repaid the brutality many times over.

The police found them lying side-by-side in the snow, bloodied and unconscious. Crimson blood splatters marred the beauty of the newly fallen snow where it sprayed as each gouging strike of the brick's jagged corners tore flesh and bone from the body of Joey's adversary.

The doctors who put Joey's face back together did a credible job, but his nose would always be crooked and a half inch off center.

The filthy brick used to smash his face caused infection, which almost killed him with sepsis, and at times, he wished it had. The infection of his face resulted in tremendous scarring and would be a constant reminder of that fight. He cringed with disgust and experienced a profound sense of loss every time he looked in a mirror.

Joey grieved every day over the disfigurement of his once-handsome features. He was always upset at the initial reaction of women meeting him for the first time, who couldn't stop themselves from reflexively recoiling in horror at their initial glimpse of him.

"So, when are we going to take them?" Alex asked anxiously.

"Ain't no better time than now," Marty replied, a sadistic smile showing brilliant white teeth in the dim light. "Let's go."

CHAPTER 21

NOT SO WONDERFUL EVENING

"That was wonderful," Elena Spacek said, laboriously pushing herself away from the camping table. It was constructed of sturdy white plastic and was normally reserved for temporary outdoor use, but it had become the decorating style of choice in college students' kitchens. The fact that it was inexpensive and easily moved from apartment to apartment added to its popularity.

The simple white plastic chair Cole purchased earlier that afternoon from the local patio and garden center moved in jerky movements. Its feet jammed into the still-serviceable dull grey carpet covering the floor of the living room where Cole and Rachael had set up the table and chairs. It made it difficult to move when someone was sitting on it, but it was an inconvenience most students were used to.

It had been Rachael's idea to make an impromptu dining room in the empty living room. She wanted to avoid the confines of the galley-style kitchen where there was barely enough room for two people to slide past each other while preparing a meal.

The foot-worn, tacky carpet forced Elena to lift the chair, move back a few precious inches, then flop unladylike onto its seat. She would then have to get a better grip on its slab-sided arm rests and lift again, repeating the sequence over and over to gain the distance from the table she desired.

Elena was a well-endowed but plain looking young woman with a round, smooth face. Freckles dotted her pale cheeks. They'd been a point of embarrassment for her all her life, but the boys seemed to adore them, so she'd learned to overlook them. She'd worn her lifeless and frizzy brown hair to the shoulders since second grade. Her deep, dark brown eyes burned with the joy of life, and her heart-shaped mouth puckered into a small but pleasant smile. She frequently flashed her brilliant smile, and it accurately reflected her friendly, down-to-earth demeanor. A brightly colored loose-fitting rumpled cotton shirt that harkened back to a style from the early 1970s effectively hid a sturdy but shapely figure. A pair of faded, form-fitting blue jeans completed her ensemble.

"What do you put into your secret spaghetti sauce?" she asked Cole, thinking about having another piece of crusty bread thickly slathered with rich, golden butter.

"It's a secret so I can't tell you," Cole said, flashing her a sly smile.

"Get out of here!" she replied playfully, pushing at the air in front of her as though she were deflecting his jibe.

"OK," he said. "I give up, but you have to promise not to tell anyone."

"I promise!"

"I grind zucchini and carrots, only about a cup of grated zucchini and a quarter cup of very finely grated carrots and add it to canned sauce with a healthy dash of avocado oil."

"That's all?"

"No, after that, I add finely minced onion, green pepper, a half teaspoon of minced garlic, and a tiny smidge of Tony Chachere's Original Creole seasoning. The real secret may be to add an extremely tiny pinch of baking soda. That takes the edge of bitterness out of it. It's the way my aunt makes it and I stole her recipe."

"I swear not to tell a soul," Elena said with a coquettish smile. "So, what are you planning on doing now that you're getting close to graduation?" She was interested in keeping the conversation going because Eric was still occupied stuffing his flushed face. She knew he'd be unable to speak without spewing food particles across the table, so she talked with Cole. At least he took a few minutes between bites to swallow.

"Well," Cole said. He spoke with a stately manner because talking about himself was his favorite subject. "I have to take the Law School Admission Test and depending on how I do there will determine what I have to do next."

"That's the LSAT, isn't it?" Elena asked, knowing it was the test used by most law schools to evaluate potential students. She wanted to play dumb to bolster Cole's already inflated ego.

"That's right," Cole replied. "I can also take the Graduate Record Exam but the LSAT seems to be the best one for getting into law school."

"You'll do great on it, I'm sure," she said. False admiration was evident in her voice, but she had a flirtatious gleam in her eyes. Cole liked that. "Then you'll go off to law school, I assume. What type of law do you want to practice?"

"I'm thinking of criminal law," Cole said, his chin rising to make himself appear more important. He grinned playfully and Elena smiled back.

"Your father wants you to go into corporate law because there's more money in it," Rachael said quickly, trying to interject herself into the conversation. She wanted to sidetrack the attraction that was obviously growing between them, even though she was contemplating breaking off her relationship with Cole.

I may end up dumping this guy, but it'll be on my *terms, not his,* she thought to herself. *The problem is, I'm not sure if I really want to dump him. I think I may be in love with him, and I don't want to screw that up...*

"I'm not sure that's really important," Cole said.

"I agree with your father. It's a good idea to get the best return on the time, money, and effort you'll be putting into law school," Rachael said. She glanced at Elena, who looked away.

Ignoring Rachael's comments with a dismissive wave of his hand, Cole continued his conversation with Elena without looking at Rachael. "I want to practice criminal law because the poor and downtrodden are only a product of the environment they grew up in. The economic system is stacked against them ever getting anything decent in this world. Maybe I can have a small part in changing that to make this a better world to live in."

"And you think they should have a good lawyer to represent them because of the way society has ignored their needs and forced them to commit crimes just to survive?" Elena inquired. She'd recognized the path Cole's reasoning was taking and she wanted to say things that agreed with his way of thinking.

"Exactly," Cole said, puffing out his chest. He smiled appreciatively at Elena for agreeing with his point of view. "You seem to understand this better than many others," he said, furtively glancing toward Rachael out of the corner of his eye to see if she caught his meaning.

"Society has thrown these people away. It's up to someone like me to make sure they get a fair trial. Maybe they can get into a work program that'll teach them useful skills. That way they can enter the mainstream of society instead of merely being punished for whatever it is they did," he continued. The more attentive Elena appeared, the more animated his speech became. "It's not their fault they turned out the way they did. They need a fair chance to be rehabilitated, otherwise they'll never be able to become productive members of society."

"But your father ..." Rachael said, trying to interject herself into the conversation.

Cole rudely interrupted her and began speaking to Elena, wanting to ignore anything Rachael may say.

Eric kept his face hovering over his plate and shoveled food into his mouth, glad that the conversation didn't require him to participate.

"The lower socio-economic classes deserve our attention more than the fat-cat corporations do," he said, reiterating what his liberal professor said in sociology class. "Giving them a good lawyer is the least we can do to show we care for them since society as a whole is ready to throw them away like a useless piece of garbage."

"But ..." Rachael stammered, desperately trying to become part of the conversation. Before she could say anything more, she was interrupted by sharp, persistent knocking.

"That must be some of the guys from the gym," Cole said. He quickly stood up, and with a spring in his step, made his way to the door. He was hoping for an excuse to avoid any further discussion with Rachael. "They probably just decided to drop by to see my new apartment."

Without looking through the peephole, Cole opened the door with a flourish and stepped back to let his guests enter.

Before Cole was able to step fully out of the way of the swinging door, Marty Noorey hit it with his shoulder, shoving it forcefully into Cole's face.

Rachael heard the snap of Cole's nose breaking and watched him fall heavily back against the wall. He clutched at his face with cupped hands, afraid to touch his crushed nose. His knees wobbled but he didn't fall, and she watched in horror as three hooded men rushed into the room. She instinctively knew they weren't fellow college students.

An electrifying jolt ran through her body. In a crystal-clear flash of insight, she realized having sweatshirt hoods pulled tightly over their heads to hide their faces was an imminent sign of danger.

Elena sat with her mouth dropped open in shock and surprise. Her mind was unable to comprehend what had just occurred. While Elena sat transfixed, Rachael grabbed her purse from beside her chair, and rushed into the bedroom at the rear of the apartment.

Elena caught a flicker of movement out of the corner of her eye as Rachael bolted for the bedroom. She jerked her head to watch Rachael disappear into the blackness beyond the gaping maw of the empty room's door. With her mind in confused and uncomprehending turmoil, she swiveled her head to again look toward Cole. Her befuddled brain raced to make sense of the calamity unfolding before her eyes.

"What the hell!" Cole roared, doubling over in pain and gingerly clutching his shattered nose. The pain diminished his ability to think clearly, and the burning pain in his face felt like an out-of-control gasoline fire.

"What the hell …" Marty unwittingly mimicked when he realized that the young man who had opened the door was not the older person he expected. Marty immediately recovered from his surprise and jabbed a solid right fist to Cole's solar plexus.

Cole plummeted to his knees in a tiny fraction of a second and landed with the sickening smack of bony knees smashing unchecked onto unforgiving linoleum flooring. He was dazed and tottered in a kneeling position for a split second. His face was a graven mask of pain, horrendous anguish, and uncomprehending amazement. His unseeing eyes fixed on an invisible point on the opposite wall.

With slow, agonizing gesticulations, and looking like a peasant bowing respectfully before a monarch, Cole slowly bent forward at the waist with the fluidity of poured molasses on a cold winter day.

With an excruciatingly slow bowing of his head, he continued toppling forward until his forehead came to rest on the cold linoleum of the foyer. He rolled onto his right side and began monotonously rocking back and forth with short, choppy groans emanating from his narrowing throat.

Alex and Joey didn't waste time ogling the devastation lying before them. Instead, they bolted past Marty, jumped deftly over Cole as he laid writhing in pain on the floor, and darted into the living room of the apartment. They knew from hard-earned experience that they had to move fast and keep moving to overwhelm their prey before they lost the element of surprise.

"What the hell ..." Eric muttered around a wad of masticated buttered bread and salad greens. He promptly dropped the bread he was holding between his index finger and thumb. With his eyes fixated on the two men hurtling at him, he began hopping his chair back from the table in short, choppy stages but thin, worn carpet grabbed incessantly at the chair legs, impeding his progress.

"What the hell ..." he angrily growled a second time, still trying to stand up. His sentence was rudely interrupted by Alex viciously smashing him on the upper side of his head with the eight-inch crescent wrench.

Alex had practiced the savage downward chopping swing he wanted to use in situations like this one, and his gnarly fist gave the wrench all the momentum it needed to get the job done swiftly and effectively. With a loud cracking noise, the blow glanced off the side of Eric's thick skull and opened a gaping gash in his scalp. A spray of blood and hair spewed unevenly across the milky white surface of the paper tablecloth Cole had thoughtfully placed over the cheap looking plastic camp table. After doing its work on Eric's skull, the wrench deflected weakly off his massively muscled shoulder.

In a flash, Alex stepped to the other side, raised the wrench across his chest and backhanded the flat side of the weapon into Eric's ear with a weak but effective blow.

Eric's legs gave out from beneath him, and he crashed heavily back into his chair. He struggled mightily with all his willpower focused on the effort to regain his footing and was able to hoist himself up halfway, but he failed to stand all the way up. His buttocks smashed weightily back into his chair again.

With a vacuous stare, he hunched his shoulders forward. His eyes were fixed on a patch of vacant air six inches in front of his face.

He woozily gazed at nothing for a few seconds, then, falling deeper and deeper into a dazed stupor as time seemed to stand still, his huge blocky head plummeted with a sodden thud into his half-eaten plate of spaghetti.

He struggled as much as he could to raise his throbbing head, but it seemed to weight a ton. He wasn't strong enough to lift it and could only get it high enough so his face was able to dangle pitifully a few scant inches above the table top. His upper body was supported in a semi-erect posture by a huge but now useless forearm resting limply on the tabletop.

A piece of limp, overcooked spaghetti protruded from his left nostril and wobbled up and down with each gulping breath he took. The right nostril, on the other hand, was packed solid with red sauce, which began bubbling comically in concert with the wobbling spaghetti noodle dancing in his left one.

He remained in that static position, his reeling mind unable to comprehend where he was or what he was doing there.

Elena, taken totally by surprise and being further outside her element or experience than she had ever been, sat in stunned silence. Not knowing what else to do, she began screaming incessantly, belting out one piercing shriek after another while gazing in horror at the savagery taking place before her eyes.

Joey took two swift steps forward and viciously snatched Elena by the hair on back of her head. She sat immobilized with fear as her attacker brutally ripped her head backward. With noxiously bad breath swirling turbulently from between his tobacco-stained teeth, he viciously snarled into her face, "Where are the old people? Where are the old people, bitch?"

Elena, frozen by fear, could only continue wailing at the top of her lungs. She mindlessly bellowed one unrelenting heart-rending shriek after another with only enough time between them to suck a sharp, choppy breath into her oxygen-starved lungs before the next long, high-pitched screech issued from her gaping mouth.

Fascinated, Joey stared intensely at a dark green piece of broccoli stuck between her brilliantly white lower molars on the right side of her mouth. With tremendous effort, he shook himself out of his reverie. He purposefully made his voice as low and rumbling as possible to appear as menacing as he could portray himself to be. He huskily demanded, "Where are the old people?"

Not getting a response from Elena, he sadistically shook her head from side-to-side before thrusting his face closer to hers. With mounting tension and frenzied impatience in his voice, he menacingly whispered into her ear, "For the last time! Where are the old people?"

In a fit of anger, he wrenched her head back even farther. It was extended to the point that her screams were becoming strangled from the tension put on her vocal cords by the muscles in the front of her neck. With disgust flowing through his veins, he slowly and meticulously placed the tip of a six-inch Craftsman flat-bladed screwdriver to the hollow of her neck.

To add emphasis to his demands, which were intended to tremendously escalate fear, tension, and ultimately submission in his victim, he began putting more and more pressure on the delicate, creamy white skin of her svelte neck with the icy cold, unforgiving tip of the screwdriver.

The pulse in her common carotid artery beat wildly, causing her alabaster skin to thump up and down with Latin-beat rapidity. The jugular veins lying beside the carotid bulged with an intense purplish hue that could only be matched on an artist's palette. The tip of Joey's screwdriver danced with each pounding pulse. The sight caused him to laugh. After a few seconds, his laughter stopped abruptly, and his mood became surly once again.

"Where are the old people, bitch? Where's the dope and money?"

Abruptly, he stopped talking and froze in place.

It took him a moment to figure out what caught his attention. Even though Elena was almost totally paralyzed with fear, her eyes widened to the point where the whites appeared to be three times the size of the pupils.

That he expected, and it was the result he was striving to achieve. But her shocked gaze was not fixed on him.

She wasn't looking at him at all. Even though his terrorizing face was only inches from hers, she was looking at something behind him. With a flood of fear-induced adrenaline rushing through his veins, Joey spun around, stood to his full height without relinquishing his cruel grip on Elena's hair, and gazed uncomprehendingly toward the rear bedroom doorway to face whatever terror had captured Elena's attention.

A deafening roar and blinding flash of yellow-orange flame split the air. A split second later, his head exploded into a fine mist of cascading vapor.

The nine-millimeter Inceptor ARX High Penetration bullet was designed to transfer maximum energy to a target via hydrodynamic ram effect. Upon firing, its unique shape magnified its surface area and utilized the destructive rotational force of the projectile to wreak devastation on its target. The result was a self-defense round engineered to perform far beyond the stopping power and terminal performance of most expanding handgun bullets on the market.

The 80 grain ARX bullet struck Joey's forehead at 1445 feet-per-second and instantaneously transmitted 371 foot-pounds of energy to the anatomical structures of his head at the time of impact.

After slicing through the skin and piercing the frontal bone of his skull, it rotationally drilled through the frontal sinuses. Performing as it was designed, it bore its way in a straight line through the frontal lobe of his brain then liquefied the basal ganglia on its devastating path through the center of his head.

The bullet's blistering speed was significantly diminished by resistance offered by the various consistencies of bodily tissues it traversed. Even after it slowed down, it still had enough speed remaining to blow a two-inch hole through the occipital bone making up the back of his head.

A fine mist of blood and vaporized neurological tissue flew nine feet beyond where he had stood.

Life promptly left Joey's body and he plummeted to the ground in a ragged heap. He didn't attempt to halt his uninhibited fall because he couldn't. He was dead a nanosecond after bullet impact. If it hadn't been for the force of gravity collapsing the weight of his earthly remains onto his lungs, his final breath would have never left his body.

Both Marty and Alex looked toward the source of the horrific blast and saw Rachael standing in a Weaver stance with only her right eye and arm visible beyond the bedroom's door frame. Her black shoulder bag was at her feet, and the Walther CCP handgun equipped with a set F8 Night Sights was in her hands. With shocked horror, they saw the silvery pistol smoothly and deliberately swinging in their direction.

Without hesitation, Marty darted for the front door.

Cole was still rolling pitifully back and forth in small, jerky motions on the floor. Taking a long, single leap Marty vaulted over Cole's writhing body and headed toward the door.

In his haste, Marty overran the doorway and bounced off the wall across the hall from Cole's apartment. Breathing a sigh of relief to be out of the apartment, he turned left and bolted as quickly as his panicked feet would carry him toward the street.

Instead of immediately following in Marty's footsteps, Alex, being dimwitted, made the fatal decision to throw his crescent wrench at the shooter.

Wasting a valuable and irretrievable split second, he wound up like a baseball pitcher tossing the final throw of his career in the seventh game of the only World Series he'd ever be in. He took a long step forward as the arm holding the wrench whipped from behind his head.

He let it fly with a tremendous amount of anger-fueled force that propelled it end-over-end the short distance across the room. Its fast, arching trajectory homed in on Rachael's exposed and extremely vulnerable head like a laser-guided missile.

The heavy crescent wrench carried an incredible amount of kinetic energy due to its mass and density. It raced toward its soft, fleshy target and was fully capable of inflicting serious injury and instantly incapacitating Rachael with a horrible and potentially fatal wound if it hit her, but it didn't.

Instead, the hastily flung wrench imbedded itself in the dry wall beside the bedroom door. With a puff of dust, it stuck parallel to the floor with only three inches of its length protruding from the gaping hole in which it came to rest.

Rachael began taking the slack out of the trigger and had only moved it a smidge before the wrench left Alex's hand. Just as the wrench struck the wall, her index finger completed the trigger press. Alex was off balance and fully extended toward her, still looking like a professional baseball pitcher releasing a blistering fast ball from the mound in a World Series game.

The Walther's trigger broke cleanly and sent the second bullet she'd fire that night down the handgun's three-and-a-half-inch barrel. After traversing the short thirteen feet separating Alex from Rachael, it blasted through the fourth rib on the left side of his body near its juncture with his breastbone.

Needle-like shards of fragmented rib bone arched outward from the point of entry. The rapidly rotating bullet churned its devastating path toward Alex's vena cava, the largest vein in the human body which empties oxygen-depleted blood returning from the head, arms, and the lower portions of the body directly into the right atrium of the heart. But for Alex, the small tear in the wall of this important vessel would no longer allow it to perform its vital functions.

Alex may have been intellectually weak, but his survival instincts were exceptionally strong.

Almost of its own volition and without conscious thought, Alex's body began twisting toward the door as it followed through and righted itself from the frenzied gyrations it performed to propel the wrench at Rachael.

Without wasting any time on unnecessary movements, his legs began pumping furiously, propelling him out the doorway in an impetuous dash to safety. He bounced off the wall across the hall from Cole's apartment in almost the exact same spot Marty had hit with his outstretched hands seconds before. And just like Marty, he bolted to the left in a desperate attempt to follow his friend and accomplice to the safety and freedom of the street.

Alex savagely ripped the hoodie from his head to give himself better visibility and air. It was becoming harder to breathe. He sprinted wildly down the hallway with rapidly snowballing anxiety and increasingly longer stride lengths.

The blood pumping unimpeded from the rip in Alex's vena cava filled his chest cavity with more and more blood, taking up space normally reserved for air. Free flowing blood pooled in his chest cavity, placing mounting pressure on his lungs, reducing the amount of life-giving oxygen he could pull into his starved lungs. He expelled more air with each breath than he could suck in with the next.

As Alex neared the end of the hallway, the crushing, unrelenting pain in his chest forced him to slow his pace to a slow jog. He clutched at his chest in a futile effort to alleviate the pain. His face contorted into a tormented grimace.

Compelling himself to continue moving toward the street and the freedom it brought, he managed to get within ten feet of the door leading outside before his legs turned to rubber. He fell headlong to the thin, mottled brown carpet stained with years of grime from the soles of shoes worn by residents and their guests.

He cringed and recoiled in pain as his pig-like nose squished sideways from the tremendous impact it made with the unforgiving concrete floor that lay inconspicuously buried beneath the disgustingly soiled carpet.

In a valiant effort to regain his feet, Alex pushed himself up from the floor with trembling arms, only to fall face down again. His blood-clogged nose smashed into the unforgiving concrete a second time.

With failing strength, he tried to push himself up once again, but he simply didn't have the power or will to raise himself more than four inches above the ground before crashing back down.

His final thoughts were of his first girlfriend. A feeble smile flickered fleetingly across his parched lips as visions of joyful memories cascaded across his mind. Then his smile faded.

His mouth flopped open in a silent scream of terror as he died with unseeing eyes that stared into the turbulent depths of Hell.

CHAPTER 22

WHAT'S YOUR EMERGENCY?

Rachael's horribly trembling hands lost all traces of fine motor skills and refused to remain motionless. She began shaking uncontrollably just as her rubbery knees threatened to buckle. With tremendous will and concentration, she sidestepped and shuffled unsteadily behind the concealment of the door frame, and then dropped clumsily to her knees.

Snatching at her hastily dropped purse, she hysterically dragged it toward her. As soon as it touched the front of her knee, she madly probed its dark confines until she eventually, and with great relief, felt her frantically searching fingers land on the cold, smooth surface of her cell phone.

Yanking it from her purse, she made a gargantuan effort to keep the Walther that she still grasped firmly in her shaky hand pointed as straight as she could manage toward the front door. Rachael reminded herself to keep everyone still in the apartment, whether they be friend or foe, in her peripheral vision.

Cole was still writhing pitifully on the floor in agonizing pain.

She forced the moans and cries of the people she knew to be friends from her mind and held the phone up in front of her face, keeping it on the same level as the Walther. Only then did she allow her eyes to flit between its illuminated number pad and the front door. She reminded herself to keep the gun pointed in a safe direction with her finger off the trigger and lying alongside the frame.

Frantically dancing her thumb over the keyboard, she accidentally flubbed dialing the number for emergency services. Her jangled nerves had caused her stumbling fingers to hit the number nine key twice. "Damn!" she muttered aloud but in a hushed voice.

She managed to reset the phone, but on her second attempt her flying thumb tap danced on the number one key three times.

"Damned! Damned! Damned!" She whispered. The mounting frustration and aggravation she felt was evident in her strained voice.

With great concentration and determined effort, she managed to dial 9-1-1. After four rings a dispatcher answered. "This is 9-1-1 dispatch. What is your emergency?"

"This is Rachael Fiorenza. Three men just broke into the apartment I'm in and tried to kill me, my boyfriend, and another couple," she replied with panting, shallow breathing hindering her ability to make coherent speech. "Send the police and a few ambulances immediately!"

"We'll have the police there as soon as possible. Please don't hang up. I'll stay on the phone with you until they arrive."

Rachael made sure the dispatcher had the address correct, and with a halting, uncertain tap of her uncoordinated thumb, she disconnected the call but kept the phone in her hand.

Elena snapped out of her stupefied state and looked around as if she'd just woken up in the middle of a nightmare. Seeing Rachael, she called to her in a pitiful, almost child-like voice, "Rachael, Rachael, I don't know what to do."

Her face scrunched up in confusion and large tears began pouring down her face again, but she didn't move.

"Come back here with me. We can wait for the police to arrive. I just called them. They're on their way," Rachael said in as calm of a voice as she could muster. She kept her sentences short and distinct so Elena could easily comprehend what she was saying. "We know we're safe back here. They may come back."

Elena stood, shakily got her feet under her, took a few tentative steps to assure herself that her legs would support her weight, and then started briskly walking straight toward Rachael.

Elena was blocking Rachael's view of the door, so she gave her instructions in a calm voice. Rachael surprised herself at how calm her voice was considering the turbulent state of near hysteria she was feeling inside.

"Move to your right," Rachael said, waving Elena to the side with the hand she used to hold the phone. Her other hand kept the Walther pointed at the door. "Don't get between me and the door, I have to keep it under surveillance in case they come back. Stay out of my line of sight and don't walk in front of my gun."

"But I'm afraid of guns," Elena wept pathetically. A fresh batch of tears welled up in her panic-stricken eyes.

"Yeah, well, one just saved your life so don't be too wussy about it," Rachael replied dryly. "Sit over there in the corner behind me and stay quiet."

"Eric is still just sitting there," Elena said numbly, motioning dispassionately over her shoulder toward the massive young man leaning dazedly on the table. Eric's weight was still resting heavily on both of his forearms. He looked very much like a depressed drunk leaning over a bar in a seedy tavern after a two-day bender.

Rachael stole a fleeting glance at Eric. With an analytical and detached demeanor, she noted that his head limply hung suspended in the air but was slowly sinking closer and closer toward his smashed plate of half-eaten spaghetti.

"Leave him for now," Rachael instructed sternly. "The EMTs and police will be here shortly. I just spoke with them. They'll take care of Eric."

"And Cole," Elena sniveled. She slid down with her back to the wall and cowered on her haunches with her knees pulled tightly to her chest. She began sniffling and whimpering like a small, frightened child. Astonished, Rachael saw Elena pathetically rock back and forth in a rhythmic cadence. She stared blankly at a spot on the floor a few feet in front of her.

Rachael was not sure if Elena was capable of speaking, so she ignored her.

Remembering she still had a task to perform, she began fumbling with the contact list in her phone, all the while keeping a vigilant watch on the front door by glancing over the phone while she dialed. Her fingers awkwardly skimmed over the keypad.

Finding the correct contact in her phone's directory, she firmly pressed the button with her thumb.

After three rings she was connected with an operator at Self-Defense Helpline. It was a company Sarah and Nadine highly recommended that offers comprehensive legal protection for its members in case they are ever involved in the unfortunate situation of having to defend themselves or others from violent aggressors with the use of lethal force.

After giving them the vital information including her full name, where she was, the situation as she understood it, and the police jurisdiction that would most likely be handling this incident, she hung up.

Rachael glanced toward Cole and saw he was struggling to his feet. The agony caused by the intense effort he was putting forth was etched upon his face.

He was obviously in great pain as he placed one hand above the other on the wall and laboriously pulled himself up. Once he was standing, he leaned heavily against the wall until he got his bearing. Once he was confident that he could walk without falling, he powerfully but awkwardly shoved off the wall and moved toward

Eric. He was still bent slightly at the waist and walked with a guarded and stilted gait.

He hobbled over to Eric without looking at Rachael or bothering to ask if she was injured or not.

After checking Eric and getting an answer from his friend that he was OK, Cole painstakingly pulled out a chair and flopped down onto it. Hugging his belly, he croaked out a few words meant for Rachael even though he was not looking directly at her.

"What did you do?" He asked in a bewildered tone. His head began swaying from side to side as if the effort of talking demanded extra strength and energy he had to pull from the far reaches of his body.

"What do you mean, 'What did I do?'" she asked incredulously. She emphasized the "I" in her sentence.

"I mean …" Cole began saying, but she cut him off.

"I saved your life you flaming asshole!" she wailed. The adrenaline coursing through her veins like a runaway locomotive had started dissipating and the events of the evening began taking their toll on her.

With a deep, shuddering breath her raging emotions and relatively calm demeanor began crashing into a crumpled heap. The empty burning feeling in her gut was probably very similar to what onlookers seeing the fiery demise of the Hindenburg decades previously must have felt.

"What are we going to do now? My dad will kill me for ruining this apartment. He'll never get his security deposit back now," he cried. Tears began streaming unabashedly down his face in torrents. "You and your self-defense crap have made a mess of everything."

He began rocking back and forth the same as Elena. Seeing both of them rocking senselessly almost brought Rachael to tears.

Rachael dropped her hand to her side so the Walther was pointed safely toward the floor. She composed herself the best she could and began thinking of anything else she should be doing. Realizing that she was still kneeling, and had not moved since she'd fallen, she decided to move to a more comfortable position before trying to converse any more with Cole.

She stiffly shifted her weight to ease some of the discomfort gnawing at her throbbing knees, and in a soothing but fatigued voice, said, "I'm going to talk to the police when they get here. I can hear the sirens. They're coming, and they'll be here soon. I'll get this all straightened out."

He stopped rocking when he heard her voice.

"And what should I do?" he howled, louder and more persistently than before.

"Well, you may want to consider changing your pants before the police get here because you appear to have pissed yourself," she replied in a deadpan voice. All her energy had drained out of her. She was demoralized and had just used up the last of her energy and ability to care about much of anything.

Cole glanced down at his lap with a deliberate but vacuous gaze. He listlessly stared at the wet stain darkening the front of his tan khaki trousers

He didn't say anything for a long moment.

Then, in a low, calm voice he simply mumbled, "Oh shit."

CHAPTER 23

REVELATIONS

"Being able to see and talk with you over the Internet is really cool!" John Yates exclaimed. Sarah, Nadine, Chauncey, and William hid their smiles and tried to stifle giggles to avoid him hearing them.

"Reverend," William said tactfully. "You really have to get up to speed with computers and the Internet. There's a brave new world out there."

"I am!" he exclaimed excitedly. "Samantha, a local teenager who's a member at the church I pastor, is tutoring me. I'm paying her a paltry amount to compensate her for her time, and she's a really good teacher."

"That says a lot about any teenager," Sarah said, trying to be supportive.

"It does say a lot about her, for sure," John said. "She has a tremendous amount of patience with me and doesn't talk down to me or my ignorance. Once I get a better understanding of using a computer for anything more than simple accounting, which is all I did while I was at the mission, and Chauncey can attest to that, I'm going to take a course at the local community college."

"I can attest to you being computer illiterate. I think it's a great idea you're going to take some computer courses," Chauncey said. He put great effort into hiding his smile while he joked with his old boss.

"I was talking about only using the computer for accounting," John replied. Then he caught on that Chauncey was only teasing him. So, in the spirit of fellowship and with a delighted chuckle, he added, "You know what I mean, you rascal, you!"

"I like being able to kid around with you now that you're not my boss anymore," Chauncey replied, trying to catch a few gasping breaths. Then he and William broke down with belly-splitting laughter.

Sarah and Nadine merely smiled. They realized they weren't able to share in the male camaraderie these men formed while working together for so long.

"So, what's new in Gerty's Run these days other than you discovering the wonders of the World Wide Web?" Nadine inquired. She tried changing the subject to allow her and Sarah an opportunity to join the conversation.

"Well," he began slowly. He was obviously being careful thinking through what he was going to say. "I've met a really wonderful woman and we seem to be getting along fairly well."

"Whoa!" Chauncey replied, his eyes growing big and his interest piquing. He leaned forward attentively, then eagerly said, "Tell us all about this! I've never known you to take a romantic interest in a woman. This is an entirely new side of you I never knew existed."

"Yeah, Reverend, this side of you is new to me also, and I've known you a lot longer than Chauncey has," William added, leaning forward to be closer to the computer monitor. "Tell us about this new romance."

"And don't leave out any of the juicy details," Nadine piped in. "You know a lot more about us than we do about you, so fair is fair. Spill the beans!"

"OK y'all," he said, resigned to his fate. "Fair is fair. You're correct Nadine, but there's not much to tell, really."

"That's for us to decide, John," Sarah said. "Give us the entire story. Then we'll pick your brain for any additional information you may have held back. You know how this works!"

"Yes, Sarah, with you guys I definitely 'know how this works,' as you so delicately put it," he said. His face shined with youthful enthusiasm as the tiny camera on his computer focused tightly on it. "Her name is Gail. She has a teenage daughter from a local guy who moved on with his life without a second thought about either Gail or the baby she was carrying."

"How did you meet her, if I may ask?" Sarah inquired. She was trying to gently change the subject because she saw John's face darken. She knew that thinking about a man who'd abandon a pregnant woman to fend for herself and her unborn child without help must anger John terribly.

"She's a member of the congregation at the church where I'm the pastor. Gail has been a tremendous help with getting me settled into the community," he replied in a comfortable, conversational tone. Sarah was glad to see that he seemed to have mentally moved past thinking about Gail's situation as a single mother. "She introduced me around to a lot of the local folk and we found out that we had a lot in common with our various likes and dislikes. Her daughter Samantha, she's the one who's teaching me about computers, seems to have taken a real liking to me also. That helps bring us closer together in a very big way. That's especially good since she's my computer teacher."

John smiled at them as though he had just made a tremendously funny joke.

"It's nice to see that you not only met someone, but she's a local woman who knows the people and customs in that area," Nadine said, stating the obvious. "That can really go a long way toward you being able to make inroads into the community."

"That's very true, Nadine," he said, suddenly serious. "I just hope I'm able to shift my mind into being able to communicate effectively with a teenage girl like Samantha. That's a totally and definitely different situation than I'm used to dealing with. I really don't have much knowledge or experience coping with or handling the myriad of situations that tend to arise around young women."

"I understand that situation all too well and feel your pain," Sarah sighed, thinking about the relationship she was trying to form with a handsome widower. "The Lewis girls are definitely an enigma that haunts me even when I'm not around them."

"Speaking of the good Doctor Lewis and his lovely daughters," John said in a low voice, carefully choosing his words. "How are things going between you and him these days?"

"As well as can be expected," Sarah said, sighing again. "The girls are civil toward me, but I think that's because they no longer view me as being in competition with them for their father's affections. It may all be too little too late, I'm afraid."

"So, things aren't going so well," John said, solemn. "I'm sorry to hear that. I heard you two made a nice couple and may have been compatible."

"That may be true. Dan and I still see each other occasionally. Unfortunately, it's not the type of relationship we both hoped it could have been," she added, forlorn. "Teenage girls do change the equation in a relationship."

"They sure do," John replied soberly.

"So how is your niece, Adrien?" Nadine interjected, trying to steer the conversation in a more positive direction.

"Well, that's a good news and bad news type of situation," John said. The despondency in his voice made Nadine realize that her attempt to make more positive conversation had failed.

"How's that?" she asked.

She wasn't in a hurry to delve into the bad news side of his conversation.

"Well," John began slowly, drawing out his words while he thought about what he was going to say and how he was going to say it. "The good news is that she's graduating college with honors. She's accepted a job in Ohio at a very handsome level of monetary compensation with tons of benefits."

"That's great," Sarah said, hoping they could skip the bad news.

"It is great," John said. "Except her mother, my sister, is beside herself that her little baby girl will be moving halfway across the country. At least that's the way she views it, even though it's only a half day's drive away."

"That's understandable," Sarah said, glad that the bad news was not too bad at all.

"But that's not the bad news," John said.

Sarah and Nadine's hearts sank in unison.

"She decided to move to Ohio because she'll be living with the young man she's been seeing at college for the last two years."

"Oh," Sarah said, not quite sure how to respond to that tidbit of news, especially with John being a preacher who may have a strict view of people living together without the benefit of matrimony.

"It wasn't totally unexpected, although my sister was hoping they'd get married. This living together arrangement kind of caught her by surprise," John said. "He's a very nice young man, at least according to my sister. She approves of him as husband material, and he's going to be a teacher at an elementary school in Ohio, so he should be able to provide the finances a growing family will need. I'm just not sure how she views him now that he's merely an employed live-in with her daughter."

"Well," Sarah said, speaking hesitantly as she strove to assuage John's anguish over this situation. "Many young couples are living together these days even though statistics show an arrangement like that greatly increases the chances of divorce later if they do decide to get married."

"Of course. I know how things are done these days compared to when I was younger," John replied. "It's my sister who's having trouble with this arrangement more so than I am."

"I'm not making any judgements," Sarah said, afraid she'd somehow offended him.

"I know you aren't," John said. "Most of my experience is with various scenarios where the man merely impregnates the woman and leaves her to fend for herself and her child on her own. I think that's one of my sister's major fears. She doesn't want to see Adrien being put in the very difficult situation of being a single mother."

"Is that type of thing a major problem in the area you're in now?" Nadine asked.

"Yes, it is," John replied, his face showing his dismay. "The situation of a single mother trying to make it in the world, especially in an economically depressed area like Gerty's Run, is anything but pleasant."

"Of course," Sarah said, hoping she could change the subject. "It's tough keeping up with all that's happening with young people at this stage of their lives. There's a lot going on with the change from attending college to entering the working world. Have you heard anything new going on with Adrien's friend Rachael? The one who attended the class with her?"

"From what I heard, Rachael dumped her boyfriend, Cole, because, well, because he's an asshole from everything I've heard about him," John stated matter-of-factly. "According to Adrien, she's now dating a nice boy named Brian. They met in college when they were both involved with her campus concealed carry group."

"She's such a nice young lady and was a real asset to our class. It was a great idea having her and Adrien attend the class together," Nadine said. "It's a shame she was having so much trouble with her boyfriend giving her a hard time about her pro-Second Amendment activism. It was really weighing heavily on her. I hope things work out better for her and this Brian guy."

"Rachael called me a few weeks ago and we talked for quite a long time. She didn't mention anything about Cole other than what happened at the home invasion at his apartment," Sarah said. "She did tell me that she and Adrien went to visit Brian at his parent's place and she really got along well with Brian's mother and father. She never said anything about actually dating Brian."

"She told me the same thing when she called me. She didn't mention anything about dating Brian to me either," Nadine said. "It's really nice when students from our classes stay in touch. It means that they really had a good learning experience and a good time doing it."

"That's for sure," Sarah agreed. "She told me that after Brian returned to school a few days after Adrien and Rachael's visit to his parent's house, his folks invited them to visit again. All three of them took them up on their offer the following weekend and had a great time according to Rachael."

"I think Brian's parents may have been concerned about him returning to college after what happened to him. They were probably glad to see he had a good support group to help him return to campus life successfully," Nadine said.

"From what Rachael told me, she and Brian visited his parents for a third time at his parent's insistence. Adrien couldn't join them because she had to study for a big exam she had coming up. That may have been when they first started to see themselves as a couple, I suspect," Sarah said. "It appears that Rachael may have found not only a good guy but one who shares her concerns about personal safety. That's an important ingredient to have in a relationship if it's going to last for any length of time."

"That's nice to hear," William chimed in from the back of the group. "She deserves a nice guy. She seemed like a nice young lady with a good head on her shoulders. At least that's the way it appeared from the short period of time I was talking with her."

"That was my impression also," Chauncey added from his place beside William. "I'm glad she called and spoke with Sarah and Nadine after that terrible experience she had with those criminals breaking into Cole's apartment. Her insights gave me some important information as to what to expect after an incident of that type."

"What did she say that was so important?" John inquired.

"She said that while Self-Defense Helpline was a tremendous help with her legal situation, she's still in counseling for the emotional toll it took on her for having to act in self-defense the way she did," Sarah interjected, answering the question John had posed to Chauncey. "Her new boyfriend Brian is standing with her and offering much needed support. That's something her old boyfriend, Cole, whom I will not call an asshole like everyone else does even though I wholeheartedly agree with their assessment from what I heard about him, would not have done."

"Yes, it's an unfortunate aftermath of that type of situation. At least the legal shenanigans were kept to a minimum because the legal system can be brutal on a law-abiding person who must defend themselves or others with lethal force," Nadine said.

"It seems that you're damned if you do act in self-defense and damned if you don't," John added wryly.

"That's true," Sarah said. Her voice began quivering as her emotions started to get the better of her. Then, her tone hardened with steely resolve. "You never know what havoc predators like those three guys who broke into Cole's apartment can wreak, especially if their victims are good hearted young people with their entire lives ahead of them. But I know for certain that it's much better to be alive because you were prepared to protect yourself than being dead or maimed for life because you weren't."

"I think you've proven that yourself, and you've helped other people be prepared to deal with the evil that can touch our lives," John said.

"I totally agree with you, John," William said. "And that includes you too, Nadine."

"Thanks," Nadine said.

Then Nadine shuddered. Her head and shoulders shivered so violently that even John was able to see the motion over the computer monitor.

Everyone looked at her.

"Are you okay, Nadine?" John asked. "You look like your mind is somewhere out in outer space. Then you just shook from head to toes."

"Yes, I'm fine," Nadine said. "Do you believe in premonitions?"

"Well, I think there may be something to them, but that's never been proven," John replied.

"I was thinking about that Dark Night of the Soul stuff you told us about," Nadine said.

"That may have something to do with what we've been discussing, even though I don't see how," John said. "Is that what you're referring to?"

"Not exactly, but when Adrien's name was mentioned I got this terrible feeling like she's about to experience the Dark Night of the Soul," Nadine said. "It was such a strong, gloomy feeling deep inside me that it sent a shiver down my spine. I guess that's what you saw."

"Oh, I hope not!" Sarah said. Her lower lip began to tremble. "Adrien's such a nice girl, and I'd hate to see her have to go through an experience like that."

They all looked back and forth between each other, while John merely watched them. No one said anything.

The heads of everyone in the room swiveled in unison toward the computer monitor, and they stared at the image of John's face.

Everyone remained silent, afraid to voice their thoughts about Adrien and the Dark Night of the Soul.

The End

If you enjoyed this book…

I would truly appreciate it if you would help others to enjoy it also. Reviews of books are a vital part of helping readers find series they will love. Reviews are often what make the difference between passing over a book or finding a series that will keep you on the edge of your seat and demanding the next installment.

Your review will mean a lot to both me and to future readers. You can leave a review for Educated Justice at Amazon by visiting:
http://www.amazon.com/review/create-review?&asin=B08CF2YLXD
    or to leave a review for this three-book box set you can go to
http://www.amazon.com/review/create-review?&asin=B08J1WGYBQ
(It would be great if you left a review at both).

Or you can leave a review on Goodreads.com. Creating an account at Goodreads is very simple and you will discover a new home there with other readers who have reading interests very similar to yours. Check them out.

Thank you very much in advance for taking the time to post a review and your opinion of this book. It is greatly appreciated, and I look forward to reading your review!

Be A Beta Reader Team Member

I am recruiting willing volunteers to be members of my Beta Reader Team.

What's all involved in being a beta reader? Well, you'll be helping me flesh out my manuscripts for each book before it is published. Many authors use beta readers because you are very astute at reading and any errors will jump off the page and strike your eye as being incorrect.

What types of things might you find?

One author likes to tell the story (OK, he reluctantly tells it) of the time he had his main character flicking the safety off a pistol that does not have a safety. Whoops!

But these are the types of things I need your help with.

If you are willing to help, I will make the un-edited manuscript available for a few days on BookFunnel. You can download it, read it, email me with anything you find that is not right within the following two weeks, and I'll look over your suggestions.

This will be a tremendous help to me and will give you insights into the process of how the books you love to read are put together.

I have a standalone chapter that is just a small gift to you for joining the team.

A week or two before the launch date I will send a finalized copy of the book out to the Beta Reader Team members so they can read it then post reviews on Amazon with the story fresh in their minds. It's OK to wait to read only the finalized copy and then write a review if that's the only part of the publication process you are interested in.

You can get a free chapter for becoming a beta reader by visiting https://dl.bookfunnel.com/q1z60hf7io.

Continue the series with Book Four:
FASTER JUSTICE

2 Maniacs, 4 Guns, 13 Bombs, and 5,000 vulnerable students to protect. Piece of cake, right? Well, maybe not…

When Adrien and Lance begin life as a married couple fresh out of college, they face much the same troubles as other couples.

Well, actually, they have a ton more than most…

After Adrien is confronted by a hammer-wielding thug during a smash-and-grab robbery, her most closely held secret must come out, and Lance doesn't know where to begin helping her.

Lance's uncertainty in his new role in life is compounded by being selected to participate in Ohio's groundbreaking FASTER program.

When the school where he teaches is attacked, will he have the backbone to do what needs to be done? Or will he flounder the way he has in handling Adrien's long-held secret?

Educated Justice is the fourth part of the action/thriller True Justice series. Anguish, suspense, and loads of action take this novel by D. E. Heil to incredible new heights.

Pick it up today to rush head-long into the next episode of the True Justice series!

Delve deeper into your new favorite book series by visiting the author's website at: www.DEHeil.com/

Want even more? Sign up for my mailing list and receive a FREE copy of the Prologue for the next book in the series, FASTER JUSTICE!

No, the prologue is not crucial to what you just read in *Educated Justice* or what you'll soon read about in *Faster Justice*, but it is an interesting sidelight you may want to know about.

If you sign up for my mailing list, I will immediately send you a copy of the prologue for your reading pleasure.

Your email listing will NEVER be sold or used for anything other than an occasional announcement pertaining to this series of novels. Naturally, you can unsubscribe at any time.

To get your FREE copy simply sign up at https://dl.bookfunnel.com/c9dognsdz3 and the prologue will be sent to you in the blink of an eye!

You can see more about the rest of the books in the True Justice series by visiting the author's website at DEHeil.com.

Publisher's Note: This is a work of fiction. Names, characters, places, and incidents are a product of the author's imagination. Locales and public names are sometimes used for atmospheric purposes. Any resemblance to actual people, living or dead, or to businesses, companies, events, institutions, or locales is completely coincidental.

Book Layout © 2020 BookDesignTemplates.com

ISBN: 9798686033887

CONTENTS

Made in the USA
Columbia, SC
30 December 2020

30060465R00450